PROLOGUE: A CONTEMPLATIC

Death comes to us all. For some, such inevitability reminder to live each day as if it were one's last. To othe a life sentence mired by morbid ambiguity, the final knowingly made privy to the host. Such procrastinations plague many a waking moment, the irony of a life being consumed by death a bizarre man-made purgatory. A penance one either accepts the burden of gladly, the resolute promise of an afterlife offering some form of security or alternatively, serves instead to liberate the keenest of atheists from the burden of scepticism.

The night sky had cleared, the light drizzle now replaced with a shrill wind. As the wretched figure hunkered against the wall of the alleyway, he found himself contemplating his own mortality, a notion which determined the plotting of his next course of action. Of one variable he was certain; his next move would need to be a decisive one. The blood loss he had sustained would not permit indecision. The tears he had previously shed had done little to soften the congealed blood around his bulbous right eye, the receptacle all but swollen shut.

A sadistic twinge of pride welled within the silhouetted figure. The amount of torture he had endured yielded little in the way of intelligence for that of his captors. He had divulged nothing, an unremitting sense of moral duty throughout the long hours only serving to further temper his resolve.

Torture, if he were to be discovered, was inevitable; he had known that from the start. Regardless of whether or not he had succumbed immediately to his captor's barrage of questioning, torture was a beloved pastime of the group and they would not let the truth stand in the way of their own personal gratification.

The London backstreet was eerily quiet, the buzz of traffic replaced now by a relentless ringing in his ears, a dull static that yearned for Hawkins to rest his head against the wall, to give in and embrace the warm lull of sleep and ultimately what came with it, death. A self-diagnosis of his various injuries ended in the realisation that he was profoundly concussed, the blood loss only serving to further sap his body of any strength. The short alleyway afforded a view of the adjacent road at both ends; to his right, the lane he had dragged himself away from and to his left, possible refuge.

The pungent smell of the refuse bin he now found himself propped up against did little to dispel his nausea, his clothes already flecked with blood and vomit, his skull swimming. It did however, afford some cover should any of his captors arrive at the mouth of the alleyway to his right, a wayward inspection revealing little more than the gloomy outline of an overfilling bin surrounded by broken glass.

The broken glass had been Hawkins doing. As he had groped his way along the alleyway, using the wall for support, an external security light had sprung into life, illuminating the alleyway. His crippled right hand, which had been rendered useless by his captors, came up to shield his eyes, temporarily blinding him in the process. In a panic Hawkins had removed his belt and had taken to swinging it blindly in an effort to shatter the glass with the pewter buckle. After several unsuccessful attempts, he succeeded; the alleyway once again plunged into darkness, a scattering of splintered glass cascading across his shoulders.

The exertion had taken its toll. Hawkins had grasped at the bin in an effort to steady himself but regretfully had failed in his agonising stupor to observe the wheels at the base of the metallic structure. With a harsh noise it had given way, bringing him down hard upon his side. It had taken his last remnants of strength not to scream out as his right hand instinctively shot out to break his fall, the mangled limb crumpling under his weight. After having been beaten for a significant period to no avail, they had taken to pulling out his fingernails, the nails upon his right hand completely removed. They had started on his left hand, removing the nails upon his thumb and index finger before he had managed to escape.

Exhausted, he had shuffled his cold and sodden back against the brickwork, cradling his mangled appendage, rocking in agony. When the pain finally subsided, Hawkins had begun to take in his surroundings, noticing that his legs and buttocks were wet also. It had been raining when he had first escaped from West Acre Point and he deduced that he must be sat in a puddle.

He shifted his weight to his left arm in an effort to raise himself before collapsing backwards, the effort excruciatingly futile. Slowly and with some effort, he dipped the tip of his finger, absent of a nail, into the puddle. It felt warm to the touch. He rubbed the alien substance between his thumb and forefinger. It was thick, syrup-like in consistency.

At first, he presumed it to be some miscellaneous liquid that had leaked from the bin beside him. He raised his index finger to his left eye, squinting. The alleyway, devoid of light, offered little in the way of scrutiny, his left eye now growing dim at the periphery. His inspection proving fruitless; Hawkins instead diverted his attention to that of his sense of smell. Although his nose had sustained substantial blows, it had not been broken, just violently swollen.

With a cursory sniff of the substance his mouth ran dry, the distinct smell of iron hanging heavy in the damp December air. Panic began to rise within his chest. He probed his torso, groping at his flesh in an almost comical fashion before his fingers finally came to a rest, all subtlety lost. He let out a feeble moan, instinctively retracting his hand, the area around the wound tender and warm. In his haste to escape he had left himself exposed. In an effort to calm himself he began to recall his escape, seeking out a cause to the effect.

When he had broken free of the restraints that shackled him to the sturdy chair, his captor had been brandishing a Stanley-knife, the blade mostly retracted or so he had thought. He had desperately beaten at Hawkins' chest before he was felled, the cutting implement discarded and thrown aside. He had come down heavy upon his attacker, using the last of his strength to pummel the man's head clean off of the hard, concrete floor. With a fevered bloodlust he had continued longer than necessary, the base of the man's skull bouncing hard off of the surface until it was replaced with a repulsive, squelching thud.

It was during this period, fuelled by his desire to fight in order to instigate his flight, that his captor must have tagged him. When he had finally come to a rest, chest burning with euphoric labour, the man's head had lolled sideward exposing the inner workings of his skull, a Rorschach style pattern of vibrant blood adorning the floor beneath. Hawkins, concerned only with his desire to survive was unmoved by the sight, the events of the day having tarnished

2

any sympathy he had for his fellow man. Hobbling, he burst through the service door that led him out and away from the West Acre Point shopping centre, the myriad of wet London streets before him.

That had been ten minutes ago. The notion of any form of advantage a head start may have afforded him now ebbing away by the second and with it, precious blood. He began to wheeze heavily. The wound was small but deep enough for him to place the tip of a finger in. If he could not stem the bleeding or find medical attention soon, he would bleed to death. His body began to shake extensively, the cold December air chilling his damp clothing more so. An intense nausea crept along Hawkins' spine, a numb feeling beginning to churn at his temples.

He made to get to his feet once again, the prospect of being upright now all too alluring and with it the possibility of more oxygen. A black veil descended across the vision in his left eye as he began to black out. His movements faltered, his limbs losing all rigidity. As he lost consciousness, he mentally berated himself. His previous vocation had placed him in some compromising positions; Afghanistan, South Africa, Sierra Leone and here he was about to die on the streets of the very capital he had been brought up in and adored so much.

A plane murmured overhead, the drone somewhat soothing. All that was visible in the night sky were the white lights blinking on the plane's wings. He imagined the pilots, making their final alterations before their descent into Heathrow, their passengers expectant and eager to once again be firmly on terra firma. Had it really only been three days ago since he had stepped off of that plane at Heathrow? Blackness enveloped the rhetorical sentiment.

(CHAPTER BREAK)

He had always wanted a career in the Armed forces, ever since his father, an ex-serviceman himself, had bought him that replica of a World War Two Hurricane. The plane was intricately painted in green and brown along the fuselage and wings, the iconic concentric red, blue and white discs under the wings and along the side of the plane. His father had remarked that these were called roundels, or as he had referred to them as a six-year-old, 'Randal's'. His Father had of course forgiven him this indiscretion. After all, the innocence of youth permitted forgiveness for most things.

He remembered how the canopy could be slid back to reveal a tiny pilot, plastic and painted in full military fatigues, which could be removed from his cockpit. He used to dream of swapping places with that pilot. However, the bank holiday air shows that he attended with his family as a young boy were as close as he ever came to achieving such a dream.

Those Bank holiday weekends in the summer when everybody flooded the beach to witness the Red Arrows finale or to witness the iconic flyby of a lone Spitfire or as his Father had referred to it, "The Usurper." The same lecture each year, his Father adamant that the Spitfire had wrongly received much of the credit during the Battle of Britain in 1940 over that of the Hurricane, an aircraft that was accountable for four- fifths of all enemy aircraft destroyed between July and October. How his father used to comment on the life lessons that could be extracted from the Hurricane.

"Son," he would recant. "The Hurricane might have been slower, larger than and not as glamorous as the Spitfire but pound for pound it did the business. It could outlast the Spitfire any day of the week and my God, could they take a beating. They had durability and got the job done, unlike that pretty boy flying up there," he would point at the Spitfire and stare at it, as if he were waiting for it to open fire in an effort to quell his protestations. "The Hurricane," he would summarize, "is a lot like life. You never give up; you run things at your own pace and although you might not be the best looking or most attractive on show, you always get back up, battle on."

(CHAPTER BREAK)

Hawkins jolted awake, the steady sound of water as it pattered upon the concrete retrieving him from his blissful nostalgia. How he missed his father, his mother, his beloved brother. The pattering was suddenly replaced by the clinking of a bottle. Hawkins raised the cumbersome weight of his head and drunkenly inspected his environment. His trouser leg was sodden, a tepid liquid gathering around his ankle.

Presuming it to be blood, he assumed that a substantial period of time had elapsed since he had blacked out. He swallowed back the panic before it had time to surface and through dry lips, his parched throat removing much of the onus from his words, recounted his Father's words, "You always get back up ...battle on".

A loud belching sound came from his right, fear immobilising Hawkins instantaneously. He held his breath listening intently for any further noise unaware as to whether the person on the adjacent side of the refuse bin was friend or foe. He tensed his body in an effort to assess his faculties. An all but extinguished fire singed his nerve endings. It would have to be enough; he had remained immobile for far too long now. He had begun to gather his resolve when the acrid smell hit him. He sat up marginally, inspecting his lower body. The liquid that had gathered around his ankles was clear in the moonlight, the fluid too free moving to be blood. No, instead it was a very different by-product of the body, urine.

A clearance of the throat was followed by the shuffling of feet, glass cracking underfoot. The glass upon the floor began to part as the silhouette shuffled forwards, a bemused grunt causing Hawkins to flinch. He traced the source of the noise, deciding reluctantly to maintain his position. Although prone, the darkness afforded him some cover amongst the various bin bags he found himself uneasily perched upon. He daren't move for fear of displacing the contents of the bags.

A solitary foot edged out from in front of the refuse bin. Not moving his head, Hawkins lowered his gaze, taking in the figure's footwear. Although he could not make out much, one thing was clear, the obscured character was not wearing military- issue boots as his attackers had done so. Not wanting to become complacent, Hawkins maintained a strong mental grip on the ember of hope that flickered within his chest, the fearful expedited beating of his heart now calming slightly. He continued to hold his breath, his lungs burning, the pain coursing ever more so from his innumerable wounds.

The figure stepped forwards, now no more than about two metres or so from the refuse bin. The shadow was disjointed, no clear outline visible, a mass of clothing dispersing any hope of identifiable characteristics. The mass swayed slightly, its knees weaving. A seasoned click of the joints came followed by a groan of ecstasy as the figure stooped down and retrieved what Hawkins presumed to be his discarded belt. Was this one of Thompson's men, examining his trail?

After close inspection Hawkins fears dissolved as the character pulled the belt around its waist and inspected the find, ascertaining whether or not it fit. Hawkins evaluated his situation, he felt as if he were about to black out again, his lungs yearning for air. His need for oxygen now overtook his need for stealth and finally after a deep exhalation of air, he spoke.

"Please... I need your help... I've been injured... badly," his throat was cut off by the exertion of articulation.

The silhouette in a blatant movement retreated quickly from the location of the sound, completely taken off guard.

"Jesus! Who goes there?" the distinctly masculine voice hissed. The pronunciation was slurred, a thick East-End accent punctuating the question harshly.

Hawkins' head once again began to swoon. With a concerted effort he shoved himself away from the wall slightly, holding out his left hand pleadingly, "I need to get out of here... right now. Please... phone an ambulance..."

The figure retreated slightly, his exasperated gulping of air representative of his panic. He began to fumble in his pockets before finally withdrawing what he had been looking for. Even in the pitch blackness of the alleyway Hawkins could see that the man was visibly shaking. After several attempts the man struck a match. When his eyes fell upon the wretched figure before him he brought his hand up quickly to his mouth. Not quick enough however. A torrent of bile erupted from between the gaps in his fingers, his eyes wide with horror. From his free hand, an anonymous brand of vodka fell to the ground, the heavyset bottle harshly clinking off of the hard cement and to Hawkins relief, not breaking.

The man steadied himself against the neighbouring wall, the flame of the match snuffed out. For what seemed like an eternity, Hawkins listened intently as the man retched, his appearance now of grave personal concern. He could only imagine what a shock he must have been to the inebriated man. In the seconds of light the flame afforded, Hawkins observed that the man was homeless, his attire forlorn. The trench coat he wore was threadbare, seasoned by years of grime.

"Who... who did that to you?" came a strangled tone, bile most likely scolding the man's throat.

Absurdly, Hawkins remembered the advice given to those in in the event of being sexually assaulted, to instead call out 'fire' instead of 'rape', the likelihood of someone coming to your aid all the more likely. He was cautious of frightening the already terrified man any further. Regaling him with the arduous hours of torture he had sustained or the identity of his captors would only serve to ward the gentlemen off further, his judgment already impaired by alcohol.

"A bar fight," he replied with agonised embellishment.

"They beat you with a bar?" the homeless man interjected hastily, not having fully processed the information. His tone was lightened somewhat by his ignorance, if only he knew of the events that had transpired earlier that day.

Hawkins was beginning to grow weary, the heady cocktail of blood loss and trepidation rendering him impatient. He shook his head briefly before halting harshly, his head laden with agony, "No, a fight, outside of a bar."

The gentleman's alarmed tone had now shifted to that of a rather inquisitive one; he seemed welcome of the conversation, the dire situation at hand in need of no hurry or expediency. The shadowy mass of the vagrant stooped down, the grating of the bottle of vodka as it was retrieved causing Hawkins to wince, his senses heightened by adrenaline.

"You wanna learn how to handle your drink fella or at least your fists, rough area round here," the man guffawed, his silhouette juddering. "Look at me lecturing you like a hippo, one of those hippies that are critical... whatever the fuck you call them anyway. Which bar squire? Aha hold on a mo. Let me guess... the Carpenters Arms or was it the White Hart?" the question was finished with a substantial gulp of vodka.

"The Hart," Hawkins countered hastily.

Another swig of vodka followed by a large belch, the smell of which filled the immediate area, his tone suddenly turning entrepreneurial. "An Ambulance is going to cost money, there's a payphone up on Chancellors Grove. I hope they didn't mug you to boot, on account of me being somewhat strapped for cash."

"It's free to call 999," Hawkins plainly responded through gritted teeth.

"Oh it's not for the payphone petal; I'm not running a charity here or a marathon for that matter. Talking of which, it's bound to take me double the time what with me zig-zagging completely all over the gaff and all, might as well make it worth both our whiles, hey? Plus, how many good Samaritans have passed you on the road to Dam... da... Dominoes?" he gleefully chortled, his brand of inebriated humour of much personal entertainment.

"Look, I don't have my wallet, I..." Hawkins rummaged through his brain for an explanation, knowing full well where his wallet was, "I left it on the counter of the bar".

"I see," the man replied with an exasperated sigh. "I'm sorry to hear that fella. I feel for you I rightly do...that being said as I alluded to earlier, I am brassic, I mean the moths come out of my wallet with sunglasses on... at least they would if I actually had a..." the drunkards false sympathies were cut short.

Hawkins grew tired of the man's opportunistic outlook, his pain not an entrepreneurial conquest to be capitalised upon.

"For fucks sake!" he blurted out. "I'll give you whatever you want, you've got my bloody belt for starters, take that as a down payment, a sign of goodwill." The ferocity of his tone brought with it a new threshold of agony, his suspected broken ribs jarring with each syllable.

"How do I know this is yours?" the vagrant raised the belt slapping it across the palm of his right hand.

Hawkins opted for a change of tact. "Look, that's a hundred-pound belt in your hand."

The homeless gentlemen comically held it out for inspection in the pitch darkness of the alleyway, stricken with surprise.

"Regardless, it's yours... the way I see it, whether you help me or not, I won't be needing it. You can either have a belt in one hand and a tidy sum in the other later on..." a sharp intake of breath, "or my death on both of your hands. Let's see if your conscience holds up as well as your trousers will..." an agonising prang of pain spread across his chest, "Your call."

Several seconds passed as the destitute shadow before him weighed up his options. At first, Hawkins worst fears were realised when the man plunged the belt into one of the deep pockets of his trench coat and made to leave. His heart sunk, his father's mantra angering him now, the sentiment rendered hollow. He had given everything in his final moments, the whole day for that matter and for what?

Abruptly, the homeless gentlemen halted three feet shy of Hawkins and began tossing sacks of rubbish aside, clearing a clear footing around the circumference of Hawkins. For the first time, the homeless man's eyes were evident in the gloom of the alleyway and Hawkins locked gazes with them. His weight shifted as the bags around him were displaced and yet still, a prone Hawkins focused on the man's eyes, his own gaze demonstrating the thanks that his throat could no longer muster.

The man hunched down and wrapped his arm around Hawkins. His mangled hand briefly brushed against the man's torso, Hawkins distressed tones stopping him momentarily.

Finally, the gentlemen's line of sight settled upon Hawkins steady gaze and he winked, "With a hundred notes or so in my pocket I doubt anything will be able to hold me up, if you catch my drift. Talking of which, this probably isn't going to be pleasant...sorry," he grimaced empathetically, a series of discoloured teeth housed within swollen, grey gums.

"On the count of three: One," his grip grew tight around his mid-drift excruciatingly gathering the flesh around his wound. Hawkins fought to stay coherent. "Two," the man's feet parted in preparation for the weight to come. "Three," and with a large heave the man brought Hawkins upwards.

Hawkins, now devoid of energy, allowed himself to go limp, the man taking the full burden of his frame. His head lolled back, the stars above now of more importance than ever as they distracted him from the numbness below his shoulders. His pointed feet cut a course through the broken glass as his rotund saviour dragged him with halting advances, his exertion admirable.

Hawkins inhaled sharp and fast, his mid-drift clammy, his lungs seemingly full of the same shattered shards of glass as that on the floor. The air was sweeter now, less stagnant. Thankful, he ignored the body odour that also emanated from every pore of the homeless gentlemen, his clothes soiled and stale from months of rough sleeping. Grunting, the gentlemen advanced towards the mouth of the alleyway now no more than ten feet away.

"Name's Billy by the way," he wheezed, "although everyone around this neck of the woods calls me Buffalo Bill. The cops know who I am, felt me collar a few times. If they ask about who helped you, feel free to use my name... only if there's a reward in it of course," he distastefully propositioned.

"There's a payphone just up the road," he stopped and hefted Hawkins sinking bulk higher. "On the left, I'll use it to phone you an ambulance and that's where I'll leave you. No need the both of us wasting our time with statements, I've got a full diary tonight," the man erupted with light-hearted glee.

Drunkenly, Hawkins eyes rolled back, his head lolling on the shoulder of the man who had come to his aide. For the first time, assisted by the weak orange glow of a streetlight near the mouth of the alleyway, Hawkins was afforded a closer inspection of the morally defunct Samaritan who currently cradled him.

It was no wonder that people referred to him as Buffalo Bill. His shoulder length hair was wildly matted and indicated that in some glorious yesteryear it had been blonde. Presently however, like the aspirations and dreams the man must have once had, his hair was faded and of a straw like consistency. The bottom half of his face was completely obscured by an overgrown beard of the same straw like discolouration, the hair wild and untrimmed. Those features not obscured by hair were weathered and established an appearance which had been tempered by the elements it had long been subjected to.

To Hawkins' advantage, the man's physique was broad and bloated yet strengthened by hardship; a network of strength concealed under his crude trench coat, a powerhouse of deprivation. Hawkins had been lost in a dazed evaluation of the man's strength, reinforced all the more so when a light from behind traced across the wall to his right, enlarging the man's girth so his saviour's shadow was distorted and looming upon the brick wall. The screech of brakes broke him from his trance.

Painfully, he craned his neck backwards, the alleyway behind him now sealed off by a white van that was drawn across it. The side panel revealed the emblem of Harpers construction LTD, an insignificant detail to those unaware of those the vehicle housed. The vehicle idled lazily. Hawkins began to quake. He attempted to work his legs but they proved to be unresponsive. He squeezed his bicep harder against the base of Bill's skull and the man halted.

"Careful," he squawked and turned to face the bundle he was trying to manoeuvre. His ear suddenly twitched and the man began to turn backwards, the noise of the engine suddenly registering. His eyes squinted as his eyes adjusted to the darkness they had seemingly left behind and he scanned the exterior of the vehicle. He turned back to face Hawkins. His eyes narrowed at first before widening with realisation. Hawkins squeezed the man harder, the look of abject fear etched across his face was the only proof Bill needed.

Assuredly and with a stern validation to his voice Hawkins had not yet witnessed in his inebriated state, he harshly stated, "They're here for you."

Hawkins shook his head, his eyes pleadingly protruding from their sockets. Impulsively the man sought to remove himself from the situation. He began to push against Hawkins, shrugging him off violently. A booming noise reverberated from within the vehicle, the chassis rocking on its axels. Hawkins tightened the crook of his arm around the burly man's neck.

"Get the fuck off me," Bill hissed, arms now clawing at Hawkins head and upper torso, his body now turned in towards Hawkins. He dropped the solid bottle of vodka once again, pledging both hands towards Hawkins.

"They're going to kill me," Hawkins petitioned.

"That's your problem," Bill barked as his clawed fingers found Hawkins wound.

With a bloodcurdling squeal Hawkins crumpled to his knees, his upper torso soon following, once again flung into the darkness of the unlit section of the alleyway. He feebly hung onto Bill's shins with his left hand but it was soon batted away, Bill kicking at the doomed figure. All he could do was adopt a foetal position, absorbing the blows to his upper body, his cheek pressed against the cold, wet ground.

"This is on you, you lied," he snarled, trying to detach himself from any guilt.

Suddenly from behind Hawkins, the door to the van was brought along its runners before coming to rest with a metallic thud. A substantial beam of light from a torch shone directly into Bill's eyes. He shielded his eyes, wincing at the brilliance of the white light; his features were desperate and apologetic. Not sure of himself, Bill raised his hands in the air and he quickly began to back out of the alleyway

"Hey, he's all yours," Bill smiled nervously, shrugging his shoulders. "Thought I could nab his wallet or something, don't mind me."

As he progressed backwards the heel of his shoe caused his half empty bottle of vodka to spin, skittering across the cement. The beam of light came away from Bill momentarily, investigating the noise. With the inhabitants of the van momentarily distracted, Bill seized upon his chance. Stumbling slightly with hands still aloft, he bolted. Immediately, there came a hastened movement of feet at the other end of the alleyway as someone gave chase.

"Leave him!" a level voice sternly ordered.

The footsteps abruptly halted a metre or so from Hawkins, the inhabitant of the van breathing harshly sending a shiver down Hawkins' spine.

"Is it our man?" the nettled East End accent demanded.

A click of a button as the beam of a torch fell upon Hawkins, scanning his upper body, "It's him alright," the voice closest to him returned in a strong Scottish accent, the relief resonant in his voice.

The answer received an authoritative grunt. Hawkins turned onto his front and began to weakly crawl, the remaining nails upon his left hand clawing him agonizingly onwards. He advanced at a snail's pace, the blood from his wound leaving a trail in the vibrant light of the torch. His mangled right hand flailed limply behind him and through gritted teeth, a low whimper emanated upon each exhalation. Glass crunched underfoot. His vision had once again begun to swim, the glow of the streetlamp ahead blurred but ceaseless in its role in spurring him onwards.

A foot came down vehemently upon the small of his back, the substantial size of the sole and the taut crack of leather indicating they were military-issue. Hawkins, pinned face down, yelped out in pain as the boot rotated from left to right, the wound sustained to his torso spreading wide open. To no avail he still opened and closed his left hand, reaching for the next inch of pavement, the line of light afforded by the streetlamp no more than a foot away.

"Stop!" the familiar voice of the group's leader sternly ordered.

Hawkins stretched his left hand as far as it would give, the socket of his shoulder cramping immediately, quaking under the exertion. This time, the heel of the boot twisted. With a shudder of pain, Hawkins devoid of any will to proceed yielded in his attempt.

"Good. Now, I'm going to remove my foot and sit you up so that we can continue that little chinwag between the two of us that you so rudely interrupted earlier. You try anything and it ends right here, right now," he paused. 'Do you understand?"

No response came. Fearing that his prey had blacked out or worse still was intentionally being insolent, the boot clad figure pressed down harder, demonstrating to Hawkins once again that its owner was in full control of the situation. Hawkins ground his teeth biting down hard, spittle flying from his mouth, eyes widespread with anguish.

"Yes…" he breathed out in a manner that conveyed both his pain and surrender.

Just to be sure as the figure removed his foot, he twisted the heel of his boot, which registered another weak groan from Hawkins.

"Now that I have your full co-operation, I'm going to move you. You've lost a lot of blood," a harsh sniff followed, "and it smells like you've voided your bowels to boot. Now the guys are going to be as delicate as possible, which is more than you deserve, however, the vaguest hint that you're not co-operating and they snap your spine in two," the exacting voice asserted.

The foot came free of Hawkins back and the heavyset figure clicked his fingers. Two sets of feet scuffled forward, frenzied hands soon grasping at Hawkins. After being rolled onto his left-hand side, the two obscured figures dragged him towards the wall he had first found himself propped against, all ground gained previously now lost. Hawkins' head bobbed upon his chest as the two men propped him up against the wall.

"Now that you're comfortable, we can continue, Private," the last word delivered with menacing disdain. The large stature of his principal captor stepped forward, eclipsing the remainder of what little light remained.

"Jones, take point and keep a look out," he calmly instructed. Jones acted instinctively and hurriedly set off to the left of the alleyway. "Greaves is keeping a lookout in the van so Mc Allister, so you're on me, you never know you may learn something. Keep your mouth shut and keep the torch pointed in his vicinity," a flourish of venom concluding his order.

The familiar figure hunkered down before Hawkins, glass cracking underfoot, the heat emanating from the man's body palpable. The torchlight now illuminated Hawkins' torso.

"Is that ok, Thompson?" Mc Allister queried, ever the jobsworth. He received no answer, Thompson instead settling upon a conceited scoff.

"Good help is so hard to come by. Wouldn't you agree Private Hawkins? But then you'd know all about that…" he pulled harshly at Hawkins hair raising his entire head in a sharp and fluid movement. He now fixed his gaze upon Hawkins, smiling slightly "… wouldn't you."

Thompson reached out and with a meaty, glove-clad hand grabbed Hawkins' jaw so tight that Hawkins envisioned the fingers puncturing the flesh of his cheeks. Hawkins looked dazedly at the man who had been present for much of his interrogation, an active participant in fact, not letting rank get in the way of getting his hands dirty. Although his vision was beginning to wane, now dotted by black spots and the intensity of the torchlight in his eyes, Hawkins would never forget the face that met him. Like a new-born baby Hawkins struggled to support the weight of his head, his eyes shifting uncontrollably in their sockets. He no longer wanted to fight the cold.

"Look at me when I'm talking to you!" Thompson spat.

Hawkins went to instinctively wipe the spit from his eyes but had no reserves of energy left. His arm raised a centimetre or so off the ground before it retreated. His eyes focused slightly. Thompson raised his other hand and grasped Hawkins' bicep within a vice-like grip.

"Come now, Private. Don't die on me, not after all we've been through today... not just yet," he squeezed tighter causing Hawkins to inhale sharply. "You'll miss the best part and what I'm about to propose is a once in a lifetime offer... granted, that's not very long for you in the grand scheme of things but needs must, I'm on somewhat of a schedule."

Thompson removed his hand from Hawkins' bicep and peeled back his jumper, the congealed blood which had fused with the material finally relenting painfully. Thompson's eyes darted across his torso and the unmistakable twinge of a smile parted his lips. He replaced the material.

"Now, I know you must be in quite some pain by now, it's been at least twenty minutes since your last little show of force."

Hawkins eyes began to close once again. Thompson brought his hand up with brutal speed and enclosed it around Hawkins ear, twisting it with satanic ferocity. A jolt of pain coursed through Hawkins' head, stabbing at his temples. He twisted weakly away from Thompson, however to no avail.

"I want to know where it is and I want to know now, no more games. I know it's somewhere in there..." he lifted a pointed finger indicating back towards the direction of West Acre Point which was still visible even though it had been partly obscured by the van. To emphasise his point, he twisted Hawkins's head firmly by his jaw so that he could view the postmodern oddity.

"You tell me now and this goes no further. Now, you know I can't let you live but I can make it quick and that's a whole lot better than you should expect or deserve. I'll make it quick and your family, now that we know who you are, don't need to fear any form of retribution. They'll not see one of us; we'll even leave you somewhere that someone can find you. That, way your family can give you a proper sending off. Fair is fair, remember what you've put us through today! It's more than you're owed and I'm a man of my word."

Hawkins cleared his throat, swallowed hard and replied with such clarity and conviction, that it shocked the two men, "Ok."

Thompson smiled, relieved. "That's it, you know it makes sense. No need for any further unpleasantness."

"I put it somewhere you'd never be able to find..." He opened his mouth, taking in a deep rasping breath. Thompson licked his lips expectantly, leaning in towards Hawkins so that he could make out his victim's trailing, whispered speech.

Hawkins diverted his gaze from the shopping centre and finding a last morsel of adrenaline twisted his head back to face Thompson, fighting against the solid stance of his grasp. He smiled a grotesque profile of blood lined teeth, two of which were missing after having been removed with pliers earlier. Hawkins's cheeks were squeezed up to his ears. His wound was losing blood rapidly; he felt the sudden eerie warmth of death envelope his body. He began to go numb.

'See out the clock,' he considered, resigning himself to the fact that with his death would also come his unconditional silence. They would never find what they were looking for.

"I..." Hawkins halted, gathering the last remnants of strength in his parched throat, wanting the next fragment of speech to sound as convincing and unimpeded as possible. "I left it with your honour. Good luck trying to find that, you delusional fuck."

With that he cocked his head back and spat in Thompson's face. A darkly crimson, congealed substance that resembled marmite, dripped from Thompson's forehead to the bridge of his nose.

A siren could be heard off in the distance which prompted an incessant appeal from Mc Allister, "We need to hurry this up, Thompson."

Thompson rounded slowly, methodical and exacting in his movements. With a thousand-yard stare he gawped back at Mc Allister, Hawkins' blood rendering the man inhuman, the molasses- like substance leisurely thinning out across his features. Still holding his quarry, he continued to glare back at Mc Allister, his shoulders heaving, short, sharp inhalations and exhalations coming only via his nostrils.

Mc Allister cautiously and most likely unknowingly, took two steps backwards, the torch in his hand cutting a swathe of light across Thompson's features. The intensity within his eyes was immense, ablaze with a concoction of anger and uncertainty as to how to proceed. Mc Allister diverted his gaze, his body quaking. When his eyes finally came back up to meet his superior, Thompson still glanced back at him, however his vision had shifted, a resurgence of clarity. He seemed to almost be staring straight through his underling.

Slowly, Thompson broke his gaze with Mc Allister and devoid of any emotion twisted back to face Hawkins. Motionless, he stared back at the fleeting prey before him, a fragment of respect stabbing at his better judgement. Hawkins held his gaze, still smiling in a taunting, macabre statement of defiance.

"You're done..." Hawkins wheezed, "I gave you... nothing."

Thompson let go of Hawkins' bicep and chin simultaneously. Hawkins' head lolled slightly but came to a rest upon the damp brickwork. Mc Allister's torchlight silhouetted Thompson's shoulders.

"You see that light Boy Scout? Walk towards it for me," Thompson spoke plainly, his body rattling with anger too long suppressed.

"I'll see you soon," Hawkins grunted.

With lightning precision Thompson's docile state burst into life. He angled his thumbs towards Private Hawkins' eyes, thrusting his gloved hands into the white, egg like flesh.

"No Thompson, we need him! Stop!" Mc Allister yelped.

Hawkins flung his hands up defensively around Thompson wrists, alternating between clawing and grabbing. Thompson persevered, spurred on by Hawkins' shrill screaming.

"You just couldn't fall in line could you? You morally defunct Boy Scout! I knew you were trouble from the start. Today might not have opened your eyes wide to our cause..." a pleasurable groan of exertion halted Thompson momentarily, "so allow me one final demonstration."

Thompson's thumbs, encased in leather, thrust through Hawkins's eyes with a stomach-churning squelch. With a final scream, blood curdling and high pitched, Hawkins grasping movements faltered and were reduced to little more than the twitch of his left foot.

For several moments the scuffle of Hawkins' left boot mixed with the excretion of bubbling saliva was all that filled the alleyway. Thompson lingered over the body for what seemed like an eternity, thumbs still placed firmly within Hawkins eye sockets, using his substantial weight to ensure the job was done. He was breathing heavily.

Jones had now joined Mc Allister at his side. Dumbstruck, the two men looked at one another, their superior's actions coming as no surprise to them. It was instead the predicament of how to proceed without Hawkins that concerned them; he had already delayed their plans quite substantially. Jones made to speak and Mc Allister fervently motioned with his hand for him to cease. Jones ignored him unadvisedly, miming an obscenity.

"Thompson," Jones spoke, his voice suddenly pubescent. "Thompson, what do we do now? We needed him; he was the only one who knew where it was stashed away..."

It was at this very moment that Thompson came to. The red mist beginning to dissipate; the realisation of what had transpired took hold. Uncharacteristically, he removed his thumbs in a quick yet delicate manner. He inspected the bloodied slime like substance on his fingers which was barely visible in contrast to the dark leather of his gloves. He stared at it, his face a picture of pure concentration. He rubbed his left forefinger against his thumb, almost savouring the texture. Thompson, from his crouched position began to stand, a majestic predator whose hunger had finally been sated, the spoils of victory ingested.

"I mean...the big man; he's going to string us up for this. If we can't deliver, we're as good as dead," Jones continued feeble-mindedly.

Mc Allister's nervous eyes crossed back and forth incessantly between Thompson and Jones. Thompson had most definitely assessed and evaluated every conceivable contingency as to what may or may not happen, regardless of the day's failures, many of which fell squarely upon his leadership.

13

Thompson further lorded over the body of Hawkins for several moments before he turned in a pivot like motion upon his right foot. He was still inspecting his hands admiringly as he approached the man who had dared question his authority and judgment. He did so until he was scarcely a metre away from the man. He raised his hands bringing them level with Jones' torso. Jones flinched ever so slightly and desperately tried to maintain a regimented stance, eyes forward.

Thompson began to move his hands from left to the right wiping the substance upon his gloves across the cotton of Jones' black t-shirt. All that was visible on the dark material was a jelly like substance that dampened his torso slightly. The man continued to look ahead, desperately urging himself to remain composed. Thompson knew he was scared. He could sense his adrenaline, no the fear, as it coursed through the man's body.

He could feel the man's heartbeat rhythmically pulsating, the thud expedited by terror. Thompson savoured the moment, cleansing his hands like a surgeon scrubbing up after an operation.

Rather abruptly Thompson's hands came to a rest upon his quaking torso. Finally, he looked up, Jones' gaze shifting uneasily from left to right, his eyes betraying his false bravado. The man had arched his head ever so slightly away from Thompson, finding it hard to maintain eye contact.

"You know what the difference between you and me is Jones?" Thompson probed in a lifeless tone. "Hmmm?"

Jones shook his head from side to side, ever so slightly, the movement of his Adam's apple slow and fidgety.

"No?" Thompson asserted bemused. "Well allow me to enlighten you. You have been and always will be, afraid to get your hands a little bit dirtier than the rest of us. The last few days have shown me that. You are a follower, a sheep in a herd of indifference. You are not an instigator of change. You might as well be like him," he rounded, pointing at Hawkins before returning his gaze, wild eyed and venomous.

"Lying on a rubbish heap destitute, a totem of the very modern contagion we seek to cure, to eradicate. A man so willing to die for an ideological institution that didn't give two shits about whether he lived or died, as long as he got done what needed to be done. A task they were all too incapable of doing themselves. We are living in an age of pure unadulterated, debris. The system is failing. Granted, what we have done thus far, what comes next, it's dirty, make no mistake about it, dealing with his kind always is. But do it we shall. If it's what is required of us, we will gladly continue to reach down into that very detritus, to sully our hands and do you know why Jones?" he gobbed.

Jones shook his head in a composed motion, "No Sir."

"Because we love this country," Thompson cooed with pride, jutting his chin out slightly as he did so. "We were getting nothing out of him. Nothing! He was brainwashed and indoctrinated like all the rest, trying to save Pierce, the hostages, people he didn't even know, who would likely not even have given him the time of day on any other given day. So answer me this, are you one of the initiated or are you just another sheep? Are you a shepherd or one of the hegemonic flock that plight this land? Because I'm starting to think you don't have the nerve for the next step."

An upright Jones decided to stare at Thompson's forehead rather than absorb those piercing eyes once again. He admired Thompson and his dedication to the cause but his methods recently, especially today, had been unorthodox and at times reckless. His mind snapped back into focus. He cleared his throat, now aware that his throat was parched. He exhaled finally, aware that throughout Thompson's condemnation, he had barely taken a breath.

What really worried him however was the fact that he already felt as though the day's events had rapidly spiralled out of control. He had felt himself becoming more expendable to the cause, in Thompson eyes, as well as those around him. After all, he had largely been complicit in Hawkins ability to exact the damage he had thus far. He should never have…

"I'm waiting," Thompson pressed.

Jones registered the silence, in his stupor unable to piece together what Thompson had just asked. Flustered slightly he replied, "I am sir. I was just worried about how the plan would proceed from here… that you know…that our client would be unhappy with an incomplete job. I would give my life to the cause. No question about it, sir'.

Thompson looked searchingly into Jones' eyes before settling upon the steadfast air of honesty within his voice. He removed his hands finally and let them hover before Jones. For several uneasy moments Jones was unsure as to how Thompson would proceed. Having kept him waiting long enough, Thompson lightly patted him on the shoulder.

"We can't afford any more mistakes. The next stage of our mission goes ahead as planned. This country's future rests upon our very shoulders," he patted firmly upon Jones shoulders once again to emphasise his point. "Now if there's no further questions gentlemen," he paused, as if he needed his men's approval. He had it, willingly earned or not.

"Let's proceed then, as planned. Jones, pick up that sack of shit and put him in the van. Our employer may want proof."

With that he began to walk towards the van, Mc Allister already stepping into the van's cabin, muttering something to Greaves in the driver's seat. As Thompson reached for the side door of the van he stopped, resting his hand upon it.

"Oh and Jones, never question me in front of the men like that again. Make no mistake; if I wasn't already an explosives and tech expert down because of the Lone Ranger over there, this situation would have played out very differently."

"Yes sir," Jones replied, chilled to his very core, in no doubt whatsoever about the legitimacy of Thompson's threat.

With that, Thompson slid the door open. Jones felt an icy breeze as the wind caressed the sodden contents upon his t-shirt. As Thompson stepped up into the van, he twisted around to close the door. Just before the door slid shut and still maintaining eye contact, Jones could have sworn that he saw Thompson wink at him, momentarily.

Jones waited for the metallic click of the door's lock to be heard before he deemed it safe to relax. He glanced over at the body of Hawkins and came to the sobering conclusion that it could have very easily have been him lying there. Thompson was pure, undiluted evil and regardless of the horrors that had been committed today or that would be in the not too distant future, it was Thompson's reckoning he feared the most. He would debate the validity of his cause with his maker when it came to it; he just hoped they did not meet under circumstances expedited by Thompson himself.

Jones looked up and heaved a sigh of relief, the intensity of the moment lingering, his procrastinations doing little to ease his conscience. Stopping a second, he observed the full moon, now largely covered by cloud. A drop of rain landed upon the bridge of his nose, quickly trailed by several others upon his arms and upper torso. A storm was coming.

CHAPTER ONE: GHOSTS OF CHRISTMAS' YET TO COME

Heathrow airport was in the thralls of utter chaos. It was the season for it of course. Christmas. Good will to all men, so long as you didn't cut ahead of said man in the customer service queue or lose his baggage, both of which had happened to Tom Hawkins. As he stood there, growing increasingly disgruntled, his hand luggage draped uncomfortably over his shoulder, he maintained that if at all possible, he would not return to an airport in the foreseeable future.

The clothes he wore were stale and stuck to every orifice of his body, his underarms sodden. As a Private in the Army he had always taken great pride in his appearance and personal hygiene, the two interconnected disciplines paramount foundations when building any serviceman. It had of course been drummed into him by his Platoon Commander time and time again during basic training and as with most ex-servicemen; it remained with him instinctively within his own daily routine. He remembered his Platoon Commander's mantra with a wry smile, *"Our first and last battle is germ warfare, a war you yourself must declare. For a man, who washes when he pleases, welcomes sickness and diseases."*

He rubbed his eyes dislodging some sleep. He had had very little sleep on his connecting flight from Singapore to Britain, his initial journey having started in Australia. A day's travel already extended by a further seven hours sat in Singapore Changi Airport, a few hospitality tokens to keep him and the rest of the passengers on board his flight someway docile, the endless slew of complimentary drinks dulling notions of mutiny.

To make matters worse, when he finally arrived back in Britain he had been forced to wait for an additional hour at the bag carousel as the other passengers upon his flight slowly began to dissipate, their own luggage retrieved and in hand. When he approached the attendee on duty at the time, an excitable gentleman by the name of Stuart, he was infuriatingly informed that if his bag had not come out after all this time it had most likely been misplaced or worse still, lost.

Stuart's nonchalant attitude provoked Tom further; the veneer of his hospitality spread all too thin, rendered almost transparent by the burdens of the festive season.

He was a short, slim man, dressed in a one size fits all uniform provided by the airline, the shirt, trouser and waistcoat combination matching that of the plane's branded colours, blue and yellow. The shirt, cheap polyester, clearly highlighted the large sweat patches forming under his arms. His high forehead, due to a receding blonde hairline, also visibly showed beads of sweat. The airport was ridiculously full. Whether it was stress related or due to the stifling heat created by the mass of people, Stuart looked flustered. Hawkins knew the feeling; he too was losing his ability to maintain a friendly façade. He steadied himself with a deep breath.

Whilst discussing next steps, both Hawkins and Stuart had needed to sidestep other passengers on a frequent basis, the throng of people only accentuating Tom's annoyance, the claustrophobic environment airless now. He longed to exit baggage reclaim, with his bag ideally and meet his Father in Arrivals.

Finally, Stuart had ushered Hawkins to the nearby customer services desk and that was where he had stood for the last forty-five minutes, one attendant on the counter, dissecting Stuart's farewell over and over again in his head. On any other given day the comment would have been received with no ill intent, a friendly response or courteous gesture given. However, today was not one of those days.

"On behalf of the airline I am very sorry for the predicament this may have placed you in Sir. I do hope that this hasn't put you off flying with Regency airlines too much with regards to any future travel plans to Australia or any of the other various locations we fly to. The best of luck with your bag and we do hope to have you flying with us again, very soon."

With that, Stuart smiled, retreated into the swarm of other passengers and was gone in mere seconds. Stood alone with his thoughts, arms crossed, bag strap digging into his left shoulder, Tom's opinion towards Stuart had altered significantly throughout his time in the queue. His initial assessment had been that of pure unadulterated hatred of the man before arriving at his current stance which bordered frankly on the homicidal.

He transferred his bag strap to his right shoulder, revelling in the pleasure of removing it from his inflamed arm. He continued to procrastinate over the seemingly harmless provocation.

'That prick might as well have been reading that comment from the staff handbook, the self-inflated, cardboard cut-out'. Tom began mockingly quoting Stuart, engaging in a conversation in which he played both parts.

'I do hope that this hasn't put you off of Regency airlines too much with regards to any of your future travel plans to Australia or the other various locations we fly to'. Hawkins clenched his fists. His bag slipped from his shoulder ever so slightly. He repositioned it. *'Where else do you fly to, Purgatory? Is that where I am now? Because this might as well be it Stuart! One endless customer service queue-'*

He was interrupted by the desk clerk, her face substantially made up with blusher and lipstick, her natural beauty side-lined in favour of company policy. She looked questionably at Tom.

"Can I help you Sir?" she smiled in a manner that indicated the question had at least been asked twice now. Tom took a confident and forceful stride towards the desk, mentally listing what he intended to say and how best to deliver his tirade.

"As a matter fact," he petulantly began, dumping his hand luggage on the blue plastic coated desk, sliding the rucksack ever so slightly to the right so as not to obstruct his or the clerks view when he laid into her verbally, "Yes, yes you can."

The clerk's smile slipped ever so slightly round the edges of her mouth. She knew what was coming, just as she had known with the thirty-odd other passengers she had encountered thus far when her shift had started four hours ago. She straightened slightly, subconsciously preparing herself.

"What seems to be the problem sir?" she heartily replied.

Tom took a considered pause and bit down upon his lip. *'Bite the bullet and air your grievances in an email later,'* he mentally urged himself, his head clearing somewhat. *'It's not like it's her fault. She wasn't the person who mislaid your bag. Who knows, a bit of tact here could help me get out of here sooner'.*

He needed to keep a level head. He, like every other person in the airport, just wanted to be on their way, towards whatever destination they had planned. He placed his left hand on the desk, boarding passes and passport extended to the clerk. She took them delicately observing that there was no wedding ring evident.

"I'm sorry..." he dropped his gaze, reading the clerks name badge, "Anna, I didn't mean to bite your head off. It's been a long day, you know?" he forced a smile which resulted in a mellowing of the clerks features, her posture no longer rigid.

Anna nodded knowingly and swept a stray strand of brunette hair behind her right ear, her hair curled slightly at the ends. The vibrant green of her eyes juxtaposed the blue and yellow of her uniform impeccably, her figure while athletic was still curvaceous. The burning anger at the pit of his stomach along with the desire to berate an employee of Regency Airlines, subsided, quenched by his growing attraction for the woman.

In an effort to validate his urges Tom afforded himself a glance at one of the women sat across from Anna on an adjacent desk belonging to a different airline. He was met by a woman who looked as though she had had a fight with her make-up bag and had lost badly; her life spared so that she could go forth and recant her near miss in all its technicolour glory.

"You can talk," he thought.

He suddenly felt rather paranoid about his appearance, the air conditioning that circulated throughout the vast terminal cooling the clammy sweat across his back and forehead, his haggard appearance rendering him hypocritical when commenting on others appearance.

He smoothed down the gelled hair at the base of his skull feeling rather bashful, unsure as to how to proceed, his attraction making him second guess even the most basic of pleasantries. He was uncertain but there seemed to be a mutual attraction, the clerk still smiling her head flirtingly tilted to the side, hair falling on a heap upon her shoulder.

Tom mentally berated himself for coming across on first impression as just another impatient traveller. He tried to reconcile with the fact that Anna would of course be accustomed in her line of work to many a disgruntled customer using her as a conduit for their anger.

"That's more than ok..." she slid Tom's passport and boarding passes in her direction and inspected them, "Mr. Hawkins. I see you were on the connecting flight from Singapore, if I'd been delayed for over seven hours I would be the same way," she paused and laughed, "I'd probably be climbing the walls by now."

Tom laughed, his smile dissolving his frowning features instantaneously; a smile that Anna observed made him look all the more attractive. She held his gaze, his eyes a dull yet transfixing blue, a twinge of sadness inconsistent when compared with his pristinely white porcelain smile. His gelled, brown hair had recently been cut and was accompanied by a consistent coverage of stubble.

Her line of sight dipped slightly taking in the rest of his well-maintained physique, his tall stature not threatening in any way. The broad shoulders underneath his navy polo gave way to a torso that tapered down towards his waist in a v shape, the short sleeves of his polo framing his biceps in a tight yet tailored fit. A man behind Hawkins coughed and shot Anna an impatient expression. Deliberate of course, Anna thought. She returned to her original train of thought.

"Right, where were we, oh yes," she playfully asked. "What can I help you with today?"

"My bag," Tom quickly declared, "It didn't come out at the carousel and your colleague Stuart said to come here. He said it had most likely been misplaced or that it might not have even been on the plane. It's a black case, Samsonite. It has my details on the tag."

Anna sat transfixed throughout Tom's brief description of events, still mesmerized by those eyes. She found herself desperately wanting to help this man.

"Well," she said, clearing her throat, pulling her keyboard closer. "Let me look on the system and see if we can't find out where it was last."

She began tapping away, her face slightly illuminated by the screen, her red lipstick glistening. While Anna busied herself, Tom took the opportunity to take in the surroundings behind her, desperately trying to maintain a composed exterior. The desk was full of cheap, corporate Christmas decorations. He loved Christmas but always hated the tackiness of businesses who were realistically only interested in the corporate profits to be made. It was as if the decorations were deployed as some form of smokescreen, a blatant masquerade on behalf of institutions such as Regency Airlines to cover their crass desirability for monetary gain during the festive season.

What immediately struck Tom was the sign, rimmed around the edges in silver tinsel. A yellow placard, with blue writing which read *'Regency Airlines: The only way to travel around the world quicker than Santa's sleigh.'* Not bloody likely Tom brooded.

He briefly inspected the crowd behind him, the disgruntled line now fifteen or so people deep. Tom's attention was drawn to a man who held a newspaper aloft, the front cover of which was exposed. The headline was unsurprising and mirrored the sentiments of the complimentary newspaper he had briefly skimmed through during his flight. 'DIVISIONS GROW AS GOVERNMENT WATCH ON FROM THEIR PARLIAMENTARY IVORY TOWER.' He had kept up to date with current affairs whilst on his travels, the international community fully aware of Britain's current financial and social predicaments. He returned his attention back towards the desk.

The tapping stopped. "Oh," Anna started bemused, drumming her chin slightly in a bemused fashion. Tom straightened, preparing himself for the worse. "That's unusual. It says on the system that the bag was checked in on your connecting flight from Singapore Mr. Hawkins. That being the case, no pun intended, it should be in baggage somewhere."

Anna picked up the phone headset built into her cubicle which was also blue and dialled a solitary number. She put the phone in the crook of her neck and looked up at Tom.

"I'll just ring down to the baggage team and see if they can't find your bag. Here's hoping," she added, crossing the fingers on her free hand, her nose wrinkling ever so slightly with her wide smile.

Tom reciprocated, crossing both his fingers, a regrettable gesture that he immediately rebuked himself for, having looked so immature.

"Hi, Regency Customer service desk here. I was just wondering if you could check on a bag for me. I have a Mr Hawkins here, first name Tom, who did not get his bag off of his flight." She paused listening to a question. She lifted Hawkins's boarding pass and scanned it before replying, "It was the 8.45 connecting flight from Singapore." Another pause 'Yes it was checked in on the flight. I checked the manifest. It's a black Samsonite case. It should have a luggage tab with his details."

Another break came in the conversation, reciprocated by another nod. "Ok, no problem." She turned the receiver into her shoulder and smiled at Hawkins.

"They're just going to have a look for you now Mr. Hawkins. Apparently, the plane had no luggage left on it but he's going to check the lost and found for any bags."

Tom desperately wanted to check his watch but did not want to appear rude, simply nodding. Two minutes or so passed. Anna was listening intently for a response. When it did come, Tom could tell from the look on her face that it was not good news.

"Ok, thank you. Please let me know if you find anything," she responded pleadingly before placing the phone back into its housing. She paused; head tilted down before she looked up.

"I'm sorry Mr. Hawkins but we are having some trouble locating your bag at the moment. The baggage team have looked and cannot seem to find it. Are you situated near the airport?"

Tom sighed and with both hands now on the desk, lowered his head for a few seconds. He looked up, "Yes, reasonably so. About thirty-five minutes away. So, there was no sign of it?"

"I'm afraid not sir," came Anna's genuine reply.

Tom stood slouched and dragged the palm of his hand down across his face. "So, what do we do now?" He asked, too tired to vent his anger, too tired to demand reparation.

"Well sir, I've logged your details and a description of your bag. Do you still reside at the address on your passport?" Anna queried.

"Oh… that's my old place; I'd don't live there anymore. I'm…" he cleared his throat. "I'm staying with my parents, temporarily, that's their address," Tom let slip, blushing slightly as he did so.

Anna smiled kindly, "Same here, London property prices hey. The nearest I'll ever get to owning a place of my own at this rate is playing Monopoly." She finished with a titter, her laughter intoxicating, dispelling any uneasiness.

"Anyway, I'll send a report to head office and we'll continue to search for your bag. I'll also get someone up in head office to contact Singapore Changi Airport and double check that they got things right on their end. If it has been placed on another flight, we should know within a day or two if it boarded the wrong flight. I really am sorry Mr Hawkins, I apologise on behalf of the airline. I'll do everything in my power to…"

Tom looked up and smiled wryly, "It's ok Anna," he replied, his strong London accent sincere. "You've been more than helpful. It's not your fault." Tom's statement made Anna feel a sense of relief, stoking her desire for him further.

"So where do we go from here?" he questioned.

Anna had to stop herself, briefly evaluating whether the wayward comment was a come on or not. *'He's a customer Anna!'*

She cleared her throat, "Well Mr Hawkins, the moment we hear any news we'll let you know. If we do indeed find your bag, we'll get a courier and forward it out to you, free of charge of course. I'll just need to take your temporary address and some other minor details."

Tom nodded and so began ten minutes of information sharing. He gave his parents' address, still slightly embarrassed at having to do so; he covered his tracks further by maintaining that it would just be for the Christmas period only. A lie, he was effectively homeless and his parents, of the many Christmases he had missed recently, would need his support this year more than any other.

Anna stopped typing. She looked up and smiled again. There was something very reassuring about that timid smile, Tom thought. He longed for female companionship. It had been so long since he had had a meaningful relationship, a bond external to that of family or his unit.

"Right Mr. Hawkins that should do it," she handed him back his passport and boarding pass. Her hand lingered as she did so. "I'll hold on to you no longer, it wouldn't be very festive of me," she smiled, a sad tenor to her voice.

"I really am sorry about this Mr. Hawkins, especially at this time of year. If you have any further questions or need to reference who you spoke to," she pulled out a Regency Airlines information pamphlet from behind the desk, letting go of his documents.

Tom's view was obscured but when she handed it back to him he noticed that she had scrawled her name across the top "Here's my name." She slid the pamphlet across the counter.

Tom picked it up, his hand quaking slightly. He read her clear and feminine penmanship, the name Anna Burrows clearly legible.

"Thanks Anna," he turned to leave and stopped abruptly. He had felt as though there had been chemistry between the two of them. He too had noticed that she had no ring on her finger. The overweight man behind him, fist on his hip looked at Hawkins impatiently and raised an eyebrow. He ignored him and turned back, Anna looking up expectantly, happy to see him once again.

"Look, Anna. I know this may seem a bit forward," he leaned on the desk lowering his voice "but..." he paused; he could hear his heartbeat in his ears. His hands had become clammy, "I was wondering... if you were free sometime, after Christmas of course. If you may like to..."

He had come too far to fall at the final hurdle now. He stopped. He had sworn to himself that his new life would be different upon his return, a fresh start, one that could only be attained with his departure from the Armed Forces. He would be different, seize upon every opportunity. The Army had provided him with a daily insight into the futility of man, a perspective he intended to maintain now in the doldrums of daily life. Life and death were not one and the same; they were exclusive, devoid of one another. He chose to live; he owed himself and his family that.

"Erm if you'd like to..." He rubbed the back of his neck, coy and nervous.

Anna leaned forward ever so slightly, sultry in her movements yet not so much as to alert anyone external to their conversation. She could see his difficulty in constructing his thoughts, a twinkle in her eyes.

"My number's on the back of the card for just such an occasion, Mr Hawkins," and with that came another intoxicating smile.

A wave of happiness and masculine bravado came over Tom momentarily. He returned the smile, feeling as though he should say something charming.

"Well," he remarked, "You'll be glad to know I carry very little baggage."

Anna giggled, covering her mouth so as not to alert the impatient customers behind Hawkins of her unprofessionalism. She straightened the blouse of her uniform and cleared her throat gently, brushing back the stray hair that had once again loosened itself. Tom grinned; thankful his attempt at humour had hit its mark.

"Oh," Hawkins suddenly remembered, "My name is Thomas by the way...well," he laughed, still feeling rather embarrassed, "Tom, Tom Hawkins." He resisted the urge to state his name like some form of suave James Bond. He had only narrowly escaped his previous joke.

"I know," Anna beamed, relishing Tom's brief, perplexed appearance. "Your passport," she giggled pointing towards his travel documents.

Tom smacked his head playfully, "It's decided! I'm definitely going to have to go through anything to declare now; I think I need to declare myself an idiot."

Another inebriating titter emanated from Anna, her professional facade once again slipping.

"We'll just chalk it up to jetlag, shall we? Keep in touch Mr. Hawkins,' she said, the business-like tone slightly returning yet still steeped in playfulness.

"Here's hoping," Tom countered.

With that he smiled, tapped his burgundy British passport upon the desk and turned on his heel. It didn't take long for the plump man behind him in the queue to launch into a diatribe about baggage allowance costs.

CHAPTER TWO: THE BRIEFING

A disgruntled Gerry Taverner entered the stuffy room with an exasperated look upon his features, closing the heavyset door behind him in a fluid and singular movement. He paused, pressing his back against the cool, varnished wood and heaved a sigh of relief, glad to have distanced himself from the pompous entourage of advisers and assistants that bustled on the opposing side of the door.

The ornate room, although lavishly decorated and furnished, was small and claustrophobic. The entirety of the left-hand wall of the room was occupied by a floor to ceiling bookshelf. The shelves were lined with a broad range of literature which Gerry concluded, were most likely present for decorative proposes as opposed to serving in any functional capacity. The back of the room held a mahogany cabinet, a range of tea and coffee making equipment lining the top of the lavish unit. Two of Gerry's team stood either side of the cabinet; a playful football related debate could just be overheard, both heavyset gentlemen looking rather out of place cradling delicate bone china teacups.

The centre of the room held a hefty, circular mahogany table which was currently occupied by the other three members in Gerry's team, two of which were playing cards, the remaining member, Jack Wright, obscured by a tabloid newspaper. Both his highly polished shoes straddled an adjacent chair, his posture relaxed.

"He's already getting on my bloody tits and we've only just started," Gerry proclaimed, wiping sweat from his brow, sweat that had largely accumulated within the last ten minutes. He removed his grey suit jacket and placed it upon the back of the chair Jack rested his feet upon.

'Big mistake on the shirt front,' Gerry mused, catching his reflection in the full-length mirror that sat propped up against the wall adjacent to the bookshelf. His light blue shirt had succumbed to the onslaught of perspiration that the last three hours, a close emphasis on the last ten minutes, had inflicted upon him. He lifted his arms above his head inspecting the darkened sweat patches under his armpits before tilting ever so slightly, arching his back to catch a glimpse at the damage. That was peppered with sweat also.

Coincidently, it had also been just ten minutes ago that he had left for his meeting with the principle, a term given to a primary client or employer in need of Gerry and his team's specialist skillsets, namely that of protection. On previous assignments, both the public and employers who had enlisted his services such as foreign dignitaries and celebrities of varying statuses oversimplified Gerry's chosen profession, arrogantly equating his line of work with being that of a bodyguard.

There was however, so much more to his job than just standing in front of a principle or VIP. He had trained hard to be where he was today and felt that such a term was derogatory, discourteous. It had been a hard-earned position, a position that relied largely upon reputation and his ability to conduct himself in a manner which satisfied him and his client, his professional conduct and track history of great importance both to him and any future career prospects. Clients often proved difficult, uncooperative and unpredictable which when it came to Gerry's line of work, complicated matters significantly. No more was this evident than with that of his current employer.

"I'm guessing he took our advice on board one hundred and ten percent then," Jack countered, the query heavily laden with sarcasm.

"Did he fuck, why break a habit of a lifetime, hey?" Gerry sighed, kneading his forehead. "The protection detail is a go gentleman. Nothing changes. We're here to do our job the best we can and if he doesn't like that, well he can go and bloody sing," Gerry abruptly summarised.

"Or cop a bullet" Jack jived. "God knows there are plenty of people out there with him firmly in their sights...half of them are in this bloody paper."

For the first time, Gerry caught the headline emblazoned in bold letters across the front page of Jack's newspaper. No photo accompanied the text and with a headline like that, there was no need. 'DIVISIONS GROW AS GOVERNMENT WATCH ON FROM THEIR PARLIAMENTARY IVORY TOWER'.

A mob of rowdy demonstrators had taken up permanent residence for the past three weeks in Parliament Square, the space reduced to that of a ramshackle maze of tents and placards festooned with various imagery and incendiary sentiments. What made matters worse was the oversaturation of news coverage, with the entirety of the left and a large swathe of the right-wing media, echoing the sentiments of those who camped out on the green. The tension in the air had been palpable, the news crews making sure to capture any and all signs of unrest, of which there had been plenty. Extra police officers had been posted to the area, a precaution that only served to provoke the demonstrators further; their presence regarded by many as yet another show of force orchestrated by the current, totalitarian regime.

Gerry laughed to himself. The Whitehall elite were watching on alright. The principle had himself been watching the protests on a large television screen when he had entered his office. In fact, he had been so immersed in the current news report, a feature detailing a protest that was currently taking place at Canary Wharf, that he did not notice Gerry as he was ushered into the room by a personal assistant.

The information bar at the foot of the news report had established that over four thousand people were present at the protest of which had largely been orchestrated by various social networking sites. Before Gerry had cleared his throat to attract the attention of the Prime Minister, he caught a man being interviewed by a reporter on the news network.

He was dressed in a black pinstriped suit, complete with vintage umbrella, briefcase and a bowler hat, which sat at a jaunty angle. Though he replicated a banker from a bygone era, he looked rather out of place in front of the imposing skyscrapers of Canary Wharf. While the contemporary glass and steel structures dwarfed the demonstrators, the legitimacy of their message was bolstered somewhat by the humongous structures, the grandiose architecture serving as symbolic testaments as to what could be accomplished with money, with capitalism. It was after all the heartbeat of the financial sector, a statement paradoxical in nature as the buildings that cocooned the protestors on all sides, as impressive as they were; seemed lifeless and cold.

The man on the television seemed rather animated and irate as he raised his briefcase and pushed it towards the camera. The side of his briefcase bore an all too familiar message, the writing scrawled in red paint in an effort to simulate blood. The epitaph read, *'Prosperity favours the rich. Humanity cannot be taxed or bought. R.I.P. Government'*.

Gerry cleared his throat. The Prime Minister flinched slightly, startled from his mesmerised state. He finally caught Gerry's eye, a toxic hue to his stare. The Prime Minister's body stiffened ever so slightly. He turned and placed his arms behind his back, puffing out his chest slightly. He seemed to be reasserting his dominance, afraid that someone outside of his political party had seen his true face, the theatrical façade of optimism slipping slightly. A face in which he had so repugnantly paraded to the cameras and journalists for quite some time now, prostituting himself to the media, seeking the nation's affection time and time again.

"Mr Taverner take a seat," he said, indicating to a nearby chair with a nod of his head, hands still clasped behind his back. The statement came across as more of an order than that of a gratuitous sentiment.

"Thank you, Mr Prime Minister," Gerry responded.

He made his way to a red, leather backed chair and sat down. He unclasped the button upon his blazer, making himself as comfortable as the impending conversation would allow. Many others would be nervous within this sort of situation, sat before one of the most powerful men in Britain. However, Gerry had been sat on the adjacent side of many a familiar desk in his time; the only thing that seemed to change was the person that occupied the other side of the desk.

"Before we start Mr Taverner, I wish to make one thing abundantly clear. Like myself, I know you have a job to do. A job with a great level of importance, namely protecting myself," the Prime Minister stated in an unvarnished and sobering tone.

Gerry pre-empted what came next. He had become an expert in debunking the self-inflated, political jargon of which he had been frequently subjected to many times before. The Prime Minister moved across the room now, the desk now between the two men. He remained standing, his hands firmly clutched behind his back, chest still puffed out. His head was held slightly aloft, so much so that it appeared to Gerry that he was almost looking down upon him over his wired rimmed glasses.

"I, as I am sure you are aware, am under significant media scrutiny at present. Many within the media and the general public do not think I have the stomach for this job. They think that I am hiding away, neglecting my duties, my itinerary."

It was true. As of late, the Prime Minister had needed to re-arrange and even cancel some of his state visits and meetings largely due to the ever-increasing death threats that he had been receiving, as well as the mass protests across the country. It seemed wherever he went at present, no matter the scale of the function or appointment, there waiting when he arrived, were angry mobs, placards held aloft.

It had only been last week that Gerry, whilst in charge of co-ordinating and leading the Prime Ministers protection detail, had advised that the Prime Minister not attend a local market whilst out campaigning over issues surrounding the economy. To the public, the Prime Minister and his cabinet were seemingly incapable of instigating any worthwhile policy that resulted in anything other than the taxation or ceasing of benefits, the people of Britain taking the burden of the nation's debt solely upon their shoulders.

It had been an impromptu effort on behalf of the Prime Ministers, wanting to be seen supporting independent business, his change of heart occurring whilst in transit to another engagement, the change in schedule most likely proposed by his moronic aide. Jeremy Grant was a bloated man with an even greater regard for his service to the Prime Minister than that of his waistline. Gerry had adamantly advised that this was not an advisable detour, he and the unit not being able to assess the area or recce it prior to his arrival. The Prime Minister had declined his advice outright, demanding that Gerry and his team execute his wishes. What ensued was an incident that Gerry, overcautious as ever, would not soon live down.

(CHAPTER BREAK)

The Prime Minister, accompanied by the close protection team headed up by Gerry, had arrived at the market in Oxfordshire. Upon Gerry's first initial inspection, his fears were instantly justified. The market was a myriad of intricate stalls, scattered in an irregular fashion. The place was a maze and what made it all the more concerning, were the avenues between the stalls which seemed to follow a one-way system. The market was busy, heaving with causal shoppers. If anything were to happen, the constant throng of people surging in one direction may present issues to the safety of the principle, all the more so if panic ensued.

Gerry established with the rest of the team that they would be taking a low- key, overt approach. This meant that although the men were armed, they would not brandish their weapons opting instead for maintaining a tight perimeter around the Prime Minister. They were there to be seen, a presence, yet they did not want to unintentionally come across as too heavy handed.

The Prime Minister, in true character, had once again established his protestations. Gerry had ensured him that it was the safest approach, an approach that both guaranteed his safety as well as allowing him to maintain the façade of appearing comfortable and undeterred amongst the crowd.

'A man of the people,' Gerry cynically considered.

The team had approached the market, instantaneously engulfed by people on all sides. They had attracted the attention of the crowd, many of whom the close protection team kept at bay. They kept a closed box formation around the Prime Minister, a rehearsed position where the Prime Minister was encased in a box shape by Gerry and his men. Each member of the six-man team made up a corner of the box respectively; with Gerry offering further protection at the Prime Ministers shoulder, Jack Wright waiting in the car. Gerry was there as both a deterrent and as body cover, should he have to intercept an oncoming threat such as a potential knife or gun attack. This formation not only allowed the team to surround the Prime Minister on all sides but it also afforded them a three hundred and sixty degree angle of the market.

The team were alert to the potential threat of a breakaway assailant, the likes of which these kinds of situations bred. All it took was a split second, a lapse in concentration and the Prime Minister could be assaulted or worse, fatally wounded. Gerry kept in constant radio contact with his team. He had a transparent earpiece that relayed audio to the rest of the team. The headpiece travelled from his ear and down his sleeve, to a presell pad, which Gerry and the team clicked to open communication with one another. Concealed inside the collar of his suit jacket was the miniature microphone that he relayed his orders from, the device hidden and obscured.

Gerry like many before him, often had to resist the temptation of lifting the collar to his mouth for better audio, the constant fear that his team may not be able to make out his orders, especially in a loud environment, ever-present. This however was a massive mistake. A man talking into his suit lapels or a shirt collar would undoubtedly raise suspicion within the average passer- by, never mind a trained insurgent or assailant. To an expert in the field, trained in intelligence gathering and surveillance, this was as good as an alarm bell, an indicator that they were being surveyed by undercover operatives.

A chorus of camera flashes began to illuminate the Prime Minister and those surrounding him. The press had always made Gerry uneasy; his previous career in the Special Air Service had been dependent upon him keeping his identity a secret, being an omnipotent, faceless operative that could blend into any crowd. Old habits die hard, habits which he carried with him into his current occupation, the desire at not having his face plastered over the cover of some tabloid rag, still of high personal priority.

Moreover, assailants often preferred to hide in plain sight, blending into the crowd. The prestige and access a journalist was afforded provided the perfect cover. The right forged credentials could afford them admittance to areas that general members of the public were not made privy to. A muzzle flash could easily be disclosed by the blinding bombardment of camera flashes, rendering the location and identity of the shooter unknown, the panicked crowds concealing the assassin further, their getaway made all the more viable.

The paparazzi were quick to respond to the photo opportunity and were on the scene within minutes. It had always surprised Gerry how fast, no matter how sudden the change in the Prime Ministers itinerary, that the press were on the scene. They had been alerted of course, Grant never missing an opportunity to garner free publicity.

The Prime Minister had stopped at a stall where he had engaged in a discussion with a local stall owner specialising in cooked meats and conserves. He offered the Prime Minister a sampler of some meat unknown to Gerry or his palate, which the Prime Minister gratefully accepted and tasted. Gerry mentally cursed the Prime Minister. He had specifically told the Prime Minister en route to the market not to sample any food or drink offered in case of foul play, the possibility of the food being tampered with a stark possibility.

It had been at this point that the man behind the stall went to shake the Prime Minister's hand. The Prime Minister reciprocated, leaning further into the stall. The man held his outstretched hand for a substantial amount of time, the length of which unnerved Gerry. He informed his team of a potential situation via his mic.

The stall owner, still holding the Prime Ministers hand in his, began to question Pierce on his parties' latest reforms to the Healthcare system; a set of unpopular reforms that had seen massive cuts to the National Health Service, its staff and the services targeted, bearing most of the financial burden. Gerry reached for the baton attached to his belt, pre-empting the scenario of having to direct it forcefully at the man's wrist, thus breaking his hold upon the principle.

The metallic baton was telescopic and with a flick of the wrist, could be extended to its full length, around thirty centimetres. This was and always had been Gerry's first line of defence when it came to the public. A drawn firearm in the public eye could cause no end of problems for the men as well as the principle and was never the preferred strategy. The unwarranted brandishing of a gun, whether serving as a deterrent or not, could result in a loss of faith within the public, worse still, it heightened the chance of a weapon being discharged accidentally, a case befalling many an efficient, well-trained man in the past.

The stalls proprietor was currently mentioning something about his Mother and his inability in being able to find her a suitable hospital. The rural area with its local hospital could not cater for her needs, his line of questioning now becoming quite stern. The camera's continued to flash. Gerry observed the Prime Minister trying to withdraw his grip somewhat. He was nodding along to the man's line of questioning, feigning interest, yet slowly trying to slip his hand from the clasped hands of the stall owner. The mood was beginning to turn rather sour.

Someone off to the side of the stall shouted, 'Stick your reforms up your arse, you elitist pig. Good luck finding a local hospital to treat that', which received many a cheer, a wave of raucous laughter reverberating throughout the crowd.

Inquisitive patrons of the market started to surge towards the periphery of the crowd. The people were no longer moving along the stalls but had instead taken to forming a circle around the envoy. Gerry took a step closer towards the stall owner and the principle. In an authoritative voice, which exhibited his thick Sunderland accent, he calmly asserted, "Let go of the Prime Minister now, sir."

As he did so he slowly moved his suit blazer away from his belt in an effort to show the man that he was carrying a weapon. At the same time, he stepped closer to the stall, instinctively stepping in front of the Prime Minister. The stall owner looked petrified and instinctively dropped the Prime Ministers hand, shaking his head quickly from side to side in a display of innocence, accentuating his lack of desire in wanting to bring any harm to the Prime Minister.

The man, now devoid of colour in his face looked from Gerry to the Prime Minister, "I'm sorry, I was just asking a question," he turned to face the Prime Minister. "No harm intended. It's just my Mother, she's really sick and I don't know what to..."

Gerry, slightly alarmed by the man's panicked state stepped ever closer to the man. He could practically hear the man's heartbeat racing. The Prime Minister shot Gerry a scathing glance, one that displayed utter disgust at what he believed to be an excessive display of force. The Prime Minister turned back to the terrified man before him.

"That's quite alright," the Prime Minister calmly responded.

It had taken Gerry aback ever so slightly. It had seemed quite sincere, a trait that Gerry believed the Prime Minister lacked in his character. After all, here stood a man that had ruthlessly cut financial swathes throughout the public sector without mercy. He knew he should not let his own personal opinion compromise his judgement of the principle but this man was a heartless bastard.

The Prime Minister continued. "We all get passionate about those we care about. Let me be the first to assure you Mr...?" His voice trailed off in a questioning tone.

"Kevin... Kevin Aylesbrook Mr Prime Minister," he blurted out.

Kevin, it seemed, had calmed down significantly. He was no longer shaking and had opted to look at the Prime Minister instead of Gerry. That said, Gerry noticed that his eyes, every once in a while, would flit back to the unobscured baton attached to his belt.

"Well, Mr Aylesbrook, let me be the first to personally assure you that, your Mother, regardless of her condition and geographical location, will be afforded no less care than a person within closer proximity to the hospital. There are various schemes, many of which my party and I are looking into at present that I guarantee you..."

He was halfway through his sentence when a severe crack rang out. Gerry immediately shielded the Prime Minister and brought his full, all-encompassing body weight across the Prime Minister. The Prime Minister tried to protest but Gerry knew he was scared, his body had gone taut and a low shiver had surfaced. He knew the feeling all too well, that delicate, hybridised mixture of fear and adrenaline coursing through your veins. The only difference between Gerry and the Prime Minister at that precise moment in time was that Gerry had signed up for just such a feeling.

Gerry's men had closed defensively around the Prime Minister, creating a cocoon. They had now withdrawn the MP5 Kurz sub-machine guns that they had been carrying all the while concealed under their suit jackets. The German made gun was renowned amongst Special Forces across the world, especially in that of Europe. Kurz, meaning 'short' in German, was a modification on the HK MP5, which was a longer barrelled weapon. This particular model was a thirty- round, lightweight sub-machine gun and when held under the lining of a suit jacket upon a strap, was practically undetectable to the untrained eye and many a trained one also.

The men provided cover whilst Gerry, his Glock pistol now drawn, negotiated the Prime Minister away from the stall and towards their vehicle convoy. All the while he communicated with his men and the getaway vehicle, the engine of which had never stopped running.

"Charlie three to Charlie one, we are foxtrot. Potential engagement. Proceeding to the RV," he sharply barked.

To the uneducated ear of those within the market, who themselves had heard the noise and had reacted with surprising speed; the orders issued by Gerry were unfathomable. However, to the team around him and the final team member in the car, Charlie One as Jack Wright had been codenamed, it was crystal clear. Gerry, codenamed Charlie three, led the principle towards the vehicle or foxtrot as it was known for short, the remaining team members covering their exit.

The car, along with the two other support vehicles in the convoy, had positioned themselves to the side of the market, which Gerry had earlier identified as being the clearest exit as it was unoccupied by stalls and consisted of an area where rubbish was stored. The area was deserted and was consequently designated as their chosen rendezvous point.

From the RV, Gerry and the Prime Minister would then proceed to the ERV or Emergency Rendezvous point, three and a half miles away, in a closed off and concealed area of woodland Gerry had spotted on their way to the Market. Here they would wait for the rest of the team to meet up with them after they had secured the area at the market and had terminated any known threats. Their job, first and foremost, was to cover Charlie One's exit and ensure that they were not pursued.

When they reached the car, a black Jaguar X type, Gerry bundled the Prime Minister into the back seat of the leather interior and sprawled himself over the Prime Ministers upper torso with the Prime Minister practically in the foot well. As soon as Gerry closed the door, Jack Wright sped off. Jack was the best driver in the team and had proved himself not just on the test track but during previous scraps the team had found themselves in. Jack or 'Wright turn' as he was known in the team due to his ability to turn a corner at high speed with an unnatural accuracy, did not speak; instead, he concentrated on the task at hand, the road ahead. The car dashboard, which was also connected to the coded radio, allowed Gerry to listen to the chatter as the remaining members of the close protection team methodically secured the market.

"Get off of me you idiot," the Prime Minister spat.

Gerry, engrossed in the radio, had not registered that he was still atop of the Prime Minister. He instinctively slid off the Prime Minister and settled into the passenger seat beside him. The Prime Minister crawled up out of the foot well, his face and neck crimson from the rush of blood to the head at having been thrust downwards.

The Prime Minister readjusted his well-tailored suit, unclasping his buttoned-up jacket. His regular and immaculate slicked back hair was now sticking up precariously in several places. He caught sight of himself in the rear-view mirror. He smoothed his hair down fiercely as he looked intensely into the mirror, always concerned about his appearance, his vanity sickening Gerry further. The Prime Minister caught Jack's eye line in the rear-view mirror and fixed upon his gaze. Jack instinctively diverted his view.

Gerry glanced cautiously out of the back window. They were not being followed. He faced forward, still catching his breath.

"Can someone tell me what that was all about?" the Prime Minister insistently barked, trying to regain authority. His voice betrayed him however, his voice still shaken.

"We'll know more once we've done a full sweep and contained the market Mr Prime Minister but we believe a shot was fired," Gerry stated plainly.

"A shot? There was no gunshot you bloody moron. The most dangerous thing in that market was the risk of salmonella." The Prime Minister was irate now. His chin flecked with spittle, his head still crimson.

"As I said sir," Gerry replied in a more assertive manner, "We'll know more when we regroup with the team at the ERV." He diverted his attention, leaning over the driver's seat slightly. "Jack get on the radio to the team and see what's going on," Jack nodded and picked up the radio from the dash.

"Mr Prime Minister, I need to check you for any injuries, can you please remove your suit jacket."

This had become standard procedure when protecting a high-value target. In 1981, President Ronald Regan had been involved in an assassination attempt carried out by a lone gunman. He had just finished a speech to a group of trade unionists at the National Conference of Building and Construction Trades Department, when upon exiting the conference via a side door, six shots from a .22 calibre revolver, had been fired.

The President had been immediately bundled into the back seat of the Presidential limousine by the secret service. He had not noticed at first that he had been shot; initially thinking that he had broken a rib when he had been shoved into the limousines back seat.

However, when he began coughing up blood, such thoughts were cast aside. A round had made its way through, regardless of the best efforts of the secret service, with one member, Tim McCarthy who had shielded the president, being hit in the abdomen. The bullet, which had ricocheted off of the highly armoured vehicle, had entered just under Regan's left arm, entering his torso and narrowly missing his heart. Luckily for Regan and the American public he had survived but by sheer luck alone.

Gerry had reviewed the footage repeatedly for both practical and training purposes, as had many others within protection agencies across the world. If the Prime Minister had been hit unknowingly, the quicker he could establish this, the better. The Prime Ministers features distorted in a macabre fashion. He seemed disgusted at the proposition.

"Excuse me! You are not touching me you cretin. Do you have any idea how bad this is going to make me look? How weak this is going to make me appear? The press are going to have a field day with this."

"Sir, the press are of no concern of mine, your wellbeing and safety is my only…" Gerry was not allowed to finish.

The Prime Minister, flustered and with wild, grasping hands, pulled his jacket flaps up and over his head, rotating so that Gerry could get a good look at his pristine white shirt. The movement of his giddy arms moving in an arc displayed a pure loss of control. The adrenaline was getting to him. He was in mild shock.

"See, see!" He shot round and looked at Gerry intensely, still holding his blazer aloft.

Gerry diverted his eyes away from the Prime Minister's contemptuous, gaping eyes and analysed his torso. No blood splatter. Gerry returned to Jack in an effort to change the subject. As he did so he re-holstered his Glock, adjusting his own suit jacket. He had heard the transmission from the team and knew that they were not far behind but he desperately wanted to change the subject.

"How far out?" Gerry fixed his eyes upon the rear-view mirror, meeting Jacks stare, he seemed anxious.

"ETA is three minutes. The team identified no assailant at the site." He paused, briefly checking the road before him. He once again met Gerry's gaze in the rear-view mirror for what he was about to say. Gerry had not picked up on the last bit of the transmission as he had been transfixed by the Prime Ministers gaze.

Jack cleared his throat. "All signs at the scene point to a car backfiring sir. No assailant found. Quick inspection by the team before exfil found no shell casings or evidence of foul play."

Gerry lowered his head slightly. He could feel the eyes of the Prime Minister boring into the back of his skull. He waited in anticipation for the haranguing he was about to receive.

"A car backfired! You manhandled me through a busy crowd of potential voters because a car backfired," Gerry made an effort to speak. "No," the Prime Ministers unrelenting tone rattled on. "I am going to write a full report on this. You and your team have done nothing but hinder me as of late and this is final proof of your incompetence. The camel's back is well and truly broken. You're done; your team along with you are finished."

(CHAPTER BREAK)

The Prime Minister threw the brown file onto the desk. He pointed with his index finger at the document with a thrusting flourish of pure maliciousness. Gerry returned to his original train of thought not looking at the dossier in front of him but rather at the finger of the Prime Minister. How easily he could snap it in two.

"In that folder, effectively, are you and your unit's unconditional resignation papers. I have already insisted that you not be assigned to my detail again, after tomorrow's visit that is. The new team assigned with my protection will arrive the day after next and as much as I would quite frankly like you and your men out of my sight at the quickest available convenience, this it has been brought to my attention, is not possible."

Gerry met the Prime Ministers gaze, his features remained neutral. It had taken all the resolve he had to bury the anger he was currently feeling. It was almost as if the Prime Minister had picked up on this, as after three seconds he retracted his finger.

"Permission to speak freely, sir?" Gerry inquired, the anger rising in his chest.

The Prime Minister turned back towards the Window. "What makes you think I have any desire to listen to what you and that bunch of miscreants have to say? You will ensure that my visit tomorrow goes as smoothly as possible. Then as soon as I step foot back in this building, you will be dismissed, permanently."

"Hold that thought, I'll tell you what," he stated with false enthusiasm, "let's practice ahead of tomorrow shall we? Just so you don't cock that up too. You are dismissed'. He continued to look out of the window.

Gerry made to leave then stopped, standing his ground for several seconds. The coward did not even look at him, his masculine front a façade just like the rest of him. Gerry rounded and walked towards the door. He pulled the door open, looking down the corridor. Freedom. He made to leave.

"Oh and Taverner," Gerry stopped at the door and twisted, the anger in his throat now.

"Yes, Mr Prime Minister," the detest in his voice palpable now.

The Prime Minister twisted his head slightly away from the window. "Try not to step on any crisp packets in the shopping centre tomorrow. We wouldn't want you mistaking a bag of salt and vinegar for a full out assault, now would we?" He smiled, looking sideways, holding his stance.

Gerry clenched his fists. He had to play the loyal house dog and it repulsed him. Men like Pierce knew that. Gerry was effectively chained and muzzled, unable to lash out, Pierce firmly holding the chain. Pierce hid behind that hierarchy, using it to facilitate his own lack of masculinity. Gerry felt his skin crawl; he despised the man before him. Not for this moment, nor for the moment at the market. No, he hated him because he was single handidly bringing this country to its knees. A country Gerry loved. A country he had been willing to lay his life on the line for. What did this man know about the true world outside of these four walls? He was a spoilt, privately educated, political time bomb waiting to implode. He was a socio/political hermit, out of touch with the very problems that stood upon his very doorstep.

Gerry bit down hard, swallowing his rage, "Yes sir."

With that he turned and closed the door, walking back towards the safe confines of the room and his team ahead. Real men, men who would sacrifice their lives for the very man that ensured that they were continued to be paid low wages, separated from loved ones and poorly equipped in some far-flung hellhole in the world.

Men who knew true struggle, men that had tasted desperation, a taste which still lingered in the mouth of many a veteran. He reluctantly decided that he would keep the news of their approaching unemployment until after the mission was complete. The last thing his men needed now was that distraction. They would fall in line, take orders and persevere. After all, was that not what all soldiers did? Fell in line for the greater good.

CHAPTER THREE: HOMECOMING

Brian Hawkins awaited the arrival of his son with a boyish glee, his eyes never leaving the automatic glass doors before him. He surveyed the glut of passengers as they exited Customs, their tired and forlorn trudge a complete juxtaposition to that of the festive decorations that adorned the Arrivals court. He drummed his fingers upon the metallic barrier draped in tinsel, his son's lengthy delay only serving to bolster his excitement at finally being reunited with his son.

The state of affairs in which he had last seen his son had been far from ideal. Brian along with Tom's Mother Pam had come a long way since those dark days, the funeral of their youngest son Anthony taking a significant toll upon the family. Brian looked down at the tinsel barrier and coiled an end around his thumb and forefinger. His thoughts as they often did so began to turn morose. He played over the conversation he and his wife had had before he had left to collect Tom all those hours ago. Pam had been in a fevered state of preparation, ready to venture out to the shops one final time for last minute supplies before the big day.

Tom's arrival home had changed his wife's demeanour markedly for the better, a sense of maternal purpose doing her the world of good. They had both discussed the importance of regaining a sense of normality, the past year having been especially turbulent for Tom. With his dramatic change in vocation eleven months ago, Tom had decided to go travelling with some friends, with the money he had saved over the years. A trip that both Brian and Pam had wholeheartedly endorsed, although were at first taken aback with. What with Tom's previous career, they had assumed that he would be reluctant to travel again so soon, let alone as far as New Zealand and Australia

Tom was a huge Rugby fan and if possible had stated that he wished to catch an All Blacks game regardless of the fact that he was a staunch England supporter. *'Sussing out the competition for the summer series'* he had joked with his Father before leaving. Brian had missed his son greatly but both welcomed and understood the reasoning behind his son's impromptu expedition. Brian wholeheartedly bought into the philosophy that travel broadened the mind. It afforded the unique privilege of perspective, even the briefest periods of time allowing one to assess and garner a new appreciation for what they had left behind, both mentally and figuratively.

Brian had come from humble beginnings and had always invested in his two sons a deep sense of work ethic and self-worth. Originating from the London borough of Hackney, Brian who had been born in 1953 had himself had a very loving and enjoyable upbringing unlike many others upon his estate, post-war Britain along with its rationing and loss of life, still a visible scar upon his community.

His father, Anthony Hawkins, an ex- serviceman who had fought in the Second World War was a stern yet fair man, rare of the time. He showered Brian, his Brother Arthur and his two sisters Florence and Ellen with affection and more than made up for what he and his family did not have, with his kind natured disposition. His mother, Eileen who stayed at home to maintain the household and ensure the children were clothed, fed and watered, worked tirelessly and like many at the time, was extremely devoted and house proud. They had lived in a small yet bright tenement house upon the second floor, the building housing five other families.

Brian idolised his father immensely and often pestered him when he was younger, curious to know about his service during the war. His Father could not fathom why Brian took such an interest. As he saw it, he had just being doing his duty like millions of other men had. His Father was steadfastly humble and as Brian often concluded when describing his Father's character, had the uncanny ability to appear humble when being humble.

It had all began around the age of seven, when he began to become increasingly aware of his Fathers service within the war. Many a time he sat by his Father's armchair, asking him to regale him with stories of far-off lands and adventure. His father had served in the Army, posted in North Africa during the height of fighting against Rommel's forces in the desert. His father would often tell him abridged versions of stories and events within the war, masking what Brian would later discover for himself to be the true face of war.

He remembered once, when he was eleven, sitting opposite his father on a hard backed wooden chair. He had asked his father a simple question, one fuelled by the inquisitive nature of a young boy.

'How many Germans did you kill Dad?'

He remembered his Fathers reaction to this day. His Father had been sitting in his armchair by the fire, the afternoon paper draped across his lap. A look of sadness which Brian later recognised via hindsight to be a look of shame, washed over his features. His father simply cleared his throat, stood up and left the room. When he returned, nearly an hour later, he ruffled Brian's hair and settled back into his chair with his newspaper, turning the wireless on. It was not until Tom had asked Brian that same question over thirty years later that he truly emphasised with his Father.

When Brian was seventeen, he had decided that he himself, like his father, would like to enlist within the Army. It would take him a further two years to bolster up the courage to act upon his decision. He remembered the argument clearly that they had had on the night he told his Father and Mother that he had enlisted. Brian, then Nineteen and an apprentice butcher alongside his Father, knew that this news would come as a shock with regards to the plans his Father had intentionally laid out for him.

His father, who had saved what little he could to support the household after expenses, maintained that with their joint salaries and some graft, they could both invest in and open their very own family butchers. 'Hawkins and Son Family Butchers' he would often remark, his voice laden with hope and determination. It was his intention that they would train up Arthur also when he came of age.

Brian had promised his Father that he was only to be enlisted for a compulsory fixed term of six years and after that, once the itch had truly been scratched, he would return to establish the business. This eased his Fathers dismay ever so slightly but as he had remarked at the time, 'A lot can happen in the world in Six years'.

As ever, his Father's sage words rang true and Brian would in fact serve in the Army for a sum total of Eighteen years. A service which brought him much in the way of adventure and discipline yet left him with feelings of intense guilt, largely due to his abandonment of his Father's dream. His Father realised his dream before he died sixteen years after Brian had enlisted, however with his Brother Arthur instead.

Brian had carried that same guilt with him for year's right up until the very day that his first-born son stood before him and Pam and established that he too wanted to enlist. It had been at that very moment that Brian felt the pain and worry that his father must too have felt.

Brian was now the same age that his Father had been when he had died and he felt every one of those years laden upon his shoulders, the death of his youngest son having aged him considerably. Brian was a healthy man; he had always maintained his fitness and he looked remarkably youthful both in his features and physique. He made it part of his daily routine to walk every day, alternating his routes every other day, old habits dying hard, habits that had been ingrained in him from his military service.

Whilst serving in Northern Ireland during the Troubles and on his first assignment as the newly appointed Corporal of his platoon, he had been given a piece of advice from one of the intelligence officers on hand. He made sure to heed the advice; the end of his six year stint in the Army was to be extended, the familiarity of home and his Father's wishes falling by the wayside. Spurred on by the prospect of Platoon Corporal, the rapport he had with his men and the love for the career, he decided to proceed with a life in the Armed forces.

That said, the advice he had received upon starting his new post had done little to ease his decision. The Chief Intelligence Officer, Mike Garrick, had stated upon his arrival that to survive the Guerrilla warfare that would ensue under his watch; he would have to abandon any and all forms of routine for the personal safety of both his men and himself.

Garrick, who would have been about Brian's current age back then, was a short, overweight man, who had been balding severely. His cheeks always looked flustered and ruddy which to the unobserved eye gave him quite a jovial disposition. He was well liked both within the regiment and the Royal Ulster Constabulary. Many saw him as a fount of all knowledge, a man always happy to impart wisdom upon you, especially after a few whiskeys, a good many in Garrick's case.

However to Brian, the main feature that distinguished him from being jovial in the slightest was his eyes. When Brian looked into them, he did not see the reassurance of an older man bestowing his wisdom upon a man his minor. No, he saw within those grey eyes a dedicated resolve tempered by weary sadness. Garrick, who was a strict Protestant, had little allegiance to either side in the conflict. He was a proud patriot that strived to distance himself from the socio, historical and political background of Ireland. All he truly wanted was an end to the whole thing. He loved his country dearly but was quite frankly tired of the violence. The need to remain ever watchful, regardless of your surroundings, had taken its toll. His words still rang true to this day and whenever Brian mused over them, usually when getting the daily newspaper or out on one of his walks, he reminisced, the words coming back to him in that thick Belfast accent.

"The one thing that'll surely get you killed out here within an instant laddie is routine. Routine is only the friend of your enemy. Simple day to day actions like going out for the paper at the same time, to the same shop every morning or leaving for work at a regimented time, will make the enemy privy to your movements and schedule. The minute your schedule is made apparent to them, all it takes is a hit squad to plant an IED on your vehicle or organise an assassination attempt when you're at your most vulnerable. And do you know when that is?" Brian remembered that he had shaken his head at the time, transfixed by the man before him.

"Well let me tell you. It's when you're carrying out a day-to-day mundane task, away with the fairies. When something as simple as buying a newspaper, can turn out to be the biggest mistake of your life and most likely it'll be the last one at that. Remember, routine and familiarity only helps you to arrive on time to one place, the undertaker."

Garrick had died three years later. It turned out that he had frequented one local Protestant drinking establishment too many times. In his drunken stupor, on his short walk home, a walk he had traipsed a thousand times, he had had little chance against the four IRA members that had pulled him into their car. The Royal Ulster Constabulary later found Garrick in a wasteland, half a mile from his house, situated in the neighbourhood that he had grown up in and in turn had raised his three Sons within also.

Brian would often walk around the neighbourhood that both his sons had grown up in. However, as of late, he had stopped. He was tired. The walks he had once taken, that afforded him a solitary hour alone with his thoughts, now haunted him. His mind when unoccupied would flit to thoughts of his son's death, his last dying minutes.

He was actually starting to contemplate something he never thought he would, early retirement. Pam had often said to Brian that they should retire sooner rather than later, with the pension age growing ever higher. Brian had dismissed this theorem a variety of times, preferring instead to continue until he was at least Sixty- Five, when he would receive his pension. He desperately wanted to keep busy.

He had used Pam as an excuse also. As Brian had remarked, it was not economically viable to retire five years early and maintain the same quality of life they had strived and toiled for all of their lives, not with Pam's reduced hours. He had been disgusted at himself for using her as an excuse. She had reduced her shifts, as had he. The death of their son had sucked away her desire to work, a desire that had fuelled her for much of her adult life.

Brian, who was currently working as an Emergency medical dispatcher, also loved his job and felt as he had done in the Army, that he was helping people. When he had left the Army he had tried his hand at a myriad of jobs ranging from a postman to a security consultant, however, he never sustained the buzz and excitement that he so craved, one not felt since his service. All that changed however when he started his job as a dispatcher, his regimented style and first-hand experiences went hand-in-hand with the real-time pressures of his career.

He was once again responsible for those in his care, their very lives depending upon his clarity of thought and his ability to maximise the resources at hand. The ambulances across the capital, out on the front line, were his platoon, death and illness their only enemy. Well, that and the severe cuts the NHS currently faced. He was well liked in the dispatch centre by the team around him, more so when he spoke out against a set of redundancies that threatened his department. Three under Brian's command had already been culled and he had tirelessly used his rank to curry favour with the powers that be, ensuring that for now at least, the redundancies were halted.

The team now looked to him more than ever, their very careers in a constant state of flux. The team respected Brian's ability to remain unshaken and firm footed in any given situation but that had recently changed. He found that he had been slipping, second guessing himself. As he saw it, indecision was the biggest killer. Although to his knowledge, no severe or irreparable damage to any patients had occurred, he feared it was only a matter of time. He often looked at those around him, younger and more technologically savvy and considered whether or not to sacrifice himself in the next wave of redundancies, sparing the youthful aspirations of those around him, the last in, first out policy making the redundancies all the more untenable.

This was never more apparent than when he heard from one of his colleagues and oldest friends at the Ministry of Defence, who phoned him personally, to break the news that his youngest Son, Anthony, had been killed whilst on patrol. A local militia group, the remnants of which comprised of oppositional forces left over from the civil war in Sierra Leone, were to blame. Brian did not need his medical training or prolonged stint in the Army, to reassure himself that his Son's death had been a painless and instantaneous one.

The armoured Land Rover, second in the convoy that his son had been travelling in had been hit by an RPG and had all but been destroyed, resulting in the death of his son and two other Privates, Private Wayne Evans and Private Martin Keeler. All that had been left of the men in the burnt-out carcass of the vehicle were their dog tags and other various items, one of which being a crucifix, which hung charred from the rear-view mirror. Consequently, one of the hardest aspects of their son's death was that there was no body to bury. Anthony was afforded a funeral with full military honours and an empty coffin was buried on the day of his repatriation.

Anthony's coffin instead consisted of personal effects such as an England Rugby shirt, kindly signed by the Elite squad upon hearing of Anthony's death via the news and various other personal items from friends and family; family photographs, letters and his toy bear Alfie, which he had had since he was small. Pam had insisted that he be buried with Alfie, the bear that Anthony slept with every night as a young boy, insisting that just as he could not sleep without him when he was younger, her little boy could not now rest in peace without him.

Anthony's dog tags were all that remained of their Son from that fateful day which now took pride of place on a table beside the couch in the living room. The dog tags, which were slightly blackened from smoke damage, hung on the corner of an oak picture frame that encased Anthony's regimental cap badge. Beside it was another frame that contained a photograph of Anthony in full regimental regalia, a huge smile etched upon his face. The frame sat atop a Union Jack flag that was draped over the tabletop. That would become the enduring image that Brian and Pam would often conjure up when thinking of their Son. Brian had caught Pam once or twice, whilst cleaning the house, lifting the photo and kissing the frame, before ever so delicately dusting it as if to remove any sentimental evidence.

Anthony, their beloved son. A fine example of patriotism and a man held in such high esteem not just in the family but within the local community also. Anthony like Tom had never caused Brian and Pam any unnecessary pain. The two Brothers were inseparable throughout growing up together and were the same as adults. They associated with the same group of friends, received glowing reports from their local school and were never returned home in a Squad car. They were so inseparable that it was of no surprise to Brian when Anthony announced that he wished to enlist in the Army, he did so within the Rifles, the same regiment as his Brothers.

Regulation stipulated that the two could not serve together in the same company, therefore Tom, who already belonged to A company and had so since his service started two and a half years prior to his Brother's enlistment, was proud to see Anthony join B company. This had overjoyed the two Brothers no end and Pam and Brian were also happy that the two were to be stationed in such a way that they could look out for one another. This, as Brian now pondered, was to result in his son's death being all that more unbearable.

Confirmation of his son's death came in an abundance of ways; although there emerged one witness account that was truly indisputable, rendering Brian and his wife devoid of any doubt. Regardless of there being little in the way of anatomical remains for the coroner to examine or confirmation via the regiment's manifest, their son's sign-out sheet for vehicle number two in the convoy signed by his very hand before he left on patrol. No. The true confirmation came via their eldest Son Tom, who had also been travelling in the same convoy.

Tom meticulously narrated the events that had taken place, filling in many of the blanks for Brian that had been left unanswered by the MOD's account, the Official Secrets Act coming into full play.

Anthony had been on a routine patrol of a neighbouring village. It had been just four miles outside of their barracks, located just outside of Freetown, Sierra Leone's capital. Reports were flooding in of civil unrest within two parts of the township, one to the Northwest of the local township, the other in the heart of the town.

Both A and B Company were to leave the barracks and follow the road down into the town, breaking up when they reached the outskirts of the village. B Company was to break away and travel to the North-Westerly point of the village to quash a group of rioters who were reportedly causing civil unrest. This was largely seen as a co-ordinated effort with that of the RSLAF known officially as the Republic of Sierra Leone Armed Forces, who had become highly confident and skilled in their reestablishment of the country.

The Army, who were offering support to the humanitarian efforts of the Red Cross and UN task forces, had been stationed within Sierra Leone for the last decade, just outside of the capital. Although the Civil War had ended back in 2002 bringing an end to a decade of civil war, the British Army remained within Sierra Leone, offering training to the RSLAF. So far the RSLAF, restructured and retrained by the Army, were self-sufficient with regards to the running and maintenance of their own Navy, which now monitored the country's fishing grounds, with the Army offering force elements to both the UN and African Union as well as infrastructure.

Subsequently, the British armed forces had gradually decreased their support due to the ever-rising competency of the RSLAF. Anthony and Tom had been among those selected to join the International Military and Training unit (IMATT) tasked with assisting Sierra Leone. They had also offered support during the Ebola crisis, helping build camps and maintain security. Due to their training within the Rifles regiment, they were seen, along with 28 other men from their platoon as instrumental in training the Army in Sierra Leone.

As Tom stated to his father at the time, the routine intervention in the local civil unrest was seen as the perfect opportunity to assess the men that they had been training in the RSLAF and they felt confident in the abilities of the men they had trained, having taken them out on manoeuvres before. Nothing, however, compared to the real thing.

Largely, their capacity as both soldiers and as instructors had been relatively routine. However, around a month and a half before Anthony's death, there had been an increase in the rebel factions and their hostility towards the British and UN forces. They were becoming more incessant in their attacks which were largely orchestrated by a rebel faction of men who had served in the oppositional RUF (Revolutionary United Front) during the conflict. The RUF had become extremely resentful towards that of the Sierra Leonean Army as well as the international aid and support it's townships had been provided with during the Ebola crisis and with its educational programmes.

These men were the last remnants of members not arrested and tried for their appalling acts during the Civil war. It was common for UN forces to be captured and executed by the RUF, however, ten years later the resurgence of factions, mainly comprising of ex-members of the RUF, had led to Various UN and Army convoys being attacked. This was of course a constant threat to the IMATT and the men aiding in the continued logistics training and establishment of Sierra Leone, which many saw as a positive intervention. On the 12th January, like every other day and night on active duty within Sierra Leone, the fear of attack had not escaped Anthony and Tom's conscience.

B Company had been at the head of the convoy, as they would have to bear left ahead of the convoy as they entered the township. A company would continue forward towards the centre of the city. Along with the other two Privates, Anthony was in the second armoured Land Rover, three cars ahead of the Land Rover that Tom himself was sat in. They had left the barracks in a single formation, four vehicles in B Company and five in A Company. They progressed at a reasonable speed down the rutted road that led away from their regiment's complex. Tom stated that from his position in the convoy, situated in the back seat of the armoured Land Rover, that he had a clear view of his brother's Land Rover. It had been a quiet night and the visibility ahead was clear, a full moon drenching the landscape.

As the Convoy reached the township, the head of the convoy began to slowly turn the bend ahead. The radio crackled into life and B Company confirmed that they were proceeding to their objective. It was at this point that a lofty and gaunt black man had stepped out in front of the Land Rover in which Tom was sat. He pushed ahead of him a stall on wheels, battered, containing rugs and second-hand clothes. The driver, Private Ray Jenkins, slammed down on the brakes and violently drummed on the cars horn in short regular blasts, ushering with his right hand for the man to move. The man transfixed by the headlights of the Land Rover stopped and stared back into the canopy of the Land Rover for several seconds. Jenkins had continued to sound the horn and had now, Tom established, taken to swearing under his breath. Tom's hand had tightened around the handle of his service weapon, prepared for any hostilities that might ensue.

He tried to look past the stall so that he could fix his eyes on the convoy ahead and in turn, regain sight of his Brother's vehicle but his view was obscured. Private Phillips in the passenger seat picked up the radio and informed the rest of A Company and B Company that they had been halted by a civilian, who at present was not identifying any signs of hostility.

Soon, the man, a look of understanding upon his face, began to move the stall forward until it was on the adjacent side of the road. Tom relaxed his finger from the trigger slightly. Recently, the attacks from the local militia, in particular from one group that called themselves 'The Peoples National strike force', had become more frequent. However, as Tom considered at the time, the man in front of them posed little threat. Suicide bombers were not the local militia's style. They instead preferred full-frontal attacks upon convoys using Ak-47's, grenades and...

The whistle of an RPG up ahead was just audible over the noise of the engine. The man with the stall immediately cowered behind the protection of his stall and covered his ears. The whistling noise was then replaced by the unmistakable noise of an explosion, soon accompanied up ahead by an orange jettison of flame and twirling acrid, smoke. Private Phillips immediately got on the radio to establish if the convoy had been hit and established that they were advancing towards their location.

It was at that stage that the radio crackled into life and Vehicle One or Bravo One as it was known in the convoy, stated in a panicked and blood curdling fashion, that Bravo Two had been hit by an RPG and that they were under heavy fire from armed insurgents with fully automatic weapons. Deep down, as if he had a psychic link to his brother, it was at that point that Tom knew that his brother was dead. The road ahead gave way to vehicles Bravo Three and Four as they reversed back around the blind bend in the road, Bravo Three's bonnet aflame. It had been behind Bravo Two, behind Anthony's vehicle. He recalled what Tom had said next with utter...

Brian's train of thought was interrupted by an announcement over the intercom, the message informing those in the airport to report any unattended luggage. He found himself which a substantial length of tinsel wrapped around his knuckles. Awkwardly, he unwound the tinsel from his enclosed fist and strategically twisted it around the barrier once again.

He scanned the crowd for Tom before quickly checking his watch. He had received his Sons text just as he was about to leave for the airport to collect his son. The text had informed him not to leave the house until he received word from Tom. His Son's message had been lacking in detail but he had established within his message that it was something to do with his luggage. That had been almost two hours ago. Due to his close proximity to Heathrow and it being Friday, his day off, he was able to wait at home on stand-by, awaiting word from his son.

Brian had been waiting at home all day, giddy with excitement not quite knowing what to do to occupy his time. As soon as he had received the text from his son forty-five minutes ago, he was able to put down the cup of tea he had been nursing and jump into his car, arriving at the airport twenty- five minutes later. Had he really been alone with his thoughts for that long, staring into space?

He continued to survey the crowd. On his forth sweep, as he turned his head back towards the double set of doors, he caught sight of a man matching his Son's profile. The man before him necessitated further inspection. He was broad and bronzed and he too had halted to search the crowd. The confirmation came when the man stopped scanning and locked onto Brian's line of sight before breaking into a smile. He began to stride towards the barrier and raised a hand to wave. Brian lifted the newspaper in his right hand in acknowledgement, returning the smile. Tom walked around the barrier and embraced his Father. They said nothing for several moments. Brian pushed his son back ever so slightly, not in an effort to be rid of his Sons embrace; he had of course longed to see his Son in the flesh for months but instead, so that he could get a better look at him.

"Struth," Brian laughed in a mock Australian accent. "What have they done with you down under?"

It was a genuine question. It had not just been the deep mahogany tan that had taken Brian by surprise. His Son resembled a bronzed Adonis. Tom had always been physically fit and muscular, largely due to his passion for Rugby from a young age and his service in the Army but his son looked as if he had put on extensive muscle.

Tom laughed, "Let's just attribute it to all that healthy living and a beach lifestyle. I'm just glad to be back. What a bloody trauma today has been."

"It's great to have you back Son. I know your Mother is chomping at the bit to see you, so we better not keep her waiting," he made an effort to turn towards the door then suddenly registered the absence of luggage, Tom's rucksack only visible. He stopped.

"Where's your luggage Son?" he enquired, noticing his son's posture slump ever so slightly.

"I wish I knew myself Dad, looks as if the airline has lost it in transit or something. They're going to phone me if and when they find it. I'm not holding my breath though. Can we get going? I am dying for a cuppa."

"Well to be honest Son, I can't say I'm surprised. Everyone at the moment either seems to be on strike or protesting. It's a wonder the country is still in one piece," Brian suddenly stopped himself.

He did not want to talk politics now. His son was back.

He decided to change the subject and tutted, "Bloody typical. You go all the way around the world, end up in the country that invented the boomerang and your luggage doesn't come back. That's irony if I've ever heard it." They both laughed. It was good to hear his Son laugh. It felt as if it had been a lifetime since his Son last seemed genuinely happy.

"Well at least you're back in one piece Son," Brian said, enthused with joy.

However, when they both fixed upon one another's gaze both of their minds turned to the family member who had not returned. Brian scolded himself for not considering the implication of such a statement. How could he have been so stupid? Tom immediately identified his father's change in expression.

He raised his hand up to his father's shoulder and patted it. He was desperate to change his father's train of thought. He could only imagine how his Father had felt these past few months. He had been quite reserved, displaying minimal signs of emotion when last they spoke. Not for lack of trying Tom understood but instead as a defence mechanism, a coping strategy, always keeping strong for his family.

"So where are you parked Dad? I've seen enough of this airport to last me a lifetime," Tom chimed.

CHAPTER FOUR: LIVING SHRINE

Although it had only been four months since he had left, Tom felt as though he had been away for a lifetime. As soon as the cold, drizzle laden air hit his nostrils; a nostalgic euphoria washed over him.

"I bet you've not missed this," Brian quipped as he weaved between travellers and discarded baggage trolleys.

"Wouldn't be home if it wasn't chucking it down," Tom returned, struggling to be heard over the rain.

He followed in his Father's meandering path as the pair negotiated the various patrons of the airport as they ran past and back into Arrivals, sodden and dishevelled. The deluge was relentless, the squall causing the rain to lash the pavements at a canted fashion. The short distance between the exit and the carpark serving as a stark reminder to Tom, his bare legs sodden, his limbs frozen.

The two arrived at a zebra crossing, the wind relentless in its assault. With the road devoid of traffic, Tom stepped into the road. Brian hung back briefly stopping at the curb to aid a Chinese tourist who was struggling to lift her suitcase over the truncated domes of the sloped pavement. The woman thanked him in broken English; Brian simply smiled graciously in return.

'Ever the gentleman', Tom considered proudly.

They finally made it to cover and began to ascend the concrete stairs of the carpark to Level Two where Brian had been parked.

Brian rounded at the top of the flight of stairs and tossed his car keys to Tom, which he caught one handed, the Cricket on the beaches of Brisbane having only improved his dexterity.

"You get in Son, while I go pay the metre," he pointed towards the car before hurrying towards ticket machine located in the opposite corner of the parking complex.

Tom did so graciously, pressing the key to the silver Volkswagen Polo. The central locking clicked and he pulled the door open, dumping his bag in the foot well behind his seat. He pulled the door shut, his body trembling. Brian was at the ticket machine now, staring intently at the palm of his hand, manoeuvring change around it.

Tom reached over and put his father's keys into the ignition, twisting it so as not to start the engine but to engage the radio and heating. He twisted a dial on his Fathers dash and a warm, steady breeze hit his face instantaneously. He closed his eyes, the warm current of air reminiscent of the balmy wind that had hit his face on many an Australian beach. Tom's head began to swim with jetlag, his muscles relaxing blissfully.

Suddenly, off in the distance a car door slammed shut, the noise of which reverberated around the solid concrete structure of the carpark. Tom violently flinched, the noise startling him. He brought his hands up to his face and massaged his eyes intently, a forceful circular motion.

"Get a fucking grip," he rebuked himself through gritted teeth.

His hands shakily descended into his lap before forming clenched fists. Ahead through the windscreen his Father pumped change into the ticket machine. With a sigh he reached upwards and pulled down the sun visor, he could only imagine what he must look like after that flight. His eyes switched from his Father to the visor, the face that met him stopping him dead. Anthony.

Tom pulled at the visor gently not wanting to disturb the photograph that was precariously sticking out of a pouch upon the visor. Tom looked back towards the ticket machine, his Father still fiddling with change. Slowly he reached towards the picture and pulled it from its makeshift domicile, his Brother's face giving way to that of his own face, younger, happier.

A fond smile broke across Tom's face. It was a picture of Tom and Anthony when they were boys; Tom was about seven which would have had to have made his Brother around the age of four. They were in a field of some sort, stood before the wing of a plane. Tom could not decipher the model of the plane but he concluded that it had most likely been taken at one of the various air shows they attended as children. Tom had never seen this photograph before. He felt the bitter twinge of a tear form.

The two boys were stood in mock salute, squinting somewhat in the sunlight. Anthony was close by Tom's side as they both stood to attention. Anthony was much smaller than Tom which Tom had compensated for slightly in the photograph, as he was bent at the knees, still ensuring that he was upright. Perched on their heads and at a jaunty angle, were the unmistakable crimson caps that belonged to the Paratroopers. Anthony had not gained all his teeth yet which gave him a comical, almost goofy demeanour.

He had always been the joker of the two. His matted blonde hair shot out from the sides of the cap. The two were both dressed in shorts and sandals, accompanied by t-shirts emblazoned with various children's characters; Anthony's bore the familiar Batman emblem, a hero of his growing up. Tom was transfixed by the photograph. They looked so happy, so natural playing mock soldiers. If only they had known back then what they knew now, would things have been any different? Maybe for Anthony, Tom pondered but not for him.

A knot twisted in his stomach. He had continued to play soldier for nearly nine months after Anthony's death. After he had attended the funeral of his Brother, things had been different when he returned to active duty. He had begun to second guess himself. He thought nothing of it until the panic attacks began to settle in. He had hidden these as well as he could but his friends in the platoon had started to notice. He was no longer fearless, as he had been previously. His friend Gary Nichols had found him crying one night in bed, inhaling and exhaling deeply, fighting for air.

He had calmed him down, firmly grabbing him by the shoulders, regulating Tom's breathing. Unbeknown to Tom, Gary had simply put it down to a bad nightmare, one most likely attributed with the loss of his Brother, some recurring flashback of that night. But Tom knew what it had really been about. He had lost his nerve. He feared the danger he may put those around him in and for his life or rather the prospect of subjecting his parents to the potential loss of their only remaining child.

An unnatural hate had manifested within him for the indigenous people, the very same people he and his Brother had so wanted to help in the first place, the ideology of hearts and minds now sickening him to his core.

However, the thought that truly haunted him during his pitiful slumber each night was the guilt he felt for his Brother's death. How could he ever tell his Father, a man who served with distinction in the Army, that the only reason he was sitting in his car seat now, while others in the Armed forces around the world were being shot at was because...

The light above Tom's head came on and the door clunked open. Tom quickly shut the visor and pretended to wipe the sleep and tiredness from his eyes, instead clawing away the tears. Brian settled into the car and pulled the door to. He looked across at his son. Regardless of his bronzed skin, the entirety of his colour had seemed to have drained from his skin.

"Are you aright Son, you look a bit peaky?" Brian questioned, resting an arm on Tom's shoulder.

Tom turned to look at his father staring into his eyes. Those heavy eyes that bore the combined weight of loss, age and the distinct love that still resided within them for his surviving offspring. He so wanted to tell his father why he had gone to Australia and what the months after Anthony's passing had taken from him. That he had lost not just his brother but his very soul. The tightness intensified in his stomach. His father did not need this. Not now.

'Play up your role one more time,' he internally berated himself.

"Yeah," he managed a fake smile. "I look bloody awful. That flight must have taken more out of me than expected."

Satisfied with his son's response, Brian's inquisitive demeanour melted into a smile. "No doubt, you're probably jet lagged up to the eyeballs. Why don't you get some sleep? I'll wake you up when we get home. It won't take us too long."

Tom nodded and repositioned himself in his seat, pressing his head into the corner of the headrest. He let the hot air of the heating wash over him. He shut his eyes and feigned sleep, the prospect of addressing the real problem at hand proving all too much in his current state.

(CHAPTER BREAK)

The wind had increased quite significantly on the journey home and the car now felt far removed from the internal shelter of the concrete structure at Heathrow. Brian's Volkswagen swayed slightly whenever a new gust of wind crossed the A40's carriageway. It was now the tail end of the work commute home and the distance between the cars bumpers had widened. A marked improvement from when Brian had set out a second time to collect his son. Every so often, Tom would afford himself a glance at the road from the slits of his eyes, trying to keep up the charade that he was sleeping. He had found himself returning to the guilt of his brother's death as well as his own shameful secret and instead, rather cowardly, decided to shut himself off. Instead, he had taken to berating himself for his drowsy facade.

'You wait over months to see Dad and you can't even look him in the eye. You prick!' He clenched the handle of the door frame out of sight of his father.

The car turned a sharp corner. Tom felt such anger in himself. The plastic handle begun to creak under the exertion of pressure his hand forced upon it. He released it.

Tom flinched as he was tapped on the arm. To his father, it appeared that Tom had just been startled from a deep sleep. But he had not been. He was on edge and had been so lost in his thoughts that he had dropped his defences somewhat. Tom opened his eyes. Brian, eyes still fixed firmly on the road, was waiting at a set of traffic lights.

"Sorry to wake you Son, ETA three minutes. Thought you'd want to see how the neighbourhood has changed," he smiled, looking from the road ahead, up to the traffic lights and back again.

"I've been gone for four months Dad; I doubt it's changed that much."' Tom slid up the seat, pulling the seatbelt ever so slightly away from him.

"Well, I don't know if I told you this when we last spoke but it's all been a bit lively round by us as of late. Let's just say, a lot of people aren't in the Christmas spirit."

With that, the lights changed and Brian applied more pressure to the accelerator, switching the car into second. Tom was about to ask his Father what his last statement had meant when upon rounding the next corner, his question was answered. West Chester Street, Tom knew it well from his paper round as a boy.

Up ahead, huddled against the wind were a set of people, struggling to keep their placards under control in the onslaught of the wind. One woman clutched on to her hat in a macabre dance as she alternated from ensuring that her hat remained firmly on her head whilst also maintaining that her sign was held aloft. There were easily a dozen people, their backs turned against the easterly blowing winds.

"What the?" Tom was gob smacked by what he saw.

He turned in his seat as the car passed the group and when he could see no longer via his peripheral vision, reverted to looking at the crowd in the wing mirror. The group disappeared around the bend. Tom was still somewhat bemused by the whole thing. He had caught one placard as it blew upwards from the coven of protesters which read, *'NO TO CON'* but before he could see the rest of the sign it was swept away from his line of vision. Brian cocked his head slightly.

"I don't know what you kept up to date with down under, I know you've never been one for politics Son but to put it quite frankly, the neighbourhood's been in a bit of an uproar these last two months. It's been on the regional and national news channels and radios nonstop."

Brian came to a T- Junction and stopped. He looked left then right and left again before turning into the junction.

"What was all that about Dad?" he gestured with his thumb back in the direction of the protestors. "You couldn't get me out in this weather for all the tea in China."

"It's that bloody new shopping centre. The one they built last year, you know the one off Albany Cross road?" Brian looked at Tom questioningly. Tom nodded. They had started construction on it just before he had left for the Army.

"Well, it's kicked up a right palaver. Turns out that as well as being extremely successful, the bloody owners want to extend it and build a new wing onto the place. They haven't even finished the last extension they commissioned and they want more, typical business men," he scoffed. "Anyway, to do that, they need to spread further out into the community. If completed, it's going to result in a further extension of the site and that means one thing."

Tom looked back at his Father, the puzzle pieces not fully slotting into place as of yet. Brian analysed his son's face and surmised as much.

"They need more space. They're trying to buy up the surrounding property. Twelve or thirteen I think... or is it eleven?" Brian trailed off.

Tom spoke, now in full grasp of the situation, "No way are they going to get away with that. You can't just ask people to up sticks and move elsewhere because of a shopping centre."

"That's what your mother and I said but it turns out the resettling fee and offers for the properties the owners are getting, have been sky high. Several have already accepted the offer. To be honest I can't really blame them. A woman that works with your mum was talking to her about it in town the other day. She was saying that she inherited the house off her mother, when she died, only child."

Brian looked at his Son and diverted his gaze. He cleared his throat.

"Lovely three bed semi it is but she's not married with no fella either. She can barely keep the place running. What with her shift work at the hospital, she was barley in the place. Well, until she was made redundant that is. Have you heard about all of these cuts in the NHS? Your mother is like a cat on a hot tin roof at the moment. She doesn't know whether her job is secure or what. We discussed it and if the axe does fall, she'll take early retirement. They'll be a good redundancy package and pension in it for her, which is a lot more than I can say for a lot of poor sod's out there at the moment," Brian shook his head.

Tom assessed whether this was an intentional statement taking into account Tom's current unemployment. His current position was like that of many people in the public sector, getting sold off piece by piece. However, he was different to those people. He had not been made redundant, far from it. He shook such thoughts from his head. It wasn't his father's style. He knew that his father and mother were highly supportive and would keep a roof over his head until he found his footing. He cheered up ever so slightly, safe in the knowledge that he should count his blessings. Other people out there did not have the same luxury. Tom mulled over what his father had told him and broke the silence.

"That's madness. I heard snippets on the news while I was away but I thought that was just the usual political mudslinging that surfaces during the run up to elections. I'd heard about the cuts, hell I saw it first-hand in the regiment, we lost a few to redundancies."

Brian tutted and shook his head at this, appalled. "The lack of investment in Britain's men and woman abroad and on home soil is disgusting. Not surprised you guys got hit by the cuts out in Sierra Leone. International aid, always one of the first things to go, costs four times as much when we have to go back out there and clear up their mess though. To think, we used to finish wars and conflicts."

Tom spotted the Old George Inn ahead to the left; they were growing ever closer to home. He suddenly felt a pang of excitement. In an effort to change the subject, Tom decided to offer his closing statements on the matter.

"Well Dad, to be honest, whether she's falling apart or not, I'm just glad to be back in good old Blighty. Politicians come and go and as per usual we'll be the ones left to pick up the pieces and deal with the fallout of the next out of touch, Eaton wide boy."

Brian laughed, "Couldn't have put it better myself Son. They'd be dangerous if they had half a brain cell among the lot of them," and with that Brian hit the indicator and turned left into the street where Tom had grown up, Wrenley Close.

The street was comprised of a combination of both detached and semi-detached houses. His father and mothers house was a little further down the road on the left. The street was illuminated by the fluorescent, orange glow of lamp posts strategically placed at ten metre intervals to afford the best visibility for pedestrians, one of whom was currently walking his jet-black Labrador.

The houses on the street had been built back in the 1930's and were a juxtaposition of vintage architecture versus modern commodity. The houses mostly had their brickwork painted white, the black guttering contrasting the pale elegance of the houses in a prominent and refined border. Tom counted along the house numbers as they passed, decreasing in increments of two.

He could see his mother's car ahead. The indicator clicked briefly for one final time as his father pulled into the space behind his mother's car. In an excited motion Brian pulled on the hand brake, knocked the car out of gear and turned the keys to a stationary position. The car juddered slightly as the engine shut down.

Brian turned in his seat, unbuckling his seatbelt. "Right, well let's not keep your poor mum waiting any longer."

In a singular movement Brian opened his door and exited the vehicle. Tom sat there for a moment; a wave of excitement mixed with a mysterious twinge of nervous energy eating away at his stomach. He collected himself and took a breath. Whether he knew it or not, his eyes cast unconsciously over the sun visor as he reached for the door handle. He decided to dismiss any and all thoughts, content on enjoying the moment. With that he thrust the door open and stepped out of the car, the solid pavement reinforcing his convictions further. This was where he should be right now, this was what he needed.

Brian stood beside the passenger door patiently, already having retrieved Tom's bag from the back seats foot well. He watched on as Tom stood looking up at the house, his eyes never leaving the structure as he closed the car door behind him. The boys had always loved the house and no matter where they were, away on a school trip or upon active duty, they loved coming home. Brian stepped forward and patted Tom affectionately upon his left shoulder.

He felt his son flinch violently under the thin material of his polo. His hand froze. Tom looked down bashfully before turning to his father, a weak smile eventually mustered a smile that Brian reciprocated. Smiling he held Tom's backpack aloft.

"You've already lost one bag today," Brian jokingly commented as he handed Tom the Rucksack, "We don't want you losing this one as well."

Tom took the bag and slung it over his right shoulder, strikingly aware of the fact that his father had not taken his eyes off of him since exiting the car.

"Right, lead the way Son," he gestured towards the house.

Tom smiled back at his Father and sauntered up the path to the front door. He instinctively waited until his father was at his side to open the door, the only thing at present standing between him and a fresh start. Brian grasped at a singular key and shook several others free. He winked at Tom as he placed the bronze key into the lock and twisted the key in a singular motion, pushing the door with the edge of his palm.

The welcoming smell of home hit Tom's nostrils immediately, a smell unique to each and every house in the world, made all the more welcoming by the smell of his mother's cooking, beef stew, his favourite.

Brian stepped aside and let Tom shimmy past him. He stepped into the hallway, dropping his bag by the skirting board, the wall framed with various photographs. The wall served as a family timeline. Nearest the door were both sets of grandparents both on their respective wedding days, both looking formal yet utterly enthralled, their joy captured forever in black and white, resigned to the annuals of history.

Next along was his own parents' wedding photo, Tom's mother in a reserved yet beautiful white dress. Holding his mother's hand was Brian, a large toothy grin etched across his face, framed all the more so by the prominent moustache on his top lip, kitted out in full regimental dress. He had gotten a lot of stick from Tom and Anthony about that moustache. Anthony had always said that his father looked like, 'The lost member of the YMCA'.

Tom smirked at the memory, the next photograph taken at school of Tom and Anthony intensifying his nostalgia all the more so. Tom looked directly at the camera with a level of serious dedication, his forehead slightly furrowed. Anthony leant slightly in towards Tom, a beaming smile upon his face. The smile of a young mischievous boy, cheeky and absent of many a tooth, still so much growing to be done and so much time ahead of him in which to do it. Tom shuffled his weight slightly in the hallway.

Tom's gaze instinctively traced along the final five photographs, a space upon the wall that he been freed up over the years to accommodate the Hawkins military lineage. A strand of service that had begun with Brian's grandfather, a strand abruptly terminated with the final photograph, that of Anthony the day of his passing out parade.

Tom's focus was broken by the distant noise of shuffling feet, hurried and expectant. His mother rounded the corner and stopped dead in her tracks. It was evident that she was pleased to see Tom, rather taken aback. She scanned his torso and with that, like a missile homing in on its target, buried herself into his chest. As she did so, she gave a muffled whimper; one of relief and happiness at being reunited with her Son. Tom instinctively put his arms around his mother, almost smothering her with his biceps. He could feel the tepid tears slowly soaking through his polo. He leant down and kissed his mother's head.

"Hi Mum," Tom whispered.

A sucking back of tears emanated from his mother as she pushed away from his torso and held him at arm's length, still holding on to his shoulders, as if she were going to lose him. Her features were a portrait of pure juxtaposition. Her face, still youthful for her age, displayed a warm and radiant smile however, her mascara and damp, swollen eyes, told a different account.

"How you been Mum?" he inquired, knowing quite well that at this precise moment in time, no matter what had occurred before this moment or would precede it, that she was currently the happiest woman in Britain.

She giggled somewhat and reached within her sleeve for a tissue, still holding on to Tom with her left hand. She raised her other hand to her face and dabbed away the tears from her cheeks, analysing the tissue afterwards and the black hue of mascara caked upon it. She tutted in realisation and laughed again, gesturing that she was being ridiculous.

"What must I look like?" she corrected herself, standing slightly more upright.

"A panda," Brian quipped peeping over Tom's shoulder, before quickly adding, "but a lovely one at that."

Pam rolled her eyes and looked at Brian in a mocking yet stern glare, hands on her hips before she broke into a smile. "Is that the best line you've got? I hope you don't take after your father with flattery Son."

Tom's mind bizarrely flitted back to Anna.

Tom twisted at the waist and pulled his father in closer. Brian was about a foot shorter than Tom, still of average size and build for a man of his age. But against Tom, Brian almost seemed to be swallowed up under the upper torso and arm of his Son.

"Nope Mum, I learnt from the best. After all he did manage to bag himself you," he raised his voice at the end in a jovial and playful manner, prodding his mother for a reaction, a shrouded complement.

Pam rolled her eyes again and planted her open palm to her forehead, before closing her eyes, in a theatrical display of disappointment. "That does it then. A chip off the old block if ever I saw one"

They all laughed. Tom stepped forward, releasing his father from his vice like grip, Brian stumbling slightly forward with the sheer momentum of his son stepping away. Tom put his arm around his mother and turned them both delicately.

52

"I don't know about you two but I've been dying for a decent cup of tea ever since I left sovereign soil. One thing we obviously didn't teach them Aussies when we were out there, was how to make a decent cup of tea."

Mother and son stepped through into the kitchen. Brian edged into the living room and placed Tom's bag on the edge of the tanned leather sofa. He withdrew from the room quickly not wanting to miss any of the tales his son would no doubt regale them with. He was savouring every minute of this. As he did so he knocked a photo frame from the side table next to the sofa. Brian grimaced as he did so, making a reach for it but proving too slow. It was only after he saw it lying there on the carpeted, beige surface before him, that he registered it was not damaged in any way.

He picked it up and turned it over in his palm. Looking up at him was Anthony. Noticing some fluff from the carpet, he brushed it delicately away. He turned back to the table, draped in a folded Union Jack and placed the photo down with a careful precision, angling it slightly away from him and into the centre of the table. The material of the flag gathered somewhat, which required Brian to slightly tug at the material, straightening out the kink.

He stood back and inspected the table for any discrepancies since he had entered. Pam meticulously arranged the table, cleaning any dust from it every other day. Every Sunday she would place fresh flowers into the vase situated adjacent to the photograph. On days when the England Rugby squad played, she would always place a single English rose into the vase.

On the table were two frames, both turned in towards the vase at a slight angle. They were both parallel to one another and in perfect symmetry. Brian smiled and touched the table ever so slightly, being careful not to disturb what he had once wrongly referred to as a shrine to Pam, when his wife had first established it. He had been angry at the time and still regretted his caustic choice of words. He knew it had upset his wife and so soon after their son's passing. Brian lingered for several moments before realising that he had been absent a while. He lifted his fingers from the tabletop and instead used them to turn off the light.

When he entered the kitchen, both Pam and Tom were sat at the table, Tom bringing his mother up to date with a story that seemed to have her captivated. Brian stood in the doorway. The kitchen, which was rather spacious, allowed both for a dedicated area for cooking as well as a large enough area for a table that could seat six. It was oak and had been a permanent feature of the kitchen since the two had moved in many years ago. Many a family meal had been had around that table in past years. It was an institution and a practice that Pam and Brian had prided themselves on. No T.V. dinners or missed dinners allowed.

Tom had always lovingly referred to it as 'The Boardroom' when he was a teenager. An area dedicated to catching up on one another's day, for spreading out across to analyse bills or do homework. It was that very table that Brian had nervously sat down at to have 'The conversation', with his son's. The same table both parents had been made aware of their son's intentions of joining the Army. In fact, where Tom sat right now, facing away from the door, had been were Brian had sat when Pam had received the phone call in the living room, that Anthony had been killed in action.

Placed on the table between Tom and Pam who was currently sat at the head of the table were three ceramic mugs of mahogany coloured tea. Brian took this as his chance to step forward and sit down opposite his son. Tom looked up grinning as he did so not breaking his trail of conversation. Brian took a sip of tea and listened intently, trying to pick up on the general gist of the story.

"And Sydney Harbour Bridge Mum, you would love it. Maybe not walking up it but the view is amazing. We couldn't get Stuart up it in the end, so he just sat in a pub. Still can't hack heights."

"Can't say I blame him, I get vertigo just standing up too fast," Pam snorted. Her face cleared ever so slightly and her eyes focused with a warm glow. "It's great to have you back son. You sound like you've had a great time and most importantly are in one piece, that's the main thing. And there was me worried that you were going to starve out there without me or the Army providing you with three square meals a day," She chortled as she prodded Tom's bicep.

Brian interjected, wanting to re-enter the conversation, "He's bulked up hasn't he Pam? Looks like you'll be playing more of a forward position for the club now son."

The club in question, the local Rugby team, was where Tom had played Rugby before joining the Army and during a conversation home whilst in Australia, Tom had mentioned that on his return home, he would like to re-join the team, all be it in an over twenty-five capacity.

"Well, I'll have to wait to get my kit back first before I do that Dad, otherwise I'll be playing in my boxers... and I've only got one pair at that," Tom stated swallowing back the laughter with a sip of his tea.

Brian joined in but Pam's features seemed somewhat confused. Brian looked over at his wife and recognised her utter bewilderment at having missed out on the joke.

"The airline only went and lost his bloody luggage didn't they Pam," Brian tutted, as he thrust his thumb towards Tom.

Pam bit her bottom lip, eyes raised once again to the heavens before shaking her head, "And sod's law it had to be my boy's bag that got lost," she responded, patting the top of Tom's hand upon the tabletop. She noticed that his hand withdrew ever so slightly when she did so. Tom caught her eye and smiled, reassuring her to an extent.

"It'll be alright Mum, I've sorted it. They're going to get in contact with me when they find it," he paused slightly, looking downward in a somewhat pessimistic fashion, "If they find it."

Pam was about to speak when the timer on the oven went off. She shot up and opened the oven, an amalgamation of fragranced steam hitting Tom like a culinary sledgehammer.

"Well hopefully this goes some way to cheering you up Son," Brian chipped in, indicating to the oven.

Brian stood up and walked over to the cutlery drawer and began removing knives and forks. Tom made to move, in an effort to help but Brian indicated with an outstretched palm to remain seated.

"Sit down Son, you just relax. I'm sure you've worked up a right appetite travelling. You just focus on devouring this meal. That's an order," he smirked.

Tom thought it better not to argue and relaxed back into his seat. His mother was dishing up dinner, his Father now placing the cutlery on the table along with three place mats, all emblazoned with their names. Tom picked them up and leant across the table distributing them. They had always sat in the same seats. It had been instinctive, traditional. Just as he was about to place down his mat, his name emblazoned across it in navy blue, the bottom mat appeared. There in a sweeping, crimson font was Anthony's mat. His mother had always referred to him by his full name and regardless of protestation from her son when she had bought the mat.

Brian placed a beer down in front of Tom. Tom turned to his Father, who was looking intently at him with a smile, before he took the place mat from him. He patted his son on the shoulder and walked over to the drawer in the kitchen unit where the place mats were kept. He opened the drawer and placed the mat inside carefully before pushing it shut.

Pam had witnessed what had happened and saw her son, looking somewhat reticent, picking at the label on his beer bottle, made flimsy by the dew. She was grateful that the dinner was ready.

In an effort to break the silence, she took a step towards Tom, plate ready in one hand. His suspicions were gratefully confirmed, it was homemade beef stew. She had always been surprised that even from an early age this had been her son's favourite meal. After all most children at a younger age were put off by the merest indication of vegetables but then again, her son had always been easily pleased and grateful of what he had.

She placed the plate, trailing a column of flavour-induced steam, in front of her son. Tom looked up and smiled at his Mother.

"Now I'm officially home," he announced in a grandiose fashion, a beaming smile on his face as he picked up his fork. Pam put her arm around his shoulder squeezing him delicately.

"Yes you are," she replied in a thankful manner. As she did so, she turned to face Brian and smiled. Brian reciprocated conscious of her pure, untainted happiness.

(CHAPTER BREAK)

Pam registered the omission of surrender in her son's face and understood that although he felt rather awkward about his mother doing his laundry at the age of twenty-five, he would relinquish his power and allow her the small victory.

She smiled, taking a step further into the room, indicating back to where she had just been, "When you've finished in the shower, just dump your clothes outside the door and I'll bung them in the washing machine. Your father and I were talking and he thought it would probably be a good idea to get a few clothes and toiletries, while you're waiting on your bag."

Tom had checked his phone earlier before his mother had come in and he had still had no response from the airline. It could be days, weeks even, before he was reunited with his belongings. He had toyed with the idea himself and had also seen this as a perfect smoke screen for going out and getting his mother and father their Christmas presents. He had bought them various trinkets from Australia but nothing substantial; a miniature boomerang with Sydney emblazoned across it in yellow and green, a few bottles at duty free, which were thankfully in his rucksack and an All Blacks t-shirt for his Father.

"Yeah Mum, I was thinking I might pop out to that shopping centre up the road and get a few bits. Haven't been in there yet, it'd be interesting to see what all the hype is about."

As he said this he walked over to his rucksack and the unzipped it, the zipper straining against the bulging contents within. He pulled out the multi-coloured Duty-Free bag and held it out towards his mother.

"It's just a little something from Down under. Nothing big," he grinned, taking a step towards his mother, the bottles clinking.

Pam held out her arms and took the polythene carrier bag. She peeked inside, "You shouldn't have gone to the bother Son, this stuff's not cheap to come by at the best of times," she remarked, pulling a bottle out for closer inspection before placing it back carefully.

"Ahhh it's only a couple of bottles of wine mum. Plus, it's the least I could do. Thanks again for putting me up while I get back on my feet. I'm going to get on the web tomorrow and start looking for jobs. As soon as I get something..." Pam cut him off, slinging an arm around him.

"Son, only one thing matters and that's that you're home. Rent free and jobless makes little difference to me and your dad. You and your brother have always done right by us and we're so proud of you both. All we care about is getting you back on your feet. I know it's been hard lately, a massive change... but try not to let it affect your Christmas. I went out and got the full works today, turkey and all the trimmings, so we're all set, presents and all so don't you go buying anything tomorrow for me and your dad. Besides we have the best present money can't buy, you home."

Tom smiled mischievously at his mother, "You do know I'm going to ignore that and get you both something anyway?" They both laughed in unison.

"Just don't go going mad on our account. Are you alright for money? Dad and I have-"

"No Mum I'm fine for money at the moment."

Pam looked at him intently after this statement, head slightly cocked in a manner that indicated to Tom that she was evaluating the validity of his statement.

He laughed, pushing his mother back slightly to look at her. "Honestly Mum, I have some Australian dollars to change up tomorrow and I still have plenty of savings."

Pam's face relaxed, satisfied with her son's financials situation.

"Right, well shall we go down and crack open a bottle? I'll get changed quickly, I'm sure I can cobble something together."

Brian emerged at the door not yet crossing the threshold, "Did I hear someone mention alcohol?" he questioned comically.

Tom laughed and looked from his mother to his father, "Cohhh," he exhaled, "your hearing's still as good as ever. Did you hear the bottles clinking from downstairs?"

Brian took an almost theatrical step into the room, holding a finger aloft, "Correct me if I'm wrong... Chardonnay 2001 I'm detecting..." a jovial sniff, "grapey undertones?" he mockingly teased nose held aloft, a mock upper-class drool to his tone. He walked over to Pam hugging her.

"I know you two are catching up but I'm feeling like the lad at the party that no one wants to dance with here," he chuckled. He looked at Tom questionably, "You not showered and changed yet Son?"

Tom went to reply but was cut off by Pam, "He's going to have one before bed, so that I can wash his clothes."

Tom sensed that his mother had been quite fast in her response, as if she were covering her tracks somewhat. Brian looked on still further, confused.

"Doesn't he have anything in the..." he turned inspecting Tom's empty wardrobe before stopping abruptly. He turned back, "Well I was saying to your mother downstairs that if you didn't have anything, bar wearing your old man's gear that you could take something from Anthony's room."

The penny dropped. Tom looked to his mother, who now ashen faced, looked down at her hands which were now joined in a weak, prayer like gesture. His mother had been adamant about washing his clothes as she had not wanted Tom to take up his father's offer, not that he would anyway. He would feel awkward wearing his deceased brother's clothes. He turned his eyes to his father establishing that it would be unnecessary but by the time he did so, his father had turned and was exiting the room.

"Come on Son, let's see what we can dig out," decreed Brian in a voice that radiated helpfulness. Tom looked back at his mother. A solitary tear ran down her cheek. It stopped for what seemed a lifetime at the crest of her cheek. Brian called again.

"Tom!" his voiced trailed down the landing.

Tom rested his hand on his mother's shoulder. She did not look up. She went to speak but choked back the sentence, all her concerted efforts currently focused on restraining the tears that Tom knew would inevitably come. Tom bent down in an effort to try and meet his mother's eye line.

"I'll tell you what Mum. Have you got one of Dad's old bathrobes?" A slight nod. "Well how about you grab me that and I'll get out of these clothes and you can bung them in the washer tonight. They'll be dry by tomorrow won't they?"

He asked the question in feigned earnest. He knew full well they would, he just wanted a response. Something, anything to draw his mother out of this downward spiral, so desperately wanting to preserve her son's memory in one of the only ways she knew how. Pam nodded her head and raised it slightly.

She cleared her throat and forced a weak smile. "Yes darling," another clearing of the throat, "I think there's one in the airing cupboard, I'll just go and..." she pointed in the direction of the bathroom and set off. She arrived at the door avoiding the direction of Anthony's bedroom.

Tom stood for several seconds before realising that his father would be waiting and briskly walked from his bedroom onto the landing. He stopped. Ahead lay the bannister, leading downstairs. To his left the bathroom and his mother. He observed that she had shut the door, most likely to shield the noise of her swallowed sobs. He turned right.

Tom took a deep breath and stepped towards Anthony's bedroom door ajar at the end of the landing, a sliver of light protruding from the doorway into the hallway. He had not been in this room since the week after his brother's funeral service when he had helped his father sort through some of his brother's possessions. He touched the door frame, white and cold to the touch and pushed it open.

Tom was immediately taken aback. The room was exactly the same as when he had left it nearly ten months ago. The room was pristine, an indication that it was regularly cleaned. Tom stepped in and in an effort to justify his assumptions ran his fingers across the top of the wardrobe located to the right of the door. When he brought his hand up for inspection there was not a speck of dust upon it. The resonant thump of a shoe hitting the inside of the wardrobe startled Tom. Brian poked his head out from around the corner of the wardrobe door. He registered Tom's look of awe and took a step backwards, a Brown suede boot in his hand.

Brian considered how his son must be feeling at this stage. He had probably expected to see the room emptied or perhaps turned into a study or an area in which to store excess possessions. Instead, what confronted him was the uncanny sight of his brother's room frozen in time.

The room was of average size and consisted of the usual fixtures and fittings: an MDF wardrobe, a single bed, a bureau with a TV placed on top, surrounded by multiple aftershaves, deodorants and trinkets. Tom had even observed that still, placed on top of the bureau, was a ten-pound note and an assortment of change left, untouched. Tom smiled slightly as he traced his eyes around the room.

Just visible under the light blue exterior of the painted wall were the unmistakable outlines of assorted children's characters from their youth. Brian had unknowingly painted over the existing wallpaper when Anthony, being eleven at the time, had protested that the existing wallpaper was too childish. Brian had assumed at the time that the thick layers of paint, three coats in total, would cover up the tapestry of youth. Over the years they had gradually returned with the fading of the paint, like some distant memory, a fragment of some past reminiscence fighting to make its presence known.

Anthony, like any teenager finding himself in the world had at first been horrified by the spectre like wallpaper returning but soon shrugged it off, instead turning it, as was his way, into a family joke. He did however try to cover much of the wall space with posters of bands, films and to their mother's disapproval, semi- naked women. Tom was taken aback by the memories that the room brought back. The room even smelt the same; the tiniest hint of Anthony's chosen brands of deodorant and aftershave still pranging his nostrils.

"Your mother cleans it twice a week, religiously. Every Tuesday and Sunday," Brian interjected, breaking Tom's trance.

Tom looked at his father, managing a weak smile. A smile he intended to come across as warm however to Brian, it mirrored that of his own feelings on the matter, a feeling of pure heartfelt concern for his wife at how she was coping with her indescribable grief. Tom felt he should say something.

"Mum seems better. Seems like her old self again." Tom felt rather awkward at this statement.

"She's doing better, taking it day by day, as we all are. The last couple of weeks have been a bit tough you know, what with Christmas on its way and the anniversary looming". Brian moved back, shoe still in hand and sat on the edge of the bed.

"Dad, I wasn't going to say anything but..." an awkward clearance of his throat, "when I was talking to Mum there, she said that you had discussed and agreed upon me buying clothes tomorrow." Tom could see that Brian registered what he was driving at and sighed.

"I've put my foot right in it there, haven't I?" he shook his head. "When we were downstairs, she did seem a little off when I suggested that you borrow some of Anthony's stuff but I thought nothing of it at the time. She's obviously not ready to part with any of this stuff yet, all be it temporarily."

He turned and delicately placed the shoe at the foot of the bed, groaning slightly as he sat back up. When he returned to his original position his posture was immaculate and militarily straight, as always.

"Look Dad it's not your fault. We're all coming to terms with this in our own way and Mum being the only woman in the house, as blokes, we're bound to put a foot wrong here and there. She knows we mean nothing malicious by it."

Tom looked intently at his Father taking two steps towards the bed. He still remained at enough of a distance to ensure that he was not encroaching on what was, his father venting.

"Look Son, the main thing for us all at the moment is to maintain some form of normality or resemble it as best we can. Your Mum and me for that matter, are just happy to have you back home and want to make it as relaxing and as stress-free as possible. Whether you admit it or not, I can tell that you're finding it hard back on Civvy Street..." Tom made to interject but Brian stopped him with a motion of his hand. He looked at him sternly.

"Son you forget, I've been there. I just want you know that we're both extremely proud of you and that you were an absolute rock during Anthony's passing. Your mother and I are here for you no matter what, financially, keeping a roof above your head...whatever you need." Brian stood up, placing his hand in his back pocket. He produced a handful of crisp notes.

Tom knew what was coming, "Look Dad I'm honestly alright for..." Brian shoved the money into Tom's hand, turning it over and shielding it with his own. "Son, don't be so bloody proud. We both wanted you to have a great time in Australia and between you and me; we wanted you to blow every bloody penny you had. You've worked hard for it and God knows if anyone deserved a respite it was you. Now I won't take no for an answer."

He smiled and held his hands over Tom's until his son's features relaxed. Tom turned the money over in his hands before placing it in his pockets. It was futile to argue. He put an arm around his Father.

"Thanks Dad, that's too much."

Brian patted his back, "No more than you deserve Son. Now listen, how about you help your old man clean up this cupboard. God bless her, your mother will go through it again like a dose of salts but…." He paused trying to find the right wording so as to not sound callous "…it's her way of dealing with it you know? We'll mention none of this to your mother."

Tom nodded, understanding that the matter had been well and truly resolved and to Tom's relief with as little exploration of their emotions as possible. They cleared the floor of the wardrobe, Brian placing Anthony's shoe back into the cupboard with a delicate finesse once again. He closed the doors.

In an effort to reassure his father Tom concluded, "I'll go and get some stuff tomorrow at West Acre. I suppose whether we like it or not, it's here to stay, so instead of establishing a trade embargo, we might as well benefit from it."

Brian laughed. They both made to leave when Brian stopped. He turned to Tom.

"I almost forgot," he slapped his side and turned around, hastily approaching the bureau.

He opened the top drawer having to slightly edge the drawer out on either side to manoeuvre it out. He reached in and pulled something out. It was the box that Anthony had made during Year Eleven Design Technology. Brian opened the lid and revealed a mass of train tickets, the edge of recruitment leaflet poking out other assorted receipts and papers.

Brian riffled in the box for several seconds, mumbling away. For the briefest of moments Tom believed that his father was trying to offer him more money until, over his shoulder he glanced the money atop the bureau, unmoved.

"Ahhhh," Brian announced triumphantly, holding the folded piece of paper aloft with gusto. Tom looked back baffled.

"Son, I need you to do me favour when you go for your bits tomorrow," he looked at his son then back at the piece of paper.

"Yeah of course Dad, what do you need?" Tom replied instinctively.

Brain unfolded the receipt. It was crumpled slightly but was still legible:

In the Frame LTD.

33-42 West Acre Point Shopping Plaza, London

Manager Peter Hensley

www.intheframe.co.uk

Telephone: 0208 7846743

Card Name: VISA DEBIT

SEQ Number: 02

APP. Crypt.: A0000004579363

Xxxxxxxxxxxx7156

TOTAL £39.97

CASH £39.97

CHANGE DUE £0.00

No. Items sold: 1

Ref number: 00529

"You name it, we frame it. Picture perfect every time."

Today you were served by Malcolm

Tom winched at the cheesy nature of the slogan at the base of the receipt.

"Your mother found this by your brother's bed when she was cleaning, must have fallen out from under the mattress or something when she was making the bed."

Tom looked back at his father; curiosity etched upon his face. "Your mum phoned the number on the receipt and talked to a man at the shop. He said that when the shop opened along with the shopping centre that they were having a sale and that your brother had placed an order. When your mother asked what it was, the man stated that it was a Birthday present that had been specially displayed for a Mr Brian Hawkins. However, that was all that it stated on the system." Tom was transfixed by where the story was headed.

"Now understandably he didn't say what the gift was even after your mother explained that your brother had died... plus it was gift wrapped. The man said that if the receipt was brought along with a form of I.D that they would hand it over. They've had it since just before Anthony left for his tour with you." Brian looked at his son expectantly, partly checking whether his son was following his train of thought.

"So, what do you need from me Dad?" Tom enquired.

"Well two things Son and you'd be doing your mother and me a solid for doing it. Firstly, if possible, when you go shopping tomorrow could you take this and your brother's Driving Licence downstairs in the lock box and pop in and get it from the man. Your mother was understandably upset and adamant that we get this back but she couldn't face going herself. I would go but…."

Tom understood, quickly blurting out his understanding, "No, no Dad I understand. I'll get it no problem. Plus, Anthony would have wanted you to open it as a surprise. I'll get it first thing."

Brian's features softened with love for his son. The sentimental value of opening a gift knowledge-free from his departed son, for once last time with Christmas days away, would make it all that much more special.

Brian straightened, the smile melting away marginally. "There is one more reason that I need you to go Son." He turned the receipt over in his hands and revealed, in blue ink, that there was writing scrawled upon it. It was Anthony's handwriting, no mistake about it. The way he scrawled his Y's had always got him into trouble with his teacher at Primary school. He had remembered the battles his parents had had with his brother's handwriting when they were younger.

The message read, in slightly illegible writing, "Hawker 8 21 18 18 9 3 1 14 5."

Tom instinctively took the receipt from his Fathers hand and inspected it closer. Brian watched on intently, hoping for some light to be shone on the matter.

Tom met his Fathers gaze, "Well that's my nickname at the start, from when we were younger, even called me it when we were in the regiment. But as for the numbers, I haven't got a clue. Maybe it's the number of the credit card he paid for with it?"

Brian shook his head slightly at the explanation his son had just offered and dove back into the box this time revealing a wallet, drawing out a blue debit card. He handed it to his son. Tom held it in his other hand, comparing the card and the receipt. His Father was right. The number was not even close to matching along with the fact that for a Debit card number, it was three digits short.

"Huh," he remarked, turning the receipt over for any further clues, finding none.

"Your Mum and me thought that it might be some kind of reference number for when he collected my present or a phone number but when we called it, the line said that it was an unrecognised number." Tom stared at it further.

Why was his name on it? Had his brother intended for Tom to do him a favour and intentionally left it in his name for collection? Or was it meant to be a gift from the two of them for their father's birthday.

"To be honest Dad I haven't got a clue," he said folding the paper before holding it up, "Don't worry Dad, I'll get to the bottom of it tomorrow. Probably a reference number as you said. It's all paid for and everything, so there shouldn't be any issues picking it up. I'll bring Anthony's wallet along just in case I'm asked for anything else."

Brian nodded and Tom took his brother's wallet from his father. He opened it and held his breath when he saw what was inside the plastic pocket within. It was a picture of the two of them on a lad's holiday they had taken to Malia when Anthony had just left College. So as not to bring attention to it, Tom shoved the receipt into the note section of the wallet and quickly placed it in his back pocket.

"Right, well that wine isn't going to drink itself," he laughed and Brian indicated for Tom to lead the way.

They both stepped out onto the landing and as Brian did so he afforded a look back at his son's room. He flicked off the light, a slight smile on his face. Tom caught it as his father shut his brother's door. A reminiscent look of joy twinned with an air of expectation framed his features. An excited expectation as to what his son had bought his father for his birthday, a birthday that marked another year of life. Another year he had outlived Anthony, a bittersweet fact that no father of any age, should have to endure.

CHAPTER FIVE: SHOP 'TIL YOU DROP

Tom awoke to the smell of bacon before the incessant drone of the fire alarm. The same alarm that went off whenever the merest hint of a fry-up was detected, which usually also indicated that breakfast was about five minutes from completion. The morning chorus of the Hawkins's household. The familiarity brought a smile to Tom's face as he turned on to his right-hand side, propping himself upon his elbow as he did so. He gazed at the alarm clock on his bedside table through sleep laden eyes. 9.45 AM. He had slept for well over ten hours.

Quite embarrassingly enough, fifteen minutes after he had gone downstairs to spend an evening in the living room with his parents for a catch up and a drink, his jetlag had taken hold. After snapping from his slumber several times, his father in mid-conversation, his mother had finally demanded he go to bed as if he were a six-year-old boy again. Unlike he had when he was a child, Tom did not argue.

Tom stretched, contorting his body into an almost unfathomable shape in an effort to ease some of the stiffness sustained from his deep slumber. Even after all this time he still found it hard to sleep on anything over than the taught canvas bed he had grown accustomed to whilst on Active Duty. At least, that was the excuse his brain often arrived at as he lay awake during one of the many frightful nights of sleep he had endured of late. He could not remember the last time he had slept in so late or so well, his Army morning routine still proving hard to shrug off.

Before he had left the Army his assigned counsellor had been candid when he had stated that his recovery would take time. Tom had initially declined the offer of counsel, a culmination of some deep, entrenched masculine pride at not wanting to be seen as damaged in any particular way rendering him arrogant, uninterested in support. He had just wanted to carry out his job as normally as possible. However, it soon became apparent to Tom that even the most mundane of daily tasks took their toll upon him both mentally and physically. Tasks he had carried out methodically and with distinction for the two years or so prior to Anthony's death.

As he had quickly discovered at the time, the decision to talk to the Unit's Physiatrist soon became a necessity. Tom swivelled upon his bottom and thrust back the duvet. He caught a reflection of himself in the full-length mirror opposite his bed and gazed back at himself, a look of utter detest etched across his profile. There he sat for several moments in his black boxers and three-day old stubble, arms placed slightly on his hips, fists clenched. Fists that grew ever tighter.

His father and his mother had been right; he had grown substantially in stature. He had always been broad but had never been toned. In fact, he had been slightly out of shape before enlisting; a slight potbelly having developed largely from his years at University, a stark contrast to the man that sat looking back at him now, more chiselled and muscular. One would be forgiven for equating his appearance with that of vanity; it could not be further from the truth.

After Anthony's death, Tom had forced upon himself a strict regime of exercise. It kept him distracted, gave him a purpose. The complex that he and his friends had inhabited for the last leg of their trip had a gym that stayed open throughout the night, which was where Tom would often slink off to every night at around one o'clock in the morning, the embrace of sleep once again eluding him. The rhythmic clang of the weights and the intense workout of cardio, free-weights and machines would tire him adequately enough to grab a few hours' sleep, enough to get him through the next day.

Sleep had become an enemy to Tom, alcohol replacing it as a welcome companion. It became for Tom another form of sedation as opposed to his friends who saw it only as a tool in which to get drunk, chase women and partake in the follies of youth. Tom would often accompany his friends to various parties, clubs and pubs in an effort to self-medicate his insomnia. These forays were used as one of many smoke screens in which Tom would retreat within himself, a façade to hide his true mental anguish.

His friends who were staying out in Australia for another month and a half had seen him off at the airport, none the wiser. Instead, they commented on the adventures they had had and how they would miss him for the final leg of their trip. *'A man down, down under'* as they had put it, not realising the insensitive nature of their phrasing.

Tom continued to stare back at the man in the mirror. That airline clerk yesterday, Louise was it? Anna? He couldn't even remember. Tom mulled over whether or not to phone her. *"Sure she was gorgeous and really nice but... are you really going to call her? Why would she be interested in you anyway? You're mess, all over the place. Just like that sodding bag."*

Tom's knuckles were now a pale yellow. They were starting to sting with the pent-up energy. He would just let her down. Just like everybody else. Just like his unit. Just like his mother and father. Just like Anthony. His counsellor had called it 'survivor's guilt' but he knew the truth and he was ashamed of it. One of the many truths he had kept from his parents, the one detail he had deliberately overlooked when recalling the series of events to his father. It had been him that had originally meant to be in Anthony's vehicle. A last-minute change in the vehicle itinerary had seen Tom pushed further to the back of the convoy.

He had felt unworthy of such dumb luck. He would have willingly taken his brother's place had he known, sacrificed himself. To this day, Tom was still unclear as to why he had lost his place in that Ridgeback armoured personnel carrier. Had it been divine providence? Some form of heavenly intervention. He was religious, a catholic.

The tingling in Tom's hands was now noticeable. He released the pressure and ran his hands through his hair, gathering the hair at the back of his head tightly. A dull trio of taps came upon the door.

"You decent Son?" came the unmistakable voice of his father.

"Yeah Dad," Tom replied, his throat dry.

He instinctively pulled the duvet across his lower body. Brian opened the door and stepped into the room, a steaming mug of tea in one hand.

"Thought I'd bring you this up," he smiled passing Tom the mug of tea.

Tom gratefully accepted, the heat from the mug slightly stinging his palms after having clenched his fists so tightly.

"Cheers Dad," he smiled before taking a cautionary sip of the mahogany liquid.

"Breakfast is going to be about five minutes. The full works, so I hope you've worked up an appetite counting all those sheep," Brian chuckled.

"I could eat a horse and go back for the jockey. Wow, that jet lag really knocks you for six," Tom remarked, turning to face his father.

Brian laughed again, more heartily this time. "Yeah your mother and I noticed. One minute we were talking about how your mother and I had seen your Auntie Jo the other week and that she was asking after you. Next thing we know, you were spark out on the couch. I know your Auntie Jo can bore the socks off of you but..." They both broke into laughter.

Brian held his right index finger aloft as if he had just remembered something. "That reminds me. Your mum has put your clothes, washed and ironed by yours truly, on the bathroom side. If you want to have a quick jump in the shower, I'll slow breakfast down."

(CHAPTER BREAK)

When Tom finally pushed the plate aside, he felt all the better for it. Recently showered, clean clothed and fit to burst from the Full English Breakfast and two mugs of tea consumed. He pushed his chair slightly back from the table in a reflex action that indicated that the meal had been exceptional and that he was full. His mother realising this, walked over to the plate and picked it up, kissing her son on the head as she did so, her lips lingering longer than usual. She was still in awe at having him back.

Brian looked up at his son as he lightly dabbed at the corner of his mouth with some kitchen roll. He smiled. "There was a pattern on that plate before you started."

Tom laughed and his mother looked up at her husband. As if trying to justify her son's hunger, she spoke up.

"The poor lad didn't know whether he was coming or going yesterday. Big lad like him needs feeding. I'm just glad we had dinner for you when you came in. Honestly, you pay all that money for a plane ticket and all they can afford to give you is a packet of crackers and a meal that wouldn't look out of place in a prisoner of war camp."

Brian tutted and rolled his eyes at Tom who also reciprocated, ensuring that his mother did not see.

"It's hardly Belsen Airlines Pam. I'm sure they accommodated them for the delay. Right," Brian clapped his hands loudly. Tom shoulders flinched. "I better go get ready for work. Tom said he was headed to the shopping centre to pick up some bits Pam."

Tom's mother had walked back to the sink in the kitchen now and was running the tap. She turned to face Brian, a warm smile registered. Brian warmly winked back at his wife. Tom looked from his mother to his father. He found himself transfixed for a moment. There was no doubt in his mind that his father, as awkward as he could be sometimes emotionally, was trying in his own way to mend the heartache he had inadvertently inflicted upon his wife the night before.

Brian turned to Tom. "I'll drop you off before my shift starts at Twelve-Thirty if you want. Save you from walking or getting the bus there," Brian offered.

"That'd be great thanks Dad. I won't be long there, just going to pick up some clothes and toiletries, see what the place has to offer," Tom stated in a jovial yet mysterious tone.

Pam toted a knife that she was currently washing and inadvertently pointed it at Tom reinforcing that the point she was about to make was of high importance.

"That place is an absolute eyesore. I'd say not to go at all for all it's taken from the area but what good will you not spending money there do? You've got a genuine reason on account of only having what's on your back." The knife turned in a circular motion, gesturing at Tom's ensemble. "You want to see the people coming in and out of there, place is never empty. When it opened loads of residents in the area embargoed the place, me and your Dad still haven't set foot in the place."

Brian nodded in response. He took up the conversation, rising from his chair as he did so. "A lot of good it did though in the end hey pam? I saw Marguerite Anders walking out of there the other day, two bags in each hand, shuffling out of the place and she's the one that started the petition. Talk about sticking to your guns." He moved over to Pam and kissed her delicately on the cheek.

"Well I wouldn't be seen dead in their mum if I could help it but it's convenient just this once." Tom was now on his feet also. "Right, well I'll get my stuff ready Dad, when are you thinking of setting off?"

Brian looked at his watch, his eyes widening slightly, "Coahh, its Ten past eleven, I'd better get a shimmy on." He looked from his watch back to Tom, "Aim to be gone by twenty to?" Brian's dialogue peeked slightly at the end in a questioning tone.

"Sounds good to me," he turned to his mother. "Mum do you need anything while I'm out?"

"No thanks lovely, when you're finished just give me a ring and I can come and get you," Pam instinctively offered.

"You don't have to do that Mum I can just…" he started.

"Son, it's no bother plus I could use your help getting the place set up for Christmas when you get back. The tree is still out the back waiting to be decorated and I need all that stuff coming down from the loft," she gestured upwards.

It suddenly became apparent to Tom that, with a mere three days to go until Christmas, the house was devoid of any festivity. He had not considered it the previous night, his jetlagged miasma in full effect.

Anthony had died in November of last year, a month ironically set aside for marking those who had fallen or would inevitably fall in future conflicts. Tom had phoned home on his brother's anniversary on the 23rd. Tom's parents had not had a Christmas last year. Tom had returned to Sierra Leone two days after his brother's funeral, his parents left to console themselves with the fact that their only surviving son was about to return to the very place that had taken their youngest.

Tom was under no illusions that this Christmas would be tough for everyone and at times contrived for his own sake, the festive veneer cracking slightly under the resounding realisation that there would be all the more turkey left over this year.

"And don't you go spending all of your money on us whatever you do. Having you back is better than anything you can get in that place," Pam sternly asserted.

"Get in and out if you ask me Son," Brian stated as he was walking out of the kitchen door. "This close to Christmas, it's going to be murder."

Little did he know as he uttered that fleeting statement that before the day was out, mourning would once again return to the Hawkins household.

(CHAPTER BREAK)

"And you're sure you have enough Son?" Brian queried as they pulled up to the curb side of Tudor Court Road, a side street located about three minutes' walk from West Acre Point.

Brian sat in his uniform; deep green shirt and trousers, finished off with perfectly polished shoes. The uniform, the same one as the paramedics in the field wore, was perfectly ironed and emblazoned with the usual logos belonging to the Emergency Services. The blue and white NHS logo to the right as well as the London Ambulance Service badge to the left, the snake coiled around what looked like the spokes of a wheel. Above the logo sat Brian's name badge which was perfectly aligned like the rest of his uniform.

"Yeah Dad, more than enough thank you. I don't intend on being in there long enough to spend a fortune, it's going to be a madhouse as it is. In and out with military precision, that's me."

Brian smiled lightly at this, "Well alright then Son."

Tom observed that his Father was holding something back. "Look Dad about this present from Anthony, don't worry I'm on it, I..."

Brian held his hand up and cut Tom off. "It's not that Son, you're a good lad and I know you won't forget to get that," Brian replied slightly exasperated.

Tom had checked several times, two of which while in the car, that he not only had his wallet but also his brother's wallet also which he had transferred to his hip pocket as an extra layer of security from pickpockets.

Brian sighed and looked out of the windscreen. Tom noticed the faintest gimmer of tears begin to well at the base of his father's eyes. Tom instinctively placed a hand upon his father's shoulder. Brian gathered himself, obviously slightly embarrassed that his son had seen him this way. He turned and looked rather solemnly at Tom.

"You see, to be quite honest with you..." a clearance of his throat. "Me and your mum, God bless her... well we've been finding it very hard lately, dealing with the loss, that is. I thought while I had you alone for a second, I'd have a word because the next couple of days, they're going to be especially hard on your mother... me included and to be quite honest with you Son..." Tom noticed that his Father seemed to be building up to something that he was finding hard to yield.

"Look Dad, I understand-" Brian raised his hand once again. Tom shifted slightly in his seat, embarrassed at once again having interrupted. Whatever his father needed to say, it needed to be said by him.

"When your brother died, I felt at the time that we had lost him forever. I mean, physically we knew he was gone but emotionally we felt like we'd been cheated out of a lot." Brian looked at his son in a manner that sought understanding. Tom reciprocated with a slight nod of the head, encouraging his father to continue.

"There are only so many pictures and trinkets that one can keep hold of to rekindle one's memories of a loved one. I mean we'll always have memories of your brother... of you and him, of us. Him growing up," his face broke into a reminiscent smile. He turned excitedly to Tom, the anguish slightly falling away from his eyes.

"Like that night, when he was fourteen, he came home late from his mate's birthday and your mother and I were worried sick. It was because he had been walking around our block because he'd forgotten to get your mum flowers for Mother's Day," his brow furrowed once again, the memory not aiding his explanation.

"You remember everything; all the grazed knees, plasters and tears but nothing can prepare you for that phone call or knock at the door. The thought creeps into your mind every so often, plants its seed but those memories you have, help to alleviate all that."

"Every time you or your brother returned from a tour or we received a letter, a Satellite call, an email, it was one more time that we could breathe a sigh of relief. Sometimes it felt like all we did was hold our breath. But it's the memories that you know you'll never get that hurt the most. The ones that all parents look forward to: Marriage, Grandchildren, just... just seeing your child grow.... Outlive you."

Brian rested his hand lightly on Tom's shoulder. "I've tried to move on as well as I can Son. Your brother's room last night... the way it's kept by your mother."

"Dad honestly, I understand," Tom abruptly interrupted. He wanted so desperately to be there for his father but this was a side to his father that he had not seen. Hell, a side that he rarely exhibited himself.

"No Son, please," he pressed on; finding this just as difficult as Tom was.

"Look, I allow your mother to keep Anthony's room like that as it helps her, I don't know how but it does. I know that may come across to you as a little weird... even morbid, but it helps. I guess what I'm trying to say is, the reason... the real reason that I can't go in there myself," he pointed towards West Acre Point, "It's because that's just one more bit of your brother, a memory, a fragment that I don't know if I can handle. So, when you go in there, into that shop, I want you to open whatever is in there."

Tom was taken aback by his father's instruction; Anthony would have wanted his Father to open his gift. He was always the kind of person who gained much more satisfaction at Birthdays and Christmas from giving gifts to others rather than receiving them himself.

"But why Dad, I mean, this is the last loose end to tie up with regards to Anthony. Maybe it would be beneficial for you to open it; you know… it might help with the grieving process?"

"That's just it Son," Brian sighed and leant over Tom. He flicked down the sun visor. "This is how I remember your brother."

He pointed towards the image Tom had stared so intently at the night before.

"I don't want to remember your brother as the man, the soldier anymore Tom. Your mum, the flags, the medals… you know it took your brother dying for it all to really hit me. All those years I served, that you and your brother served, what was the point? What difference did we really make?"

"Dad, you can't really mean that. Sure it was a job at the end of the day but we all entered into it, wanting to serve the greater good, we knew the risks."

Brian rubbed his eyes. He sighed and flopped his hands down into his lap before bringing them up several seconds later, holding them up in a showman like gesture.

"And what good did it do us Son? Honestly? Look around you. Is this what we fought to preserve? The country is going to hell. I won't lie to you, the Army made me the man I am today and I have a lot to be grateful to it for but whatever it gave me, it took double back. I have lost sleep to it, heck your mother must have had countless sleepless nights. I have lost a son to it and now my one remaining son has been side-lined by it, discarded because some jumped up politician thinks they're the true instigators of change."

Tom looked at his father with a pang of scepticism. Did he know? Was his father privy to the real reason that he had been discharged from the Army?

"I mean, you and your brother gave everything to those people out in Sierra Leone and what did your brother get in return…"

Both Brian and Tom knew that he did not need to finish that sentence. Tom squeezed his eyes shut, self-erasing the image of the inside of that armoured Land Rover. It would often pop into his thoughts, like a fog descending, the intoxicating smell, the air thick with smoke and flesh.

"I'm sorry Son. It's just hard to look lovingly upon something that you dedicated so much of your life to and to have it take away such a large chunk of it. What I'm doing now, that's benefitting people and it makes me feel validated again. It feels like I'm helping the everyman out on the street as opposed to taking orders from some politician somewhere. The day you said you were leaving the Army, I had never been more grateful. I want you to know, that whatever you decide to do now…"

He looked Tom straight in the eye and in a loving, yet conclusive way Brian continued.

"Don't turn out like me. Live your life for you and the ones you love. It's important that you look out for those around you but there is nothing more precious than family. I spent my whole life working my way back to your mother, you and Anthony. That was the real battle I faced daily. Don't feel that you've let yourself down or me or your mother for that matter by leaving the Army. You made the decision that I was never man enough to make myself. To be honest, it petrified me when you both wanted to enlist. I wish I'd said no."

Tom swallowed hard. It finally fell into place. His father held himself, in some morbid and self-deprecating manner, solely responsible for both his children enlisting. The two of them sat in silence for what seemed like an eternity. Brian finally broke the silence.

"Anyway, I felt I should say my bit. We're all dealing with this in our own way and to be honest with you Son, I feel like shit having to ask you to be the one that goes in there to pick this parcel up but it's just one battle I can't face. So please, open it for me. If it is part of the Anthony I know and love, the boy I raised, bring it home and if not...keep it yourself or give it to your mother."

Tom nodded. He wanted so desperately to console his father, to tell him that none of this was his fault. Just like his grandfather recognised when his father enlisted against his wishes, deep down the choice had never really been his to make. He went to speak but no words came.

"No problem Dad. If you change your mind, just let me know. If not, I'll open it."

Brian smiled sincerely and squeezed his sons' shoulder, a gesture that demonstrated that he was proud of the man his son had become, a non- verbal, typically heterosexual display of love and warmth.

"You better get going or I'm going to be late for work. It's always mad busy this time of year. If it's not Christmas parties gone wrong or Christmas dinners going up in flames, it's the suicides. We really are glad to have you back son. Not a lot of other people are as lucky as us at Christmas; some have it worse off than even us at the moment. Anyway, look at me getting all morbid and philosophical, be on your way and remember, don't go overdoing it on the Christmas front."

Tom smiled back at his father, "I can't promise anything."

"Well I can promise you that your mother will have both our guts for garters if you splurge too much."

His warm demeanour returned once again. Tom unbuckled his seatbelt and stepped out of the car, bidding his father farewell as he did so. As his father pulled out and disappeared down the road Tom exhaled heavily. How he longed to unburden himself, to confide in his father. With that, he turned up the collar of his jacket against the biting wind, thrust his hands into his pockets and began to approach what the locals had lovingly referred to as Contagion Tower's.

Tom muttered some words of bravado to compose himself for the madness that would ensue. "Bring it on West Acre, I'm ready for you."

(CHAPTER BREAK)

Before Tom even looked up, he knew that he had arrived at West Acre Point on account of the throngs of people shuffling outside on the street. There seemed to be a strange concoction within the melee, a mixture of impatience at being kept out in the blistering wind twinned with the excitement brought on by the flash of cameras. He swayed on his feet as someone to his left, a heavily packed carrier bag, barged past. He regained his stance and angled his shoulder slightly into the direction of the crowd.

'This isn't Christmas shopping,' he moaned to himself solemnly, *'It's a bloody scrum'*.

About twelve metres ahead, Tom could see the pristinely polished glass doors standing at around ten foot in height, four double doors in total. Tom's height afforded him a good view of the crowd, huddled in an effort to keep warm. He locked onto a man towards the front of the crowd; Santa hat adorned upon his head at a jaunty angle and logged him as a waypoint. Tom sighed; the mass of people was at least ten people deep.

Spluttering patrons and wailing children made up most of the crowd's chorus, the unmistakable mumblings of irate consumers palpable. He pulled back the sleeve of his jacket which currently, was affording little in the way of warmth. The store should have opened around an hour ago.

"What's with the hold up?" someone heckled from within the bowels of the crowd just ahead of Tom to his left.

"Come onnnn," another exasperated response erupted, long and distinctively fed up at having been kept waiting in the abrasive conditions.

Tom had failed to notice it previously but there was a substantial gathering of men ahead in high visibility jackets, standing out against the crowd in all their fluorescent splendour. They too were stamping their feet for warmth looking impatiently at one another, disgruntled at having to hold back this many people. And that's when he noticed it, metal barricades.

Tom scoffed to himself. *'The security can't think there's going to be that much trouble, we're only shopping for goodness sake'*.

One of the men in the fluorescent jackets spoke into his radio and nodded his head in a fashion that indicated he was being given orders, most likely from the head of security, watching the crowds from a monitor room elsewhere, afforded the luxury of warmth.

A woman turned towards Tom and spoke in a lowered tone, largely due to the fact that she only came up to just below his shoulder. He angled his ear towards her so that he could hear her better.

"Pardon?" he replied feigning interest with a smile.

"I was just saying I bet this is all because of that visit today. Saw it on the news before I came out, probably another PR stunt," the woman rattled off.

Tom looked back at the woman, perplexed. She soon registered the befuddled expression etched across his face and sighed, getting quite agitated now.

"The Prime Minster, he's visiting the centre today," she exclaimed.

It must have been a recent announcement as his father and mother had not mentioned it. No doubt they would have warned him off going to the shopping centre on day as chaotic as this.

"Oh right. I didn't know about that. Do you still think the shop is going to open today?" Tom was more concerned by the prospect of being put out over that of the Prime minster visiting; he cared little for politics or the people who presided within the government.

"Oh, it'll be open all right," the woman scoffed. "How else is he going to pull a crowd in? That's why they've done it."

Tom sniffed back a dribble of snot. "Done what?"

The woman's face indicated all the signs of someone who was immediately regretting engaging Tom in conversation. She had wanted Tom to serve as a sounding board for her own political agenda but had instead found herself explaining the events.

"Obvious isn't it? The countries going to pot, the bankers, politicians and elites are getting richer by the minute and its Christmas time. What better opportunity to demonstrate to the people that the economy is going all hunky dory than a visit to a thriving shopping centre and three days before Christmas no less. All against the backdrop of the most wonderful time of the year," she finished with a flourish of disgust.

"Seems like overkill to me. I mean what's he here to do, pick up some last-minute bits?"

The woman laughed to herself quite smugly, seemingly having engaged the young man. "Probably, there's enough cameras and security in there if he wanted his own personalised shopping spree. He's doing a speech as well." The woman rolled her eyes and tutted. "He is a politician after all. They love to talk but talk isn't going to buy my two kids diddly squat. I'm losing money as it is just taking the morning off to be here and the sodding place isn't even open. I tell you…"

The woman was cut off by the high-pitched metallic ringing of a megaphone being switched on. Many in the crowd winced, the noise going straight through them. Tom turned his attention back towards the barriers and saw a portly, robust gentleman standing on a heightened platform. The man, who had very little in the way of hair was ruddy faced, a pair of squared, rather outdated, glasses occupying much of his bulbous profile. He too had grimaced at the noise of the megaphone and in an awkward fashion, fumbled with the dials.

He held his hand up in apology and began to speak into the megaphone. No words came. He seemed to be reassuring the crowd from what Tom could gather, his hands moving in calming arcs. Some in the crowd erupted into laughter while others tutted impatiently. Finally, someone spoke up.

"We can't hear you mate."

The bloated security guard cupped his ear. Tom located the man to his right and saw him raise his cupped hands.

"I said we can't hear you. The megaphone is off!" The man turned and rolled his eyes at the person next to him, who returned his glance with a snort of laughter.

The bloated security guard once again set about fiddling with the megaphone and brought it up to his mouth, shouting.

"Good morning ladies and gentlemen," his nasally tone washed over the crowd. He pushed the oversized glasses up onto the bridge of his nose further. "We would like to apologise for the wait and I am pleased to announce that we are about to start admitting you into the complex."

A large, jeering cry swept across the crowd, framed by someone off to the back of the crowd shouting, "It's about bloody time."

The security guard looked flustered and pushed the presell switch on his megaphone. "As you know we have a very special guest at the centre today and we were late setting up some last-minute security but are ready to admit you now. Please have your bags ready to be searched at the doors where the security team and members of the police, will usher you through as quickly as possible."

The security guards that stood behind their overweight superior stepped back in a regimented fashion, satisfied with the signal to open the doors.

"Here at West Acre Point we would just like to say welcome and thank you for your continued support and have a very, merry..." He did not finish as the throng surged past him towards the doors, he stumbled and dipped below Tom's eye line, swallowed by the mass of frenzied consumers

Those at the head of the queue were through the barriers in no time, already through the high glass doors. As Tom got closer to the doors, about ten metres away now, he could see the scene that was to play out once he and the crowd entered the centre. Tom, regardless of his size and stature, seemed to be getting pushed towards the periphery of the crowd. He focused on the glass doors and edged himself back towards the centre of the melee, exerting force with his right shoulder. His early metaphor about it being like a scrum was now fully realised. Along with another rather tall gentleman, broad and bearded also, Tom anchored his position and the crowd began to move in a more linear fashion.

Tom focused on the doors. The crowd were being merged into four lanes, one for each set of double doors. Tom could now see what the man with the megaphone had meant. Although still slightly jostled, Tom could see the unmistakable black and white uniform of the Metropolitan Police, finished off and adorned by the world-famous Custodian Helmet, festooned with highly polished silver crest.

From his current position he could see that two officers stood at each set of doors and behind them, a metal detector. To the left of each metal detector was a table whereby a member of the shopping centre security and another police officer, halted the potential customers and searched through their bags. Tom considered turning back; this was going to take a while. He crooked his neck and could no longer see the street he had just entered via. The only way was forward.

Tom soon found himself being angled towards the second queue from the left, about twentieth in line. He sighed once again checking his watch. He had now been in the crowd for around forty minutes and like many within the crowd, was starting to become irate. He understood the level of security when such a high-profile target such as the Prime Minister was visiting, however, it did not help the fact that regardless of the Prime Minister's visit, he cared little.

Tom was close to the doors now and was glad of it. A light drizzle hung in the air and with it, the distinct iciness of the wind. He shuffled forward, herded like cattle, the slaughter of long checkout queues and irate shoppers fighting over products they had little need for ahead. The distinct authoritative voice of a male police officer ahead could now be heard.

"Empty the contents of your pockets into this container please sir and remove any metallic items."

The officer's tone displayed the monotony that he must be feeling at having to state the same demand repeatedly. Tom and those ahead of him were handed a plastic bowl for their possessions. He thrust his hands into his pockets and begun emptying his contents into the bowl when he was inadvertently thrust forward suddenly by the crowd behind, bumping into a smaller gentleman in front. The man lurched forward before steadying himself against the barrier that separated each of the four distinct lines on either side. Tom grasped at the man and helped steady him, pulling him upright by the shoulder.

"I'm really sorry, the crowd …" Tom started not wanting to appear animalistic like those thrusting and surging around him.

The man turned and afforded Tom a warm smile. "Not to worry mate, largely my fault. Not as steady on my feet as I used to be."

Tom smiled back, unaware as to what the man meant by this. He was far too young to be in need of a walking stick by all intents and purposes and seemed in control of all of his bodily functions.

The man, in his mid-thirties Tom approximated was wiry in frame and seemed quite hunched in his appearance. He had short brown hair that was combed back with grease rather than any type of product. He wore blue jeans and black boots, finished off with a thick Barbour style jacket, green like his eyes.

The man removed his hand from the barrier and seemed to read Tom's uneasiness, "It'll be a Christmas miracle if we get out of here before the big day. I've never seen anything like it."

Tom acknowledged this statement with a low laugh, grateful that any possible tension between the two had been averted. He just wanted to get in and out of this place. The woman in front of the gentlemen was ushered through and handed back her possessions which including the shoes she had been wearing. The man in the green Barbour jacket shuffled forward, handing his bowl over to the police officer.

It contained a set of keys, a wallet, watch and his belt. The police officer nudged his hand around the contents of the bowl and flicked through the man's wallet. Satisfied he asked him to remove his shoes. The man straightened slightly and Tom observed that the man appeared to suddenly become a little defensive in his stature.

"I'm afraid that might be a bit of an issue Officer," he responded coyly.

The police officer straightened. One of the hands behind his back now rose instinctively up to his radio, his other gripping the strap of his stab proof vest. He was cautious of the man before him.

"And why would that be sir? I assure you this is for safety purposes only and that if we do not have your full co-operation you shall not be permitted into the centre today."

Tom observed that the officer, tall with strong features, was being rather forceful. He had a job to do but there was no need for a lack of courtesy. Tom also observed that an officer on the other side of the metal detectors, armed with an MP5 and holstered sidearm, had now stepped forward slightly taking an interest in the disturbance.

"I can't take them off you see because…" the man stopped talking as the officer in front of him turned and talked into his radio. On cue, the armed officer strode over.

The man in the green jacket seemed to become quite flustered by this and tried to explain, "If you'll just listen officer."

The officer seemed disinterested and turned to meet the armed officer, happy to let him take over.

The armed officer stepped forward and spoke in a broad London accent, "What seems to be the problem here sir? This is routine and you're holding up the other shoppers."

"I was just saying to…" he struggled to find the words; his nerves were now getting the better of him, "… explain to your colleague here that I can't take off my shoes."

The armed officer, now also visibly flustered, seemed to have reached the same level of tedium that his colleague had before. The armed officer, the MP5 now level with his waist, traced the outside of the trigger guard slightly with his index finger.

He sighed and angled his head. "And why would that be sir?

The man turned and locked eyes with Tom; he seemed rather embarrassed, slightly awkward. Tom shot him a reassuring smile. The man turned back and faced the two officers. He did not answer but simply reached down and grabbed the hems of his jeans. The armed officer tightened his grip upon his MP5 and raised it a centimetre or two higher. His colleague placed his hand instinctively upon his belt, conveniently next to his can of mace. The man raised his jean legs to that of the height of his knees and Tom saw both Officers look down, their stern demeanours now replaced with that of discomfort. The officers shared a loo, the officer who had first stopped the man growing crimson in colour.

The gentleman in front of them began to explain, "You see, I can't take my shoes off as it takes some effort to put them on in the first place and it wouldn't make any difference as…" he indicated to his legs and tapped upon one "… well because they're not mine. I lost mine five years back."

The man sheepishly looked at the officers. Tom afforded himself a closer look at the man before him. The man was wearing not one but two prosthetic legs, black in colour made of what looked like a metallic, carbon fibre. Stuck to one was a Union Jack sticker and to the back of his left leg where his calf would once have been, was a painted crest, gold in colour.

It was a winged dagger with the infamous motto, *"WHO DARES WINS"*, the clear and synonymous crest that belonged to the Special Air Service.

The armed officer gestured with his hand for the gentleman to drop his trouser legs. He cleared his throat, the confidence his gun had initially afforded him seemingly sapped away.

"Very well Sir," another clearance of his throat, followed by a shift in the level of his gun, "through you go."

He tapped the other officer on the arm and gestured that he hand back the bowl containing the man's possessions. The man took the bowl and made to leave but not before he was afforded one final piece of indignant abuse from the officer on the metal detector.

"Next time sir, I suggest you comply fully with any demands made to you by an officer of the law to avoid such circumstances. Through you go."

He gestured for the man to go through, which he did so with the unsurprising beep of the metal detector. Tom could not help but tut, a reaction that the officer noticed and returned with a scowl, jutting his hand out expectantly for Tom's bowl. Tom passed through with no trouble, furious at what he had just witnessed.

As he walked through the detector he internally screamed *"Prick!"* in the direction of the officer. Ahead, stood the gentlemen, jacket thrust up to chest height as he placed his belt back through the loops of his jeans. He caught Tom's glance and smiled.

"I only came in for a pair of tap shoes," he quipped.

Tom laughed respecting the man all the more for his resilience and unfazed nature.

Tom gestured with a thumb back towards the officer. "That was completely out of order, the jumped-up little Hitler. Tom by the way," he smiled extending his hand. The man eyed Tom's hand hesitantly, slightly taken aback by Tom's courteous nature.

"Don," the man replied, firmly reciprocating.

"Well, Merry Christmas Don and I wouldn't worry about him, he's probably just pissed because he's on overtime, not that he won't be getting paid double bubble for it," Tom announced with a substantial note of disgust, still internally furious at the events that had just occurred.

Don smiled, "That or he's on the naughty list. No gift-wrapped truncheon or riot horse from Santa Clause this year." They both laughed. "Well, I better be off. Plenty to do and plenty to buy and the quicker the better I say, Merry Christmas."

He raised his hand in a gesture to say goodbye and with that he was off. Tom returned the gesture and watched as Don drifted off and mingled into the crowd, no longer visible.

'What a salt of the Earth bloke,' Tom concluded as he stepped forward, intent on getting out of the shopping Centre as soon as possible. He strode forward and once again collided with a man in a bright orange fluorescent set of overalls. The man had been carrying a roll of wire and an assorted mixture of chains and padlocks. The items exploded from the man's reach

and he made a concerted, if not futile effort, to grab them. They hit the floor with a sound that reverberated upon the unforgiving marble.

Tom stepped forward to help and was halted by the raising of the man's hand, an indication that he wanted no help from Tom.

"I'm really sorry, that was my fault, in too much of a rush. I'm sorry."

"You wanna watch where you're bloody going," a deep and jagged voice returned.

The man still had his back to Tom; all that was visible was the blue boxed logo with yellow font emblazoned upon his back establishing that he belonged to a contractor called, 'Harpers Construction LTD.'

Tom was taken aback by this. He knew that it had been his fault for bumping into the man but he had apologised for it, which was more than he would likely get form many of the other shoppers.

He decided to make one more concerted effort to apologise. The man was now pulling the materials he had dropped close into his body. He had missed one padlock and chain that had slid off to his right. Tom picked it up and turned it over in his hands. The lock and chain were new, still highly polished and displaying little in the way of scratches or dullness.

"I really am sorry. Here, you dropped this," Tom held out the chain.

The man, barely turning, glanced over his shoulder. Tom observed that he had dark brown eyes, almost black with a tuft of black hair that protruded from the rim of his orange helmet. He inspected Tom with a singular glaring eye as his olive paint flecked hand snatched the chain. He mumbled something, repositioned his hands to accommodate his items and threw the spool of wire over his right shoulder and with that, briskly marched off.

"Well stuff you then," Tom responded under his breath.

He turned and looked for a help desk. It was not hard to find as it was located near the main entrance he had just entered and was accompanied by four members of staff, all smartly dressed in black suits, accompanied by name badges and smiling faces. As Tom approached a woman on the desk looked up from a computer and smiled.

"How can I help you today sir?" she cordially offered.

Tom, not wanting to be too much of a bother smiled, "No thank you, I just need a map." He reached down onto the glass top and picked up a palm sized foldable map.

The woman nodded and reeled off the final bit of her repertoire: "Merry Christmas sir and don't forget the Prime Minister's speech will start in exactly..." she looked at her watch "...forty-five minutes, whereby all of the shops will be closed for a thirty-minute period." And with that, she looked back down at the monitor of her computer screen and began a rhythmic typing.

Tom pondered asking why the shops would be shut during the speech but thought better of it. After all, how else was the Prime Minister expecting to draw a crowd? He would be hard pressed to find may people in Britain at present that remotely liked him, let alone wanted to stand for half an hour and listen to him.

Tom unfurled the map and surveyed the shops on offer. He scanned the pages of the map, about the size of an A3 sheet of paper and mentally sketched out his battle plan. The shopping centre consisted of four levels: the ground level, first floor, second floor and the third level which was referred to as the 'Food Hall and observation deck'. Tom had established that the main motive of his visit, the shop his father had wanted him to visit, 'In the Frame', was located on the second floor to the west of the shopping centre.

This would be the second to last stop on his route around the centre. He would end it in the homeware section of the department store Osborne's, where he hoped he could find his mother a gift or two within his budget. Tom also noticed that on the map it stated that the West Plaza was still under construction and reliably informed him that it would be completed and ready for admittance by early March.

Looking up he could see to his right that the whole of the bottom floor upwards had been boarded off with wood and various blue, white and yellow construction signs establishing 'Construction in progress' and 'Hard Hat area only'. Although the shops to the West of the centre were still visibly open on every level, it was quite the eyesore. Other than that however, the centre in itself, was quite stunning. Tom was taken aback by how grandiose it was, the centre constructed of white marble throughout. The whole foundations of the building were held up by sentinel like columns of thick stone, which were at present adorned with a holly bush finish.

Above, the ceiling tapered into a pyramid of glass, emblazoned on all three sides with a stained-glass finish of the West Acre Point logo. From the ceiling, more decorations were draped down to Ground level. Squinting, Tom could make out that the objects were large, novelty presents, gift wrapped in purple, red, green and gold. A novelty Santa, about six feet in size also trailed from the ceiling on a length of lighting.

The place was decked from head to toe in Christmas decorations. Even the glass barriers that partitioned the edge of the concourse on each floor were festively festooned. From his quick analysis of the map, Tom established that the shops were located to the left and right of the reception area on all floors. There were also shops to the north end of the centre that rose upwards to the very top level of the precinct.

The magnitude of the task that lay ahead of Tom was beginning to dawn upon him. He had wanted to be in and out of the centre, ideally, before the Prime Ministers speech but was swiftly coming to the realisation that he had a snowball's chance in hell of accomplishing that personal victory. The place was mobbed.

Looking up Tom could see that the steady throng of people lined the concourse walkways on both sides. The Ground level comprised of an open area that would usually be used for general congregation and seating. However, in its place, to the North of the centre, just in front of Santa's Grotto, was a stage.

The stage was framed by a further quadrant of barriers, a containment area for the audience to stand in mass congregation. Upon the stage stood a podium, behind it six chairs, three on either side, were located to the back of the stage. The podium bore the party's logo as did the back of the stage which consisted entirely of a giant banner, again with the political logo and their mantra, "Keeping the Great in Britain." The area could easily hold over two thousand people and was already about a third of the way full, largely due to the press junket located towards the front of the barriers.

The area would have housed more if it were not for an ornate and beautifully crafted water fountain in the middle. The water feature, about eight metres in diameter, was made up of the same pristine white marble as the rest of the complex. In the middle stood an elegant golden statue of Britannia, the feminine personification of Britain since the Roman era.

She, like all of the symbolic incarnations that Tom had seen before, sat astride a Lion, complete with a shield baring the Union Jack, robustly etched upon the metal. In her other hand, a trident which allowed three flumes of water to jut from each point. The water surrounding the mosaic base of the statue captured this and no doubt contained many a discarded piece of change from passers-by, many a wish willingly cast. Tom made to move on when an announcement over the centre's intercom system sounded out.

"A very festive good morning to you shoppers, just a polite reminder that our very special guest at West Acre Point today, the country's very own Prime Minister, Andrew Pierce, will be visiting the centre today and will be giving a speech on the Ground level. Those wanting to gain a closer look are welcome to attend the designated cordoned off area in front of the stage."

"In addition, we would like to reiterate that all shops will be shut for the duration of the Prime Minister's speech and that those not situated on the Ground level may view the speech from the various concourses situated on levels one and two. However, you will not be permitted access to the Restaurant level. All those wanting to get those last minute Christmas bargains before the shops close for this short period are invited to attend Richmond and Bakers festive happy hour where everything is 25 percent off in store. Hurry though, because when those doors close, so does the discount and in about... twenty-seven minutes. From all of us here at West Acre Point have a great day in store and have a very Merry Christmas."

The message was cut off by the distinctive festive favourite, 'I Wish It Could Be Christmas Everyday' by Wizzard.

Tom rolled his eyes and scoffed, "I bet you do you greedy bastards."

CHAPTER SIX: SLAY RIDE

The plastic dust sheets hung from the walls in the yet unfinished West Plaza like spectres, swirling in the light breeze the open roof provided. The room located on the upper level of the centre was sealed off to the public and was a death trap to anyone not supervised to be there. This was largely due to the unfinished completion of the ceiling, at present covered by scaffolding and tarpaulin as well as a substantial uncompleted section of flooring. One misguided step upon the structurally unsound floor would result in a substantial drop down into the level below, a fall of at least twenty metres. Certain death would be all that waited.

Although it was early morning the room was shrouded in darkness. At present much of the space and the contents that occupied it were unrecognisable masses, outlines that did not give away their true identity. Much like the room, both the investors and the foreman's superiors had largely been kept in the dark, the extension of the West Plaza alarmingly behind schedule. The planning and materials needed had been significantly underestimated and to make matters worse, materials seemed to have gone missing. At first it had been basic materials such as the odd bag of cement or a tin or two of paint but as of late, a rather substantial amount had gone missing: tools mostly.

The foreman, Terry Hill, had taken an itinerary of all materials and had even reviewed both the internal and external CCTV footage of the complex. Currently, due to the construction work in progress, there were no cameras currently set up inside this section of the building. Hill had sat every morning with the Head of Security for an hour or so mulling over the slightly sped up footage of the night before in an effort to ascertain when the thefts were taking place.

Since his investigation had started little under a week ago, he had discovered absolutely nothing and this morning had been no different. As if that wasn't bad enough, he had been seconded away from overseeing the wiring of one of the outlets towards the end of the West Plaza, to respond to a noise complaint he had received from the Night Security Guard when he had entered West Acre that morning.

The Security Guard had stated that when he had been patrolling the Third Level, he believed he could hear a repetitive clunking noise that would stop briefly before starting up again. He could investigate no further on account of the door being padlocked from the outside. Hill had immediately dismissed this as a loose bit of scaffolding most likely blowing in the breeze causing it to collide with another bit of scaffolding or wall. After all, without the approval of his superiors no work would have been sanctioned at such an unsociable hour. The security guard, frankly not bothered either way, accepted this explanation and signed out, grateful to have ended his long shift.

He arrived at the wooden barrier that sealed off the area, a singular door to the left of the thick wood. The chain was looped between two holes in the thick plywood which he tested with a cautionary tug. As he suspected the passageway was still firmly secured. He fumbled momentarily with the key before entering; pushing aside the plastic sheeting that was draped across the entrance. He was immediately met with a strong gust of wind and the unmistakable smell of powdered cement.

He reached for his torch and flicked it on, instinctively arching it to his left where he knew he would find the nearest portable floodlight to switch on. When he did so, he stepped back and took in the entirety of the room. It was largely illuminated now except for a partial piece of the room to his right that was still cloaked in shadow. He ventured further into the room the floor littered with crisp packets and empty bottles of water.

"What messy bugger's left this up here?" he muttered, disgruntled that the men had been eating on site.

Large swathes of the floor were still incomplete on the Third Level and he made towards the scaffolding with concerted trepidation before tentatively reaching out and testing it at strategic points. Then using his torch, he traced the beam along the ceiling, from corner to corner, looking for any loose scaffolding. Satisfied he lowered his torch and made to leave when he suddenly froze.

A week had elapsed since he had last ventured into this section of the construction or any man for that matter, the brunt of the work having taken place on the three levels below. Curiosity peaked, Hill advanced into the unlit section of the room, clicking his torch on once again. With a look of pure confusion, he placed his fingers upon the wall. It felt cold to the touch and was made of sturdy plaster board.

It was his job to know the specifications of the build inside and out, so much so that he barely had to consult the blueprints anymore. It was for this exact reason that he arrived at his conclusion instantaneously; this wall was not supposed to be here. As if proving to himself that he was not hallucinating, Hill rapped his knuckles upon the wall.

'Hollow!' he mentally confirmed.

He had not authorised this wall to be built and what worried him more so was the fact that it had not been here last week. The coat of white paint was unlike the hue of the other three walls and was covered in a spattering of dust. It was fresh. Hill trained the torch upon his thumb and forefinger as he rubbed the two together.

He was so engrossed in his examination that he was oblivious to the shadow that now framed the plastic sheeting of the doorway. So much so that when he heard the rustle of plastic sheeting he nearly jumped out of his skin. He veered round aiming the torch at his assailant, who instantly covered his eyes from the glare of the torch. Hill relaxed. It was one of the new workers, Gary. Hill put his hand to his heart in a mock gesture.

"Bloody hell Gary, you nearly gave me a bloody heart attack."

"Sorry Guv. I was just coming to find you. We're out of plug sockets downstairs. Thought it best to come and ask you where they were."

Gary took a step into the light and removed his hard hat, placing within the crook of his arm. He was a slender man with cropped brown hair sodden with sweat. His work overalls always seemed to hang free off of him as if trying to avoid physical contact.

Gary had impressed Hill although not at first. Upon hiring him a month ago he rather biasedly wrote him off, largely due to his emaciated physique. However, Hill had been surprised by the way he fulfilled his duties. He could heft bricks or heavy machinery as good as the next man and his plastering technique was both quick and efficient. He had equated his slightly hunched back and hobbling gait down to years of wear and tear, the physicality of the job taking its toll as it did on many a builder. Hill gestured to Gary with his hand, signalling for him to come over, completely ignoring the question he had been asked.

"Here Gary, come and have a look at this," he ushered, pointing at the wall.

Gary walked over and looked at the wall. After several seconds he turned to Hill perplexed.

"Not the best bit of plastering I've ever seen if I may say so. It wasn't me before you ask," he added defensively.

Hill rolled his eyes and knocked on the wall. "No, no, no. Not the plastering, the wall. Something very strange is going on here." He prodded at the wall now, accentuating each syllable, "This wall was not here a week ago and I sure as hell didn't authorise it."

Gary scratched his head. "That sure is a doozy Guv. Damned if I've heard anything about it, I've been down on Level..."

"That's just the point, no one should have been up here and look," he gestured to the empty pile of bottles and crisp packets. "It looks like someone's had a bloody banquet up here." He looked intently at Gary. "I think whoever has been stealing our materials, has been using it up here. God knows why and to what end but it would explain where all that stock has gotten to."

"Have you asked anyone else about the wall? Did Head Office have anything to say about it?" Gary enquired.

"Just noticed it myself, had the night shift tell me that they heard a racket up here, a clanging noise. I thought it was a loose bit of scaffolding but it's all secured. No one could have got in here without my key anyway. I'm going to get Head Office on the phone sharpish, see if we can't shine a bit of light on it."

Hill made an effort to leave but stopped.

Gary reached up to his ear and pulled free a roll up, placing it into his mouth. He began to pat his pockets, looking for a lighter. Hill's face was a portrait of procedural rage.

"You don't think you're going to smoke that in here do you? And put that bloody hardhat back on! Head office would kill you if they found out and let me remind you that as your foreman, I..." Gary held his hand up in a gesture that cut Hill off.

An orange and blue flume of flame lit his cigarette. He took a drag upon the cigarette and proceeded to blow the smoke into Hill's face. Hill coughed and fanned it from his face, growing more crimson by the second. Gary replaced the hard hat, only this time at a jaunty angle, further mocking Hill.

"This is an active worksite and that sunshine is a disciplinary offence. You are violating more health and safety regulations than I would even care to explain. So, either stub it out or get off my site toot sweet. Your choice," Hill spat.

Gary took another drag upon his cigarette and held it for several seconds, eyes closed in apparent ecstasy. He shot them open suddenly, a devilish grin now replacing his motionless expression. Hill felt his skin squirm.

"Health and safety," Gary scoffed taking a step towards Hill. "Health and safety!"

Hill retreated several steps before making contact with a worktable in the centre of the room, knocking a handful of nails to the ground. They jingled and bounced momentarily, briefly penetrating the silence.

Gary grinned further, holding up a reassuring hand. "Be careful there now Tel, we wouldn't want you having a work-related accident, now would we?" He laughed demonically.

Hill held his torch aloft, his hand evidently shaking as the beams motion was erratic. He continued to retreat backwards. Gary surrendered no ground, advancing with each step, predator- like in fashion.

Gary adopted the bravado of a salesman, extrovert and shouting.

"Had an accident at work? Want to know if you're entitled to compensation? Then why not give our ace legal team a call. No win no fee. No case too small."

He was now about three feet away from Hill. He lashed out with the torch but Gary simply arched his back, dodging the slow, half-hearted attack. "I'm warning you, you fucking loon. Stay back or I'll cave that thick skull of yours in."

Gary held his index fingers aloft and moved them from left to right, as if rebuking a mischievous child.

"Ah, ah, ah. Abuse in the workplace will not be tolerated. That is a disciplinary offence. But don't worry," Gary said as he picked up a Stanley knife from the work bench. "... It comes with a great severance package. It truly is head and shoulders above the rest."

Gary abruptly lashed out with the Stanley knife, a swiping action that missed Hills torso by inches. Hill lurched back and ran to the other side of the work bench, using it as cover. The two began to circle the work bench, keeping their eyes permanently fixed upon one another.

Shakily, Hill grasped at a hammer and raised it level, affording himself a smile. Gary could see that Hill had grown overconfident, the misguided belief that he, quite literally had the upper hand. He took advantage and grasped a handful of nails out of the foreman's line of sight.

Gary burst into fits of laughter. "Now is no time to table a meeting Guv," he mischievously snorted.

Suddenly, Gary lashed out with the Stanley knife once again, catching Hill off guard. He did so again, Hill waving the hammer as a warning, knowing his aggressor was too far to mount any form of decent attack. It was this false sense of safety that was to be his downfall.

Gary timed the moment perfectly. Just as Hill lurched in for a counterattack Gary threw the obscured nails at Hill with accurate force. Hill defended his eyes, bringing the hammer across his head, shielding himself.

It was all the time Gary needed to administer his attack. With lightning ferocity, he leapt forward and leant across the table, slicing Hill across the forehead. Hill lurched back, the emission of crimson blood instantaneous. He brought the other hand up to shield his forehead as well as in an effort to apply some pressure to the deep wound, his hardhat dislodged, clattered off the cold cement. He began to breathe heavily and a whimper crept from his throat.

Gary calmly walked to the side of the table. Hill, now blinded by the relentless flow of blood, swung wildly with the hammer, hoping to strike his attacker a lucky blow.

Gary stood and watched Hill flailing his arms, enjoying the spectacle. He placed one fist upon his hip and used the other to rap upon Hill's helmet three times.

In a mocking, stern and authoritative voice he menacingly jived, "This is a hard hat area Mr Hill. You really should know better. But that's ok, you can have mine," and with that he took off his own hard hat and swung it with such force that it lifted Hill straight off his feet, his hammer flung from his grasp.

Hill was now crying, not that one could tell from the constant stream of blood smeared across his features. He turned onto his front and began to crawl for the door. Gary allowed him to do so, walking calming behind him. He picked up Hills' discarded hammer and began swinging it in a Chaplinesque manner.

Hill blindly grabbed at the floor with one hand as he dragged himself along, the other groping for the plastic dust sheet that would afford him the knowledge that he had made it to the entrance. Gary began to whistle 'Heigh Ho' in a concerted effort to let Hill know he was close.

"Heigh Ho, Heigh Ho, it's off to work we go," a hammer bounced harshly off of the cold cement nearby, Hills terrified yelp causing Gary a shudder of pleasure.

After what seemed like an eternity, Hill reached the plastic sheeting and grabbed at it. It shot taut with the effort. The whistling stopped. For a brief moment Hill listened, arching his ear wildly trying to ascertain his attacker's location. He could only make out his own whimpering. He used the arm of his sleeve to wipe at his slashed forehead, a wave of nausea and searing pain racing through the gash. He was completely blind. He listened intently, hoping, praying that Gary had gone.

He had not. The hammer came down about several inches from his head, the sound of the blunt metal bouncing off the solid concrete sending tremors throughout Hill's body. Hill's convulsed state twinned with that of the tarnished and bloodied sheeting, afforded little in the way of purchase. He could now taste blood in his mouth. Out of sheer desperation, he decided to make an attempt at negotiation.

"Puh… puh… please, don't hurt me. I won't say anything, to anybody," he implored.

"Now we both know that that's just not going to be possible Mr Hill. This is a disciplinary hearing and you are being charged with serious offences, full disclosure is advised."

Hill made an imploring grab for his attacker's ankle, grabbing it in a weak, begging fashion. Gary allowed him to maintain his weak purchase, the foreman of little threat in his current state.

"Grave offences I'm afraid, Mr Hill. I mean for starters there's the verbal abuse of another member of staff..."

The hammer swung down striking Hill's wrist. He cried out loudly in pain yet not so loud as to mask the sound of breaking bone. Hill's sobbing became louder. All manner of tools and machinery continued to buzz off in the distance, reducing the chance of him being heard.

"And then there's the matter of not reporting a potentially dangerous and structurally substandard wall to Head Office."

The hammer came down again, this time on the hand that held the plastic sheeting. Gary just missed the back of the hand but instead got three of Hill's fingers. Hill instantly let go, his chin impacting hard upon the cement floor. A heavy release of exasperated breath dispersed a dusty cloud from the face of the felled foreman.

"And then Mr Hill, there is the significant and unforgivable act of not wearing a hard hat on site, a piece of equipment that may have prevented you a serious accident today and for that..." Gary put a leg either side of Hill, standing over him, "... Mr Hill, Terry my old mucker, as judge, jury and executioner I must make an example of you, bring down my gavel as it were. You must understand," he stooped slightly so that Hill could hear, "this is not my preferred weapon of choice but hey, a good workman never blames his tools."

He laughed again in a high pitched and giddy fashion. "Now where was I? Oh yes, I sentence you to..." The first hammer blow bounced quite forcefully off of the base of Hill's skull, his whole body twitching instantaneously. Gary brought it down again, this time entering the skull and with it, completing his sentence, "... death."

He stood over Hill for several seconds, breathing heavily from exertion. Blood had splattered the plastic sheeting and the surrounding wood panelling of the entrance. He wiped the hammer on Hill's trousers before lightly placing the hammer next to Hill's lifeless frame.

"You know Terry; this could have all been avoided. I mean for starters, your vetting process needs some serious work. My name isn't even Gary. Greaves is the name," he offered his hand mockingly as if to shake Hill's. It was flecked with blood and miscellaneous chunks.

Greaves retracted his hand, wiping it briefly upon his overalls. "No problem Guv, we can hammer out those details another time."

Greaves smiled to himself. The first of many to come he considered gleefully. He bent and clutched Hill by the ankles dragging him away from the door frame. He then walked back to the door and with a concerted tug pulled the plastic sheeting down. He looked out onto the concourse maintaining that no one was outside or that no blood had seeped outwards onto the marble. Satisfied, he pulled the door shut and strode back towards the centre of the room. He bent down and seized his helmet from the floor, being careful to diligently wipe the blood off with a scrap of cloth before he repositioned it atop his head.

With that, he began wrapping Hill tightly within the sizeable roll of plastic sheeting. When complete, he dragged Hill over to the shaded area to the right of the room. He wiped his hands upon the floor and walked towards the door. Before flicking the portable floodlight off, he afforded himself a glance over his shoulder and nodded content with his handiwork.

He exited and re-padlocked the door. He did not need to worry about retrieving the key from the foreman, they already had a copy. He tested the door with a strong tug and turning right, set off down the gradual slant of the concourse. He glanced down at the lower levels of packed with people and smiled again.

Another construction worker approached holding a spool of wiring. Greaves simply tipped his hard hat in a greeting and started up a fresh chorus of 'Heigh Ho'.

(CHAPTER BREAK)

The wind and rain had picked up quite considerably as the Land Rover pulled up to the back entrance of West Acre Point. Visibility was a nightmare. For all Gerry knew, there could be a would-be assassin standing right next to the side of the car, waiting to take his chance. All he could see of the building ahead was through the occasional arched movement of the window wipers as they sliced through the rain, only for the windscreen to be instantly engulfed by deluge once again. The windscreen wipers were going at full pelt, the car's central heating helping to get rid of some of the condensation that was forming on the inside of the windows. Gerry wiped his hand across the passenger seat's window, trying to survey the surrounding area.

Gerry had next to his right leg, in the foot well, a large black umbrella. He fiddled with the handle in a slightly nervous fashion, not that he dared mention this to the Prime Minister in the back seat. Besides, he had previously been concerned little by his anxieties and was currently sifting through his speech with his aide. The visibility was awful and although the team had pulled up close to the precinct's doors, complete with a police motorcade consisting of four bikes in the motor unit, flanking each side of the Land Rover in a diamond formation, Gerry felt rather exposed.

He had an uneasy temper, whether he liked to admit it consciously or not, concerning the conversation he had had with the Prime Minister the previous day. He would most likely never work for the Prime Minister again, any Prime Minister or form of dignitary for that matter.

Gerry kept turning it over in his head, asking himself the same questions; *'Why can't he see I was just trying to do my job, why is he being such a prick? It would have been a different story if it had been a bullet or that stall owner had stuck him like a pig?'*

But he always arrived at the same conclusion; it was because he was a prick. A man so self-inflated and the damage limitation that his PR team and spin doctor's afforded him, that he thought himself untouchable and as Gerry knew all too well, no man was untouchable.

Gerry glanced up into the rear-view mirror, deciding to break the silence.

"One minute Mr Prime minster, the team is just surveying the area to ensure it is safe to proceed."

Still watching the Prime Minister in the rear-view mirror, Gerry noticed that Andrew Pierce had barely acknowledged that someone had spoken to him. He turned and shot Jack Wright a grimace, clenching his teeth in a display that demonstrated to Jack that he was using every fibre of restraint that he had at his disposal. Jack smirked and covered his mouth with his hand when he noticed that Jeremy Grant, the Prime Minister's aide, had caught his eye line.

Grant locked eyes with Jack and in a pompous attempt at establishing dominance, maintained it for several seconds. Jack accepted the challenge graciously; he had had just about enough of this runt.

Grant withdrew his gaze first. Rather impatiently he spoke up, "What is taking so long?"

Gerry turned in his seat to face Grant. He was raging now, *"Unbelievable! These jumped up snobs have barely acknowledged us this whole time."*

Gerry decided to shelve his internal monologue yet maintained a stern tone, infuriated that had Grant or Pierce bothered to remove themselves from their personal political bubble, a response would not have been needed.

"As I was just saying a minute ago," Gerry asserted, Grant's smug features clouding over with contempt at Gerry's forthright attitude, "The team are just doing a sweep and will be ready within the next couple of minutes. I assure you Mr Grant, we will not keep you or the…"

Grant cut him off, venom dripping from every syllable, "Who do you think you are talking to Mr Taverner? I asked a very simple question. The Prime Minister is a terribly busy man; he does not have time to-"

Gerry held his finger up stopping Grant mid-flow, the aides face turning crimson. The radio had crackled into life. Grant in his internal tirade only heard the word 'proceed'.

Smiling, Gerry turned round in his seat and stepped out into the rain, shutting the door behind him. He opened the umbrella and took a deep breath. His patience was well and truly being tested today. He stepped towards the set of twin warehouse bay doors and approached the firearms officer on duty, who had taken up position under the cover of an overhanging height restriction. As he approached, he noticed from the man's lapels that this must be the superior on duty, the Superintendent. Gerry shook the man's hand.

He raised his voice above the relentless drumbeat of rain. "Gerry Taverner, I'm the head of Prime Minister Pierces close protection team."

The Superintendent smiled and grasped Gerry's hand in a firm handshake.

"Superintendent Garson. Everything is in order. All those entering the centre have been searched at the entrance and have been made to pass through our metal detectors. We have a heavy response on show, twenty men in total, positioned at key points at ground level, by the stage and on the upper levels. The stage and audience area have been cordoned off with barricades. The stores as well as all entrances and exits will be shut before and throughout the duration of Mr Pierce's speech."

Gerry nodded in understanding; the Superintendent seemed to have things well under control.

"Very good, well we're going to bring the Prime Minister in through the warehouse and out to the staging area. Throughout the speech, ensure that your men maintain a presence on all levels. I, along with the rest of my team will establish a close perimeter around Pierce. What is the capacity looking like?"

Garson smiled lightly, "It's busy. This close to Christmas, with the capacity of the building, there are a lot of people in there."

Gerry had feared as much. "Ok, I'm going to keep in constant contact with you. If things were to go south, instruct your men to cover the Prime Minister's exit. We'll aim to exit back through to this area where the motorcade will be waiting. If that goes all goes to pot, we will exfil through the staffing area to the right of the stage."

The Superintendent nodded in agreement.

"Ok then, let's get the Prime Minister inside," Gerry announced.

Gerry turned and approached the rear passenger door and held the umbrella above it. He clearly established over his radio that the Prime Minister was on the move. Not that he had to pester his men however, they would be in position. All four members, including Jack, who would wait in the vehicle, were in position. He knew that his team always operated at the height of professionalism, his back as well as Pierce's were well and truly covered. He pulled open the door and Pierce stepped out, adjusting his black trench coat as he did so. Maintaining a forward line of sight, he adjusted his glasses.

"Try not to completely balls this up, Taverner," Pierce casually sneered before momentarily locking eyes with Gerry, a wry smirk accompanying the proclamation.

He indicated with his hand that he wished to proceed. Gerry took a step forward holding the umbrella above Pierces head and led him towards the warehouse. Gerry pondered, *"If I make it through today, it'll be a bloody miracle."*

(CHAPTER BREAK)

'Right, we've got the ok,' Greaves chirped up. "Get the others in here, say it's a foreman meeting or some shit like that. The boss said he wants them all done at once. That's twelve men... well eleven now that the actual foreman's been taken care of."

He smiled at the statement, indicating with his gloved finger towards the corner where the foreman now lay, still shrouded in shadow.

Greaves was talking to five other men, all dressed in the same overalls as him, head adorned with white hardhats that bore the 'Harpers Construction LTD' insignia. The men, a motley crew of short, tall, slim and heavy-set men listened intently to what Greaves had to say, knowing full well what was at stake here today.

"Now is everyone clear on their positions?" Greaves scanned the group.

He knew full well they did: four months of reconnaissance, meticulous planning and dummy runs in an East London warehouse set up to resemble the West Acre Point had seen to that. They all nodded solemnly.

"Right," Greaves pointed towards a bearded man with protective eyewear on. He was well built, wearing a high visibility jacket over a set of overalls that were visibly two sizes too small for his gargantuan frame. "Shaw, radio it in. We need them in here pronto."

The man took off his hard hat in response and revealed a sizeable skinhead peppered with sweat and concrete. He wiped the perspiration from his forehead before tossing the hard hat aside.

"About time," Shaw scoffed.

He reached into the back of his belt and unhooked a walkie talkie, bringing it up to his mouth. His eyes darted over the men before him. This was it. The moment they had planned for was upon them. He pushed the button on the side of the device.

"This is Shaw," he said matter of fact.

"Yeah Shaw, we hear you. What do you want?" replied a slightly exasperated reply.

"Guvnor says he needs us all to down tools and meet him on the top floor. He said something about going through the structural integrity and design of the floor."

"Bloody hell, we're not supposed to be starting work on that area for another three weeks. What's he got us fannying about up there for?"

"Hey, hey," Shaw motioned with his right hand as if the voice on the other end of the line could see him. "Don't shoot the messenger, just relaying the order is all."

A long pause followed before being punctuated by a long sigh. "Right I'll round up the lads. We'll be up in five."

Shaw smiled and tucked the walkie talkie back into his waistband. Greaves looked at the men before him.

"Right gents, act like you're working. Shaw over by the wall, Jones you're with me over there. You boys, stand by the entrance."

Once in position Greaves had one last order to give. "Shaw, switch on that radio, full blast. Keep this as silent as possible lads, quick and fast just like we practiced."

Shaw turned round and rotated the dial of a beaten-up portable radio. The signal finally settled and the distinct sound of *'Yesterday'* by the Beatles filled the room.

'Fitting,' Greaves considered.

A minute or so later the sound of burly laughter emanated from the concourse, just outside of the door. Greaves swung his index finger round in a circular fashion, indicating to the men that it was time. He and Jones stood at the workbench that he had earlier manoeuvred around with Hill. They gestured at blueprints and muttered as if talking over the schematics. Shaw acted as if he were tuning the radio. Two of the other men stood either side of the doorway, propped up against the wooden wall on one leg, whilst the remaining member acted as if he were on his mobile. The light at the door was partially eclipsed as the first of the men stepped through, Scott Denson as he would later be referred to in the Police report, soon trailed by the other men, one by one, lambs to the slaughter.

Denson adjusted the hard hat on his head, looking around inquisitively, a bemused look upon his face as he looked searchingly around for Hill.

"We getting on with this or what?" he pressed rather irately.

Greaves veered round smiling. "Well blow me down lads, a builder who's actually in a rush, never thought I'd see the day."

Denson did not know how to take this and made to counter when one of the two men beside the door closed it. The room descended into sheer darkness, the partial glow of the portable floodlight offering minimal illumination. The mass of men shuffled looking back at the door then back to their colleagues, baffled.

In the next instant Greaves and the rest of the men under his command produced an assortment of silenced weaponry from the small of their backs, safely secured within their waistbands. Greaves, holding a silenced berretta, pinched off the first shot with a sound reminiscent of bubble wrap, all be it with a metallic tenure.

Denson took the round to the centre of the forehead. He stood there, eyes wide, mouth gaping open with shock. His left hand twitched. Still he remained upright, rooted to the spot, his back slightly arched. The workers behind him spun around and made for the door but had barely taken a step before the chorus of metallic thumps followed by the illumination of muzzle flashes, rhythmic and deadly, punctured their bodies; an orchestra of the deceased with Greaves as the conductor.

Some of the workers whimpered but by large and large their deaths were quick, not out of any sense of compassion but rather as a hallmark of deadly professionalism and accuracy. After all, the men had a deadline to keep. Unbelievably, one of the men had only been superficially wounded both in the thigh and arm. Against the dull light of the floodlight, he stumbled over the bodies of his fellow workers, finally felling Denson as he shoved past him towards Shaw and remarkably, in his anguished state, further into the room away from the sanctuary of the entrance.

Shaw took a bounding stride forward and grabbed him from behind by the neck, knowing full well what he intended. He pulled the man towards him, back into the darkened corner of the room, all the while his victim clawing and thrashing wildly at Shaw. His quarry had intended to take his chances, the sheer drop that the gaping floor ahead afforded him favourable to the death his co-workers had suffered.

In a fluid motion Shaw arched his body round, twisting at the waist, the muscles in his arms contracting as he extended his grasp around the construction worker's neck and plunged it right through the thick plasterboard that Hill had been inspecting earlier. The wall gave way easily, the combination of a blunt object and Shaw's strength proving too much for the construct.

The workers head had all but disappeared into the recess. Shaw yanked the man out by his neck once again and turned him round by the hair to face his colleagues. The man was caked in dust and plasterboard held in place by the blood now issuing from the various lacerations he had sustained. He whimpered and thrashed out with his arms weakly.

Greaves was in fits of laughter by this stage. Shaw afforded himself a smile too as he held the man by the scruff of the neck, scanning his teammates for approval at the anatomical trophy he held before him.

Shaw brought his left hand across the man's face and in a jerking motion, with a noise that resembled gravel underfoot, snapped his neck in a fluid movement. Almost gracefully, like a ballerina pirouetting, Shaw extended his arm to the left and let the lifeless body fall away from him. Greaves wiped a tear from his eye, the moment of macabre choreography appealing to his morbid sense of humour.

"Well that saves us having to use the sledge hammer I suppose," he sniggered.

Shaw turned with a grunt and plunged his hand into the recess of the wall, grasping a side of the plasterboard in each. Greaves flicked a pocket flashlight that he had from his pocket on and focused it upon the jagged cavity. Shaw turned his head to the men, smiling.

"I hope you've been good little boys this Christmas," he beamed.

Pulling hard at the plasterboard, the material coming away effortlessly, Shaw exposed the true nature of the wall's existence, a secret that if it had not been for Greaves earlier would have been unearthed by the Foreman. A secret that had been encased in plasterboard, constructed two nights previously by a select collection of the men.

"Because Santa has brought you boy's lots of goodies to play with," Shaw finished with a flourish as he stepped away.

The remaining men turned looking rather smugly at one another. They had known full well what lay behind the wall but seeing it in person, was another matter entirely. For inside the cavity of the wall lay an enormous cache of stashed bags, the unmistakable barrel of an M16 assault rifle protruding from one.

Greaves whirled round to face the men almost theatrically.

"Now gentlemen, you can open one present before the big day and only one, "he took a step forward, a glimmer of undeniable fear breaking through his jovial malevolence, "because the boss gets first dibs."

CHAPTER SEVEN: IN THE FRAME

Tom looked at the screen of his Smart phone and sighed. Not only had it been an hour and a half since he had started shopping but his phone was at twelve percent battery. He had forgotten to charge it the night before. He tutted and decided to power it down, at least until he was out of the shopping centre. The screen went black and he replaced it back into his jeans pocket, composing himself for what needed to happen next. From the second level he observed the endless masses below and most notably, the exit, an exit he longed to depart through. He gritted his teeth knowing full well that this may be the last morsel of closure he himself could afford his father and mother.

He stooped down picking up the two heavily laden bags of gifts that he had purchased. Their contents: a variety of wrapping paper and bows; a book on the history of the England Rugby team and a bottle of single malt whiskey for his father as well as a bath set hamper and coffee maker for his mother. He had also purchased a gift experience for both his mother and father to go on a river boat cruise down the Thames with dinner and a complimentary glass of champagne. He had not yet purchased any clothes for himself.

With a determined stride Tom sidestepped two West Acre patrons and entered the store. He took in his surroundings, the layout of the room somewhat claustrophobic. Frames adorned the entirety of the walls to both his left and right, the myriad of frames housing a consortium of staged photographs to be disposed of after purchase. Ahead, a counter stretched along the full length of the store, topped with a cash register and an assortment of brochures. A door stood ajar behind the counter, most likely leading to an office or workroom of some kind. Above the door hung an ornate, golden frame which momentarily provided Tom with a welcome distraction. Unlike the frames around him, this one housed a place card with writing upon it.

He smiled, muttering the words to himself, "A picture speaks a thousand words. We only need two, no refunds."

The last two words were capitalised and written in a dark crimson font. Tom was so taken with the mantra that he did not notice the shop assistant that now stood before him. He cleared his throat, startling Tom.

"Sorry I didn't see you there," Tom apologised.

The man behind the counter looked disinterested.

"What can I do for you, sir?" he enquired, wiping his hands on a rag.

The assistant, in his mid-fifties Tom surmised, was squat with a comb over the likes of which Tom had never seen before. He stood before him attired in a yellow polo, chinos and red apron on which was emblazoned with the store's logo. The bright colours of the uniform completed juxtaposed his monotone demeanour.

"Oh," Tom fumbled in his pocket for his wallet, temporarily forgetting why he was there. "I erm, I'm here to collect a package, a present actually. The store phoned. I'm picking it up for my Brother, he couldn't make it himself... he's no longer with us."

He held out the receipt, the man accepting it rather limply. He briefly scanned over the receipt before laying it atop the counter.

"Wait here please, I'll check out back," the assistant drawled.

As he turned round, Tom noticed his name badge, an indignity that most likely stuck in his craw, given his age. His name was Malcolm, a more apt name Tom could never have imagined. The assistant shuffled into the next room. After a minute or so of clanging and the slamming of cupboard doors, Malcolm reappeared holding a box wrapped in blue tissue paper, sealed at the edges by stickers adorned with the store logo.

The box was quite sizeable, about the size of a biscuit tin, squared in its finish. Malcolm rested it upon the counter and tentatively slid it towards Tom, glancing up at him, his eyes moving in a rolling, almost tired motion.

"It's paid for already, all I need is the receipt for the records, I'll write you up a transaction and a receiving of goods slip now."

He slid a duplicate book out from beside the cash register and began filling it in. Tom lifted the package. It was not as heavy as he thought it would be, definitely not a picture frame due to its width and diameter. He turned it over in his hands and raised it to his head, giving it a tentative shake.

"I wouldn't do that if I were you," a quick and abrupt response came from the assistant followed by the ripping of the receipt from the duplicate book. He held it out to Tom. "It's partly made of glass."

The plot thickened. Tom accepted the duplicate slip and smiled, sliding the receipt over to Malcolm, who picked it up and pierced it upon a receipt holder spike. Tom continued to stare at the package in his hands.

"Will there be anything else sir? It's just we're closing up soon on account of the speech."

Tom still intrigued by the gift did not look up and instead shook his head from side to side, "No... no thank you."

He placed the box in the crook of his arm, picked up his bags and walked out in a dazed-like state. The concourse was thriving. Tom stepped aside and took refuge by a set of lockers he had spotted earlier. He observed that they operated on a metre-like system whereby, depending on the size of the locker, you could leave your shopping. He made the decision there and then to store his bags, along with his brother's present, so that he could go and purchase some clothing.

Tom read the sticker on the front of the blue finished locker door and noticed that for two hours it was around three pounds. Tom nodded to himself, placed the bags into one of the central lockers on the bottom row and wrestled some change from his wallet. The sign further warned that if he were any longer than the time purchased, he would incur a five pound fine.

"I bloody hope I'm not here in two hours," Tom muttered to himself.

He pumped the correct change into the recess inside the locker before closing it, twisting the key on the outside. He observed that a digital clock just above the panel had begun ticking down, alerting Tom as to how much time he had left before he either had to remove his items or top up his time.

Tom took the key and placed it around his wrist, tucking the blue band as well as the key under the strap of his watch. It reminded Tom of the type of key one got at the local swimming pool. Tom closed his wallet navigating it past Anthony's wallet in his pocket. The realisation finally dawned upon him. He had given his brother's receipt to the assistant in the shop.

He whirled round, plunging back into the shop, his eyes immediately drawn to the space occupying the receipt tidy. The spiked accessory was gone and to Tom's surprise, he began to panic. Something about that receipt was important, whether for sentimental reasons or for the set of numbers Anthony scrawled upon it. Tom went over to the counter and looked searchingly through the door behind the desk.

"Hello, excuse me," Tom beckoned.

Malcolm emerged from the back of the store, an assortment of keys in his grasp, his facial expressions displaying all the characteristics of a man who had been put out. In the background, Tom made out the loudspeaker announcing that the Prime Ministers speech was to begin in around five minutes. Malcolm eyed Tom guardedly.

"Yes?" he enquired.

"Yes, hi, I was just wondering if I would be able to get that receipt back that you took, for my brother's purchase."

Malcolm looked perplexed.

"I'm afraid I can't, sir. Store policy stipulates that we keep the original copy. You have the duplicate copy do you not? That is more than legible as proof of purchase."

Tom clenched his fists slightly and bit down upon the inside of his lip, *'Great, just my luck I picked the Jobs worth on duty,"* he internally cursed.

Tom chose to reason with the shop assistant instead.

"Look, I wouldn't ask generally, it's just that... that's one of my brother's last possessions and he's dead now and it has a number written on it and..."

Malcolm cut Tom off abruptly.

"If it's the writing on it you want, I can bring it out and you can copy it down but that is the best that I can do for you."

He looked at Tom in a way that almost urged him to argue back.

Tom attempted to meet his visual challenge, getting rather more defiant in his tone, "It's just kind of sentimental, you know?"

Malcolm's disinterested look indicated that he did not. To reinforce this, he repeated in an almost identical tone as before, "Store policy stipulates that we keep the original copy. Now I can bring you out the other..."

Tom cut him off this time in a rather exasperated tone, "Fine, I'll copy it down."

"You'll have to be quick though sir as I am about to shut the store, we can't be open when the speeches start. Security is very..."

Tom held up his hand and nodded imploring the man to just stop and go get the receipt. Malcolm once again disappeared into the back office. The distinct sound of Marc Bolan's 'Children of the Revolution', drifted into the store. Tom cringed. He surmised that this was in some way connected to the Prime Minister and that he was most likely now, preparing to walk out on stage.

Tom, a fan of Marc Bolan, mused that Bolan would be turning in his grave right about now at the knowledge that a devious wretch like Andrew Pierce was using his music to make a political statement, devoid and paradoxical when compared to the ones that he himself had set out to make. Malcom reappeared; panic stricken.

"That's our cue, the Prime Minister's on," he hustled round the side of the counter and handed Tom the receipt and a pen that he produced from his apron. "You'll have to hurry, sir. I need to shut up the store."

He ran over to the door and stood outside, placing one of the many keys he had into the shutter release. He stood there arm outstretched, key in the lock, waiting for Tom. He looked around nervously, bouncing slightly on his heels like a young child in desperate need of the toilet. Tom shoved his hand into his pocket for some paper and ironically pulled out another receipt from one of his earlier purchases and scrolled the numbers down on to it. Tom looked at his brother's receipt and felt a pang of reluctance at having to leave it behind as he turned back towards the door.

As he did so Malcom turned the key and the shutter juddered into life and began to descend forcing Tom to duck slightly under it as it came down. Tom observed that the concourse before him and the one adjacent were dotted with fellow shoppers, watching the crowds below. Tom held the receipt aloft for Malcolm when a hybridised chorus of cheering and jeering rose up from the Ground floor. The Prime Minister had emerged.

(CHAPTER BREAK)

Andrew Pierce strode across the stage with an air of defiant arrogance, walking as if he were some pantomime villain accustomed to the heckling masses. He gave an automated wave before coming to a rest at the podium and began shuffling some papers, adjusting his glasses unfazed.

He made to speak, the crowds dying down slightly in their protestation. The barriers ahead of Pierce were lined with police, some of whom were armed. On either side of Pierce were large screens which bore the announcement, *'Please remain silent for the entirety of the speech, live recording in progress.'*

The Prime Minister cleared his throat, taking the crowd in. Before he even spoke his hands began punctuating the points he was about to make.

Gerry stood towards the back of the stage, approximately four metres from Pierce. The two other men in Gerry's team were located on either side of the stage just to the wings, out of sight. The other member of Gerry's team, Paul Green, was located to the left of the stage by the exit. If anything were to happen, Gerry would cover the Prime Minister's exit, while Green ensured no one followed them through the exit into the waiting car, where Jack Wright would have the engine running in case a quick getaway was warranted.

Gerry scanned his surroundings. An additional police presence had been allocated to the ground, first and second floors of the precinct, with more officers situated by the main entrance. The place was sealed up tighter than a barrel, Gerry assessed. Unbeknownst to Gerry however, the malicious plans of a second party were already well under way high above the stage.

(CHAPTER BREAK)

The control room was the epicentre of the vast structure and housed CCTV monitors, the centre's speaker system and the external shutter controls. After the London riots, which had occurred whilst plans were being finalised upon the structure of the building, a last-minute addition had been added to the specification in case of any repeat unrest in the future. The centre, as the investors had stipulated, needed to be impregnable in case of looting or burglary.

The external shutters were constructed from a sheet of solid, reinforced steel, designed to encase the vast, glass entry points in and out of West Acre Point. The shutters were strategically designed; the metal not even grated for fear of potential assailants being able to reach through the slats in the shutter and potentially break the glass or start a fire, causing damage.

The architect, Stuart Fields, had truly designed an impregnable building that if needs be, could be completely shut off from the outside world, made inaccessible to any external threats as well as any within the structure. Both were design features that the man who currently sat in front of the CCTV terminal was counting on.

The current CCTV operator lay to the right of the insurgent, his throat brutally slit. The ever-growing pool of blood now gathering before the vast bank of CCTV monitors. Any threat of someone contacting the outside world or those entrusted with the Prime Minister's safety within the structure being alerted, were now significantly reduced. He sat patient, awaiting the command that would come via his encrypted comm's link. At the touch of a button, any and all exits out onto the street would be sealed off, cocooning those inside from outside interference.

The man cracked his knuckles and returned his hands to the monitor's keyboard, poised and ready to execute his next order. It was crucial that as soon as the barriers came down, he switch both the monitor system and his radio off before the device was used. The man sat back and watched Pierce's speech with a voyeuristic malevolence.

"That's it, do what you're good at. Keep on talking, while you still can anyway."

The man's radio suddenly beeped into life, the harsh London accent unsettling him.

"This is Team Leader to all positions. Execute your orders with extreme prejudice, over."

With that the man at the console activated the shutter release and watched as the action played out across the monitors as the shutters descended. The numerous cameras throughout West Acre Point illustrated the utter confusion of those within. A pair of armed police officers on the street outside turned round in utter confusion, the shutter denying them re-entry.

The man swivelled in his chair and monitored the deserted third level of the precinct, the sniper team currently getting into position. It was their job to take out the Armed Police and the five members of the Prime Minister's Close Protection team. They were armed with Enfield Enforcer sniper rifles, a gun ironically designed by the British for use by the police. Each held ten rounds expertly selected for the job at hand.

One of the men, Ollie Frazier, had initially questioned their team leader as to why they did not just take the Prime Minister out there and then live on TV. Team Leader had immediately and rather abruptly, cut him off.

"There was more at play here than simply killing a politician," he had stated.

The man at the console was once again shaken from his thoughts, the confiscated radio he had taken from the dead operator abuzz with chatter. It was the man on the stage behind the Prime Minister.

"What do you mean the shutters are coming down, over?" he queried.

Smiling, he surmised that the voiced belonged to Gerry Taverner, a name he had grown quite accustomed to, his name significant within the dossier they had been provided with to study verbatim.

The man at the panel located Taverner on one of the monitors, recognising him instantaneously from the photograph attached to his dossier. He zoomed in on Taverner's expression, savouring the man's bewilderment. He could visually make out the internal dilemma currently going through his head. Should he evacuate Pierce? Was this a cause for concern? He checked the monitors. All exits were now sealed. The operator's confiscated walkie talkie burst into life once again.

"Control room, do you read, over?"

"I read you loud and clear, over," the intruder responded.

"Control, the shutters are down. All routes are blocked if this goes south. Get those shutters raised now, over."

The intruder laughed slightly before pressing the button on the side of walkie talkie.

"My fault, I pressed the wrong button by mistake, raising them now, over."

Gerry seemed to visibly relax on the monitor; he lowered his arm to his side and surveyed the crowd. He had made his decision; waywardly entrusting the unknown voice. The intruder flicked another switch and powered down the monitor. He pressed the pressel switch located on his neck and spoke.

"All powered down here, ready to proceed on your mark, over."

The harsh voice came over his earpiece, "Power down now men. Device activation and engagement will commence after the first wave of the shooting as planned. There's live television cameras down there gentlemen, be sure to put on a show for the Great British public. Roger and out."

The intruder switched off his comms link as well as the operator's walkie talkie. He needed no technological advantage in visualising how the scenes would play out below. No, he could do that all by himself. He only wished he could be down there himself.

(CHAPTER BREAK)

"These numbers, are they some kind of reference number?" Tom quizzed.

Malcolm was flustered now.

"Look, I really need to..." he started.

Tom shoved the receipt slightly closer, all, the while the shutter slowly juddered downwards, about mid-way now. Malcolm exhaled and rolled his eyes, looking around once again. He was obviously concerned about being caught by a supervisor or security guard not having shut up shop. He snatched the receipt from Tom and scanned it. His response was all-encompassing in an effort to be rid of Tom.

"It's not a reference number that's for sure," he pointed to the lower part of the receipt. "As you can see that's your brother's reference number, 00529. All our reference numbers are 5 digits long. It's not the card he paid for the purchase with either as his last four digits as seen here do not match the code either. And as for the word Hawker, I don't have the foggiest."

He handed the receipt back to Tom who solemnly took it.

"It's ok, I know what the writing means," Tom revealed dejectedly.

Malcom sarcastically chipped in, "Great, now if you don't mind Sir I really need to..."

But Malcolm never got to finish his sentence. A loud crack fragmented the ambient atmosphere, forcing both men to jolt. Tom scanned the surrounding area, searching for the source of the sound. He may have dismissed it if it had not been for the chorus of shots that followed afterward. He had heard the sound often enough, gunfire. Tom surmised that they were automatic weapons, the velocity and rate of fire that the reverberating sounds created unmistakable.

Tom ran to the glass partition at the edge of the concourse and surveyed the levels below. The screaming had already started, a melee of men, women and children running in the opposite direction to the stage. Some fell as they got caught up in the crowd; others pushed and surged towards the exit located at the back of the partition. Tom's heart was beating in his ears; he swung round to inspect the stage which was now empty all be it for two men in black suits, lying face down.

Tom spotted a police officer step forward in an attempt to raise his firearm only to be cut down by a loud singular shot that came worryingly from above his head. He looked up towards the top level of the shopping centre. A second shot was fired, of which Tom only caught the distinct bright white of a muzzle flash.

Tom whirled round, tracing the path of the second round as it took out a man wrestling with another balaclava clad man holding an M16.The masked man tugged the M16 from the limp hands of the dead man as he slumped to the ground, instantaneously re-entering the melee, firing wildly at passers-by. A coating of blood coated the marble underfoot, the clatter of spent shells clattering upon the cold surface.

Hysteria gripped those to Tom's left as well as those on the opposite concourse as they ran in the direction of the escalators. This only served to bring attention to those parallel to Tom as a swathe of machine gun fire punctured the bodies, sending the seething throng of panicked shoppers into a convulsing and stuttering dance before falling to the ground. The thud of bullets entering flesh turned Tom's stomach, snapping him from his sedated state.

Tom turned back to Malcolm who was stood motionless, his hand still holding the key in the shutter release panel. He was ashen faced and in shock. The shutter was now about a quarter of a metre from the ground too small for either man to fit through. Tom looked about him. The second level was now completely abandoned. Tom spotted some people running down an escalator, two steps at a time. Tom turned and grabbed Malcolm by the shoulders, shaking him hard. Malcolm continued to stare in the direction of the cluster of fallen bodies over Tom's shoulder, oblivious to his existence.

"Listen to me Malcolm. We need to get this shutter up quickly."

No response. Tom gripped tighter with his fingers, his nails now digging into the thin material of Malcolm's polo. Malcolm winced and came to, meeting Tom's gaze.

"Are those... Are those gun shots?" he stuttered rather timidly.

"Yes Malcolm. We need to get to cover, now open the shutters."

Malcolm swallowed hard and nodded slightly. The shutters had now shut and were flush to the ground. Both men jolted again as a shot came from just below. Tom took a tentative step towards the partition once again and observed a man wearing jeans and a black jumper topped off with a tactical vest complete with spare magazines as well as various other militaristic necessities, weaving through the dead upon the floor. His face was shrouded, a Sig Sauer handgun in his grasp. The spectre pinched off two shots into the chest of a woman erratically dialling a number into her mobile.

Tom retreated in horror and backed up against the marble wall next to the shutter. It was only now that Tom observed how slow and noisy the shutters were. Tom peered over the railing slightly, following the path of the masked man as he stepped over the body of a police officer, who in a grotesque freeze frame was still grasping at the radio on his shoulder, most likely using his last visages of breath to try and radio in for help. His uniform was splattered with blood and his head displayed all the characteristics of a headshot, half open, exposing his cranium and soft tissue. The man looked at the wound as he stepped over the policeman, undeterred by the macabre sight.

The metallic whir and juddering of the shutter seemed louder than the symphony of rounds about them. Malcolm was looking over his shoulder, engaging once again in that nervous urine inducing dance that he had done so before.

'Perhaps he's pissed himself,' Tom absurdly pondered, *'who could blame him?*

Just as the shutter got to about half a foot from the ground, the shopping centres electricity abruptly cut out and the shutter halted. Malcolm looked searchingly from Tom then back again at the key, turning it from left to right, willing it to work. Tom looked across to the escalator and observed that the balaclava clad man was making a slow and steady ascent up towards the second level.

Tom grabbed Malcolm and whispered urgently, "They must have cut the power; we're going to have to crawl under."

Malcolm was in shock, Tom needed him functioning or they were both dead. He brought him down with him as he kneeled and he shoved Malcolm towards the base of the shutter. It was a tight squeeze as Malcolm was no longer in control of his body, paralysed by fear. His size did not help either. Tom afforded himself a glance back at the escalator as a man darted away from behind the cover of a flowerpot. The man in the balaclava turned with blistering speed and opened fire, felling the man with a single shot.

Tom turned back to the shutter and edged himself under. He got about half-way in when he became jammed, his physique poorly designed for such a gap. He gripped the shutter on either side and pushed his body inwards.

He could feel his stomach edging along the frame at an agonising rate, millimetre by millimetre. The second shot rang out. The insurgent had obviously finished off the man with another round, must likely to the head. With that sound Tom found a new abundance of strength, sucking in his stomach and pushing with all his might, he slid into the store and immediately was up on his feet, grabbing Malcolm by the scruff of the polo as he did so. Malcolm, who at the time had been cowering behind a swivel display holding fridge magnets, looked devoid of reason. He bundled him towards the back office.

(CHAPTER BREAK)

The operation as of yet could not have gone any more smoothly had it not been for one thing. The Prime Minister had fled into the throngs of his panic-stricken electorate, vanishing in the horror. The man who now looked on as the devastation fluctuated around him grinned beneath his balaclava. He knew the Prime Minister was going nowhere. All of the exits had been sealed; all bar one of his close protection team were still operational and the last remnants of the Police were being taken care of. He had been impressed with his team. They had drilled this course of action repeatedly and had planned for every eventuality, even the Prime Minister absconding in the first wave of their assault.

The man brought up his leather-gloved hands and discharged two rounds into a woman who lay crawling before him, whimpering as she did so. She looked to be in her early thirties, caked in blood having sustained a bullet wound to her left leg and abdomen. She served no threat to the man. No, instead in a warped sense of morality, like a veterinarian with a lame animal, he decided to put her down, not wanting her to suffer any longer. The instigator of this plan, his superior, had referred to those like her as 'collateral damage' and he knew full well that many more would die before their mission was deemed complete.

The man removed one hand from his Beretta pistol and lifted it into the air, clear for all to see. He made the universal signal of a phone receiver to the men around him, who in turn nodded and flicked their comm's units back on. He looked around making sure that everyone had switched their comm's back on. Having done so, he relayed a message. Those still alive looked on in shock, the broad man before them rendering them paralysed with fear.

"I want one cop left alive, female if possible. Neutralise any and all others. And find me the target, one bogey still operational."

He was of course referring to the remaining member of the close protection unit. By this stage the remaining shoppers on the Ground level were being herded back into the security barriers. Anyone who tried to run, no matter their age, gender or ethnicity were executed, each execution rallying a chorus of screams and tears from the surviving patrons. All exits were now locked down and those that had reached them, oblivious to the futility of their efforts, either continued to thump on the barriers or turned back looking for alternative methods of escape. There were none. The man casually reached behind him and produced a megaphone that was clipped to his belt. He brought it up to his obscured mouth.

"Can I have your attention, please," he asked in a distinctly robotic accent, modified using some form of voice altering technology.

His demand seemed mocking in its observed politeness. The crowd of people, who had been kettled, did not heed his demand and continued to cry out, holding on to strangers, creating a human cocoon, which he now observed at its core, comprised of all the surviving children. The children understandably seemed the most frightened. Some men and woman had taken to reassuring them, grasping them close and soothing their cries but they continued, just as the gunshots did so as he took a step closer to the group.

A man, leaving the safety of the group, broke away right, running for the stage. The man with the megaphone whirled round and shot him in the ankle, sending the man hurtling towards the smooth, marbled surface of the floor. The man raised his Beretta aloft and punctuated his previous demand into the air above with five more blood curdling rounds.

A hush came over the crowd, about hundred and fifty or so in size. There was still the sound of children sobbing but it was now at an acceptable level for the masked man to be heard. The megaphone was once again raised. The crowd fearing what came next.

"As of this moment, you, unlike those who lay around you, are my hostages. As I speak, my men have already secured the building and all exits in or out. Any persons entrusted with the Prime Ministers protection have or are currently, being neutralised."

This last point was heavily emphasised by the metallic and cold augmentation of his voice. The man was regionally and culturally unidentifiable, although quite vividly through the slits in his balaclava, bright green eyes were visible. The skin around his eyes was heavily laden with black camouflage paint, which served both to reinforce the intensity of his gaze and along with the other men, cover any skin on show, their ethnicity an enigma.

The man twisted round, holding his Beretta at his side, turning in a 360-degree circle like that of a theatrical ringleader. This was a statement that he wanted everyone to hear within the precinct, high and low.

"This may seem hard for you to understand at this particular moment in time but you are lucky. Me and my men wish you no harm and of that you have my assurance," he touched his chest whilst saying this, indicating his sincerity, paradoxically with gun in hand.

"But if you do not comply with my orders or with that of my men, well..." he snorted slightly "...let's just say that my men and I have plenty of bullets to go around."

This registered a slight shuffle amongst the crowd.

"Now in a moment my men will come around with a sack into which I want you to all place your possessions. That includes the following: your wallet, your phone- which many of you will have realised by now, have been remotely disabled and have been rendered useless. Also, any keys, handbags, rucksacks, sharp items or purchases today from this fine establishment. We shall be conducting random searches throughout the duration of your stay, so don't bother concealing anything you wouldn't want us to find."

The men began to circulate throughout the crowd, four in total and all the while three men stood guard, with guns raised in sentinel-like stances in case anyone made a break for it or tried to injure one of the masked men. The crowd looked hesitantly at one other before starting to place their belongings into the sacks.

"When this is done, I invite you to make yourselves comfortable by taking off your shoes, any jewellery and or belts and remember ladies and gentlemen, these can be replaced." he took a step forward once again and jutted his Beretta towards the crowd "... you cannot."

"To repeat, if you act in accordance with the demands put before you, you will not be harmed now or for the duration of your duress. However, any act carried out against me or my men that fail to comply with the specific orders I have just outlined will result in your death."

He strolled over to the man that he had previously shot in the ankle and discharged a round into the base of his skull. The man ceased in his agonisingly slow advance and sickeningly twitched for several seconds.

"So, no heroes, this isn't an action movie, you are not bulletproof," he callously remarked, as if the cadavers around them did not emphasise the point clearly enough.

The man waited for the men to gather in the valuables which proved to be a long process. The men took all shopping bags full of presents and assorted goods and threw them to the side of the crowd by one of the armed insurgents, who on more than one occasion, had to sidestep a bag.

The man who had done all the talking tentatively moved the sleeve of his black jumper up his arm to expose a watch, before replacing it. After what seemed like a lifetime, one of the men nodded towards their supposed leader. What knelt before him now was a sorry, disjointed group of people, barefoot, many of whom were either sobbing or keeping their heads low. One man, grey and in his mid- sixties, clung to his loose waistband, his belt now confiscated.

At that moment, two more armed men, complete with balaclavas and AK-47's, entered with around 30 more hostages. Another hostage taker to the right of the gentlemen forcibly led a female police officer by her blonde ponytail. She had been handcuffed with what appeared to be her own standard issue cuffs. He brought her over to the man with the megaphone and with a shove, brought her to her knees. The subordinate immediately began untying her shoelaces. The man in charge looked down at her and ruffled her hair like that of a child's.

"Nice of you to join us little piggy, I do believe you will be the only member of her Majesty's Police Force in attendance today."

As he said this the female officer looked down, a single tear rolled down her cheek. The balaclava-festooned man holstered his sidearm before detaching his comm's device. He held the megaphone aloft once again; however, this time he also brought the device up to his mouth also. The result of this was that his voice could now be heard throughout the whole of the precinct, via the PA system. His men had already set about relieving the freshly reinforced hostages of their possessions and shoes. Some were even beginning to secure the hostages with a mixture of plasti-cuff restraints and duct tape around their wrists. When they were securely detained, they were pushed to the floor, so their captors could focus on the next unwilling volunteer.

"Now, I understand all of you must be very scared, a human response I can fully appreciate. So, I say this to anyone else who may still be in hiding. As I speak, my men are scouring the area. I for one want no further bloodshed and for no more harm to come to anyone. But if you do not make yourselves known to either myself or my men, you will be treated as hostile."

He paused once again for effect, a showman of the highest order having most likely rehearsed this speech on many an occasion before today's assault.

"However, rather ironically, that brings me very swiftly to my next point. There is one man out there, who can end this right now. The only man that can truly bring your ordeal to a swift and bloodless..." he looked at the bodies strewn before him. "Well, mostly bloodless, end. He is your much cherished, silver-spooned- sucking wonder boy. The one you all came out to see today, Great Britain's very own Prime Minister, Andrew Pierce."

He allowed a moment for this to sink in, many of the hostages looking worryingly at one another.

"Now unfortunately, the Prime Minister along with one of his security team, are unaccounted for," he tutted.

"I know you can hear me Mr. Pierce. Even now I envision you like the rat that you are, trying to scrabble at doors, desperately trying to find a way out. I assure you; it is a waste of your time and mine. In the interest of sportsmanship and good will, I offer you this. I will give you twenty minutes as of now, to turn yourself in. After that deadline has elapsed, I will take it as a personal indication, that like a rat, you continue to conceal yourself as well as your whereabouts, from me and my men."

The man's gaze, although largely shrouded by the balaclava twinned with the tone of his voice, registered pure venom at the potential of being kept waiting. He shook his head dumbstruck.

"This Mr Prime Minister would be a very grave mistake on your part. So here is an incentive, should your bile ridden, self-infatuated, pompous self, need it. For every twenty minutes my men and I are kept waiting… I kill a hostage."

The crowd burst into an audible panic. The man with the loudspeaker pushed the speaker towards the direction of the two hundred or so hostages and allowed their shrieks and mumbled prayers to be relayed via the PA system. He did so for several seconds before turning back to look up at the upper levels of the complex.

"I repeat Mr Prime Minister, as I know you are not the brightest crayon in the box. Escape is futile. All stores and exits have been sealed and are impregnable. All communications, bar ours, are dead. Let me be so kind as to paint you a picture as to the scene before me just in case you cannot see it from your burrow. Around me, lay the bodies of roughly one hundred and fifty or so, men and women. Some lay trampled; some shot, others wounded beyond any help that I can afford them. I only thank Allah, praise be upon him, that as unpopular as you are, many vacated the building before you had a chance to spout more of your bile." A fearful look of arrogant understanding seemed to wash across many of the hostages faces.

He shifted and retreated several steps away from the crowd, which led to a collective sigh from some within the inner sanctum of hostages, all of whom were now bound. All in all, the assault, from start to finish, had taken around twenty minutes. The shopping centre was vast but when locked down with no shops to filter through had now become a sealed box.

"Think upon those who huddle before me, not as potential voters, nor as people that are lower down the social standing than you are and instead ponder this one and only question. For once, in your short but wholly damaging stint in office, will you step out and stand up for your people? Will you evolve from that of a lowly rat to that of a proud lion, willing to do what is right? Will you for once in your whole fucking miserable existence do the right thing? Or are you going to make me come and find you? Are more people going to have to die because of your cowardice and false bravado?"

The barrage of questioning was so loud that many within the group flinched at the pronunciation of certain syllables. Once again, he pulled up his sleeve and checked his watch.

"I guess we'll all have twenty minutes to find out. Oh and… Mr Prime Minister?" he said questionably, as if checking that the Prime Minister was still listening. "Better make it quick, time waits for no man, woman or child."

CHAPTER EIGHT: SHAKEN AND STALLED

The 'SHAKE ATTACK' stall, located in its usual underwhelming position at the back of the shopping complex, stood undisturbed from the outside. The structure, weather-beaten and painted in an ocean blue hue was designed to resemble a beach shack that would quite frankly, be geographically out of place on any beach in the world, let alone one located in Australia.

On the outside of the eight-foot by six-foot boxed frame stood an assortment of artefacts commonly and rather stereotypically associated with the country, nailed to the outside of the shack: boomerangs, a didgeridoo and with some intended play on the title, an inflatable shark. A large piece of driftwood was hung above the serving hatch of the stall which bore the establishments name in a wave like font, all be it for the word 'ATTACK' which was painted in a dripping red font, resembling blood.

To the casual passer-by looking through the opening, the structure consisted of a work bench below the serving flap, covered in various cooking implements: chopping boards, an industrial blender, cartons of fruit juice, milk and a large bowl of fruit. Nailed to the back wall of the structure, above various shelves containing more fruit and a fridge, stood an assortment of coloured chalk writing, indicating what was available on the menu. A variety of parodied milkshake and smoothie names with their listed ingredients were displayed ranging from the poorly contrived, 'Bruce Juice', a pun on the mechanical shark's name in the film 'Jaws', to the rather formulaic 'Sheila's Shake' and 'Bonza Berry'.

Below the workbench, Gerry Taverner set about removing his suit blazer. The right arm bore a slash which was caked in congealed blood around the edges. During the assault he had sustained a flesh wound when he had dived across the Prime Minister, shielding him from the onslaught of automatic fire directed towards the front of the podium. Luckily for the Prime Minister and Gerry, they had both taken flight reasonably unscathed, which was more than could be said for Gerry's team and the rest of the poor, unfortunate souls that the two had stumbled over as they sought cover.

Gerry inspected the wound unimpressed; it was a flesh wound as he had suspected no need to linger on it any longer. After all, those caught in the hail of bullets had sustained much, much worse. He reached up from under the relative safety of the workbench and grabbed at a clean tea-towel. He reached into his pocket and retrieved a tactical knife, which he flicked open. Andrew Pierce flinched at this and looked at Gerry, eyes ablaze with fear. His face was devoid of colour and there was the distinctive watering of eyes and caked, crusted snot around his nostrils that indicated he had been crying. Gerry held up his free hand in a reassuring fashion.

Whispering he attempted to calm Pierce, "I'm just making a bandage. We're safe here for the moment."

Pierce must have recently come to as he had fainted seconds after they had both entered the shack. Gerry knew all too well that shock could kill and at present, Pierce was exhibiting many of the signs: the confusion, the rapid and shallow breathing as well as the weak pulse, which Gerry had tested whilst Pierce was unconscious.

The floor of the shack was sodden with spilt liquid and various fruits that had been squashed into the wooden floor. An assortment of broken glasses further indicated to Gerry that there had either been a struggle or that those inside had dropped what they were doing when the gunfire started and had sought refuge. Gerry ascertained and hoped that it was the latter as there was no indication of blood or more notably, bodies.

Pierce had now taken to mumbling to himself, something about a report that needed to be turned in the next day. As he continued his solitary conversation, Gerry tore a strip from the tea- towel and tied it around his wound, barely grimacing. All the while he kept an eye on Pierce, monitoring his condition. If they had any chance of both making it out of this alive, Pierce would not only have to come to but would also need to pull his weight. Gerry reached out grabbing a bottle of water. He used the remnants of the tea- towel and poured half of the contents onto the material and set to washing his own blood off his hands before draining the other half of the bottle in three thirsty gulps.

Pierce was using his hands to count off something. They were shaking uncontrollably. Gerry looked around the shack for anything that may help Pierce. He spotted a carton of fruit juice to the left of him and reached for it with a slight groan. He turned back and tentatively used his uninjured arm, to twist the lid off. Around him lay individual sachets of sugar. He swept up three and emptied the sugar into the carton. Gerry only hoped that the sudden rush of energy provided by the juice and sugar may help alleviate some of Pierces angst, if not it would serve as a welcome distraction, keeping him quiet long enough for Gerry to speak to him.

Gerry held the carton under Pierces nose but Pierce continued to stare of into the distance, oblivious. Gerry used his good arm and gently squeezed Pierce's shoulder, shoving the drink once again in his direction. Pierce shuddered slightly and with glazed eyes, turned to look at Gerry.

Gerry looked sternly at Pierce and whispered in an authoritative tone, "Drink this, it will help."

Pierce nodded in a zombie-like fashion and began to gulp down the contents, the liquid spilling down one of the lapels on his suit. Gerry touched the top of the carton.

"Take slow sips, not all at once," he instructed, feeling rather like a parent instilling good table manners into a young child.

After a few cautionary gulps from Pierce, Gerry decided to test the water. Pierce had stopped talking to himself but continued to stare at a fixed point on the opposite side of the shack. He had reverted to taking slow sips at spaced- out intervals.

"Mr Pierce…" No response. He decided upon a different tact. "Andrew?"

The Prime Minister veered round appalled at the indiscretion of being referred to by his first name and by a subservient no less. Pierce made to protest and from the movement of his head and the flared nostrils, Gerry instinctively shot out and clasped his hand around his mouth, stopping him from audibly protesting, alerting any enemy sentries to their position.

Rather optimistically, Gerry's choice of words had led to some colour returning to Pierce's cheeks.

"Now listen to me Mr Pierce. We are in a situation here and I need you to remain quiet and listen to what I have to say. Now if you understand me, nod your head and I can remove my hand," Gerry held his hand sternly until Pierce nodded.

Slowly he removed his hand and Pierce, rendered bashful by the whole exchange, straightened his tie in an authoritative manner.

"Here is how it stands Mr Pierce. My comm's are down, so at present we have no contact with the outside world. Apart from myself and hopefully Jack out in the car, I think it is safe to assume that the rest of my team are either dead or are holed up in a position, unreachable to us at this present time. When the shots started, I saw two of my boys go down. All exits are sealed and our various planned exit points for extraction are either manned or locked down."

Pierce looked wide-eyed at Gerry once again and asked the question that Gerry had been pondering for the last five minutes.

"So what you're saying is we're sitting ducks?"

The question came whispered but with no less venom and anger than Gerry had expected. Gerry needed to save some face. Rather sternly, in an effort to alleviate Gerry's fears rather than Pierces, Gerry reverted to protocol.

"No sir, I didn't say that. At present, we are approximately ten minutes into this siege."

This calculation took Pierce by surprise. Gerry continued.

"Now that's ten minutes of radio silence. Jack or any number of the police switchboard will be waiting for regular situation reports and updates. Jack himself will be tuned in to all of the radio chatter via the vehicle. The police will be waiting on updates. If they aren't getting them, they are going to realise quickly that something is wrong and possibly..."

"This is all based however, on the fact that your man Jack hasn't been killed himself. As for the police, what's to say that by the time they scramble to our rescue we haven't already been discovered and executed ourselves?"

Gerry bit down on the inside of his cheek. He should have known not to engage Pierce with protocol, he was taking a decidedly half-glass empty approach here, an unfavourable approach that one should never adopt when faced with unsurmountable odds of survival. Any flicker of hope, no matter how small, needed to be kept from being extinguished.

"Listen, Mr Pierce. I'm going to level with you. Our chances of survival are slim at best. We're heavily outnumbered, outgunned and I have twelve rounds left. Our exits are all sealed off and the only logical step is to go up, which presents its own problems. There is also the large chance that you are in some way the catalyst of today's events."

Pierce looked baffled, his face demonstrating conflicting emotions, "And how do I factor into this abject slaughter?"

Gerry readjusted his position, his arm beginning to slightly go numb with pain.

"Sir, you're the Prime Minister of the United Kingdom. We get numerous threats on your life daily, thousands yearly. There is a very real chance that today's attack, on the day of your speech, is all in a hostile effort to get to you."

Pierces features finally settled upon understanding. He reached into the front pocket of his suit blazer, unfurling a polka dot hanky and took to dabbing at his forehead. His hands had started to tremor again. Gerry attempted to reassure him.

"There is a small chance that this may all be coincidental sir but if not, they will come looking for you. And if they do, then we have to look at the very real chance that this has all been staged with your harm... possibly your death, being integral to their aims."

Pierce turned to Gerry just as the megaphone came to life. He froze and burrowed his back further against the shack. And so, began what Gerry could only imagine to be the most terrifying four minutes of Pierces life to date or was likely to ever be.

Gerry afforded himself the briefest of prayers. He did not pray to any God or deity but instead to that of his fellow team member, Jack Wright.

(CHAPTER BREAK)

The safety of the back office was rendered steadily more and more sub-standard as the footfall of the masked gunman grew ever closer. The sound of steel- capped boots on marble heightened Tom's senses to such a degree that he could hear his pulse rhythmically beating in his temples.

It had been around five minutes since the man on the speaker had delivered his ultimatum and since then there had been no follow up or confirmation of the Prime Minister's surrender. Tom had at first struggled to hear what was happening until the message had started to be relayed through the PA system. Malcolm had tried to ask a question but Tom had hushed him with a flurry of his hand, urging him to remain quiet.

It was now, after five minutes of deliberation, that Tom turned to Malcolm. He settled upon utter transparency with the shop assistant. Although he did not want to scare him unjustly he knew if they were to survive he needed Malcolm to keep his wits about him.

"Listen to me Malcolm," he whispered, ever conscious of the nearing footsteps. "This isn't going to end quickly. Most likely this is going to turn into a full-blown hostage situation. Now we're safe for the moment but we need to think of an exit strategy. Now think. Other than the lower levels are there any other exits we may be able to use on the upper levels?"

Malcolm was still shaking violently and Tom had briefly considered leaving him at one stage but had immediately and rather ashamedly, dispelled the notion.

"All those people... the gunshots... what do they..." Malcom whimpered.

Tom put his hand on Malcolm's shoulder in an effort to both console and silence him at the same time. Tom felt as if he could hear a pin drop.

"Malcolm, you need to listen to me. I need you to look me in the eyes when I say this."

Malcolm looked up, his eyes sodden and swollen.

"The longer we leave getting out of here, the tighter they're going to shut this place down. Now we're safe at the moment and I promise I am not going to leave you but if we don't come up with a plan, other than just sitting here, we're going to be stuck. Now think, are there any other exits out of here?"

Malcolm straightened slightly, wiped his eyes and considered in-depth the question he had just been asked. A brief spark shot across his eyes and he once again met Tom's gaze.

"There's the roof, it's on the floor above third. Some of the other employees go up there to smoke. It's operated by coded entry."

Tom's heart fell. He had noticed the flux in the electricity just before all of the carnage had started and the man on the megaphone had confirmed his suspicions. Somehow, they had managed to lock down the building's security and with it, any methods of contacting the outside world. If the door was electronically operated, it would be a dead end.

"Malcolm, you're doing great. I have one more question and it is crucial you think about this before you answer. Is the lock mechanical or electronically operated?" Tom wiped his mouth twitchily in anticipation. Malcolm answered instantly.

"It's electrical. I'm one-hundred percent sure of it. I don't smoke myself but I have had to go up there on numerous occasions to fetch staff that have taken too long on their breaks. Not for the last few months though, as Level Three has been cordoned off, building site up there you see, no access to the level above. They can only be used for access to the warehouse and in case of emergency, a fire. The door gets unlocked automatically and staff are supposed to direct the customers to them... for evacuation."

He was starting to become more talkative which Tom viewed as a positive. He could use that.

"Great Malcolm, you're doing fantastic. Now do you remember the code to the door?"

Tom thought it best to positively praise Malcolm. Those who felt as if they were contributing in these types of situations tended to become more focused on the task at hand and were less likely to fester on their mortality and the impending doom of a bullet to the skull.

"Yes of course it's..." Malcolm put his hand to his chin in contemplation, "If I remember it correctly its C89D."

Tom muttered this to himself a few times to let it sink in. He looked at Malcolm and patted him on the shoulder. Malcolm smiled back contently, happy that he had been of use. The elation did not last, however. It was only now that Tom realised that the sound of steel capped boots had stopped. He raised his finger to his lips warning Malcolm to be quiet. Malcolm's features melted back to a state of unadulterated panic. They listened for what seemed like an eternity. The shutter began to shake. It was being tested. Tom heard a groan and presumed that the masked man with the Sig Sauer was trying to lift the shutter from the gap at the bottom. Tom turned to Malcolm and simply mimed one word, *'Hide'*.

A forceful kick shuddered against the outside of the shutter which was followed in quick succession by three further vigorous hits. Each drove deep like a knife into the ears of Malcolm and Tom. Malcolm had retreated into a corner behind a shelving unit, covering himself slightly with a large ornate frame. Tom was starting to panic now. He looked around the room and established that there was little in the way of cover. The back room consisted of a shelving unit full of frames to his left and to his right a desk with reports, receipts and a sizeable safe beside it. Apart from that there was absolutely no cover whatsoever.

His heart rate began to quicken. The masked man wanted in and the small matter of a shutter would not stop him. Tom surmised from the size of the armed attacker's stature that he would not be able to squeeze through the gap but that would only buy him minimal time. Suddenly Tom's eyes focused on the only place he could hide. It would not be ideal but it would hopefully serve its purpose.

(CHAPTER BREAK)

"Dreyfus here, over," came the voice on the other side of the shutter.

The radio came to life with a static crackle.

"Control room hearing you loud and clear Dreyfus, proceed, over," came the reply on his comm's unit.

Dreyfus looked searchingly through the shutter and pushed it with his hand in a final futile effort to breach the shutter.

 "We've got a shutter a quarter of the way open on Level Two, over."

The reply took a couple of seconds to filter back, "Is it big enough for someone to fit through, over?"

Dreyfus turned his head in a canted manner and inspected the gap for a second time.

"I'd struggle but I could manage. It could definitely allow easy access to someone smaller. There's also a key in the shutter release, over." Silence again. The response this time was directed at a third party.

"Team Leader come in," the voice from the control room asked.

"Receiving Control, over," came the robotic voice, his voice still carrying a menacing tenor that dehumanised him all the more so.

"Team Leader do we have your permission to precede with the initial start-up of the system, over?" control enquired.

It had been agreed upon that all queries and updates be directed at Team Leader for confirmation.

"You have permission to divert basic power to the shutter system only, control. Once Dreyfus has secured the unit and locked it down, shut off power again. Dreyfus, over?" the booming voice enquired.

"Dreyfus here Team Leader, over," Dreyfus replied promptly.

"Enter with care. Search and eliminate any hostiles inside. We gave them their warning. Then exit and lock down the unit. Do you require back- up, over?" Team Leader ascertained.

Dreyfus cupped his hands over his eyes and put his face to the shutter once again. He could make out the inside of the shop through the slats in the shutter. It all seemed abandoned in the shop however, the back office proving a possible area of probability.

"Shop appears to be empty. There's a small office located to the back of the store which will need inspecting, happy to proceed on my own Team Leader, over."

"Approach with caution Dreyfus, Team Leader over and out."

Dreyfus raised his Sig Sauer in his right hand and placed his left upon the pressle pad located upon his neck.

"Control, I am located outside of the In the Frame outlet and am ready to proceed on your mark, over."

Dreyfus stood ready to storm the store. He removed his left hand from his neck and placed it on the key, poised and ready to respond.

"You are clear to precede Dreyfus. Godspeed, control over and out."

And with that the radio channel fell silent. Dreyfus turned the key and the shutter shuddered into life. It rose at an agonising pace and rather annoyingly for Dreyfus, required him to stand with the key turned counterclockwise. He let go when it reached halfway before ducking away from the panel, pistol raised.

Dreyfus ventured into the outlet silently. He swung from right to left checking his corners. Satisfied the store was empty he preceded cautiously towards the partly open door ahead, tracing an arch with his gun, covering the entirety of the space. His two main concerns were the back office and behind the desk. He reached just shy of the door, a sign above reading "A picture speaks a thousand words. We only need two, no refunds." Unimpressed, he swung his pistol round with blistering speed. Empty. He briefly eyed the cabinets under the cashier's desk, quickly establishing that they were far too small for even a child to hide within let alone an adult.

Dreyfus diverted his attention back towards the door, all the while walking with his feet slightly apart, a side on angle reducing the noise of his footfall further. He swung into the room and pushed his back against the door. The room was empty apart from a set of shelves to his right, a desk and what appeared to be a safe to his left. His shoulders relaxed slightly; his gun dipped a centimetre. He made to turn when he heard the distinct sound of a wooden object grating along the floor ever so slightly. To Dreyfus's attuned ears however, it might as well have been a stampede of startled elephants.

Dreyfus whirled round and focused his attention on the far side of the office. He scanned it for any cubby holes or hiding places and surveyed his surroundings. The only perceivable gap that could house someone was a gap between the shelving unit and the wall that lay directly ahead. There was a hefty frame propped up against the gap. Dreyfus trained his gun towards the centre of the frame before thumbing down the hammer on his pistol.

"I'm going to give you three seconds to come out, hands raised, from behind that frame or I'm gonna give you some air holes to breathe through... not that you'll need them," he paused, flexing his trigger finger slightly.

"One… Two…"

A pair of chubby hands shot bolt upright, which in turn resulted in the frame falling flat. The glass inside shattered, sending pieces cascading across the floor. Dreyfus smiled to himself. Ahead of him was a middle- aged man wheezing heavily, an employee, he deduced from his attire.

The man began to whimper, his entire body was quaking. His arms dropped slightly under the pressure of his convulsive state. Dreyfus reciprocated raising the gun towards the centre of his forehead.

"Keep them nice and high," the store assistant raised them higher instantaneously, his arms unnecessarily extended. "I want you to interlock your fingers and put them on top of your head."

Once again, the man complied.

"Ple… please… don't shoot me… I didn't mean to…" the store assistant was begging now.

Dreyfus stepped towards the store assistant. He outstretched his left hand, the gun in his right hand still levelled at his skull. He indicated in a fanning motion for the man to calm down. He paused, taking in the pitiful sight before him. He stooped slightly, grasping the assistants name badge. Malcolm flinched.

"Malcolm, is it?" Dreyfus nodded.

The man nodded in reply, a single tear rolling down his cheek.

"Good. Now Malcolm, I really don't want to hurt you. The fact that you gave yourself up there indicated to me that you want to cooperate. Now, am I right in assuming that Malcolm?"

Malcolm nodded furiously, "Oh yes, I'll do… do whatever you say. Is it money you want because I have the code to the safe and-"

Dreyfus abruptly cut him off, once again raising his left hand.

"Excellent, now we're both happy. I'm not going to shoot you and you're going to cooperate. Everybody's happy. Unfortunately Malcolm, I'm not here for money, so don't go worrying your little self with any of that."

Malcolm smiled back weakly, happy at the softening of the man's demeanour.

"What I will need though Malcolm, is for you to turn around and face that wall, keeping those hands firmly on that head of yours. Is that ok with you Malcolm?" Dreyfus enquired, the condescension dripping from each syllable.

Malcolm looked unsure with this demand; his features puzzled.

"Oh, don't worry Malcolm, I'm just going to put some of these on you," he pointed to a pair of plasti- cuffs hooped around the left strap of his tactical vest. "I'm going to take you downstairs with everybody else."

"But the man said he was going to kill someone every-" Malcolm was cut off again.

"Now Malcolm, do I look like I'm going to let that happen after all of this. I could have shot you already and been done with it. No Malcolm, you co-operated. Now unfortunately, if the Prime Minister doesn't show himself then we will keep to our word, like clockwork. But think about it. All of those other people tried to run, put up a fuss. You complied. Now where do you think that's going to put you in the pecking order hey? I'd say safely right at the bottom, wouldn't you?"

Malcolm nodded and relaxed in his posture slightly. Dreyfus nodded in agreement; his painted eyes only barely visible under his balaclava.

"Now I'm going to holster my gun now Malcolm and put these on. I feel like I can trust you Malcolm, so don't go breaking that bond."

Dreyfus replaced the hammer of his gun back into its stationary position and holstered it within his leg holster. He stepped towards Malcolm, plasti-cuffs in one hand, the other held outwards in an unthreatening display.

Malcolm turned, nodding to himself in agreement. He felt all the better for the gun no longer being aimed at him. He faced the wall, the frame and its broken shards cracking underfoot. He could now hear the man behind him breathing. Suddenly, he felt a hand upon his shoulder; he recoiled ever so slightly and was met with more words of assurance.

"It's ok Malcolm. Now before I put these on and we go downstairs, I need you to answer one question for me, ok?"

Malcolm nodded.

"Good. You're doing great fella, honestly. Right, is there anyone else inside here with you?"

Malcolm let out a noise that indicated to Dreyfus that his hostage felt as if he had been rumbled. Malcolm quickly recovered and shook his head from side to side, rather too enthusiastically for Dreyfus' liking. Dreyfus patted him on the shoulder.

"Ok Malcolm. Thank you for shining some light on that for me," he replied with mock respect.

Malcolm nodded.

"I really do want to comply in any way possible," Malcolm started.

He was so pleased with having not offered up Tom that he did not hear Dreyfus slide his knife from the scabbard located on the front of his tactical vest.

"I know you do Malcolm," Dreyfus blankly stated before plunging the knife into the base of Malcolm's skull.

Malcolm's body shot bolt upright, his limbs locking. He made an effort to clutch at the back of his head to no avail, his arms wind milling in agony. Dreyfus responded by manoeuvring the knife in a fashion that resembled scrambling eggs, his wrist rotating several times in quick succession. Malcolm remained rigid for a moment or two longer before and with a blood curdling death rattle, he collapsed in a mound upon the floor.

"Either way, you were fucked," Dreyfus callously stated aloud.

He stooped down and wiped his bloodied knife on the yellow polo of the deceased store assistant, before replacing his knife into its scabbard.

"Now I wonder, who is to be our next contestant on you've been maimed?" Dreyfus clapped his hands.

As if in reply, the door behind Dreyfus swung open with significant force. He spun round to see the door reverberate and rebound backwards away from its frame, a sizeable gentleman hurtling towards him. He gritted his teeth instinctively reaching for his sidearm.

(CHAPTER BREAK)

The man Dreyfus and control had referred to as Team Leader checked his watch. Roughly seventeen minutes had passed since he had issued his demands. Consciously, he decided that it was now time to begin preparations for the next stage of the plan. He ushered over one of the men situated towards the periphery of the cluster of hostages. He indicated that he wanted him to come close enough for him to whisper. The man, small in stature, he too dressed head to toe in black, complete with tactical vest and green balaclava, leant in.

"Start preparing the set, select two of the men. Whilst they're doing that, I want you and a spare man to go outside and pay a visit to our friend out in the Land Rover. Take the cop. Use the working radios in the Land Rover and in one of the police vehicles to radio in."

The underling nodded along in agreement; he had heard it all before in the various briefings they had sat through.

"That should buy us some time. Once it's done, scupper them both. The Prime Minister is scheduled to be here for another forty-five minutes but when that times up, we're going to become flavour of the month."

Team Leader pointed at the police officer and in a voice audible enough for her to hear, spat "And if she doesn't comply, start removing body parts."

The female officer looked down at her feet once again. She had been stripped of her stab-proof vest, radio and belt complete with mace, telescopic baton and keys.

"You've got it boss. What should we say regarding the news stations and their cameras going down?"

Team Leader's balaclava gathered at the edges of his chin and it was visible to all that he was smiling under his balaclava.

"The feed wasn't going out live; Pierces speech was being pre-recorded for the evening news. If anyone asks, tell them that the press are having a field day with the speech and that they're hanging around after it for an impromptu question and answer session afterwards. Make sure you maintain radio communication. CCTV isn't going into operation yet, so control won't be watching your back. Keep us updated."

The subordinate grunted his understanding and turned on his heel. He methodically corralled two of the men on hostage duty and in hushed tones, explained what they were to do. He then walked over to the warehouse door and spoke to the sentry on duty for several seconds. The sentry nodded before the two briskly disappeared into the warehouse.

Team Leader once again spoke into his radio, "Control, over."

"Control here Team Leader, proceed, over," came the voice from above.

"Divert power to the warehouse doors. I'll let you know when they're safely inside and then on my mark seal the place up again, over."

"Roger and out," control responded.

Team Leader checked his watch again. One minute until the Prime Minister's deadline. He strode forward scanning the crowd; many within the cluster intuitively diverting their gaze, whilst others clamped their eyes shut in meditative prayer. However, for those who did not, a new, more horrifying scene was unfolding upon the stage. Two of the masked men busied themselves setting up a makeshift set, placing a singular metal chair within the centre of the stage, a sizeable sheet of tarpaulin underneath.

Next to be set up was a camera and tripod, one of the masked men adjusting the camera several times to achieve the best framing and line of sight. As he busied himself with the positioning of the camera, the other subordinate furiously tapped away on a laptop, which via a cable, was connected to the camera. For many, the stark realisation of what was being prepared on stage began to set in. Their darkest fear, a fear that had been publicised and cultivated by the media as well as many a politician, had finally hit home.

The two men walked to the back of the stage and placed a further set of chairs a metre or so apart from one another. One reached into a small pouch located on his belt and handed the other man an end of the material. They both stepped back away from one another and carefully, whilst unfurling the material, stepped up onto the chairs.

The gasp was instantaneous causing those who had been avoiding Team Leader's eye line to finally break their charade. Those within the cluster who had a basic grasp of geography and current affairs recognised the tricolour flag consisting of red, white and black. A singular line of Arabic occupied the centre of the flag, a mantra that to many within the Muslim community, had been bastardised and weaponised. 'God is great'.

However, what unnerved the assortment of hostages more so was the image that occupied the space beneath the text. For those linguistically challenged by the text, the symbol was all too abundant in its message; a geographically accurate globe slightly obscured by two black scabbards, malicious and curved. Rather alarmingly, western countries such as the United States of America, the United Kingdom and the entirety of Europe had their lands emblazoned with red.

Rather innocently, a sobbing child looked up at the flag and in an effort to understand a situation as of yet left unexplained by those in seniority, read out the only legible line in English, located towards the top of the flag. The girl's voice could just be heard over the hammer blows as the two masked men nailed the flag securely in place.

"The Islamic Brotherhood for Righteous Judgement," the young girl recited, faultless in her pronunciation.

The young girl met her mother's tearful gaze in a manner that sort approval, her curious nature wanting to ascertain whether she had read the text correctly. The mother let out a brief sob in response before pulling her daughter close, holding her tight. Team Leader's eyes shifted from the flag and fell upon a man in a suit. He raised a leather clad finger like that of death himself.

"You'll do," his modulated voice dully indicated.

(CHAPTER BREAK)

For the entirety of the minute or so Tom had shielded himself behind the door, his mind had been awash with fear and a steady realisation that whatever happened, he needed to act.

The way he saw it, he had three options. One, he could remain hidden behind the door and pray that the gunman left, unaware of his presence. This option was quickly dispelled however, when he heard a rather unconvincing Malcolm, paralysed by fear and misplaced trust, lie unconvincingly to his captor.

Two, he could make a bolt for it. He had glimpsed a brief look at the shutter before he had sought refuge behind the door and surmised it was about halfway open. He would now be able to fit under the shutter with hasty ease. However, if he were successful, two further problems presented themselves; what to do when he made it outside of the shop and could he reach the shutter before being shot in the back. He briefly conjured a heap of mutilated shoppers; his body being tossed onto the pyre. He shuddered and diverted his attention back to the task at hand. There was no doubt about it, these men were highly trained. After all, they had managed to eliminate any and all threats whilst at the same time securing hostages.

Only option three remained; an unfavourable course of action but a necessary one all the same. He would need to launch a full-frontal attack on the gunman. He would need to be quick, stealth not a viable option in the confined space. His hands had clammed up substantially now, the space behind the door claustrophobic. He made sure to moderate his breathing so as not to be heard, his lungs longing to expand further, the plywood door not permitting such.

Tom needed to break from cover at speed before the veiled hostile had a chance to draw his sidearm. He suddenly heard the gunman assuring Malcolm that he was holstering his sidearm.

The robotic tenor of the gunman's voice suddenly delivered a question that rendered Tom motionless.

'Is there anyone else inside here with you?'

Slowly, Tom raised his hands, placing his palms lightly upon the door frame so as not to move it in any way. Regardless of Malcolm's response, the hostile would mercilessly slay Malcolm as he and his co-conspirators had done so with the other shoppers. He needed to act. Option three it was. He readied his stance, the muscles in his shoulders taught, ready to thrust the door free of its frame.

He prepared himself, counting down from three in his head. He hadn't even made it to two before the panicked gargling began. Tom's stomach shifted violently as if he were going to vomit, a cold sweat crept along his back. He listened intently, the thump of Malcolm's body finally confirming it. No shot had been fired. Instead, Malcolm had been made to suffer, most likely stabbed. The realisation was instantaneous, the words of the man on the megaphone authenticated. If he were to surrender or be captured, he would share in Malcolm's fate. The nausea within the pit of his stomach hardened as fear gave way to anger.

The hostile spoke out aloud, clapping his hands. Tom cared little, the man's words inaudible, worthless. He would aim to knock the assailant unconscious and subdue him. All being well, the severity of his actions would end there.

Tom burst forward, the door swinging away from him violently. He covered the distance between he and the gunman with blistering speed. The masked man was quick to react; although slightly taken aback at what he was seeing, most likely internally berating himself for not having checked behind the door when he had entered the office. The gunman reached for his sidearm but was flung off balance momentarily by Tom. The gunman righted himself and whilst holding Tom back with his forearm, once again began groping for his gun.

Tom, who currently had his palm in the gunman's face, was thrashing at the man's torso with his other free hand, a clenched fist which drove rhythmically into the man's ribcage. Tom's knuckles bounced off the uneven contours of the tactical vest, at one point even hitting a spare magazine, which sent a pulsating shot of agony up and along his forearm.

The gunman's eyes, which were still visible through the layers of paint and Tom's clawing hand, never left Tom's. The gunman seemed calm and collected, his movements quick with a calculated choreography. Unlike Tom, he was not burdened with uncertainty, all too aware of what needed to happen procedurally. He had no intention of letting Tom walk out of this shop alive or allow him the upper hand.

Tom's attacks were proving superficial. He felt an urge of panic creep up within his throat before formalising the panic into a question, *"What if I can't stop this man without killing him?"*

Tom of course was no stranger to death but that was in the past, he had left that life behind in Sierra Leone. The gunman gained purchase of his sidearm and began to withdraw it from his holster. With lightning speed Tom diverted his free hand and locked it over his assailant's grasp, forcing the gunman's hand back into the holster. The two wrestled, swaying like inebriated ballroom dancers. The gunman's index finger was still curled around the trigger, the pistol moving an inch in its holster before being shoved an inch back. Both men quickly shared the realisation that this was now a battle of strength and longevity, the first to weaken would be the first to die.

Tom decided to make his move; he removed his outstretched palm from the gunman's face and clenched it into a fist. He directed two successive jabs to the area he presumed to be the bridge of the masked man's nose. The first blow visually registered tears within the man's eyes. The second however, resulted in the man's nose compacting under the force of Tom's knuckles. The gunman sniffled momentarily, a wet sound from under the balaclava indicating to Tom that it was most certainly bleeding, perhaps even broken.

Both the man's hands instinctively shot up to cradle his nose and that was when Tom seized upon the first opportunity afforded to him in the current stalemate. He made a grab for the gun and successfully pulled it from its holster. Tom felt the cold, textured grip of the handle and was suddenly overcome with a sense of dominant self-assurance. He pointed it in the direction of the gunman and cocked the hammer back.

Still holding his nose, a muffled set of expletive phrases followed. The hostile falteringly met Tom's eye line, holding his palm upwards in a gesture that warranted mercy. With great difficulty the man spoke. He seemed to be swallowing back blood as he spoke, a distinct nasal whistle punctuating the end of each word.

"Stop, stop, stop," he ushered with his free hand, his tone still shrouded with a mechanical hue.

Tom was taken aback by the gunman's plea. He stood rooted to the spot, legs slightly apart, gun trained at the centre of the man's chest. He felt unsure how to proceed, instead waiting for the gunman to compose himself. His heart was racing, his palms clammy around the grip of the Sig Sauer. He had never shot one of these handguns before but had no doubt that if it came to it, he could shoot this man. The man crouched down and lifted his balaclava as he spat out blood; his gloved had obscuring his lower jaw. He replaced it before standing up again. His hands came to a rest upon his hips, as if in an effort to gulp in some air but Tom read what he was trying to do.

"Make a grab for anything and I put one in your chest, hands in the air, now."

The gunman froze. He nodded his head in understanding before slowly raising his hands. The room fell silent, all be it for the whistling exhalation of the gunman.

"It doesn't need to be this way. No one here has to get hurt…" the gunman stated in a manner so condescending that even the device he was using to alter his voice could not conceal it. Using the gun, Tom indicated to the body of Malcolm.

"Try telling him that, you lying sack of shit," Tom asserted.

Rather abruptly, the façade dropped, and a low, stunted laugh came from the gunman. Tom tightened his grip upon the gun.

"He's the liar here. After all, he did say no one else was in the room and in my book that warrants…"

Without due thought and clouded by anger, Tom took a large step towards the gunman and placed the end of the Sig Sauer centimetres from his forehead. Tom was beginning to feel a deep resentment for the man who stood before him.

"What gives you the right to say that? He was just an employee. He didn't deserve to die like that… none of those people you killed did," Tom pressed harder, bile rising in his throat.

"You can't make an omelette without breaking some eggs," the gunman shrugged. "Talking of which, you do know that gun is empty right?"

Tom felt a stab of uncertainty strike at the core of his stomach. He raised the gun slightly higher in a show of force that indicated his distrust.

"That's bullshit and you know it. You were reaching for it…"

"Of course I was. How were you to know it was empty? If the tables were turned and I had pulled that piece, would you have known whether it was loaded or not? I mean, why do you think I gutted porky pig behind me there?" He thrust a pointed thumb over his shoulder, arms still above his head. "No bullets."

Tom felt as if the walls were closing in on him, the man presenting a perplexing dilemma. In a matter of seconds, Tom had gone from a position of superiority to nervous bystander once again.

"I'll prove it to you. Unload the magazine and check for yourself. If it still has bullets in it, you'll have a round chambered, enough to finish me off. If I'm right, well let's just say," he moved his eyes down towards his belt buckle, the knife visible in its scabbard. "You brought a gun to a knife fight."

Tom swallowed hard. The man had a point. He had already planted the seed of doubt; both he and the gunman knew it. Every fibre of Tom's being urged him not to be intimidated by the man's trickery. The weight of the pistol suddenly felt lighter. Against Tom's better judgement he took a step backwards and using the button on the side of the gun, discharged the magazine from the handle of the gun, never taking his eyes off the masked man.

He freed his supporting hand from under the handles casing and grasped at the magazine. He brought it up slightly, breaking his line of sight with the hostile momentarily. It was all the time the gunman needed. To Tom's immediate horror, the visible glint of brass was evident. The gunman was upon him. He violently struck out at Tom's right forearm, now unsupported at the base by his left hand, the gun spiralling to the floor.

Tom was flung against the shelving unit. A frame became dislodged by the impact landing squarely upon his left shoulder. An intense bolt of numbness spread across his shoulder. He let out a heavy grunt, the grasp upon his attacker weakening considerably.

The panic-inducing sound of the knife being drawn slowly from the hostiles scabbard punctured the silence. Tom was doing everything in his power to fend the gunman off, his arm angled deep within his attacker's upper torso. The knife came up and Tom instinctively snatched at it with his numb arm. The knife came down a considerable distance, stopping several inches from Tom's shoulder. Tom had the height and weight advantage, the gunman around five-foot-nine and of average build. Tom on any other occasion would have found it no great effort to overpower the man but his shoulder felt as if it had been bathed in liquid nitrogen.

The blade twisted in his grasp and nicked the palm of his hand, sending a steady dribble of blood trickling down the hilt. The knife lowered another inch. The gunman's breathing was heavy now, the effort of laboured breathing erratic and excitable. His eyes, brown and fiery with dedication, bore into Tom's. Tom tried to sway the man's stance but he was rooted to the spot. The knife came down a further two inches, perilously close to his face.

He was not strong enough, his legs either side of the gunman creaking under his attacker's substantial lunge. He decided to chance the only play he had left. If it proved to be unsuccessful, he would have sacrificed his footing for nothing, his attackers blade soon following suit.

"You dumb fuck! You're gonna die for breaking my nose. I'm going to enjoy slicing…"

The man's grunting voice, heavily laden with exertion was cut short by the knee that forcefully drove into his groin. Unsurprisingly, the man arched his back before doubling over in distress, the knife trailing off to the side. Tom took his chance. His right hand shot out finding purchase upon a sturdy frame for support. With all his strength, he pushed the gunman away with his left leg.

The man stumbled backwards, a hand clutching at his groin, the other held up in defence. Tom quickly gathered himself and heaved the frame from the shelving unit, bringing it down hard upon his attacker. The first blow slightly cracked the glass, forcing the attacker to drop the knife. The second however, led to the gunman's head poking through the slightly concaved MDF backing of the frame. His legs turning to jelly as he fell to the floor.

Tom observed that on the wall, towards the edge of the door frame ahead of him, was a roll of duct tape hanging from a nail on a piece of string. He moved towards it, his intention being to gag and bound the assailant while dazed. He stepped towards it, his fingers briefly brushing it, when he heard the sound of broken glass shifting behind him.

Tom spun round ready to defend himself but was instead barged through the open door. He came down heavily upon the stores counter, winded, the entirety of the air in his lungs expelled. He made to get up but the man was upon him once again. His attacker grabbed at the material of his t-shirt, hefting him closer. Tom instinctively shielded his face. The two successive jabs were delivered to his stomach instead. His knees went weak, the barrage continuing. Tom feebly lashed at the man's shoulders but the masked man, intoxicated with bloodlust, was all but invincible.

Tom held out his left arm in an effort to steady himself against the counter like a boxer in the corner of the ring, holding onto the ropes in an effort to weather the storm. That was when he fingers grazed over the object. His vision began to swim as his head lolled to the side, his attacker alternating between his torso and his head. His vison blurred the item his hand had made contact with barely visible. Desperate and in a laboured, clawing motion, he edged his fingertips over it.

The gunman had now taken to clamping his hands around Tom's neck, his thumbs at such an angle, that Tom felt as if they would penetrate his neck. He could smell the leather of the man's gloves, the tightening of the material unnerving. Black dots began to appear at the periphery of his vision, his lungs jerking in a slow, jarring deflation. He felt his hands close around the object.

The gunman, his speech broken with effort, brought Tom back towards him.

"Time to… pay the piper…" he howled.

Tom inhaled deeply, using the last morsel of air he had left at his disposal. He was damned if he was going to go out without a fight.

He brought the desk tidy up towards the gunman's shoulder. To his surprise, the gunman reacted with ferocious speed. Removing a hand from around Tom's neck, he brought up his hand in an effort to bat away Tom's attack. It was a pitiful attempt and instead diverted Tom's vigorous attack. The desk tidy instead penetrated the leather clad hand, Tom's momentum carrying it further onwards.

Wild-eyed, the man faltered backwards, his hand rather comically held in place by the spike which Tom now observed, had been driven all the way through and out the other side of his neck. The masked man began gasping for air, retching like a cat trying to bring up a fur ball, blood beginning to seep from the wound. The man's eyes rolled in his head before he fell back against the wall and then to the floor, a crimson swathe spread smeared across the wall.

Tom begun to panic, "Oh my God, I didn't…"

He had not meant to kill the man just simply fend him off, superficially wounding him. Tom dropped to his knees. He noticed, under the counter, a roll of sugar paper used to wrap items bought in store and began wildly unfurling the material. The wound made a slight sucking noise as he pulled the desk tidy free from the man's neck, flinging it aside. The man, overwhelmed by fear and pain, grabbed at Tom as he placed the bundled sugar paper against his neck. The man's eyes penetrated Tom's very soul framed by pure hatred and the realisation that he was not long for this world.

He made a last grasp for his comm's unit but Tom seized his hand. The man looked back at him brazenly before tugging slightly at Tom's substantial grip. A moment or so passed, the wounded insurgent attempting to speak, his face returning to a defiant hatred. His body began to convulse erratically.

"No, come on," Tom pleaded.

However, upon finishing the sentence, he observed that the man's eyes had already rolled backwards into his head.

The sickening panic Tom had felt earlier, returned. Self-preservation or not, he had not intended to kill this man. Pitifully, he pushed upon the man's chest, his other hand still firmly held over the crimson-soaked sugar paper covering the small yet mortal wound in his neck. He could no longer hear the masked man breathing; only the gargled bubbles of blood exiting his wound. Tom readied himself, ready to administer the kiss of life. He pulled the man's balaclava back, revealing a tuft of black hair and the strong features of a man in his mid-thirties.

What he saw resulted in his jerking away from the body, forcing him to his feet. The man's features alerted him to the very real threat of what was happening. All attempts to save the hostile quickly replaced by a transfixed look of utter shock.

CHAPTER NINE: HOUSE OF COMMONERS

The room had an aroma that if blindfolded, one's nostrils would immediately attribute with class and elegance. The study, a large room, framed on all sides by mahogany panelling and various political portraits was extravagant in every sense of the word. To the left of the room sat a bookshelf which consisted of row upon row of leather-bound books, assorted in regal crimsons and emerald greens. At the head of the room sat a large ornate table complete with lamp, blotter, tray for incoming papers, a phone complete with an intercom direct to the secretary and a twin set of fountain pens. The blotter, along with the pens, were both emblazoned with the unmistakable crest of the Houses of Parliament. Behind it stood a high backed, leather office chair which lay unoccupied before an open laptop.

The door suddenly opened and a man walked through holding a bundle of documents under one arm. The man, who was slightly greying at the temples, looked to be in his mid-forties. He still had a full head of hair, ruffled and set into a quiff. His face bore minimal wrinkles and his eyes, green, seemed youthful and enthusiastic. He had dispensed with his suit blazer and instead had the sleeves of his crisp white shirt rolled up to his biceps, his red tie complementing the navy blue of his trousers, finished off with brown brogues.

He exuded the demeanour of a personable, relatable person, which was partly why Pierce had chosen him for the job. The two had little in common, recently more so than ever, yet he was under no illusions as to why he occupied his current post within the cabinet. He was a political prodigy, an unknown variable. He was the state educated son of two working class parents from London, part of a family of four, two brothers and a sister. He had become involved in politics at school and had always been very left- wing.

However, when he had been offered the chance to come on board in Pierce's campaign for Prime Minister, he had jumped at the chance. Although Pierce, a staunch right- wing politician, was his polar opposite, he had become disillusioned with his own political party; a party that seemed more content with mudslinging than actually implementing any worthwhile policies. His defection and crossing of the benches had seen a mass of news coverage and he had been worried that it would lose him much in the way of support. Unlike many others within the chamber, Jonathan Benley had not been born with a silver spoon in his mouth nor educated in the likes of Eton. That said he was especially popular on both sides of the political divide and often received favourable coverage from the media.

When he had been elected as the MP for his constituency, one newspaper had read the following morning, 'House of Commoners', a headline that may have offended those less thick-skinned but not Jonathan Benley. No, the mantle was one he embraced wholeheartedly. He was proud of his upbringing, of the hard work that had made him the man he was today. He was a politician for the people and was viewed as such. To others, a move from a left-wing party to a right-wing one would have been seen as political suicide but to Benley, a man of the people, it had been very easy for him to turn in his favour.

The electorate generally seemed to like his political style and had indicated as much in various opinion polls. He had also been instrumental in signing and pushing through the landmark Endurance Act, a piece of legislation the likes of which had never been seen before in Britain. The act dictated that for the first time in British history and politics, the death or illness of a

Prime Minister would result in the Deputy Prime Minister assuming the role, until a general election could be held. In the event of an attack where both were incapacitated or killed, it would move successively down the line of high-ranking politician's within the party.

Benley, third in the pecking order, had remarked that it was a necessity, as he deemed it they were living in, *"An age of ever increasing uncertainty with terrorist plots set to demean and underwrite Britain's security."*

The legislation had persevered through various redrafts and discussions and had in fact been put forth by the oppositional party in power before Pierce was elected Prime Minister. Pierce had been reluctant to put it through at first but under mounting pressure from high-ranking MP's such as Benley as well as others within the opposition, it was finally passed with a majority.

A woman trailed behind Benley jotting down notes upon a notepad, Molly Cartwright, his secretary. Molly was in her late thirties but could have easily been mistaken for being in her mid- twenties. She was an extremely good-looking woman and to her annoyance often rendered people aghast when she was introduced to them as the Home Secretary's personal assistant. Her brunette hair, a deep curled mass, hung loose around her shoulders and rather comically bobbed wildly in the air. She had been Jonathan Benley's secretary for the last three years and relished her time working in Downing Street. She was the mother to one daughter, Poppy, aged five. She had been married to her husband Stuart, a financial adviser, for coming up on seven years.

Jonathan threw his papers onto his desk and continued speaking to Molly or Mol as he affectionately referred to her.

"No, no, no. If we move the immigration review that's going to put us back on the passports and the public is already calling for our blood on that!" Jonathan emphasised in his strong yet refined East-London accent.

"What about this?" he turned to Molly, a finger held aloft. "Swap my one o'clock with my three o'clock, Daniel Smith can wait and put my conference call with Borders and Immigration at one."

He looked almost pleadingly at Molly. She scanned her notepad, flicked one page, scanned it again then looked up at Jonathan Benley with a smile.

"I believe that's feasible Mr. Benley, just don't forget that if you don't talk to Daniel Smith today, it may hold up plans on the..." Jonathan Benley held his palm up; his shoulders shuddered with a low laugh.

"Mol let me have this small victory. I might actually be able to eat some lunch today, well that is if this conference call doesn't go on forever like the last one."

Molly laughed at this and continued to write upon her notepad, striking something off. Benley turned round to his desk and sieved through the scattering of papers. Presently, he found the one he was looking for and handed it to Molly.

"If you can type up those notes from earlier and swing that past Richard Avery's office, I would be forever in your debt," he said with a smile.

Molly nodded and made to turn away, "Another debt. I'll have to start calling these in," she wryly chuckled, "Anything else while I'm here, sir?"

Benley who had returned to sifting through his papers and an assortment of folders looked up in consideration and thought for several seconds. His finger shot into the air once again and he span round.

"Yes! There is one more thing. Could you patch me through to Scotland Yard on line one please as well as the Deputy Prime Minister on two. Better check in on the PM's visit."

"I'll do that right away, sir," Molly replied instinctively.

There was very little that Molly would not do for her employer, which is a lot more than she could say for many others within the party, Pierce included.

"Mol, I don't know what I would do without you," he exhaled joyfully as he sat behind his desk.

Molly smiled. That was one of the many reasons she loved working for Jonathan Benley. He was passionate, hardworking and ruthless when it was demanded of him in the House of Commons but he never overlooked anyone. No matter the size of the cog in the general order of things, you were made to feel appreciated and instrumental in the running of things.

She slipped out of Benley's office, shutting the door as she did so before walking over to her desk which was located in a room to the left of Benley's door. She began flicking through the rolodex upon.

Jonathan Benley slumped down in his high-backed chair with a sigh, cradling his forehead. The Prime Minister's growing unpopularity had kept him busy as of late and the opinion polls were looking as if he would soon be out of a job in the cabinet. Many within the party and the electorate had cried out for Benley to put himself forward as a candidate within the election race although he had quickly dismissed this prospect. As he had explained to a radio presenter interviewing him three weeks previous, he was not in the business of *"Spearheading coups."*

That said it was becoming increasingly more difficult to ensure the safety of both Pierce and the nation as a whole. Each day brought with it a new death threat or a declaration of terror levied upon the people of Britain. The government's recent foreign policy, of which Pierce had largely overseen, had also ruffled many international feathers, the deployment of British troops around the globe seen a profitable enterprise to many in the Middle East and Africa. As if matters were not dire enough as it was, the party had been rocked by several scandals, three of which involving members of the cabinet. Insalubrious expense claims, tax avoidance and a good measure of sexual deviance had led to the party becoming besmirched.

Benley leaned forward and picked up the telephone's receiver, pushing the button for line one. A brief conversation with Scotland Yard maintained that Pierce was currently finishing up his speech and that afterwards he would be fielding questions from the press. The series of events were described in a not too dissimilar account to the one he had received prior to entering his office from a Jack Wright, the driver in Pierces' close protection unit. All seemed to be going according to plan.

"Yes, very good, thank you. As mentioned, keep me informed of any and all possible incidents or changes to Mr Pierce's itinerary," Benley signed off, bringing the phone down swiftly.

He rubbed his eyes before tentatively looking at the flashing light that indicated there was a call waiting on line two. He cleared his throat and pushed the button. The Deputy Prime Minister's secretary answered.

"Yes, can you put me through to James please Janet," Benley graciously enquired in a familiar and friendly manner.

"Yes Mr Benley, I'll put you right through to Deputy Prime Minister Braham now. Please hold."

"I'll catch you out one day," Benley muttered to himself.

Although rather immature, Benley liked to play a game with the staff whereby he referred to the person he wanted to speak with by their first name, even the Prime Minister. It was his intention that one day the veneer of formality would momentarily slip and a personal assistant or aide would refer to their superior by their first name. Benley knew it was a silly game but it kept a spark of his rebellious working class attitude alive. No one had caved as of yet but he was ever hopeful of when the day would come.

He heard a phone being jostled from its base and awaited the reply.

"Good morning Jonathan," came the upper-class drawl of James Braham, his demeanour and often jovial nature juxtaposing his refined manner completely.

"Morning, James. Just thought I'd check in and update you on the Prime Minister's visit."

Benley heard a sniff on the other end of the line followed in quick succession by a grunt.

"I see. I don't suppose that you're phoning me to inform me that the Prime Minister has done us both a favour and has dropped dead or has decided to elope with a mistress or some such?" Braham stoically jived.

Benley, amused by Braham's forthright condemnation of Pierce, chortled audibly which in turn registered a slight guffaw from Braham in return.

"Afraid not Mr Deputy Prime Minister, you're stuck with your job I'm afraid, not quite in the hot seat yet," Benley prodded.

Braham feigned mock disappointment, "Ahhh well old boy that's a shame. I suppose we'll just have to settle upon political suicide instead. I gather he arrived safely?"

"Oh yes, no issues. We've had both Scotland Yard and his close protection team call it in. No doubt we'll be getting coverage filtering through within the hour," Benley establishing, swivelling slightly in his chair.

"Well let's hope he hasn't made a spectacle of himself. That's the bloody last thing we need this late in the election campaign." Braham's tone suddenly shifted and bore the tact of a man seeking reconsideration on Benley's part. "Talking of which Jonathan, I must urge you to reconsider my earlier proposal."

"James we've talked about this at length. Look, I'm not Andrew's biggest fan myself. You know that, the cabinet knows that... hell even the public knows that but at the end of the day I am not about to put all our jobs at risk and take part in some kind of hostile takeover. This country's already in enough of a state as it is, it doesn't need us jostling for the Prime Ministers head on a pike."

Silence followed. Benley could tell that Braham was considering his next advance with a degree of calculation.

"Jonathan, you and I are friends are we not?"

"Great here come the violins," Benley's internal monologue surmised.

"Yes of course we are James," he reassured his colleague.

"And you know what I am like as a person first and foremost, over my responsibilities in politics, my title?" Braham pressed.

"Yes?" Benley answered unsure of the direction in which Braham was headed.

"Then you'll understand me when I say enough is enough. We have rallied behind Andrew for as long as we possibly can and in doing so; to our own detriment, have tarnished our own reputation within the political forum. We can no longer amble on behind him. His approval ratings and popularity are at an all-time low, he has done little to improve the state of the economy or the country's infrastructure for that matter and he seems generally happy to disregard the party's stance, yours and mine included."

"He's a political nomad Jonathan, a man with no clear direction. He is in a tailspin sport and whether you like to admit it to yourself or not, we're going down with him. The question you need to ask yourself Jonathan is, will you accept the parachute I'm handing you or would you rather go down in flames with Pierce?"

"Very metaphorical of you James," Benley wryly retorted. "No matter what happens there'll be a career in poetry at the end of all this for you."

Braham's brash undertone abruptly came to the fore.

"Now is not the time to be flippant Jonathan. This is a serious offer on the table, one which I would myself feel all the better for if you were on board with. I know you are a man of principle and this seems rather, well, Julius Caesar of us to do but this is more than just stabbing a man in the back. This is a country on the brink. If I have to play the part of Brutus within the grand forum that is contemporary politics, then so be it. Raise the bloody curtain I say."

Jonathan sighed. He did not have time for this conversation, especially on today of all days.

"Here is my standing on the matter James, Shakespeare analogies and historical forays aside. Neither I nor you are going to become the next Brutus or any other conspirator for that matter. This is not the forum and it is most certainly not Ancient Rome. Now you are a dear friend and as I have gone on record to say many a time before, I support your opinions as well as your position when it comes to Andrew and his shortcomings as Prime Minister. But what I cannot condone is being the first in line to plunge the knife into neither his back nor any of the other seven who did so to Caesar."

Jonathan Benley sat awaiting Braham's response and found himself staring at the portrait of Winston Churchill, on the wall to his left. The silence on the other end of the line indicated to Benley that James Braham was all but done trying to convince him. He respected James greatly and wanted desperately to bring an amicable closure to the conversation.

"James, are you still there?" Benley pressed.

A dejected voice replied, one fraught with disappointment, "Yes Jonathan, I'm still here."

"James, whatever the outcome, you will always have my backing. I just think on this matter, your tactics are a little skewed. After all, who needs a Brutus when we have our very own despot who is more likely to stab himself in the back! I mean it took twenty-three stab wounds to fell Caesar; Pierce has nearly that amount in political faux-pas and poor policy alone, mostly instigated by his own hand."

"So you're content on waiting for him to land the killing blow himself? Let him be the instigator of his own downfall?" Braham queried; his intrigue reinvigorated.

"Men at some time are masters of their own fates: The fault, dear Brutus, is not in our stars but in ourselves, that we are underlings," Benley smugly quoted Shakespeare's Julius Caesar.

He had himself played the role of Cassius in his school's production of the play and had never forgotten the lines he had learnt with such dedication. His mind trailed back to his friend Jamie Wiseman who, on the debut night of the performance, had referred to him as Casio, the popular brand of calculator, instead of Cassius, which had caused his friend a great deal of embarrassment. He smirked at the memory.

Braham snickered with great gusto. Benley smiled, safe in the knowledge that any threat evident within Braham's voice earlier had now been extinguished.

"Beware the ides of March, my good man. Underlings we are and underlings we shall remain for the foreseeable future."

"Well, here's hoping it won't take as long as March," Benley hastily added.

"Well let's wait and see how Pierce's proposals on tackling terrorism in the Middle- East go down. The last thing the country wants right now is more of our men sent to the abattoir that is that country" Benley sniffed, his patriotism once again resplendent, he himself having served as an officer in the Royal Marines for nine years prior to entering politics.

"I hope it won't come to that. The last thing we want to be doing is giving the extremist cells in the Middle East anymore fuel to heap upon the propaganda pyre. Besides, it's the home-grown brand of extremism that keeps me awake at night, not some deplorable in a backwater somewhere."

Benley had campaigned strongly on this matter. Every day he received various Intel from both MI5 and MI6, pertaining to warnings and threats of various severity. Only last week, a raid upon a house in Bexley Heath had unearthed a terrorist cell that was planning to use homemade pipe bombs as part of a co-ordinated and simultaneous attack on military recruitment offices across the country.

"Very true Jonathan, very true. Well, I must be going; I have an interview on Talking Politics at three. Oh joy," he stated sarcastically.

"You make sure to put that smoke screen up good and proper. Wouldn't want the people of Britain knowing how really up shit's creek we are now would we?" Benley prompted Braham, semi-serious.

"I'm so used to pulling Pierce's arse out of the fire I'm an old hat at it now. I doubt Talking Politics or that loathsome host Richards will have anything in their arsenal that I haven't already had to contend with. Think over what I said today Jonathan, just promise me that much," Braham finished pleadingly.

"Of course, just don't move on anything without at least using me as a sounding board first," Benley sternly asserted.

"Agreed," Braham concurred with honest bravado.

"Just remember James, Churchill was also disliked by his cabinet and look what he achieved. A given, he wasn't re-elected after the war but to quote the great man himself, 'You have enemies? Good. That means you've stood up for something, sometime in your life."

"I would hardly class Pierce as anywhere near his calibre would you Jonathan? Come now," Braham chuckled once again.

"No James," Benley stated as he continued to stare at the imposing portrait of Churchill on his wall, "But then again, Rome wasn't built in a day."

CHAPTER TEN: A POLICY TO RALLY BEHIND

"If you think I'm going out there you must be more delusional than previously thought," Pierce hissed from the confines of the Shake Attack stall.

"Sir, there is a very real chance that we are not going to get out of here in one piece. Hell, staying hidden from them for this long has been a feat in itself," Gerry admitted submissively.

"The job of you and your men is to protect me whatever the cost, sacrificing your lives should the occasion deem it necessary and here we are, you wanting to hand me over to those mad men. I am not going out there to be prostituted before the masses for them just so that they can put a bullet in my skull or worse," Pierce protested caring little for anyone but himself. He was willing to sacrifice countless men, women and children to save his own skin.

"Mr Pierce, I am well aware of the responsibilities that fall under my job title. The same goes for the rest of my team, the very men that put your life before theirs. This isn't some run of the mill assassination attempt. I honestly think if they wanted you dead, they would have taken you out during your speech. I'm just laying out the facts here. In about a minute someone is going to cease to exist, based on the decision you make here, right now."

Gerry was aware that his tone was slightly pleading in nature.

"Collateral damage, that's what you military lot call it, isn't it? We do not negotiate with terrorists and we most certainly do not barter with barbarians of their sort when a Prime Minister's life is the currency."

"Sir, with all due respect this isn't the time to start lording policy about, there are lives at stake. We have one man on the outside and for all we know, he's most likely dead," Gerry paused at this, the inner fears he harboured for his good friend of seven years verbalised for the first time. He pushed it to the back of his mind. Mourning would have to wait.

"There must be some other way, a Plan B or something. You prepare contingencies, don't you? In case of compromise" Pierce was displaying all of the characteristics of a man coming to terms with the insurmountable odds stacked against him.

"Sir, my comm's are down, I'm low on ammunition, all power has been cut and all exits sealed; I saw them come down before the bullets started to fly. I'll level with you, there's a very real chance that you could die but the fact that they have taken hostages, most likely chalks this up to money. They probably want a ransom from Downing Street for your safe return. It could buy us the time we need, for our guys to formulate a strategy to extract you, me and the hostages. You need to think about the people out there, Sir. Not just as their elected official but as human being. It's in your hands-"

The gunshot rang out, reverberating around the marble structure of the shopping centre. The gunman had intentionally placed their gun near the megaphone to achieve maximum resonance. What followed was the most blood curdling medley of screaming and hysteria that Gerry had ever heard. He looked down at his feet and sighed. Pierce looked ashen faced and pulled his knees up to his chin, cradling them like a frightened child.

The megaphone shrieked with static before settling.

"The next one only gets ten minutes," put forth the unmistakable, distorted voice of the man who had spoken earlier.

The Prime Minister gulped and looked at Gerry with a forlorn sideway glance, aware that Gerry had now taken to staring at him.

(CHAPTER BREAK)

Team Leader motioned with his hand for one of his men to take the body away. The man left a trail of blood that coiled before the group of hostages, many of whom were sobbing lightly, probably so as not to identify themselves as the next potential viable suitor for execution. One woman dared to look up, inadvertently locking eyes with the ringleader. He was talking to one of his subordinates. He caught the woman's eye before twisting away from the woman, shielding his lips from being read.

"Sir, we can't get Dreyfus on comm's. We've been trying him for the last couple of minutes. I'd like to take some of the men and search for him."

Team Leader nodded, bringing his arm up higher around the man's shoulder. He felt the man quiver slightly as he did so. He spoke into the man's ear.

"Chances are he has gone silent while he takes care of business. That said, take two men and check what's taking him so long," he squeezed the man's shoulder, savouring the man's body as it tightened instinctively with fear.

How he relished the power and dominance fear granted. He whirled round and pushed the presell switch connected to his comms.

"Alpha Team, Team Leader here, over," he said firmly.

"Alpha Team hearing you loud and clear Team Leader, over," came the reply.

"Any sign of the PM yet, over?" he asked rather faint heartedly, knowing full well that the minute his men even had the slightest of inclinations that they had found Pierce, he would be the first to know.

"First sweep of the ground and first floor yielded nothing sir. We found a couple of employees hiding out in the Santa's Grotto but we neutralised them, over."

"Very well, Dreyfus has gone dark. The subgroup is checking the second floor, so proceed with another sweep of the first floor and then the Ground floor again. He's in here somewhere; we just have to smoke him out."

Team Leader did not bother to state 'Over', a deliberate indication that emphasised the severity of the situation at hand. He adjusted the voice changing device beneath his balaclava. They had been a cheap purchase from a novelty shop but as of yet had been instrumental in maintaining their cover. He knew the building was locked down. It was airtight. That said, he could not help but consider whether or not his well-executed plan had hit a snag, perhaps some tradesmen's entrance not on the blueprints or an unknown access route out of the complex.

He turned back to the crowd. It was five minutes until the next execution and he was growing impatient. If he wanted to expedite the process, he was going to have to up the ante. He settled upon the woman who had caught his gaze earlier. She looked up, her eyes sodden. He approached the woman and kneeled before her pulling his gun from its holster as he did so. He cut an arc across the group with his pistol before bringing it to a rest just shy of the woman's forehead. Her shoulders began to quake uncontrollably, a low sob emanating from deep within her throat.

Team leader raised his spare gloved hand and lightly stroked the woman's head several times, the contact causing the woman to recoil.

"Be still," Team Leader stated.

The woman looked up, meeting her captor's gaze, a gaze which was held for several seconds. Finally, he motioned with his gun for her to get up. She shakily began to rise to her feet, Team Leader following suit. When she had gotten to her feet, Team Leader indicated for her to stop.

"Don't move," he sternly ordered in his robotic drool as if the woman had any choice.

Team Leader's eyes shifted momentarily from the woman. He clicked his fingers and pointed a gloved finger behind her. The woman made to turn but Team Leader withdrew his pointed finger and instead placed it under the woman's nose, venom returning once again to his eyes.

"That's your first and last warning," he simply stated.

The woman shook her head lightly indicating that she understood. She stood rooted to the spot. Team leader returned his attention to the scene playing out behind the woman. Suddenly an agonised howl broke the silence. It was not until the person responsible for the scream began to plead with an unseen captor that the woman before Team Leader realised the owner was female. The woman daren't look. Instead, she focused her eyes on a column behind Team Leaders head, a fixed spot in which to channel her terror.

The pleading intensified and it was not until a man's outstretched arms appeared at the periphery of her vision that the realisation of what was about to transpire dawned upon her.

First came five stunted, slightly pinkish chubby digits, followed by a stick-like arm encased in a blue jumper. As if she needed any more clarification, the various assortment of Thomas the Tank Engine characters festooned upon the jumper's arm indicated the true horror of what was to come next. As the child passed her eye line, she caught sight of the child's face, a milieu of utter confusion, framed by sodden eyes.

The masked man tugged at the boy and for the briefest of seconds the child resisted, his lip beginning to quiver.

"Please not my son. Take me instead, not my boy. He's innocent, please. Take me," the mother shrieked from behind.

Mumbles from others within the group began to also plead. Team Leader pulled the boy up and as he did so, holstered his weapon. He pulled the boy up and cradled him, bouncing him on his forearm. The child, no more than about two looked questionably back at him sobbing slightly. The man cooed the child in a metallic crackle and swung slightly at his hips making an effort to calm him.

In a sickening turn of events Team Leader grasped his megaphone with his free hand and angled it towards the crowd, the cries of the mother now amplified around the complex. The mother was now in a state of frenzy. She grasped at the air as if trying to grab her son's hand. In a demonstration of pure innocence and infancy the child turned in Team Leader's arms and waved back at her, open and shutting his hand. Team Leader brought the megaphone back round.

He stooped slightly and spoke into the child's ear, all the while making sure the megaphone captured the conversation.

"You want to go back to your mummy? Huh?"

He continued to sway the child, who was squirming slightly, twisting from the masked man back towards his mother. Others in the crowd were crying now.

"How much do you want to go back to your mummy?" he questioned.

He lifted the megaphone towards the child. After ten seconds or so the child uttered a single word quaking with imminent tears.

"Mumma."

The singular word echoed around the complex. Satisfied, Team Leader twisted the megaphone back towards his own mouth.

"Do you hear that Prime Minister? This little boy, who I must note is about fifteen or so years shy of being one of your registered voters, wants his mummy."

He raised his wrist slightly to look at his watch. He nodded to one of his men who stepped forward, unsheathing his gun in a fluid motion that expressed no conflicted feelings over what was being asked of him. He came up behind Team Leader and raised it to the child's temple.

"A bullet travels faster than the speed of light. Lucky for you Pierce, knowing full well how inept you are at making decisions hastily, you've still got... around fifty seconds to give me your answer before my man beside me with a gun pointed at this young boy's head, executes my order. Let's see if your principles are as quick to surface as a bullet is to be fired, shall we?"

The man wielding the gun cocked the hammer back. The child looked from Team Leader back to the gun and unaware of the situation lightly gripped the barrel of the gun playfully. The gun wavered slightly but the insurgent held firm, sating the child's fascination.

The mother's cries were inaudible now due to the convulsive state she now found herself in. Shock having taken hold, she made to stand, bound hands outstretched in a pleading manner. An insurgent to her left forcefully shunted her to the ground.

One of the other insurgents approached, coming close to Team Leader's ear and muttered, "Sir, do we really need to..."

He was cut off.

"If you can't handle this, then you're of no use to me," he stated calmly, eyes still firmly focused on the woman before him.

The subordinate, his own interests quickly taking hold, nodded solemnly and took three steps back.

The woman before Team Leader murmured something, chin upon her chest.

Team Leader brought up the megaphone using it to lift her chin upwards. Her eyes met his, a steely determination having now replaced the fear.

"You need to get something off your chest?" Team Leader rasped.

Stuttering slightly, the woman replied, "Take... take me instead."

Team Leader cocked his head slightly, intrigued by the woman's noble if not futile deed.

"I'll take you all if needs be," Team Leader replied. "Now shut you fucking snivelling before I give you something to cry about."

The woman once again lowered her head dejectedly but not before breaking her gaze slightly to give the child a look of reassurance, her sodden features doing little to comfort the child. Team Leader focused on the crowd once again.

"Well Mr Prime Minister, looks like this little boy can tell the time better than you. Times up I'm afraid. This boy's life is on your conscience..."

He turned to the gunman and nodded, holding the child outwards so as not be to close when the deed was done.

"Stop," a shrill Northern shriek reverberated throughout the Ground floor. "We surrender, just stop, and let the boy go."

Team Leader turned to the man with the gun and indicated for him to holster his weapon before ironically handing the boy to the same gunman for safe keeping. He turned towards the direction of the command, dropping the megaphone as he did so. It clattered harshly upon the marble.

He scanned the complex before his eyes fell upon a shack like structure. Two hands, one bloodied, rose above the service hatch of the structure. Two of the men instinctively whirled round and trained their automatic weapons upon the structure. The hands assuredly gave way to arms, which were in turn followed by the missing member of the close protection team. Team leader stared back in disbelief at the man, his regimented stance intact.

"Where is he?" Team leader said firmly, stepping forward slightly, his hand resting on his holster. The man turned and pointed down.

"Very slowly and with two fingers, throw out your sidearm and any other items you may have," Team Leader instructed.

The man reciprocated and very slowly withdrew his firearm free of its holster between his thumb and forefinger. He tossed it through the open hatch before raising his arms aloft once again. Team leader indicated to his men to move in. They stepped slowly towards the shack; their movements cautionary, methodical.

"Let me see him," Team Leader barked.

Dejected and beaten, the bodyguard crouched slightly and hefted Andrew Pierce up by the lapels of his suit. Pierce's eyes darted from the advancing insurgents before settling upon Team leader. His face was sodden with sweat, his shoulders and arms shaking. He collapsed slightly but was held firm by the surviving member of his security detail.

A low, audible laugh erupted from Team Leader and he started to clap slowly. He held out his arms in a grandiose fashion taking several steps forward. His men's weapons were trained on their newfound captives, one of the men having already gathered up the surrendered gun upon the marble floor.

"Welcome Mr Pierce, so nice of you to finally bestow upon us, the pleasure of your company. If my religion dictated that I celebrate Christmas, I would say that this was truly the greatest gift I could ever receive." He patted his head slightly in mock ignorance

"Where are my manners? Come now Prime Minister, you can't stand there all day. After all, I may have gotten what I wanted for Christmas but there are countless people who have not yet received the gift of your company."

Unbeknownst to the Prime Minister, Team Leader's gaze subconsciously diverted to that of the mocked-up stage and with it, the empty chair located within the centre.

(CHAPTER BREAK)

The news channels were quick to acquire the live stream but not as quickly as those at the London headquarters of MI5. The situation room, a space full of assorted monitors and rows of employees typed furiously away. The screens were awash with footage and live updates on internet chatter. When Richard Miller had arrived at work earlier that morning, he did so with the usual perspective, one that had been instilled in him for the seven years he had been in the job. The perspective that, every day was different and had the potential to present all manner of variables for the United Kingdom and her interests.

He always started his day with the belief that everything and anything could happen; he along with the rest of MI5 had contingencies for every fathomable threat. Nuclear attacks, biological crises of varying extremes, even the one that was being played out before him now on the screens. It was naïve to deem anything out of the ordinary or too implausible. But this, this was one of the contingency files that no Director of MI5 ever wanted to have to open.

Miller appeared the epitome of calm. He was cool and calculated at the best of times and had mastered his poker face over his vast tenure to such an extent that even now as those around him awaited his next order, he knew they believed him to be level-headed enough to see them through this crisis. However, unbeknownst to those around him, inside he was wrestling with a palpable inner panic.

Out of a sense of practically over comfort he kept his blazer on, the dampness of sweat under his armpits, cool and catching the breeze of the air conditioning. The sweat would be a tell-tale sign of weakness, an indicator that he was feeling the strain.

Miller, fifty-two years of age and a married father of two, prided himself on keeping himself fit. He ran every morning before work on Hampstead Heath, a five-minute saunter from his three- storey house. He looked over the wire rimmed glasses that sat low upon the bridge of his nose, arms crossed across his torso. His hair, a deep shade of black speckled by grey, was uncharacteristic for a man with a career marred with such a high threshold of stress.

"What do we have Susan?" he questioned; eyes still firmly fixed on the centre monitor.

"Analysing the footage now sir." Furious key commands ensued upon the keyboard. "It's a live feed being uploaded remotely, most likely internally, using the shopping centre's internet connection," Susan established.

"How could they have access to the centre's system?" Miller thought out loud, knowing the answer yet wanting to regurgitate the information at hand. "Can we cut their connection?"

"We've dispatched units to the centre but we have to assume from what they've said thus far and from their set of demands that as well as locking down the building, they have access to the security protocols. We can cut the connection but from an analysis of their signal, they're bouncing their live feed through a variety of different servers. It would take forever and a day to locate them all and shut them down and even then, we would probably only be looking at the tip of the iceberg. Also sir..." she paused.

"Precede Susan," Miller urged.

"We have to presume that those on the ground protecting the PM are either all dead or incapacitated in some form or another."

Miller broke his eye line with the central screen for the first time and looked rather solemnly at Susan. What he said next would sound callus to the casual outsider, even slightly insincere but to Miller it was simply a point that needed to be addressed.

"I would operate under the assumption that they have all been neutralised. They clearly have a large number of hostages on show. The video shows three men, two grunts and what appears to be their leader. We must also deduce from their threats that there are more of them off-screen, presumably quite sizeable in force from what they have managed thus far."

Miller massaged his eyes under the lenses of his glasses and under his breath he muttered, "What a mess."

Promptly, he composed himself and spoke up so that the whole room could hear. The rhythmic clatter of keyboards was replaced by that of swivelling chairs and over thirty sets of expectant eyeballs.

"Ok ladies and gentlemen, we all have more than enough to do, so I am going to keep this short and sweet." Miller pointed forcefully at the freeze frame upon the central screen, that of a bloodied Pierce, absent of all colour. "Our priority is that man right there. He cannot and will not die today. This is likely to be one of the biggest scenarios many of you have ever faced in here today, if not the biggest. But I wish to remind you that we receive this very threat on an hourly basis, day in, week out, yearly. The only difference today is that this isn't a dry run, we ladies and gentlemen, are severely on the back foot. No amount of intel or prior threat status could have prepared us for this, we are officially flying blind."

Miller dropped his finger and surveyed the room, scanning the personnel at his disposal as if they were a captive audience awaiting a Shakespearian sonnet. Whether they believed in his performance or not, the only review that would certify and validate his performance was that of the newspaper front pages, headlines ablaze with the averted chaos that was likely to ensue over the next few hours, possibly days.

"Now, I need intel, blueprints of the centre and I want their demands looked into. In half an hour, I want all contingencies surrounding how this may play out in my hand and most importantly, I want to know who this Islamic Brotherhood for Righteous Judgement is and any leverage that we can get over them to even the playing field." He whirled his finger around like a helicopter. "Now let's hustle people, the clock is ticking. We don't go home until Pierce does."

The banks of analysts swung back to their consoles, various staff hastily moving around the room clutching documents and relaying messages to others. Miller leant upon the desk overlooking the space and stared at the banks of monitors before him.

"Susan, play it back for me one more time."

(CHAPTER BREAK)

The speech bore all the trademarks of a man that had rehearsed over and over what he would say in his head but had not submitted it to paper. The words, spoken forcefully, gathered much of their momentum from the fact that they were both whole heartedly believed in by their speaker as well as the untold millions watching the live stream on the internet.

The stage quite literally and figuratively set, held the Prime Minister in centre frame, flanked by two masked men wielding AK-47s. The leader stood behind him, his right hand resting upon Pierce's right shoulder and juxtaposed to this, a resting machete in his left, all the while trained and rested upon Pierce's other shoulder, angled towards his neck. The flag and insignia had also deliberately been positioned in frame. Arched around the edge of Pierce were twenty hostages: men, women and children of assorted ages and ethnicities.

However, what was most unsettling was the way in which the hostages were arranged. They knelt before Pierce, bound by plasti cuffs, facing in towards Pierce instead of outwards for the benefit of those in Whitehall and the intelligence services analysing the data. In a macabre display of prearranged proxemics, they looked as if they were praying to Pierce or more aptly, begging him. The masked man spoke firmly and with gusto.

"What you see before you is a sight that the citizens of Britain have seen daily upon the front pages of this nation's newspapers and via an assortment of other partisan, biased media. As I have rather figuratively displayed for you by those before me, for quite some time now many have turned towards men like Pierce, elected officials, supposed pillars of society, those that they have themselves blindly elected, for guidance. Like sheep in a flock the people of this country carry out and upheld many a politician and law makers ideologies, in fear, a fear of being imprisoned or considered socially abnormal for voicing concerns or rallying against the social order."

"Many will argue that what takes place here today is all on Pierce's shoulders but they would be wrong. Do not be mistaken. On this day he will feel the mighty and righteous hand of justice, the strength of which will be tempered by those in this land and afar, those he has sought to enslave. No, if you truly seek out the guilty," he raised the machete momentarily and pointed it towards the camera relaying the live feed "simply look in the mirror."

The machete returned to Pierce's shoulder which registered a sizeable shudder from the Prime Minster, his head lowered.

"Yet unlike the man before me and those who blindly follow him, I give you, the people a choice. Located somewhere in the capital, is an explosive device that will yield an explosion of such magnitude, that the cost to both life and property will leave a scar, the likes of which the people of this country have never experienced before. Today, I stand before you, a man forged by the violence and bloodshed that this man and those of his ilk have brought down upon many a man, woman and child. I am a product of this man's design, his imperialistic hunger. So, why you may ask, am I giving the citizens of this country a choice? How can you trust a man who is clearly devoid of any feeling for Pierce or for the inhabitants of this country? What do I have to gain from not killing everyone in this building right now?"

He clicked the fingers of his free hand and the sentries flanking either side of the hostages raised their Ak-47's, cocking them as they did so, training them at the cluster of hostages.

"The answer in short is...you don't. But know this; if I wanted to, at the merest click of my fingers these men would open fire. A knick of this blade, Pierce dies."

The leader motioned his free hand slightly and the sentries lowered their guns.

"As you can see, although the power is literally in my hands, I instead entrust you with this blood debt, you the people. Now, although today will end in death, I, with these very hands, offer you, the public a chance to make a decision, finally for yourselves, one that will directly impact upon your country. Who lives? Who dies? Unimpeded by politicians or social commentators which if I may add is a lot more than was afforded to those in Britain's imperialistic conquests. So, to you the people of the United Kingdom I ask you to consider the following carefully."

The masked figure reached into his pocket and redrew a stopwatch. He clicked it, all the while ensuring it was in frame.

"In five hours, I either kill Pierce, letting all those within the walls of this disgusting monument to capitalism, live. No retaliation or backlash will be exhibited by my men. We will simply permit them to leave. Or I push the button on a kill switch and take out a sizeable chunk of Rule Britannia's already fetid carcass."

He afforded those around the world a moment for this to sink before indicating downwards with the hand that clutched the stopwatch.

"Below this video upload are two icons, one reads save, the other sacrifice. I simply ask you to make a choice, a public ballot if you like. Will you save Pierce and sentence those in an undisclosed location to die an agonising death or will you sacrifice the one man who has brought us here to this very place in time? While I allow you a moment to consider, I must also take this opportunity to warn the government and policy makers of this country that, attached to this live stream is a fail-safe".

"If you cut the feed or tamper with the site in any way, the device goes off, along with the execution of all of those in this building. I hand you, the electorate, the power to determine your own fate, create your own policy. Vote or no vote, you, the citizens of this country, will be complicit in whatever transpires in your nation this day. You are consistently patronised with the metaphor that a miscast vote is a wasted one. I am not here to judge. Your inactivity will serve just as much as a vote in its own right."

The lead speaker draped the stopwatch, attached to a circular, noose like bit of string, around Pierces neck. He pulled out his sidearm and held it aloft. From the periphery of the stage, one could just make out via the live stream a person being bundled forward, a female, a police helmet sat jauntily upon her head. She was ashen faced, her shirt untucked, her eyes darting from that of camera, to that of the crowd of hostages. Tears streaked her cheeks. An armed man to the right of the speaker pushed her to her knees, her hands bound. The officer was shaking uncontrollably now; she seemed to be mumbling a silent prayer to herself.

"To both set proceedings in motion and highlight the severity of our demands..." the leader rounded and in a hazy motion pinched off a singular shot, the muzzle of his sidearm emblazoned with light, the muscles along his arm recoiling.

The Police Officer fell instantaneously, a crimson mushroom spouting from her skull as she did so. The thump of her body audible to the millions who watched on in silence around the globe, news networks across the globe thankful for the delay in their live coverage, ceased their airing of the feed. The leader holstered his sidearm.

"If we even sense that this building is about to be breached or taken in any way, everyone in here, including me and my collaborators, will die in his almighty name. This I decree in his name and by the will of the Islamic Brotherhood for Righteous Judgement."

The men either side of the leader repeated this last line in chorus before the live feed was severed.

CHAPTER ELEVEN: LAST NIGHT A DJ SAVED MY LIFE FROM A BROKEN HEART

Tom stared back at the lifeless body before him. Any consolation or need for self-preservation surrounding the fact that he had just killed a man had swivelled to the rear of his conscience. His knees wavered and he slid down the wall. He pressed his back firmly against the cool construct; the only strength that remained aided by the man-made construct, an irony that Tom was all too aware of. Regardless of the contorted expression of his attacker Tom instantaneously placed the face. He knew nothing of the personality that once inhabited the lifeless vessel but felt the loss all the same. He brought a quaking hand up to his mouth and stifled a panicked sob.

He found himself unable to divert his gaze from the builder he had bumped into earlier that morning upon entering the complex. The man's anger at the time had seemed disproportionately rude but he had simply written it off as someone having a bad day. His brain set about piecing together the puzzle to a mystery he barely had any of the pieces to. Was this some kind of disguise?

Tom finally forced himself to look away from the corpse's brown eyes, devoid of life. The camouflage paint smeared across and round his eyes as well as the edges of his mouth only emphasised his deceased state all the more so. His skin glistened with sweat and congealed blood.

Tom went to touch his head before suddenly withdrawing his hand with a stomach lurching realisation; his hands were caked in blood. The by-product had dried around his wrists but was still damp and warm to the touch. On closer inspection, his mid-drift looked like a butcher's apron.

Tom's breathing became erratic and in his confused stupor his training abruptly edged to the foreground. He decided to divert his attentions, a cautionary inspection of the body a welcome distraction. The alternative was allowing his brain permission to articulate what he had done, an unacceptable moral quandary that would have to wait.

Tom shakily adopted a squat-like position and tentatively patted the man's pockets. Nothing. He slipped his right hand into both pockets to be certain bringing out nothing but a stick of chewing gum. For some unknown reason, possibly out of shock, Tom placed the stick of gum into his own pocket, trying as hard as possible not to bloody his clothes any further.

With that, Tom leant forward and began to slowly unzip the man's tactical vest. It was not all too dissimilar from the ones that he had himself worn in the past. Attached to it was a leg holster, which he unclipped first. He slipped one of the attacker's arms out of the vest and tugged. The dead body flopped onto its front. Tom suddenly felt quite exposed, a graverobber weary of some passer-by. Tom grabbed the vest and slowly peered over the counter. The coast was clear. He decided rather than crawl over the body that he would make a dart for the door to the back office and did so with an advanced degree of stealth.

He violently halted at the mouth of the doorway nearly tripping over the body of Malcom. Death via the hand of another was always unsavoury and horrific but at this time of year, it only served to reinforce the feeling of loss, a sight far removed from the tinsel and festivities that adorned the period. Thankfully, Malcom's eyes were closed unlike that of his attacker's. He still bore a pained expression on his face, a tributary of tears etching the wrinkles around his eyes. Tom, currently unsure of what his next move would be, did the only thing he could at present. He removed a dust sheet from one of the canvases and draped it over the body. Upon contact with his upper extremities, blood started to seep through the sheet.

Tom leant down and picked up both the Sig Sauer and the discarded magazine that had been knocked out of his hand earlier. He registered a pleasurable shiver; the gun feeling natural in his grasp. He inspected the magazine once again cursing his gullible lapse in judgement. Three rounds, more than enough to subdue his victim with non-lethal force. Tom drove the magazine back into the gun's butt and afforded himself an expletive. He stepped over the body and began lightly removing items from the desk not wanting to make any sound. He placed the vest on the desk and began to search it, placing the pistol flat upon the tabletop.

The first pocket gave way to an I.D. card. The picture on the card bore his attackers expressionless face glaring back at him. The name on the card stated that he was Robert Boyd which Tom immediately dismissed as an alias. The company indicated that he worked for Harpers Construction LTD. Tom placed the I.D. face down.

In the same pocket he also found a set of three keys which he immediately placed into one of his trouser pockets. There was also a small black device, which Tom surmised was a replacement should there be a fault with the initial device used to modify and disguise his voice. Attached to the vest also were two spare magazines, holding twenty rounds each. Tom's mind flitted back to the gun on the desk, one round in the chamber, three in the magazine. How many people had the other sixteen bullets mown down?

He unzipped two more pockets finding nothing. Tom turned over the vest and to his shock noticed something he had previously missed, black and round, a set of grenades. He carefully unclipped one and tentatively turned it over in his hands. He repeated the action, and instead repositioned the grenades upon one of the shoulder straps, first removing the torch that was housed there. The other strap held a radio and earpiece. Tom stared at the vest and the contents atop the table. He reached for the radio, unclipped it and placed the earpiece within his ear. He registered that it was switched off and shakily flicked it on, a relentless static buzzing within his ear. He hooked the radio to his belt and stood, transfixed by the silence.

He slid open one of the drawers before him and riffled through it for a moment or two before retrieving a Stanley knife. He unsheathed it from its housing before placing it with the other items upon the desk.

"Sub team finishing the final sweep of the first floor, over."

Tom froze; the metallic drone of the insurgents all the more robotic over the comm link.

"Dreyfus, you there, over?" Tom listened back none the wiser.

Static replaced the sound of his breathing.

"Dreyfus? Have you finished checking out the unit on the second floor? Over," the voice demandingly pried.

Tom's blood ran cold, his earlier suspicions realised. Robert Boyd had indeed been a cover.

"Dreyfus, I repeat has the unit been secured? What's going up there?"

Tom's hand automatically reached for the gun, his hands clammy and cold.

"Right, we're coming up, over," stated the voice.

Tom hastily placed the gun down upon the desk with a thud and picked up the voice modifier. He paused, trying to muster some saliva. He had no idea what this man had been like or what relationship or association he had had with those on the other end of the radio. All he knew was that he had to try something, anything.

Tom cleared his throat and spoke up, holding the black device over his mouth. Before he spoke, he ensured that the device was on before pressing the presell switch to the comm link with his free hand. The sound of his own voice took him by surprise.

"Dreyfus here, all clear up here, over," he stated with audaciously, awaiting the reply with trepidation.

"Blow me down, took you bloody long enough. Did you encounter any hostiles, over?" replied the ominous if not irate voice.

Tom's eyes instinctively fell upon the dust sheet, the halo of blood now crested around the helm of the makeshift shroud.

"No issues, over," Tom replied quickly.

"Roger that. We're on our way up to sweep the rest of the floor; we'll converge on your location, over."

The last morsels of saliva all but dried up at this. Tom was thankful for the voice changer as his voice was now audibly shaking. He surveyed the weaponry before him, his last resort quickly adopting pole position.

"No need, I have it all under control up here. I'll check out the rest of this floor then come down and RV on your position, over," Tom responded calmly.

This was the last card that Tom had left to play. If it failed, he did not fancy his chances. He longed for the static to cease and for those at the other end of the line to reply.

"Alright Dreyfus, we'll get onto control and get him to open up the shutters for you. Stay frosty up there and converge on our position in twenty. We'll be outside Reilly's Diner, over and out."

Tom's heart filled with hope and all he could muster was a, "Roger and out."

Unfortunately, this hope was soon replaced with abject fear. He checked his watch marking the time. He now had twenty minutes to either hide or escape. He was, however, a realist and made a pact that if it came to it, he would not surrender. Surrender was as good as putting a gun to his own head and pulling the trigger himself, Malcolm had proved that.

He reached for the vest and set about pulling it across his sizeable torso. He zipped it closed, clipped the leg holster to his leg and picked the pistol up. He ejected the magazine, pulled the slide back and watched the chambered bullet exit via the side of the gun. He picked it up between his thumb and forefinger and thumbed it back into the magazine. He slid the all but empty magazine back into the tactical vest and loaded the Sig Sauer with a fresh magazine. He holstered the pistol before picking up the Stanley knife. He needed to get to an exit. He favoured stealth over digging in and waiting for the hostiles to come looking. Time was now Tom's biggest enemy and unlike the sizeable amount of men occupying the building, it was in short supply.

Quietly, he moved towards the doorway, peering slightly around the edge of the door. All was clear. Tom could now see across to the other side of the second level and he was relieved to see the shutters rising on the adjacent store fronts. The shutters belonging to In the Frame also began to rise with a shuddering whine. Tom tentatively stepped forward until he was flush with the edge of the store front. He drew level with the marble façade and surveyed his environment.

The coast was clear both to his left and his right, Tom quickly ascertaining that the latter was the more favourable direction in which to head of the two, the escalator and dead body to his left causing the hairs upon his forearms to stand on end. In a fluid motion he shimmied out onto the concourse in a crouched position and began to edge away from the ill-fated outlet.

Up ahead, he spotted what he was looking for. As he understood it, as the man had said over the intercom system, all doors had been locked down. He had quickly come to the realisation that if he were to breach one of the emergency exits it would take a considerable amount of force. He paused briefly and set about inspecting the exit Malcolm had mentioned earlier complete with coded keypad. The door along with its frame was wooden and should the code given to him by Malcolm not work due to a lack of power or the employee not recalling it correctly, Ton believed it was weak enough to be pried open.

That said, he would need something sturdy and more importantly, relatively quiet, to prise open the door. He looked ahead and noticed a sporting goods and camping store named Pennywhites. He quickly edged towards it; momentarily stopping at five second intervals maintaining that the coast remained clear.

When he reached the storefront to Pennywhites it took all of Tom's self-restraint not to leap up from his haunches and pounce through the open doorway. He gave the store a cursory scan, committing the layout to memory before entering. The store was laden on either side by a variety of sporting paraphernalia: balls, golf clubs, sports strips and footwear. Finally, he stood up, feeling decidedly exposed. He settled upon walking to the back of the store first, that way he could work his way back to the exit hopefully after having found what he was looking for. It was not long before Tom found the section he had hoped to find, the camping section.

Tom's eyes scanned the extensive selection of products and immediately set about evaluating their functionality and the decibel level they would emit. First came a small hatchet; sharp and lightweight but would require the loud act of hacking at the doorframe. Next came a sturdy looking, foldable spade. Tom unfolded the spade, doubling it in size. He turned it over in his hands, pressing against the metal before stopping abruptly, a bolt of pain pulsating deep within his shoulder, his earlier altercation with Dreyfus most likely having bruised his upper torso. Irrespectively, the handle was far too short and would afford him little in the way of leverage.

Tom scanned the shelves for several seconds before finally settling upon a mountaineering pick; a slim yet sturdy implement both sharp and of substantial in length.

Tom tried to snap the tubular frame of the handle with all his might, his knuckles turning yellow. Satisfied, he judged it to be robust enough. The handle had a looped piece of twine strung through a hole in the handle. Tom grabbed a carabiner from the shelf adjacent and slid the catch open, placing the twine within the carabiner. He then clipped the pick to the front of his tactical vest not wanting to attach it to his belt where it was more likely to knock against his leg, stealth his main objective.

Satisfied with his find, he made to leave when a black blur cut a swathe across his vision. He immediately crouched down, his heartbeat thumping through his temples. He skulked forward entering the centre of a circular rack of waterproof jackets, tentatively spreading the jackets apart like a set of curtains.

He focused his attention on the concourse ahead so lost in his voyeuristic surveillance that, when the radio he had confiscated from Dreyfus came alive, he nearly fell forward with panic.

"I don't know where the fuck you are Dreyfus, but you better get your arse over to the music store now. We bumped into some people that decided to play hide and seek with you… and won. I thought you said you were searching this floor. Come in, over."

Tom quickly set about adjusting the volume dial on his radio before checking his watch. He still had twelve minutes left. His mouth ran dry, his timetable inextricably brought forward. He made to reach for the voice changer and froze for a moment before lightly punching his leg in anger. He had left the device in the very outlet he had just come from, upon the desk of the backroom office.

Tom's eyes never left the store opposite, his vision largely obscured by jackets. He needed to get a closer look. He carefully pushed the hangers aside, making sure to be as quiet as possible. He crept forward before adopting a prone position. He crawled forward three metres or so before stopping just shy of a display piled high with discounted hiker's boots.

He adjusted the volume once again, lowering the volume more so, the insurgent clearly visible now on the adjacent concourse.

"Team leader, come in," came the voice from the other end of the radio.

"Team Leader here, over."

"Dreyfus has gone dark. We can't get through to him on comm's. We've also found some stowaways up here."

It was hard for Tom to distinguish between the two metallic voices. That was soon rectified with the unhinged response from Team Leader.

"What do you mean he's gone dark? He's not a bloody faulty flashlight. Search the area and find him now. Or do I have to come up there and educate you in…"

Tom didn't need to hear the fear in the other man's voice to register that he was scared.

"No, no. No need for that sir, we'll do a sweep now. He's probably just turned his radio off again, that's all. What are your orders concerning the hostages up here sir? We have one female, a teenager and a…" he halted abruptly aware that he was blathering.

What came next sent a wave of nausea throughout the entirety of Tom's body, the level-headed delivery of the command only serving to magnify Team Leader's callous demeanour.

"No Frazier, what you have there are three drains on our resources. Use you knife and slit their throats; I don't want any gunfire setting the hostages off again. They had their chance, now go and find Dreyfus and finish your fucking sweep!"

Tom chanced a closer inspection, peering further out from behind the mound of shoe boxes. He saw a man, whom he presumed to be Frazier, touching his ear. Kneeling before him and another armed insurgent, were the terrified shapes of a woman, a teenage store assistant and an elderly gentleman.

"Ok sir, I'll be back in contact when we find Dreyfus, over and out," the insurgent nodded, holstering his sidearm as he did so.

Due to the responses of Team Leader having come via the insurgent's earpiece, the hostages were completely oblivious to the death sentence that had just been sanctioned. Distressingly enough for Tom, the woman at the feet of the insurgents seemed to relax somewhat, misinterpreting the holstered sidearm as an indication that she and the other two hostages were to be spared.

The man removed his finger from his earpiece. He unbuttoned the sheath of his knife and withdrew it. Without hesitation, the elderly gentleman immediately made a bolt for the man but was soon dispatched by a violent boot square to the centre of his face, Frazier's partner delivering the forceful swing. Tom felt his whole torso tighten with rage. He clenched his fists and felt the veins within his forearms protruding. Rotating the knob upon the radio fully now, he switched the device off. He crawled out from his hiding place and reached for the first thing that came to hand.

The smooth contours of the varnished wood sent a shiver down his arm and all the way up to his shoulder. The ergonomic handle felt like an extension of his very being. The red mist had truly descended. Tom inspected the baseball bat tightly grasped within his right hand, the realisation that it may serve to demystify the haze overriding all other coherent thought. He stood up, no longer afraid of being discovered, longer in control of himself. With tunnel vision he stalked onwards and at the very end of that tunnel was the sight of that man's bloody face, unconscious and slumped, flanked by a screaming woman and whimpering teenage boy. His strides were relentless and instinctive. Although on autopilot, he was deadly silent, focused and unfeeling. Instinct and training had resumed.

The woman contorted her body trying to break free from the man's ironclad grip, her attacker's thumb driven deep into the recess of her collarbone. He held her in a kneeling position. The other masked man pressed the teenager against the wall with barely the minutest bit of strength exercised. The boy did not resist and was rendered lifeless with fear. The armed man could smell the cold, dull smell of sweat from the boy nuanced with that of urine. If he were ever asked to describe the smell of fear to anyone after this day, that would be how he would define it. He kept one eye trained on the boy, the other on the woman.

It was largely due to this shared concentration that when the briefest glimpse of a shadow dropped across the teenagers flinching face, he was too distracted to react. The object first struck the top of his shoulder, which forced him to expel an almost soundless, internal groan. The knife fell to the ground and made a loud clacking noise upon the marble. As the man stumbled, all the strength sapping from his thighs, he caught a glimpse of his would-be attacker. He instinctively reached out for the first thing that came to hand. He snatched at the boy, gathering the material of his uniform and a sizeable handful of flesh within his grasp. The boy grimaced.

The attacker, believing the man to be using the boy as a human shield, grabbed him by the strap of his vest. With an unnatural level of strength, the man with his free hand, wild eyed and furious flung the man three metres or so, into a set on speakers. His radio unintentionally came away within the man's spade-like grip, the earpiece harshly yanked from his ear. The insurgent threw out a hand to break his fall but was too off-balance only mustering an inch of movement before the full momentum of his fall came to a crescendo. With a thud that resembled a bowling ball being dropped upon the floor, he was rendered unconscious and lay spread eagled on the floor.

The altercation, which must have taken around four seconds, had only briefly incapacitated the man's partner with disbelief as he was upon Tom within the blink of an eye, a knife held aloft within his left hand. Just as soon as the other man had hit the floor, the armed insurgent launched himself at Tom, knocking the petrified woman down as he did so.

The man was roughly both the same height and width as Tom but had a marginal weight advantage. His movements were deliberate, honed by some practiced fighting style. He moved in close, successfully driving a boot squarely into the centre of Tom's knee, the impact forcing him to drop his stance, the bat faltering just above his waistline. The man reacted with blistering expediency grabbing for the bat with his spare right hand, the metallic knife, fifteen centimetres in length swinging down.

Tom pushed the man back slightly, finding a new reserve of strength at having been set upon by an instrument that could render his internal organs non-salvageable. His attacker, grunted heavily through gritted teeth and leaned in again, using his additional weight to keep Tom's arm, along with the bat he held, wedged between the two men's torsos. The two engaged in a macabre waltz neither wanting to relinquish any ground.

The attacker came down with the knife again. Tom edged his trapped forearm towards the man's neck, the blade two inches from his own face now. Reluctantly, he made the active

146

decision to drop the bat. It bounced once before rolling between the two men's feet. Tom now slipped his free hand upwards and grabbed the man's wrist, slightly knicking the knuckle of his right index finger as he did so.

Tom inhaled deeply; the sound of salvia being sucked down the inner workings of his jaw. The attacker, now reinvigorated by the sight of blood, leant back and leveraged his body for the next exerted barrage of strength. So confident was he, that he afforded himself a gloating expletive. The knifed hand raised above his head, gave the man a feeling that he had the upper hand both figuratively and literally.

"Come on you fuckwit, Santa's got your stocking filler right here for you," the comment made all the more absurd and dreadful when delivered through the voice changer.

Tom's eyes never wavered from the knife, which unfortunately was more than he could say for his arm which shook like a rattle. He resolved to push the man back one more time but had barely settled upon his plan of action before the knife plunged about a quarter of the way into his flesh. Tom's stature protracted with the agony of the blade entering about an inch or so from his right armpit. The dampness, which had previously been sweat, was now replaced with the unmistakable ambient trickle of warm blood.

Tom yelped out as he dropped to his right knee, his left soon following. His left hand still gripped listlessly around the knifeman's wrist, a grip so weak and unthreatening that his attacker allowed it to rest there. The knife had still not left his shoulder. The man began to twist it by the hilt, his eyes ablaze with pleasure. Tom's lower back began to cave as he began to slump backwards, the last remnants of his strength feigning. He looked up at his attacker, the thought of pleading for his life, crossing his mind momentarily. The man withdrew the blade, Tom's back arching with the departure of the cold steel. This was to be the killing blow. Tom readied himself.

It never came. The attacker's pleasure ridden pupils were soon framed by a new sensation, one of deflation and suffering. A metallic release of pain came from the man's voice altering device beneath his mask. Tom dropped his gaze, the warm trickle of blood down his right side somewhat comforting.

The woman, who had previously been barged aside, was lying between the gap in the man's legs, both hands gripping a blade that protruded from the man's inner thigh, a position one could only hope was absent from the karma sutra. She whimpered, still holding the blade, unsure of what to do next with the instrument she had acquired from the other hostage taker upon being felled.

The insurgent fell to his knees, dropping his knife as he did so. He landed atop the woman's head, who quickly using all the power in her buttocks and thighs, shimmied out from under him. The two knelt before one another, the attacker gripping Tom by his wounded shoulder, half with deadly intent, the other out of support. A bolt of pain demanded Tom act. Reaching out, he gripped the man's inner thigh, making sure to plunge his thumb as deep into the wound as it would go. The man straightened with pain, a shaking judder rising up from his torso. Spit flecked Tom's chin. The realisation soon took hold that the victor of the ensuing melee would be the one with the higher pain threshold.

The man dropped his hand and began probing for the discarded knife that he had stabbed Tom with. Tom, quite delirious with pain now, afforded himself a look at the man's groping hand. The teenager, motionless with fear, flinched and tried to lightly push the man's hand away when it came near him or the knife but the man soon made contact with it. His fingers lightly touched the end of the hilt. He began strenuously groping at it in a laborious motion.

Tom looked back towards his attacker, the woman quaking and rocking, just visible over his shoulder. The attacker's hand was still weakly trying to push Tom's hand away from the edge of the blade in his leg, a surface area Tom was rhythmically working with his thumb, maximising the area of suffering. Tom lifted his weak arm and made a grab for the knife, he too now probing. The attacker leant in, obscuring the blade from Tom.

"You don't… you don't need to do this," Tom pleaded.

His voice was shallow, each word felt as if it were being spoken under water, the pain rising in his throat. His aggressor ignored him; the only reply that came was the scraping of metal on marble floor; the blade now found, being worked into his palm.

Tom mustered a more defiant plea, "Please. I just want to get out of here, I don't want to…"

A motion danced across Tom's eye level; he quickly slumped back onto his knees, the blade skimming past his face. The masked man followed up his attack with another. He angled the knife edging it towards his injured right-hand side. He briefly felt the man's hand slip away from the blade lodged within his inner thigh.

It was now or never. The blade lay exposed. Tom quickly moved his hand away from the blade protruding from the man's leg and instead grabbed it by the handle. He withdrew it, registering a scream from the man, a flume of blood preceding the arc of the knife. Tom brought the knife up above his head.

"There is no way out," the insurgent howled and with that his body jerked upwards in a last-ditch effort to gain the extra proximity need to wound Tom once again.

But Tom was first. He pulled the man closer, angling his body away from the blade and thrust his own knife between the man's shoulder blades, giving the blade a quick, sharp twist for good measure. Tom felt the man's body contort and arch at the entry point of the blade. He weakly thrashed for several seconds before succumbing, dying face down in Tom's own inner thigh. Tom sat motionless for a moment panting with exhaustion and blood loss. He used the last remnants of strength that he could muster to push the attacker away. The last remnants of bloodlust within the tank expelled, the stark numbness off realisation once again returning.

He cast an eye over both the teenager and woman. The teenager, wild-eyed and devoid of colour gawped back at Tom as if he were some untamed beast, ravaged by retribution. Tom made to speak, to offer a reassuring platitude. Unsuccessful, he instead dropped his gaze, ashamed.

Once again, he had had no choice, deep down he knew that. That said, unlike Dreyfus, he had murdered a man in an all too public display, in front of a woman and a teenager. He himself had been conditioned for war, trained to deal with the formality of taking one's life, they had not. Tom could still feel the eyes of the teenage boy boring into his very being.

Here he was for the first time, a young man only accustomed to such violent displays of this magnitude upon a screen or during videogames. Now here he was witnessing the true, unholy majesty of death at the hands of another and all in the most glorious HD of them all, one's very own eyes. Tom looked imploringly back at the boy, seeking his understanding, of what had needed to be done. The boy instead recoiled, a new fear gripping the boy as his pupils contracted. Tom drunkenly followed his gaze before they came to a rest upon the speakers. The unconscious insurgent was gone.

(CHAPTER BREAK)

The documents that landed in front of Richard Miller were lighter than he would have hoped. He picked up the dossier and thumbed through the sheets, all of which were covered in an assortment of official stamps and markings. The documents had just come over the wire, straight from Langley, Virginia, provided by the Director of the CIA. Miller hated contacting other intelligence agencies around the world. He viewed it as a sign of weakness, an omission that his house was not in order, that he had been caught on the back foot. But as he had always hypocritically chanted to his staff, *'Information, no matter the source, from ally or foe, is knowledge that was not known a minute ago."*

He scanned the pages before dropping them lightly upon the table, uninterested. He knew little more than he did a minute ago. One of his analysts, Rupert Benz, approached, a slight young man who served as a daily reminder that in this digital era of cyber terrorism and online threats, this was ever increasingly becoming a young man's game.

"Not much to gleam from that," Miller unenthusiastically remarked.

Benz, or 'Merc' to his friends, shirt sleeves upturned to his elbows, cradled an electronic tablet.

"No sir, not much. That said there are one or two things to be gleamed from the information."

'Ever the optimist,' Miller reflected before rotating his finger, urging Benz to proceed.

"Well sir, here are the highlights. The CIA establishes that they have heard little chatter surrounding this particular organisation. Intel is pretty light on the ground as that document indicates but the consensus seems to be that this is a fairly new group. Our contacts at Langley stated that the contents of that file were compiled based on two hits. One was an intercepted message over a well-known terrorist webpage."

Benz tapped an icon upon the tablet in his hand and the webpage dominated the various screens within the situation room. Miller scanned the screens looking for anything out of the ordinary. After all, he had seen countless sites of this nature before.

"The Americans haven't shut down the site as of yet as the intel gathered from it has been gold dust, helping with numerous operations and even thwarting an attempted bombing of the U.S. embassy in Egypt. The users don't know that they've been rumbled. Anyway, the Islamic Brotherhood for Righteous Judgement was used as a username by one of the sites followers. They left one message on the site as well as a You Tube link to a news report on the Prime Minister's visit to the Middle East last year. The message simply read, and I quote, the West continues to defile our land with conquests they know little of."

Miller pondered this for a second, his forehead furrowing.

Benz continued, "They tried to trace the web address but came up empty. But the second source of intel," he chortled briefly, "well that was a doozy of the highest order, from the mouth of a prisoner captured during a covert operation out in Sierra Leone."

Miller's ears pricked up. Benz took this as an indicator that his superiors' curiosity was now well and truly stirred. He followed up with a flourish of raps upon his tablet screen, a series of mugshots of the same man now filling the screens. The orange jumpsuit he wore did little to bring any life to the unresponsive gaze that gawked back at Miller.

Benz continued, "The man, a Hamza Al Masood, was a well-known arms trader, a frequent staple upon the CIA's most wanted list as well as our own. He has been responsible for trading and dealing with a cornucopia of terrorist organisations around the world for over a decade. Christmas came early when the Americans captured him; you may remember we received some crucial intel from them regarding the arms deal that was due to go down involving a splinter cell in Leeds?"

Miller nodded; he remembered the case well. It had concluded with five known terrorists and a partner of Al Masood's being incarcerated for life, a cache of over fifty Ak-47's and three crates of grenades being confiscated.

"So, what affiliation did he have with the Brotherhood?" Miller queried.

"Well, that's the thing sir, none. He divulged to the CIA that he had been due to meet with the group in Sierra Leone two days after he had been captured. By this stage in the interrogation, he was leaking information left, right and centre. My contact at Langley said by the end he was more of a well of information as opposed to a leaky bucket."

Deadpan, Miller looked at Benz and stated rather matter of fact, "A couple of hundred volts of electricity to the bollocks will loosen anyone's lips."

Benz nodded and preceded, "Indeed. The weird thing is though; he informed them of where the meet would take place, gave them a time, a location, the works. The Navy Seals tasked with the mission cased the place out the day before the meet was to go ahead, ready to intercept the group."

"And?" Miller probed.

"They were a no show. The Seals waited thirty- seven hours after the drop was actually supposed to take place before they finally aborted the mission."

"Misinformation to save his skin?" Miller thought out loud.

"Possibly," Benz nodded. "Maybe they got spooked or were waiting for a call from Al Masood that never came so they backed off. For what it's worth, having been at the U.S. government's leisure for that amount of time, I highly doubt he would have lied," Benz made his opinion known.

"Did this Al Masood say what they were buying or why they might have not made the drop? Any info on whom or what organisation he thought he might have been selling to?"

"Unfortunately, sir, that's where things get pretty patchy. He stated the Brotherhood were who he intended to meet and that they had mentioned their organisation, by name, on at least two occasions during their preliminary communications. He stated that they had heard about him through a third party, one they did not disclose. He also stated that they seemed rather clandestine in their approach, wanting everything to be on their terms, not that he thought this unusual, that being the very nature of the beast when dealing or buying illegal arms. All he stated was that they were interested in explosives and automatic weapons, high velocity. They had asked him to bring a selection for their consideration."

"Discerning bargain hunters by the sounds of it," Miller muttered massaging the right arm of his glasses.

"To summarise sir, I think it's highly likely that we may be dealing with an organisation situated in or around Sierra Leone, most likely having crossed the borders from Sudan or Libya. When pressed further by the Americans, let's just say they reacted badly to the aborted mission; Al Masood had one last titbit to offer. He stated that they seemed professional and that he only ever spoke to one person, a man who did not disclose his name or any further details about the organisation."

"I would presume at this stage that this 'Brotherhood', as they call themselves, are most likely from a military background given their knowledge of ordnance, from a Muslim background and have links to or have members from or within, Britain. They would need someone this side of the water to co-ordinate and relay information while they busied themselves with their little shopping spree."

Miller turned away from the screens, deep in thought once again. He did so for around thirty seconds before turning slightly to Benz, not instigating eye-contact.

"These men, no matter their creed or allegiance, are not going to be talked down. Ready the SAS and set up a direct line with the Police's armed response unit. We are well and truly in the dark on this one. Monitor any known terrorist communications and let me know if we ping anything on this Brotherhood."

Benz shuffled slightly and asked a question that had plagued him since the start of the siege.

"And what of the hostages sir?" he probed timidly.

Miller looked at his wristwatch. Four minutes until the next hostage was to be executed. He sighed, turning to Benz.

"I guess it would be too much to hold out for a Christmas miracle?" he bluntly stated, the last morsel of humour that he had left.

Benz smiled weakly before looking down. Miller sensed the man seemed to be seeking more, some level of reassurance. He had little to offer.

"We do what we always do Benz. We observe, we case the building and when we get the opportunity, we make our move, quickly and efficiently. Those people in there," he jabbed, "they are down the pecking order, an inconvenience to this scum. If we have the Prime Minister die on our watch or worse still a bomb goes off in London, it will be the worst terrorist attack on British soil that we have ever or will ever likely see. I fear the collateral damage is going to be high on this one. God help them all in there."

(CHAPTER BREAK)

The woman took off the thin cardigan she had been wearing and placed it between the arm of the tactical vest and Tom's wound, before zipping it back up.

"That should stem some of the bleeding," she stated ashen faced, "But you're going to need that stitched up before long. It's not too deep but left too long it could present problems."

Tom groaned and managed to crouch inside the store behind a pile of packaged plasma televisions.

"You a nurse?" he optimistically enquired.

She shook her head, flicking tears from her curling eyelashes. "I'm a vet. Two years now."

Tom turned and looked back at the teenager. He was kneeling now, head in his hands, rhythmically rocking to-and-fro. The elderly gentleman was still passed out beside him. Tom had his gun drawn, poised for a possible counterattack from the other insurgent. There was only one way in and out of the outlet. The terrorist had no radio and as Tom had repeated to himself in a soothing fashion, probably no mobile. No, he was still in there.

He mustered a quip in the interest of relieving some of the pressure, never taking his eyes off the inside of the store.

"It's ok, I've had all of my shots...been neutered also," he smiled weakly.

The woman before him only peered past Tom towards the entrance. He settled upon an alternative course of action; the woman needed a structured plan not a one-liner.

"We can worry about me later. What's your name?" he said as he lightly touched the woman upon the arm. She flinched. Her features displayed all the indicators of someone unsure of her surroundings or those who inhabited them for that matter.

"Michelle," she replied matter-of-factly.

"Ok Michelle, I need you to look at me," he squeezed her arm lightly once again.

She did so with a somewhat lobotomized expression.

"My name is Tom...Tom Hawkins. I'm pretty dinged up here Michelle and the other man that tried to attack you, well he's still in there," he motioned to the open doorway behind her.

She nodded slightly, wiping tears from her eyes.

"The way I see it, we have two options," he continued in a hushed tone. "Now you're doing great Michelle but I'm going to need your help. Here are our options; we can either make a break for it, head for a Staff exit an employee told me about earlier, if its unlocked that is..." he gave the woman a cursory glance before proceeding, "or I enter the shop and try to subdue the man that attacked you, forcefully if needs be."

She finally met Tom's gaze, her face gaunt, a look of pure fear framing her features. He hushed her with a calming motion of his hand.

"It's ok Michelle, I'm not going to ask you to do anything dangerous, all you need to do is stay here," he pointed at their current location.

Michelle's posture relaxed slightly.

"Now, I have his radio but the big dilemma is...are you still following me Michelle?" Tom smiled reassuringly.

Michelle nodded in response.

"Amazing Michelle, you're doing great, honestly. My biggest fear is that as soon as we make a break for it, even if we do manage to escape through the Staff exit, radio or no radio that man is going to contact his friends or worse, come after us and he will try to kill us again."

Michelle nodded weakly once again, averting her gaze, her upper frame trembling slightly.

"Now I'll need you to stay here if I go back in," Tom declared.

Those wild, fear laden eyes shot up to meet Tom's once again. He gave her a reassuring squeeze of the shoulders.

"Michelle, I need to make sure no one else comes after us. I'm sorry you had to see what you just did but you need to understand that if it wasn't for you Michelle, we'd all be dead. You saved my life. All four of us are still breathing because of you Michelle and I want to make sure it stays that way, but these people... these men, they don't want that."

He placed the knife back into Michelle's open hand as he finished the sentence. She stared back at it numbly before stifling a whimper.

"I don't want you to have to use this Michelle. Not again but if anyone comes out of there that isn't me, you need to either run or defend yourself."

With that he closed her hand around the knife softly and made to stand.

She grabbed his wrist with a vice like grip; the only words she knew at this particular junction were, "I'm scared."

"It's ok Michelle, I know," he stooped slightly, stroking her hand. "Believe me, fear is good. Fear keeps you alert, on your toes. I'm going to go in there and I'll be right back out, I promise.

He lightly peeled her hand from his.

"Stay here, anyone comes, run and hide. If I'm not out in two minutes, go across to that sports store and hide. Take the lad, leave the other man."

He considered what he had just said. He felt as if he were betraying all that he stood for. After all he had wholeheartedly believed in the military mantra 'No man left behind', he had lived by it for long enough. He winched slightly as a jolt cascaded down his wound.

He straightened and mentally recited to himself the other mantra that had seen him through his various tours, 'Survival of the fittest', the irony of his battered state not lost upon him.

"And this is really important Michelle," he said as he holstered his sidearm. "If you hear a gun go off, run. I am only going to use this as a last resort. The minute my gun or his goes off, we're going to have merry hell rain down upon us. Do you understand?"

A solitary nod once again. He was hoping, praying in fact that the man had fallen unconscious once again, after all that had been a sizeable blow to the head that he had sustained.

"Stay here out of sight. They may already have seen us on the cameras but we have to hope for the time being that they haven't. Remember, if anything seems off, you take the boy and run for the sports store," he reiterated this demand by pointing a finger towards the sports store before giving her a pat upon the shoulder as he past her.

"Thank you," Michelle whispered sheepishly.

Tom paused and looked upon the woman with her back towards him, an unbearable pity rising in the pit of his stomach. He took a deep inhalation of breath. This was it. He entered and past the store's threshold, picking up the baseball bat as he did so. He was terrified, the darkness of the outlet all encompassing. He held the bat at eye level, primed and ready. His eyes fell on a light splattering of blood, most likely Tom assumed, from the assailant's nose. Unfortunately, it left no discernible trail for him to follow.

Thoughts of his parents surged through his mind. Had they seen the siege on the news? They would be beside themselves with worry, scenarios of the worst degree considered.

(CHAPTER BREAK)

His name, for all intents and purposes, was of little importance. He had been warned by the unit's leader not to use first or last names. Although some members of the squad had done this over the radio, he had not, not wanting to incur the wrath of their leader. How he wished now that he had his radio. His head felt as if it had been caved in with a sledgehammer, his arm, although regaining some sensation, throbbed with each beat of his heart. He had no idea who the attacker with the baseball bat had been but concluded that he was a dead man walking. Either his partner had finished the job or he would but as time ebbed away he feared the worse. He decided to wait a further two minutes before investigating. Most likely if his partner had been killed, the man and the other hostages had made a bolt for it.

'Let him run, there's nowhere to go' he thought to himself.

When he came to, he had seen his partner kneeling before the man, both having a purchase upon a blade, plunged deep within one another. He had felt no sympathy for his partner, fight or flight had truly taken hold. He had crawled at first, the static in his head still strong. Fortunately and due to the extensive hours of well spent analysis prior to the operation, he knew about three-quarters of the centres structure off by heart.

Thankfully, 'Stereo-Hype' had been one of the outlets securely filed away within his memory. The music store had jumped out at him when revising the schematics of the shopping centre and at the time he had used it, along with three other outlets, as a reference point for navigation in case he became lost or disorientated. He longed to use his sidearm but was out of ammunition. He had intended to take a magazine from his partner after they had slit the throats of the three shoppers taking refuge within the store.

Currently hidden behind a row of Hi-Fi systems, he listened intently. He could see the register from where he was presently hunkered as well as the red standby light belonging to the cashier's scanner. His heart jumped. That meant that the appliances, when the outlet had been locked up, must have been switched off. When his partner up in control had redirected the power to open the shutters, he had also given the store power. Thankfully the EMP had not taken out all of the electronics within the store.

Come to think of it, as his eyes scanned the dark rows before him and to his sides, he could see the unmistakable glow of various standby lights. A karaoke machine complete with television and a set of tablet devices were clearly charging. He crawled towards the register a plan already germinating.

He knew exactly what he was looking for before he even arrived. As he crawled, his eyes never left the metallic outline of the control box. He reached the cash register and afforded himself a cursory glance over his shoulder; still all clear.

He opened the metallic box, his smile gathering the material of his mask at the corners of his mouth. Inside, the switches were all flicked off; various labels above each switch indicating its function. His plan brought with it two possible advantages: one, the prospect of alerting the rest of his team far below and secondly, the advantage of disorienting his prey.

The masked man placed his hand limply on a switch and muttered, "Let there be light."

(CHAPTER BREAK)

Tom crept onward using the cash register ahead as a waypoint. He moved silently, as he had been taught in the Army; feet at an angle, bent at the knees, slow and steady. He concentrated on the sounds around him, breathing through his nose in an effort to reduce any sound omitted from his own body. His senses were so attuned to his environment that when the lights burst into life, accompanied by an assortment of screens displaying a multitude of muted music channels, his heart nearly imploded. Doubt began to settle in, his chosen course of action suddenly feeling foolish, misguided.

He raised the bat marginally gripping it tightly with both hands, his eyes scanning the environment. A disco ball hung above casting a multi-coloured aura across the walls and floor ahead, the silence now replaced with an electronic whirr of devices. If he needed any further clarification that his attacker was conscious, this was it. Still, he advanced.

He grew closer to the cash register, a metre away now, the safety the shelves provided on either side all but exhausted. It was then that he felt the slightest brush of a foreign object as it became dislodged from the shelf. Instinctively, he swung round, making a grab for the dislodged item before it fell from its stand. It had taken a significant amount of effort not to yelp out, his wound sending a fresh bolt of pain down his arm. Thankfully, he caught the object just in time. He held the remote control tightly before placing it upon the carpeted floor, hoping the material would muffle any sound.

As he straightened, he inspected the shelf upon which the remote had been perched, a CD entitled *'Make- ups and Break- ups: Volume Two'*, also propped precariously upon the ledge. He afforded himself a moment of composure before advancing. He had not yet taken two steps when he froze, his instincts detecting another presence. A static shiver cascaded across his back.

(CHAPTER BREAK)

He lay just ahead. A brief clatter of items had disclosed his location. He slyly crept forward keeping his eyes fixed on the back of the man's head. That was where he intended to thrust the pair of scissors that he had procured from in a pencil pot atop the cashier's desk. He was two metres away now, breath held. His body urged him to strike but he subdued the impulse. Feet apart with a low centre of gravity, he progressed. One metre left. He raised the scissors, angling his body away from his quarry so as not to cast a shadow.

He made to strike when his foot came down upon something hard and plastic. It creaked under his weight momentarily before being drowned out by a nearby speaker ahead. Rapidly, the surrounding stillness was replaced with music, his target instantaneously whirling round, bat held aloft.

(CHAPTER BREAK)

Tom had never been so happy to hear Sonny and Cher in all his life. *'I Got You Babe'* rang through his ears forcing him to instinctively whirl round. The eyes of his attacker bulged with surprise; the disco ball's light accentuating the pointed shears of the raised scissors. Tom swung the bat instinctively at his attacker who easily sidestepped the blow.

'They say that we're young and we don't know...' in a fluid motion the insurgent launched himself at Tom and so commenced a macabrely choreographed ballet of jerking movements and evasion. Tom parried his attacker's advances with defensive swings of the bat; all of which his attacker shuffled past and sidestepped. His attacker finally went on the offensive, reciprocating with downward, slashing angled motions of the scissors. His attacks alternated between Tom's head and upper torso. Tom bobbed his head, the frenzied dedication of the insurgent unnerving.

The attacker, feeling his senses obscured by his mask, yanked it off. A flume of blonde hair fell out from under his balaclava, blue eyes following and with it the device in-built into his balaclava. He hopped back, putting three metres or so between Tom and the arcing motions of his bat. He grinned. The man, like Dreyfus, had a liberal smearing of paint around his eyes and jaw so that any visible skin not covered by his balaclava, was obscured. This only served to frame the intensity of his attacker's piercing blue eyes further.

"I suppose this means my partner back there is dead?" he sneered in a West London accent.

Tom held firm, still swinging the bat as a deterrent. His attacker raised his eyebrows indicating his query warranted a response.

Tom feared the man's reaction yet understood that the longer he allowed the man to toy with him, the longer this macabre theatrical display would go on. He longed to claw back some morsel of dominance. In a rash response, rendered all the more futile by the dulcet tones of Sonny and Cher, he settled upon impromptu bravado.

"Let's just say he was on Santa's naughty list," Tom smirked.

He cringed as soon as the statement had left his lips. His attacker's features drooped with condemnation completely unimpressed by Tom's quip.

"Funny man, huh? Well I can't speak for my partner back there but all I know is, within the next minute or so, you're going to be another fatality chalked up on the list when they pick through the ruins of this place."

With that he lurched at Tom once again, breaching his guard. The two both hit the ground bitterly. Tom shimmied, the edge of the remote edging further into his back as the two rolled and contorted their bodies seeking to gain a superior purchase over the other. Tom held firmly onto the bat with both hands, the varnished wood thrust vehemently into the insurgent's neck. He could feel his heart beating through the searing pain of his wound, additional weight only agitating the wound further.

For the moment he held the gnashing, rabid physique of the insurgent at bay, his attacker gripping at the bat with his left hand. The right hand came down in relentless, hacking swathes, the scything chunks of wood displaced unnerving to Tom. Yet the bat held, the insurgent resembling a lumberjack felling a tree to no avail. Tom once again came down upon the remote; briefly staggered by how the pain of the petite, plastic item in the small of his back was taking precedent over the leering man atop his frame. Abruptly, Sonny and Cher ceased and 10CC's *'I'm Not in Love',* now narrated the fray.

The man straddling Tom was smiling; a perfect smile, one speckled with spit at the exertion of supporting his body weight.

"Hardly a death chorus..." he pushed further and exhaled with effort, acquiring a few precious centimetres "... but it'll do."

He was now about a foot away from Tom's face. The jabs of the scissors varying in their proximity, one falling a centimetre short of Tom's right eyeball.

'It's just a silly phase I'm going through. And just because, I call you up...'

Tom's chest was heaving now. With each expelled breath he felt himself relinquishing another inch or two. His elbows were starting to concave, the distance between his hands becoming closer. To make matters worse the assailant above him had decided to change his tact now bringing the scissors down towards the back of Tom's right hand. Luckily, he saw the attacker's eyes as they darted towards his hand with a fevered intent and he pre-empted the attack, withdrawing his hand as the blade sliced deep into the wood.

Tom utilised the momentum and drove his knee upwards into the man's crutch. The attacker rolled off, his head now a crimson red. He grunted, breathing hard against the pain. Tom rolled the man off and got to his feet, never taking his eyes away. He backed towards the cashier's desk, transferring the bat to his uninjured yet weaker left arm. Blood now trickled down his right wrist.

The attacker sucked in a final pant before using a shelf to steady himself. He rose slowly. When his head finally came up the attacker's cadaverous grin had returned, his blue eyes burning with intensity, the pleasure of overcoming the pain within his groin euphoric.

"My name's Ollie Frazier by the way," the attacker stated as he smoothed down his clothes.

In a rolling motion he exported the scissors to his right hand, the blades of the scissors pointed in towards the man, a technique that shielded the blade from the victim. Tom did not intend on becoming the man's victim yet currently, the burden of a third life outweighed his desire to attack. He knew deep down that he had had no other option on two previous occasions, instinct had kicked in.

"Why are you telling me that?" Tom roared over the music, bat raised once again, his footing strong, calves taut, waiting to transfer as much power to the swing of the bat as possible.

Frazier smugly turned down his lips in a manner that highlighted the pure pleasure he was going to get from the next sentence. Unlike Tom, he was relishing every moment the altercation brought with it.

"Two reasons. One, so that you know the name of the man that is going to gut you," he confidently asserted.

Tom dreaded having to prompt the man but did so against his better judgement, trying to match the bravado in Frazier's voice, "And the second?"

Frazier advanced three steps, his arms held outwards, scissors all but obscured but for the handle protruding from the top of his clenched fist. He sniggered.

"Because you needed the push, you need to feel this, to be in the moment fully. You see your biggest mistake wasn't following me into this outlet. No, your biggest mistake Sundance, was walking in here thinking you had alternatives, that you could reason with me, hell possibly even subdue me," he abruptly began sniffing violently at the air like some feral creature. "If not for the fact that I can smell the hesitation on you, oozing out of every pore and most likely every orifice by now, it's written all over your face. You could have had me when I was on the floor back there but you hesitated."

"And what makes you think that that was a sign of weakness? That I wasn't just mustering up the energy to finish you off, cave your head in," he emphasised raising the bat defiantly.

"Don't go giving it the big I am! You followed me in here because you knew that I didn't have my radio and that as soon as you bolted, I would have alerted my team as soon as possible. That left you two options; subdue or kill. But you committed the cardinal sin."

Tom slightly entranced by the man's calm magnetism dipped his bat marginally; his vision blurring slightly, Frazier's face now distorted and fuzzy, his words lolling him slightly into a catatonic state. Frazier proceeded.

"Don't get high on your own supply!" he barked. "Your arrogance was your biggest downfall. You entered here, cornering me like some kind of wounded animal, thinking you held all the cards; that you had the gumption to do what needed to be done. I mean fuck me you drew first blood. You took down my partner most likely by accident or against your better judgement. You were high on your own victory; I mean you've gotten this far. That's a lot further than many of the people downstairs I can tell you. I appreciate that, I really do."

He took another step forward, his blackened eyes never leaving Tom's. Like a wild animal he stared down his prey, showing little sign of weakness, regardless of his physical state. The terms of war had changed and whether Tom liked to admit it or not, Frazier was gaining traction. He smiled briefly before replacing his grin with pure malice, underlining all the more the mistake Tom had made in entering the music store.

"You came in here thinking you were King of the bloody jungle, that you had me cornered, injured. What you failed to do however was enter with the balls to finish the job. See unlike you, I know what I have to do to survive. Killing you is my first and last resort; it'll be a bloody pleasure if you must know. And all because of one barrier I overcame years ago. One thing I don't fight, that I give in freely to. Do you know what that is?"

He jutted his head forward expectantly, awaiting a response. Tom held firm desperately trying to maintain focus.

"My base instinct, that same Instinct that allowed me to kill sixteen people downstairs when the bullets started flying; two of them were cops, one an elderly woman, I could go on. It was that very instinct that was going to steer my hand when I slit that bitch's throat along with those two poor excuses for men out there. And instinct…" he raised his bladed hand, "… is what is going to help me kill you and any other fuckwit who wants me to punch their ticket for 'em. I'm just as nature intended. When nurture came knocking, nature won out, as it should always do"

"Simply put, you've gone from predator to prey; you're the one who is cornered, on my turf. And the only way you're walking out of here," he pointed at Tom, "is with that bat."

Frazier motioned towards Tom, urging him to make a move. Tom stood inert, unsure of how to proceed. Frazier was right; he had felt a slight advantageous air about him when he had walked into the store. Frazier shifted his feet so as to get a better footing amongst the debris on the floor. His foot, one final time, came down upon the remote, the previous song cut short to make way for his Father's favourite song. The thought brought stinging tears to the edges of Tom's eyes.

Frazier repressed a laugh, poorly.

"Fitting…well come on then Mr Jungle VIP. Predator or prey? Alpha male or bottom of the food chain? Come at me and see."

Tom burst forward, urged on by the man's retorts and jives, the music only helping to drown out his criticisms. Frazier braced himself ready for the attack. Tom came down heavily upon him; his strength more than doubled now. Frazier was impressed.

He threw Tom against a shelving unit which consisted of an assortment of radios and whilst doing so, flicked one of the scissors blades from his enclosed palm. Tom moved his head dodging the swathing motion of the blade. Frazier once again changed his tactics and went for Tom's injured shoulder. He drove his spare fist into his wounded shoulder.

Tom yelped out and faltered, sinking slightly. Frazier stepped back and made ready for the killing blow. Tom swung out instinctively with the bat, mustering up all of the remaining strength he had left. His head spun a heady cocktail of pain and blood loss. His vision began to grow dark at the corners. Tom looked up, raising his bat limply, readying another attack but was met instead by a swaying Frazier, his fist clenched tight against his chest.

A steady drip of blood cascaded down the edge of his hand, a look of shock and confusion etched across his furrowed brow. He took two undetermined steps backwards. Tom's vision cleared slightly and instinctively began to piece together what he was seeing. He must have driven the scissors into the man when he had lashed out with his bat, driving the blades of the scissors deep into the man's chest.

Frazier stumbled against the shelves and began to slide along them, knocking various electrical appliances to the floor as he did so. He was panic stricken now, gulping for air. He turned and in a jaunty fashion, began moving back towards the outlets one and only entry point. Tom reached up, grabbing at one of the shelves, the ramifications of Frazier escaping pulling him from his stupor. If Frazier communicated with his colleague's downstairs in any way, he along with Michelle, the teenager and the elderly gentleman were all as good as dead.

Tom held out a hand still trying to reason with Frazier, "Stop!" he beckoned after him, his voice weak and far from authoritative.

Frazier clearly in pain yet still overwhelmed with the need to be the author of Tom's demise, glared back, a laboured smile returning.

"You're a fucking dead man," he boomed and with that threat he began to shout as loud as he could, his feet breaking into a quickened pace.

Every so often he would afford himself another look back at Tom, who was now rising to his feet. He became distracted with blood lust, Tom's death now more likely than ever forcing him to ignore the application of putting one foot in front of the other. He smiled. Although the man had gotten to his feet, he was bent double, the shelves which held blood streaked vinyl's on either side, his only support.

Frazier screamed out again, "Up here… anyone!"

Tom steadied himself; his fingers closed around the bat and rather painfully, lifted it above his head mustering the singular phrase, "Stop!"

Frazier was all but two metres away from the store's entrance, the warm light outside welcoming. There was no stopping him. Reluctantly, Tom arched the bat backwards, twisting painfully at the hips and swung, the bat rotating through the air with sufficient force.

The bat fell short of Frazier's torso, Toms desired target and instead collided with his ankle. As Frazier made to raise his left leg it came down upon the bat causing the handle to flick upwards, catching his other foot. Knocked off kilter he was sent tumbling forward. Ironically, if it had not been for the sizeable pool of his dead partner's blood at the threshold of the store, Tom surmised that Frazier would have fallen just short of his final destination.

Instead, Frazier wind milled his arms, trying desperately to regain his balance. He finally broke a foot away from the bat's handle but to no avail, instead stepping into his partner's blood.

The loss of balance combined with his unsteady footing sent Frazier over the edge of the balcony's metal and glass partition, the fluidity and speed of which was dizzying.

Tom looked on, instinctively stepping towards the man, as if he would somehow be able to reach the man in time, catching a wrist or stray limb. His arm lingered for several seconds, outstretched, offering futile aid. He was thankful for the final lines of Elvis' ballad, the volume and intensity of which doing much to mask the bloodcurdlingly scream that most likely emanated from Frazier before he succumbed to gravity.

'Take my hand; take my whole life too, for I can't help falling in love with you'.

CHAPTER TWELVE: HOW THE MIGHTY HAVE FALLEN

Alpha team, who had been tasked with sweeping both the ground and first floor, had just been finishing their sweep of the first floor, about to proceed to their final sweep of the Ground floor, when one of the armed men saw it. Luckily the mirrored glass structure of the building allowed those within to look out but for those outside, no discernible way of looking in. Team Leader had of course warned the team that any tactical units outside would most likely be using heat signature technology to map the building and all those within it but even this would have its limitations.

Plus, as Team Leader had remarked, at this early stage in proceedings, they would not take the risk of eliminating a member of the team for fear of hitting a hostage or endangering those within. After all, at this stage they would have extraordinarily little intelligence in which to base a full out assault upon.

The streets were deserted. Police vehicles were scattered along the street in an arched pattern, affording those behind the vehicles cover. Every now and then a crouched figure keeping low would run across the open front of the building most likely to discuss something with a colleague or alter their position. All roads leading into the precinct were closed down within what one would safely assume was a sizeable block radius. The leader of Alpha team watched on smugly safe in the knowledge that for all their planning and intelligence they may or may not have already gathered, they had no idea what would transpire this day.

He had just been about to turn around when he saw it. His cheekbones rubbed roughly against the material of his balaclava. How he loathed having to wear it.

"That's a new one on me," he muttered to himself, a bemused smile breaking across his face.

He pressed his face against the glass and peered out, a low laugh emanating from within his throat. Still laughing, he hit the presell pad to his radio. Before he spoke, he afforded himself a moment to regain his composure remembering to whom he was about to speak.

"Team Leader, over," he asked.

He waited several seconds before the reply came.

"What is it?" the cantankerous reply came, all radio etiquette now abandoned.

"We have a new development out on the street, over," he turned over his shoulder and saw his men clearing the last of the units.

"What kind of situation?" Team Leader's interest had been piqued.

"Well, they have a message out there sir. They're trying to make contact, over," he continued to peer out.

"Oh for fucks sake Alpha Leader spit it out; this isn't Close Encounters of the Third Kind. I don't hear anyone playing a keyboard, do you?"

The dry wit of Team Leader made Alpha Leader feel all the worse. It was Team leader's most unnerving trait as far as he was concerned. It encapsulated his unhinged psyche more so. He shuffled uneasily and cleared his throat. He peered out of the window once again.

"Yes sir. Sorry sir. They are communicating via an electronic road sign. It's cycling two messages on about a ten second interval. The first one says… Allow us to open communications…" he waited for the screens display to change "…sat phone left by entrance. No tricks, over."

He waited for Team Leader's response, transfixed by the orange glow of the writing displayed on the sizeable screen.

"They're trying to re-establish some resemblance of control. That phone stays where it is. I doubt they'd pull anything even if we did grab it. Proceed with sweep Alpha team; I'll concern myself with opening up communications."

"Understood sir, Roger and out," he replied, not wanting to push the situation any further.

He rested his clenched fist upon the cool glass of the window, repressing his anger. He hated taking orders from that prick. Raising his shotgun he stepped away from the window and set about re-joining his team and their final clearance of the first floor.

(CHAPTER BREAK)

"Going live in one minute sir, sound check needed," the voice established.

Team Leader nodded and positioned himself behind Pierce once again; a demonstration of power married with intimidation that he revelled in. He whispered into Pierce's ear, unnerving his prisoner more so.

"You politicians pride yourself on your opinion polls," he came close to Pierces ear and raised his voice in such an audible level that Pierce flinched, "well let me tell you, I've just had a look at our little social experiment online and I'm sorry to be the one to break it to you Mr Pierce but I don't think you'll be securing that second term."

Team Leader withdrew, leaving a weeping Pierce to mull over what had just been said. He stood upright and adjusted his vest slightly, wanting to achieve as high a level of formality as possible. He was flanked once again by two armed guards at the back of the stage, their guns still trained on the hostages.

Gerry was knelt before the insurgent to the right of the stage. His hands were bound behind his back, a vicious gash above his right eye. He was hunched over in pain rather than in a display of defeat, his breathing laboured. Two of the masked men had had some fun with him earlier in the warehouse, their bloodlust seemingly not sated by the bodies of those strewn around the centre. He had no doubt that he was being displayed, prostituted before the cameras for all those in the secret service and Whitehall to see.

The man behind the camera held up his hand and motioned that they were going live in three, two, one…

"I wish to make the following abundantly clear. There will be no contact. No negotiation. No open channels of communication. We have made our demands very clear and it would appear your nation has begun to do likewise. We will communicate with you, if and when we deem it-"

The camera man looked up. The hands that had been steadying the camera fell limply to his sides. If he had not been for the balaclava his face would have been a canvas of pure astonishment. He, along with those of the remaining hostages not positioned around Pierce, did the same, moving their heads quickly from an elevated position to a downward one.

A woman shrieked making Team Leader pause, the hairs on the back of his neck standing to attention. He felt all his muscles tighten as he turned slightly to reach their gaze. He did so just in time to see the body of a man falling about a metre above the stage. Team Leader watched on in utter amazement for a millisecond before he raised his hand and made to utter a warning to the armed guard positioned to the left of the stage. All he managed was one word.

"Move …" he started but had been too late.

The guard briefly looked up before the body came crashing down upon him. The guard let off a flurry of bullets as he was brought to the ground. Team Leader hit the deck, taking Pierce with him, inadvertently shielding him. The sickening thud of the falling body crushing the unsuspecting guard, amazingly, registered louder than the stuttering of the man's AK-47. The sound was a sickening concoction of breaking bones and the splintering of wood as the stage gave way slightly.

Team Leader quickly gathered himself and realising he was holding onto Pierce, shoved him away in disgust. He observed the two men on the floor. The one that had fallen was in military attire, one of his. The hostages were screaming and were covering their heads; one was writhing around the floor holding her ankle, grasping at a seeping gun wound. Another lay prone facing upright his back arched, hands still bound, half of his face missing.

Team Leader faced back towards the camera and shouted three words, "Cut the feed!"

His cry was of such magnitude that it audibly shook the tone of the voice changer, the level of decibels emitted through the device unfathomable. The hostages were whimpering. Team Leader let out a blood curdling howl at the disorientation of what had just transpired. He turned and withdrew his holstered sidearm. The woman on the floor continued to writhe about and scream away to herself. Team Leader put a singular shell into the woman's skull, the round automatically hushing the hostages. With unflinching expediency, he stepped over the body of the dead woman and in a dazed like state, approached the bodies of his two fallen conspirators.

He turned and faced his men who now gathered around the front of the stage, alternating between inspecting the scene that had just taken place and their primary objective, the guarding of the hostages. Team Leader's eyes were ablaze with anger and the unmistakable temperance of something else, something new. Uncertainty. He looked down at his feet before reaching up and grabbing the top of his balaclava.

He pulled hard upon it. The balaclava sat in his hands for several seconds before it came loosely to his side before falling to the ground. He looked up; his face drenched with sweat. His eyes grew black, shark like in nature as they soullessly scanned the crowd. They all looked back in fear and confusion, trying to formulate and evaluate what they were seeing.

Team Leader wiped his brow and holstered his sidearm, leaving the strap unbound, there was more killing to be done yet. He hit the presell pad to his microphone.

"The ruse is up gentlemen," he stated rather dejectedly. "Masks are optional. As of thirty seconds ago we are now compromised. Alpha team, get the fuck up to the second floor and let me know if any of Bravo team are still breathing."

Team Leader glowered over the hostages, many immediately breaking their gaze when his eyes feel upon them. A trickle of sweat zig-zagged down his stubble, his white, pinkish skin sporadically visible in those areas not covered by camouflage. His jaw was strong, much like his sizeable frame. The intricate criss-crossed lights that hung festively above were reflected in his perfectly shaved head, a demonic festive red. The men around him looked unsure and turned to their counterparts, uneasy whether to remove their masks or not.

After thirty seconds or so the man to the right of the stage, who flanked his now dead partner, removed his hood. He was on his knees; he held his nose as a steady drip of blood hit the ground. Pierce's last remaining bodyguard, the one who had so quickly surrendered the Prime Minister, was missing. Others around him soon followed, their white skin standing out against their dark tactical attire. The bloodied man approached. He looked Team Leader straight in the eyes, on edge and sweating profusely. His confusion and pain formulated itself into a singular question.

"What do we do now, Thompson?" a whistle came from his nostril as he said this.

'Probably broken' Team Leader pondered. He weighed up the merits of grabbing the man by the nose, punishing him for his sloppy indecisiveness; twisting the appendage ensuring that if it was not already broken it soon would be. Instead, he absorbed the question and for the first time in recent events, an eerie calm descended upon him, he almost looked as if he were back in familiar territory.

"It appears we have an intruder or two Jones and because of you and the colossal fuck up that is your life, one unaccounted member of Pierces security detail," he held his gaze as he accentuated this final line. "Go get me Remy," he commanded.

(CHAPTER BREAK)

Tom sat with his back perched against one of the store's shelving units. He stared deeply into his open palms, fascinated by the intersecting creases which now ran red, like tributaries of suffering. Some held the belief that one's palms could tell much about the owner they belonged to; character traits, emotional state, their psychological make- up. Most people, Tom had once read, were usually most interested in the lifeline, the line that started between the index finger and thumb before ending at the base of the thumb, just above the wrist. It was also, he had read whilst sitting in a dentist's waiting room, a common misconception that it indicated longevity of life or the date of one's death.

Tom knew that to those practiced in the art of palmistry; this was instead an indicator of life encounters, health and emotional well-being. Tom stared deeply into the creases. Although he dismissed palmistry as nonsense, he could not help but contemplate his own mortality. His own lifeline was stained with blood. Was this a precursor for what was to come? Was his own life to come to an abrupt end with the cessation of blood at the base of his wrist?

He flinched; his train of thought interrupted as he heard the crunching of plastic under foot. As soon as he registered that it was Michelle he eased. She looked terrified. Tom rose to his feet shakily, stumbling slightly. Michelle rushed towards him and helped prop him up, a gesture Tom was all too glad to accept. He was battered, bruised and losing blood by the minute.

"You've lost a lot of blood. We need to get you back to the sports store. I can try and…" Tom shot Michelle a look that cut her off, it was one of abject defeat and self- loathing.

Tom swallowed hard, "Michelle, you need to go. Take the boy and the man if he's awake and go."

Michelle stared back at him intently, "I… I don't understand, I thought we were…" she faltered.

Tom leaned back against the shelves and sighed hard. "So did I Michelle. So did I but with that man going over the top we have about a minute or so max, before they're up here. You need to hide. I'll draw them out; get them as far from here as possible."

Tom shakily retrieved his sidearm and held it aloft, flicking the safety off. It was a half- hearted display at best. He set off towards the stores opening, Michelle guiding him.

"They're probably going to be looking out for us on the cameras now. Run as fast as you can to the shop. When I entered the shop there seemed to be a blind spot to the left by the exit. Head that way, God willing, if they see you come out, they won't be able to see where you go. I have the code for the door; if it works, I'll gauge if the coast is clear and then I'll come right back and get you straight away."

"If not, I'll tamper with the exit; try to make it look like we got out and resealed the door. If I do make it out, I'll try to get help first… I won't leave you behind I promise," Tom declared.

"And if the door is broken or the code is wrong?" Michelle worryingly mumbled.

Tom for the first time began to register what he was proposing and the magnitude of what came with it.

"If I can't… well, they'll think you all escaped through the door. I'll cover the exit and act like I'm covering your escape out of the building. Hopefully, that will fool them."

"And if not?" she questioned as they reached the teenager and the older gentlemen, withdrawn and white with fear.

"Then we gave it our best shot," he said half-jokingly, mustering a smirk.

Tom looked at the teenager and the older man suddenly aware of the fact that he did not even know their names. He propped himself up against the marble beam of the stores entrance.

"Now go, exit left, run around the concourse and come back on yourself. Keep as close to the wall as possible. Hide in the sports store, try to arm yourselves; don't go down without a fight."

They readied themselves for Tom's command.

"On my mark," he held up three digits "Three, two..." Michelle held out both hands and grasped Tom's free hand. She had tears in her eyes once again. Fear and gratitude etched across her face as she mouthed the words through choked up resignation.

"Thank you".

Tom nodded and squeezed her hand.

"One," he grunted.

The barely conscious older man, now propped up by the teenager, burst from the stores cover, Michelle bringing up the rear. They did not afford themselves a backward glance. Tom watched on as he unlatched the ice pick on the back of his belt. He regained his composure and pushed himself away from the column. All three were now in the store, safe he hoped.

He fixed his sights on the Staff exit and began to shimmy tentatively towards it, all the while staying close to the wall. The red LED that indicated the door was locked mockingly taunted Tom as he reached out his hand towards it. He mouthed the code Malcolm had given him and methodically punched it in. The light remained red.

Tom swore and scanned the concourse behind him ensuring he was not being crept up on from behind. The concourse remained deserted. He typed the code in once again, slower this time. No reassuring click came. The code Malcolm had given him was wrong or it had been changed most likely by the insurgents. Tom leant against the door testing its strength, gripping the ice pick tighter now, testing the rigidity of the tool once again. He would not be able to barge it, not with the condition his shoulder was in.

"Well Tom, this is going to take some doing," he muttered to himself.

(CHAPTER BREAK)

Gerry's upper torso ached. His hands were still bound and each step jerked his arms from left to right, his bones grinding in their sockets. After he had head-butted the guard with all the effort he could muster, he had rolled off of the stage, using the fire of the AK-47 and the general confusion to make his escape. He had headed for the nearest escalator located closely behind the stage, putting the stage as firmly behind him as possible, affording some level of cover. He had bounded up the escalator steps two at a time, difficult in nature due to the fact that after the power had been cut, they had stopped at differing heights. He had acted out of instinct but even now, as he made his way to the second floor, he cursed himself.

He felt like some dumb teenager in a horror film, the type that always runs upstairs when they realise an intruder has broken in. It was stupid. It narrowed options and any hope of escaping. Sure, you could hide, maybe even arm yourself but the killer had one luxury, usually that of time. Luckily for Gerry he had viewed the schematics of the building and had memorised them. He even had a folded blueprint of the shopping centre hidden in his belt. All he needed to do was unfree himself and if possible, arm himself.

There was of course another reason why he had gone up, a variable that his torturers in the warehouse had failed to keep hidden. Gerry played this over and over again in his head. Alpha team had been tasked with a job before it had all gone belly up with Bravo team. Gerry mentally played the message over and over; the one that had been stated as he lay huddled in a pile of packing crates, believed to be unconscious. He could hardly blame his captors for thinking it; after all, they had beaten him with boot clad feet and clenched fists for an extended period.

Gerry, hands bound, could not even protect his head as he had been taught to do so growing up on his council estate if he were ever to go to ground. His Dad always used to say, *'Never kick a man when he's down; leave that to the coward who started the fight in the first place'*.

Gerry reached the foot of the escalator that led up to the second floor. His chief torturer had said little between the flurries of punches he had landed but when Gerry was all but dead to the world, he let the piece of intel slip to his partner. He had to get the message out. He breathed heavily, his blood finding its way to his cuts and bruises, pulsating both from exertion and pain.

"After we're finished with him, we'll go see if we can help Alpha Team set up the charges on all of the possible breaching points. The clock's ticking and if we don't find the package, we're all up shit creek without a paddle."

Gerry once again mulled the omission over. It meant two things. All doors, all possible breaching points by a tactical unit, were to be booby trapped. Anyone entering would be a sitting duck. They would be too concerned with breaching quickly, blinded by the ignorance that the hostiles had only brought down the shutters out of necessity, for defensive purposes.

Secondly and all the more puzzling, was the fact that they were here for something other than the Prime Minister. They had referred to it as a package that still needed to be found. Well, the Prime Minister was in their grasp, so was he just a diversionary tactic or was he a secondary goal?

Gerry made it to the top of the escalator. Just a few more steps and he would have the biggest distance between the men below and himself that he had had all day. His heart sunk when he reached the top, ahead of him stood a tall figure, his torso encased in a tactical vest. He seemed to be busying himself with something, his broad frame obscuring the task at hand. Gerry instinctively crouched.

'He must be preparing the door for a trip wire,' he mused, knowing full well that that the door only leads upwards to the roof via two flights of stairs and through Level Three, a caretaker's room on the middle flight.

Gerry scanned his environment. He could not risk entering any of the shops for fear of bumping into any of the other men. Plus, even if he could find a weapon, his hands were bound and he held out very little hope of finding anything in the music and electronics shop ahead to his left.

He weighed up his options and decided upon his next course of action swiftly. He would strike quickly; knock the man out with a forceful barge to the floor, possibly using his thighs to snap the man's neck once he had done so. He assumed the man would have a knife or some sharp object in his tactical vest with which to cut himself free. It had to be now. If he waited any longer, the fluidity of the situation would shift dramatically, one assailant was better than the untold hordes most likely making their way up the escalators presently.

He advanced keeping low, his feet quick and his centre of gravity solid. He focused on the man's back and moved forward systematically.

Absurdly, only one thought now stabbed at his conscience, *'Where is his balaclava?'*

(CHAPTER BREAK)

The man in control was now pacing. He had lashed out at anything and everything that he could lay his hands upon. A pencil pot full of stationary was thrown at a wall; his office chair was rolled precariously against a wall. It had been done out of a composition of fear and personal failure. Rather ironically given his role in the grand scheme of things, he had lost control, not just in his brief barrage of destruction within the control room but also in his failure at having missed any possible intruders. Consequently, two men had died, two live on T.V. Worst still, he held out very little hope for Dreyfus and the rest of Bravo team.

His breathing was erratic; his fists came down clenched upon the desktop of the security console. He was twitchy, shaken.

"Fuck, fuck, fuck. He's going to kill me for this," he slapped himself on the head repeatedly, cursing himself. "You had one job. You idiot, you fuck..." his blood froze when he heard the voice at the other end of his earpiece.

He wiped his upper lip; he was sweating profusely. As he withdrew his hand, he noticed that for the first time today, he was shaking. Killing unarmed people and storming a building had all been child's play compared to the situation he now found himself in, being in Thompson's bad book. He cleared his throat, swallowed hard and took a deep breath.

"Control, come in over!" Thompson boomed.

"Control here, over," he replied, mustering all the strength and resolve that he could.

"You better start giving me some good news up there control because right now you're about as useful as a fucking waterproof teabag!"

He swallowed hard. Thompson had spoken in a threatening tone but was still maintaining some level of decorum with regards to operational procedure. If he had uttered any iteration of his name, Ian Carling would have been worried. Thompson tended to refer to the men, even outside of operational capacity, by their surname. It had always been impersonal and distanced and that was the way Thompson liked it. The mission was all and had been so ever since their days together in the Royal Marines.

"Not as yet sir, nothing seen on the monitors. All shop fronts are shut down; only those requested by Alpha team are open along with those that Bravo team requested. I think we can safely assume that whoever threw Frazier over the top came from the second level. I'm looking at Alpha team now, they have converged at the bottom of the escalator on Level One awaiting you to join them, over," he had tapped the screen reassuringly as he said this, Alpha team now congregated in an arc of fire at the bottom of the escalator.

Thompson began a barrage of swearing that lasted for several seconds. Carling winced at this and gripped the edge of the console desk.

"Are you fucking stupid or are you just here to completely sit on your backside? Shut the shop fronts on all floors. Lock this place down you fuckwit!"

Carling stuttered, cursing himself in tandem, "Yes sir, right away."

He furiously tapped away at the keys before him and watched as the shutters on the first and second levels began to shudder towards the ground.

"And while you're at it, as soon as I come off of comm's with you, get the men to switch off all communications and use the device. I don't want anything getting out of this place, no phone calls, no text messages, not even a sodding Facebook update. If Frazier and Bravo team were taken out by an outside party, they will have fully operational comm's."

All Carling could muster was a, "Yes sir, sorry sir, over."

Thompson sighed heavily, "I don't want apologies or excuses. Just know this. If I have to tell you how to do your job again," a new air of malice descended upon the emphasis of this next line, "I will come up there personally and shove that office chair right up your fat arse before I put a bullet in your skull. Understood?"

Carlings mouth grew devoid of spit. He replied, knowing all too well that he was effectively signing a verbal contract that put his neck on the executioner's block, the metaphorical axe most likely inches above his head.

"Yes sir, it won't happen again. I'll keep my eyes peeled, anything comes up and you'll be the first to know, over."

Radio silence hung in the air for what seemed an eternity.

"Keep them peeled Carling or I'll be up there to peel them for you. Roger and out," he barked.

With that threat, reinforced by the use of his surname, Thompson's open line went dead. Carling ran his hands through his hair, his fingers instantaneously moist with sweat. He exhaled, his nerve endings afire with pent up fear and anxiety. He wiped his forehead and did as always and followed Team Leader's orders.

"All units switch off Comm's, one-minute interval burst of device commencing in two minutes. When I turn the lights back on, it is safe for you to proceed with cycling them back on, over and out."

Carling went over to the upturned office chair, brought it back onto its wheels and rolled it over to the console desk. He slumped down into the seat and watched the clock on the console's monitor.

(CHAPTER BREAK)

Gerry was now no more than five metres away from the figure in the tactical vest. He had reduced his movement and was currently holding his breath. Gerry had decided that he would give himself around a three-metre run up, giving himself enough momentum to barge the man to the ground.

He had taken the left-hand side of the concourse after observing the fixed CCTV camera above him, passing under the camera which was located to the edge of the Stereo-Hype store front. He had ascertained that this area was a CCTV blind spot along with the sports store opposite.

Gerry hoped that whatever transpired, as long as it did not cross the threshold of the camera's visibility and arc, he should remain concealed, as long as he hid the body afterwards. As he saw it, at his current pace and calculated movement, he should avoid the CCTV's arc altogether.

His shoulders stretched his chest so taut that he could feel his heart stabbing away at the inside of his shirt. The man before him had the height and weight advantage but he had the element of surprise, the Goliath to his David.

Four metres. Gerry angled his shoulder now. The man had still not diverted his attentions away from the door, his back towards the Stereo-Hype outlet. He was putting his full body into the ice pick that he was using to pry the door open, his left foot pivoted for leverage.

"That will make it easier to knock him off balance," Gerry mentally calculated.

He could feel the body heat eradiating off the man; he could even smell his aftershave, which hung damp in the air with his perspiration. He could see the contours of his back straining under the exertion of opening the door, his upper torso covered in some innocent's blood; the thought of this reinforcing his desire to end the man before him. Gerry tensed his muscles, they ached under the beating he had been subjected to earlier but he dispelled such thoughts, replacing them instead with the pleasure he would have at snapping one of these murdering scumbag's necks.

That however, was when it all went to hell. The lights behind him started to flicker out in a linear fashion. The insurgent before him whirled round, ice pick at the ready. His eyes fell quickly upon Gerry's and rather embarrassingly Gerry froze, uttering an absurd sentiment.

"But you're white?" he said in an almost questioning tone, as if he were expecting some form of affirmation from the ice pick wielding stranger before him.

The man raised the ice pick in a motion that snapped Gerry out of his daze. He instinctively plunged himself into his mid-drift, forcing the man to drop the mountaineering tool, driving his attacker against the door. The blackout was nearing ever closer. However, what came next completely took Gerry by surprise.

171

"Wait, wait, wait. You need to stop," the man resisted, almost pleading, shoving Gerry away from him slightly.

Gerry made to drive into him again but instead had his own momentum used against him. The man took him by the shoulder and overturned him. He came down hard upon his coccyx and he groaned loudly. With brutal speed the man recovered the ice pick and followed up by kneeling upon his chest, his full weight bearing down atop of him. The dying winter light of the skylight built into the ceiling was all that illuminated the second levels upper third and barely at that. The last sets of lights were about to flicker out, the third floor above now completely shrouded in darkness. They locked eyes. Gerry defiantly spat at the man hitting him squarely in the left eye. The man did not even flinch, nor did he wipe it away.

"Do it you murdering piece of-" Gerry started.

"Shut up and listen. I'm not one of them. My name's Tom, Tom Hawkins and if we don't get this door open in the next thirty seconds or so, I've got a feeling that we're going to have some serious company."

Gerry's face softened with confusion. Truth be told, the man could have killed him in a variety of quick and efficient ways in a quarter of the time it had taken him to deliver his speech. Gerry's body weakened slightly as he weighed up his options. The man who called himself Tom rose to his feet and twisted Gerry onto his front as he did so. If this was the killing blow, the man could not face to look him in the eyes.

He felt a blade being withdrawn before being placed between his wrists. The man pulled back in an angled fashion and severed the binds. He rolled Gerry onto his back and held out the knife, hilt facing towards Gerry. Gerry snatched it away and pointed it at Tom. It had been a sign of trust. A sign that demonstrated Tom had no ill intent for the man. Gerry decided to extend the same courtesy. He got to his feet and placed the blade into his belt strap.

"I'm Gerry," he stated, eyeing the still slightly raised ice pick before pointing at it, "and you won't need that, on me or the door. When those lights go out, the door will open."

Tom lowered the pick and nodded at Gerry, a non-verbal sign of trust. Gerry braced himself against the door. One hand grasped the handle, his other shoulder against the centre of the door. Gerry gave Tom a readying nod, Tom stood adjacent to the side of the door frame. Gerry focused his eyes on the steady red light of the keypad. The lights flickered above them and to Gerry's relief; a clicking sound was heard as the red light faded on the keypad. They were plunged into darkness. Gerry put a hand upon Tom's shoulder which registered a grunt; Gerry feeling the warmth of what he perceived to be damp blood.

"Through the rabbit hole we go Tom," he half joked. There would be time for questions later; all that mattered now was putting the door and the gunmen behind them. If the man now known to Gerry as Tom was telling the truth, *"Well,"* Gerry mused *"I might just have an ally in all of this."*

They both plunged through the door into utter darkness, fluid in their motion. The door closing just as Alpha team reached the top of the escalator, night vison goggles brought down. They had waited until all the lights had gone down in the hope of affording themselves cover. Moreover, if the night vision had been used with the lights on, it would have rendered all those wearing the equipment prematurely blind. They scanned the area, the enormity of the silence dwarfing the darkness.

CHAPTER THIRTEEN: THE CHANGING FACE OF EXTREMISM

Carling was staring intently at the concourse on the central monitor. He had at the time been monitoring a screen located on the periphery of the monitor unit; the first floor. He had been watching Alpha team get into position and had out of the corner of his eye, glanced what he had thought looked like an arm roll into focus. He had tried to adjust the angle of the camera but it would pan no further. He had just been about to review the footage when the monitors began to power down, the blackout nearing its completion. He gave a literal shake of his head, dispelling the apparition not wanting to bother Thompson unintentionally.

If there was anyone on the second level, Alpha team would find them. Carling flicked on his torch in preparation. He hated the dark. The dark brought with it viscous flashbacks, flashbacks of that night in Afghanistan three years ago. Diagnosed with and discharged with PTSD by the Royal Marines, a mere label to them, a life sentence for him. He counted down the seconds; a desperate attempt at keeping his mind occupied. It already seemed like a lifetime ago since he had been bathed in the artificial light of the control room.

As was often the case it was a futile effort, thoughts of his previous life resurfacing, a life he had so desperately sought to distance himself from. Initially he had tried to bury his past and it had worked at first, painful reminiscences suppressed under layers of cerebral mud. However, the roots had burrowed deep within his subconscious. Snubbing his pain only fed the cancerous roots all the more so, anchoring them further within the inner recesses of Carling's brain. How he longed for the memories to take the form of a tumour, something that could be cut out, removed or failing that, a source of death.

The memory finally seeped into his conscience as it always did so in the dark, a single wound, clean and central to the upper torso. How he wished the wound had occupied his own body instead.

(CHAPTER BREAK)

Tom hated the dark. It had been an irrational fear of his since childhood. He had always been told by his mother that he would grow out of it but years sitting in Fox holes, on stag, had quickly dispelled that theorem. The other men in the unit were more than accommodating when Tom would offer to take extended lookouts or on the odd occasion, not wake the next man on night patrol, at all. He would sit alone with his thoughts and ponder what had been and what was yet to come, a variable all too real to him at present as he groped his way up the metal staircase.

"Hold up," Gerry whispered abruptly. Tom froze. "I'm going to need that ice pick".

Tom's back tightened with uncertainty. Was this a play to disarm him? Had he not earned his trust? Tom pondered this briefly before concluding that it was in his best interests to unlatch the ice pick. He held it out blindly, brushing Gerry's hand slightly. Gerry grasped at it and turned back towards the door.

"What are you doing?" Tom questioned, eyes still firmly fixed forward, regardless of the fact that he could not even see his hand in front of his face.

Gerry had advised they not use the torch in case the beam were to be seen from under the crack of the door. Tom heard the slight scraping of wood followed by a slight grunt of exertion.

"The space before the bottom step and the door is slightly smaller than the ice pick. I'm wedging the door. That should buy us some extra time if we need it," he followed this up with a pat upon Tom's shoulder wanting him to proceed up the stairs, using Tom's shoulder as a reference point.

Tom sardonically mused to himself, *"Talk about the blind leading the blind."*

He fondled the corner of the wall and registered that they had reached the first flight of the staircase. He made to turn around and proceed up the staircase but Gerry squeezed his shoulder slightly rendering him motionless once again.

"Roughly three steps ahead, there's a door to a caretaker's room," he whispered, his hot breath on Tom's neck. "We're going up, not down. There's nothing down there for us, it opens out onto the Ground floor concourse which is sealed and well-guarded".

Tom advanced clutching at thin air. After several agonising moments, his forefinger touched upon a cold, metallic frame. He reached lower to where he guesstimated a door handle to be and was grateful to find it reasonably quick. He twisted it and pushed the door inwards. It creaked slightly but not so much to unease the two men. They both entered, Gerry lithely closing the door behind them with the palm of his hand. Tom let out a sigh of relief. Gerry finally removed his hand.

"We're not out of the woods yet," he stated in a rather condescending manner.

Tom fumbled for his torch, his hand grasping it tightly.

"Not yet. Wait a minute," Gerry urged.

"Why?" Tom pressed.

"Because I want to test out a theory, give it a minute," Gerry said rather hastily.

The temptation for Tom to speak, to fill the silence was all too desirable. Instead, he fixated upon his breathing. It felt like they had waited a lifetime and then, a single red light flicked on in the ceiling. Tom once again attuned his ear to the sound of movement, a hand being slid over plasterboard, then the flick of a switch. A bright bulb shone above. Gerry grasped his forehead in his hands and clenched his teeth in anger.

"Mother..." he started.

Tom was baffled, transfixed by what could possibly be going through Gerry's head at this present in time. He stepped towards him slightly and Gerry shot him a look that was a canvas of insight. Gerry slid down the door and sat with his head between his knees.

"The bastards, the absolute..." he was working his way up to something.

He shot his head back fixing his eyes upon Tom. He smiled slightly, amused by something unfathomable to Tom, who for the first time noticed that Gerry's eye had now swollen to a Quasimodo like, purple hue.

"They had us from the start. They had us bent over a barrel before we even got here. How? How did they get hold of that kind of hardware?" he probed rhetorically.

Gerry registered Tom's look of complete ignorance and tapped his head slightly.

"Think about it Tom. Lights go on, lights go off. Communications go down. It all happened after the shutters came down," he finished this with a questioning glare.

When Tom did not reciprocate, he continued.

"There's more to this then someone flicking a circuit breaker or a switch on and off. No, this is being controlled. I'd heard rumours and hearsay but I wrote it off as some sort of tin hat conspiracy bullshit made up by people who had watched too many films."

Tom still looked on baffled. Gerry released a sigh and decided it best to proceed towards his conciliatory point.

"A lot has been said over the years about Electromagnetic pulses or EMP, as they have become more commonly known."

Tom had heard of the term before and nodded, "They disrupt electronic devices, right."

Gerry nodded, "And up until now, that was it. However, the armed forces, governments, people in charge of important systems around the world have always had one fear; what if it were ever to be weaponised."

Gerry rose to his feet and pointed up to the steady red light built into the ceiling. Tom observed that it was a smoke detector of some sort.

"When that light came on, the power came back on," Gerry said adamantly.

Gerry brought down his palms slapping them upon his thighs. What came next was reminiscent of a teacher who had exhausted all avenues with their students and had instead settled upon condescension.

"Right, now this is just a theory, so hear me out. I am by far no expert on this but I know an EMP fries anything electrical inside the radius it is used within. Electronics are disabled, rendered inoperative, useless. However, as far as I was concerned, they were still developing such tech. There is no way they could have that type of technology on this site. Hell, it might not even fit into a room. When I made my way upstairs, I noticed that the streetlights were still on outside. I think we can safely determine that the EMP has come from within the building."

Tom nodded as he lowered himself onto a nearby workbench. He grimaced as he propped his wounded arm against the metallic surface. He leant back shakily, the unsurmountable odds the two men were facing only growing in stature and looked up at the ceiling.

"We are so fucked!" he said angrily still maintaining a hushed tone.

He locked eyes with Gerry once again.

"Two questions; how are the lights still on, if they've used an EMP? And what do we do now? I mean, it's not like we're going to be able to push all the doors open like we did the last one."

Gerry nodded; the look of sheer incomprehension replaced now by resignation.

"They must be operating on some sort of cycle, a loop. Any electronic devices switched off are not affected."

Tom clicked his fingers and pointed at his earpiece.

"That would explain the chatter on the radio. The guy in charge keeps telling them to turn off their comm's at intervals. And that generally coincides with…"

Gerry finished his sentence reluctantly, "The lights going off. That sure would explain a lot." Gerry wavered slightly as he rose to his feet, the pain creeping up his battered body in waves. And in answer to your second question, I was hoping you'd be able to help me with that?"

Tom's skin suddenly felt icy cold. He found it hard to muster a singular phrase let alone an orchestrated plan. Terrified, he had not expected to still be alive. He had earlier reconciled himself to the fact that the insurgents would most likely give chase after his little escape attempt.

Rather ashamedly, his thoughts drifted back to Michelle and the lie he had told her that his primary objective would be to seek out help. It had not been. No, he wanted to save his own skin first and foremost. He was no hero; he had killed out of necessity. After all, look where his heroic interventions had gotten Malcolm.

Gerry must have detected Tom's apprehension because he ushered him to calm down with his hand, stepping closer.

"Look, Tom. I understand you're slightly overwhelmed at the moment and I'm right there with you matey. I don't know who you are, what you do or what you have had to do to get to this point but I'm going to go out on a limb here and say that you're military, most likely ex. Am I right?"

Tom nodded momentarily slacked jawed, "How did you know?"

Gerry's features flickered slightly; a macabre smile framed by a swollen lip and bloodied incisors. He rested his hand upon Tom's good shoulder. Tom noticed for the first time that, much like himself, Gerry had also sustained a wound to his arm, his shirt encrusted slightly with blood.

"Well, first of all, you've gotten this far and you've picked up some souvenirs along the way to boot," he pointed at Tom's tactical vest. "You can't pick them up in your local shopping centre. My guess, you've ran into at least one of those whack jobs," Gerry's features suddenly became rather excited. "So, is he still alive and kicking or has the poor sod realised that there weren't seventy-two virgins waiting for him?"

"You haven't seen it yet, have you?" Tom cautiously inquired.

"Seen what?" Gerry's reply came, his Sunderland accent peaking slightly.

Tom sighed and rubbed his eyes.

"I don't know how long we're safe here but a lot has happened, so I'll try to make this short and sweet."

And with that, Tom began to recant the sorry series of events that he had been subjected to within the past two hours or so.

(CHAPTER BREAK)

Benley appeared as if he were about to arrive at the crescendo of his verbal bombardment directed at the man on the other end of the line, Richard Miller. Miller thought it better to let Benley run out of steam or rather as he saw it, run out of swear words or items, most of which could be found around the office, that he wished to shove up or down any given orifice upon Miller's person.

"I'm going to see that you choke on the assurances you made us about the Prime Minister's safety and as for the current plan of action that your team has drawn up, well you can shove them right up your arse!"

Silence at last.

Miller took his opportunity, "Sir, all of the above aside, it's the best we have to offer at the moment. Intel is scarce on the organisation that orchestrated this attack and any efforts to open communications have, as yet been unsuccessful."

"I'm hearing a lot of problems here Miller and very little in the way of solutions. Now I want the Prime Minister out of that building and I want any other potential targets narrowed down and I preferably want it done before another hostage decides to take a swan dive."

Miller paced the room, tapping at his thigh impatiently.

"Sir I know you don't want to hear this but that's just not possible. Moreover, we don't know if that was a hostage that landed on that insurgent or not, we're still reviewing all of the footage and we think that-" Miller was once again cut off.

"No Miller, what isn't possible is you keeping your job after all of this, that my deluded friend is a foregone conclusion. If we didn't have anyone to fill your place right now, I'd have you trussed up in stocks in the middle of Parliament Square. Let's not detract away from the fact that the biggest victory we have had in killing any of these pricks has come via a hostage with a penchant for dive-bombing. And you know what else is going to happen today Miller?"

Miller swallowed; he hated acting the lapdog. Reluctantly he answered, forcing the bilious anger back down into the pit of his stomach.

"No sir," he replied unenthused.

"Seems to be a bit of a pattern with you today Miller, my spelling things out for you. Well let me put this into words you can understand," he spat before pausing for extra gravitas. "The Prime Minister does not die, that is simply not an option. If he does, we are all going down in a political tailspin of shit and fire the like of which has never been seen before. What's more, we will effectively be declaring open season on any British Prime Minister or foreign dignitary for the foreseeable future. Not on my watch. Now, am I crystal clear Miller?"

Miller swallowed hard; his voice broke slightly, not from fear but from the anger he stored away in reserve within his throat.

"Yes sir."

Benley's only response was to hang the phone up.

(CHAPTER BREAK)

Gerry exhaled heavily not yet fully processing what he had just been told. He too had filled Tom in on all that he had witnessed: the killing of dozens around him, a slip of the tongue from his would-be torturers, breaking the nose of one of the insurgents. He paused after Tom had finished, digesting what he had just heard. He slowly patted Tom upon his back, like a father praising his son.

"Well, at least that's three less we don't have to worry about," Gerry half-jokingly quipped, kneading a jaw that seemed to have grown substantially more swollen during Tom's account.

"Listen Gerry don't get me wrong, I'm ex-military but that's all behind me now. I'm no crusader; I'm just a man that was in the wrong place, at the wrong time. I got backed into a corner and my hand was forced."

Gerry looked intently at Tom, weighing up the statement with a wry smile.

"Tom, I'm going to level with you, those guys downstairs, they're good and when I say good, I mean cold-hearted killing machines. I don't know what their agenda is but you can be damn sure about one thing, this place is sealed up tighter than a virgin."

Tom made light of the situation, "What is it with you and virgins?"

"Misspent youth," Gerry winked before straightening, the stern demeanour once again returning.

"This might come as a shock to you but that man down there, Pierce, I loathe the very ground he walks on. Never liked him, never will. As far as I'm concerned, the papers have been too nice to him, he's an even bigger prick than they give him credit for," he shook his head lightly.

"All that said and done, it's my job to protect him and what's more we need to look at the bigger picture here. He dies; the country will be whipped into frenzy. I mean fuck, they're practically complicit in signing his death warrant as it is and all at the click of a mouse."

"What are you suggesting here Gerry? We're hardly the Lone Ranger and Tonto right about now are we?"

"No...we most definitely are not. What we are however, are two discontent members of the public with a fuck off axe to grind. As I said, I don't care much for Pierce; it's those poor sods down there that I care about," he thrust his bloodied finger downwards.

"I hear you about escaping, about getting help but I don't see it as a workable option lad. I mean you heard me, right? They've set charges on all possible breaching points. Even if we did leave this room, make our way down the stairs instead of up and exit via the Ground level, chances are it's wired up like a Christmas tree. Then there's the fact that the doors are all on electronic locks."

Tom started to feel an uneasy feeling rise within the pit of his gut, one of reluctant agreement. He got up and walked to the side of Gerry. Gerry countered his thought process before Tom verbalise it.

"Say we do nothing, wait for a breaching team. Those poor buggers have no idea what's waiting for them. They'll plan for booby traps of course and resistance, probably expect to lose a good old chunk of the hostages but what they won't be prepared for is how well these guys have utilised their time. They're stalling Tom, this whole Islamist charade, the online judge, jury and execution malarkey. I mean come off it; don't you find it a tad suspicious that they've given the people of Britain and the Government a deadline?"

Gerry sniffed, shaking his head from side to side.

"No, whatever it is they're planning; it's going to go down well before that deadline. They're here for something else, hell they even said earlier that they're searching for something and let me put it this way," he locked eyes with Tom, "It's not this Christmas' must have buy."

"We're already pretty dinged up, my shoulder's buggered and you..." Tom began.

"I'm fine, never felt better. Either way, I know this place like the back of my hand and I sure as hell couldn't live with myself if I just hid in a cubby hole while innocents are slaughtered. They're not going to let anyone live lad. All these choices they've proposed, what kind of terrorist does that? You mark my words, if we live to see tomorrow and we do manage to escape, I'd wager all I had on this place looking like the inside of an abattoir along with a substantial part of London looking like the inside of Pierce's pants right about now."

Tom saw the complete honesty in Gerry's eyes partnered with the intense flicker of hope. Since he had left his regiment Tom had honestly lost any hope of being of any use to anyone let alone within an operational capacity. He was barley holding himself together as it was. He reached down and withdrew the Sig Sauer upon his hip. He held it out to Gerry, the man meeting his gaze dejectedly before accepting it reluctantly.

"Well shit. I guess I have my answer," Gerry said staring at the gun.

"I'll help you as much as I can, have your back and I'll even help you formulate a response but if there is even the remote chance of me getting out of here, I'm going to take it, with or without you. I think it's only fair that you know that."

Gerry nodded his understanding. He could not conceal the plastered across his face but he appreciated Tom's honesty.

"You said you had a man out back, in a car. You think he's still alive?" Tom broke the silence.

"Jack? I bloody hope so; he's a tough old prick. If he is dead, you can bet your bottom dollar that he's taken one or two along with him. He would have radioed it in as soon as it all started to hit the fan. For all I know he might even be heading up the cavalry."

"So, what's our next move?" Tom asked nervously.

Gerry eyes flicked right. Tom followed his gaze and saw a turquoise first aid box on the wall.

"I'm no Florence Nightingale but before we go anywhere, we need to get you patched up, that wound looks like its pissing blood."

Tom had not wanted to admit it to Gerry but his legs felt hollow and his head was in an intermittent state of nausea and sickness. He mustered a nod and Gerry gestured to the workbench. Tom did not argue. He carefully lifted the blueprint free of the table and placed it carefully upon the floor. What little blood he had left rushed to his head as he stood up. He wavered, holding onto the edge of the table. After steadying himself, he lay upon the table, the room spinning.

Gerry went over to the first aid box and detached it from the wall. He opened the kit and put a surgical glove on; the effort of which seemed to take an age over his swollen knuckles. He looked down at Tom before moving a desktop light closer to his shoulder.

"Before we start," he let go of the rubber and it thwacked off his wrist. "I just want to say sorry."

Tom, feeling quite exposed lying on the table, shot him a worried glance, "For what?"

"Well, this is going to hurt and well you know..." Gerry shrugged.

"No problem," Tom exhaled, grasping the edges of the workbench.

"Oh and one more thing," Gerry added as he began to open a sterilised wipe.

Tom mustered a quizzical raised eyebrow.

"I'm sorry for spitting in your face earlier, its well... not the best first impression" he smirked through a crimson grin, his lips mangled.

Tom squeezed his eyes shut and laughed weakly. Gerry set about removing his tactical vest. He used the knife and cut a right-angled flap within Tom's clothing just big enough for him to manoeuvre. He pushed the wound together. With a brief, stifled grunt all Tom could do was black out.

(CHAPTER BREAK)

Tom awoke in a dreamlike state. He knew he was alive and that he had not died on the workbench. Unless it was hell he now found himself in. It certainly had been the last time he was here, the site of his brother's death. The smell of charred flesh, the groaning and spitting of the vehicle's frame as it yielded to intense heat. He stumbled forward, always onwards. Rounds whistled past his head, those around him screaming for him to take cover. Still he moved onward, unperturbed, pulling away at the wreckage of the vehicle, the flames intense through the thick material of his gloves.

Tom was fearful. Not of what he would find within the wreckage, he knew all too well what he would discover having endured this dream dozens of times, always with the same outcome. No, what truly terrified him was the futility of having to endure this endless mental theatre again and again knowing the outcome would or could never be altered.

Empty. His brother's body like that of the others within the canopy reduced to a hybrid of melted flesh and charred clothing; their limbs in no way discernible from one another. The tears that gathered around his eyes stung as they were boiled by the flames, the choking gag within his throat brought about by the stench of fetid flesh. The tears that welled in his throat were all that stopped him from projectile vomiting over the vehicle's carcass. The sweet, acrid smell of melting flesh combined with petrol hung heavy within the dry, desert air.

With that a hand grabbed at Tom's shoulder, pulling him back as a cloud of smoke swept across the canopy, shrouding all within.

When it cleared, he was in an office. Cold, modestly furnished. A room meant to facilitate an interview as opposed to affording a man counsel. Tom sat opposite a stern looking gentleman, bald, rimmed glasses, military uniform under that of a white doctor's coat, a juxtaposition that still struck Tom as absurd. Two opposing forces, the ability to both save a life as well as take it.

He gripped the arms of the chair, the wood yielding slightly under the pressure of his grasp so much so that he imagined it splintering. The man's voice came via an echo, solemn yet comforting knowing full well what he had endured. He heard the same sentence ring out again, always the same, bringing a natural conclusion to his nightmarish limbo.

"With immediate effect, we are serving you with an honourable discharge. In light of your efforts and your brothers passing, I along with the rest of the Army would like to officially express our gratitude and…" he trailed off.

Tom dazedly looked to his left and stared through an open window at the world outside. He strained against the muscles in his neck, knowing what would inevitably come next. The light shone bright through the window almost blinding him. However, no amount of light emitted through that window could ever shroud the solitary figure that now stood beside the window.

Tom knew he was not really there and that if he had disclosed the apparition to the Army Psychiatrist that he had been offered upon his discharge, they would have corroborated this. No, Tom had not told a soul about what haunted him every night. For there, standing to the right of the window, stood Anthony. His body was ablaze, his skin blackened, cracking and spitting as the fire consumed him further. His face was still partially untouched, his eyes burning with the intensity that they had often done so for much of his life. He locked eyes with Tom and for the briefest of seconds Tom thought he detected the briefest of cheeky grins, the type he gave Tom when they were young boys, just before Anthony would declare a plan or some new adventure to be ventured upon.

This, however, was one adventure that Tom could not follow him on, all be it for his parents, it was one he had contemplated many a time. The intensity of the light came to a crescendo but not before Anthony rose his hand to salute his brother, uttering one single phrase, one reminiscent of their childhood.

'Hawker'.

(CHAPTER BREAK)

Gerry held Tom's good shoulder and slightly shook him, his hand drenched in perspiration. Tom's eyes shot open and rolled upwards towards Gerry. His body jerked violently and for the first time Tom recognised that Gerry's hand was clasped over his mouth. He was breathing heavily through his nose.

"Easy, easy, it's ok lad, it's just me, Gerry," he cooed.

He removed his hand and Tom shot bolt upright, sucking in air. Gerry stared back at Tom, before he reached back towards the seat he had been sitting on whilst he waited for Tom to come to. He held a hip flask up to Tom's lips and tilted his head back.

"Have some of this," he stated as he tipped the flask further.

Tom began to gulp down the potent liquid and Gerry withdrew it quickly.

"Easy there, we don't want to impair those senses too much. You were just having a nightmare."

Tom's breathing began to slow; the heaving in his chest alleviated. He swung his legs free of the workbench and rose unsteadily to his feet.

"How long was I out?" Tom probed, his throat warmed and slightly parched by the whisky he had just swallowed.

"Only about ten minutes or so, not long. You passed out when I started closing the wound up. Found some whisky in the draw there, thank God for the underpaid and overworked masses hey? I disinfected the wound as best I could then put a fresh gauze and bandage on it. I'm no surgeon but that should keep you going for a while."

All the while he whispered which brought Tom back to the reality of the situation. Tom rotated his injured arm. It felt remarkably improved.

Tom's blurred vision began to clear slightly and he observed for the first time that Gerry had also rolled up his sleeve and had administered a bandage to his injured arm also. He caught Tom's gaze.

"Not a bad little first aid kit they had on standby for me to turn my hand to. Now, bragging rights aside, we have a bigger problem."

Tom looked towards the door and was alarmed to see that Gerry had dragged a heavy filing cabinet in front of it. Gerry followed his gaze and maintained it also, he spoke, all the while keeping his back to Tom, he had the Sig Sauer grasped in his hand.

"About five minutes ago, not long after you passed out, I heard gunfire, from the direction we came in. I barricaded the door and then came back to you. You were making too much noise, so I held you down and covered your mouth."

Tom instinctively unsheathed the knife that had been returned to the scabbard located on the tactical vest behind him. Gerry heard this and turned.

"How much good that will do I don't know," he sardonically murmured.

"Well, we need to defend ourselves," Tom stated unconvincingly, the fear clearly resonant.

"That's not the point Tom," he gripped Tom's shoulder.

Tom gazed at his hand nervously, then back to Gerry.

"Tom… when the shots came," he paused again.

Tom looked deeply into his eyes, a look that urged Gerry to continue. Gerry sighed and continued begrudgingly.

"There was three shots Tom. They came in roughly two second intervals. They sounded grouped, organised. It sounded like an execution."

Tom fell against the desk slightly and steadied himself, evaluating what he already knew to be true.

"I… they were supposed to…" he could not find the words.

"I'm sorry Tom. I really am. You did the best you could under the circumstances," he made to grab Tom's arm but he batted it away.

Gerry knew all too well what he was feeling, he had been there himself many a time both in an operational capacity and within everyday scenarios. Futility, death and loss were all too familiar to those in the Armed Forces, an unwelcome bedfellow. He had not allowed himself to linger too long on the thought of his own team as they lay slaughtered below his very feet.

Tom's bladed hand was shaking, Gerry eyed it with caution. He took a step back, not out of fear but to give Tom the space he needed.

"We should have stayed. I should have stayed. They didn't stand a chance. I could have done something," he raised his free hand to his head, a shaking set of fingers probing at his forehead.

Gerry knew he shouldn't but it was a formality in these situations. He had never been great with dealing with other people's emotions but he thought he needed to attempt one last roll of the consolation die.

"I know Tom but you did all you could. They wouldn't have gotten as far as they did if it hadn't been for you. You can't-" Gerry was cut off abruptly by Tom, his voice now too loud. Gerry ushered him to calm down, to lower his voice.

"That's just it though isn't it! You, me, we're always too late. Everybody always is. Too late to stop the problem before it begins. Too slow to offer help, we're always on the back foot."

Tom thrust the knife in the direction of the door.

"We were out there in Sierra Leone and it's the same back here as it was out there. I'm fucking sick of it. I'm sick of all the death, the personal sacrifice and I'm sick of bastards profiteering off of innocents."

"Tom, you need to calm down. Lower your voice," Gerry pleaded, his monotone state beginning to crack. Tom rounded and brought the knife down hard upon the workbench, before pulling it free again, pacing on the spot.

"Let them come, I'm done with all this waiting. I've fucking had it with being on the losing side," he made to budge past Gerry but he proved immovable.

Tom made an effort to free himself from Gerry's grasp but he pulled him back forcefully. Tom writhed in his grasp.

"Tom," he held him firm, "Tom, that's just the thing, we're not on the back foot here."

"Tell that to Michelle and…"

Gerry brought a heavy open palm across his face. It rattled Tom's jaw and he staggered slightly. He looked back at Gerry in a look of pained anguish and confusion.

"Stop trying to get yourself killed and listen to me for a fucking minute," Gerry hissed. "I hear you mate; I really do. I'm just as pissed off as you are. Don't forget my team are down there too; not just my team but my friends and you can be as sure as hell that no matter what happens, I'm not going in there half-cocked. I'm taking as many of those terrorist cardboard cut-outs with me as possible or I'm going to die trying."

"Now I do have a plan and if we both play our part, we may just be the only chance those people down there have. Now as hard as this is going to be for to hear mate, you need to hear it," he looked at Tom demanding his co-operation.

Tom nodded. Gerry gradually released Tom and helped him to lower his knife.

"As I mentioned earlier, those people you helped, they may have just returned the favour. Now with a bit of luck and I use that word in the loosest sense of the term, they may just have served as cover."

Tom made to protest but Gerry pressed on.

"Just listen. Now as I said, with a bit of luck they've heaped the blame on them for the death of some of those men they lost. It's a long shot but with the make-up of the group and all I've managed to gleam thus far, it points towards the fact that they're on a schedule, which means they may just be happy to take that as an explanation, they've got bigger fish to fry. It's a long shot sure but it may be one of the few advantages we have. Added to that they're going to be wasting time looking for me and if I were to be captured; any of your involvement would be heaped on me. They'd have no need to look for anyone else."

Gerry's callous discourse turned Tom's stomach briefly but had the desired effect. He calmed somewhat.

"You said you had a plan?" Tom impatiently interjected.

Gerry sensed Tom's persistent need to detract away from the deaths of the three unfortunate souls that most likely lay slaughtered within the sporting goods store.

"Yes Tom. Yes, I did," he returned.

CHAPTER FOURTEEN: BACK FOOT JUSTICE

The plan, in its most simplistic form, was a straightforward one. What made it risky were all the variables that could go wrong. As Gerry had surmised all be it rather callously, if Michelle and the others had in fact already been discovered, it could prove to be rather fortuitous as far as Tom was concerned. They may proportion the death of Bravo Team with that of the ragtag group, shifting their attention to Gerry instead. It was unlikely of course; a teenager, a middle-aged woman and an OAP overpowering and murdering three highly trained insurgents.

Tom had of course been disgusted with this reasoning but could not help but recognize the twinge of realism in Gerry's reasoning. Any advantage, albeit at the suffering of another, was a possible step towards Tom getting out of the centre alive. That aside, Tom was impressed with the remainder of Gerry's plan and if it were to succeed, it would allow Tom to offer support in an offensive capacity as opposed to that of a defensive one.

In their brief time together, Gerry had impressed Tom and whether he liked to admit it or not, had reignited a miniscule spark of hope within him. Gerry, Tom considered, had to have had a photographic memory as he barely needed the schematic spread out before them. Access points, air ducts, crawl spaces, locations of strategically important interest, he knew them all and that had all been before he had taken his belt off. When he flipped it over there had been a small incision within the leather, barely noticeable to the human eye. Tom observed that he pulled out of it two items: a map and a folded photograph, of what he could not be certain.

The plan would heavily rely upon the two working together in close proximity as they would have no way of communication. As Gerry had noted earlier, *"Even if we did get another radio, the line would not be secure and if they do have an EMP, we could be hit by it at any time."*

The map was spread out on the workbench that had served as Tom's operating theatre earlier. It was kept open by the knife, Tom having since lowered it and a pencil pot tactfully positioned in the upper left-hand corner. Gerry turned to Tom and clapped his hands together in a ready or not fashion.

"Right, run the plans past me one more time so I know you're singing from the proverbial," Gerry insisted in a manner that took Tom back to the briefing rooms he had sat in whilst enlisted. Tom breathed in and verbalized the breakdown of events within his head.

"We go out through the door, propping it open with the mountaineering tool that's currently wedging the door shut. We make our way to the sports shop, you'll cover me. I'll keep to the edges to avoid the line of sight of the cameras. If the store is open and the shutters aren't down, we grab some climbing gear. We then re-enter through the door, wedging it shut again with the mountaineering tool. We make our way up to the roof, where you'll kit up with me on rope duty..." he paused and creased his forehead in thought.

Gerry patiently waited an expectant look upon his face. After a moment or so Tom continued.

"I'll lower you to the construction site, which due to renovations should afford you easy access. When all is clear, you'll sway the rope from side to side which is my greenlight to follow you down. Once inside, we will both approach the comm's room, located to the left of the construction site. We then breach the room, which you have stated is not electronically locked, hoping the door is unlocked, forcing it if necessary. We then overpower anyone inside before raising the shutters and destroying the controls completely," Tom inhaled deeply after his tangent, Gerry nodding his approval.

"Good. And if we exit this space and encounter any hostiles?" he deliberately paused waiting for Tom to finish his sentence.

"If possible, we'll silently incapacitate them. If not, you either drop them with the gun or if possible, we retreat back up the stairs silently," Tom replied nonplussed, following up with a look that stated, *'Are you happy now?'*

Gerry was and set about folding his map up into eighths again. There was however, still one thing that Tom was unsure of and it had been nagging him. He knew that Gerry was both far too well trained and wily for him to overlook such a detail.

"What about snipers? The Police or the Army are bound to have them set up on every adjacent building by now. I don't know about you but I don't fancy getting my head blown off whilst dangling at the end of a rope."

Gerry carefully replaced his map into the slit of his belt and tapped Tom on the arm rather smugly.

"I'm counting on it lad."

Tom afforded himself a smile, "And why's that Gerry?" he asked, growing more and more impressed by the man.

Gerry turned round and pulled a toilet roll out from under the workbench holding it aloft proudly; a wry smile followed.

"Is that to mop my brains up with afterwards?" Tom queried, half serious.

"Not gonna come to that," he stated as he unfurled a piece of the paper.

Now it was Tom's turn to smile.

"You bloody genius," he smirked.

"Well, it has been known. Had to keep myself occupied while you were doing the hippie hippy shake on the tabletop earlier," he quipped, all the while maintaining a humble composure.

Scrawled on the toilet roll was the start of a message, scrawled in thick black marker. Parts of the paper were smudged with bloody fingerprints.

"Now someone up there must love us as its triple-ply, so it's pretty durable, I've even saved some to wipe Pierce's shitty arse with after this is all done. You'll hold one end and we'll carefully roll it out. The message isn't long but it'll be windy up there, so keep it taut," Gerry reverted back to his natural role as leader.

"What if it blows away?" Tom asked in earnest.

"Well then, we have this," he reached into his pocket and to Tom's utter shock and annoyance; he noted Gerry was holding his phone.

"You really were busy when I was out weren't you," he countered rather sternly, hand outstretched for the phone. Gerry pulled it back slowly.

"Had to be sure you weren't having me on. I searched you, knew you were on the up and up, didn't doubt you for a second. All that said though Tom, I'm going to need this for the moment and your pin of course," he plainly stated, reinforcing his point with an uncompromising look that invited no further discussion.

Tom sighed and nodded.

"So, what are you going to do with a dead phone exactly? You said it yourself, all electronic devices that were on during the EMP were…" he answered his own question mid-sentence. "Unless the phone was switched off, when the device was used." He smiled remembering that he had turned the phone off before the attack, as it had been low on battery.

"I checked your battery. It was on twelve percent, took another one percent once fully power up. It's off now, to conserve battery. That all being said and done we should have enough to make a call or two; one of which needs to be to my people. I'm guessing that if there are snipers, they'll be in direct contact."

"It's not like we'll have any trouble getting a signal that high up," Tom replied straight-faced.

Gerry smirked, grimacing slightly at the pain in his jaw. He placed the phone back in his pocket and patted it.

"Right, once more into the breach," Gerry stated.

He once again methodically discharged the magazine from the Sig Sauer and inspected it. Satisfied, he drove the magazine back into its housing and readied the sidearm.

"I guess so," Tom acknowledged, standing upright and ready.

Every nerve in his body vibrated with morbid anticipation. He ran the plan over in his head once again. There really were a variety of variables that could go wrong; he just hoped that none of them resulted in the loss of any more life; his or theirs.

(CHAPTER BREAK)

Brian had heard the call come down the wire several seconds before he had glanced up to see the Live TV report, muted, above the rows of emergency personnel sat at their desks. The reporter stood in front of a police cordon, a substantial distance from the shopping centre. The ticker at the bottom, festooned with the words 'BREAKING NEWS', bore the headline, *'Prime Minister taken hostage at gunpoint, numerous hostages presumed dead."* It had started at first with an excited wave of murmuring between staff members who flanked him on either side.

Suddenly, the various scattering of people diverted their attention back towards Brian. He had at the time thought that they were skiving, checking that their supervisor was not looking. That thought soon dissipated when their eyes held his gaze. That was around the time that the boxed message appeared upon his screen. A series of codes and numbers, pure gibberish to the naked, untrained eye but to Brian, who along with his team, had attended the anti-terrorism awareness and response course, meant one thing, the address confirming the location.

He had of course, immediately phoned Tom's mobile via the landline before him, his own phone in his locker as was policy. He was violating procedural policy by using the landline for a personal call but these were extenuating circumstances, they could bill him for all he cared, not that the thought had even entered his conciseness at that particular instant.

Tom's mobile provider alerted him that *"The customer you are trying to reach is unavailable."* He glanced at the picture of his two sons upon his desk and he nervously bit down on his lower lip, smoothing his hair back before grabbing it in tufts of frustration.

"Please God, not again. Please don't let me lose another one," were the only words he could muster.

He swivelled quickly around in his chair. One of his team quickly approached but Brian ushered him to wait with his hand. He knew what his team member wanted to know, however at this particular junction he had himself given it little thought. He had always been punctual with issuing instructions, quick to act but this involved his family, this was unknown territory. He waited for his wife to pick up the phone, slowing his breathing; he did not want to come across as too urgent, panicking his wife further. The phone was retrieved from its dock, Brian beating Pam's inquiry as to who was phoning.

"Pam it's me. Is Tom home? Have you heard from him," Brian reeled off, automatically cursing himself; he could tell by his wife's dramatic pause that he had scared her.

"Brian what's happening? Is Tom ok?" her voice was erratic.

She had every right to expect the worst; after all, she had had it delivered to her once before. Brian wiped his face and pulled the phone away from him slightly, he was shaking now, a glacial sweat spreading across his back. Brian steadied himself and cleared his throat. He knew of no better way to say it and thought it best not to keep his wife waiting any longer.

"Pam you better turn on the news," he prompted, his voice solemn.

Brian heard a stifled groan of angst and the scrabbling of what sounded like his wife looking for the remote control to their television. This was followed by muffled audio in the background, the changing of a channel and then a dull thud. Brian swallowed hard and listened intently. No answer came.

"Pam? Pam are you still there? Love I need you to pick up the-" he was cut off by the sound of disjointed speech.

Brian now felt tears sting his own eyes; his colleague beginning to pick up on Brian's aura, retreated. Brian waited for the next question, the answer to which, he would once again be unable to answer. Pam's stuttering gave way to basic articulation.

"Is… is Tom ok? Is he…" she halted as she thought better than to conclude the sentence with so morbid a possibility, "Is he still in there Brian?"

Brian glanced up at the bank of televisions. He scanned the screens, taking it all in. He continued, not knowing what to say; only that something needed to be said, to fill the silence.

"I don't know Pam. I just saw it on the news. I tried to phone him but got no answer. That's why I phoned you. We've been put on alert here, to be on standby," he stopped at this final word, lingering on it. Evil, inconceivable thoughts began to creep into his conscience.

"Be on standby for what Brian? What do you need to be on standby for?" Pam was modulating her thoughts via questions she already knew the answers to.

Brian knew that all she needed were some reassuring words but he had none. A single tear rolled down his cheek. He breathed in deep wanting only to be with his wife.

"I need to stay Pam in case of..." he could not finish. "You need to ring your Sister and get her over now Pam. Phone her right away and then leave the line open in case me or Tom phone again."

"You need to come home now Brian," Pam pleaded, stern in her tone.

The statement made what Brian had to say all the more difficult.

"I'm needed here love. If Tom is in trouble or others are, I need to be able to direct the team. As soon as I can, I'll leave I promise," he left the statement hanging, awaiting a response.

He knew where he was really needed was at home. His stomach fluctuated between a knot of nerves to that of self-repulsion at the callous nature of what he had just said.

"You listen to me Brian Hawkins. You do what you need to do but if Tom gets through to you or you to him, you tell him to hide, to run if possible, just get out of there. Do you hear me Brian? He isn't in the Army anymore. It was the Army that took..." she broke down, any rigidity in her command now betraying her.

"I will love. I love you so much; now phone your sister, I'll be in touch as soon as I know anything. Keep the faith Pam; he's a strong and resourceful lad. Best case scenario is he left beforehand and got waylaid".

Another hollow statement. Several more seconds of tears and the sucking in of breath travelled down the phone line before it went dead. Brian put down the phone and slumped lower in his chair.

Brian's colleague, Terry Paisley, looked from the picture of Tom and Anthony then back to his supervisor. He knew all too well what had happened to Anthony, he had worked under Brian for just over five years know, he himself having a son currently serving in the Navy. He placed his hand on Brian's shoulder; the nerves seemingly penetrating through Brian's body into his hand. Brian looked up and gave him a look that depicted pure desperation and fear.

"Brian you don't need to be here. The details are still sketchy. I'm sure the Police or the government have a plan in place. I'm sure Tom is..." his comforting words faltered. Brian straightened.

"Whatever has happened, I need to be here" he stated with a strengthened resolve as he stood.

He wiped the tears from his eyes and straightened.

"Right listen up, here's what we're going to do."

(CHAPTER BREAK)

Tom's hand gripped the mountaineering tool; Gerry had decided at the last minute not to use it as a wedge between the door and the foot of the staircase as he felt it was not sturdy enough. He had instead ventured back up the stairs and had returned with a fire extinguisher which he used to prop the door open. All being well, the mountaineering tool would be used to breach the door to Control, leaving Gerry to take out anyone inside. Tom was glad to once again be reunited with the implement.

Tom's other hand touched the cold marble to his left, he traced his hand along the wall as both a reminder to keep as close to it as possible, avoiding the arc of the camera, as well as a means to steady himself. His heart had skipped a beat when he and Gerry had peered out of the Staff exit seeing that the coast was clear, the sporting stores front still open. He ran through the shopping list in his head: rope, two harnesses, two carabineers and a set of repelling gloves if possible, to assist against rope burn.

Tom knew all of the equipment intimately having experienced repelling in his basic training as well as from a mountaineering activity day he and his friends had taken part in when in New Zealand. What they were going to attempt was quite simple. There would most likely be a cavalcade of other repelling gear within the shop but as Gerry had stated, he wanted to, 'keep it simple and functional'.

Tom loved to repel. He knew of and had even learnt how to set up the technique of descent that Gerry had suggested. It was a quick method and would allow them to hastily set up their descent whilst relying on minimal moving parts.

Gerry pressed his back to the left of the store front and indicated for Tom to do the same. Tom did as he was told, keeping the mountaineering tool held high. As of yet, there had been no sign of any of the insurgents and eerily, no sound from below. Gerry rounded the corner of the store front and scanned the outlet. He held his hand up and indicated for Tom to wait. He entered the store, the Sig Sauer at torso height. Tom's whole body was taut with fear and as he unhelpfully kept reminding himself, this was the easier part of the plan. To make matters worse, the thought of his brother's burning carcass kept stabbing at the fringes of his mind. He kept clamping his eyes shut, swallowing hard as if he could digest the vision that was seared across his corneas.

After around thirty seconds Gerry reappeared, he looked ashen faced. He lowered his gun slightly and whispered to Tom never taking his eyes off of the surrounding area.

Gerry sighed, "It's all clear mate but ... it's pretty grim in there, I'm sorry. I understand if you want to take the gun and cover me while I go back in and get the stuff."

Tom swallowed hard and with a shaking of his head, pushed past Gerry. He had seen more than enough death in his lifetime and held no macabre penchant to see anymore but his foolish pride spurned him on. He needed, no wanted, to see this. He had to verify to himself that it had been those three innocent souls that he had both been rescued by and had in turn aided. He fixed his eyes on the back of the store and the display of mountaineering gear, all conveniently grouped.

He walked to the back and grabbed what he needed. It was thankfully all there, he even took a bag to put it all in, grabbing two spare head mounted torches as well as a hand-held torch. He took a deep intake of air, swung the bag over his shoulder and turned around. He no longer focused upon a singular point and it dawned upon him that what had seemed like an obscure black mass upon Tom's entry, now revealed itself to be a sprawled set of legs and the unmistakable arm of a woman, petite hand and painted nails at the end.

Gerry was ahead, still inside the doorway using it as cover, never looking back.

Tom moved in the direction of the mound. He kept looking forward right up until he drew level with the lifeless mass. He reluctantly shot a cursory glance and instantly snapped it back again. He began to salivate heavily as a full wave of nausea crept up his throat, craving to be out as if he had ingested sea water. He steadied himself against a shelf. The bodies were piled on top of one another. The old man lay at the base of the pile, only his white hair visible under the teenager who had been stacked above.

Michelle lay at the top of the lifeless totem-pole-like structure, her hair flung back, largely covering much of the teenager's torso. Her head was concaved and bloodied. Brain matter hung free from various sections. Her one remaining eye still encapsulated the fear she must have felt, a tear still gathering at the bottom. Tom reached out bringing across two all-weather jackets, draping them over the bodies.

The pool of blood that had gathered towards the centre of the pile welcomed the jacket, another substance to stain with its unwelcome crimson plight.

"I'm sorry I couldn't get you out of here," Tom rasped, choked up.

With that he bowed his head and briskly walked towards the store front, stifling another urge to heave before tapping Gerry upon his shoulder. No words were needed, Gerry knew he wanted to proceed and be free of the place.

They once again stuck close to the wall and made their way to the Staff exit, Gerry covering the rear. They entered the staircase and Gerry pressed the door shut lightly. When he turned, he was met with Tom sat on the stairs, head between his knees in the weak light. Gerry squeezed past him and gave him a pat on the shoulder.

"We need to getting going partner," Gerry grudgingly interjected.

Tom straightened reluctantly and made to follow Gerry up the stairs, once again using the stairwell bannister, although this time for support as opposed to guidance. It was at this stage that Tom realised he was still holding the mountaineering pick.

"Gerry are you sure we shouldn't wedge the door shut again" Tom whispered.

"We stick to the plan, no last-minute changes, no matter how small. You're going to need that to breach Control's door. Plus, I heard the electronic lock when I closed the door. That confirms it; they've got the system locked down electronically. Only way someone is coming through that door is via someone in Control unlocking it, which if the plan doesn't proceed as planned, we won't need to worry about…" he deliberately let the sentence hang wanting bringing Tom back to the severity of the task at hand.

"Because we'll be dead," Tom said dejectedly.

They reached the caretaker's room and pushed through. Tom placed the bag of mountaineering supplies on the workbench and set about removing the contents. What followed was a methodical series of non-verbal commands whereby both men assembled the equipment. Both men placed their harnesses around their hips and buckled them tightly. Next came the head mounted lights. They both tested them almost in sync, quickly switching them off to conserve battery. They unscrewed their respective carabineer, fed it through a loop in their harness and screwed the clips shut. They would set up the ropes when on the roof. Gerry handed Tom the knife.

"If I get into any trouble, you might need to cut me free," he stated nonchalantly, giving little consideration to the ramifications that such a scenario would create. Tom took it and placed it within the scabbard on his tactical vest, buttoning it closed.

"It's now or never. Keep the head mounted lights off until we start repelling. If we do have some trigger-happy snipers out there, we don't want to give them a clear indication of where our heads are at," Gerry stressed, frivolity now in short supply.

Tom nodded and adjusted his harness slightly; it was cutting tightly into his groin. As far as he was concerned when hanging from a rooftop, tight was good, even better was not getting your head blown off. They both turned around to leave. Gerry paused at the door; hand poised an inch above the handle. Gerry nodded to Tom, flicked the torch in his hand off and with that opened the door, slipping out into the great unknown.

(CHAPTER BREAK)

"One OAP, a woman and a pre-pubescent runt threw Frazier off of the third floor. Is that what you're telling me?" Thompson spat.

"I sent you to find and take out the Prime Minister's bodyguard, the one you let break your nose and get away. Remember him? I did not send you to eliminate the three stooges of the bloody life cycle. You know, I was wrong Jones, you must have some almighty balls on you to come back down here and spin me a bullshit yarn like that," Thompson growled.

Jones knew that he had been deliberately sent to reconcile his earlier misdemeanour at having let the Prime Minister's guard escape and he had failed. All he could do was look awkwardly at his feet.

A short and scrawny man, he had often been overlooked in many aspects of life: sports selection, women, and respect from his peers; at least that is what he blamed his unpopularity upon. Truth be told, a fact his alcoholic mother had often heaped upon him, it was because of his shortcomings in character over that of his height and physical attributes. She had always belittled him, a failed single mother seeking great pleasure in belittling her son at any given opportunity, her plaything to keep her occupied when the bottle was empty.

He was one of the only men on the team that had not actually served within a military organisation. He had instead learnt much of his trade, that being arson, explosive ordnance and disposal, via a far right-wing militia group with affiliations to various terrorist factions and militia groups across Britain. The group, the Albion Templar Movement or ATM, attracted and coerced Jones quickly. He had always been suggestible and was highly delusional; his need for gratification and validation far outweighed the morals and initiatives of the organisation, that being to render Britain an immigrant- free zone via the re-establishment of the British Empire.

At first Jones had paid the order lip service but he soon found himself immersed in the party's ideologies, staging bombings on high value locations and targets, attending marches and parades, inciting hate wherever possible. However, once he had learnt all he could from his handlers, when he had been headhunted by Thompson; a truer sign of validation had never been bestowed upon him before, he decided to be rid of the order, an option only afforded to those who left via natural causes or execution at having been disloyal or breaking one's oath to the movement. A staged gas explosion at the local gathering of the party's forty-seven members had seen to that.

All of the members were wiped out in one foul swoop, much of the group's paraphernalia destroyed along with the blast. Many of the bodies were deemed unidentifiable by the Police and when they did discover it was a far-right fascist group sifting through the evidence, they quickly dismissed it as a gas leak. In doing so they avoided the embarrassment of having had little to no evidence on the hate group's existence.

Quite amazingly what helped corroborate the Police's story all the more so was that there had been a similar gas explosion less than three miles from the site of the blast; on a local housing estate at the home of an elderly woman. An alcoholic by all accounts or so her neighbours stated when interviewed out on the street, their houses deemed unsafe in case of a further leak; a heavy smoker also they had pointed out.

When the blaze was finally put out and the Fire Department could finally enter to conduct their investigation, the cause of Gail Jones death was deemed an obvious one. A cigarette butt, a smouldering couch, a discarded bottle of whiskey and a gas cooker left on.

It had been case shut and closed as far as the Fire Marshal had been concerned. As he had told one of the Policer Officers on duty at the time, "We see this sort of stuff all the time; so much so it's like the beginning of a bad joke to me and the lads now. A destitute chain-smoker decides to switch on the hob and fry themselves up a quick snack. They leave the gas on, the hob unattended and think hey, why not go for a crafty fag. "

"And you know what; while I'm at it I've only had three-quarters of that bottle of whiskey, be a shame to let that go to waste as well. Victim drifts off, cigarette lit in one hand and boom. Good night Vienna. Jesus, from what the neighbours said I'm surprised she needed the gas as a catalyst, enough empties in there to plug up a landfill. Doubt they'll need to even embalm her at the funeral home".

There had not been much left to bury and little money to bury her with, a blessing considering the pauper's bank account she had left behind along with her only surviving relative, an estranged son.

Jones's lack of a service record had taken the team by surprise when Thompson had hired him. He had tasked Frazier with training Jones in the use of firearms and hand-to-hand combat. Frazier was displeased with the menial task but did not protest, Thompson was too volatile for that. That said, behind Thompson's back he made it all too apparent to Jones what an inconvenience he was to him and the rest of the team.

'Story of my life,' Jones had thought at the time.

Nevertheless, he vowed not to wallow in his inability to connect with the team on either a social or personal level. Instead, he had decided to give Frazier a taste of his own medicine, ostracising him instead. He had rigged up Frazier's bed while he slept. When he awoke, he did so to a pair of pliers in his hand and a sign stuck to his head which read, *'Move and you die.'*

He lay motionless while Jones lay in the bunk opposite him, his features awash with contemptuous glee. As he took great pleasure in telling Frazier at the time, he was the only one capable of setting up such a creative myriad of trip wires and ordnance and as of yet, he was currently one of only a handful of men in the world that could disarm it.

Upon hearing this, soaked with sweat and trembling, Frazier let fly a variety of verbal demands. From threat maker to apologist. However, Jones held firm, stating that if he wished to reverse roles that he instead wanted to play the role of the teacher, Frazier his unfortunate muse. As Jones had stated conclusively to a blathering Frazier, he would teach Frazier a lesson he would never forget or one that he would die in the process of learning.

What took place was forty-five minutes of soul shredding fear as, using the cable cutters in his palm; Jones talked Frazier through disarming the wires one by one. Upon the last wire being cut, Frazier had leapt out of bed and had beaten Jones within an inch of his life; yet another non-verbal form of communication his mother had rendered him accustomed to.

The severe beating had been worth it however for two crucial reasons. One, he had had an audience. The rest of the team except for Thompson had watched the whole thing. The team had found it hilarious and after the event he had earned himself notoriety and respect amongst the men.

Secondly, an air of uneasiness at crossing Jones in the future was now firmly established, especially from Frazier. Unbeknownst to Frazier there had actually been no explosives under his bed. It had all been a bluff. However, the man that now stood before him knew nothing of the meaning behind an empty threat. Like orders, he carried out all threats with extreme prejudice.

"They were all we could find up there sir. It must have been them; the bodyguard was dinged up. We'll find him I promise, his hands are bound, he couldn't have taken out Bravo team, or what was left of them after Dreyfus went black, anyway," Jones spluttered all the while trying to maintain a tone of respect for his superior made all the more difficult by his broken nose. At the end of each sentence, it resembled a poorly played recorder.

"I swept the other floors Jones. There was no one, which leaves me with a certain quandary. Did you screw up or did I?" Thompson took a step closer to Jones. "Are you saying that I didn't do my job right? Is that it because that would be a mighty big accusation to band about?"

Jones was fixed to the spot staring at his boots, cautious of how to proceed. Thompson expediated his response with the end of his Remington pump action shotgun or as he lovingly referred to it as, 'Remy'. They both locked eyes, Thompson's intense stare demanding a response to his question, the barrel burrowed into the crook of his neck. He shook his head and Jones dumbly followed suit. Not finished, Thompson rose the barrel of the gun higher, lifting Jones chin to a level that required him to peer down upon his superior.

"I didn't think so. Now as I've always said, if you want a job done right, you need the right tool. Shaw, here now," he barked clicking the fingers on his spare hand.

Jones heard a heavy footfall from behind, the unmistakable girth and muscular stature of Shaw stepping into his eye line. The long, cold barrel never left his chin. Shaw eyed Jones up and down with a level disdain that he reserved only for men of Jones' stature. He was a fitness freak, a poster boy for weightlifting, a pure specimen if ever there were one for the definition of a powerhouse. After all, his burly prowess had permitted him earlier to crush a man's skull through a reinforced plasterboard wall like it were a grape.

Every item of clothing fought to contain his physique, so much so that a ricocheting button would have been of no surprise to Jones. His shaved head gave way to an even more impressive beard, bushy and unkempt. His nickname amongst the team was 'Valhalla', a bringer of death to many a man, expediting their journey to the afterlife. All his six-foot five physique needed was an axe to wield and the namesake would be complete. He looked down at Jones, arms behind his back, clothing straining at the seams.

"Yes sir," Shaw stated with a military air that came a close second to the discipline and pride he afforded his own physique. He was Thompson's right-hand man and he revelled the additional stature it afforded him.

"I want you to take the rest of the charges and set them up on the roof, sweeping the third level before you do so. If they are planning an attack, the roof is going to be their best option. I'm guessing that's where our man is headed also, up," he eyes briefly scanned the hostages, he lowered his voice accordingly.

"And take a hostage with you. A child ideally," Thompson ordered returning his attention back to Jones, Remy still prodding into his skeletal chin. Shaw now broke his gaze with Jones and looked at Thompson in a baffled manner. Thompson saw this via his peripheral vision, alert as ever.

"Tie the child to your back," he stated plainly, "making sure that he covers your upper body and head if possible. That way, if our friends out there do have any snipers, they're not going to risk shooting you with a high calibre bullet for fear of a round passing through."

This registered a massive smile from Shaw. He looked up to his superior's genius, he the brawn to Thompson's unrivalled intellect.

"Yes sir," Shaw beamed.

"You are dismissed, keep in radio contact and wear a mask," Thompson stated, never leaving Jones' gaze.

Shaw grunted his understanding before bounding over to the group of hostages, once again it was the child in the Thomas the Tank Engine pyjamas that attracted his gaze. He hefted the child from the crowd; his mother once again hanging onto him, screaming. A swift and echoing backhand from Shaw put an end to that, the mother knocked out cold. The force with which he lifted the child nearly dislocated the child's shoulder before he smothered him in the arched crook of his bulging arm. The child's eyes darted around in confusion; no more tears left to be shed. The bound hands of hostages made to grab at the child. A futile effort.

Thompson traced the barrel across Jones' cheekbones and up along the bridge of his nose. Satisfied and with a bloodcurdling smile, Thompson lowered the shotgun.

"Remove the notion from that empty vessel you call a skull, that you're not expendable because we've lost men. You are expendable, as we all are to the main objective at hand. You've been demoted to hostage watch; Palmer will take over Alpha team. You ever try to undermine me like that again in front of my men Jones and I'm going to introduce Remy to your colon," he stated calmly before turning back to the crowd of hostages, their sobs once again serving as an aphrodisiac to Thompson.

(CHAPTER BREAK)

When they reached the roof's access door, it worked on a push bar action, just as Gerry had stated. They pushed, Gerry once again sweeping the roof with the Sig Sauer. They were instantly pushed back slightly by the wind that whistled through the cracked door. To make matters worse it was raining, only lightly at this stage but enough to cause issues. Tom couldn't believe his eyes; he even double checked his watch. It was three- fifty and almost pitch black, the cold winter's night had closed in fast. He had felt as if he had been in the building for longer than he actually had been but he was amazed by the day's transition.

"Shit, that's going to make our little venture that bit more of an ordeal," he shouted over the wind.

Gerry shut the door again, largely assisted by the wind. He made to wipe the rain from his cheeks and grimaced at having touched the grazes and bumps that lined the contours of his face.

"You weren't expecting to be cut any breaks, were you? There goes any chance of you using your toilet roll trick," Tom blatantly declared, starting to unfurl the rope from the bag.

"We proceed as planned, if they see the message, good. If not, they'll probably think it's us trying to wave a white flag. The weather's picking up though, so visibility is going to be poor, which may help slightly with regards to any snipers positioned out there," Gerry stated with hopeful purpose.

"We'll have to take all that we can get," Tom countered.

"Right, we'll wait until we get out there to tie the rope. There's a solid pipe to the right of the door or an air duct closer to the edge of the building. I vote for the pipe."

Tom nodded in agreement.

"No chance the rope will get us to the bottom?" Tom chanced, registering a smile from Gerry.

"If only mate, Rapunzel I am not," he stated tapping his smooth head.

"Right, we tie the rope, we bring it down through the carabineer, then pull slack and wrap under the carbineer, bringing it back through the clip, tightening the clip after. Make sure you test the rope and maintain that it goes in the direction that we're going down. If it rolls back up, redo it. You got that?"

Tom methodically nodded his understanding once again.

"Now, you said you've rappelled before but I'm going to hazard a guess and say you've never done so with a wounded shoulder. Lucky for you, you're right-handed so use your right hand as your break hand, behind you, left hand on the rope to guide you. Now I'm not trying to tell you how to suck eggs but if you let go of the rope it's going to slip out of your clip and unless you grab on, you're dead."

"Got you," Tom returned, loosening the rope ready to go.

"Oh and one more thing," he pointed at the strap of his vest, "I'd feel a whole lot better if your stowed them in that zip-up pouch on the front of your tactical vest there."

Tom looked down and remembered that he was carrying the set of grenades. He nodded and carefully removed them from the shoulder strap, tentatively placing them within the pouch located just above the belly of the vest.

Gerry nodded his thanks, "Last thing we need is one of them getting caught on something and sending you sky high Well... higher than you already are"

They bundled through the door. Tom handed Gerry the rope and he took to tying it around the pipe. As Gerry busied himself setting up the rappel line, Tom stepped forwards, waving his hands, highlighting himself as unarmed and of no conceivable threat. Gerry tested the knot he had tied and walked backwards, feeding the rope towards the roof's ledge. He gave it another trying yank, satisfied, he threw it over the edge. He walked over and joined Tom. He produced the toilet roll from a plastic bag that was intended to keep it dry should it be raining.

"Always prepared," Tom muttered, his voice swallowed up by the wind.

Gerry handed the toilet roll to Tom and gripped the end of the paper. He said something to Tom but his voice was absorbed by the wind and rain.

They unfurled it, keeping it as taut as possible the wind already lashing at the paper. They held it there for several seconds before weakened with rain and the gust, the strip of toilet paper, along with their message, disintegrated in the middle and flapped listlessly in the squall. Gerry threw it to the ground, Tom following suit. Gerry came in close to Tom's ear and shouted, just audible over the wind.

"That's that, all we can do now," he blinked heavily against the rain.

Tom patted Gerry's shoulder indicating that he had heard him. Gerry made his way to the rope and began setting it up. He was methodical and quick, testing the line twice in quick succession. He walked to the edge, pulled on the rope once again ensuring it was taut and stood beside the ledge. He then peered down over the ledge before nodding in confirmation.

Both men put on their rappelling gloves. After kneading the material tightly into his hands, Tom kneeled by the rope and held it.

Gerry leant in once again, he jabbed his finger down.

"The scaffolding is around the window. There's plastic sheeting blowing in and out of the window, means it's not been filled in yet since I last checked it during my sweep of the premises yesterday. Aim for there, get inside."

Tom caught most of this in the wind, the odd word swallowed by the wailing onslaught of rain and gust. Once again all he could muster was a nod, his face stinging with the stabbing rain, the gust pushing against his injured shoulder. Gerry stepped off the edge and half leant out away from the building. He slightly swayed in the wind and steadied himself quickly.

One hand behind him, the other on the line he began to feed the rope out behind him; a slip of his guiding brake hand and he would not be able to halt the rope or its quick escape from his carbineer. He soon disappeared over the edge and Tom, steadying his feet against the edge of the roof's lip, leant back, keeping the rope as taut as possible. Tom could feel Gerry's jerking motions on the rope which came to a halt after a minute or so. The rope swayed slightly and grew slack. The temptation to sacrifice his stance and peer over the edge was almost unbearable.

That was until Gerry tugged heavily on the rope four times, before swaying it forcibly. It was now clear and ready for Tom to proceed. He began feeding the rope through his carabineer; his hands noticeably shaking now, not from the cold, not from the wind but once again from fear. He turned his back to the edge of the ledge and tested the rope.

Tom interlaced his fingers, squeezing the gloves deeper into his hands once again. He afforded himself a glance over at the adjacent buildings. The wind was blowing the rain in a sideways motion largely obscuring his view of those below. He saw the rain framed against the blue flash of the sirens below, the odd black shape the size of a car also evident. Tom diverted his gaze now to the London skyline. A crane off in the distance alerted low-flying aircraft to its position via a red light upon its arm. A series of skyscrapers etched the horizon, some windows illuminated with light, late workers unaware or seemingly uncaring as to what was currently happening to London and the current residents of West-Acre Point.

Tom looked over his city. How beautiful it looked, the stars separating the skyscrapers from the unknown veil above. Tom turned back, urging himself to hurry, not wanting to worry Gerry. He rotated his injured shoulder and leant back against the concrete ledge. He lowered himself and began slowly feeding the rope through his right hand, located behind him. His harness cut deeply into his groin, which registered a pained intake of air. Tom's biggest fear was not of letting go; it had instead been slipping on the glazed windows, now basted in rainwater. He would have to descend slowly, keeping his legs apart.

His arms burned under his own bodyweight, the blood finding its way quickly to the gash in his arm, seeking to be out of Tom's body like he wished to be free of the shopping centre. The wind whipped at the back of his neck. A loud bang rang out above. Tom seized up inside. He pushed thoughts of thunder and lightning from his mind, not wanting to consider being hit by lightning atop of a goliath-sized building. He afforded himself a look down between his legs. The scaffolding was around two metres away now. The urge to expedite the process eroded his mettle but he dispelled, not wanting to rush. His heart was beating heavily now, he longed to wipe the rain away from his eyes as it dripped down via his hairline, the smell of his hair gel filling his nostrils.

The rope suddenly swayed and Tom pulled down hard upon the rope held in his braking hand. He leant out pushing against the building to steady himself, his calves almost popping from his legs. He breathed a nervous sigh of relief at having not lost his footing and stood firm for several seconds. Content, Tom made to lower himself further when suddenly, the rope gave a heaving jerk and Tom found himself lifted ten inches or so higher.

He held firm, clasping ever tighter onto the rope. He looked up; his vision obscured every few seconds or so by drops of rain forcing him to shut his eyes. Before he could even open his eyes again, he was hefted further upwards.

Tom looked down, his heart in his throat. He was growing further and further away from the scaffolding quickly arriving at the horrific conclusion that he was being pulled back up. His mind was awash with what to do next. He had two options; one was to let go of the rope and attempt to grab at the scaffolding as he fell, an undesirable scenario with the current state of his shoulder and the sodden metallic bars.

Yet, the second option seemed less desirable; allowing himself to be dragged up the building's edge, left to confront whoever was reeling him in. Tom weighed up both options, panicking as the scaffolding grew further away. He deduced that there was more than one person above as he was pulled effortlessly up the glass structure.

"Gerry!" he screamed, his throat filling with wind, his words muffled and carried away.

He was now no more than two metres away from the rooftop. Tom pressed against the building with his legs and countered hard, trying to halt his upward momentum. His limbs were on fire now, his pectoral muscles felt like they were going to squeeze out of his body via his armpits. The rope tugged taut once again and he yielded no distance. Spurned on he leant harder against the rope. He made to adjust his right boot for a better footing when he slipped slightly. It was all he had in him not to fall as he came free of the building's foothold.

His braking hand slipped slightly behind him. He tried to use the momentum to rappel slightly further down the rope but when he looked down to his horror; he became aware of the distance between the end of the rope and the top of the scaffolding. He swung around giddily, his back hitting the triple glazed glass behind him sending an explosion of raindrops showering down upon him. Tom had lost all purchase, his first option to drop to the scaffolding now gone, ripped from him like that of his footing. He hung on, trying to turn his body to no avail, slipping on the smooth, wet glass.

Tom finally settled upon a course of action and removed his hand from the rope behind him. He dropped slightly but caught the rope with his spare hand, now gripping the rope two-handed. His weakened shoulder offered him little in the way of strength. He removed a hand from the rope and began to unclasp the button on the compartment of his knife. The rope dangled free below him hitting the back of his heels. He glanced up gauging the distance now left, weighing up whether he would have enough time to unsheathe his knife.

He saw a pair of gloved hands pulling at the rope; the forearms bulging under Tom's weight. One over the other, they hefted Tom further back the way he had come. His hand fumbled round the hilt of his knife, groping for any purchase. One metre away now. He had just begun to draw the knife from its housing when a hand closed over the forearm of his spare arm, the other grasping the back of his tactical vest.

The knife was instead withdrawn by the shadowy assailant before being cast aside. With a final heave and a dizzying flip, he was upturned, his head making contact with the concrete ledge behind him. His head exploded in a culmination of pain and nausea. The star laden sky came back into focus once again before a heavy-set figure eclipsed them, reaching down towards Tom's neck.

CHAPTER FIFTEEN: A MOONLIGHT TANGO FOR TWO

"Hold your fire! What do you mean there's movement on the roof, hostiles or friendlies?" Miller interrogated the Commander of the SC&O19, the Metropolitan Police Services elite firearms unit.

The OCU Commander for the SC&O19 was currently relaying information back to Richard Miller who was at present, uncharacteristically irate.

"The two Rifle Teams with eyes on corroborated it sir. Both teams believe them to be friendlies. They came out on to the roof, waved their hands then they pulled out a toilet roll," the Commander trailed off.

The Police marksmen were a branch of SC&O19 and were currently situated at strategic points both on the ground and along the adjacent rooftops that surrounded West Acre Point. Each team consisted of a marksman and a spotter and it had been the two teams situated at the front of the centre, atop a building opposite, that had noticed the two men.

"They pulled out a what?" Miller questioned, having heard the statement but not quite believing it.

"A toilet roll sir, they said it was pretty choppy up there, poor visibility due to all the rain and wind. Both confirmed that the two men unfurled a toilet roll with was a message written on it. They caught some of the message just before it blew away. It said..."

Miller heard the turning of a page on a notepad.

"Friendlies. Twelve hostiles. Four hostiles down. Hostiles are not..."

"Hostiles are not what?" Miller pressed.

"That's it I'm afraid, that's all either team got. They also said there were eight numbers on the paper but they didn't have time to make them out," the Commander paused, waiting for the next question he would undoubtedly not have an answer for.

Miller digested the information, rubbing his forehead again as if he were trying to massage an answer free. Miller jubilantly brought a hand down upon his desk.

"Eight digits, it was most likely a service number. Can you describe what either of them looked like? What are they doing now?" Miller retrieved a notepad.

"Two white male's sir, one tall, one shorter. The taller one was wearing a tactical vest, the other armed with a handgun. Chatter currently states that they are currently setting up what appears to be a rappel of some kind. The shorter one is proceeding to the edge," the Commander reeled off in tandem with the live audio his teams were reporting back.

"A rappel? How did they? How long is the rope, over," Miller requested, his interest piqued.

Miller could just make out the Commander in the background forwarding the question to his team, drumming his fingers upon his desk expectantly.

"No visual on the length of rope sir but my man says it looks nowhere near long enough to reach street level," the Commander reported back.

Miller brought his fists down upon the desk in anger; the chance of insider intel simply shimmying down a rope too good to be true.

"How do you want us to proceed sir?" the Commander requested.

Miller momentarily mulled over his plan of action before outlining his thought process.

"Right Commander, here's what I think. They are poorly armed, have made an effort to open communications and are currently at the highest point of the building. As stated on your previous call, your intel revealed that many of the thermal hotspots are situated on the bottom floor, where we believe the hostages and insurgents to be. My guess is that these two are friendlies, most likely trained, military possibly. One armed, one in a tactical vest, those are hard to come by in a London shopping centre the last time I checked".

"Then there's the message. I would deduce that they have most likely taken these items from those they have incapacitated. Now it is of paramount importance that we do not proceed under the assumption that the four hostiles mentioned are neutralised and out of the picture for good. We may still be dealing with the full pack."

"We saw one fall on the live feed and land on another member of the team. I think it's safe to conclude that he is dead and the one he landed on is either dead or incapacitated, so we're potentially looking at ten hostiles," Miller took a deep inhalation of breath.

"I agree sir. Hold for a second sir," another secondary conversation with his tactical unit ensued, mumbled and undecipherable.

He came back curtly, "Sir the shorter man has just repelled down the side of the building and has entered a window framed by scaffolding on the third level. The second is fixing himself to the rappel now."

"That seals it, "Miller excitedly blurted out. "I think we may have some inside help here Commander. I highly doubt a terrorist would pop out for a breath of fresh not unless he was on a suicide mission. I'm making the call," Miller sternly concluded, "Let them proceed. I repeat…"

"Hold sir," the Commander abruptly interjected.

Miller sensed the unease in the Commanders voice and his blood froze the Commander's voice muffled. He could, however, sense the heightened speed in which he was speaking, slightly elevated now. Miller began to pace, ensuring he never left the radius of the hands-free landline atop his desktop.

"Sir relaying it as it happens," the Commander's voice disrupted the quiet line. "Another man has stepped out onto the roof. He's armed, masked and… repeat again Sniper Team Echo…?" Another pause ensued.

"Commander! Commander, what is going on? Respond, over!" Miller barked.

The silence continued for several seconds.

"Sir, the man looks like a hostile. Conditions are poor; Echo team cannot get a decent visual. He is armed, masked and approaching the rappel line. Hold sir…" the Commander trailed off once again.

"Come on," Miller muttered to himself.

When the Commander finally did return, Miller sensed the dread in his voice.

"Sir, the hostile is apparently pulling the rappel upwards along with the taller, second man back towards the roof. The taller man is hanging on," the Commander's words came thick and fast, relaying the chilling live account.

"Does your team have a clear line of fire on the hostile?" Miller pressed.

He looked out at the situation room and the news channels that were already capturing the footage live. A long shot captured the man hanging from the line before it tried to zoom in closer, his features could not be made out, the camera blurring under the strain of both the focus and the weather. That was when Miller heard a surprised tone come via the Commander's mutterings. A repetition of the question followed. Miller bit his bottom lip.

"Sir, the hostile has a young child strapped to his back. I repeat he has a young child strapped to his back. Line of fire is poor and we may risk the bullet taking the child out also, the man is right on the ledge. The child being mortally wounded or the hostile falling from the ledge would be highly likely. How do you want us to proceed, over," the Commander hastily probed, seeking the clarification to act.

Although he had tactical carte blanche whilst in the field he seemed to value Miller's input.

Miller glanced quickly at the screen adjacent to his glass-fronted office. A myriad of calculations and collateral assessments ran through his mind. The man on the rope was perilously close to the roof's ledge now; he now faced the camera, his face still out of focus. He hung on with a singular hand, his guiding rope trailing behind him.

If he were to order the taking out of the hostile, it could prove the catalyst that would tip the scales ever more so against their favour. The order may result in the man falling over the side of the building with the child still attached and all on National and International news outlets. In addition, visibility was poor and the man on the end of the rope was hanging on for dear life. By taking out the hostile holding his literal and figurative lifeline, he would release the rope and with it the man on the other end, who to all intents and purposes seemed an ally.

"Hold your fire. I repeat, hold your fire. Do not engage the hostile, over," Miller bellowed.

Another mumbled relaying of orders from the Commander to his men.

"Holding fire over," the Commanders formal response shaking the lines audio.

Miller slumped down into his seat and peered up at the bank of various news outlets just as the man on the rope disappeared over the ledge. Miller looked down at his desk, a pang of guilt rising within the pit of his stomach, one question plaguing him.

'Have I just sent that man to his death?'

"How should we proceed sir?" the Commander pressed once more.

Startled from his musings, Miller stared back at the phone upon his desk with resentment. If there was one luxury his chosen career did not afford it was adequate time in which to mourn.

"Hold fire. No one is to open fire on anyone. Serve only in an observatory capacity. I repeat, do not fire. Observe only. We cannot risk hitting the child or the other friendly. An attack on a hostile at present could instigate a chain of invents within the centre. Relay back all live information to me as it transpires, I am keeping this line open."

Miller looked up once again at the screen and the empty ledge still being filmed. The press were lining up like vultures, waiting for the body of an innocent man to be cast off of the lurid structure. Miller knew he must remain impartial in such situations, level-headed but right now he felt sick to his core. Not only were they massacring innocents and threatening his country's very way of life but they were exploiting their youngest hostages, using them as body armour.

Miller suddenly found himself doing something he had not done for a while; he found himself praying for the man on the roof. A solitary figure he had only been made aware of mere moments ago, a man he hoped was trained, capable of the instinct to defend and if needs be, kill.

(CHAPTER BREAK)

Gerry shielded his eyes as he leant out from the cover of the open window. The patter of rain lashing tarpaulin served as the only thing louder than his breathing. He gazed up; all that was visible was the drunk like movement of falling raindrops. He feared that Tom had either lost his nerve or that something even more sinister was transpiring. Whilst he had not heard a gunshot, he began to fear that Tom may have been taken out by a sniper. Upon observing that there was still movement upon the rope as it swayed from side to side, he pushed such fears aside.

"Nice and easy, that's it lad, take your time," he whispered to himself by way of comfort.

The swaying continued for several seconds and then to Gerry's horror began to ascend, he made to grab for the rope but it trailed outwards and away from the building. He thrust his head out of the building once again, looking upwards. Thoughts of Tom's betrayal came to the fore, the cold realisation that maybe Tom had been playing him all along, biding his time to be rid of Gerry. For all he knew, Tom was in conversation with the hostage takers now, returning to his unit.

He beat the wall with his fists, rebuking himself for having had such a thought. This situation hinged on hope not cynicism. Tom had had his chance to kill Gerry and had not followed through, he had even entrusted him with a loaded gun, one which he gripped all the more tightly now as he focused on the ajar wooden door to the building site behind him, a sliver of light breaking through into the room. No, he believed in Tom.

"Come on lad, you can do it," he pressed, willing him to descend, hoping he had hoisted the rope to readjust his line or carabineer, arrogant to the horror of the figurative and literal battle of David versus Goliath that now played out above.

(CHAPTER BREAK)

The metallic taste of blood lined Tom's mouth. His head felt heavy as if he had had concrete poured into his ears. All thought processes were fluid, his reasoning intangible. Although his vision had not fully returned, his hearing was alarmingly attuned; the sound of a crying child piercing through the wind and rain like a siren. At first he assumed that he must be concussed, the noise of a crying child not gelling with the scenario in which he currently found himself.

In a state of delirium, he made to stand, his palms planted upon the sodden shingle. The notion was soon dispelled, however. Between his wavering posture and the heavy clad boot that now came down viciously upon his side, his efforts proved to be futile. Any deferments as to whether he was concussed were quickly abandoned. This was all too real. As the agony worked its way along Tom's body, he afforded himself a glimpse at his aggressor.

Between his blurred vision and the squall, he at first supposed the figure to be disproportionate in size, a trick of the light or lack thereof. However, a crack of thunder soon brought figurative illumination to that miscalculation. All Tom could do at present was take in his unforgiving stature as he lay prone, fixed to the spot.

The masked assailant was gargantuan, a mountain of a man that dwarfed even Tom's lengthy stature. The man obviously took great pride in his appearance, every muscle strengthened and attuned to within a pinnacle of physical perfection, an Adonis of the terrorist world. Tom made to scuttle backwards but his purchase upon the shingle roof made slow progress. The wind and rain had picked up quite substantially now, coating the surface with a constant film of saturation. In return, the masked behemoth grunted under his infrastructure and cocked his head slightly in wonderment, intrigued by his prey. He remained stationary.

Tom too found himself in a state of bewilderment. Although his brain still found it difficult to latch onto a cogent thought, he found himself repeating one patient question to himself over and over, *'Why hasn't he finished me off yet?'*

Tom adjusted his gaze, his breathing heavy, elevated. He had put three metres between himself and the masked man when suddenly his hand fell upon a gantry. Never breaking eye contact with the shadowy figure, a thought shot to the fore; it was a set of stairs that led to another section of the roof. He had observed it when he and Gerry had been setting up their harnesses.

He reached up and groaned as both his shoulder and his heavily bruised ribs contorted with exertion. He hefted himself upwards which in turn registered a sickening smile from his attacker, the expression visible via the slit in his balaclava.

A crack of thunder and lightning illuminated the roof and his attacker; the rain lashing off of the man's broad shoulders as they heaved with anticipation and excited exhalation. Tom's head was warm and wet, the unmistakable combination of rain and a head wound bleeding. His legs felt hollow. He rose to his full stature and puffed out his chest. It was fight or flight time; the latter most likely a result of him being tossed over the side of the rooftop. He made to ready himself when another burst of lightning disclosed a revelation that turned Tom's stomach inside out. He took the sight in, his hands clenching at the railings on either side of the gantry.

The man had attached to his back a harness not to dissimilar to that of a baby carrier fashioned with rope which was woven and intertwined via his tactical vest. Tom stumbled slightly when the head of a young toddler, crying and sodden with rain, protruded from behind the man's substantial shoulders. The child was exhausted and with no words to formulate his abject fear, flailed legs that came level just above the man's lower back.

The fear within the pit of Tom's stomach hardened; tempered by the righteous inferno that was his rage. Michelle and the others mistreatment earlier resurfaced only adding more fuel to the fervour, dissipating any concerns for his own personal safety entirely.

He weighed up his options quickly. His attacker was his physical superior in every sense of the word; in stature, weight, reach and unfortunately for Tom, that old mantra 'The bigger they are, the harder they fall' was utter bollocks in this scenario. Heaped upon this was the fact that he had an innocent strapped to his back both serving as a human shield. If he were to fell this mountain of a man, a tumble to the ground would result in said child being suffocated or worse still crushed, of that Tom was certain.

Tom acted quickly, feigning a slip on the steps, grabbing a handful of gravel from behind him as he did so. He did have one advantage however, his attacker's arrogance and ego. It would have to be brain over brawn. Grey matter versus body mass. Rather abruptly the man seemed to grow tired of Tom's retreat; his weakness seemingly an insult to him. He was unlike the men Tom had engaged earlier, Dreyfus and Frazier. They had been show boaters, talkers. The man before him might as well have been a mute, a single word not yet exchanged.

However, like Frazier and Dreyfus earlier, they got off on this kind of thing; it was a blood sport to them. The masked man bounded over to Tom, showing Tom the courtesy of allowing him to get up, which he did so, accentuating his weakened state, playing to the gallery. The man grew closer and reached out for Tom; Frankenstein-like in posture. Tom allowed him to get in close, eyeing up the intricate series of knots attached to his thighs and shoulders ensuring the child stayed in place.

He eyed up the large gun strapped to his right knee, a sizeable weapon like its owner. Tom waited until he was almost upon him before lashing out with the gravel, knowing full well he only had one shot at this. His own safety was secondary now, the plan he had formulated was going to be pretty for him. It concerned him little; the child was all that mattered.

The gravel hit him straight on. The man's head jerked back, his eyed blinking in confusion. Tom reached down and made as if to grab the man's gun. Through intermittent vision he clamped down upon Tom's hand and held the gun firm in its holster, a bulbous, spade like hand enveloping his. No worry, Tom had achieved what he had set out to do. He backed up the gantry steps, never taking his eyes from his attacker. When the steps levelled out onto the gantry, about ten metres in length, he reached into one of the vests pockets and pulled out the keys he had taken from Dreyfus earlier. He placed them, facing outwards, in-between his fingers, creating a makeshift knuckle-duster.

What he had in mind would require his attacker to feel as though he had the advantage, parrying half-hearted blows. However, what occurred next threw Tom's plan into disrepute. Tom waited until the man reached the head of the steps, wanting him to be on the same level just in case he stumbled. A tumble down the stairs would result in the child being severely injured or worse.

The metallic steps groaned under the man's weight. Viciously, Tom swung his makeshift knuckle-duster, aiming for the man's crutch. He did so as hard as possible, putting his full weight behind his stronger right arm. To Tom's amazement he hit the man squarely in the crotch, even turning his fist as he did so, intending to achieve maximum injury. The man faltered slightly his legs weakening as he doubled over.

Tom took his advantage and grabbed for a knot on the man's shoulder, acting as if he were following up his attack. The assailant, to Tom's utter shock, grabbed him by the neck, standing upright as he did so. He shook his head from side to side and smiled. The shot to the groin had done nothing.

Tom writhed in his grip. The man was big but no matter how big a man, a clean shot to the groin should surely double anyone over, especially one sponsored by Yale. He raised his arms slightly and Tom felt his feet leave the ground slightly. Still, he maintained his grasp on the knot, blood rushing to his head. Tom saw the man bring back his spare fist and knew he would need to accept the blow willingly if his plan were to succeed. The blow was like a cement block being dropped onto his torso from seven stories up.

All air exited his body, his vision darkening. He was bent double just like his attacker should have been. Still Tom held onto the knot, all he could do as the man supported his body weight. His keyed hand left the man's grip. He pulled it back and lashed out weakly at the man's eye, drawing blood. Yet the behemoth barely flinched.

Then, to Tom's horror the man turned around on the gantry, still clasping Tom by the neck, his other hand gripping at his torso. His girth just allowed for him to turn one hundred- eighty degrees. He gritted his teeth, Tom's stature and weight more awkward than the superior weight that he could deadlift in a gym. He strained and brought Tom in closer before he shoved him out and away from him, letting go at the last second. Tom flew backwards and away from his assailant, gratefully unravelling the knot as he did so.

He just had time to observe at the height of his arc, the child slightly slip lower upon the man's back, the harness now missing another knot. Nevertheless, Tom did not have long to revel in his small victory. The floor rushed up quickly to meet him; he instinctively shielded his head as he came down hard upon the shingled roof, sliding a sizeable distance along the sodden surface. He was severely winded, gasping for oxygen, black dots punctuating his pupils like full stops. He exhaled painfully, sucking in air. His position afforded him a perfect view of the staircase though he cared little at present, the fear of a lack of oxygen his prominent concern.

The masked man descended the stairs slowly, methodically. He could have landed a killing blow with his sidearm but instead he reached the bottom of the stairs and stood motionless. His attacker turned slightly and barked an order at the child, one which Tom could not decipher, his ears struggling to hear over the rush of blood coursing through his head. His attacker ogled Tom as he writhed around on the floor. Now, no more than four metres away, he finally broke the silence: his voice deep and guttural yet loud. His tone was nearly as unsettling as his stature. Nearly.

"You take your time," he growled, "not like you have a lot of it left now anyway. I'd wager you've cracked a rib or two there, possibly even broken a few. It must hurt…not that I'd know much about that," he mockingly diagnosed as he begun pacing around Tom.

Tom sucked in air "What… what the fuck are you made of?" he snatched for air.

No man could take the level of punishment he had sustained without showing at least a morsel of pain. Blood coursed from the substantial wound above his eye. The man simply blinked it away as if it were rain. He let out a bellow, the question seemingly orgasmic to him. He took a step closer to Tom.

"Doctors call it a congenital insensitivity to pain or to the uneducated, an insensitivity or inability to feel pain," the man said pompously.

Tom rolled onto his side and spat blood from his mouth, mustering a sneer. He held his ribs, playing up to his role. He was hurting yes but down and out? Not when the stakes were this high.

"Doctors might have one or two things to say about you," a deep inhalation of breath married with the formation of a low snigger. "But invincibility, that's nearly as feeble as your punch was back there."

The man straightened, his features turning from a smug bystander to an emasculated one. Tom rose shakily to his feet, his back facing the man. He afforded himself a smile; regardless of the world of pain he was in, he had touched a nerve. The man reacted to his insult, just like anyone else Tom had encountered with a little or a big man complex. The constant need for dominance and approval reared its ugly yet advantageous head. Tom took the brief respite to scan the rooftop both for the location of the knife and to ascertain whether the door which led out onto the roof had been shut behind his attacker. He observed that the rope was still intact. Gathering himself, Tom rounded to the sound of the masked man cracking his knuckles.

"I hope that medical history of yours is all make-believe," Tom sneered.

"And whys that runt," the insurgent spat.

"Because I'm going to be really gutted if you can't feel me kicking your deluded arse all over this roof," Tom grinned, raising his guard.

The insurgent laughed and wiped something away from one of his eyes; a tear, a raindrop or blood, Tom could not be certain.

"I'm going to savour every second of this and when I'm finished, I'm going to string you up from this building as a reminder, a reminder to all those sheep down there that weakness is a cancer. You're just another pothole in the road to progress, one that needs to be tarmacked over. You, them, it's all futile," the masked man growled in a disdainful tone.

"Look at the moral steamroller over here. You think what you've done here today is just? What you're doing now, using a child as body armour? I mean, what the hell has that boy or any of the other people down there ever done to you or your cronies?" Tom fervently put forth, biding time.

The masked man briefly glanced back at the child, hefting him slightly higher upon his shoulder.

"What we do here today is for the good of this country," the masked man jabbed.

"Oh cut the bullshit! You're not even who you say you are. You're cowards; spineless liars prepared to smear another faith, another culture with the blame because you're too afraid to show your true face. That's, why you hide behind a mask!" Tom shouted above the wind using this as his prompt to start navigating the rooftop.

The man let out a guttural guffaw and clapped. He turned slightly and pointed out at the London skyline.

"Out there, that's the true sham," he spat with venom. "You know what's more bankrupt than this country? The morals of those who run it and we're just as guilty because we vote them in. We bitch and we moan when they don't do what we elected them to do and then, we do it all over again. No, I hide my face as after today, what comes next; it will need me to remain anonymous, a silent warrior with no face. What we do here today is not for some form of moral gratification or self-fulfilment. We are going to be instrumental in shifting the balance, of being the spark, the flame that ignites the fires of revolution, the furnace in which to cultivate a new social and imperial order".

"We are here to put the Great back into Great Britain. You question why we wear the masks? It's simple. We are fighting fire with fire. Politicians today, every day, hide behind the mask of empathy and spin. We are not a figurehead; the country has all too many of those as it is. We are devoid of classification, of a manifesto. We instead only serve to highlight to the people that they have a choice, that they have a voice. They always have. We are just a concept, an instrument in which to retrieve what has been muted for so long now."

Tom was taken aback. He had underestimated the man before him, arrogantly typecasting him as just another muscular giant devoid of any rational thought. Although he maintained his exterior composure, the man had substantially progressed up the scale of terror for Tom. He was both brain and brawn. Worse still he had an unshakable, all be it a deluded, belief system. The man before him may have taken personal offence to the insults banded his way by Tom but at no stage was he going to let it interfere with his mission.

'A soldier till the end, after all, one man's freedom fighter is another man's terrorist' Tom surmised.

Tom was battered, bruised and hopelessly vulnerable but he could no longer delay the inevitable, he used his attacker's moment of moral procrastination and made to charge. The masked man snapped from his train of thought and raised his guard. At the last moment, Tom fell to the floor using the wet shingle as a direct track towards the man's legs. He hit the insurgent's shins full on felling him like an enormous tree. Thankfully and due to Tom's quick-witted instincts at having rolled away, the masked man fell in Tom's direction, the crunch of bone integrated with shingle.

Tom was up quickly. He unlatched another knot on the man's other leg, fumbling with the moist material. He hushed the child who looked back at him with abject panic; the child's body heaving up and down with the masked mans laboured breathing. He directed his attention to another knot largely loosening it, all the while praying that his attacker had been knocked unconscious.

No such luck. Just as Tom made his way to the final knot, the masked man began to rise. He grabbed the back of Tom's heel with lightning speed and pulled the feet right out from under him. He came crashing down, perilously close to the roof's ledge, his injured shoulder taking the full brunt of the impact. He yelped out in pain and felt bitter tears sting his eyes.

"How sweet it must be to feel pain. To feel the exhilaration as you must do right now, death creeping its way up your body, to have that indicator, that last morsel of being."

As he rose to his full stature, Tom afforded himself the briefest of victories as the child slipped from the intricate pulley system upon his back. His attacker surveyed the child unenthusiastically, still attached by the last knot around his shoulder. The child had served his purpose, their umbilical link now only serving as additional weight to be dragged.

He unsheathed his knife and cut the cord, stepping out of the makeshift harness as it hung loosely from his body. He smiled at Tom laid prone upon the shingle, relishing the pain he could see etched across his quarry's features. He stared at the knife considering whether to finish Tom off there and then but thought better of it, sheathing it instead.

"I want you to know that this is not easy for me. Quite the opposite in fact. For me this is a no pain, no gain situation. Your efforts, whilst admirable, are wasted upon me. Whilst inflicting pain comes naturally to me, sadly experiencing it for myself, does not. So, I'm afraid you're going to have to do that for me".

Tom remained spread-eagled. He grasped another set of gravel and the masked man brought an ample boot down upon Tom's clenched fist, grinding it into the shingle. Tom gritted his teeth in pain; stuttered gasps were his only reply as the masked man twisted his boot. Tom lifted his head against the pain, maintaining the small boy was ok. He afforded himself a brief smile when he saw the toddler errantly walking back towards the roof access door. The boy stumbled once but rose precariously to his feet and preceded, his calls for his mother lingering on the wind.

His tormentor followed Tom's glance, angered that he was not being paid the attention he felt was warranted. Pivoting at the hip, he forcefully brought his fist squarely into Tom's face twice in quick succession. However, as he brought his clenched fist back for a third blow, the grin remained.

Incensed, he glanced at Tom's bloodied shoulder, his bandage slightly visible. He lashed out at it, Tom's nerve endings erupting into life. Whilst his smile faded to that of a saliva laden smirk, still he persisted. Unsatisfied, the man hefted himself clear of Tom and instead diverted his attention towards the child. He took a step towards the boy. Tom weakly grabbed at his calf, which he shook off easily. Tom made to turn onto his side but was all but paralysed.

"Stop," he pleaded weakly.

The insurgent was oblivious, growing ever closer to the child. He took another two steps towards the child before another crack of lightning illuminated his gargantuan frame, the steaming sweat leaving a snaking trail behind his body.

Tom outstretched his hand feebly, his eyes still focused on the man's calf, an impossible distance away now. He panicked, unable to act. The thunder cracked again only this time the man's feet violently gave way beneath him. He did not have time to put out his hands, his chin and upper torso taking much of the sizeable impact as a cascade of raindrops spattered Tom's face and extended hand.

Tom looked on in pure bemusement unable to fathom whether the assailant had simply fallen or by some act of God, had been struck by lightning. He made to withdraw his outstretched hand when he noticed it. Tom brought his palm up to his face in the dim light to inspect the foreign object further and immediately swallowed back the desire to vomit. A jagged chunk of flesh about the size of a fifty pence piece clung on at the base of his thumb. It hung there for a moment before the molasses-like blood lost its purchase and dislodged, the flesh hit the surface water with a light splash.

Seeking further clarification, Tom dumbly turned his attention back to his attacker, his calf now bleeding out. Disorientated and in a substantial amount of pain, Tom's head lolled sideways as he looked towards the ledge of the roof as if tracing the trajectory. No Gerry. The crack that he had heard had instead been from that of a gun at some distance.

Tom raised a weakened hand to the ledge and elevated himself further. Still no sign of Gerry, that confirmed it. Using the ledge as cover, he poked his head out from behind the recess, afraid that the next bullet may be for him. He scanned the series of high, silhouetted buildings opposite.

Suddenly a brief movement demanded his attention. He traced his eyes sideways and saw it directly opposite the shopping centre, a rooftop slightly higher than that of West Acre Point; Telrange communications the imposing electric sign divulged. He had almost given up hope, feeling as if he had imagined it, when it came again; a double flash of light, a short pause and then another two flashes. Tom dumbly observed the light for several seconds, transfixed by the signal. Finally, he arrived at the conclusion that it had to be a signal establishing that they were aware of his presence and that he was ok to proceed, free of the retribution of a sharpshooter. They would not fire on him. Taking a deep breath and making sure not to ponder on the variables of what he was about to do for too long, he decided to be put his theorem to the test and shakily got to his feet, his hand nearly slipping on the lip of the ledge in the process.

The masked man's gloved hand grasped at his leg; a clean in and out. It was gushing blood profusely. The man held it not out of pain but out of confusion, trying to stem the flow, Tom wondering if he could feel his consciousness slipping away also. He walked towards the man, deliberately blocking the sniper's line of fire; he could not risk the child being hit. The masked man's eyes were framed by shock as he locked gazes with Tom. He fumbled for his sidearm, taking a bloodied hand from the wound and set about fumbling with the latch on his holster. His eyes momentarily left Tom's in an effort to divert attention solely to that of freeing his sidearm

Tom, who was noticeably limping, crippled by the stabbing pain in both his ribs and lower back, sped up his gait, each step a jolt of newfound agony. He was roughly a metre away when the man spun round with the gun, a Beretta. Reacting instinctively, Tom diverted all his power into his right thigh and swung his leg squarely into the side of the man's head, his boot driving forcefully into his temple. The man collapsed backwards, the Beretta sent flailing two metres or so away and, in the process, answering Tom's earlier question; he could indeed be knocked out.

He shuffled past the floored insurgent towards the child who now looked up at him; innocent confusion still peppering his features. He picked the child up; grabbing the empty rucksack they had left on the roof earlier as he did so. He cooed the small child whom he cradled in his stronger arm and began the arduous process of moving towards the edge of the roof. The child squirmed slightly. He was sodden and heavier than expected Tom's purchase uneasy.

"You did so well, do you know that?" he hefted the child slightly higher in his arm, "so well. What's your name little guy? Huh?" he grinned.

The child stared back at him in open-eyed wonder. It suddenly dawned upon Tom that his face must be utterly grotesque by this point, a tapestry of abuse.

"Not a talker, hey? Well that's ok."

He put the child down before removing the rucksack from his shoulder, keeping his back towards the masked man. He set about adjusting the straps on the rucksack, securing them as tightly as the material would allow. He knelt down and threaded the child's arms through the rucksack one at a time, grinning as he did so. The boy sniffed before letting out a gratifying giggle.

"You know what…that's the best sound I've heard all day," Tom said as he pulled the straps over the boy's tiny shoulders.

The straps interlocked via a sturdy clip which Tom clipped shut, tugging it three times for good measure. Ruffling the boy's hair, he seized the end of the rappel line that lay to the edge of where he had himself been dragged and fed it through his carabineer.

He intended to use himself as an anchor, his course of action spontaneous, the parameters formulated on the spot. He then fed the rope through the handle at the top of the bag and wrapped it down through the straps, intertwining it around the child's torso as well as his shoulders, doubling the support. Next, came a multitude of close-fitting knots, testing them individually. As an additional precaution, he lifted the light frame of the child via the rope, free of the ground and was glad to see that the rope cut delicately into the child's frame. It was sturdy. He looked at the child and shot him one final smile.

"OK little fella. I'm going to lower you down to my friend Gerry now. We're going to get you back to your Mum."

The child smiled at the sentiment, registering the word Tom had used. With a reassuring nod he gave the line a final test. Satisfied, he grabbed the child and placed him upon the roof's ledge. He peered down and adjusted his position, aiming for the top of the scaffolding. Before he began the process of lowering the child, he afforded himself a cursory glance over his shoulder. The insurgent was still comatose.

Cradling the boy's body, he lowered the child over the ledge, the child's hands grabbing at the empty air. Another laugh. Tom stood firm and placed one foot upon the ledge, using his knee as a guide for the rope. He began lowering the child slowly, the scaffold now his only focus. Regardless of the boy's light frame, the rope was assuredly taut which made guiding the rope all the more easier.

"Not far now little man just a few more metres," Tom consoled the boy, raising his voice to be heard above the hostile elements.

His eyes snapped front and centre; a series of random flashes came via the building opposite. Tom continued to lower the child, his eyes never leaving the barrage of light.

"What the hell do they…" Tom started.

It was the crunch of shingle underfoot that initially pricked Tom's ears. His elbows shook slightly, the blood in his very veins practically glacial. Reluctantly, he turned slightly; first observing the empty pool of blood and then the shadow of an arm. Before he could even react, the masked man's body engulfed Toms nearly forcing them both over the edge. Tom steadied himself; a momentary loss of control upon the rope quickly rectified, his hand clamping closed around the blistering movement of the rope's fibre.

He violently shoved backwards against the lumbering figure which afforded him suitable time to glance over the ledge. The boy was about a metre and a half short of the scaffolding. Tom observed a set of pale arms reaching out, trying to grasp at the child. All he could do was pray that it was Gerry. He willed himself on, just wanting to hold out long enough for the boy to be secured.

The mass of muscle finally advanced inwards once again but Tom held firm, his stance rooted to the rooftop. Which is more than could be said for his attacker; the rhythmic tap of shingle underfoot indicating to Tom that the man was hopping on his uninjured leg. He was off balance.

Again, something glinted in the corner of Tom's eye. At first, he believed it to be torchlight. However, the malicious curvature of the knife as it edged its way into his field of vision and towards the rope, soon put an end to that. He made to peer over the edge again for any indication of the child's safety but the hooded man instead pulled him ever further backwards.

Tom held his breath, angling his neck away from the blade as it came ever closer; the steel lightly prodding at the rope. He shot his weakened left hand upwards, clamping it around the man's wrist. He could no longer rely upon the snipers, his attacker once again shielding his extensive frame with the use of another. That was how he had crept up on Tom without being fired upon, he had used Tom's body to block the sniper's line of sight, hence the flashing of the torch.

"Please… just stop. He's just a child," Tom pleaded through gritted teeth.

The masked man's breathing was heavy now; exerted by the effort of bringing the knife in towards Toms guideline. It made contact once again, this time fraying the strands slightly.

"What greater pain is there," an exerted heave "than growing up condemned to a life of servitude? He will only grow up to be another sheep. Better he dies young… a lamb spared of the slaughter."

Tom felt the rope sway in his hand, no discernible indication of weight on the other end. He retracted the rope with his free hand, gathering the extra slack. As sure of anything as he could be at present, he attributed this to Gerry having retrieved the child. This spurred Tom onwards and mustering his last reserves of strength, he thrust his back as far as it would go into the torso of the insurgent, using it as a ballast to heft the man off of his one good leg.

Tom's whole body quaked; a heady cocktail of adrenaline twinned with exertion. His back bowed slightly, concaving under the man's mass. Yet he held firm, the man's comments about harming the child only serving as a scaffold of resolve for his spine.

"Not nice is it? Being worn as a human backpack, is it you sick fuck," Tom winced, the man's substantial girth bearing down upon his already weakened frame.

"If I go…I'm bringing you with me," the insurgent growled.

Tom made to reply when he heard another crack quickly followed by the whiz of a bullet and the final punctuation of a splat. The man upon his back cried out in shock rather than in pain and shifted his body weight dramatically.

'*Most likely a flesh wound,*' Tom considered not wanting to squander the advantage he had gained to that of misplaced optimism.

Remarkably however, the knife grew closer to cutting the already frayed rope. Tom had to act and quickly. He lifted the spool of slack rope, sacrificing his purchase upon the attacker's grip to do so before swinging it blindly behind his head. The rope made contact with what Tom assumed to be the base of his aggressor's head and he set about wrapping the rope several times around the masked man's neck, never taking his eyes off of the knife that bobbed now with the masked man's panicked fervour.

For the first time, the masked man altered his course of action, now adopting a policy of self-preservation. His vice like grip left Tom's torso and reached for the rope but Tom shot it taut. He gripped firmly onto the rope below him, pulling forward slightly giving himself some additional slack. He now put both feet on the ledge and gathered himself pushing down with his full bodyweight. The man let out an asphyxiated gasp, his breathing panicked and sputtering.

It was his intention to choke the man out, for the behemoth to pass out from lack of oxygen. If he was pressed and more extreme measures were needed, an extra forceful tug or two upon the rope may be enough to snap his neck. Tom was just coming to terms with the options at hand quite literally, when out of the corner of his eye, the juddering jolts of the man's knife-clad hand once again began to descend. However, this time it was angled inwards, towards his ribcage.

An unwelcome but necessary realisation crystallised at the forefront of his mind; a notion that was absurd and just as equally suicidal. That said the situation he now found himself in, blocked off from retreat, was just as dubious. He tightened his grasp upon the rope. The knife was about four inches away now. He kicked the rope free ahead of him and watched as it spiralled down the edge of the glass fronted exterior. He took a deep breath, deliberately paying no attention to the frayed strands of rope not wanting to assess its resilience.

And with that, Tom leapt from the buildings edge, a metre or so of rope between him and his attacker trailing behind. He transferred his hand from the rope around the man's neck and instead favoured the rope before him. He slid wildly down the rope before clamping down tight. The rope spun him hard slamming him against the building's sodden exterior before it snapped taut.

Still the rain came, the rope slippery before him. He was now essentially supporting his own bodyweight, directly facing the street, the wind whipping at his vision. One slip and the rope would slide from his carabineer and he would fall to his death. He spun his guide hand around, gathering a loop of rope around his grasp for extra support. He began a slow walk down the building, feeding the rope slowly. He directed himself towards the barely visible scaffold; its surface area looking wide and inviting. Even over the intense squall Tom could still hear the choked gasps of his attacker above; his only concern was whether the rope would hold under their combined weight.

His thighs were shaking substantially now, his whole upper torso felt as if it would upend any moment, his attacker serving as a weighted anchor. If that were to happen, he would flip upside down, his chances of regaining an upright position all but impossible. Dispelling such morose reflections, he persevered the shaking in his lower jaw and upper arms excruciating now. His only solace was that with each step he put more distance between him and the behemoth above.

His foot finally came down tentatively upon the scaffolding which registered a creaking groan. With an exasperated release of exalted air, he laid belly first upon the structure. It held strong. He turned onto his side and glanced upwards, the rain falling in angled motions. A drop of blood cut a swathe through the rain before it hit Tom's cheek. The lightning flashed once more, revealing Tom's attacker above. Tom's entire body ceased up. The masked man still had one horror left in store for Tom.

In the flash of the lighting, Tom saw the slow, agonised movement of a bladed hand reach above his attacker's head, the other hand holding the rope, trying to ease some of the pressure from his neck.

Tom's eyes shot down towards the rope in his carabineer. He pulled at it and felt a resistant weight still at the end. The boy. Gerry was most likely inside struggling with the intricate web of knots, desperately trying to free the child from his makeshift harness, not wanting to cut the rope should Tom need the additional slack.

Tom shielded his eyes against the rain and observed with horror the scene playing our above. If his attacker cut the rope, he would take both Tom and the child with him as he fell. A man of his size, at the speed he would fall and with Tom in the condition he was in, he would have no hope of stopping his descent. Tom swore and began fumbling with the rope, his fingers were numb, not his own.

"Gerry." he screamed. "Gerry, cut the kid's line. Gerry!"

The wind swallowed up his words. His heart was in his throat. The man began severing the the rope. Tom made to grope for his own knife and cursed himself, recalling it was still on the rooftop. Instead, he gripped the rope with both hands. Even if he unlatched himself from the carabineer, the child would still be dead. With all his effort he pulled down upon the rope. Rain spat out from the rope as it shot taut. He pulled the rope back and lay astride it, tilting his head up towards his adversary. The masked man's legs began to spasm and dance like a puppet at the end of a string, his hand momentarily dropping slightly. However, not for long as the knife began to rise again.

Tom changed tact, pulling the rope outwards, away from the building. The man swung slightly. Tom brought the rope inwards. The man moved slightly away from the building. Tom swung him back in, groaning against the weight. Once again, he swung the body out, then back in, building momentum. The man's shoulder lightly touched the window above. Tom attempted a larger, more concerted pendulum attempt. Groaning in severe agony, his muscles ablaze, he mustered one more concerted swing using the man's weight against him. The masked man's elbow struck the window and the knife fell from his grasp.

Tom could not help but howl with rapturous elation before stopping abruptly as the knife swished a metre or so by his head. Spurned on, he leant his body against the structure for support, keeping the rope taut and did so until he felt the tapping of the masked man's leg against the rope cease. He glanced up in apprehension. The body of the giant swayed lifelessly.

By way of further clarification, it was several moments before Tom finally let go of the rope. His arms felt as if they had been yanked from their sockets. He continued to look up, his eyes filled with water, the joy now exuding from his very pores. It continued to rain heavily, Tom's tears merging with the deluge. He held his hands out before him. The gloves material had yielded to rope burn, a pink rawness to his palms spattered lightly with blood. All he could do was stare back at them; the movement below not even sufficient in breaking him from his trance

"Is that you Tom?" Gerry's voice shouted. "I have the lad."

Tom's heart swelled with pride and ecstatic jubilation and brought with it more tears. He sniffed heavily.

"Can you hear me Tom? Are you alright?"

After several seconds, he spoke.

"Yeah, it's me," he mustered.

"What the hell took you so long? Get your arse in here and stop hanging around out there," Gerry berated leaning out of the window slightly just below the scaffolding.

Tom glanced up at the body swaying upon the rope. He traced the rope upwards until he located the sizeable swathe of frayed rope. He assured himself that it would hold his weight giving it another reassuring tug.

"I ran into a problem," Tom shouted back, halting slightly, "A big one."

His tears gave way to a supressed smile. He had saved a life; all be it via the taking of someone else's.

(CHAPTER BREAK)

"That's unacceptable! I gave the specific order that no one was to interfere. That was a direct contradiction of my order, Commander. Operational carte blanche or not!" Miller spat, fearful of the consequences that might now befall those within the complex.

"Sir with all due respect, our man on the inside, he was getting his backside handed to him up there, we didn't have a choice, there was a child involved. Added to that, the shots barely slowed the insurgent down," the Commander spoke with an air of disbelief to his voice.

He had disobeyed a direct order from his superior but deep-down Miller knew it had been the right call. He would reflect that in his report, when and if, this all came to a head. He diverted his intentions to the likely retaliation those within West Acre Point would now have to endure.

"And what do you think is going to happen when they discover we played a part in this? It doesn't matter if one of the friendlies landed the killing blow, they will start to execute hostages!"

"Sir, with all due respect, given the circumstances, they have bigger problems to deal with. Irrespective of the fact that we contravened the terms and conditions laid out, I doubt they are going to want to poke their head out after what has happened to inspect the body," the Commander verbally drummed out.

Miller massaged his temples and once again looked out upon the bank of television screens.

"Thank God I got onto the news teams when I did and had them cut the live feed," he half muttered to himself, "we need to contain this and quick Commander."

"We're doing all we can down here sir. We're holding the perimeter and awaiting further orders concerning your entry plan," the Commander replied.

"Entry is currently being finalised on our end. We have two SAS teams on standby running scenarios and devising an entry plan as we speak. They will run point but we will need you and your team in a support capacity; those are your orders at present, you'll be updated when and if, we decided to breach," Miller asserted.

He heard the distinct sound of indecision on the other end of the line. The Commander sounded as if he were contemplating whether to ask a question or not.

"What is it Commander?" Miller pressed.

A sigh fluttered down the line.

"Well sir, it's just... you said earlier that you believed these men, the ones who set up the rope, were trained. Well...what if they're doing our job for us?" The Commander reeled this last statement off swiftly.

Miller was astounded by the misplaced omission of hope.

"Our job, Commander, is our job. No one will be doing it for us," Miller barked uncharacteristically.

"That's not what I meant sir," the Commander continued level-headed, "I just thought that they may have just given us two more options."

The Commander let this statement hang in the air intentionally piquing Miller's curiosity.

"And what options would they be Commander because God knows, I need more options," Miller impelled.

"Well, the way I see it sir and this is just my opinion but they'll either serve as a distraction for us or they might actually be trying to help. You heard the message yourself, four hostiles down, with another one dangling from the roof. If there were twelve, that means we're left with seven potential hostiles now. I think they're trying to help the hostage's sir."

Miller paused and pondered the Commanders thought process. Although he did not what to admit it, the Commander had a point. Miller hated variables; he saw them as potential disasters waiting to go wrong but he was running out of options. He knew Benley was going to ring him at any moment and that what he would have to say to the Home Secretary would not fill him with an abundance of assurance and goodwill.

"Either way Commander, unless we get some form of contact from our mysterious dynamic duo and soon, we'll have no option but to breach. We have little over three hours until Pierce is dead, either way. They are on high alert and the fact that they are losing men is only going to make them jittery, their trigger fingers all the itchier. We proceed as planned; the Regiment will breach when we have a better lay of the land. Then and only then will we act. Keep your men frosty up there and update me on any and all new developments," Miller countered in an authorial tone.

"Yes Sir," the Commanders dejectedly responded.

"Oh and Commander," Miller probed.

"Tell your man up on the roof, your sharpshooter," he paused, trying to sound as humble as possible. "Tell him he... he did the right thing, bloody good shooting. No doubt they'll be a commendation it for him"

"Will do sir, Roger and out," the Commander returned, his voice laden with pride.

(CHAPTER BREAK)

Thompson did not need to be told by Carling up in the control room. He had become transfixed by the live stream of results, the public voting away busily, the Prime Minister haemorrhaging votes by the second. Not that he was surprised. After all, it seemed a no-brainer that one life should be sacrificed for the majority. As far as Thompson was concerned it was operational necessity, the reduction of collateral damage and what made it all the sweeter was the fact that the British public were voting in their droves.

The smile upon his face was facilitated by that comfort, the knowledge that the British people were being forcefully shaken from their political slumber by the very same technology that enslaved them on a daily basis. It was rather ironic then that the very same technology now abruptly wiped the grin from Thompsons features also or rather, the minimised window in the bottom right corner of the laptop. The small window relayed a live news stream, the contents of which serving as an emotional low blow.

Involuntarily, Thompson's fist came down heavily upon the table jolting the laptop slightly. Greaves heard the commotion and quickly set a course for Thompson; his superior now hunched over the laptop, his body afflicted with pure fury. Greaves proceeded with caution, maintaining as much of a militaristic aura as possible.

"Sir, I thought I'd let you know that all of the preparations have been made. We're airtight. Anyone tries to breach; they'll be peeling them off of the walls for weeks. I suggest we start moving the hostages now."

Thompson did not reply. His shoulders were drooped, his hands clasping the sides of the table. Finally, after several agonising seconds, he lifted his head slightly and turned back to face Greaves. The stare he fixed Greaves with froze his very soul.

"Sir, what's... what the problem?" Greaves stuttered.

Thompson stepped away from the screen and stared back at Greaves. It was at that moment that he caught the headline on the now maximised online news feed, the picture anchoring the text at the bottom of the screen. It spoke a thousand words. Greaves hands shot up to his head. A solitary figure, shaded and substantial in girth, hung from the side of the building.

"Shaw is dead and it would appear," Thompson swallowed hard, driving the anger back down his gullet in preparation for what he was to say next, "We have two assailants."

"How the fuck did they take out Shaw? The guy was a beast. He was..." Greaves could not find the words although not out of some sense of grief.

Just as Shaw had been absent of all physical feeling, Greaves had been born with a lack of empathy or emotional sentiment. In addition to this, Shaw was Thompson's right-hand man, the hammer in his clenched fist. Yet, he was no blunt instrument. He was fiercely loyal to their cause, a true enforcer of their beliefs, both physically and verbally. The plan after all, had largely been formulated by the duo.

Thompson pressed on; he had no conceivable answer for Shaw's demise. Shaw had been one of the founding members of the militia group along with Thompson and he had been a fierce associate.

"The plan proceeds as normal. Place the hostages in that empty outlet across the way; it's being gutted for a new store. Ensure they're all bound. It's time for a united front. The news reports state there are two hostiles, so assume there are more. Take a team and search for the package, Alpha team can take out the threat; I'm going to watch Pierce."

"Yes sir," Greaves quickly replied, unnerved by the reserved demeanour Thompson now adopted.

"I guess we can safely assume that one of those hostiles is his personal bodyguard. I don't know how he took down Shaw in his state but no one else dies here tonight, the plan can't sustain any more losses," he jutted his finger downwards, emphasising this last proclamation.

"Absolutely sir, I'll take the rest of the men after we secure the hostages and start turning the gaff over for the package. If it's here, we'll find it," Greaves assuredly put forth.

Thompson looked back at Greaves searchingly, weighing up whether Greaves was being insubordinate, the man seemingly questioning the validity of Thompsons plan.

"It's here, of that you can be sure," he gobbed, "now square those hostages away. Anyone resists, execute them."

Greaves nodded, turning back to the remainder of his men. They looked towards him for orders and for the first time, Greaves no longer felt the confidence of safety in numbers. He pushed the thought back, his split personality snapping back into the fore, Mr. Hyde once again dominating Mr. Jekyll.

"What the hell are you staring at me for? You heard the man. Load up the cargo on the double, we're going hunting," Greaves sneered.

He moved over to the hostages and produced a tubular baton more like a cattle prod than a Taser, due to its menacing length. He brought it up close to a man's eye level and made sure everyone could see what happened next.

"And just so any of you don't get any ideas," the blue pulsation of electricity sparked into life at the head of the black device.

Greaves grabbed the man by the shoulder and dug the device deep into the man's ribs. The man shook and convulsed, spittle flying from his lips, his eyes rolling back into his skull before he flopped down beside a woman who was shaking uncontrollably. Greaves scanned the group and nodded to himself. Message received, albeit via fifty-thousand volts of seizure inducing power, made all the more deadly by the man it was wielded by.

(CHAPTER BREAK)

"Oh, I'm sorry for coming across as inconsiderate but there was me thinking you were going to be at the end of that rope, not a bloody kid! What are you, some kind of part-time stork or something?" Gerry rambled on over-excitedly, having not stopped pacing the joint since Tom had re-entered the complex.

Tom ushered Gerry to lower his volume both out of covertness and not wanting to upset the child who was now sat on a workbench, content playing with a loose piece of sandpaper.

"Gerry, it was hardly planned. What the hell could I do? That guy was reeling me in like a bloody fish; the kid was strapped to his back. I mean come on mate, what would you have done differently?" Tom punctuated this question, with an expectant glare.

Gerry sighed and rubbed his eyes. He maintained Tom's gaze and any feelings of resentment or diversion from their original plan, melted away. He ruffled the child's hair before patting Tom's arm.

"Nothing lad I'm sorry, just a bit highly strung that's all," he broke into a grin, "not as highly strung as him outside, mind. Thank God. You did well, no doubt about it," Gerry relinquished.

Tom swallowed hard and turned away from Gerry, detached from Gerry's jives. He had not told his newly appointed partner but right after he had spoken to Gerry out on the scaffolding, he had violently vomited over the side of the metal rigging. He had done so twice, before dry retching. If it had not been for the rain, his mouth would have been caked in sick.

For the briefest of seconds, Tom detected the acrid smell of burning flesh. The image of a canopy engulfed in flames, resurgent once again. He had shakily lowered himself using the remainder of the rope, wrapped tightly around the metallic structure, Gerry hands outstretched, ready to receive Tom. He now had his hands thrust into his pockets; they were shaking uncontrollably, the muscles in his shoulders quaking wildly.

"So, what are we going to do with the boy?" Tom questioned looking at the boy who was still transfixed by the sandpaper.

"Well, it's hardly a crib but..." he pointed to an overturned wooden packing crate, "it's big, sturdy and as long as he stays quiet, he won't be heard."

Tom nodded in approval and stepped over to the box. He made to upturn the box when his body stiffened. He reached back behind him and unclipped the mountaineering tool. It suddenly occurred to him that he had not thought to use the tool on the roof earlier. Cursing himself he focused on the task at hand, promising to berate himself later.

He held his other hand up in a gesture that told Gerry not to move. Gerry froze also all be it for the releasing of the safety upon his Sig. Tom took a deep breath and violently prodded before him with the tool before lurching back slightly. He turned and looked solemnly back at Gerry.

Gerry reached within the rucksack and produced the torch. He strode forward, reaching Tom in two strides. He waited until he was next to Tom before flicking the torch on. The torch's arc reached the blood-stained cement first. Gerry traced the light inwards, following the puddle's source. Gerry's beam fell upon an orange clad shoulder. He traced the beam upwards towards the neck and immediately inhaled in disgust. Tom soon followed. Gerry knelt lightly, removing the glove on his right hand as he did so. He touched the cadaver's neck, the icy feel upon contact maintaining that he did not need to bother with checking for a pulse.

"Must have been one of the foremen, bastards snapped his neck like a twig. Haven't seen a neck that twisted since..." lost for words, Gerry didn't finish.

Instead, he moved the torch down and away from the body and stopped abruptly. He shot the light up and Tom followed his gaze. Gerry stepped towards the wall, a gaping hole speckled with blood, hung open. Gerry reached the wall and stuck his hand in, the torch placed in his mouth. He fished around, his face bearing the exertion of stretching his arm. His features quickly relaxed in shock, his eyes shooting up to meet Tom's. Tom too nervous to speak stared back in bated breath.

"Fuck me sideways," Gerry whispered.

Gerry pulled and with a clatter of metal, produced an MP5. He passed it to Tom who took it, mouth agape. Gerry thrust his hand back into the inner wall's cavity. He produced three magazines for the MP5, which he placed on top of the MP5 huddled in Tom's arms. He moved his hand from left to right and further produced a Glock 18. Satisfied, Gerry withdrew his hand and looked back at Tom in shock. Gerry took the MP5 from Tom, shoved the three magazines into his pockets and paused. He held the Glock 18 out towards Tom. Tom looked unsure and shook his head but Gerry pushed the gun into Tom's hands.

"Tom lad, you need to be armed. If what's just happened has taught us anything, it's that these guys are just as handy with their other nine digits as they are with their trigger fingers."

Tom stared at the gun for three seconds or so, weighing up Gerry's evaluation. He reluctantly nodded discharging the magazine out of a force of habit and cocked the weapon, keeping the safety on. He holstered the weapon, trying to hide his adrenaline infused hands from Gerry. Gerry pulled a large sheet of tarpaulin from a wall and draped it over the corpse on the floor.

"That poor bugger had a family, a mortgage, paid his taxes just like anyone else. No one special, no threat to anyone," Gerry let the statement hang in the air like the start of a eulogy.

"These guys must have been planning this for months, hell, maybe even longer. They've hunkered themselves in good and proper, brazen as you like and even set themselves up with a cache that could arm a small militia, guessing by the size and depth of this recess. They even left weapons behind that's how bloody well tooled up they were. We were like fish in a fucking barrel down there, me and my team. Not to mention those poor bastards down there, all dead. Outgunned and caught with our bloody trousers around our ankles."

Tom looked back at Gerry; he needed this release. Gerry turned his back to Tom and away from the dead body. Tom was wrestling with his own demons at present, the weight upon his right leg making him feel uneasy, the gun strapped to his leg feeling as though it were closing of his last avenue of free choice. It was his choice to use it of course but when faced with someone who would not relent, who would not hesitate, who were armed themselves, there was no choice at all, Tom knew that all too well now. He turned to the small boy atop the workbench, still content with his piece of sandpaper. He turned back to Gerry who was fixed to the spot, staring off into the distance, MP5 cradled in his forearms.

"We need to get moving Gerry. I have no idea if he managed to get a message through to his team or not," Tom pressed.

Gerry flinched slightly as he was pulled back from his trance. He nodded, cocking his gun in reply, a noise that reverberated off the surrounding walls.

"Talking of contact lad, I tried your phone just after I entered the window. Still couldn't get a signal to my people or anyone for that matter. All the satellites and what not in the world, a phone that takes pictures and can get email and here's me waving it around for a signal," he scoffed.

"Well we hardly had time for that on the roof. We'll keep trying" Tom reconciled.

Gerry bowed and picked up the upturned box, he brought it over to the shadowed corner, keeping it out of sight. Tom smiled at the small boy and picked him up, the child content flapping the limp sandpaper. Tom made to turn right and abruptly stopped, arching on his feet slightly. Gerry shot a wary look towards him.

"What is it?" Gerry whispered, fear pranging his voice, MP5 readied.

Tom stepped backed and walked around the left-hand side of the table. He embraced the child in his arms tighter, turning his head away from the body as he approached Gerry.

"There's a huge hole in the floor over there," Tom thumbed back in the direction he had just come from.

Gerry nodded and walked over. He knelt slowly, obscured by the workbench. Tom heard the click of his torch quickly followed by a second click, turning it off. He turned and traced the rope that lay on the floor, a substantial amount of slack left after Tom's overzealous wrapping of the harness around the boy. He took the end and strolled back slightly, feeding it through his palms, judging the length. He nodded to himself, coiled the rope up and left it by the hole, testing it with a final tug. He stepped lightly back towards Tom.

"There's a store below, on the second floor, deserted. If it all goes tits up, we RV back here and climb down. It might be sealed up but even so, that has to be better than climbing back up. If you get back first, wait a minute behind the workbench and provide covering fire should I need it. You'll know it's me, I'll be shouting my head off for you," he nodded to Tom for his understanding, which Tom returned.

Tom carried the boy over and lowered him into the box, the child smiled back up at him and laughed. Tom smiled back and shook his tiny little hand.

"You stay here little man. We're going to go open up the doors so you can go home but you need to stay put, ok?" Tom reasoned but the child had already returned to playing with his sandpaper, content.

Tom grabbed some tarpaulin to cover the box then thought better of it as it might rustle, alerting someone. Added to that, it was a suffocation risk. He bent down and lightly brushed down a dust sheet. He laid it carefully over the box and turned back to Gerry. Gerry held up his hand and indicated for them to both move slowly towards the door. They both set a course for the crack of light under the door flanking either side of the door. Gerry raised his MP5 and indicated with his eyes, that he expected for Tom to do the same. Tom bunched his fist slightly, before withdrawing the weapon, flicking the safety off; the red dot indicating that the gun was live barely visible in the gloomy surroundings. His weapons training instructor's mantra echoed in his ears, 'Red is dead, men'.

Gerry lightly pulled the door back and Tom squinted out, momentarily blinded by the light. The coast was clear. Tom gestured to move forward, covering Gerry's exit. Gerry peered out to his left, the direction of the control room. Tom stepped out, facing right. He stepped back slowly, both men affording the other cover. They kept two metres apart from one another, close to the wall, keeping out of the arc of the cameras. Tom heard a camera whir above and instinctively hugged the wall a little tighter. Up ahead, the corridor which led to the control room began to come into focus. The marble floor had a substantial incline and although technically on the same level, meant that the control room was elevated slightly.

Tom briefly glanced back and saw Gerry hold his hand up. He indicated for them to stop. Gerry groped his way to the edge of the empty doorway, pressing his back against the wall. He peered round the corner and shot his head back quickly. He turned back to Tom and ushered Tom to follow, motioning with his hand towards him. Tom slowly raised a thumb, all clear. He unlatched the mountaineering pick and silently joined Gerry. Gerry rounded the corner in one movement, once again angling his feet to minimise sound, his knees slightly bent. They both crept forward slowly. Tom's heart was in his mouth, his temples throbbing. He dared not breathe at this stage.

Gerry reached the door keeping as close to the edge of the door frame as possible, aware that his shadow may alert someone on the other side via the crack under the door. Tom replicated this on the left-hand side of the frame. He prepared the mountaineering tool; it hovered several inches from the crack between the door and its wooden frame. He peered sideways at Gerry who motioned for him to wait. His heart nearly exploded when the radio piece in his ear, burst into life.

The tool swayed closer to the frame and Tom jolted his hand back just in time, pulling the tip of the tool towards him. Gerry's whole face was frozen with pure terror. He mimed wiping his forehead in mock relief upon seeing the tool inch away from the door. Tom touched the earpiece further into his ear and held up his hand urging Gerry to wait. He listened intently, craning his neck slightly. Satisfied, the conversation over, he shot his eyes towards the door and held up his free hand in a symbol that indicated the man on the other side of the door, was speaking on the radio and Tom was receiving it.

The faintest sound of a tapping keyboard could be heard, the buzz of monitors also. Gerry raised his MP5 slightly and tightly gripped the handle. Tom cringed at the minute sound. His muscles were primed, ready to breach the door just above the single lock. The conversation ceased and Tom shot Gerry a nod of his head. He repositioned the bladed implement, turning it inwards. Gerry's hand lightly caressed the handle of the door as he lightly tested it. It was locked, which was of no surprise to both men. He met Tom's gaze once again, his hand still on the handle, just above the lock and mimed a countdown: three, two...

CHAPTER SIXTEEN: LOSING CONTROL

"And you're sure this is the outlet with the best visibility on the monitors," Thompson probed.

"The unit is locked down sir. I'll have an eye on the hostages via three different angles. One guard to be sure, McAllister would be best. I can't foresee any issues, over," Carling maintained, feigning confidence.

"Well, we didn't foresee a rogue bodyguard and a mysterious good Samaritan did we Carling? But here we are. Keep me updated of anything remotely out of the ordinary. If one of those hostages so much as breaks wind, I want to know about it straight away, over," Thompson stressed.

"Will do sir, over," Carling pushed, yearning to be off the channel with Thompson.

"If it's not kosher, you let me know right away. No more mistakes. Roger and out," Thompson spat, the line finally going dead.

Carling exhaled loudly and picked up a pack of post-it notes from the desk. He peeled off three slips and placed one under each of the monitors that he needed to watch. The shop front of Brenton's Curtain shop was shown via three angles: head on, to the right and a high angled shot from the first floor. He took a sip of tea provided from a machine located to the left-hand corner of the office, free to employees. He sucked in and winced as he burnt the end of his tongue.

"Shit," he cursed under his breath as he covered his mouth in pain.

He placed the cup heavily onto the monitors desktop and thrust himself back into the swivel chair, grimacing further as the handle of his gun dug into his side. He sighed and sat on one buttock, unclipping the latch of his holster, removing the sidearm. He slapped it down heavily upon the desk's counter before him. His jaw was soured with tension and anguish. He smoothed his hair back and returned to his viewing of the three monitors. He had not admitted it to Thompson and never would but what he had seen Shaw do, with that child, had sickened him to his very core.

He had seen Shaw march up towards the Staff exit on the second floor. When he had turned to the camera just above his head and swivelled his finger in indication to open the door, Carlings finger had lingered slightly.

Carling had zoomed in slightly on the child's face, staring back at him for several seconds. It was Shaw's second forceful swirl of his finger that had snapped him from his trance. He had buzzed Shaw through unknowingly sending him to his death and most likely the child's. Carling had himself seen the news footage, one of the monitors screening a live news broadcast. Having scoured the footage, he had seen no sign of the boy and believed him to be dead also.

Paradoxically the cessation of his conversation with Thompson had given way to something even more terrifying, time alone with his own thoughts. Time in which to recall the petrified expression upon that boy's face, a face that now set about unravelling Carling's festering subconscious. Every time a memory was subdued, the pain momentarily stemmed, another memory reared its head anew. Carling would often visualise the repressed memories as scabs, given little time to heal before being picked at again, mentally, his brainwaves the sharp nailed finger, pick, pick, picking away.

The room was dimly lit now but Carling still propped the torch upright affording himself another column of light, the steam from the tea intertwining with it. He focused on the light, trying to slow his heart rate. He swallowed hard, urging himself not to be coerced by the darkness to his right. But the voice was begging him now. He forced his eyes shut and rocked slightly in the chair.

"Get a grip you coward, there's nothing there. Just like there wasn't anything there the last time or the time before that," he chanted to himself.

How he longed to quench his thirst with the scolding tea. It felt as though he had swallowed a Brillo pad. His hands gripped the arms of the chair, the hinges creaking slightly. He longed to authenticate his hypothesis but feared the result so instead resigned himself to a quick glance. He immediately wished he had not. He broke into a barrage of expletives and thumped down on the arms of the chair. He whirled round in the chair, spurred on by a frustrated anger and a need to absolve himself of his solitary penance. His bravado faltered and he began to slowly whimper. He began to thump the side of his head, hands shaking, the low chant beginning once again.

"You're not there... you're not there... you're gone," he glanced up again, the spectre unmoving.

He knew it was PTSD and he had the official diagnosis to prove it. He knew it was a hallucination, the child before him; olive skinned, with black matted hair and a youthful exuberance. The boy smiled, my God how he always smiled. His hand behind his back, a twinge of boyish deviance etched upon his features. His hand whirled round quickly, his outward grasp clutching a cluster of poppies, a gift to someone who had ventured into his land, uninvited. A symbolic paradox in itself; the Poppy, a symbol that meant so much to the Western mentality, a symbol of remembrance and respect. To the boy and those who ran the Poppy field he had most likely plucked the bunch from, it instead served as a revenue stream, crucial in funding their war of terror. An opiate, a hallucinogenic totem that brought with it only death and false visions. The irony did not escape Carling as he stared back at the apparition.

The poppies dripped blood; the deep jagged cavity of the bullet wound where his heart should have been now visible. A hole located where a patriot would themselves wear a singular poppy in remembrance. Was this his remembrance? He had often deliberated upon that same question. No, it was his penance, his life a walking purgatory. The singular word once again rang out. He had sought out the meaning of the Pashto word months later, hoping it would bring him closure. It had not, the word *'Gift'* encapsulating the boy's innocence evermore. He stared back at the boy, sobbing, transfixed by his solidity. He did not notice at first the splintering of the door, not until the wooden shards flew through the spectre, the door yanked outwards. The vision ceased and for the briefest of milliseconds, Carling savoured the respite. It did not last for long.

(CHAPTER BREAK)

The man had been staring intently at the wall before him, transfixed by it. Tears had swollen his cheeks and he sat trembling with a thousand- yard stare that Tom knew all too well. Gerry had put his full weight behind the door, pulling the door outwards and free from its locked frame. Tom also found himself momentarily off kilter but Gerry soon righted himself and levelled the MP5 in the direction of the insurgent. Tom darted for the man nearly stumbling over the body of another casualty, his uniform indicating that he was part of West Acre's security detail. The insurgent's features melted from a transfixed glaze to one of venomous realisation. He dived sideways for his gun, his chair falling to the side heavily.

Tom heard Gerry call over his shoulder, "Don't you fucking dare."

The man's hand fell on the gun and he made to pick it up. In a singular movement, Tom spun the mountaineering tool around in the palm of his hand and directed the blunt, hammer like end of the pick towards the man. He brought it down heavily upon the back of the man's hand, with more force than one would have considered necessary. Tom had panicked. He had expected him to yelp out but instead the hostile sucked in his scream, not seeking to verbalise it. He grabbed his hand and made a silent, inverse screaming motion before relenting, moving slightly backwards. Tom kept the mountaineering tool primed and ready for the next attack, switching it to his left hand. With his right, he waved it down in a calming motion.

"Don't do anything stupid, we just want to..." the man abruptly lashed out pushing Tom backwards slightly.

Tom instinctively thrust him back forcefully, using the mountaineering tool. Tom heard Gerry shifting closer behind him, the metallic gun clattered slightly in his grasp. His right hand instinctively shot out and his hand clasped around the hot polystyrene cup. He gripped it, winching as some of the hot liquid splashed onto his skin. Tom flung the cup in a linear and forceful fashion towards the man. His assailant instinctively covered his face, ironically with his crippled hand, many of the bones most likely broken. The tanned liquid exploded in a cacophony of scalding droplets. Most of the liquid hit his hand, some striking his exposed forehead.

This time, the man yelled out loudly. Gerry shoved past Tom and silenced the flailing man with a right cross that caused the man's knees to buckle beneath him as he fell over the chair behind him. He hit the floor hard, rendered unconscious. Gerry shook his already swollen hand in pain.

"Shut the door, then..." his eyes darted around the room before falling upon a toolbox under the monitor's desk.

He thrust his hands into the box and rummaged around. He soon produced a spool of cable wire and handed it to Tom. "Tie it closed with these. Wrap it around the handle and then spool it around that table leg. Things are going to get a whole lot louder."

Tom nodded and returned to the splintered door frame. He wrapped the cord round the handle three times before tying a knot. He then replicated this twice more, before trailing the cable back into the room, tying it around a table bolted to the floor behind the monitor bank. If they were breached, it would not be the table he feared of not holding out but the cable instead. He gave the cable a cursory tug. It did not yield.

Gerry was looking upwards tracing a water pipe which ran halfway along the ceiling, above the monitor room. He nodded to himself and plunged back into the toolbox. He pulled out a sprig of cable ties wrapped in an elastic band. He then created a circle with one, feeding the end through the clip. He placed it around the wrist of the unconscious man and pulled it tight. Gerry repeated this again on the other man's wrist. He then turned the man onto his front and picked up the swivelled office chair, placing it back on its wheels. He hefted the man into the seat, placing a forearm on each of the chair's arms. He took two more cable ties and fed one through each tightened cable tie around the man's wrists. He looped them shut, making a pair of makeshift handcuffs on each wrist, like those the assailant and his partners had used on the hostages.

Gerry tugged them tight, stood upright and rolled the man's head backwards. There was a rag in the toolbox also. Gerry grabbed the back of the man's head, fed the rag in-between the man's teeth and tied it at the base of his skull before stepping back to admire his handy work. He grabbed one more length of cable and wrapped it around the man's shins, securing it tightly. He then turned back to Tom, eyed up the door and nodded approvingly.

"So, what do we do now?" Tom pressed, stepping towards the console of monitors and keypads.

He stared at one of the screens; three of the insurgents were discussing something on the Ground floor.

Gerry exhaled and scratched the back of his head.

"For starters and before we make our next move, we need to extract any information we can from Osama Bin caught out over there, by any means necessary. It's one thing hitting the right button, it's another once the shutters actually start to rise. When that happens, we're gonna have the world and it's fucking wife descending upon us."

"Not to be the bearer of bad news or anything but we're sitting ducks in here. Boxed in. It'll be like shooting fish in a barrel as far as they're concerned" Tom anxiously postulated.

"Fuck me, I hope your handier in a gunfight than you are at metaphors mucker," Gerry quipped before once again shooting him a knowing smile as his eyes shot up towards the pipe above their heads.

Tom's gaze followed his. Gerry pointed upwards, never taking his eyes off Tom.

"Water service pipe. I remember it being on the schematics. It ran into this room, it was going to be my indication as to whether we were in the right room or not, a waypoint."

"The right room for what, exactly?" Tom pressed.

Gerry stepped away from the unconscious man, following the pipe to the furthest wall. Before him, a small filing cabinet lay against the wall. Gerry hefted the cabinet sideways between his legs; his back bent, sharp, panted breaths brought on by the weight. He stood back and Tom saw a squared, metallic hatch about the size of a manhole. He motioned for Tom, asking for the mountaineering tool. Tom leaned over the unconscious insurgent and handed it to him.

Gerry grabbed it and placed it within the doors seam. After three downward tugs, the corner peeled back. Gerry placed the tool on the floor and bent the corner downwards, placing his full body weight upon it. The frame of the door yielded, creaking ever so slightly. With three backwards tugs the doors lock relented and swung open. Gerry peered back over his shoulder and smiled.

"That should take us right back to the room we've just come from if memory serves. As we're still technically on the third level, there's a slight drop in one of the shafts. Nothing too substantial I would have imagined but it should get us back to the boy and our ERV".

Gerry rose from his crouched stance with a grimace, more out of old age than out of pain. He picked up the mountaineering tool and placed it on the monitor's desk, next to their hostage's gun. Gerry then hefted the toolbox onto the desk and began removing tools, placing them methodically upon the desktop. Tom shot him a worried glance. As a soldier Tom had never condoned torture, largely because he knew he may possibly be at the receiving end of it one day, if captured. He firmly signed up to the Geneva Convention and its rules surrounding the treatment of captives and prisoners.

"Don't worry, it's largely for show," Gerry pre-empted, rifling through the tools, "largely," he continued rather unconvincingly.

"Ok, he's going to come around any minute. Go over to the machine and grab three cups of coffee, put four teaspoons of sugar in each, we're going to need all the energy we can get".

"And the third cup," Tom questioned, fearing the answer slightly.

Gerry was eyeing up a tube of heavy-duty superglue.

"Well he can either drink it or wear it. Depends on how he wants to play this. The last cup didn't go down so good," Gerry quipped as he kicked the discarded cup that Tom had thrown at their captive.

The man in the chair let out a groan and dipped his head upon his chest. Gerry turned and looked at Tom.

"No matter what happens here, we've got a small window of time. We need to be quick and extract as much from him as possible. Keep your eyes on those monitors for me and if anyone gets near that door, use the gun I gave you and fire a few warning shots through the door."

Gerry leant closer to the man and squeezed his chin. The man's head lolled back; his eyes rolled deep within his skull. Gerry shook slightly and moved his head from side to side.

"Wakey, wakey, eggs and bakey," Gerry mocking chimed.

Tom noticed a guttural change in Gerry's voice; he sounded more like Clint Eastwood than a man from the North East of England.

Tom had to admit it, although they had needed to come across as threatening, willing to do anything to the man, whether that be true or not, he did not like this side of Gerry. Gerry, like Tom was a trained killer of sorts, Gerry at the very pinnacle having served in the SAS.

The man's eyes began to focus upon Gerry and a heavy, panicked whistle emanated from his nostrils. The gag in the man's mouth moved in and out with the man's flustered breathing. His eyes shot wildly around the room then settled upon Tom before moving back towards the door and then back to Gerry again. He tugged at his makeshift restraints and shook in the chair to no avail, a futile but necessary attempt. Gerry did not move, staring back intently with a smile.

Gerry blew on his coffee and took a sip, before sucking in deeply, acting as if he had burnt himself upon the coffee.

"Damn, that is like liquid magma. Hotter than Satan's arsehole that," he turned back to Tom and gave him a wink.

Slowly, he diverted his attention back to his captive and began to wipe the man's forehead with his shirt cuff, wiping the remnants of the coffee away from his face, the man noticeably tremoring now.

"But you'd know all about that now wouldn't you, Carling? That's your name isn't it? The guy in the control room, the monkey to the organ grinder downstairs," Gerry pressed.

The man nodded violently. Gerry stood up, the man following him all the while. He danced his fingers over the tools upon the tabletop and stared intently at them. What he said next, was delivered to the tools.

"Now don't be deceived by my partner's boyish good looks and my honest eyes. We are both highly trained and the extent of our skills goes far beyond a mean right cross and throwing a cup of Nescafe. No, no, no, our talents stretch far beyond that."

Gerry picked up a wrench and turned it over in his hands. Carlings eyes fell upon the blunt object with feverish dread before turning his gaze back to Tom.

"Now, you and your cronies have done some abhorrent things today Carling, my sick, deluded chum and you will have to answer for that," Gerry turned back and locked gazes with Carling, resting the wrench on his cheekbone.

Carling instantaneously flinched and tilted his head away from the tool, the vein in his neck protruding and pulsating with an elevated pulse.

"Whether that sentence comes by way of a judge, your maker or for that matter, from your own conscience," Gerry mulled over, "well, that falls outside the realms of these four walls. What is within your control is the choice I am going to afford you now".

Slowly Gerry removed the wrench from Carling's quivering cheekbone and placed it upon the tabletop. He slid the cup of coffee into view and gestured to it.

"A choice that centres solely around this fine, Incan blend of brown, coffee goodness".

Carling looked confused as did Tom in the background as to where this line of questioning was headed. Gerry sighed and playfully put his head in his hands.

"Look at me droning on. I can read the room, the pair of you think I'm as daft as a brush. Why is this knobhead banging on about a cup of coffee like come aficionado? I mean, I'm more of a Bovril man myself, what the fuck do I know anyway. And at any rate, the pair of you will need a cup of coffee just to stay awake if I carry on," Gerry chuckled.

Carling let out an uneasy, muffled laugh in return. Gerry abruptly ceased his laughter and glared back at Carling. Carling quickly fell silent. After several seconds, Gerry methodically picked up the polystyrene cup of coffee and rotated it aloft, transfixed by it.

"I'd forgive you for thinking that. No, indulge me this once the opportunity to continue with my little metaphor. You see this is no ordinary cup of coffee. You know what it is? Hmmm?" Gerry asked Carling who returned with a fervent shaking of the head.

Gerry turned back to Tom "You?".

Tom shook his head, rather embarrassed now.

"This is reckoning in a cup is what it is gentlemen. Pure, filtered and bitter as fuck. What blend? Judge? Jury? Executioner? Well, there lies the rub. So, let's find out shall we. I can remove that gag and allow you to sip at this fine blend of coffee and we have ourselves a nice little chat..." he shot Carling a knowing glance, "...and of course, it goes without saying that if you scream or call out for anyone, well, just like the last cup of coffee you sampled it's dying to be introduced to your face. Are you keeping up sunshine?" Gerry cocked his head awaiting his captives reply.

 Carling once again nodded his head overenthusiastically.

"Good... and then of course there is option two. Just out of transparency and in an effort to come across as mutually understanding of one another, I feel it is crucial to explain in detail, what that entails. So to start with, that nice, welcoming cup of coffee..." Gerry tipped the cup slightly towards Carlings crotch, the liquid perilously close to the lip of the cup "... well, let's just say, we'll be roasting a different type of beans".

Tom folded his arms, his nails digging into his upper arms.

"Then, once we've gagged you again and you've simmered down a bit, I'm going to try my hand at a bit of DIY, with you as my personal flat pack. Unfortunately for you, I'm running on a bit of a tight schedule, so we won't be starting off slowly, never could stand all that torturer's foreplay stuff myself. No, just like every good man and a flat pack, I'll be ignoring the instructions and losing parts. So, the choice rests solely upon the next movement of your head and the question I am about to ask."

He leant in closer.

"Either DIY stands for drink it yourself in reference to this cup of coffee I hold before you or well, in the good old words of MC Hammer..." Gerry reached down with his spare hand and raised a hammer, lightly tracing the bridge of Carling's nose "... well I'm sure you're old enough to remember the rest."

Gerry took a step backwards. He held the cup of coffee in one hand, the hammer in the other.

"So, are you a coffee drinker or..." up came the hammer in the spare hand "... a closet glutton for punishment?"

Carling stuttered slightly but Gerry interjected, ramping up the tension. Carling froze and rigidly held his head firm.

"This coffee's going cold and with it my one time offer".

Tom shifted uneasily behind Gerry reeling at his partners newfound persona. The man in the chair seemed to look through Tom and back towards the door, assessing his chances of escape. Carling's eyes returned to Gerry's and he nodded towards the cup of coffee, three single nods of intention.

Gerry nodded and placed the hammer down in a deliberately loud fashion, Carling recoiling at the noise.

"Just remember Carling, just like you, those tools aren't going anywhere."

He pulled at the rag free keeping his hands clear of the man's mouth for fear of losing a finger. The man panted and swallowed in air. Gerry held the cup to Carling's lips and allowed him to take a sip. He did so and Gerry took the cup away just as soon as he had given it.

"As I said, we're on a tight schedule. So, this is how this is going to work; I ask a question, you answer it promptly and honestly. Now me and my friend here, we might as well be sponsored by polygraph. If you pause or we even think for a second that you are fobbing us off or leading us down a merry path, you lose more than our confidence. Once we've asked all our questions, you get to live, hopefully intact, all extremities accounted for and me and my partner leave. I'm sure I can find a set of shelves or something to put up at home to quench my DIY craving," Gerry remained monotone throughout.

Carling cleared his throat and spoke lightly, "I... I understand, I'll tell you whatever you want to know, just please... please don't hurt me anymore."

"Well it sounds like we have a mutual understanding and for that, you get another sip of coffee," Gerry asserted as he once again briefly held the cup to Carling's lips.

Tom, satisfied that his coffee was now cooled, drained his cup in one go, the heavily sugared beverage making his taste buds burst with static.

"Question one: what's your true agenda here? One of your men mentioned a package, not in reference or pertaining to the Prime Minister. What are you really here for?"

The man swallowed hard and seemed to be fighting with what words to choose. All that subsided when he afforded himself a sideways glance at the tabletop laden with tools of various menace. He cleared his throat again.

"We're here for the Prime Minister but he's only part of our objective. We're here for..." another pause filled the room.

Gerry picked up the hammer and drove it down hard upon the monitors desktop. Both Tom and Carling jumped, startled by the threat.

"We're here for a set of schematics," Carling blurted out.

A wave of disgust and realisation spread across his face.

"My God he's going to kill me when he finds out I told you."

"Be more concerned with the here and now and what I might do to you if you pause like that again. Question two: this he, you mention, I'm guessing you're referring to the big cheese running the show. Who is he and why does he want these schematics? Would I be correct in guessing that they might have something to do with the EMP device you're using?"

Carling's mouth dropped open in shock.

Gerry smugly nodded. That was as good a confirmation as Gerry was going to get regarding his theory surrounding how they were controlling the buildings power and its sturdy shutters.

"How did you...?" Carling started.

"Lights go on and off at your will, electronic devices fried and you're cycling your radios, switching them off just before the lights go out," Gerry shrugged, "it doesn't take a rocket scientist to work that out."

"You're correct. We have sole control of the building's electricity supply. The man's name is Thompson, Russell Thompson. He's the man in charge."

"And I'm guessing this group you and he are part of isn't the Islamic Brotherhood for Righteous Judgement?" Gerry probed, knowing full well he was correct.

"No, that was just a smoke screen," Carling clarified.

"Well, don't keep us in suspenders. What do you go by?" Gerry pressed.

Carling swallowed hard. He looked quite embarrassed by what he was about to divulge.

"We call ourselves PATRIOT. It stands for Protection against the Rise of Ideological Occupation and Terrorism."

This pranged a sense of wonder in Tom. He stepped forward; Gerry glanced over his shoulder and followed him with a questioning glance.

"Your man up on the roof, Shaw, he mentioned that you were going to be a force of rebellion, that today was just the start of things to come. He said you wore the masks so that you could continue to do you work afterwards. What's the endgame here?"

Tom was playing over Shaw's monologue in his head. Carling afforded himself a laugh and diverted his gaze from Gerry to Tom.

"Not much chance of that after today is there. We're dropping like flies, if we keep going at this rate, we'll have no one left in the movement."

"Well if you'd put as much effort into your plan as you did into acronyms, you'd be laughing. You terrorists are all the same, you love a bloody acronym," Gerry huffed, disgusted.

Carling ignored Gerry's statement and began to lay out the organisation and their plans.

"The first thing I want to say is, all bullshit aside, I have no idea what we're looking for here."

This registered a suspicious look from Gerry.

"Honest to God I don't know, I swear," he spluttered.

"Well seeing as you don't know whether you're batting for Team Allah or the bloke with the long hair and sandals, I hardly think we can..." Gerry started.

"There are only two people that know; Thompson and Shaw," he revealed, a look of realisation etching his features upon the mention of his fallen comrade.

"Chalk that down to one," Gerry said in a far from humble fashion, shooting Tom a brief, immodest wink.

Carlings eyes darted nervously between the two.

"I suppose so. Look, all me and the others know is that the package is of a military nature and that it's on a memory stick, a blue memory stick for all the fucking good it's done us," he followed up with a petulant leer.

"Why's that? Come to think of it, why is what you're looking for, being militarily related, in a London shopping centre?" Tom pushed.

"As I said, the Prime Minister was our secondary agenda. We'd been planning that one for months. Once we had formulated a strategy as to how to grab the Prime Minister, we quickly recognised that our numbers were far from what we needed to execute our plan".

A pained sigh was released.

"So we cast the net wide; I said it was a bad idea at the time. We started enrolling people into the group that weren't trained, they were sloppy. Sure, they believed in what we were doing, they lapped it up in fact but they weren't ex-military like us, the founding members. Nah, they were like cardboard cut-outs compared to us".

He shook his head.

"Many of us had met through Thompson. Some of us were fresh out onto civvy street whilst others plied their trade doing mercenary or close protection work. The organisation was Thompson's idea. As he put it, we were fighting other people's wars and although work outside of the military had the ability to make us financially better off, it made us ideologically impoverished. We were ignoring the biggest battle of all."

"Which is?" Gerry dug deeper.

"The battle at home, the one many of us had at sought to escape in the first place, moving from place to place. Many of those who make up the group have been discharged from the Armed forces, mostly dishonourably, me included. When we got home there was nothing for us," he spat.

"I mean fuck, it's hard enough getting a job when you're an ex-serviceman let alone when you've been chucked out. A lot of us were lost, left numb by the whole thing. Hell, even when we were enlisted, we didn't feel like we were fighting for Queen and country."

Carling continued to gesture with his hands even though they were bound.

"We were sent here, there and fucking everywhere, fighting for Britain's business interests more than anything else, all the while the cuts came quick and fast. As the money dwindled so did the men around you. More died, the equipment got worse. It soon got to the point where we didn't even have the tools to do the job."

Carling paused and swallowed deeply using up the last remnants of spit he had left. Gerry gave him another deep sip of the coffee. He nodded back in thanks.

"Anyway, as I said, the nets were widened a little too far. We were on a mission out in Africa when we came across two Brits in a bar, mercenaries like us. They had approached us, apparently, they had heard about what we stood for and wanted in. They too had been ex-Army, discharged like us; they had an axe to grind, finding whatever contract work they could.

We verified their story, it all checked out...maybe a little too well, if we'd known that at the time. Anyway, to cut a long story short..."

"Please fucking do. It's like a sodding episode of Jackanory in here" Gerry scoffed.

Carling continued, a petulant look upon his face.

"We were assigned a job, strictly black ops, off the books. It was big and we needed the bodies, so we let them join. Thompson saw it as the perfect opportunity, thinking it would be the best way to assess their skillsets for the mission ahead, the reason why we're here today".

Tom and Gerry shared a glance that demonstrated neither was sure of what was about to come or of what to make of the revelations that had come thus far.

"We were tasked with hitting an installation in Sweden, all very hush hush, no government wanting to acknowledge it was there, plausible deniability and all that bollocks. The installation was a coalition operation, various countries including Britain all joined together with the soul intention of creating advanced tech that could be used both to counter the rise of cyber terrorism as well as within a battlefield capacity."

"We were sent to retrieve such a device, top shelf, state of the art. Thompson never told us who our generous benefactor was and to be fair, none of us gave a shit, as the pay-out was big and I mean big. All Thompson said was that it was directly linked to the Prime Minister's capture, our employer, being the same person who put today in motion also."

"The EMP device," Tom said aloud, Carling nodding in agreement.

"A state-of-the-art EMP device, portable with a strong range, the only prototype of its kind in the world; as I mentioned, top shelf. Anyway, we took out the site, it was heavily guarded, no one was left alive and then we burnt it to the ground. We lost one of the new guys we had signed up at the bar in Africa but the other one survived and was a regular star pupil. Thompson took to him straight away. Robert Townsend was the fucker's name."

"As an additional baptism by fire, Thompson had even assigned him his own solo mission that night, which turns out, was to retrieve the memory stick of data I mentioned earlier. He was proper handy with a gun; he took out more guards than any of us that night. So, Thompson brought him into the inner circle, making him an integral part of the plan. Long story short, he was a rat, worked for the government, it was all a cover. He..."

Tom shot his hand up and stopped Carling from speaking; he drove his finger into his ear. Gerry tensed and stepped towards him.

"What is it?" the fear in Gerry's voice more than evident.

Tom listened intently before turning back towards to the bank of monitors, scanning the rows of screens nervously.

"Tom what the fuck is it?" Gerry grabbed his arm.

Tom whirled round to meet Gerry's gaze, "Thompson's checking in, he's asking for Carling."

Gerry reacted by slamming his hand against the wall, the monitors shaking slightly. Gerry's face began to crumple with anger, he turned back to Carling who was now smirking away to himself. Gerry held his chin firmly.

"What did you do?" Gerry spat, his fingers digging into his chin, Carlings skin turning yellow under the impression left by his fingers.

"Nothing and that's just the point," he giggled menacingly.

Gerry stepped away from him and began pacing, swearing under his breath. Tom began to feel the icy fingers of fear grope at his spine again. Gerry stopped pacing and faced Carling, a dark demeanour descending over his features, the anger having taken hold. His hand shot out for the first thing that came to hand, the wrench and he swung it at Carlings head. It made solid contact with his cheekbone; a thud followed by the unmistakable crunching of bone. Carling was rendered unconscious instantaneously. His head bobbed back quickly, before falling flat onto his chest. Gerry made to swing the wrench again but Tom intercepted his wrist mid-air.

"Enough Gerry! We need to get the shutters up and running, leave him!" Tom screamed.

Gerry's eyes were wild with disbelief, Tom could literally see the process of resolution furrow his brow. He was battling to keep his anger under control, wrestling with his desire to land the finishing blow.

"The little fuck was stalling. He sung like a canary, feeding us all of that bollocks without telling us what we really needed to know," Gerry dropped the wrench and glanced drunkenly off into the distance, his body language registering defeat, the resolve in his voice sapped.

"A canary! Gerry there must be a bloody donkey somewhere in the world missing its hind legs but that means nothing right now," Tom reached Gerry's shoulders and pulled him back towards him, making sure to dig his thumbs deep into Gerry's upper torso.

It worked, Gerry's hazed like state faded and he whirled back round to face the monitor, he began wildly scanning the buttons. Tom did the same.

"We need to find the button that releases the door before he..." Tom stuttered and stumbled backwards; eyes locked on the central monitor.

His body, stricken with fear and a state of foreboding, rooted him to the spot. He heard the radio go dead in his ear and knew what was about to come. Out of instinct, he switched the radio off. Gerry was tapping randomly at buttons as he focused his eyes on a monitor that displayed the shutter doors. They were still firmly closed.

"Come on Tom, press anything. Those doors aren't going to bloody open themselves," he pleaded as he furiously danced his fingers over the monitor's unlabelled array of colourful buttons and dials.

Tom laid a hand on Gerry's shoulder which prompted him to turn briefly back to Tom, wanting to ascertain why Tom was no longer helping. He followed Tom's transfixed stare and his fingers came to a rest over the keyboard.

Gerry first glimpsed the three men who were bounding their way up the second-floor escalator. Gerry and Tom were both in no doubt as to where they were headed. His eyes then focused on the central screen, his blood instantly running cold. Thompson stood staring back into the camera; a sizeable smirk filling the lower half of his face. His hand was aloft, an object in his hand, his thumb primed.

"Turn it off!" Gerry screamed, which resonated a degree of shock within Tom, enough to snap him from his trance.

Tom began to furiously scan the keyboard; Gerry began pressing the bigger buttons on the console. Lights flicked on and off around the centre as they lost and gained their power. Tom felt a glimmer of hope as parts of the lit-up monitor board began to die. The doors however, remained sealed.

"It's working, keep pressing buttons. Even if the power is fully off, we can switch it back on, work the doors," Tom urged, transferring his eyes from the keyboard to that of the monitors.

Still Thompson stared back. There were now only two sections of the keyboard left active, mockingly lit up.

Tom and Gerry both turned their attention to this area, pressing a series of buttons. A command flashed up upon the screen and Tom's heart leaped into his mouth.

'Do you wish to open gate system? Y or N."

Gerry glanced over at Tom and smiled. Tom fervently scanned the keyboard until his eyes finally fell upon the letter Y. He made to shoot out for it, his index finger primed. He was about an inch from the keyboard when they were both plunged into all-encompassing darkness.

Gerry let out a guttural groan and started tapping at buttons. Tom's breathing, erratic and exacerbated by the darkness filled the air. He began groping at his vest, searching for his torch. Gratefully, he found it and switched it on. The beam fell upon Gerry who was hunched over the console, his hands tightened into fists.

"We need to go Gerry, they're coming. That door won't hold for long," Tom omitted.

"We were so fucking close," he said to himself.

"I know but we need to go, now Gerry," Tom reiterated more sternly this time.

"If they don't kill us here, they're just going to corner us somewhere else," Gerry muttered to himself.

Tom saw in Gerry the very thing that every solider was told to avoid in a survival situation, that being succumbing to the odds. Omissions of doubt, no matter how small, soon flourished into the one thing you did not need in a survival situation, namely, another mountain to climb.

Tom reacted fast.

"You don't get to say that Gerry. You do not just get to give up. You know why?" Tom let the question linger.

Gerry turned to Tom, his face a canvas of utter defeat and remorse.

"Because there's a child we, together, rescued and a shedload of hostages down there whose lives are riding on us getting them the fuck out of here. I sure as fuck didn't throw myself off of a building to die in here, no way. We move to Plan B."

"We're outgunned lad. That was our only hope. The place is a fortress, no one is getting in or out," Gerry petulantly recanted.

"So, we bring it down from the inside. Gerry, those people down there need you, hell I need you. You and me, whether we like it or not, are their only hope," Tom stopped, the sound of heavyset feet slapping on marble beginning to trail down the hallway.

Gerry nodded and with it the self-doubt cleared from his face and the bulldog spirit manifested itself once again in his intense glare.

"Sod it, he who dares wins, hey lad? Today's as good as any to cop it but not before taking some of them with us. I'm not doing anything better today," Gerry joshed.

"Amen to that," Tom replied, a guilty cocktail of excitement and fear resonating in the pit of his stomach.

Gerry reeled round picking up the MP5 from the desk.

"Get to the hatch, I'll cover you. Move in about five feet then stop. There are two shafts, the one on the left should lead straight to the room with the boy, the other to the floor below. Wait there for me. I'm going to try and pull the filing cabinet across the hatch once we're both in, that should bide us some time. Oh and Tom, I'm going to need one of those grenades on your shoulder there."

"But what about the console, we might..." Tom started, beginning to remove one of the grenades from his vest.

"If we can't have it, I'll be fucked if they're having it," Gerry concluded defiantly as he carefully received the incendiary device.

"That reminds me," he reached into his pocket and handed Tom his phone back, "if all goes belly up here, the last thing we want is that getting hit by a stray bullet."

Tom nodded his agreement, took the phone and ran to the hatch, pushing Carling out of the way as he did so. He squeezed through the hatch ensuring he followed his training, going shoulders first; if the widest part of his body fit, so would he. He had no idea how wide the shaft system was and he did not wish for his broad frame to get stuck. If the shaft were too small, he could back out, not that his options were much better back in the control room.

Gerry took position behind Carling. He swung him around in the chair and angled him towards the door. He crouched behind the office chair, making himself as small as possible, crouched, MP5 at the ready.

"Remember lad, Plan B if it all goes tits up," Gerry reiterated in a wayward fashion, largely to himself.

Tom backed into the shaft and felt the heel of his right foot teeter over the edge of the left shaft, the control room seemingly slightly higher than the room with the boy in it. He made sure to steady himself, giving Gerry enough room should he have to quickly manoeuvre into the shaft entrance. Gerry's fingers flexed over the MP5's fore grip. His head was dipped low as if in genuflection.

Tom drew his own gun, the safety flicked off; he fixed his line of sight beyond Gerry. From his vantage point he could just make out the bottom third of the door. The breeze from the room below teased his fringe. He wished so much to break the silence, to alleviate his bodies urge to explode with nervous tension. Amazingly, a thought forced him to break into a smile; he nodded to himself and repeated the absurd recollection, a line from a favourite, childhood film.

"Now I know what a TV dinner feels like," he whispered to himself in a defiant hybridised state of levity and anger.

He grimaced as the key band around his wrist dug into his flesh, the key protruding at a scathing angle. Tom eased the band from his wrist and placed it within his back pocket, not wanting the band to cause his dominant hand any discomfort whilst firing.

(CHAPTER BREAK)

Thompson was flanked by Jones and Greaves, having ordered McAllister to maintain his hostage guarding duties. Pierce was knelt before him cowering, a black hood over his head. Thankfully, the shutter securing the hostages had remained sealed but at least a third of the lights on the bottom floor had gone out. Thompson had been alerted to the incursion when the lights began flickering and two of the shop's shutters rose slightly before lowering again. It was at that stage that he had attempted to establish contact with Carling to no avail.

At first, he had pondered if the random flash of the lights was some form of Morse code. After staring at the lights for several seconds he maintained that if it had been Morse code, it was absolute gibberish. He had acted fast, lifting the EMP from his tactical vest, acting as he had briefed the men before the attack, should their communications be breached in any way.

McAllister had seen the EMP device within Thompson's gloved hand rise with purpose scrambled to switch off both his radio and the laptop keeping them abreast of the voting online with regards to Pierces life. When the laptop had been powered down, he had nodded to Thompson, establishing that the laptop was powered down and that it was safe to proceed. McAllister had been tasked two simple tasks; film any and all hostage videos and secondly, to ensure the live feed was not tampered with in any way, as Thompson had warned the authorities earlier. He now kept a watchful eye fixed on the outlet housing the hostages.

McAllister, who was as Scottish as shortbread and had been one of the founding members of PATRIOT. He had joined at the age of twenty-five, not long after completing a computing course at University which he passed with a First Honours degree and thusly, making him the youngest member of the team. No surprise, as he had begun hacking from a young age, content to stay in his bedroom throughout much of his formative years as a teenager. He had always been an awkward boy, his school had maintained that he was on the Autistic spectrum and as McAllister had pragmatically surmised, they were right to some extent.

However, whilst some wore their diagnosis with a level of embarrassment, even shame, he embraced and treasured his label. It acted as cover, allowing him to spend extended periods of time on his own without being questioned, allowing him to both focus on his daily routines as well as his online, extra-curricular activities. As McAllister saw it, the world was full of labels and overzealous-diagnosis', his label served as camouflage, his fellow students and even his parents to some extent, expecting very little of him with regards to criminal deviance.

He was a loner at school. His parent's well-founded yet ultimately futile attempts at assimilating him with fellow classmates at school and with friend's children from a young age had yielded little. Nothing truth be told. Many considered him devoid of any interpersonal skills and chalked his future up to an unremarkable one of loneliness and solitude which he found all the more ironic for if they were to review his online friends, granted they were faceless but friends all the same, they were in the thousands. This was echoed by the screensaver he had upon his desktop which read, 'Online friends don't byte'.

McAllister was a slight man with prescription glasses; his wiry six-foot-four frame resembling that of an anaemic praying mantis. He carried himself awkwardly and was to many a surprising addition to the team, no one more shocked than he. His long mousy hair, scattering of post-teenage acne and gaunt features made him blend into the crowd, a feeling he had openly welcomed his whole life. Thompson had observed his comments on numerous revolutionary and far right-wing chatrooms and often joked with the rest of the team that the dark web was like his very own interview room.

He had seen McAllister's comments and observed that when fellow members of the groups poked fun at him, he did not retaliate verbally. Instead, what struck him was that one week after a man with the domain name 'Union Hack' had referred to him as a *'Virgin concerned with socio/political issues that were far above his limited understanding',* said man, a Wayne Leighton as was later named by the News networks, wound up facing consecutive life sentences and extradition to America, when it was discovered that he had hacked into both the Pentagon and a reputable American bank, syphoning off several million.

Apparently, he had sloppily left a traceable IP address, which right up until his guilty verdict he vehemently denied, adamantly establishing throughout that he had been set up. Thompson agreed with Mr Leighton, he had indeed been set up, by McAllister no less. He had paid a fellow mercenary contact to get in touch with McAllister under the radar and had been pleased when McAllister had decided to jump at the opportunity of being part of PATRIOT. And why wouldn't a man in a dead-end IT job working for a banking company, unfulfilled and tasked with mundane jobs do so? A twenty-something still living at home due to the ever-increasing London property prices, his University loan a financial albatross around his neck.

Thompson was a ruthless judge of character and had vetted McAllister and his dedication to the cause stringently. He was angry at the world and alone, vulnerable and unaware of the qualities that made up friendship. The perfect mailable mound of clay for Thompson to mould to his ideological ends, the technological ace in his pack that could do more damage left alone with a laptop for five minutes than Thompson could do with a fully automatic weapon in say, a shopping centre.

McAllister watched on as Thompson spoke in a hushed, animated tone. He admired the man and hung on his every word, wishing he could be as forceful and competent at giving orders. He was like the father he never had, his real father suffocating him with demands to go outside and socialise, quoting books he had read on autism. It had made it all the more easy to leave home when he had been given his starting fee of eighty- five thousand pounds by Thompson as an advance for both hacking the shopping centres schematics and for designing online covers for the men to infiltrate the centre on the day of the speech, alter-egos that ranged from building contractors and foremen to that of general members of the public, all remarkably authentic and untraceable.

He had told his parents that he had received a job working for a programming company that required him to travel. He maintained the ruse, making sure to send home pictures of him in various locations around the world; unbeknownst to his parents these were either Photo shopped or staged whilst on missions in deserts that posed as beach fronts. He did not hate his parents, nor did he yearn for their company. As he saw it, their minds were put at rest whilst the primary objective of avoiding suspicion was upheld. Everyone was a winner.

Many would attribute that to being on the spectrum but as he and Thompson both saw it, it was not love or company that he craved, it was the desire to be noticed on as large a scale as possible, to leave a mark, a mark often represented by an untraceable IP address or programme. As a person he was a nobody, a faceless entity but online he was more than just an avatar or a domain name, he was everything he had ever wanted to be.

"The radios are compromised, so radio silence until I give the order. Palmer is leading the remainder of Alpha. They are going to breach the comm's room and take out the hostiles. I have given specific orders that they be taken alive if possible, for interrogation, for all we know they could have been working with our inside man. Now all of this has moved our plans forward slightly. The priority now is to release another message, we've been inactive for too long. Then, we move to extraction, taking Pierce with us."

The men surrounding Thompson nodded along with this, absorbing his every word.

"Right, now Alpha set up over three- quarters of the charges on all the possible breaching points, the only area not covered is the roof. Here is my proposition, Jones and Greaves you two go up to the roof, hoist up Shaw, and then cut the rope loose. Masks on, ensuring you stay in cover. If the media or the police get a whiff of the fact that Shaw isn't a raghead in any discernible way or cross reference his face with their database, our little charade will well and truly be blown.

"Then I want you to exit back through the roof access door and set a charge on it, that way if our boys do escape again, they can only go down. At that point, you'll converge on the extraction point with me and McAllister, where we'll await Alpha."

"What about the hostages, sir?" Greaves questioned, a slight smirk of knowing anticipation framing his mouth.

"You'll set charges on the door there too before you make your way upstairs. There's only one way into that outlet and that's through the shutters," Thompson smugly answered which raised a demented giggle from Greaves.

"Well there's always option two but that involves them being peeled off of the walls, don't it boss," Greaves chirped in a way that sought gratification.

He did not receive it; instead, Thompson rolled his eyes slightly and turned back to Jones, continuing with the plan.

"When we're all down here, we will set a charge on the site Bravo prepped earlier. After that we execute the last phase of the plan," as Thompson said this, he glanced over at Pierce and smirked shrewdly.

"The clock is ticking gentlemen; our primary objective may be lost. Alpha Team have orders to sweep one final time on their way down, if they have the insurgents all the better, they may know something. If we cannot retrieve the memory stick, we revert to Plan B earlier than expected. Are we all clear?"

Thompson stood to attention having given the order. Both Jones and Greaves replicated this, clapping their boots together, saluting Thompson.

"Yes sir," they stated in unison.

"Dismissed," Thompson stated uninterested, a level of distain evident in his tone.

It often seemed that he tolerated those within his team, elevating himself above them. Small cogs within the overall scheme, juxtaposed to that of his superior ingenuity and tactical knowledge. They were as much a necessary evil as they were a potential liability, as were all human beings.

"Get out of the way you berk," Greaves scolded McAllister as he and Jones approached.

Jones set about unclipping a charge from his tactical vest and began setting it up, McAllister stepping aside passively. Thompson also approached; he raised his gun slightly as if to further establish his commitment to sentry duty.

"At ease McAllister, you and me, we're on the move. No need to watch those hostages any longer, the charge will see to that," Thompson stated nonchalantly.

He kicked Pierce lightly in the side which registered a muffled anguished groan. Thompson knelt and crept in closer to his ear. When he spoke, Pierce flinched violently.

"Time to go check on those approval numbers of yours Pierce. I'm afraid I have a feeling it's going to be a hung parliament myself," Thompson mockingly toyed with his quarry.

He nodded at McAllister to grab Pierce, before turning and sauntering towards the cordoned off area located on the Ground floor, to the right. He approached the blue wooden structure adorned with the various signs warning of construction and produced a key, unlocking the fresh padlock on the door. He stepped through, McAllister and Pierce soon following.

CHAPTER SEVENTEEN: REMOVING THE CIVIL FROM CIVIL WAR

Tom steadied himself, one hand pressed hard against the cool metal of the air duct, the other held tightly on to the Glock 18. He breathed lightly through his nose, trying to minimise any noise. Tom watched on in horror as the wire wrapped around the table leg agonisingly became taut. They were testing the door, tentatively at first, just as he and Gerry had. Satisfied the door was not locked but rather wired shut, a heavy yank proceeded the initial testing of the door. The wooden frame creaked as the light testing of the door gave way to a heavy and rhythmic wrenching motion. Tom saw the top and bottom parts of the door warp slightly, moving away from the frame, the pressure being exerted upon the door pulling it free.

When it came, the splintering of wood made his heart stab at his chest. He watched the wire go taut and then limp between each barrage, beating in time with his heart. Another crack could be heard and the distinct echo of exerted voices. Then, it went deadly silent; the wired lifeline Tom had fashioned going limp. Tom entertained the idea that the wire could not be broken by brute strength, that it would hold. He soon drove it from his thoughts. As if to reinforce this belief, Tom heard the distinct roll of metal on cold, hard marble.

Tom remembering his training opened his mouth instinctively as wide as possible; clenched teeth and the force of a grenade could lead to a mouth full of shattered teeth. He hunched his shoulders and burrowed his ears as deep into the recess as they would go in a vain attempt at muffling much of the sound; his upper arms and chest beginning to quake.

It did not take long for the concussive blast to swing the door inwards and away from the safe housing of the frame, an orange and white flume of fire and smoke licking at the door frame as it was jutted into the room. The seat Carling occupied was swung aside with him in it. Gerry himself was flung back slightly but quickly righted himself. The room started to fill with choking smoke and to Tom's amazement, the sprinklers came on, soaking the floor in heavy cascades of water.

An already sodden Gerry edged back towards Tom, affording himself a flick of his head to displace some of the water streaming down into his eyes. The blast had awoken Carling, who was screaming out to his men. Tom, who had managed to stay upright, maintained his original stance. His ears rang and his vision, although impaired by smoke and the disorientating blast of the grenade, could just make out the nozzle of a gun as it poked around the door's frame and let fly a flurry of bullets from blind cover. Tom heard as several rounds bit into the surrounding concrete wall at the mouth of the shaft. He reciprocated and fired off two rounds, unsteadying himself with the recoil. Gerry also retaliated, letting off two short blasts of covering fire as he reached the mouth of the shaft before letting loose another flurry of bullets.

With that he let the gun hang around his shoulder by its strap and reached for the grenade he had taken from Tom earlier. He pulled the ring of the spring-loaded grenade that allowed one to hold onto the grenade for an eternity so long as the lever was not released. The floor of the metal shaft was saturated with the additional water that dripped from Gerry and every time he shifted his feet, the squelching of rubber on metal could be heard. He turned slightly to Tom and made to say something. The firing had started up again and he ducked slightly, firing off a volley of shots with his spare hand, his MP5 aimed at waist height. He made to turn again but was unable to finish his sentence.

It was as if all of the atmosphere had been sucked from the room, time now advancing at a lethargic pace. The last thing Tom saw was the distinct hexagonal shape of three flashbang's as they trundled towards the prone figure of Carling who was remarkably untouched by the dozens of rounds exchanged thus far. As one drew level with his head, the distance between him and the concussive device about three metres, he made to turn away. He grasped at the handles of the chair and tensed every muscle in anticipation of what was to come. He had only just expelled a scream when he was quickly enveloped by the concussive blast of the grenade as it both deafened and blinded all three of the men in the room simultaneously.

Tom slipped slightly upon the water in the shaft and was sent momentarily off-kilter. He collided with Gerry who fell away to his right. Dazed, Tom felt a round metallic object hit his knee as he windmilled his arms before succumbing to his own momentum. His stomach lurched, blood rising to his temples as he was thrown backwards and carried quickly down the left-hand shaft, violently thumping his head and elbows off the sides as he did so. It was not long before he was spat out onto the hard-concrete ground of what he assumed to be the room with the boy from earlier. His eyes were covered in a static firework display; his ears ringing with pulsating agony. The fall had been quite sizeable and had resulted in Tom landing hard upon his coccyx, causing him to howl out in pain.

After several moments of lolling from side-to-side, Tom's vision had just began to return when he heard a hollow thud emanate from the shaft and a flume of smoke twinned with an intense sulphur-laden heat, bellow from the opening he had himself just been ejected from. The boy to his right began to cry out, a shrill confused euphoria of fear and terror.

Tom groaned and turned onto his side, groping at the floor like a blind man. His back spasmed as the extent of the fall worked its way from his coccyx along his back. He blinked hard, trying to regain his sight, slipping slightly on the dusting of concrete upon the floor. For all he knew at this time, it might as well have been flour, all senses blitzed from his very skull.

When his vision finally halted its canted swoon, his head clearing somewhat, he drunkenly rose to his feet. He felt as if he had just stepped off a roundabout in a child's playground that had been travelling at one-hundred miles per hour. He winced; the child's cries coming like the impact of a hammer. No hangover imaginable could be as bad as this Tom had bizarrely pondered. When his eyes finally adjusted to the darkness and the effects of the flash bang, he scanned the room and to his utter dismay and horror, made two stark assessments. The sound accompanied by the smoke and heat meant only one thing, the grenade had gone off.

Tom tried to reason with this, when a singular thought came hurtling back, hitting him harder than the flashbang had. Knocking Gerry off balance. The metallic thud upon his knee trailed by an explosion four or so seconds later. The final piece in the puzzle was Tom's uttering of one singular word.

"Gerry".

(CHAPTER BREAK)

Palmer rounded the broken door frame and let off a cautionary blast of his M16, cutting a swathe across the mouth of the vent shaft. The sprinklers downpour continued unimpeded.

He advanced deeper into the room, the other two members of Alpha team trailing behind him, guns raised also. They passed Carling, not even affording him a second glance. Palmer flicked the mounted torch on his M16 and shone it into the scorched and jagged mouth of the shaft.

"Empty," he declared in a tone of personal clarification before turning back to address his men, ignoring the pathetic pleas from Carling to be untied.

"Hertz, Doc, on me," Carling's voice uttered, shrouded in thought.

The two men approached, Docherty or Doc for short approached first, eager to receive further instruction. A Belfast Loyalist, Doc joined the cause without a moment's procrastination. Thompson had found him out in Turkey of all places, in a prison for arms smuggling. He had bribed the Officer on duty for the man's safe passage, the Officer seeing that he was well paid for his indiscretion. Under Docherty's still continued disillusionment, he vehemently believed that Thompson had done so out of some misplaced patriotic duty. As he had informed Docherty at the time *'I'd hate to leave a Brit to these Fez wearing pricks.'*

The truth of course could not have been further from the truth and the more senior members of the group often poked fun at Docherty behind his back for this, Doc's naivety knowing no bounds. One only had to have met Thompson for less than thirty seconds to establish that the man did not have a sentimental bone in his body and although staunchly patriotic, he would not have seen it as a priority to part with twelve thousand Liras, if he did not have an ulterior motive.

There was also the very real threat of keeping quiet, not wanting to be the one to inform him of the truth and in doing so, break Thompson's carefully constructed hold over Docherty, a sense of eternally being in debt to Thompson for his status as a free man. The true reason was very black and white, tones hard to register when viewing the world through rose tinted glasses. Thompson had been told by a contact about the man's incarceration and had been afforded both his patriotic background and his rap sheet. Docherty was a master forger with unrivalled munitions links. He was known to many in the black market and other various clandestine organisations as the go-to man for all things forged. Legend had it that no matter the life you had led, when it came time to meet Saint Peter at the gilded gates of Heaven to attest for your various misdirection's, he had the papers for that also.

Thompson had sought his employ for various missions but had sought to embed Docherty, galvanising his future loyalties for the mission currently at hand. It had been Docherty who had established the men's physical identifications alongside McAllister's digital credentials for entering the country and all being well, leaving it. He had also ensured that all the men had the proper documentation and aliases to infiltrate the centre, Thompson knowing full well that a visit from the Prime Minister would raise issues surrounding the intelligence services. Everything from their identification passes to work on-site right through to forging the releases needed to smuggle the weapons they had attained for this mission, past the port authorities in Dover.

Ironically, Thompson had further relied upon Docherty and the very Turkish arms traffickers he had been imprisoned for dealing with in the first place, to attain the substantial bulk of the arsenal they had today. It had not been hard to achieve. The right amount of money exchanging hands, the right forged documents needed for the traffickers to conduct their various nefarious deeds under the cover of forged legality. Thompson even used Docherty's very reason for having approached the traffickers in the first place as cover, that being that they were themselves buying arms for a Loyalist group back in Belfast that he himself had been an affiliate of.

"Way I see it boys, we might have killed one of them. You heard the explosion; I reckon one of them was fixing up to throw a grenade in on us. We flashed them; stupid fuckwit drops the grenade. Goodnight Vienna," Palmer remarked in a bragging nature, his own self-inflation coming to the fore once again.

"My heart bleeds for them," Hertz muttered.

"Well, you know what they say, if you've gotta go, go out with a bang," Doc chirped up.

Hertz and Doc sniggered to each other.

"Alright Twiddle-Dee and Twiddle-Dumb, back to the task at hand, you know the boss and he ain't going to be happy with this as a reasonable cause of death. I'm going to see what I can retrieve in here and get that dumb fuck off of his arse. You two go down and sweep the stores below and neutralise anything that moves. God only knows where those vents lead. Carling and I will join you when we're finished. Stick together and don't get separated. You know the drill, if you can take them alive, do so. If not, turn them into a human pencil, no expense spared on the lead," Palmer afforded himself a smirk this time as his humour raised a low snigger from Hertz and Doc.

Doc and Hertz bundled out of the room, Hertz prodding Carling's ribs on the way out with his boot as he did so which raised a pained inhalation of breath from Carling. Palmer walked over to the monitors and started flipping switches. Several of the screens flicked into life, others lay dormant, fried by the EMP. Still not looking at Carling, Palmer began to reel off Carling's indiscretions.

"You know, you're just lucky a lot of this stuff is waterproof. I can only hope the same is true of your pants because when Thompson gets hold of you-" Palmer halted himself, the stark realisation that he himself could be in Carling's position at any time.

Palmer found a switch and managed to flick the emergency sprinkler system off. He scanned the screens that were still operational; thankfully, all the doors were still firmly locked down. Carling arched his neck towards Palmer painfully. He was still tied to the chair, a puddle surrounding his upper torso and head.

"Look, I know I messed up but we're all good, the place is still locked down, the plan hasn't been compromised," Carling seemed to be trying to reassure himself rather than Palmer.

Palmer rounded and strode over to Carling. He grabbed a cluster of hair and an arm of the chair and righted Carling; his pained protestations came quick and fast. Palmer came close to his face, uninterested by the level of discomfort he had inflicted upon him.

"But this isn't the first time is it Carling? What about Africa or Colombia for that matter? I'm not even going to go into Marrakesh. You had one job and it's a pretty cushy one at that, seal yourself in a room and be our eyes in the sky, open and close the odd door when it's needed. We're down four men here Carling and don't think for one second that just because you're the technical whiz kid around here that Thompson is going to let this streak of blunders continue. None of us and I mean none of us, come before the mission. The plan here today is going to change things, it's bigger than any of us, maybe even Thompson," Palmer spat, the evident traces of spittle flecking his dark, brown skin.

Carling was engulfed in a heady cocktail of fear and overwhelming realisation.

"Maybe that's just the problem Palmer; this is too big for us. We're just twelve men ...well eight now," Carling half-heartedly digressed.

Palmer's hand shot out and grabbed Carlings throat.

"No, it's too big for you! You're damaged goods Carling, God knows where Thompson found you, he never said. Just that you were dishonourably discharged. You're unhinged. Don't think I've not seen you, talking away to yourself, the nightmares at three o'clock in the morning like clockwork, that gimpy expression you have when you stare off into space. I've said it time and time again, you've lost your bottle if you ever fucking had it to begin with. I mean shit, you're lucky you still have a head after those two corralled you up," he said throwing Carling's neck aside with disgust. "No wonder your missus left you."

Carling ignored that his lungs screamed out for oxygen and he shook violently, several nerves being well and truly prodded.

"You don't fucking talk about Nat! You don't have the right to even mention her name. You know nothing about me. You don't get to go there you wanker!" Carling strained against his restraints, a long protruding vein of anger jutting from his neck.

Palmer tutted, "You were broken when we got you, only worthwhile thing was the discount we got you at. Found you at the bottom of a bargain basket, all dented and label free. Now the tin's open and we all know what's inside and let me tell you, its ohhh so disappointing. Thompson gave you a cause to fight for, a cause that outweighs any bit of skirt or mental breakdown you may be having. So here's how this goes; I'm in charge of Alpha team and whether I like it or not, you're with us. Finish off everything you need to do in here and then we're shutting it all down permanently."

"No more mistakes, you're answering to me now. Thompson's the last of your worries. You mess up on my watch, make me look incompetent and it won't be Thompson that gets the honour of putting you out of your warped mind," Palmer finished this barrage with the unsheathing of his knife.

He let it hover an inch from Carling's torso before he began to cut away at his binds, a deliberate statement of intent.

Carling rubbed his aching upper torso, massaging life back into his newly freed limbs. He stood up, lightly probing his face before withdrawing his fingers quickly having touched upon his scalded forehead and blistered cheeks. He was sure he was bleeding from his right ear, the headache he was experiencing indicating onset concussion. Silent in his defiance, he stepped past a Palmer who glared back at him and set about powering up the last sections of the consoles.

"We keep it all locked down, wait for Jones and Greaves on the roof to finish setting the charges, then we power it all down and you make this an obsolete, tamper-free system," Palmer ordered.

Carling stubbornly nodded back in understanding.

(CHAPTER BREAK)

Not wanting to be caught out like Shaw had been, Greaves and Jones popped four smoke grenades and tossed them out from behind the cover of the roof access door. They waited several seconds before proceeding. As Greaves had discussed with Jones as they ascended the metal stairway, neither of them was in any doubt that there were snipers on any one of the adjacent buildings. The smoke would, they hoped, afford them enough cover to winch Shaw back to the safety of the roof, before setting the charges. They reckoned they would need to toss their last remaining smoke grenades after they had pulled Shaw up, to afford them the time they needed. The thick white flumes of smoke swirled majestically in the wind; the rain slightly dissipating the thickness of the cloud.

Both men, equipped with gas masks, entered the roof quickly. The rope was tied to the right side of the door and still using the door as cover, the men began to heft Shaw's substantial girth back towards the ledge of the roof. Greaves held firm in his belief that no matter what had happened on the roof with Shaw and his would-be attackers that the sniper teams must have had some part to play in his comrade's fall from grace. He had fought alongside Shaw on many an occasion and was certain that he would not have gone down without taking bodies with him and that the only thing stronger than his physical prowess was his patriotic dedication to their cause.

Although Shaw seemed to get snagged at several points upon his ascent, it was not long before the exhausted men felt his body snag on the edge of the building ahead and with a huge heave, his body hit the gravel of the roof. Greaves indicated for Jones to discharge the remainder of the smoke grenades and to start prepping the charges. Greaves, through gritted teeth, began to pull Shaw across the roof, reeling him in like a fish or rather a whale given Shaw's sizeable stature.

Never being one to pass up the opportunity of delivering a distasteful pun, Greaves heckled to himself, "Thar she blows Captain Ahab," as the top of Shaw's head popped into focus, cutting a swathe through the smoke like the bow of a ship.

It was all he could do to hide the exertion upon his wiry frame, his non- existent upper body strength made slow progress with the awkward weight, his balance constantly off kilter on the gravelled surface. Hand over hand, Greaves methodically brought him closer, Jones rendered invisible within the thick, bilious smoke. When Shaw was about a metre from the door frame, Greaves cut the rope and let it fall to the floor. He hooked his hands around the shoulder straps of Shaw's tactical vest and began to shuffle backwards in a jaunty fashion from side to side, his breathing replicating his exerted imbalance.

Greaves dragged him in to the top of the staircase before methodically unravelling the rope from around his neck. The tangled nature of the rope had cut into his throat; a dry layer of encrusted, congealed blood came away from the wound caused by rope burn and strangulation. He pulled the door to and waited for Jones; glad his partner could not see how strenuous the task had been. Jones had offered to do it but Greaves' arrogant pride had not allowed it.

Greaves rolled Shaw's balaclava upwards and was taken aback by how passive the man looked for one who had died in such a horrific fashion. Other than the wound around his neck, a light blue tinge to his lips and the fresh blood smeared across his face which Greaves assumed came via a fistfight, Shaw seemed at peace. Greaves did not maintain his vigil over the body for long however and he took his opportunity waiting for Jones to inspect Shaw's body. It was not long before his earlier suspicions were confirmed. A substantial flesh wound to his upper right shoulder; an exit wound the size of a fifty pence piece on his left calve. Greaves knelt and lifted Shaw's left leg at an angle that would have brought tears to conscious man's eyes. He surveyed the exit wound and nodded to himself, affording himself the vocal clarification he needed.

"High velocity round, most definitely from a sniper rifle. You interfering-" the door opened and Jones nearly stumbled over the pair.

He yanked off his gas mask and sucked in vast gulps of air, wiping the condensation from his brow.

"All set, smoke's just starting to disperse," Jones swallowed.

Greaves did not look up, still gripping tightly onto Shaw's leg. Jones followed the man's line of sight and took in the entirety of Shaw's frame.

"That looks like a sniper round. The boss gave them strict instructions. He said-" Jones started.

"I know what he said," Greaves spat as he dropped Shaw's leg. "They went ahead anyway, tried to pick him off. He sustained a direct hit and a fleshy. That said, make no mistake, the defensive wounds on the hands and face, the rope around his neck, they didn't finish the job. No," he shook a finger, "it was our man on the roof."

Greaves stood up and wiped Shaw's blood on to his black jeans. He made to leave.

"What about Shaw? We can't just leave him here," Jones called after Greaves in a childlike fashion.

"You heard Thompson. He said get him out of plain sight, well we've done just that, mission accomplished. If you think I'm carrying him down a couple of flights of stairs, you've got another thing coming. Booby-trap him and leave him there, he'll make a decent draft excluder, about the only thing he's good for now anyway."

And with that, Greaves disappeared down the first staircase. Jones sighed and reluctantly unlatched a claymore mine, setting it at the feet of Shaw. He replaced the balaclava that Greaves had rolled up on Shaw's forehead and stepped away from the body glancing back momentarily.

"Be seeing ya fella," he mustered before setting off down the metallic stairway.

When the smoke finally cleared upon the rooftop, the sniper team stared on in pure amazement having been told in no uncertain terms, to hold their fire this time. It would have been pointless anyway, due to the thickness of the smoke. When the last of the smokescreen dissipated, all that was left was the furled up, cut length of rope and a shallow trail in the gravel where the body of the masked man had been dragged. The empty canisters of the smoke grenades scattered towards the middle of the rooftop. This information was directly relayed via the radio to an apprehensive Richard Miller, a man quickly running out of options.

(CHAPTER BREAK)

Tom had seen the end of the rope begin to dance and curl its way upwards and out through the fissure in the floor. He made little effort to grab at it, not wanting his position to be given away, yet knew that with it, another figurative and literal lifeline was being pulled away. He instead concerned himself with the next predicament, keeping the boy silent enough to remain undetected, a task harder than many of the tribulations he had endured thus far. The child was hunkered down in the box, screaming his lungs out, his Thomas the Tank Engine top and bottoms sodden with tears. He gripped onto his ears, shaking with frustrated anger and confusion at what had just happened.

Tom hefted him from the box and gave him a cursory glance, turning him in his arms, inspecting his body. Satisfied, Tom ascertained that the boy was physically unscathed, concluding that the noise and force of the explosion must have come as quite a shock to the young child. He patted him on the back and shushed him, bringing the child's mouth closer to his torso, thus muffling a large percentage of the child's cries. This aided in calming the boy as well as minimising his siren inducing call. As Tom patted the child's back, swaying the child from side to side, he scanned the room. He brought the child over to the workbench and sat him atop of it.

"Now you stay there," he stated in a consolatory tone, his own voice barely audible above the ringing in his ears.

Trying to keep the boy engaged, Tom grabbed a piece of sandpaper and gave it to the child who reciprocated with a cheeky gurgle of hilarity and once again set about flapping the inanimate object. Tom, desperate and without a way of reaching the floor below, ascertained that this was about to get even rougher for his body, as an item atop the workbench set the gears of an idea in motion. He reached for the duct tape and turned it over in his hands, observing that it had been practically unused, the edge tapered to afford the next user an easy purchase. Tom unwound a length of the tape, the sound causing him to flinch and the boy to jump slightly. The child observed Tom with baffled intrigue for a moment or so, joyous amazement etched across his face. Tom was grateful. Not only had the boy quietened but upon the boy hearing the noise of the tape it confirmed to Tom that there had been no long-lasting auditory damage from the concussive blast of the grenade exploding.

Tom tugged at the material, giving it all he could with his wounded shoulder. He afforded himself a wayward glance at the child and smiled back at him, all the while measuring up the child's weight. Content, he began wrapping the tape around the child's torso, aiding the child by lifting his arms. The child's furrowed brow highlighted his concentration and observation upon Tom. Tom swathed the tape around the child several times, leaving a gap at the back that he kept from sticking to the material of the child's top with two spare fingers. Into this gap, he wrapped another length around the several layers of tape, until he was satisfied that that the two separate pieces of tape were assuredly attached.

Tom then tentatively lifted the child, the end of the duct tape sticking to his palm which he followed up with several cautious wraps of the material around his right hand. The duct tape held strong and he lifted the child up and down in an effort to assess the tensile structure of the everyday material. It held. His plan was to lower the child down to the level below, then follow. However, no amount of duct tape would hold his substantial weight, therefore, he surmised that he would have to lower himself into the hole and drop from whatever height his tall frame afforded him. He kneeled by the edge and stood the child up gripping the child by his shoulders.

"Right little guy, time to go see if we can't find your Mum," he beamed.

The child fluttered the sandpaper and offered it up to Tom, wishing him to have it. Tom shook his head and pushed it back to the child.

"No, no, you keep hold of that. You can give it to your Mum when you see her, as a souvenir of our little adventure together, hey?" Tom ruffled the child's hair as he said this.

Tom then lifted the boy and began to lower him into the hole; his shoulder now shuddering with pain. He kept the roll of tape on his left hand as a form of pulley and used his right hand to guide the duct tape, peeling and rolling off slack when it was needed. The line began to turn in and stick to itself, but this only served to make the strand of duct tape more resilient.

When Tom felt the child touch down, he stepped back from the edge of the crevice and unfurled some more slack, he tied this to the workbench's table leg, wrapping it around the leg before tying it in a knot. This would ensure that the child did not wander off long enough for Tom to get down to the level below if Plan B should be needed. If not, he would simply pull the boy back up. He intended to wait for Gerry, affording his newfound ally enough time to return. He pushed all thoughts of the explosion and its repercussions from his thoughts and instead decided to concentrate on the whistle of the wind outside, a welcome distraction.

Just as Tom was tying off the last of the duct tape a heavy force came down upon the wooden door, the unsecure chain lock rattling violently. Tom hunkered down behind the table and withdrew the Glock 18. He once again flicked off the safety and waited. A second booming barrage came down upon the door; this time the distinct rattle of a screw hitting concrete could be heard. They had incorrectly assumed that the door had either been locked or barricaded, affording Tom an advantage, their breach no longer executed stealthily.

Tom once again pushed his ears into his shoulders and waited, mouth open, the fear of another flash bang or grenade causing him to tremor. Tom peered out from behind the edge of the workbench, the shadows dancing between the cracks of the makeshift door. Swiftly, the door came swinging inwards and the room flooded with light. Tom assumed a firing stance and decided to hold fire until he knew what he was up against. Two men entered, Tom made all too aware of this by the long shadow that cast its way along the floor and the wall before him.

He listened intently as the strap of a gun creaked slightly, the metallic arching of a gun being swept across the room. The men separated; one going left, the other right as they intended to flank the workbench. Tom afforded himself the briefest of glances from his disclosed position and swallowed hard when he recognised the blistered face of Carling. Satisfied that there were two men and that the remainder of the team were not here, most likely on the search for Gerry, Tom weighed up his options.

The element of surprise was the only card left to play; of that Tom was certain. That said, it was the who rather than the how, that caused Tom to pause for thought. Yes, Carling was the obvious choice. He had undergone a substantial amount of pain whilst under duress not to mention the concussive blast of the stun grenades. Whilst he felt he had some measure of the man unlike that of the unknown assailant approaching from the left, Tom knew all too well the damage a wounded predator could do. To all intents and purposes, the unknown aggressor was the unknown variable in the mix.

He lay flat on the ground and peered under the bottom of the workbench waiting for the other man to come into focus. The man's shadow edged closer, Tom's heart beating faster. The movement of Carling behind his head and to his right filling him with dread. Yet he held his nerve and waited for the man to step into his line of fire. He did not have to wait long. The size ten boot of the man's left leg came into view. Tom did not hesitate. He pinched off two rounds in a tight grouping, the first catapulting a sliver of concrete into the air, the second a splat followed by a groan.

The man fell to the floor with a heavy thump before the metallic echo of a gun, sizeable in calibre, hit the ground and slid away. The man's wild brown eyes locked gazes with Tom's from via the underbelly of the table and he shot a gloved finger up and towards Tom. Tom observed that the man was black, with short, cropped hair. He was briefly taken aback by the man's ethnicity, the assortment of the insurgents rendering their original cover-up all the more fantastical.

The non-verbal command was registered by Carling who rushed to the head of the table. In one movement he upended the heavy construct which Tom was too slow to roll away from. The table came crashing down upon Tom's lower body. He resembled a magician's assistant about to be cut in half. The intense weight of the table drove the air from Tom's chest and immobilised his upper body; the Glock 18 sent flailing from his hands, the pain in his injured and bloodied shoulder nearly causing him to pass out. To make matters worse, a variety of tools and all manner of building paraphernalia cascaded down from the tabletop, a tape measure hitting Tom squarely on the bridge of the nose.

His chest heaved as if it were trying to dislodge the table, black spots firing across Tom's vision. He was winded and unarmed. He could hear the wounded man turning and swearing to himself, however, he was now obscured by the corner of the table. Tom heard slow footsteps behind his head and he desperately pushed against the table. He looked round for a weapon and heard the tear of duct tape. He made to grab at the strand just as it tore before his very eyes but to no avail as it fluttered away from his outstretched fingers. He made to call out when a shadow fell upon him, cutting the cry off in his throat.

Carling peered down at Tom, his face a vision of pure venom and self-fulfilment at having captured one of his captors. He placed a foot upon the table and pressed down hard. Tom wheezed in pain; a rattled crackle emanated from his lungs. His right hand was pinned, his left-hand scrabbling at the loose items framing his head and shoulders.

"Got time for a coffee?" Carling beamed, his blistered face forcing him to grimace slightly at the movement of his cheekbones. Tom's eyes shot up to meet Carling's.

"Ahhh what a shame, we'll have to..." he pushed down harder on the workbench, "table a meeting for that some other time won't we?"

Tom's temples burnt and the metallic tang of blood filled his mouth. His left hand fell upon an object which he instinctively started to grope at, a spirit measure, useless for all intents and purposes.

"We need him alive," the injured man growled through gritted.

Without taking his eyes from Tom, Carling replied. "Not before I have some fun with him Palmer."

He turned back to Tom, a curious look materialising across his blistered features.

"What was it your man said to me? Just like every good man and a flat pack, I'll be... ignoring the instructions and losing parts. Yeah, that was it. Where is that Geordie bastard anyway?"

Tom muttered something. Carling did not catch it and released the pressure from the table slightly.

"What was that? I couldn't quite make that out on account of you being a human carpet."

Tom grimaced, sucking in what little oxygen he could from the slight release of the workbench. He breathed in, continuing to probe the scattering of items within his miniscule reach, the spare inch from the table affording him additional reach. Carling noticed a change come across Tom's eyes as they clouded with venom, a slight smile etching his lips.

"I said he's from Sunderland you dumb fuck."

He began to snigger, but Carling thrust the table down harder.

"Funny guy, cracking jokes although I've never seen a comedian under a table before. There was me thinking it was called stand up for a reason. Not much chance of that now is there?" he rocked the table from side to side, the edge of the wood cutting a swathe along Tom's ribcage. "We'll see how funny you are when I'm done with you. Then and only then, will I toss the scraps to the man on high."

"Stop dicking about Carling. Knock him the fuck out already and restrain him. I'll need a shitting transplant at this rate," Palmer asserted, sounding distinctively faint of heart.

Carling whirled round and looked aside towards Palmer, momentarily breaking his gaze with Tom. Tom's hand fell upon something made of rubber and metal, the thick tabletop relenting slightly. Tom tentatively caressed the items contours and immediately registered its purpose. His fingers lightly danced across the handle as he tried to claw it close enough so that he could gain a purchase on it.

"You're out of action Palmer, I'm running Alpha now. This waste of space is my ticket back into Thompson's good books and not you or anyone else for that matter, is going to take that away from me. I caught him, me! I may have screwed up in the before, in the past but this is mine. He is mine. The boy with the poppies was a mistake, missing these two on the cameras was a mistake. Don't you see that was all out of my hands but this..."

"What the fuck are you on about, what boy with the..." he sucked in an anguished bolt of pain as he cradled his injured leg, "you're nuttier than squirrel shit you are. It's no wonder your bird left-"

Carling released the pressure he was administering slightly and withdrew his sidearm, firing three successive rounds in Palmers direction. Tom did not see what happened next nor did palmer cry out. Instead, it was the wet slap of bullet upon torso that confirmed it to Tom. Carling had shot one of his own men. With that uneasy thought prominent over all others, Tom now had a full grip on the handle of the cold steel. He fondled for the button.

"I warned you. I told you time and time again not to mention her. You've always brought that up; it wasn't my fault, the boy with the poppies broke us apart. It had nothing to do with me, stop fucking blaming me for everything! We were happy. I was happy before all of this. I was a good man," Carling began to choke up, dropping his pistol slightly.

Tom never took his eyes from him. He was distracted, directing his volley of anger at Palmer, his weight upon the table faltering and with it his foundation. Tom braced the tabletop with his pinned right forearm, ready to push, a firm grasp of his newfound weapon in the other hand. He would only have one attempt at this; it had to be achieved in one fluid motion. He just hoped it had been maintained and was ready to be used.

Tom shimmied and thrust himself against the table, enough to slide round slightly to face Carling, freeing both hands, his legs still pinned. His ribs screamed out, the movement jarring. Carling instinctively drove his full bodyweight down upon the workbench. Tom grimaced but had manoeuvred himself enough to execute his plan. Carling stood with an open stance, his gun to his side.

"I'm a good man. I only wanted to help the boy, his country... my country," Carling babbled with bile and self-loathing.

The man was gone; he had taken to justifying some misdemeanour to his foe, hoping to exorcise some internal demon. Tom cared little. There was only one boy he cared about right now and he was below him, unchaperoned. He brought up the nail gun using the last remnants of upper body strength he had left, every nerve in his left arm firing off in pain.

Carlings quickly identified the new threat. His expression changing from one of anger to that of panic as impulsively rose his gun. Tom pressed down hard on the plastic button and was relieved to hear the pneumatic hiss of air followed by the thud of flesh, as he peppered Carling with several nails largely in a cluster around his right shoulder. Carling yelped out in agony and fell to the ground, his pistol bouncing through the open cement gorge.

Tom hefted the table from his torso and afforded himself a deep inhalation of air. Yearning to establish that he had regained the upper hand, in an uncharacteristic moment of crudeness he afforded himself the briefest of quips.

"Nailed it," Tom wheezed.

He sniggered slightly but his ribs shut the guffaw down, a blurting cough rising within his windpipe instead. Tom massaged his legs with his right hand all the while keeping the nail gun trained on the unarmed Carling, who flopped about in pain. He glanced over at the body of Palmer and observed the gigantic pool of blood, the lifeless stare; nothing to fear where Palmer was concerned.

Tom stood upright sucking in air, his right arm flailing by his side, numb and sodden to the touch, Gerry's makeshift closing of the wound most likely busted open. He fetched his fallen Glock 18 and holstered it before he grabbed some wall insulation, packing it in and around his wound, the tight tactical vest holding its position firm. He transferred the nail gun from his weakened left arm to his right, which had now gained sensation. Tom breathed out in ecstasy glad to be rid of the additional weight upon his weakened arm.

He kept the nail gun trained on Carling who was convulsing upon the floor and visually checked the man's torso and waist for any concealed weapons. He had none. Tom then backed over to Palmer, still training the tool on Carling's centre mass, keeping Palmer between the two. He picked up Palmers weapon, an M16 and stepped back from the corpse. He cradled the nail gun in the crook of his hand, the M16 firmly in his grasp, now trained at Carling. After transferring the M16's strap to his shoulder, he repositioned the nail gun in his right hand. He walked over to Carling and knelt beside him, pressing the nozzle of the nail gun into his shin. Carling halted his blubbering pronouncements and turned round to meet Tom's gaze. Tears streaked his eyes. Tom cut him off at the pass.

"Don't speak, just listen. Who you are and the events that have led you to where you are today is immaterial to me. I could never empathize with you, your sick cult or the reasoning behind today's attack but you've largely managed to avoid the brunt of the bloodshed up in control."

Carling dumbly stared back at Tom unsure as to what his captor would say next with the nail gun stilled burrowed firmly into his shin.

"But what I can understand, more than you will ever know, is that you are not in a good place mentally. Tell me, Carling isn't it? Have you spoke to someone about your PTSD?"

Although Carling jutted out his chin and continued to stare back at Tom, his erratic breathing rendering his false bravado weaker by the second, a slight red hue to his checks indicated to Tom that he had not.

Carling stammered, "Is this... the bit where you try to level with me? Play the good cop? You know nothing about me... about why I was discharged, about why I'm here today. You're just some civvie do-gooder living on borrowed time."

"See that's where you're wrong, I'm ex-service, Army. I know you think you've only got one play here but there is an alternative. A choice that I didn't take when I had the chance."

Carling sniggered; his eyes wild with stubborn anguish.

"That explains a lot, here was us thinking you were some have-a-go with a death wish," he shook his head, "I've made my choices, I made them in the forces, I made them up in that control room with your bad cop boyfriend and I'm sure as fuck going to make them here. I'm in control of my decisions, no one else."

"That's exactly what I said when they discharged me with PTSD," Tom conceded, leaving the statement to hang in the air.

A static tingle swept down Tom's body, one of relief at having divested himself of a great burden. Astonishingly and to no greater shock than to Tom himself, Carling was the first person he had ever divulged the truth to about his departure from the Army.

Carling scoffed, "And what, you think that makes us... two sides of the same coin? Someone to hold your hand and sing kumbaya with? Nah, we ain't the same, not even close. It's just a label, another way for the Rupert's and Whitehall elite to make cutbacks. It's all bollocks...another label to make you ashamed of your actions, of who you are. What I've done here today, what I will do... I've never been prouder of anything in all my life"

Tom looked upon the man with pity and grudgingly decided upon a firmer stance. He drove the nozzle of the nail gun harder into the man's shin, twisting it as he did so.

"OK, fine. Then its option two, bad cop as you put it. Any more of these in you and a tetanus shot will be the least of your worries. At the very least it'll make it a bitch to walk through any metal detectors, not that you'll be going anywhere anytime soon. So, I'm going to ask you this once and you're going to answer and promptly; how do I get out of here?"

Defiantly, Carling once again turned his head to the side and jutted his chin outwards like a petulant child. Tom fired a nail into the man's leg without hesitation. Carling internalised his scream and began to convulse again, his hands opening and closing trying to distract him from the real pain.

"Breathe," Tom urged the man before levelling the nail gun at Carling's thigh, "and answer the question. I have a boy down there who I want to get out, can't be any older than two. Now by the sounds of it, this boy with the poppies..."

Carling snapped his neck round to face Tom, venom in his eyes.

"You failed that child. Now, call it what you will but I'm giving you a chance at redemption. Can't you see that you dumb fuck?" Tom pressed defiantly.

Carling cocked his head back and violently gobbed at Tom, who calmly wiped it from his right cheek and chin with the back of his hand. Carling sneered.

"Take your redemption and stick it up your arse Mother Teresa. My soul was lost long before I ever met you and ..."

Tom made to fire another nail into the man's thigh when an eruption of gunfire illuminated the room; the smell of cordite proceeded by the splintering of wood as bullets peppered the workbench. Carling violently thrust Tom away and had it not been for the M16 lodging itself across the mouth of the exposed hole in the floor, he would have fallen headfirst through the recess. He dangled precariously, the strap holding firm, the length of the gun serving as an anchor across the width of the hole.

He could hear the shuffling of feet on the concrete above, the thud of bullets. The strap cut across his upper left-hand shoulder and around his neck, the material chaffing and cutting off his circulation. A man-made noose suspended him from the floor below as if in limbo, neither dead nor alive. Below him lay sanctuary and the young child, above only death.

Tom looked up to see the gun being raised from its anchor point; they were using the makeshift noose to drag him back upwards. With that, Tom made an executive decision, using his last visages of strength, the image of Shaw hanging from the side of the building spurning him on, he brought up his knife and cut the strap with one gash. He fell into the gloomy darkness below, praying the young child was not below. No such item broke his fall, instead that of a mannequin, which only served to break his fall slightly. Tom felt it come apart at the waist and he fell the remaining metre or so, landing harshly upon his side. With agonising instinct, he jolted sideways and hobbled to his feet.

A cascade of M16 fire came through the hole and briefly illuminated the room in white, staccato light. Tom caught a glimpse of the child ahead, several metres from where he had fallen, still intent on playing with his sandpaper. The gunfire stuttered on and off, rendering the room dark then light again. Tom judged where he had seen the child and scooped him up. His back and arm screaming out even under the insignificant weight of the young child. He hobbled forward, the light of the doorway twenty metres away or so. It was open. He moved towards it, shuffling like a lame man. The child flapped the sandpaper directly in his line of vision. The muffled anger of an argument could be heard from above which was quickly preceded by a thud. Still Tom powered on. His foot struck the base of a display stand and momentarily whirled sent him off kilter. He cantered at an absurd angle before righting himself.

A round whistled by his ear, a mannequin's head exploding before him. He instinctively began to run in a zig-zagged fashion, another bullet thumping into the ground beside him. The light of the open doorway seemed so bright now, Tom quite not believing his luck. The boy began to giggle and gurgle as if he knew they were close to open ground, a snowballs chance in hell of escape, a door opened by Gerry and Tom when they were up in Control possibly.

"Keep your head down little guy," Tom panted, another round punctuating his point and causing him to instinctively stoop his head.

"Stop or you're dead" howled Carling, his frenzied voice unmistakable.

Tom glanced back and made out the shuffling spectre of Carling, his grin the only thing visible in the gloom, the unhinged man having followed Tom through the hole. Just shy of five metres from the mouth of the entrance, another shot cracked out. Ignoring it, Tom stumbled out into the light, his eyes momentarily adjusting to the deluge of artificial light. He shielded the boy's eyes and heard footsteps to his left. He was on the second floor.

He instinctively bolted right, fearing the heavy footfall to his left and the prospect that remaining stationary would do for Carling's faltering aim. He stumbled onwards, his eyes fixed upon the Staff exit at the end of the concourse, surmising that it also led up just as the one he and Gerry had ventured through earlier had done. He made his way towards it, the lactic acid in his legs urging him to desist. Going up limited his chance of escape but afforded him the possibility of a hiding place or even better, if he could make it to the roof, support from the snipers.

Tom fixed his gaze on the corner of a perfume outlet up ahead where the concourse diverted right, affording him cover. He had barely formulated his next course of action when it disintegrated before him, the marble tiles falling apart before him.

"Nowhere to run hero," Carling's shrill call sounded out, followed by another wild flurry of gunfire.

Tom ignored him and made to turn the corner when he was hit by a thud, one which sent him sprawling to the floor. The boy in his hands afforded him little space to break his fall and he landed hard upon his elbows. Immediately using the momentum of the fall, he shimmed himself around the corner nudging the child before him into cover, the blood lubricating his knees, his head swaying with the dizzy pain of blood loss.

(CHAPTER BREAK)

They had argued with him at the mouth of the hole, Hertz and Doc, berating him for being stupid, that he was not thinking straight. Upon hearing the gunfire, they had rushed quickly from the Second Level back up to the Third. As Carling assured them, he had never been saner in all his life, never so in control of himself. He pushed them away, taking with him the M16 he had confiscated from the edge of the recess, firing a series of wild shots into the darkness.

Without any consideration for his own wellbeing, he had jumped through the hole, landing heavily upon his bad shin. He had not even yelped out in pain, a discombobulated mannequin breaking his fall, briefly sending him off balance. He had quickly gotten to his feet, pulling the nail out of his shin as he did so with a maniacal grunt. His target had moved quickly, his back towards him, the light ahead only serving to outline his profile further. That was all Carling needed a featureless silhouette just like the ones on the shooting ranges he had trained countless times upon. He hobbled onwards, his shin all but crippled.

As he approached the corner flecked with blood, he made sure to savour the coopery smell of blood in the air as he traced trail of blood on the floor indicating he had severely wounded his prey. He had warned him to stop, not that it would have done him any good. He arrogantly mulled over Hertz and Doc's conversation at the mouth of the hole on a loop.

"Who's unbalanced now? Knocked him off balance, didn't I? Thompson's going to hike up my share for this," he muttered to himself as his loped forward, levelling the M16 at the bend six-foot ahead.

Just as his prey had been about to round the corner so too had the child with the poppies. Without pause, he had fired, the explosion of marble replacing the phantoms head.

Carling sternly asserted to himself, "Haven't got time for you, "relishing the sound of the blood as it slapped and stuck to his boots as he swung round the corner, gun trained low towards his attacker.

And there he lay huddled before him, his back facing towards him. Carling trained the gun at his head, the column of marble smeared in blood. He manoeuvred around the man, so that he now stood before him. How he craved to look into his eyes when he administered his redemption in the form of a bullet. His ears pricked up and his heart jumped with ecstasy. His victim was crying. How he would savour this moment.

"An M16 round will do that to you! Now fucking get up and face your retribution like a man! You won't get a pep talk out of me. No. You die now you…" His blood froze.

His prey locked eyes with him, his face smeared in blood like some savage nomad. The tears had done little to wash away the amount smeared across his features. If looks could kill, Carling would have been six feet under as of two seconds ago. The M16 limply dropped to his side as the man before him straightened from his crouched position slightly. In his arms he cradled a child, a boy.

The child's head was caked in blood. As the man shifted, the child's head flopped lifelessly to the side; a piece of sandpaper falling from his chubby digits. The man's anguished scream forced Carling to drop the M16 with a clatter. The man before him stared at the child and wept. He wiped the child's fringe away from his eyes, grasping his other tiny hand close to the Thomas the Tank Engine emblem upon his chest.

Carling looked from the child, to the man and then to the third person who had now joined them once again. The child shed a single tear as he stared back at Carling. Never leaving his gaze, he crouched and placed the bunch of poppies upon the young child's chest. Before tiptoeing to whisper something into the man's ear. With that, he rested his hand upon the grief-stricken man's shoulder which registered his head to rise in a kind of drunken understanding.

The child locked gazes once again with Carling and he uttered a single word in Pashto, one which he had heard endless times before, one which plagued his every waking moment, even in slumber. Carling began to stutter, his upper torso now quaking uncontrollably.

"I...this isn't. I mean it can't... it can't be real. It's just... what did the doctors say? A hallucination...a manifestation of..."

Swaying, he harshly kneaded his forehead and temples. The man clutching the boy stared back at him; any humanity had now fallen from his eyes, his bloodlust in full control. He carefully laid the child's head upon the floor, once again sweeping his fringe from his face. He picked up the piece of sandpaper and placed it back into the child's hands, crossing them across his chest as he did so.

The tears relented; his shaking muted somewhat and through choked gulps he stated feebly, "I'm so sorry I..." he stopped and patted the child's chest, his words now devoid of meaning; the self-realisation of futility all too great.

"I'm going to get your Mum and then... we're all going to get out of here together, ok? Just like I promised. You wait here little man," he cooed before rising to his feet.

Carling continued to look past him, the child with the poppies still staring back at him. He began to slap his head hard wishing to drive the vision from of his mind. If only it had been that easy all these years.

"You're not real. You're dead. None of this is real," he babbled to himself, sobbing and shaking his head violently.

The man before him drew his pistol and stood lifeless, rooted to the spot. Carlings eyes darted sideways to meet his, a sense of clarification washing over him. This was real.

"Phuh...phuh...Please do it. I didn't mean to... not like then, like last time. I'm not in control of myself... I never meant to..." he pointed at the child.

The man held firm, his dehumanising stare wilting. The child beside him, no longer burdened with poppies touched the man's armed hand delicately.

"The option... the one you mentioned earlier, of redemption. Is that still possible, is that still on the table, I want-"

He was cut short; the man's arm came up and fired two rounds into Carling's skull.

(CHAPTER BREAK)

The content smile on Carlings face sickened Tom, one that demonstrated his being at peace. His gun, still smoking fell limp to his side, the rounds still ringing in his ears. How loud the ringing was. Tom stood, lightly swaying. He had no redemption to offer, his own having been ruthlessly stripped away. He turned his back on Carlings lifeless form and knelt before the child.

"I said I was going to get you out of here little man..." he made to lift the child, wanting to seek out a place in which to keep his body safe whilst he finished what needed to be done. "And that's what we're going to-"

The thud came heavy to the centre of his shoulder blades. An explosion of agony seized his body before the nausea began to lick at the edges of his vision. He was unconscious before he even hit the ground.

CHAPTER EIGHTEEN: TORTURED SOUL

Thompson intended for this to be his last live feed to the world outside. Balaclava once again pulled down; he brandished the Remington shotgun, training it at the base of Pierce's skull. McAllister had pulled down the Brotherhood's mock flag from upon the stage and had now draped it across the wall of their new location. The sealed off area, to the right of the main entrance was cluttered with rubble; a heavy coating of cement hanging in the air. A perilously large recess occupied the centre of the vast space, a pit with substantial sides.

All the lighting had now been positioned in a one-hundred-and-eighty-degree arc around the wall adorned with the flag along with a hooded and pitiful Pierce. Thompson stood directly behind Pierce, all the while making his presence known. McAllister stood with his back to the edge of the vast pit, a plastic bundle of tarpaulin occupying the right-hand corner of the pit.

"And you're sure this will look the same McAllister?" Thompson prodded, adjusting his balaclava.

"With the correct tight angle, the right framing, yes sir, we can make it look identical to the staging area out on the forecourt. They won't be able to recognise the difference between the stage and this construction site," McAllister boasted.

"It needs to, we're haemorrhaging time here and with it, the primary objective," Thompson omitted, disgusted at the air of defeatism in his own voice; a sentiment that was becoming all too familiar as of late.

"Right sir, the camera is all framed up and ready to go," McAllister confirmed, peeping out from behind the camera.

"This needs to be succinct and to the point. We've thrown them off enough with the false countdown; they still think they have two hours and ten minutes. The boys in 22 SAS will no doubt have their incursion plans all squared away; the charges will only do so much to hold them off," Thompson reaffirmed.

"We still have our two contingencies sir, "McAllister chipped in, trying to appear helpful.

"You don't think I know that you bloody moron?" Thompson spat the flecks of spittle made visible by the artificial lighting. "I was the one who came up with this plan, remember! No, we keep the assets as a last resort," Thompson shuffled, irritable and wanting to proceed, "Let's get this fucking over with."

McAllister, who had now returned to cowering behind the camera, held up his hand once again to countdown Thompson. He had reached one when Greaves burst in through the door which registered a barrage of expletives from Thompson.

"Halting live feed," McAllister methodically stated.

Greaves paced over to the men with a determined stride. Thompson eyeballed his subordinate as he drew closer. A second later and they would have presented yet another blunder to that of the intelligence agencies and the British public.

"This better be good Greaves," Thompson hissed, as Greaves reached his side.

"Yes sir, it's important. Charges planted; Shaw retrieved. Sir, Shaw's body, it had a flesh wound and an exit wound from a high calibre weapon, most likely a…"

"Sniper rifle," Thompson finished, nodding in disdain.

"Yes sir. Defensive wounds on the body and the rope around his neck indicate the signs of a fist fight but our guy up there was helped. I knew one guy couldn't have taken down Shaw, the guy was a juggernaut," Greaves asserted defiantly.

"So that confirms your suspicions sir," McAllister called out.

Thompson did not even justify McAllister's response with an answer. Instead, he brooded for several seconds.

"What would you have us do sir? Round up a few more hostages?" Greaves giddily interjected.

"No. It's time to get a bit more creative with this. They interfered and for that they need to be punished. That MI5 Director General in the intel dossier Carling managed to hack…Miller. Is your man still casing his house?" Thompson inquired knowing full well what Greaves response would be.

"Yes sir," Greaves promptly established.

"McAllister… alert our contact via secure comms that he is a go. I want to know the moment it is done," Thompson motioned with a steely rationale.

McAllister furiously set about typing on his laptop. McAllister stopped momentarily and awaited a response. Thirty seconds later, he looked up at Thompson.

"Asset activated and operational sir," McAllister nodded.

(CHAPTER BREAK)

Selina Miller was privy to only the essential details of her husband's career. There were certain things she had had to be made aware of in order to protect her family and in turn, her husband. Richard Miller never followed a daily regime and he had advised that his wife do the same. School runs, shopping trips and daily chores needed to be strategically planned out, the nature of her husband's chosen profession demanding nothing less. It had been strenuous at first but what with the current socio/political landscape and the COBRA threat level remaining at severe for quite some time now, it was times like these that she was grateful that her husband's unflinching pessimism had rubbed off on her.

Days were designated and set aside for their two children, a boy aged five and a girl aged eight, to arrive early and late at school, all so that their schedule was fluid and unfamiliar to anyone who may wish to surveil their household. Harry and Rosie Miller were currently at a friend's house, having fully settled into their Christmas holidays, their mother taking the welcome opportunity to catch up on some household chores for the busy period ahead.

She checked her watch observing that it was five-twenty; twenty minutes before she planned to leave to collect the children. The cold winter nights had rendered her body clock all asunder, darkness having largely closed in by around three forty-five. She had not had time that day to watch the news, as she busied herself with Christmas wrapping and last-minute groceries for the family meal on Christmas Day. Then there was the table to fetch from out of the attic, an ordeal her husband's hectic timetable could not permit her to wait for. She did not begrudge him of this. Afterall, when you oversaw the nation's domestic security, of what concern was furniture and table placements.

She was just putting the finishing touches to that night's dinner, the oven timer prepped, when the doorbell rang. Wiping her hands on a kitchen towel, she strode through the hallway and peered through the peep hole in the door. On the other side, a courier stood looking at a clipboard; she sighed and painting a fake smile across her features, unbolted the door before opening it.

"Hi there, can I help you?" she enthusiastically greeted the man, the wreath on her door handle swinging to a chorus of bells.

The rain continued to crash down outside. The man slightly curtsied with his sodden hat and smiled.

"Evening love, sorry to disturb you so late but we've got a package for..." he arched the large package in the crook of his arm and read the name out at a jaunty angle "... a Mr. Terrence Reeves."

"Oh, I'm afraid you've got the wrong house. Terry... I mean, Mr. Reeves, he lives next door," she pointed to her right and made to turn back into the house.

"I know miss but he's not in and neither was his other neighbour," the man asserted in a friendly manner, impressive due to his waterlogged demeanour.

"Oh, I see, well if you leave it in his porch, I'm sure it'll be ok, he'll be in soon from work, he usually is around this time," Selina smiled, her job list jabbing away at the back of her mind.

"I would do usually, it's just he's the last package on my route before I clock off on my holidays and its chucking it down so much out here, I'd hate for it to get water damaged, being Christmas and all. If I could just leave it with you, I can get your signature and leave him a note in his letterbox. That way he can knock you up for it later. If that isn't too much trouble," he smiled, water dribbling from the peak of his hat.

Selina Miller considered this for a moment or two, surreptitiously eyeing the man's identification around his neck, the World Courier Deliveries' logo emblazoned upon his hat and waterproof jacket. Nodding in a way that dismissed her standoffish nature she arrived at her decision.

"Why not, it's Christmas after all," she laughed reaching for the clipboard, shaking the cynicism from her head like raindrops. Signing the form, she handed it back to the courier.

"Would you like me to bring it in for you miss, it's quite heavy," he brought the package up, the cardboard covered in red fragile stickers.

"Erm no it's ok, I can manage. Might as well burn off some of those excess calories before the Christmas gorging gets too out of hand," she chuckled.

The man passed over the package and she turned putting it down with an overzealous thump, not expecting the weight. She made to shut the door.

"You have a good one miss and a Happy Christmas and New Year to you and yours," the courier grinned as he turned back down the path, bringing his collar up to shield himself from the onslaught of the wind and rain.

"And a very merry one to you too," she beamed, shutting the door against the unrelenting elements. The oven beeped.

(CHAPTER BREAK)

McAllister nodded to Thompson indicating that the deed had been done. Without pause, Thompson rotated his finger in a grandiose manner indicating he was ready to begin.

"Remember, he doesn't execute his orders until I say," he droned, his voice changer now returned, once again distorting his tone.

"Lessons need to be learnt, sir. He knows the trigger phrase and is watching the live feed via his position in the field."

"Going live in five, four, three…" McAllister's gesticulated, counting Thompson down non-verbally.

"A wise man once said, keep your friends close," he pulled Pierce closer, "and your enemies closer. A wise mantra for all concerned in today's social experiment. As I speak, the paradox that I am considered the latter is not lost on me. In fact, the reality that I am one of you makes it even more ironic. Regardless of my training, my religion, my ethnicity, I too am born of this land. A national. A resident."

"Any such thoughts would be naive, all the more so after what I am about to say. For you see, my strict and simple instructions have been defiled. I warned you. I established that if anything within or external to the confines of this structure were jeopardised, you would force my hand. And forced it you have."

Thompson whipped off Pierce's mask. His hair stood at a jaunty angle and through the slits in his tear-streaked eyes; he winced at the bright lights before him. Thompson pumped his Remington shotgun and placed it to the back of Pierces skull. He flinched and began to murmur a silent pray to himself. With his free hand Thompson raised his machete and trailed it down Pierces back. Through his gagged mouth Pierce mumbled and wheezed.

"I warned you of the consequences of interfering with the will of the people. To the intelligence agencies of this fetid land, who ply their dirty trade both domestically and abroad, I have only this to say to you, your interference comes at a heavy price."

Thompson slit Pierces bound wrists, shoving him forcefully forward. Pierce collapsed upon the ground, breaking his fall with his free hands.

Greaves, who was also masked, stepped forward from behind Thompson. He roughly thrust something into Pierces hand and closed the Prime Ministers fist around it. Pierce shakily looked upon it and made to give it back when Greaves smacked him across the head and shoved the item back towards him.

"I have here your puppet master, the very man who has overseen the pulling of many a string in his post yet, was never truly man enough to sully his own hand. No, he has subordinates for that. Subordinates such as the MI5 overseen by Director General Richard Miller."

Pierce could only look dumbly upon the device enclosed within his fist.

"And to you I ask the following," Thompson stepped forward slightly, "if I control the puppet master, who now pulls your strings? Let us put it to the test, shall we? What happens next, to you protectors of the realm and all those within it I leave in the hands of Mr Pierce here, my dancing puppet on a string."

Thompson punctuated this point by pushing Pierces head further downwards.

"Pierce has on many an occasion, to his knowledge or not, pushed a button, using one of his many strings to carry out his work. However today, he shall push the button; he shall be a string of the realm, an extension of the people. Are you following me Mr Pierce?" Thompson queried.

"Yuh... yes," Pierce stuttered.

"Very well, then let us begin. In your hand is a detonator. Said detonator is connected to a bomb which is located and attached to one of those strings you so love to pull at, a brave and noble servant of the realm. A man or woman who has sworn their allegiance to crown and country...not to mention with it their silence, their very life should the need arise. I give you the following ultimatum...a bullet to the skull or the cutting of a string. Who, what or where, I cannot say. All I ask is that you snip the string of one of the miscreants who took it upon themselves to disobey the orders of their puppet master."

Pierce brought the detonator up to his face and let out a strangled sob, shaking his head slowly from side to side.

"I leave the decision with you Prime Minister. Lessons need to be learnt. You have ten seconds to decide. Ten, nine..."

Without hesitation, Pierce pressed the button. Upon closer inspection, which the live stream would most certainly be subjected to by the various intelligence services and news outlets around the world, one could clearly see the shocked expression within the eyes of Pierce's hooded captor. Ensuring he had done so correctly, Pierce proceeded to press the detonator a second time before taking to pleading at Thompson's feet.

"Another string cut. Man, woman or child... I shall let you follow the severed strand and find that out for yourselves. You have less than two hours until the live feed decides Pierces fate, force my hand again and I shall take this as a direct act of your unwillingness to listen to the will of the people. Remember, there are many more strings that can be cut."

With that the live feed was cut.

(CHAPTER BREAK)

The subsequent minutes after the broadcast were a tense affair. Fingers disappeared into a flurry above keyboards, phones rang, the terrorist's footage already being replayed and scrutinised. Richard Miller paced behind the banks of people, waiting for the first indication of the target that had been hit. He had insisted a check of all vital landmarks had been prioritised and was told almost immediately, that they were secure, much to his relief.

Miller sipped furiously at his tea, a welcome distraction. He pulled his phone out of his pocket and checked his messages. He had none. The extremists mention of him by name had taken him off guard. He had mentioned him directly, as if he were hinting towards or acknowledging that Miller was part of some ulterior motive. He stared intently at the bank of monitors as they played the footage back, stopping at intervals, rewinding it, scrutinising it.

A hand shot up clutching a set of papers and Susan instinctively bolted towards the man located in the centre of the banks. She grabbed the papers and hastily weaved her way back through the pit of monitors, towards Miller.

"What have we got Susan?" Miller queried, biting his lower lip as Susan handed him the papers.

"An address sir. The emergency services have been bombarded by calls from neighbours. John's just running it now. He's also going to see if there's any CCTV in the area, get us a better look. It shouldn't take long for us to establish…"

Susan stopped abruptly and leapt back slightly as Miller's cup of tea landed upon the floor. Susan traced the movement of the cup back up towards Miller's eye line again. He was ashen faced, staring at the papers, his hand was shaking aggressively.

He could formulate only three words, "Oh God no."

Susan grabbed his wrist slightly and shook.

"Sir, what is it? Sir, what's wrong?" she beseeched.

"Got it! Putting it up on the screens now sir," came John's excited voice from his workstation.

The details began to formulate and materialise up on the screens. Miller looked up dazedly and stared back, his eyes harbouring tears. Susan turned at the waist in a rigid motion, still holding his wrist.

"The house appears to be registered to a…" John stopped, his hand shooting up to apprehend his gasp.

The typing and hushed muttering of the monitor staff as they busied themselves came to a halt also. A variety of windows opened upon the larger, central monitor, a mortgage declaration, a map, a road and then, a driver's license and passport. Both bared the face of a slightly younger Richard Miller staring back out at the now older proprietor of the very same face. A face that bore a completely different expression now; the concentrated stare and expressionless features one uses when taking an official passport picture, juxtaposed to that of Miller's current expression.

His mouth hung agape as it opened and closed like a fish. The words would not come. Many within the monitor room bowed their heads, avoiding eye contact with their superior.

"My children, are they?" Miller started.

Susan took Miller by the arm, gently pushing him down onto the steps that led down towards the monitor pool. She positioned him sternly and knelt before him, staring into his sodden, bloodshot eyes.

The façade of formality was now cast aside, a timid demeanour to her voice.

"Richard, we can't expect the worst. John will have units on the way if they haven't already been dispatched. I need you to tell me who would have been at home Mark?"

Susan once again shook his wrist slightly, trying to drag Miller from his stupor. He drunkenly swayed as if to faint. Susan steadied him as an operative handed her a cup of tea.

"What do you mean, we can't expect the worst?" he muttered, not actually directing the comment at Susan. "That's exactly what we do here isn't it. Plan for the worst, expect it even."

"Mark, you can't let them..." Susan started.

Miller's eyes bore into Susan.

"Can't let them what Susan?" he spat. "Get inside my head? Win? They have won! They've never bloody stopped winning!"

John had looped round and approached Ryder from the rear. He peered down at Susan. Susan broke her gaze with Miller and looked up. She shot him a look that asked if they were still alive. John looked down sullenly and shook his head slightly. A single tear cascaded down Susan's cheek. Miller spotted this and turned back to face John who stared down at his hands not knowing what to say. He settled finally upon formality, the best approach.

"Sir," a clearing of his throat, "Ambulance and fire crews are on the scene, Police have an ETA of two minutes. They..." he could not find the words.

Miller's jaw clenched and he straightened slightly, readying himself for the news that was to come.

"Proceed with your situation report," Miller sternly stated in a procedural nature.

"It appears there was an explosion of some kind sir. Fire crews are fighting to put it out now before they can go inside. The crew evacuated your neighbours and ascertained from them your children's whereabouts."

Miller constricted upon hearing this, bracing himself for what came next. John produced a notepad and scanned it.

"A Mrs Fenwick stated that her son had joined your daughter and son at a friend's house and that your wife had agreed to pick all three of them up at around six," John relinquished, in an almost stalled fashion.

"So my children, they're ok? And my wife..." Miller shot up and checked his watch, his face breaking into a smile upon observing that it was five-forty-two. "She must have been on her way to pick them up. Yes, she was taking them to their friend Charlie, he lives just shy of half an hour away," he began smoothing his hair back, some bravado returning.

He hugged Susan, who reciprocated limply.

"Mark I really think we should..." Susan started.

"Great work John, well done on keeping me updated," Miller stated ecstatically as he turned and shook the operative's hand rigorously. "Ensure a unit is sent out to my wife and my children. I have a company tracer in both cars; we can pull that up and get someone out to them."

Whether or not Miller deliberately ignored the expression upon Susan and John's face was unclear. What did become evident however, was the three-tier house of Richard Miller as it materialised upon the central monitor. An arc of emergency vehicles cradled in front of the front garden, fifty or so neighbours stood on the opposite side of the street. The footage came via a police helicopter and zoomed in and out at intervals before becoming obscured by billowing black smoke.

Miller rounded and saw his house ablaze and stumbled slightly, all life once again drained from his very core. He did not stare at the house but instead at the inferno of twisted metal and debris situated on the drive. His lip trembled and he wavered, John catching him slightly. Susan mouthed platitudes but Miller had been struck deaf, dumb and blind. The last words he heard were from John.

"I'm so sorry sir but the car never left your house. The fire crew are readying to search the property. There's still a chance your wife wasn't home," John optimistically suggested.

However, in that moment, a moment of clarity, the likes of which had never been felt before by Miller descended; he resigned himself to his fate and that of his beloved wife's. He stared back at the footage from the helicopter as the stream from the hoses dowsed the gravel drive of his once ornate home. The smoke had begun to turn white and indicated that the fire was being brought under control. The black and white footage on the screen went white briefly as the camera zoomed in too close on the flames, before Miller's vision itself turned black and he fell from his colleague's grasps.

(CHAPTER BREAK)

"Our contact just updated us on Miller, sir. As you predicted, he demanded he be kept on, wanting to still head up the operation, regardless of what we did to his wife," McAllister smirked.

Thompson turned to glance at Pierce who had been brought back to the corner of the room; his hood firmly brought down over his head. Pierces muffled sobbing was euphoric to Thompson, the mental torment he must be going through at present unfathomable.

"And the children?" Thompson probed.

"Still alive sir, at a friend's apparently," McAllister stated weary of Thompson's response.

"Pity," Thompson cruelly responded.

He wiped his hands and walked over to McAllister. Stopping side on, he lowered his tone.

"The Prime Minister and the nation have no idea that the detonator was a duff and that's the way it needs to stay. For all intents and purposes, Pierce thinks he killed Miller's wife and that will further our cause with the rest of the nation. Miller will be off his game now and we'll need to exploit that as much as possible. The house was just a demonstration of our true statement of intent."

Thompson stopped dead as Doc and Hertz entered abruptly. Between them, a man was being forcibly dragged. The figure was unconscious and was caked in blood and dust. They came closer, their faces beaming at their catch. Thompson's heart danced with excitement and he began a slow, mocking clap.

"Bravo gentlemen," he rasped, "search him, remove his possessions and then restrain him."

The men nodded. Doc maintained his restraint on the unconscious male whilst Doc frisked him. Like an animal scoping out its prey, Thompson maintained a safe distance, the site not yet secured. Hertz brought over the man's possessions. They had stripped him of his tactical vest, gun, mountaineering tool, wallet and phone. Thompson danced his fingers over these slightly before laying them to the side. Greaves and Jones stepped from the shadows, curious. Thompson shot them a look that indicated he did not wish for them to take one step further. Both men froze instinctively.

"Where do you want him sir?" Hertz enquired.

"In that chair," Thompson gesticulated, deep in thought.

His men did as he asked, Hertz dumping the man heavily onto the metal frame of the chair. Hertz and Doc both took an arm and secured the man firmly to the chair with duct tape from a nearby duffle bag. Satisfied and with a cursory tug of the duct tape, they stepped aside admiring their handy work. Safe to advance, Thompson stepped forth.

"Looks like he's been through wringer," Thompson mused as he lifted the unconscious man's chin, turning it from side to side to ascertain his identity.

The congealed blood and dust made it an unfeasible task. Thompson let his head slump back upon his chest.

"And what of the other one? The Prime Minister's man? Where's Palmer and Carling?" he prodded.

Hertz and Doc shifted uneasily, neither wanting to speak first. Thompson stepped closer to Doc, the man who exhibited his weakness more blatantly. Thompson stood silent awaiting his response. Doc nervously peeked up towards Thompson's expectant gaze.

"They're both dead, sir. This piece of shit took them both out. We heard a commotion up on the Level Three and rushed up to the site. Palmer was down, shot, Carling was raving. Completely lost the plot truth be told. He was saying something about how he'd been tortured and that this guy along with a boy had made it down through the hole up on Third and that they were on Level Two. Carling went through the hole, he was inconsolable, wouldn't listen to a word we said, honest. Didn't we Hertz?"

Doc looked waywardly at Hertz. Thankfully, he nodded back promptly in justification of Doc's protestations. Doc continued.

"He made his way through the crevice. We bombed it down the escalator; Carling was losing off shots left, right and centre. When finally caught up to him, this guy was standing over Carling's dead body, crying. Hertz knocked him out cold with his rifle butt."

Thompson took this all in; the two men could see the cog's turning.

"You said he was crying, why?" The reply was callous, the lives of Palmer and Carling already chalked of as collateral damage.

Hertz looked wearily at Doc and Thompson followed Hertz's line of vision, the two men adopting the demeanour of bashful children about to be punished for some indiscretion. Thompson now fronted up to Hertz.

"I asked you a question," Thompson expelled, venom oozing from his lips, his jaw clenched.

Hertz cleared his throat.

"When we found them sir, there was a young boy with him. He was dead... shot. The man was cradling the boy's body. Way we see it, one of Carling's stray bullets must have found their target. It was... it was the boy from earlier, the one Shaw had on his back. The one... the one you selected, sir."

Thompson nodded at this. Undisturbed, he pressed on, "One less body to worry about. Serves Carling right too for defying orders, swifter justice than he would have been afforded in a court martial by me. Dumb fuck."

Doc nodded along with Hertz, Doc letting out a nervous laugh. Thompson snapped back to face Doc and the man stopped laughing instantly.

"And what of the other one?" Thompson pressed, compelling the men to speak.

"When we found Carling, he was tied up and the two targets had barricaded themselves up in Control. They'd been torturing Carling. Just before he went down into the hole, he said that he hadn't told them anything. When we breached the room, we flash banged it. One of the muppets must have had a live grenade and dropped it. They got separated, each falling down a separate service shaft. Carling and Palmer checked out the one this guy tumbled down. It led out into..."

Thompson rolled his eyes, "I'm fully aware of the schematics shit-for-brains".

"Yes of course sir," Doc swallowed.

"And the exit shaft you checked, the Prime Minister's man?" Thompson impatiently pressed.

"When we got there, the door was red hot. The room was on fire. We kicked the door in, the room was an inferno, the sprinklers were dosing most of the fire... it's out now. So, we don't have to worry about that forcing anyone's hand outside. It's contained. We're going to go back up and I.D. the body to be sure but there's no way someone could have survived that or the initial explosion that close up," Doc stated assuredly.

Thompson clicked his fingers and Greaves approached with Jones. Thompson turned to the two men.

"I'm a sucker for a good barbeque boys. Bring me back something," he sneered.

"You a leg or a wing man?" Greaves smirked.

"Surprise me. All four of you are going up there. One more sweep for the memory stick on the way down. Radios back on, I'll see if I can extract some information from Rambo here, see if he can point us in the right direction. Understood?" Thompson callously established in a nonchalant fashion, rolling up his sleeves.

"Yes sir," the four chimed in unison.

"Good, fuck off," Thompson grunted.

Greaves turned and ushered Doc and Hertz from the room hurling hushed expletives at them as he did so, Jones heading up the convoy. Thompson turned slightly and tracked their movement as they left the room; biting his lower lip he stifled some expletives of his own. The makeshift site door closed and with it, his victim's last visages of hope.

Thompson turned back to face McAllister, "Keep an eye on the live feed; we're in the eye of the storm now. Counterattack imminent," Thompson warned.

McAllister nodded and fixed his eyes upon his laptop. Thompson grabbed a bottle of water and a cloth from the duffle bag and pulled another chair over, placing it before the dishevelled man. He sat, arms dangling by the sides of the chair as he waited. Whilst they were on the clock, he did not want to rush what came next. His body went limp, no excess energy being used up or depleted. He eyed his victim up and down. How the pathetic example before him aroused his morose curiosity.

(CHAPTER BREAK)

Tom began to come to. He did not open his eyes, fearing what awaited him if he did. Instead, he gathered his senses. The metallic taste of blood mixed with cement made his mouth dry. The base of his skull was on fire, his neck and shoulders stiff. He assessed his extremities with slow, minimal movement. Both wrists were bound by duct tape, the sticky adhesive pulling at the hair on his forearms. He listened intently. He could smell the perspiration first followed by steady, rhythmic breathing. To his right, muffled sobs.

"I know you're awake," a short, rasping voice broke the silence, causing Tom to flinch.

The voice bore a distinctive East London twang. He opened his eyes and straightened, his neck feeling as though it had been pummelled with sledgehammers. He grimaced and squinted as the bright light from a nearby source flooded his senses.

After several seconds, his eyes began to focus and the shadow before him materialised. The man was bald by choice, the shadow of his hairline evident at the forefront of his cranium, a film of sweat gleamed across it. Tom surmised that it was shaved out of necessity rather than for aesthetic purposes. His nose was horrifically broken, flattened in the middle, it twisted both right and left having most likely not been set properly. However, it was his eyes, black and lifeless like that of a shark, that garnered his attention.

"Can't say I blame you for being tired, what with all that killing you've been up to," the insurgent stated.

"You can talk," Tom muttered, his dry throat ebbing much of the confidence from his voice.

"Needs must, I'll catch forty winks after this is all over," promptly came the jagged reply.

"Well I'm sure they'll be plenty of time for that in prison," Tom grimaced, rotating his neck to ease his discomfort.

Thompson tutted and nodded. Tom maintained eye contact, unblinking. Unexpectedly, Thompson exploded in a startling flurry of speed. He grabbed Tom by the bottom of the jaw. The legs of the chair, all bar one, elevated from the ground. He was immensely strong, a wide and muscular frame. A mixture of bulk and muscle, nothing lost to fat, like that of a boa constrictor.

"Your overconfidence does not strengthen your stance here runt! Understand this..." Tom stared back, his breathing erratic.

"You think yourself a hero for what you've done here today. You're sadly mistaken. All you've succeeded in today, is in pissing me off. I hold your life in my hands; the method by which you die begin and end with these ten digits. The threshold of the agony you can endure is measured only by the distance you force my hand."

He dashed Tom's head from his grasp and returned to his seated position, all the while holding his hands before him like a magician about to perform some sleight-of-hand, a cold and calculated statement of intent. Tom sucked in air, the impact of the chair returning to the hard cement floor jolting his frame harshly.

"You think I'm scared of you?" Tom snarled, the blood returning slowly to his head.

Thompson laughed. He brought his outstretched hands into his lap, clasping them tightly.

"Fear is a very subjective and individual experience. I should know, I have been on the receiving end of it many a time. For some, the infliction of pain or the merest hint of torture forces them to crack under duress," he motioned the snapping of a twig before bringing his left index finger level with his temple, "whilst others fear what is yet to come, the unknown. After all, is there any greater canvas for fear than one's own imagination?"

He motioned with his hand as if using a paint brush; the irony of the delicate nature of the strokes not lost on Tom.

"Do you know what the scariest thing in the world is?" the bald man queried, as he removed his leather gloves, allowing the question to hang. "It's not the here and now. No that's locked in; the adrenaline takes care of most of that. No, what's truly terrifying, what keeps me awake at night and I have no qualms about admitting that to you," he wagged his finger "is what will happen tomorrow," his captor finished, placing the gloves neatly on his lap one on top of the other.

"I mean I highly doubt that sitting in whatever hovel you crawled from this morning you even for the briefest of seconds considered that in a matter of hours, on this very same day, you'd be running around a London shopping centre acting the hero" he scoffed, the last word proving distasteful and awkward in his mouth.

Tom shook his head.

"Well, if I'm the hero, that must make you and your men the villains...Thompson, isn't it?" came Tom's barbed response.

This registered a brief glimmer of surprise from Thompson.

"You know my name?" he smiled, clapping his hands satirically, "it matters little to me, for what is in a name?"

"Maybe you're right," Tom shuffled in his chair, slyly testing his restraints, "it's just about as generic and insignificant as your mission is here today. You do know Victoria isn't on the throne anymore?"

This registered a sustained chuckle from Thompson.

Tom pressed on. He had made peace with the fact that it was only a matter of time before he was to be executed. The only detail that pained him, that penetrated his inconsolable anger, was that he could not do so fighting on his feet. That and the unattended and lifeless form of the innocent child that most likely still occupied a substantial puddle of blood two floors above him. All that aside, he was damned sure that he was not going to go out quietly, submissively.

"I hate to break it to you Thompson but Rule Britannia doesn't rule the waves anymore and she sure as hell doesn't give a shit about your warped sense of patriotism. You're just another loon, hiding behind outdated and misinformed ideals, a dinosaur, a relic. The kind who kills women and children in the name of some greater good," Tom expectorated.

Thompson now burst into a raucous guffaw, mockingly wiping an imaginary tear from his eye. Mc Allister looked over at the two men bemused by the level of levity that had entered the room.

"Thank you for that, honestly I haven't laughed that hard since Pierce over there pissed himself."

This registered a sideways glance from Tom. That concluded the mystery as to the identity of the sobbing person.

"People like you have no allegiances, you change them like underwear," Tom retorted; Thompsons lacklustre reply spurning him on.

"Well let's just say I'm not as hygienic as you think, haven't changed them in a while," Thompson promptly returned.

He was enjoying the verbal chess game that was transpiring. Like a petulant child he was playing with his food.

"Until the next payday comes along," Tom sneered.

Thompson leant forward in his chair and tutted.

"If there is one thing in this world that can't be sold or bought, it's one's ideals. A man's wealth or lack thereof is not based on what he has financially but instead in what he can take! And if that's by force, then so be it. I mean don't get me wrong, it helps if the aforementioned payday does fall in line with your belief remit...a very sizeable one at that," Thompson thinly smirked.

"You think the British public gives a damn about your ideals? Good luck after today," Tom sniffed, shaking his head bemused.

"You see, you fail to see the problem because you are part of it. It's politically correct, subservient rats like you that have eaten their way to the very core of this country's ideals, the foundations that made it the country it was. It may just be a core left, brown and decaying but while there is still some of that apple left, while there are still people like me, it shall endure, waiting for its seeds to be harvested and replanted," Thompson interjected, asserting his misinformed, hierarchal stature proudly.

"More of an orange man myself," Tom quipped, punctuating his point by shifting his chair back slightly.

"Funny," Thompson paused in an orchestrated fashion, scratching his chin, "I would have put you down as more of a carrot man myself. You think that carrot they dangle helps you, helps you to see through the dark. That you are unique," he shook his head at this and snorted.

"You're a peasant to people like Pierce, a rung far below him on the social ladder. One covered in shit and detritus, stuck firmly in the mud, propping the rest of the elitist ladder up. Oh, they need you alright. They need you to keep the ladder steady, covered in all that shit so they don't have to be. But here's the thing, carrots grow in shit and mud. They grow towards an ideal, as too will the British people".

"And let me guess, you're the stick?" Tom indifferently jested.

Thompson checked his watch, "No, I'm the harvester who after months of careful cultivation decides which carrots to pluck from the mud and shit… and those that have gone to seed."

Thompson rose, pushing the chair backwards. The metal scrapped on the cement and caused Tom to writhe in discomfort. Thompson picked up Tom's possessions, placing them very carefully atop the lap of the metallic seat, so that they were now adjacent to him. Tom looked around, testing his bindings once again. They held strong. Thompson ventured over to a duffle bag and brought it over, placing it at Tom's feet.

"Leaving so soon," Tom mustered.

Thompson veered round and bared a toothy, sadistic smile.

"And miss opening up my Christmas present," he huffed bringing out a Stanley knife from the paint specked duffle bag, drawing the blade from its yellow, plastic casing. Tom's blood froze his core beginning to tremor.

"I heard you gave Carling your very own Spanish inquisition upstairs. He never did have much of a threshold for taking pain or inflicting it for that matter. Me? I love it. I am what you might call a connoisseur, a sadist. I am a person who takes great pleasure in inflicting pain upon others. However, as I mentioned earlier, I am a man dictated by his morals. What I say now, is a pledge to you. If you answer my questions, truthfully, without hesitation, I will kill you quick," Thompson put forth slicing the knife quickly through the air with expedient gusto before making his way behind Tom.

"But, if you do decide to make me work for the information, I am going make you wish you died upstairs with that dopey little kid," Thompson spoke this final threat into Tom's ear.

This registered a bolt of anger which ran along Tom's back and he bucked in his chair, letting fly a flurry of expletives. A profile of the child's face came flashing back; Tom glanced down at his bound wrists and saw the blood belonging to the boy.

"Oh don't worry lad, he'll soon be forgotten about, as will you. Me on the other hand, well, I'll go down in history, behind closed doors of course but up there all the same, with other greats like Churchill, Montgomery, Newton," Thompson swayed the knife with each name mentioned.

"Newton?" Tom sniggered, "well you know what they say...what goes up, must come down and what I've got in mind, it won't be a fucking apple twatting you on the head that you have to worry about you sick..."

Thompson grabbed a bunch of his matted hair from behind and pulled back so hard Tom felt as if his scalp would come free.

"Ah, ah, ah, there's no need for playground insults now is there?" he gave an extra tug, "I'll let it pass on account of this being your first time. Now, you know my name, what's yours?" he flung Tom's head away from his grasp.

"Try looking it up in the Yellow Pages under-"

Tom's head exploded as Thompson swung his substantial fist into his jaw. His vision exploded, a pulsating bolt of suffering erupting from within his ear.

"Not in the mood for foreplay, hey? Well let's just check one of these wallets shall we," he glanced down at the chair and turned his mouth down smugly, "two wallets? Maybe you aren't at the bottom of that ladder after all."

Tom relaxed slightly when he picked up his wallet over that of Anthony's not wanting the artefact to be defiled in any way. Thompson removed various cards from the wallet, discarding them with a dramatic flourish until finally, he fell upon his driver's licence. He scanned it before clicking his fingers. The man on the laptop shuffled over, briefly affording himself a nervous glance in Tom's direction. Without looking at the man, he held the licence up and the subordinate sheepishly took it from Thompson.

"Run a check on our guest Tom Hawkins here for me Mc Allister," Thompson grinned.

McAllister nodded and once again shuffled off; his footsteps soon replaced by the rhythmic tapping of a keyboard.

"Now that we've been introduced and we know that you are in fact a Mr. Tom Hawkins, I think its due time we move onto the more pressing matters at hand. Before you address me with another quip or wise arse retort, let me remind you that I now know who you are. I will therefore, in a matter of seconds, have your life on a computer screen. That means family, loved ones, work colleagues, all expendable if you fuck me around. Are we clear Tom?" he said, accentuating the name with a click of his tongue.

Tom began to feel the fingers of fear grope at his heart now, the last remnants of hope disintegrating. He had barely given any consideration as to how the events of today may impact upon his parents. Ashamed, he swallowed hard.

"Yes," he responded meekly.

"Good, then let's begin. Question two, why were you here today?" Thompson quizzed.

"I was getting some last-minute bits for Christmas," Tom replied.

"Say I believe you; it's all a bit of a coincidence isn't it? A bloke with the ability to take out half of my men, abseil down a high rise building with weapons training to boot. You're ex-military, aren't you?" Thompson let his point hang for several seconds, an expectant look upon his face.

Tom paused remembering his training. He was tempted to give his name, rank and serial number but thought better of it, knowing it would further antagonise what was already a very unstable man. Moreover, as Tom saw it, by doing so it would be as good an omission as any. He settled upon a nod of agreement.

Thompson elatedly clapped his hands shaking his head in disbelief. Tom allowed him his moment, once again scanning the room. Behind Thompson sat a table with all manner of various tools upon it and strangely enough what appeared to be a suitcase.

"I knew it, a fucking inside man, off the books. Shopping my arse," Thompson paced.

"This is the first time I've ever been here, I'm not even serving anymore," Tom interjected.

Thompson bound forward and delivered two haymakers deep into Tom's torso. Tom rocked on the chair, ensuring he inhaled as best he could with each blow, his head swimming. Thompson caught Tom by the upper arms and turned him towards the pit. Tom was sucking air in, winded beyond belief. Thompson hefted his head upwards once again by his hair, his head reminiscent of a block of lead. He pointed towards a tarpaulin covered mound in the pit.

"The last ex-vet to lie to me ended up where that skid mark is now and let me tell you, I made the treacherous bastard suffer. Now, I'm going to ask you this and I better get a fucking clear response. What was your mission here today?" he pressed.

"Sir, I have his details," Mc Allister cut in, "our contact even got us his military records. He's telling the truth; says here he was dishonourably discharged for..." McAllister scanned the document for several seconds.

Thompson waited patiently; his ear cocked in McAllister's direction. McAllister exhaled upon reading the report.

"Quite the rap sheet our man has got here. A Private Hawkins sir: disobeying orders, reckless behaviour in the field and it says here he was diagnosed by a military doctor with PTSD. No way he's still operational guv."

"McAllister, are we not ex-service?" Thompson teased.

"Yes, sir," McAllister answered meekly in his Scottish accent.

"And are we not currently operational?" Thompson continued.

McAllister nodded and returned to his laptop, his face crimson with embarrassment. Thompson shook his head in contempt.

"I'm still waiting, soldier," Thompson probed further, mocking Tom with his newfound knowledge.

Tom still faced the pit, a visual incentive as to what would happen if he failed to comply.

"I'm telling you the truth. I left the service nearly a year ago. Wrong time, wrong place!" Tom replied, his tone brevity laden and succinct.

Thompson was breathing heavily, muttering to himself in a considered tone. He walked round to face Tom and reproduced the Stanley knife. Without hesitation, he slowly drew the sharp blade across Tom's right arm and then replicated the action upon his left. Tom screamed out and jerked in a convulsed state, the warm blood stinging his wound upon its departure. His beating heart pummelled inside his chest now; the panic truly taken hold.

He mentally rebuked himself. He had provoked his captor, allowing fear and anger to control his actions thus far. He had always struggled with the juxtaposing emotions, the very culprits than stoked the fires of his PTSD. He had feared what the condition reduced him to and what others thought of him. It had been the sole cause of his shame at not wanting to tell his parents, especially his father. Thompson knelt a metre or so before Tom, avoiding his untied legs as they flailed and writhed.

"It's a simple question Private, even for someone like you that is clearly a sandwich short of a picnic. I bet you didn't put up this much of a fight when they discharged you did you, you fucking coward!" Thompson snarled.

Tom literally felt his life draining away from him. The wounds upon his forearms were around three inches in length, not too deep as to bleed to death but a clear indication of worse things to come. Tom clamped his eyes shut; the distant cracking of metal yielding to flame, twanging his eardrums. The sweet smell of flesh carried upon the heated desert wind. He swallowed hard.

"Not now," he muttered to himself through gritted teeth.

Thompson looked at him, a look of pure parodied confusion upon his face, he acted as if he were concerned, grabbing Tom's chin.

"If not now my white, feathered deserter, when? This isn't Butlin's, you're on my fucking time here," he reinforced this with a squeeze of Tom's forearms. Tom bit down hard as fresh blood erupted from his wounds, foaming saliva gathering around the corners of his mouth.

"It hurts doesn't it," Thompson grunted with exertion, "I can see it now, as you fade in and out of consciousness. But that's not because of the blood loss. No, that's cold, hard realisation. The stark arrival at an obvious conclusion you've avoided for so long," Thompson leaned in closer and whispered.

"The loss of hope itself as it seeps away. It died long ago though; you can tell. You're a quitter; failed at playing solider, failed to help your partner in crime from being blown to bits, failed at saving that young boy."

"Shut the... fuck up," Tom screeched, his arms numb, his whole upper body quaking now.

Thompson pressed on, unyielding in his verbal barrage.

"All that training, all that hope, where did it get you? Right back to square one, the bottom of that shit laden ladder" Thompson leered, finally letting go of Tom's forearms.

Tom wheezed heavily. He avoided looking at the damage done, his severed flesh telling him all he needed to know.

"You look a little under the weather there, Tommy boy. Is there any of that hope left? A last drop to see you through what comes next or have you finally been purged of that disease, that epitome of misinformed philosophies?" Thompson goaded.

Tom's head had collapsed upon his chest, his head swirling, unconscious bliss enticing his temples. The anger of the day's events flooded in and out, affording him the briefest bursts of adrenaline, the urge to fight on. Even now, he could feel some of the feeling returning to his upper forearms.

"I intend to purge this very country of that awful ideology, that false desire, of hope. Hope is a disease! One that leads us astray. The cure itself, we ironically beg for, instead leaving our fates in the hands of the bankers, politicians and celebrities of this world. But that too is withheld from us. It keeps us passive, like junkies craving heroin, wishing for something we cannot attain. So, we try and quell it with apathy, loving thy neighbour, a perceived and excepted moralistic outlook. But there is no hope!" Thompson began to hasten in his speech becoming more irate, fanatical.

"Hope is what is sold to us, as an assurance, a commodity like everything else in modern society. Packaged and decorated like some cheap whore. On the outside desirable but within, diseased and rotten. A dream of a better tomorrow," he snorted at this.

"A mere distraction to detract us from the very truth dawning upon us that it isn't going to get better! Things aren't going to change, not when men like Pierce are in charge," he jutted a bloodied finger in the direction of the hooded heap in the corner of the room.

"There's no light at the end of the tunnel, no better alternative within some bastardised manifesto. It makes no difference to the man, woman or child still in that tunnel, clambering towards the unknown light of idealism, of hope. Hope is the real enemy. It stops people from mobilising, from tearing down the charade of modern law makers and those that uphold them! For one to attain absolute freedom, one must first embrace the realisation that the status quo is broken, that a ballot papers only worthwhile use is to wipe your arse upon."

Thompson grabbed Tom by the chin and glowered down at him; his delirium making it difficult to maintain the pretence that he was following Thompson's tirade.

"You ask why we have done what we have today. What right minded patriot would do this to his people? Revolution is always bloody. Instigators of change are always deemed criminals, vilified by those who they seek to help like that of the French revolutionaries or the Bolsheviks and that you little prick, is the true answer to your question, the true price of hope. You see politicians lie and hide behind facades of hope dangled before the electorate. Rolled up sleeves, we're all in it together, jolly good. No, to be a true instigator of hope you must first establish that there is no hope; hope is what you make it! Hope is what you take for yourself, what you sacrifice for the greater good, a Greater Britain."

He let go of Tom who defiantly kept his head upright.

"Which brings me to my next question, what was your end game here? Place is wired to blow, half of my men are still standing, the nation is being held to account, a hostage of its very own misguided principles. What conceivable contingency did you play out in your head that saw this going any differently?" Thompson asked with genuine interest, stepping back to survey his quarry.

Tom met his captors gaze, his head swaying slightly. A morsel of adrenaline seduced his muscles and ran its way up his spine.

"They all ended with me kicking your arse back to the eighteenth century, right where you belong," Tom derided.

Thompson burst out laughing, delighted by Tom's resurgence of passion. He clapped his hands ferociously.

"Oh I'm glad to see I haven't beaten your sense of humour out of you... not yet anyway. Be honest now, it was hope wasn't it? And look where that's gotten you. The same hope I'm sure all of those government lackeys invested in you, a hope that you would retrieve both the device and the schematics, that they could use your unflinching faith to avoid sullying their own hand."

"Just like your man Robert Townsend?" Tom jived.

Thompson spat and a discerning look crumbled his jovial features, the name sickening him to his very core.

"Another man sold a lie, a dream that he was doing it for Queen and country. We accepted him as one of our own, gave him a true purpose. Another lamb blinded by the promise of hope, ironic when you come to think of it. But you've seen where hope got him, where it will lead you," Thompson puffed, pointing over towards the tarpaulin clad mound.

"Which brings me to my final question, before you too, join the same gullible rank and fate that befell him," Thompson positioned himself to the side of Tom, allowing him a full view of the pit and what lay ahead.

"I don't care who sent you, I don't even care about why they sent you, what I want to know is, where they told you the schematics were," Thompson arrogantly demanded.

Tom's heart sunk, knowing full well that whatever answer he provided next would not be satisfactory. Even if he had been on a covert mission and had told Thompson the truth, he would still torture him by way of validation.

"First I heard about your EMP device was from Carling," Tom embellished.

Thompson nodded; his mouth turned down in an expression that indicated that he half believed Tom.

"Oh, I am under no illusions that Carling divested it all like some cheap whore but you Tom, you are the unknown quantity here and I'm on a tight schedule, so..." he raised he hands in a shrug, "needs must and all that".

Thompson walked behind Tom, his footsteps echoing in the vast space. It was not long before Tom could hear a metallic object, heavy, being manoeuvred. It sounded like a propane tank of some sort. Next came the sloshing of liquid shadowed by a splashing noise upon the concrete. His ears now terrifyingly attuned, he picked up the noise of a wet cloth being whipped and began to piece together what came next. However, that was secondary to that of the smell of petrol. Thompson spoke from behind Tom at an increased distance to before by Tom's reckoning.

"They used this to run the generator down here. It's what's powering the lights, no wiring in here at the moment you see, that was going to be a couple of the other men's jobs next week, as part of our cover. Think we'll be going on strike that day," he said, rather pleased with himself.

The sound of the metal object began to reverberate around the room, a slow and loud clang as it was dragged across the concrete floor. The sloshing of liquid could be heard with each jolt of movement.

"Always loved the smell of petrol when I was a kid, couldn't get enough of it. You know, I've always wondered if that's the politicians excuse for entering countless overseas wars. That they too, loved the smell," Thompson drew level with Tom.

He held a wet cloth dosed in what Tom speculated was petrol, from the acrid smell that permeated his nostrils.

"Would sure make some sense out of all of the countless lives lost in acquiring the stuff over the years I suppose. That said, I think it's the smell of the money that heightens their senses all the more so, hey Pierce?" Thompson concluded with a raising of his voice.

Pierce flinched upon being called, instinctively covering his hooded head expecting another blow from Thompson.

"Just get it over and done with," Tom defiantly muttered.

Thompson tutted and shook his head. He placed the folded rag long ways, dripping in petrol and placed it across Tom's bloodied forearms. He screamed out in agony, driving his backbone further into the metal back of the chair.

"Always was one for giving the people what they wanted," Thompson arrogantly jived, gleeful at the pain he was inflicting upon Tom.

"McAllister, has our man here got any family? Parents, siblings, children, a bit on the side even?" he called off.

"Just checking now sir," McAllister gurgled with joy, relishing the chance to be part of the show. He continued to type, "You still living at Thirty Wrenley Close?" He smirked at Tom as his head shot up, gritted teeth and anger in his eyes.

281

"I think we have a winner!" Thompson howled with joy.

"You go near any of my family and tied to a chair or not…I'm going to…"

"Do nothing. It's easy to make threats Private, when you're tied to a chair and you know you can't back them up," Thompson sneered with provocation.

Tom quivered, shaking with anger, spittle dripping from his mouth like a rabid dog.

"He has a mother and father at this address, not finding a registered address or current occupational status for our man here, so I think it's safe to assume he's still withdrawing from the bank of Mum and Dad, sir," McAllister sounded up.

Thompson cast a raised eyebrow over Tom and began to tut.

"Even better, another freeloading leech sucking the lifeblood from this great country; well, we're going to settle the books today, clear all debts to the nation. More than a pound of flesh I should imagine."

"One deceased Brother, an Anthony Hawkins, KIA while serving in the same regiment," McAllister emphasised this last bit, slightly taken aback.

"Hmmm, let's find out a little more about our boy Anthony there shall we McAllister. After we pay the parents a visit, we'll swing by the cemetery; make sure we leave a memento for him."

He turned back to face an inconsolable Tom.

"Was there anything left to bury? Everyone's so IED happy these days, it's so impersonal," Thompson leered.

Tom breathed heavily, the pain now ebbing to the back his head, the anger bubbling to the surface once again. He could hear the crackling of metal accompanied by the charring of flesh. The petrol brought back all the sensations of being in his Brothers vehicle, the fear only serving to heighten his senses. He now took to muttering obscenities and empty threats, caring little if Thompson heard them or not. He rotated his wrists, the hair plucking free from his skin, yearning to be free like Tom.

"I bet your brother wasn't this much of a bitch when he was lying face down in some arse-end bit of the globe," Thompson poked Tom with his finger as he accentuated each word.

Tom bolted forward using his unbound legs, lifting the chair from the floor in a crouched position. Still bound, he drove his head deep into Thompson's chest, resulting in a winded exhalation. This, however, was short lived and was soon replaced by a guffaw of pleasure as Thompson recovered and connected with the side of Tom's head.

Tom fell to his knees, buckling under the blow, the chair affording him little mobility. Thompson gripped Tom's dipped head and drove his knee into his forehead. He fell backwards, blood oozing from his nose, landing hard upon the back of the chair. The chair keeled; one of the back legs of the chair now facing upwards. Tom's legs were now above him. Thompson panted heavily as he regained his breath. He watched on as his prey tried to right himself like a Tortoise upon its back.

"Turns out we did still have one last bit of hope in the tank," Thompson mused, impressed slightly by Tom's display. He walked to Tom's side and picked up the rag, beckoning McAllister over.

"Hold this tight across his face," Thompson demanded.

McAllister executed his orders faithfully. The material heaved up and down, made all the worse by Tom's erratic breathing. Thompson unsheathed his knife and picking up an empty bottle of white spirit sawed the funnel off. He then dipped this into the metal barrel of petrol and begun pouring a steady and slow stream of petrol. McAllister held fast as Tom bucked and spluttered, his lungs on fire, some of the petrol's acrid taste entering his mouth and throat.

After several seconds Thompson threw the plastic container back into the barrel and shot McAllister a look. McAllister withdrew the sodden cloth. Tom broke into a fit of coughing, petrol fluming from his lips like a fountain, his eyes darting around wildly as he looked on in desperation, his captors above him, Thompson lording over him.

"Waterboarding my boy, simulated drowning, what a bitch this is I can tell you from bitter experience. Unlike drowning, where it's sink or swim, your life isn't in your own hands but instead, is in that of your captors. We used to call this a gasoline spritzer back in my unit. Arabs loved to do it when they captured any of our forces. Paradoxical as it was what we were out there for, their reasoning behind it I suppose. Then on to the fingernails, teeth, hell if it came loose, they took it."

Tom fought to take in all the air that he could. He knew full well that his ordeal was far from over. Thompson patted his chest.

"Breath Caught? Good stuff here comes another round. Barman if you would be so kind."

Thompson looked at McAllister. The rag came back down and with it the steady and unrelenting stream of petrol. Tom's vison blackened. Constructs began to form. Malcolm, Michelle with her two nameless counterparts, the boy, his parents and finally, his brother. Tom felt a warm glow take hold. His thoughts began to dwindle, he knew it was most likely the petrol he had ingested that was burning his chest but such thoughts were soon replaced by the comfort of knowing death was near.

The central deliberation that would not subside was how his parents would cope with the loss of a second son. His eyes opened wide, stung by petrol and tears. A random quote from his childhood coming to the fore, a book his mother would read to him and his Brother before they went to bed. Tom and Anthony had loved the book, more so than the movie or the pantomime that their father had taken them to in Richmond when they were younger around this time of year religiously. Peter Pan. He remembered how he and Anthony could not comprehend the meaning of the quote, the juxtaposition of the quote an absolute absurdity. "To die would be an awfully big adventure." Tom felt his arms go numb, the meaning now evident.

CHAPTER NINETEEN: BLOOD IS THICKER THAN PETROL

"Sir, I really must urge you to reconsider this. We still have time," Susan pleaded, for the third time.

"That's just what they're expecting, us to let them run down the clock with an hour and a half to spare. We hit them now, they won't be expecting it," Miller slammed his desk.

"But sir, would it not be better to consider the other options?" Susan pressed on whilst maintaining her hierarchal decorum.

"What other options? We have teams on standby. Alpha and Bravo will both infiltrate via the roof while Charlie set charges external to the building at street level. When they get the greenlight from Alpha, they are to covertly breach along with Bravo who will enter the fray by abseiling down to the second level. We'll have them top, middle and bottom," Miller explained in an exasperated fluster as he sifted through the papers on his desk.

Susan held her tongue momentarily and sought to pick her words carefully. In the brief time since the discovery of Mrs Miller's death, both Richard Miller's children had been located and placed under protective supervision at one of the departments London safe houses. The acting Prime Minister, James Braham, had also made contact upon being informed of Mr Miller's loss.

Condolences were in short supply today, however. After the briefest exchange of the usual platitudes, soured more so coming from that of a politician, Braham dived headfirst into the task of seeking Miller's replacement. He wished for him to step down and relinquish his duties to an external candidate, one whom he could vouch for and had personally selected. Miller insisted that he was coping well and that no one knew the systems or protocols better than he did; to change leadership at this critical time could prove catastrophic. Better still, if pending an independent review into the events of today Miller was found to be negligent in the execution of his duties, who better to serve up on a silver platter should it all go awry. No. When this was done, for better or worse, so too would he be.

He had cajoled Braham into agreeing and sweetened the deal by establishing that he would immediately be setting in motion the necessary orders to breach the building; Alpha, Bravo and Charlie units waiting on immediate standby. Braham was delighted upon hearing this. He requested that he be provided with real-time updates and that he be made privy to the live feed via the operator's helmets.

Susan had been present in the room whilst this conversation had taken place and was unnerved to say the least by Miller's coolness and effectiveness at bartering his case. She felt that Braham had all too hastily agreed to his staying on.

"Look Richard, I don't wish to come across as condescending, you know I'm behind you, the whole team for that matter but are you really sure this is what's best for you in light of current events?" Susan delicately manoeuvred.

She had noticed that Miller's picture of his wife and children had now been placed face down upon his desk. Miller continued to shuffle through his papers, uninterested.

"It's not what's best for me Susan; it's what's best for the country. That comes first, always has and always will. I'm fine, really," Miller concluded with a weak smile that served to comfort Susan. It did quite the opposite.

"Richard don't feel like you have to put on a false front for our benefit, no one would blame you if you stepped down. Let someone else take the burden, be with your kids," Susan added.

"Susan I really am fine under the circumstances, thank you for your concern," Miller replied, sounding none too convincing.

"I know sir, I just think under the circumstances, you'd be better off..." Susan pressed on before Miller burst into a hysterical barrage.

"For the love of God woman, stop bloody nannying me! I know you and everyone else in there thinks this is about me going on some sort of," he stuttered before finding the sentiment he wished to express, "misguided vendetta! I'd be lying if that wasn't partly true. That said, the buck stops with me and only me. That, Susan, is what is best for me under the circumstances. Now do I make myself clear?" he finished, eyes wildly expectant, awaiting a response.

"Yes sir...my apologies," Susan meekly replied, eyes stinging from the tears she dared not shed.

"Good. Now get out there and let the team know that I want a list of all possible breaching points into the building and any potential exits; they are to be monitored and watched by the Armed Response units in case we lose any insurgents in the assault. Pierce is the priority; hostages come second, usual procedure. I expect some collateral damage in all of this but it can't be helped, our hand has been forced, all other avenues exhausted," Miller asserted, dismissing Susan with a wave of his hand.

Miller waited several seconds after the door had been closed to break down into a fit of stifled tears. He collapsed into his chair, the nausea of grief returning. All that held him together at present was his unwavering patriotic duty and the task at hand. He sobbed, not bothering to wipe his tears away with the polka dot handkerchief in his breast pocket.

His eyes fell upon the overturned picture. He tentatively turned it over and stared back through tear swollen eyes at his wife, so happy, so full of life, taken by a faceless killer. He did not know how today would end but he was resolute on one point; no matter the outcome, no prison cell or black site would be waiting. The remaining terrorists would die this day.

(CHAPTER BREAK)

The stinging within Tom's chest was replaced by a hard slap to the face. He came to, coughing, the dull light in the room proving too much for his eyes. He had been turned on his side, his airways opened.

"You die on my time Private," Thompson barked.

McAllister turned Tom back over onto his back and then with an exerted effort placed the chair upon its legs once again at a wayward purchase due to the bent leg. Tom's head was awash with nausea, the pain in his arms and chest causing his to vomit right onto McAllister's boot.

"Ahhh for..." McAllister started.

"That's it boy, vomit up the last remnants of that bile you call hope. Pure unleaded goodness, isn't it? Thought you'd take a step into the great unknown on us? No such luck, I still have a question that needs answering," Thompson snarled.

Tom breathed in hard; he bizarrely hoped that some of the boy's blood had been washed from his face by the rag. He stared up at Thompson; a slow laugh beginning to shake his diaphragm; each motion of levity hurting him beyond belief.

"You shouldn't have brought me back," Tom wheezed, causing Thompson to nod approvingly.

"You know, I'm impressed by your resolve, I'll give you that much. I will get answers though boy," he spat, "of that you can be sure. That little exercise has just served to illuminate what your threshold for pain is. That was merely an amuse bouche. Now we get onto the main course. "McAllister, search the rest of his possessions and when you're done, bring me over our bag of treats," Thompson drilled.

"The starter… comes next," Tom murmured to himself.

"What the fuck did you say?" Thompson growled.

McAllister shuffled over to the seat with Tom's possessions placed upon it. Tom made to reply when, having seen what Mc Allister was about to do, registered the briefest of panicked expressions. Correcting himself abruptly, he looked away. Regrettably however, the briefest indiscretion was all Thompson needed. Thompson turned to inspect the chair and then turned back to Tom.

"On second thoughts McAllister, you crack his phone and leave the other shit to me. Bring the bag with you also," Thompson established as he callously winked at Tom.

McAllister handed Thompson the contents and set off back to his laptop, Tom's phone in hand. Thompson set about emptying Tom's wallet onto the floor and with a knife in hand he slit the wallet apart, ensuring there were no hidden compartments. Satisfied he discarded Tom's wallet pocketing the money inside before unfastening the buckle upon Anthony's wallet. Tom jaw clenched, his eyes widening.

"Something in here Boy Scout?" Thompson demanded as he held it aloft.

Defiant and not wanting to relinquish any further advantage to that of his enemy, Tom made peace with the fact that he would not beg for his brother's possessions to be spared and simply diverted his gaze. Thompson shrugged his shoulders as he withdrew the receipt first. He looked at it with interest for a moment or two before pocketing it. Next came a worn condom from one of the inner pouches.

"I don't think you'll be getting lucky tonight pal. Quite the fucking opposite," Thompson chortled, discarding it upon the floor.

Next came the debit cards which he took out one by one scanning them intently.

"This one is his brothers by the looks of it, an A Hawkins," he turned, "you said his brother's name was Anthony didn't you McAllister?"

"Yes sir," McAllister clarified Thompson's statement abruptly,

"Tut, tut, tut. Looks like we have a grave robber on our hands. I'll have to start calling you Burke… for multiple reasons," Thompson jauntily nodded, amused.

He then came to the plastic pouch and removed the folded photograph inside, sheathing his knife as he did so.

"What's this," he held the photograph aloft, "a picture of your missus? Or in a similar vein, a picture of your pet dog? I fucking hate soppy animal lovers who carry around pictures of their-" he stopped tersely, his grin dissipating.

Thompson's features fell and he swayed slightly. He began muttering to himself, the empty wallet falling to the ground. McAllister even stopped typing and looked over with baffled intrigue.

Thompson turned the picture back towards Tom and thrust it an inch from his nose, "Who is this in the picture with you?"

"None of your-," Tom wheezed.

Thompson withdrew his gun from his holster and placed it against Tom's kneecap.

"I won't ask again," Thompson compelled, accentuating his point with more pressure upon the muzzle of the gun.

Tom grimaced, the gun shaking slightly; whether that was due to Tom or Thompson he could not be confident on account of his severe injuries.

"It's my brother, Anthony," Tom curtly replied, his voice crackling slightly.

"The one who died?" Thompson established.

"Yes," Tom replied quietly.

Thompson brought his hand across his bald head and shook it in disbelief. Erratically, he pulled the hammer back on his gun.

"I'll ask again, who is the other man in the picture?"

"I'm telling you the truth! That was taken when we were teenagers, just before we both went into the forces. A lad's holiday to Malia," Tom rushed to get the words out unaware as to where Thompson was going with his line of questioning

Thompson stared back at him intently, a sadistic fire burning within his eyes. His finger tightened around the trigger, the gun shaking more violently now. Tom's heart was in his throat.

"I'm telling you the truth you maniac! What have I got to lose by telling you about my dead brother?" Tom barked.

Thompson removed the gun and rubbed his head again backwards and forwards, as if he were trying to bring a thought to the surface. He grabbed Tom by the shoulder causing him to wince.

"How did he die?" Thompson spat.

"Routine manoeuvres in Sierra Leone," Tom forced through gritted teeth, "I was in the same convoy... I saw it happen. An RPG attack by the local militia, took out his vehicle, all the men inside as well."

"When?" Thompson abruptly probed.

"Nearly a year ago now," he sucked in air "why the fuck do you care?" Tom locked gazes with Thompson.

"Because I knew your brother," Thompson stated dazedly.

Tom rocked in his chair momentarily, his mind awash with uncertainty. Most notably, on question came to the fore; why was Thompson pursuing this fantasy? What endgame benefitted from conjuring up his dead brother and some fabricated interaction between the two? Every fibre within him was urging him to break the silence, to refute the claim.

"No way, Anthony would never have associated with the likes of you. I would have known. Let's cut the psychological bull, shall we?" Tom pressed on in an exasperated fashion.

"I'm not lying," Thompson dully underlined.

"Bullshit. Ok then, let's have it, where did you know him from? Actually, let's go one better, when was the last time you saw him? Huh? Give me a date, a location," Tom fished.

Thompson pulled Tom closer and through gritted, spittle flecked lips he replied, "The early hours of this morning... when I killed him with my bare hands."

Tom's heart stopped and he found himself glancing over towards the pit, utter disbelief shrouding the entirety of his comprehension.

Dumbstruck, he could only muster the word, "Bollocks."

Thompson turned his back on Tom and set to massaging his head once again. He wittered away to himself, piecing some puzzle together. Unexpectedly, he growled and booted the chair that had held Tom's possessions aside. He moved on to the duffle bag and swung it in Tom's direction. Tom did not even flinch as the heavy-set bag missed his head by a metre or so, tools clattering loudly upon the floor.

"Fuck!" Thompson roared, pacing around the edge of the pit.

Tom's mouth opened and closed like a fish, tears staining his cheeks; an eerie realisation starting to puncture Tom's defences.

Rather meekly and to himself he mouthed the words, "My Brother was... Robert Townsend?"

"What?" Mc Allister muttered dumbly to himself.

The mention of Townsend caused Thompson to veer round and unleash a torrent of violence upon Tom, a brutal combination of slaps and swinging fists to the head and upper torso. Tom's head bounced backwards, the pain serving as a welcome distraction. McAllister ran over and manhandled Thompson, pulling him away.

"Sir we need him. Sir, he may have further information," he pleaded as Thompson's arms continued in a flurry, the man's attempts to pull Thompson away, feeble.

Finally, exhausted and coming to his senses, Thompson stopped, his bloodied knuckles falling to his sides like a dominant Silverback, his chest fighting for air. Tom's head throbbed as it oscillated upon his neck. If it had not been for the fact that he was bound, he would most definitely have fallen to the floor. Thompson turned to McAllister, dumbfounded.

"The fucker had us all along. Today was all a set-up, a merry ruse. He hid the memory stick, left it here for his Brother to retrieve, knowing full well that trying to stop us from executing the mission today was suicide. He knew in the distraction of today, he could steal the memory stick and that when we discovered it was gone, we would be too busy to find it in time. Then all that had to happen was he," Thompson jutted a finger at Tom, "came along and…"

"I just finished checking his phone sir. He's telling the truth, he's had no communication with his brother in over a year," McAllister interrupted, confused beyond belief.

"No, he knew we'd be onto him if he tried any communications via text or call, that we'd be able to access his phone. He must have done it more covertly, a burner phone, a dead drop, carrier pigeons for all I fucking know. But how? He wasn't out of our sight for more than…" Thompsons face was immobilized by complete shock.

"What is it?" McAllister pressed, feeling excluded.

Thompson in spectral fashion, turned on his heel and dazedly strode over to the suitcase upon the workbench. He lifted it and began to walk back through the shadows. Tom came to, spitting blood from his mouth. Each movement of his head was pure agony; the concussion he had likely sustained earlier was all but certain now. His heaving chest made it even more of a challenge to support his thick head. Thompson threw the case at Tom's feet. It was his, the one misplaced at the airport.

"How…" he drunkenly began, his thoughts turned to molasses.

Thompson bent down and cut the green and white luggage tag free, holding it up, inspecting it before throwing it to the ground.

"Australia. Of course," he smiled, "the clever fucker."

"He died… I was there. What is this? My case," Tom ranted, struggling for breath.

Thompson ignored his protestations and pressed on, looking off into the distance.

"We had a mission in Singapore before our operation today. A three-man job while the others put the finishing touches to today's plan back here in Britain. Greaves, Palmer and I, thought it a good idea to use the opportunity as one final field test of the device, a test on something big, knowing full well that it would need to work on a larger scale, a shopping centre. Your plane experienced a technical fault just before taxi, did it not?" Thompson pressed.

After several seconds, Tom nodded dumbly.

"That was us, the EMP acting as part of the plan, a final dry run, a cover for the next stage of our plan. It was Greaves," he stopped momentarily, astonished. "Shit! He must have travelled back on the same diverted flight as you, the flight numbers on your tag."

Thompson shook his head and turned back to face Tom, the malevolent smile now returning. He pressed on, torturing Tom all the more so with his embellished reiteration of events.

"Due to Australia's strict rules on importing and exporting as well as, the scrutiny luggage and cargo goes through, we thought it best not to place the device into our own luggage. We reviewed other methods of smuggling the device into the country by sea, in cargo but none were feasible or trustworthy enough. We needed something quick and safe that afforded us the option of being back in the country before the attack upon Pierce. Fearing we may possibly be under surveillance, we thought this the best option," he indicated to Tom's case upon the floor.

"If we caught, we would be an early Christmas present for various government and intelligence agencies around the world. Instead, we decided to plant it within an unsuspecting traveller's bag, someone who would have plausible deniability should they be caught. We chose a man on your flight, a nobody... or so we thought. I had one of my tech guys, Thwaite's check him out, someone who would easily fly under the radar of suspicion, an average bloke, no criminal record."

"No," Tom whined.

"So, whilst the luggage and all the other passengers were being removed from your original flight to a new one, we planted the device in the bloke's suitcase, before it was scanned and checked again as a precaution by the airport. I had a personal man inside the airport that had helped me smuggle stuff back into Britain before, we paid him off and he carried out the deed. He was responsible for conducting random checks on bags. He busted the lock, preformed the random inspection, whilst unbeknownst to his men, slipped the device inside the case. He even stickered it up to show it had been searched already in case of any future, overzealous employees."

"The asset then placed the man's bag onto the wrong pile, a pile destined for an earlier flight to the same location, London. He did it just as the last of the luggage was being loaded; saw him with my own eyes out of my window seat. If it were discovered, it would be deemed a mistake, nothing suspicious or out of the ordinary. My man then sent us the details via a secure feed."

"Stop!" Tom roared. "This is all make-believe. For starters you've got my life on a computer screen. Cut the ruse, I ain't biting."

Ignoring Tom, Thomson pressed on. He crouched before the edge of the pit before scooping up a handful of cement shards.

"You see your brother had been put undercover within Heathrow, a month before hand, working as a baggage handler. We sent him the details of the suitcase, via our secure feed and it was his job to retrieve the case. It was important that he ensured that the ruse was not discovered and that the bag was not held aside as it had been put on a wrong flight. He did as he had been instructed. Your bag was placed on the carousel and I picked it up. He had ensured us that he would be on duty for a ten-hour shift, that way he would be available at the site for our flight and the next one; additional time in case there were any issues. A good job too as the flight was delayed.

"Of course, this gave us plenty of time to collect the bag before the unsuspecting victim even raised the alarm that his bag was missing. Of course, when we opened the case the device and memory stick had both been in there. What I hadn't realised at the time however, was that he had swapped out the real memory stick that contained the schematics with a duff."

"That doesn't square how you got a hold of my case," Tom maintained.

Although Thompson's ability to fabricate such a grandiose account on the spot was impressive, Tom maintained that it was just that, a fabrication. He allowed him to proceed, all the while rotating his wrists, his intention to weaken the duct tape that bound him.

"That's easy enough to rectify. Your brother returned to the shopping centre and established that he had wanted one more scan of the place before today's proceedings. During this time Thwaites, being as methodical as he was, decided to check the EMP device and the schematics one last time should anything go tits up in the eleventh hour.

"The EMP was of course the real Mc Coy; the memory stick on the other hand, well that was emptier than a hermits' address book. So, Thwaites hacked into Heathrow's servers and checked the manifests on both flights and low and behold, two bags were reported missing. Thwaite's challenged your brother when he returned from his sweep or at least," he threw a shard at one of the mounds, "that's how we think it went down, on account of him being face down in the same pit over there with his throat slit. We caught your brother trying to make a break for it. Unlike you, he escaped. Credit where credit is due, he even managed to evade us for a while, even after a few hours of torture. Remarkable really," Thompson trailed off, allowing the remaining shards of cement to fall from his grasp.

"All a bit too convenient for my liking," Tom arrogantly stated, unconvinced.

"I'm getting there you prick!" Thompson barked.

"So is Christmas," Tom sneered through bloodied teeth.

"Not for you," Thompson rose from his haunches like an apex predator as he said this, "anyhow, as I was explaining before being so rudely interrupted, I plan for every eventuality. I had a second, unknown man planted at the airport, an old Army mate who needed a few notes; a genuine employee there, hard on his luck, bitch of a wife burning through the kid's inheritance."

"I asked him to search your brothers work locker, wanting a further vetting process; the rest of my men were unaware of this, of course. He informed me that there was a bag inside; all discernible I.D. had been ripped off of the bag... all except for a luggage tag. He was under strict instructions not to open it until I had seen it. You see your brother thought it would be safe there, high security location like that, him being the only one on the team with clearance."

"My man, ever the stickler for details, also checked the shift rota. Turns out Anthony," Tom winced at the mention of his brother's name in Thompson's mouth, "A.K.A Robert fucking Townsend, had also doctored his shift at the last minute. You see, he actually finished around two hours after our flight had come in, which means for nearly five hours he was unaccounted for. You were on the later flight of course... so we know he didn't visit you then, "Thompson chewed over.

"Tell him about what else was in there Thompson" McAllister excitedly yapped at Thompsons flank.

"Oh yes, well remembered McAllister," he mockingly enthused, McAllister blushing at the genuine compliment. "Starting to make sense why it was in there now, I thought he was just some kind of closet pervert or something," Thompson turned and locked gazes with Tom.

"There was an airport courier uniform in the locker, hat and all, as well as a fake beard, wig and a prosthetic nose. Makes all the sense in the world now," he chuckled.

"Not to me, this is your fabrication after all don't forget" Tom sneered, looking sideways and away from the pit, his belief in Thompsons words all but ebbed away now.

Thompson stepped behind Tom again, the hairs on the back of his neck dancing. He drew close to Tom's ear once again and spoke.

"I'm not the most trusting guy in the world, as you can imagine. That said, I had another reason for having my own guy at the airport, the one no one else knew about. You see, my employer had turned me on to some intel, that we had a rat within the ranks. Who he worked for he could not say."

"At the time I had speculated that the rat, if successful in acquiring the device and or the schematics, would sell them to the highest bidder. Turns out however, our little rat needed to hide his contraband, most likely as an additional insurance when it came to the big day; some insider information on how to shut the device down from the outside thus rendering our plan and Pierces subsequent demise, inert. I mean, being dead for a year and having operated under deep cover makes it rather awkward wouldn't you say? To just, walk up to your front door. That is unless..." Thompson let the sentence hang in the air, prompting Tom to conclude his course of thought.

Tom paused and considered, the pieces starting to fall into place.

"Unless he delivered it to my house in person under the assumed guise of an airport employee returning my bag. Safe and completely untraceable," Tom reluctantly surmised.

"We have a winner!" Thompson snarled, "always was a smartass, glad I killed the little fuck now."

"So what did you find?" Tom questioned, keeping Thompson talking, the binds having barely yielded.

"Fucking nothing is what," he kicked the lid of Tom's case open, a pair of boxers and a trainer spilling out onto the floor.

"All we gleamed from this case was that you have a shit taste in clothes. We even sliced it open and checked for secret compartments, nothing. That was about the time," he thrust a thumb in the direction of the centre of the pit, "things got really uncomfortable for Anthony over there."

"Up until then much like that bag before you, he didn't have anything to declare. That is, until he ran out of hope; a handful of nails and a blow torch will do that to a man. He said the schematics were in the centre somewhere. He gave us a location, which of course upon inspection turned out to be a wild goose chase. By the time we got back to him, he had escaped, killing my explosives expert. Lucky I always bring spare," Thompson declared callously.

Tom's face now felt even more swollen and bruised. Whoever that poor soul was in the tarpaulin, all Tom could do was pray that he did not endure the same fate he had. He sucked in a deep death, the stabbing in his chest nearly unbearable now, the acrid smell of petrol still twinging his nostrils. That said, what came next, needed to be said.

"A nice story but if you think I'm going to just roll over and believe a word that comes out of that arsehole you call a mouth you have another thing coming. My brother was a hero, a good man. No way would he have gotten caught up with you rejects. This is all a coincidence, a name taken randomly from a manifest. Hell, your guy over there said it himself; he's read my record, making all of this all the easier to fabricate. How do I know my bag and that other guys weren't the only ones you took?"

Tom shook his head at the sheer absurdity of it all.

"Nah, reeks of mind games to me, some interrogation ploy".

Several seconds of silence passed.

"I'm too fucking jetlagged for this," Thompson sighed and indicated once again for McAllister to come over, "Grab his legs," he insisted.

McAllister did as he was told. The two men gained a purchase upon the chair and set about carrying Tom towards the edge of the pit. Tom readied himself for the waterboarding to commence.

"Put him down here," Thompson gestured with a nod of his head.

The two men positioned the two front legs of the chair perilously on the ledge. Tom could now see the body of Thompson's other man at the head of the pit, the one Robert Townsend had killed and to his left the body wrapped in tarpaulin. Tom's heart was in his mouth, he had no idea what horrors awaited him in the pit.

"I'll ask you this once more and only fucking once. Is the device still here in the building?" Thompson irately persevered.

"You know... earlier, you forgot to start your little fairy tale with once upon a time," Tom mockingly jibed.

Thompson spat upon the ground and grabbed a cluster of Tom's hair.

"Before we do this, just so you know... regardless of whether you talked or not, I would never have spared you from this moment," he cruelly whispered in Tom's ear.

Then, with a booming kick to the back of the chair, Tom's world momentarily spun into obscurity. His bound hand made to instinctively break his fall to no avail as he landed hard upon the uneven contours of the base of the pit.

A cloud of dust rose instantaneously, forcing him to cough, his already strained lungs heaving with exerted spasms. He was now on his side facing the tarpaulin, the ominous bundle now two feet away. McAllister dragged one of the construction lights over, illuminating the section of pit Tom now occupied. Tom's breathing was wildly erratic, his temples throbbing with the rush of blood to the head.

Thompson positioned himself behind the tarpaulin and pinched a section of the material, his eyes never leaving Tom's.

"You know, when he escaped and we finally tracked him down, lying bloody and battered, he still had a spark of hope truth be told. You could see it in his eyes... an ember at any rate. You tell me Tom; did I finally manage to extinguish it?" Thompson bellowed before hurling the tarpaulin back with a flourish.

Tom's waited several agonising seconds for his eyes to zero in, the blinding light forcing him to wince. At first all he could make out was the upper profile of the lifeless form. And then, he began to shake uncontrollably, the features beginning to arrange themselves into that of his brothers, irrespective of the blood that smeared his face, the two partially empty eye sockets, now black, an eyeliner effect of congealed blood around each. Tom's eyes filled with tears and Thompson howled with laughter, McAllister joining in demonically. Tom was unable to move his head, transfixed by what he was seeing. He was trying to mouth something, his jaw opening and closing in a dumbstruck stupor. All he could do was stare back in abject horror.

"Well, I guess we don't need a DNA test," Thompson howled.

Tom tried to shift towards his brother wishing to hold him but was embolised both by his restraints and the paralysis of grief, groping at his every fibre.

"Nuh... nuh," he stuttered.

Thompson knelt beside Anthony's body, nodding, gesturing with his hands like that of a parent trying to coax their baby's first words out.

"That's my boy, use your words, come on," he goaded before abruptly bringing an end to his belittlement.

Tom's outstretched hand, bound and bloodied, fascinated him. He traced the source of the blood to the wound upon his forearm before inquisitively cocking his head in wonder. Thompson observed the watch upon the suffering man's wrist, a plastic strap protruding slightly from beneath it. He made to reach for it when suddenly his radio, crackled into life. He stood bolt upright.

"What is it?" he hissed.

He listened intently for several moments, ashen faced.

"I'll be right up; you know the drill Jones. Blow the roof and maintain cover, just in case, until I call you down. Maintain procedure. The charges in the sewers should catch them unawares should they try that route," another pause, "I doubt it; however, expect them to hit us high and low, over."

He shot McAllister a calculating expression.

"They're breaching the roof, as soon as they've securely touched down, we're blowing the charges. I'm going to send down as much reinforcement as we can muster. When they arrive, take the camera and Pierce and make your way to Level One. I'm going to lock this room down. Watch Pierce and once this little family reunion is over, you have my full permission to do as you wish, getting any additional information if possible. We're moving towards extraction. You have ten minutes unless I say otherwise, to blow the charges."

Thompson made to leave, callously stepping over Tom as he did so. But not before rubbing further salt into Tom's extensive wounds.

"It's been a blast Tom, it really has but I have to go and make history, he gleefully decreed, patting Tom upon the head as he exited, his sadistic howls reverberating off the walls.

(CHAPTER BREAK)

Miller paced the walkway. The screens were connected to all three Units helmet cams as they relayed a live account of the operation on a dedicated screen each. As requested, Braham and Benley had also been hooked up to the transmission of the live feed. An open line with the two had also been established, their presence felt all the more so in the room via the speaker upon the tabletop.

"Are we all ready?" Braham asked his voice remarkably unblemished by the handset.

"Yes sir, ready to proceed on your mark," Miller replied with a detached yet operational response.

"And I have your assurance, that all possible exits are being covered?" Benley now chipped in.

"Yes sir, we have a police barricade four blocks wide, snipers on all adjacent rooftops. Charlie Unit are to breach at ground level, setting explosive charges upon the shutters, followed by an armoured vehicle which will serve as a battering ram through the debris; the shutters are rather sturdy, sir. "

"Alpha Unit will breach via the roof initially, before splitting into two sub-groups; Alpha is to secure the roof before moving down through the emergency exit covertly, whilst Bravo will rappel down the building, breaching at level two. Alpha and Charlie units will endeavour to focus much of the hostile's fire.

"We intend to drive the remaining hostiles up onto Level Two, effectively sandwiching them between a rock and a hard place. Once in position, Bravo team will breach and engage. Our attack is three-fold, covering all aspects of the building. We believe they will try to use Pierce as a hostage or possibly as a bartering chip," Miller added, his voice peaking slightly with uncertainty.

"Under what intel," Braham queried, slightly agitated.

"None sir, it's just how these things usually pan out. They have no way out, so they either go down in a hail of gunfire or surrender. It is our intention to disable option one before they have the chance to mobilise," Miller stated, bored with having to explain his actions once more.

"Hardly reassuring," Benley arrogantly deliberated.

"Our hand is being forced here sir. If you believe we should abort the operation or postpone, you may of course interject," Miller paused, letting the question hang, Miller testing Benley's metal.

"No, proceed as planned," Braham hastily cut in.

"Very good sir," Miller established before turning to face the situation room.

The various analysts and experts turned at the waist in their chairs, one or more of the group hushing fellow co-workers who busied themselves with contingencies and the breaking down of fresh intel. A soothing hush descended upon the room, one tinged with nervous anticipation.

"You've all been briefed ladies and gentlemen; you know your jobs, the procedure if things go south. This is finally it. We've been on the back foot all day. Well no longer. It's time to regain the high ground. Let's get the Prime Minister and as many hostages out of there as possible," Miller asserted with feigned confidence.

Many within the room nodded along whilst others sat poised, awaiting Miller's command, a professional composure waiting to be unleashed.

"Alpha Unit, mission is a go. I repeat, mission is a go, you are cleared to proceed. Roger and out," Miller barked into his headset.

(CHAPTER BREAK)

Tom was hyperventilating. The fear and pain he had endured throughout the day's events had taken their hold upon his frame, his heart beginning to pump at an alarming rate. He tried to calm himself; mentally ordering himself to slow his breathing, knowing full well that shock, could kill. His vision had dimmed at the periphery, the remainder of his vision blurred by tears. Tom's thoughts jumped briefly from that of his own plight to that of the tactical unit that would soon land upon the roof. They were walking into an ambush and with their breach proving unsuccessful, they would have little in the way of a counterattack.

Tom's other senses suddenly became heightened; the tap of McAllister on the keyboard, the smell of urine, most likely from Pierce mixed with the acrid smell of petrol. Tom's resolve began to fade, the pain finally overcoming his weak and pitiful figure. He began to feel a twinge of numbness descend across his limbs, his breathing becoming more laboured. He began to drift, drunkenly at first and then, more deeply, his mind making large swooping, canted motions. His vision cleared for the briefest moment of euphoric clarity, his mind taking him back to his brother. The talk he had had with his father. The wallet he had been unknowingly handed; his father unaware of what Tom's journey to West Acre Point would cost. When his parents discovered his death, he hoped his father would not harbour any guilt. Tom held no resentment towards his father for the wallet he had handed Tom, the receipt.

Tom's breathing slowed slightly, and a mental uppercut rattled his brain, subduing the shock. His vision cleared and the events that had led him to this moment surged through his brain. The wallet, the airport employee's uniform, the message upon the receipt. Tom wracked his brain and wrenched his eyes shut, trying to formulate the pieces of the jigsaw. Sluggishly, the information began to congregate in the forefront of his mind; the missing pieces of the puzzle beginning to drift from the periphery of his temples towards the centre of his cranium.

He worked his way through the message, pulling the numbers from memory, dispersing those he discovered to be incorrect or imagined. If he were to die, he did not intend for his passage to be plagued by the uncertainty of a code not deciphered. The message hardened. 'Hawker 8 21 18 18 9 3 1 14 5'.

Tom muttered away to himself, giddy with the thread that he was beginning to unravel. He afforded himself the briefest reminiscences of a life long ago, playing soldiers with Anthony in the garden. One of their favourite games when they had been younger was breaking enigma codes, a phase they went through after they had sat with their father, who at the time had been watching a documentary on Alan Turing and his efforts throughout the Second World War in breaking the German enigma codes.

Now, Brian's words echoed in Tom's ears and he vividly remembered the event; Tom sitting at his father's feet in front of the TV set, the end credits of the documentary rolling up the screen. Anthony sat in his lap, his father taking the toy model of the Hurricane from Anthony and holding it aloft so both boys could see. A singular tear rolled down Tom's cheek as his vision focused once again on Anthony. He dispelled any notions of his brother as a corpse, instead replacing his hollowed-out eyes with the ones that had shined so brightly, with such interest as their father imparted his sage wisdom upon them. They had always hung on his every word, even as men; willingly lectured as opposed to being brow- beaten or condescended. The remnants of his speech, the final evaluative statement echoing as he internally played it over to himself.

"Just like the Hurricane, Turing was undervalued, deemed obsolete, of no use to the more sophisticated members within the war effort. But boys..." he had stated as he leant forward and tickled Anthony's belly playfully, raising a giddy chortle from his youngest child.

"It's always those types of men, those unsung few, those men deemed to be the lesser of their parts that truly rise to the challenge. You see I don't idolise the Hurricane for its complexity or the beauty of it as a machine, just like I don't look at Turing's Enigma machine as the victor within Britain's war effort. No, I idolise the man behind the machine, the true underdogs of the war. Destined to fail, their downfall deemed a forgone conclusion. They are the true cogs that kept the wheels of victory turning, the unsurmountable odds, the backlash from their peers and mockery from their superiors, their supposed betters... well lads, that was the perfect oil to lubricate their gears, to keep them moving, from giving up. Sometimes it pays to be the underdog, a nobody. Sometimes that's what makes you, the somebody."

From that day they had left coded messages around the house, based on a simple cipher they had invented together, the letters pairing up in accordance with their corresponding place in the alphabet, A being one, Z being twenty-six and so on. The messages varied in difficulty and length as they grew older, a secret language only they knew off. To the untrained eye the random numbers scrawled on sheets of paper resembled that of some form of addition, perhaps maths homework or some telephone number. Tom could not quite believe that he had missed it; his brother had even referred to him by his childhood nickname, Hawker.

He felt a resurgence of hope, a desire to fight on, if not for him, if not for the hostages in the building then for his brother; one last code to crack, one last mission to accomplish. He matched up the cipher with the series of numbers he had recalled from the receipt and his breathing came to a concentrated halt, the link to the past soothing him finally. The cipher and code swirled in his head as he methodically matched the numbers to their lettered counterparts. And then, there it was.

"Hawker, in Hurricane," he muttered to himself, the formulation of letters and their symbolic link to his childhood dispelling any coincidence.

He smiled as he heard his brother's childlike voice, chasing him around the garden calling out his nickname, running with another piece of crayon scrawled paper in his hand.

"I bet you can't crack this one Hawker, not this time."

He had always met his brother's challenge. Tom shuffled slightly forward in his chair, the metal grating on the floor. His movements were laborious but after several juddering advancements, he drew alongside he brother. He strained his neck, negotiating just enough of an angle to kiss his brother's forehead where his lips lingered upon his cold forehead. He rested there for a second, unexpectedly glad of his current predicament, at being able to finally part ways with his brother and this time, on his terms.

"Mission received and understood little brother," he whispered.

He smiled lightly, the shackles of pain melting away, his hope resurgent. He forced himself to look away, to concentrate on the task at hand. Compartmentalise the pain, the anguish and use it.

He began to probe the surrounding area for anything he could use to free himself. His right hand rested upon the cold concrete and he clutched it open and shut, trying to work his hands free. His eyes scanned the pit until they fell upon a length of construction rebar, about a foot in length, sheered and pointed at one end where it had been cut. Tom contorted his spine, affording him a few more centimetres of reach. His fingers groped the end and initially the pole rolled slightly away from him. His heart leapt in his chest with anxiety, fearing he had lost his only hope. Thankfully, the pole rolled back in a circular motion, fortuitously edging slightly closer to Tom.

He grasped the metal and held it tightly, shimmying it through his palm and down into the safety of the recess between the duct tape and his skin. Delicately he began to saw away at the duct tape, the noise coinciding with his determined heartbeat. An oblivious McAllister continued to tap away.

Several seconds later, a bright light behind Tom broke through into the room. It illuminated Tom as well as Anthony. Tom drove the temptation of grabbing a more rounded look at his brother from his mind. He stared in the opposite direction and halted his sawing motion as footsteps approached. A shadow descended over him, shrouding him in darkness. It lingered for several seconds, Tom concentrating on his own breathing. The noise of feet shifting overhead.

"Boss wants you and Pierce upstairs. Bring all your shit with you as well. Hertz is waiting outside to take you up," the unmistakable voice of Doc, impatiently cracked.

"All packed and ready, the detonator is there, all primed. The boss gave me orders to extract any information out of..." McAllister began.

"You let me worry about that. Now move! Boss reckons the breach is imminent," Doc spat.

Tom lay motionless, affording himself a few slower, angled saws at the duct tape. The noise of equipment being gathered echoed throughout the room, which was soon replaced by what Tom presumed to be Pierce, as he was bundled towards the room's entrance, his muffled cries and the smell of urine stagnant in the air.

Then, rather abruptly, the light dissipated as the door closed behind the two men. Loud, calculated steps once again came from behind Tom. Doc's arms bundled around Tom's shoulders and he was hefted upright. The chair was then pulled from the pit and dragged with exerted effort, about three metres from the edge of the pit. All the while Tom feigned unconsciousness.

Doc knelt before him and tutted distastefully. Tom could smell his cheap aftershave, twinned with that of stale body odour.

"Open your eyes, I know you're awake," Doc stated and smiled when Tom reciprocated immediately.

Tom twisted his right wrist lightly and felt a decent flap of separated duct tape at the base of his wrist.

"Thompson tells us he was your brother," Doc pointed back towards the pit.

He held up a black object in his hand, a detonator, his finger hovering over the red button.

"When that roof blows, it's my job to press this. Guess what it's hooked up to?" Doc grinned maleficently.

Tom leant in towards Doc.

"Hopefully your off switch," Tom smirked defiantly.

Doc made the noise of a buzzer, indicating that it was the wrong answer.

"No, no my poor deluded friend," he held the detonator aloft, "this is hooked up to a substantial amount of C4, situated at the very centre of said pit. I push this; I blow a size in it bigger than that smart, wisecracking arsehole of a mouth and with it, you and your brother's corpses. No open casket for you two I'm afraid," Doc concluded, forcefully patting Tom's face three times in emphasis.

Tom looked past Doc, towards the pit, the realisation of the pit's existence made all too clear now.

"Your escape route, while all hell breaks loose above."

"We have a winner," Doc shouted with enthused mockery. "Now for the bonus cash prize, what do you thinks going to happen to this building? What could cause such a distraction for the emergency services above, I wonder?"

Tom did not need to consider his response.

"You blow the building up, bringing it down with me and all the other hostages inside. They presume you died in the blast, a form of martyrdom, a clean slate for you and your team."

"Bingo! Well done that man. So, here's your prize. Tell me where the schematics are and I put a round in your head right now, ending it all quickly. Withhold the information and I put one in each of your knees and let the rubble crush you. If you're unlucky enough, you'll be buried alive for an agonising hour or so before you succumb to blood loss. Not much on the options front I grant you but it's not like I was going to let you live."

Tom adopted a considering tone. He nodded after several seconds, fabricating the pretence of defeat.

"Alright I'll tell you," he muttered before bursting into a violent cough. He did so for ten seconds or so, Doc waiting expectantly.

"Come on, spit it out. You know it makes sense," Doc pressed.

"It's…" another splutter, dropping the volume of his voice. Doc edged closer, motioning to his ear.

"Speak up for fucks sake!" Doc impatiently commanded.

"It's under the table in the…" Tom's voice was deliberately inaudible. Doc gripped his left shoulder and thumbed his wound. Tom screamed out in agony. Doc came in closer.

"Under where? Get on with it," Doc spat.

Tom locked gazes with Doc and the mock defeat melted away "It'd be my pleasure," Tom growled.

His wrist broke free, the duct tape coming with it. Doc's confident features crumpled, he made to bring his hand up but instead Tom brought the tapered end of the rebar upwards towards Doc's upper shoulder, driving the metal as far as his grip would allow. Doc screamed out in distress, making to pull away from Tom. The pole was withdrawn with a triumphant fountain of blood and was brought down again, this time cutting a deep swathe across his tormentor's chest. Doc stumbled backwards, teetering on the edge of the pit. He swayed, grasping at his wound, his face devoid of all colour. Tom acted fast; the bloody shard of pole brought across to his remaining bind. With a flurry he cut it free.

He rose wearily, pulling the duct tape from his wrists. He took the lengths of tape respectively and placed them delicately over the two wounds inflicted upon him by Thompson, serving as a makeshift bandage. His forearms were on fire; from the surge of energy or loss of blood, he did not wish to consider, all fear now replaced with anger. Tom's true mission lay ahead of him now and he intended on succeeding in it, regardless. He walked towards Doc, who looked back at him aghast. He lifted the detonator in a show of force.

"Get back! I'll do it," he stuttered.

Tom was now no less than a metre away from him. He lashed out with brutal expediency and grabbed the wrist of Doc's right hand, the detonator shaking under Tom's exerted grip. He prised the detonator from Doc's grasp, following it up with a potent head-butt. Doc crumpled to his feet, yet Tom held him firm, now placing the detonator in his own pocket. Doc whimpered, grunting between fearful swallows as Tom twisted his wrist. He reached down and lifted him by his tactical vest, the man now a dead weight

"Who the fuck are you, man," Doc pleaded.

Tom pulled him closer, sneering intently. He stood firm; fuelled by bloodlust, his need for revenge, for his brother, for the boy. For himself.

"Me? I'm a nobody, an underdog," Tom defiantly replied before he drove the rebar through the man's upper jaw with a sickening crunch of bone, the squelch of flesh sucking at the metal upon entry. Tom held Doc for a moment before letting the man's convulsed movements carry him into the pit where he fell three metres shy of his brother.

Tom swayed his calves spasming slightly; the adrenaline ensuring he remained rooted to the spot. After several hesitant seconds, he stepped forward and back into the pit. He bent down and tested his brother's weight. His forearms coursed with an insatiable heat, the onset of pins and needles instantaneous. He paused, bracing himself for the pain that was to come. He would not drop his brother, he would persevere through the pain, he owed his brother's remains that much at least. Finally, through gritted teeth, he scooped up his Anthony's lifeless form, cradling him in his shaking arms. He held firm, shuffling his feet gradually but assuredly until he shakily placed his right leg upon the edge of the pit and using all his strength, boosted himself free of it.

He lumbered forwards, his upper torso shaking, a sinuous vein protruding from his neck. He fixed his gaze upon a singular point ahead and moved towards it, a mound of bubble wrap. When he arrived at the designated waypoint, Tom placed his brother down slightly upon the plastic sheeting and swaddled his brother in the embrace of the popping material. It was his intention to both conceal his brother whilst also protecting him in the plastic cocoon of the packing material.

He paused when it came to covering Anthony's face, thinking better of it. His brother had hated the dark when he was a boy. Tom draped the plastic sheet away from his face and instead pulled an empty box in front of his brother's head, obscuring him from view, his body hidden within the layers of bubble wrap, an indiscernible mound to the casual onlooker.

He knelt over his brother's body brushing his brother's cheek. He was alone with his thoughts when suddenly the familiar ringtone from his phone, the Rolling Stone's *'Gimme Shelter'*, rung out. He jumped out of his skin; his senses heightened by the tension. Excitedly, he made to walk over to the phone when a booming thud came from above. The room shuddered, displacing dust from the ceiling above which was immediately followed by the screams of the hostages. The blast seemed to have come from far above and with a wretched realisation; Tom assumed it to be the charges upon the roof.

His head dropped in a sign of respect, not quite knowing how to process the news, not having known the men who had landed upon that roof, oblivious to the ambush that awaited them. He had intended on warning the authorities if he proved successful in freeing himself, but he had been too late. The explosion, sizeable in nature had most likely taken part of the roof with it, along with Tom's only hope of an advantage. The cavalry would not be coming to his aide, the attack most likely being aborted, the authorities not wanting to chance Thompson's hand anymore, knowing full well that he would act upon his promise of reprisal, if challenged further.

Tom bounded over to the laptop and unplugged his phone from the wire that McAllister had been using to gain access to his phone. Graciously, Tom observed that the phone had gained a small but valuable amount of charge, the battery now reading seventeen percent. An unknown number flashed up upon the screen. Tom unlocked his phone with a slide of his finger, punching in the entry code. He answered the call tentatively.

"Hello?" he queried, realising the pure absurdity of his current predicament.

"Is this Thomas…? Tom, I mean."

The caller was female, nervous.

"Yes, speaking," Tom instinctively responded, impatience tempering his voice.

He searched the tabletop turning over a full magazine with his free hand.

"It's Anna, from the airport," the distant voice expanded.

Tom's heart shrouded with guilt at having not contacted the woman behind the desk. He rubbed the back of his head bashfully.

"Look Anna, this really isn't a good time... you see I..." he started.

Anna sighed slightly and Tom could detect the disappointment in her voice.

"Oh... that's ok, I'm... erm, just phoning to update you on the status of your bag," Anna stated coyly having phoned in the first place under the pretence of informing him about his lost luggage.

Tom glanced at his bag, the awkward nature of their discourse making him uneasy.

"Look, I meant to phone..." Tom spluttered.

"That's ok Mr. Hawkins," Anna's formality returning, the woman scorned by what she perceived to be rejection, "no update on your bag yet sir, it has not been found."

"Listen Anna, I..." Tom started.

"It's really ok Mr. Hawkins," she paused, considering whether to continue or not. "I don't usually give out my number, it was unprofessional and it is my intention to hand over your case to someone else... the incident that is, not your luggage," she awkwardly clarified, "I'm sorry for putting you in this position."

Tom had liked Anna and had had every intention of phoning her. He had lost so much today and had already made a hash of their conversation thus far. Rather forcefully Tom interjected, determined to lose nothing further today.

"Anna, look. I'm going to cut straight to the chase here, I like you and I would definitely like to meet up with you, if that is still on the table but I have a situation..." Tom paused considering whether to proceed.

"Oh my God, you're married aren't you?" she gasped, rebuking herself.

"No, no, no. Listen Anna, I don't know how to say this and please don't take this as some sort of excuse, largely because it would be in extremely bad taste if it were but, have you seen the news? What's going on in London? I presume it's on the news," Tom questioned, the thought dawning.

"What the attack on the Prime Minister and that shopping centre, yes, it's awful," she replied, unsure of whether this was some absurd flirtation, "what about it? Oh my God, you don't know anyone in there do you?" she fretfully blurted out.

Tom afforded himself a slight laugh and nodded, "Yes, yes I do."

"Oh sir, I mean Thomas, I am so sorry, I shouldn't have bothered you with this now. Of all the times to..." she trailed off.

"Anna?" Tom halted her ramblings.

"Yes," she stated in an exasperated tone.

"Tom is fine and..." he searched for the words before settling upon the cold hard truth. "Anna, it's me, I'm in West Acre," he paused allowing this to sink in, affording himself a cursory glance at his battery.

Another gasp, "But... Oh my God but...how are you able to... you're not one of them are you, one of those terrorists?" she rambled on, her tone toughening at the end.

"Look Anna, it's a long story. All I can say at this moment is, I am not one of them...quite the opposite in fact, I'm trying to help. I'm ex-forces and I've managed to escape. From the sounds of it they've just taken out a tactical unit up on the roof, so it's down to me now to get the remaining hostages out safe."

"No, you need to find a way out. Get out of there, they've got guns," she pressed on, rather animated now.

"So have I and there's more to it than that. Listen, my phones about to die and I have one more call to make, so I'll keep this short. Can you do something for me?" Tom inquired.

"Yes, yes whatever you need," Anna dazedly agreed.

"I need you to phone the Police and tell them that they're planning on levelling this place along with the hostages. They plan to escape, how with what they have planned, I have no idea. The leader is called Thompson, they're not what they say they are," Tom rattled on, briefly pulling the phone from his ear to check the battery again; eleven percent.

"Ok Tom but you should..." she hesitated.

"Anna, I have to finish this. If I don't make it out..." he paused, faced with his own mortality, "if I don't make it out of here... dinners on me," he smirked.

This raised a panicked laugh from Anna, his candid disposition when faced with such unsurmountable odds no doubt rendering him more attractive.

"If you make it out of there in one piece, I'll treat you to a seven-course meal," Anna quipped.

"I need to go Anna," Tom pressed, his eyes darting towards the door.

"Good luck Tom, what you're doing, it's..." she could not find the words.

"What anyone else would do in my situation, goodbye Anna," Tom hung up and immediately brought up his contacts list. He observed that he had fifteen missed calls from his father. He brought up his number and tapped the screen. Unsurprisingly, it was picked up after just two rings.

"Tom! Bloody hell. Where are you? Are you ok?" Brian hurriedly cross sectioned his son.

Tom's heart swelled with a spectrum of emotions upon hearing his father's voice.

"Boy is it good to hear your voice," Tom choked up momentarily, "Dad listen, I don't have much time, my phone is about to die. Listen, I'm alive and... I'm in the centre. It's awful Dad, what they've done, what they have planned. They've killed so many people… and I've, I've had to kill some myself, in defence, they were going to…" Tom suddenly felt ashamed.

Brian choked back a fit of tears.

"Tom…never mind all of that, you did what you needed to do to survive but you need to get out of there lad, right now. It's all over the news, there was just an explosion. Are you injured?" Brian quizzed, his emergency training kicking in.

"I know Dad, just a little dinged up," he embellished, "I can't leave Dad; they've got women and children in here. Plus, there is no out, the place is sealed up tighter than a drum and I'm all these people have left," Tom sadly appraised.

"Leave it to the Special Forces Son; they're trained for this kind of thing. Please, me and your poor mother are worried sick. Please, we can't lose you, we've lost so much already, we can't…" Brian burst into tears, a deep sobbing echoing down the phone line.

Tom could not hold back his own tears any longer.

"I know Dad, I'm sorry but… shit. I'm so bloody scared right now Dad. They're killing kids in here. I can't just let that go; they're going to blow the place sky-high, the hostages, the Prime Minister. They're going to kill them all. I'm all these people have got, their last hope at getting them out of here. I can't take that away from them. I can't…" Tom sobbed.

The line went silent for several seconds; Tom afforded himself another look at his battery, the charge six percent now. He feared his father had been cut off.

"Dad?" he called out in panic.

Brian sniffed his emotional state audible over the phone.

"You know Son… ever since you were young, all me and your Mother ever wanted for you and Anthony was the right to forge your own path, to make your own choices. We were just a safety net, here if you needed us. I like to think we had some part in making you both the men you are…the man you are today. And nothing you've done today could ever change that. My biggest fear wasn't failing you as a father or losing either of you… even when you both enlisted, it was… it was the fact that…" he paused again, composing himself, the words hard to find.

"It was that you and your Brother, you always wanted to play the hero, whether that be standing up for your little brother in the playground or fighting for your country. You've always been my hero Son, I just always feared that… that you needed more, that that would never be enough. You're at your best Son when you're up against it but what you've done already for those people, don't be ashamed to walk away from that. Don't let some moral sense of duty keep you there. Regardless of what has happened or what will happen, you'll always be mine and your mother's hero, no matter what."

Tom clamped a hand over his mouth, forcing the sobs down his throat. He suddenly had the sobering thought that this may be the last time he ever spoke to his father.

"Dad, there's a reason… a reason why I left the Army, it's…" he struggled to formulate the words.

"It's ok son, you don't need to justify yourself," Brian interjected.

But he did need to; he had needed to for a long time now. He needed to unburden himself of at least one secret, one facet of his life that brought him an overbearing sense of shame.

"No Dad, I need to…" he swallowed hard, gathering himself. "I was dishonourably discharged Dad. PTSD, after… after what happened with Anthony, I couldn't, I just couldn't take it anymore. I started to break down, see things, ghosts, people that I'd killed, Anthony… I started to miss things, endangered my unit, I… I just couldn't take the fighting anymore."

"What happened to Anthony Dad, it hollowed me out, left me empty, useless. All I've ever known is the Army. I've let everyone down Dad, too many times, that should have been me in that vehicle, Anthony should still be…"

Tom slammed the tabletop.

"I failed to protect my little brother Dad. I failed and that was my only job, that was my only mission and I fucked it all up!"

Tom was highly distressed now, his heart beginning to palpitate, his nostrils conjuring up the recollection of charred flesh.

"You can't save everyone Tom. Your brother, he knew the risks, you couldn't have known. You've done enough Son; you've completed your mission. Anthony wouldn't want you to be like this, to carry this guilt. We'll get through this together, just like we get through everything, together, as a family."

Tom shook his head, his father unaware of the events of the last thirty minutes.

"Dad it's more than that, about Anthony, about his death," Tom started.

"None of that matters now Son. All that matters now is the choice that lies before you. You're a man and a fine one at that. The Army doesn't just teach you how to kill a man; it teaches you how to be a man. It teaches you to put others above yourself. People often forget that the first man you kill, that you erase, is yourself. The man you were before. But the Army didn't make you the man you are now son, of that you can take full credit. You're not broken, you're not worthless. You're a fighter. A warrior with only one question that needs answering," Brian halted.

Tom stared over at his brother's body and longed to tell his father about his other son. That he had not died at the hands of some rebel fighter. That he had, now in this very moment, the tools in which to gain revenge for all those lost months, those sleepless nights. To kill the very man who took his youngest son from him.

"Do you want to fight because you feel like you need to or because you want to? Put aside any guilt you carry and ask yourself honestly, is the fight worth it? Win or lose, is it worth the risk, to those people, to you?" Brian clinically lay out.

"Yes," Tom defiantly stated.

Tom heard is father sigh, not out of disappointment but out of the self-resignation of pride.

"You get your stubbornness from your Mother you know that don't you," Brian stated in mock consolation.

Tom laughed momentarily and dried his eyes. He paused, his father ever the bastion of sanity.

"You know, whatever happens Dad, I love you both so much. Everything I am is because of you two. Whatever the outcome, I'm sorry I've had to put you through this again after Anthony."

"Son," Brian sternly stated with a soldierly exuberance, "the only ones that need to be sorry are the ones that did this. Keep your wits about you, conserve your ammo and leave none of them standing. Watch your six. I love you Son."

"You too Dad" Tom responded.

"Now go give em hell Son," Brian sternly ordered.

"Yes Sir," Tom countered and with that the phone died.

Tom dumbly pocketed the phone. If it were all to end now, it would be on his terms, all debts paid, parting words aired. The slate, however, was far from wiped clean. Tom wiped the last tears away from his eyes and picked up his tactical vest. Methodically, he set about pocketing the items confiscated from him and placed the vest back on. He drew his pistol and clicked the safety off with a flourish before holstering the weapon once again.

The absurdity of the situation and the insurmountable odds stacked against him came and went as his body was flushed by endorphins. Before he left, he made to turn and say something to the mound that cocooned Anthony's lifeless body but thought better of it. The time for talk, was over.

CHAPTER TWENTY: THINKING OUTSIDE OF THE BALLOT BOX

Miller watched on in horror as Alpha Team's comm's were rendered obsolete by the blast. The live feed went black, the last visage of colour coming from the bright white explosion atop the roof. Systematically the screens went dead, the live feed severed by the sheer concussive blast. Miller diverted his gaze towards the various live news reports upon the banks of screens and froze upon seeing the Lynx helicopter, still carrying Alpha Team who had at the time been about to descend the fast ropes attached to the helicopter's fuselage. A plume of white, scorching flame jutted from the roof like a steeple. The Lynx's pilot reeled in a valiant effort, banking right to avoid the blast but was raised ever higher upon the thermals created by the explosion. The Lynx lurched further right still, the helicopter now at a macabre, canted angle.

Miller was reduced to a dumb-like stupor, rendered deaf by the audio that came from within the helicopter, currently being relayed to the room through the monitor's speakers. The Lynx's console sounded out an alarm, a series of bangs and panicked cries came from within. All those within the situation room either hung their heads in dismay or held their breath, no one daring to speak. Unbeknownst to those within the situation room, the nation along with the worldwide community, too held their breath, silent prayers muttered to a plethora of Gods and deities.

Unfortunately, said prayers fell upon deaf ears. The Lynx swayed precariously as the pilot strived to right the aircraft to no avail and with a sickening downward spinning motion, the helicopter toppled, its blades clipping the building as it did so.

The screaming awoke Miller from his daze, the noise of the engine sputtering as all control within the cabin was lost by the aircraft's topsy-turvy motion. The last clear shot of the Lynx before it pitched downwards behind the northerly corner of West Acre Point, was a black object being flung from one of the fast ropes; a remaining member of Bravo unit who had been in the process of descending down the fast rope. Miller mouthed inaudible words of utter disbelief as an air of failure and loss swept its way through the room. Still the news cameras rolled on as newsreaders dove for cover, talking all the while in panic-stricken frenzy.

The second explosion came almost instantaneously; loud, abrupt and final. The newsreaders covered their ears as the London skyline was lit up in a scene reminiscent of 1940's London during the Blitz. A light drizzle still hung in the air, no match for the flames, no natural sprinkler system to douse the metallic bonfire.

Phones burst into life around Miller as Susan stared back at her superior, unsure as to how the man she held in such high regard would act. Miller sensed the expectant eyes of dozens of people fall upon him. He knew what they were all internally thinking. Afterall, the leader of Charlie Unit was barking the question down comms.

"Abort. Get Charlie Team out of there," Miller, snatched from his delirious malaise, conceded.

Susan was now by his side, "Sir, shouldn't we press on?"

Miller rounded on Susan and set about hammering the final nail into the coffin that was now his career.

"We're done here Susan! Can't you fucking see that? We're done? I'm done, you're done, we're all bloody done! Finished"

Susan's face was a portrait of timid submission, yet she bravely pressed on.

"But sir, Charlie Team, they could still…" Susan started.

"They could still what, Susan? Breach? Take out several armed insurgents? Grow up woman! They're the SAS, not some fucking bulletproof poster boy from some God-awful action movie. We are well and truly over a barrel here and we have just royally offered up the nations arse, ripe for the bloody plucking!"

Miller swayed at the end of the barrage, dozens of glaring eyelines trained on him. Susan had tears in her eyes and she hurriedly barged past Miller, who had not broken his intimidating gaze post rant. He whirled round to face the room, his spit flecked chin and wide, open eyes causing many within the room to divert their gaze.

"Don't just sit there and gawp, someone bring up Braham on the direct line, now!" he bellowed.

(CHAPTER BREAK)

"Yes, I understand… very well," Braham nodded knowingly, pacing a briefing room adjacent to the Cabinet Office Briefing Rooms where all COBRA committee meetings were held.

"It's a colossal screw up indeed but the plan goes ahead as intended," he defiantly whispered before pausing once again to listen to the voice at the other end of the line.

"No, there's no need for that," he shook his head vehemently, "we must trust the men tasked with this undertaking. After all, we need to consider the bigger picture; we do not want to show our hand too soon… yes of that I am sure, the Prime Minister is all but finished. We wouldn't have enlisted their help if we did not have the stomach to persevere. We've discussed this. This way, we're all squeaky clean and…" Braham broke off, covering the receiver's mouthpiece as a light knock upon the door made him freeze.

The door opened without command and in paced a dishevelled and loose tied Jonathan Benley. Braham motioned for him to wait and he turned back to his call.

"Righto darling, will do and I'll let you know as soon as this is all over. I'm sorry I shan't be there for his recital but needs must…" another pause as he listened and nodded, rolling his eyes in a sardonic fashion towards Benley who did not reciprocate his colleagues' jovial demeanour.

"Yes, it is truly awful but we're doing all we can. I really must go now Margot, the Home Secretary has just walked in… you too, goodbye dear," Braham tutted as he placed the phone back inside his blazer pocket.

Benley thought it unusual that Braham had referred to him as the Home Secretary and not by his first name. He had met Braham's wife on multiple occasions at many a summit or political event, not to mention the number of dinners he had attended hosted by Margot herself. Margot, Braham and he had been the best of chums, whiling the night away with a bottle of wine or a decanter of cognac after the other dinner guests had vacated their vast dining room in Mayfair, after yet another of Margot's successful soirees.

"What is it Jonathan? Any word from the terrorists yet?" Braham quizzed.

"None but MI5 expect a message momentarily, Miller is waiting on line two for you now," Benley sighed, rubbing his eyes.

Braham strode over to him and patted him lightly on the shoulder.

"What is it Jonathan?" Braham pressed, seeing the defeatism caress Benley's frame nay his soul.

Benley looked up at Braham dejectedly.

"We really dropped the ball on this one, James; me, you, MI5. We've played right into these bastard's hands and I really don't see us coming out of this intact, never mind with Andrew still in one piece. The failed offensive we just launched will warrant retribution and the timer is all but complete. Miller withdrew Charlie Team in an effort to regroup but…"

Braham observed that his close friend looked the portrait of self-doubt.

"Jonathan, I really must take this call from Miller, especially if he has withdrawn our chaps but listen my good man, no matter what transpires, no matter what happens to Pierce, those hostages or to the party, we must keep our heads about us. We must not falter and if it comes to these mad men issuing demands, using Andrew, as dear a friend to you and me he may be, we need to be objective," Braham callously determined, nodding at Benley in a motion that demanded he reply in a subservient capacity.

"My God James, what a colossal fuck up this has been from start to finish," Benley shook his head.

"We very well can't help that now can we Jonathan? Now, I need you more now than ever to call upon those last vapours of British can-do and get out there and rally the troops. It is my intention to converse with this, Head terrorist," he spat the title with detest, "see if we can't come to some sort of agreement, one that gives the illusion we are appeasing him whilst offering him nothing in return."

"Do you think that's wise James? I mean, the not negotiating with terrorist's argument aside, haven't we pushed enough of their buttons already?" Benley put forth.

"There is only one button we serve to halt them from pressing Jonathan. I will not be held to account by these men or any of their ilk for that matter. I intend on taking one final spin of the negotiation wheel. If it comes up a duffer, we'll send in our remaining unit with reinforcements and hope for the best. Now I really must take this call," Braham signed off, eager to be rid of Benley.

Benley nodded and turned on his heel, leaving him alone once again. When the door closed, Braham wrung his hands nervously before wiping his dry mouth with the back of his hand. He made his way to the desk and picked up the phone to Miller. He listened intently as Miller reeled off the situation report. All of Alpha and Bravo Unit lost, several police officers injured by the falling debris of the Lynx, substantial damage to the surrounding buildings, no further loss of life due to the four-block cordon. Braham remained eerily silent until Miller had ceased talking.

"And you expect them to make contact soon?" Braham asked.

"Yes sir. Based upon the expertise of such situations in the past, I expect it to be sooner rather than later. They'll be gathering themselves somewhat after that attack, formulating their next steps and you can be assured sir, it is highly likely that it will be reactionary rather than defensive in capacity. The execution of hostages, another bomb..." he paused and swallowed hard at this, the crater where his house once stood on his quiet street clouding his thoughts.

"Of this one thing I am about to tell you, be sure Mr. Miller. After today is through, you are done, finished. I have already found a suitable replacement for your post; they will be with you within the next few hours. Upon their arrival, you are to cease in your capacity, relinquish all duties and report for debrief. Your incompetence, regardless of what is yet to transpire, has been most unsatisfactory, most unsatisfactory indeed!" Braham signed off with a flourish of the receiver as he placed it down.

With that, he straightened his tie, buttoned up his double-breasted blazer and returned to the bustling COBRA committee mere minutes before the latest transmission came in.

(CHAPTER BREAK)

Once again, Thompson's imposing frame stood above a stooped Pierce, mask on, detonator in hand. McAllister stood several metres away on the concourse that ran adjacent to Thompson, ready to record. Situated on the Ground floor below, stood the extravagant mosaic water fountain, which trickled onwards, as it had done so all day, the ornate statue of Britannia unaware of the carnage around her. The grid of mosaic tiles lining the structure glimmered and caught the light, the clasped sceptre about ten feet in height, sharp and imposing like that of Thompsons glower. He had applied some additional camouflage around his eyes and mouth; the charade maintained to the very last, no witness left at the end to tell of their rouse.

Thompson once again adjusted his voice changer under his balaclava, hands sheathed in leather. Satisfied, he whipped the hood from Pierce's head. His prisoner blinked wildly, his bottom lip quivering like a new-born.

"The hour of reckoning is upon us Mr. Pierce," Thompson snarled his voice distorted and metallic in tone.

Hertz and Greaves, both masked, flanked either side of Thompson, Ak-47's held in a saluted manner. Pierce made to plead but Thompson brought a calming hand down upon his head, smoothing his hair lightly like a morose child being consoled by its mother.

"Will you take it like a man, I wonder? Or will you beg for me? Offer me whatever I want in return for your life? Better still, for a quick death! If only your party could see you now," he slapped his head coyly, "but of course, they will. The whole nation will see you, finally, for what you truly are, a coward, and an empty promise."

"No," Pierce sobbed.

"Do me a favour. When you get to that House of Commons down there," Thompson motioned slowly with his downturned thumb, "when it all gets a bit too toasty down there for you. When you think that things can't get any more desperate, be sure not to fall for the empty promises afforded to you by some demon or trickster. If they offer you a way out, sanctuary, atonement, remember this: no help was offered to the poor, needy and decrepit of this nation by your cruel, nefarious hand, ever the dangler of the carrot, ever the politician."

"May what you took from the people, never be afforded to you. Even the merest glimmer of hope bestowed upon you. Besides, you'll probably fit in great down there in hell, most likely be the Speaker of the House before the weeks out. Maybe you can worm your way to the top of the pyre, namedrop who your daddy is, it's worked so well for you thus far. Maybe even use that silver spoon that's so firmly rammed up your arsehole as some form of legal tender."

"Please, it can't all be laid at my feet. We did some good, we tried to make this country strong... for... for everyone," Pierce sobbed, his bound hands rhythmically drumming the floor, "what more can I do, what more can I do to end all this?" Pierce appealed.

"For you or the nation, Prime Minister?" Thompson poked, enjoying Pierces futile supplication.

"Both," he spoke rather too abruptly, "we can work something out, surely. It serves no purpose just killing me, instead you could use me; I will offer what services are needed; help push your opinions under the guise of my own voice. You'll have the ear of the most powerful man in the United Kingdom, the world even."

"What's to stop me from taking your ear right here, right now or both for that matter? Come to think about it, why not make it the hat-trick and take that forked, snake-like tongue of yours while I'm at it. Hear no evil, speak no evil..."

Thompson gripped Pierces shoulder and hefted him to his feet. He held him at the base of the skull and heavily brought Pierce's head down hard upon the safety railing of the concourse; the rebound of his head upon reinforced metal could be heard around the high-ceilinged structure. Pierce's feet buckled and Thompson caught him by the scruff of his collar, holding him firm.

"Now my man over there is going to hold up some cards for you. You must read these out convincingly. If at any stage I am unsure of your sincerity or you do not respond to my questions, as instructed on the cards, I add a minute to your death. Do this right and it will be quick, understood?" Thompson whispered into Pierces ear.

Pierces head listed drunkenly. Thompson shook him violently until he finally nodded his forehead already a crimson hue edged by a violet border.

"You'll need these," Thompson stated as he placed Pierces glasses back onto the bridge of his nose, one of the lenses cracked significantly.

Pierce squinted slightly, until he made out McAllister standing apposite.

"Can you see?" Thompson demanded.

"Yuh...Yes," Pierce stuttered, fumbling with the arm of his glasses.

Thompson nodded over towards McAllister, who nodded a reply, obscured slightly by the camera, red stand-by light blinking. All the players assembled; the stage finally set.

Thompson turned Pierce so that he was facing the camera, supporting him tightly under the armpits. He could not resist one final harrowing display of intimidation.

"Remember this and let the thought haunt your every waking moment in purgatory, whatever lies beyond the veil, that great unknown, I have no doubt that I'll be joining you in due time," Thompson taunted.

"Live feed set sir, his approval ratings on the feed stand at thirty-seven percent," Mc Allister prompted smiling at what came next, "sixty-three percent in favour of his execution, sir."

Pierce let out a strangled wail. Behind Thompson, Greaves and Hertz began slapping one another on the back, the balaclavas disguising their muffled, joyous laughter. Hertz made to step forward and pat Thompson on the back when he suddenly thought better of it, quickly withdrawing his outstretched hand. Greaves shot him a glance that questioned his ridiculous show of abandoned affection.

"The people have spoken; it looks like there's more good people out there then even I would have expected... not that it would have mattered anyway."

The support of the people made what would transpire next all the easier to control in the upcoming furore. With a final motion of his finger that established he wished to begin.

McAllister counted down non-verbally, from five once again. He looked to his left marginally believing he had seen a flicker of movement. He scanned the area to his left, the shops and the escalator about twelve feet away. All clear, he returned his gaze to the camera. The feed went live, Thompson pausing for effect.

"When this man ravaged my country, he took more than life, territory, resources. He, like many, removed our heart. We watched as our country was laid to waste, carved up amongst Western imperialists not yet satisfied with their already sizeable piece of the pie. Those like Pierce and his ilk came back for seconds, my country serving only as an appetiser on their menu of foreign policy. I stand before you, devoid of a heart. However, only in the metaphorical sense of the word, for as long as my heart still beats, so too does my bloodlust. I warned you of the consequences of what would happen if I were challenged. Your show of force from above was like that of all your other imperial conquests, a mere dent, a scratch upon the surface of larger things yet still at play. My heart may be blackened but it is still strong and for this and in his name, I offer it up!" Thompson prodded his heart to emphasise this final point.

"Attached to my heart is a transmitter connected to my heartbeat. Should this stop for any reason before I deem it fit or by the almighty's hand, there are five other bombs located around the capital, all in highly populated locations, all areas of high interest. You have once again tried to interfere with a repressed people. However, unlike my people, the repressed of this country were given a choice and they have made it. The eyes have it. Before I explain what will transpire next, I wish to remind you that as of yet, we have quite a substantial number of hostages that we are willing to release upon certain demands being met, so I urge you to think carefully on any future retaliation."

An unknown insurgent stepped from the shadows, one who had recently appeared, joining Hertz and Greaves. He carried, in a march like procession towards Thompson, a noose. He draped this over Pierce's head. The Prime Minister flinched and began to hysterically garble away to himself. The unknown man, masked also, placed the noose upon the railing before Pierce. The rope was around six feet in length; far too short to reach the waiting marble floor beneath.

"But first, I offer this man a chance to air any last words, a customary gesture that you, in the West, do not yourselves afford those upon who your bombs fall," Thompson motioned his hand and lightly, out of frame, kicked Pierce.

With a start, Pierce shakily cleared his throat, before adjusting his glasses once again and began to recite the place cards that McAllister swapped out one after the other.

"I stand before you today...the people of Britain and those around the world, with a declaration to make, an omission of guilt. As your Prime Minister, I was elected by the people for the people and with this; the trust was invested within me to also take into consideration the global community. I have now been afforded this opportunity to repent, to atone for my sins; a move I would not honestly have made if I were not being held captive, for such is the severity of the misdemeanours I am about to omit."

Pierce paused momentarily as McAllister continued to swap out the cards.

"I admit to and take full responsibility for my overzealous and brutal role within the Middle East, Africa and other countries. To those who stood in opposition to that of our foreign policy and aggressive, expansionist trade agreements. For the hundreds of drone attacks I have sanctioned, which have in turn led to high levels of collateral damage and loss to the indigenous peoples. I take full responsibility."

Thompson could feel Pierce shaking; he steadied him with a tight pinch of his shoulder. Pierce was beginning to falter slightly in his delivery. The unknown variable within the group, the executioner with the noose, had wrapped the end of the noose out and back inside of the railing, holding fast for what was to come.

"For the harsh and unrelenting taxation and austerity measures imposed upon my own people, largely due to the misdemeanours of my party and successive cabinets, I apologise. For too long now, the ..." a reluctant consideration at what was to come, "the British government has served to profiteer by standing upon the shoulders of its citizens, by pillaging others it deems below its heel, by offering little in the way of socio-cultural change, instead flouting the possibility of change through that of a closed ballot paper".

"As I have had it explained to me by my captors, the relevance of tonight's vote was to afford the people the one thing I and previous other governments before had deprived them of. In doing so, these men have not only given the British public a choice but have also posed a question that the people have long requested an answer to; when government fails, does the power really lay in the people's grasp? Tonight, is the start of a new order, a social movement, a revolution the like has ever been seen before. To the people of Britain, I say this," he swallowed hard, "Rise up. Rise up and overthrow those who serve to crush you below their callous, malice laden heel. It's as simple as pressing a button like the one I pushed this very same eve"

Pierce upon recalling the detonator handed to him by Thompson, burst into a strangled wail. Thompson gripped tighter, willing him to read on. McAllister revealed the next card and Pierce regurgitated it numbly, the damage he had done finally revealed in all its bastardised glory.

"I... I take full responsibility for the life of the woman I took. Given the option, as before... I put myself before others," he broke down once again unaware that the life that had in fact been taken had been done so by another, one of Thompson's grunts.

Pierce momentarily glanced down at the hand that had pushed the button and began to close his fist. He left his thumb extended; the believed guilty appendage in question. He began to cower, turning up to meet Thompson, snot and tears streaming down his cheeks. He brought his hands up in a pleading fashion, begging for leniency.

Thompson smiled under his mask. He was now satisfied that his employer's demands had been met. The mission thus far had largely been a success, the blueprints not likely to be recovered but all the same, the greater plan at hand had begun and in glorious, televised splendour. The one thing his employer had specified above all else, for his plan to truly work, was the loss of faith within the British people and in its government. The main piece of the puzzle in achieving this was the creation of a politician so vilified its people would be prepared through the use of social media, to vote in their hordes, an action that left many of the nation's populace sullied, tainted.

The nation would carry just as much guilt for the day's events at having both let the nation fall into such disrepair and worse still, voting both for the politicians that had caused said destruction; for being allowed to be duped by the seduction of the right to use their vote for anything but evil means.

"I can't do it..." he blubbered out of the camera's range, his body stooping, all rigidity in his frame now absent.

Thompson grabbed the man's head and cupped his chin in his hands. Dipping his voice, so as not be detected by the camera's microphone, he whispered his riposte, "But Mr. Pierce, you already have."

He slowly brought Pierce's chin up in his hands, forcing the man from his stupor. When he was upon his feet, Thompson spun Pierce around to face the camera. He withdrew his knife and freed Pierce from his plasti-cuffs. The new addition to the team bent his knees, leaning back slowly, wrapping the end of rope tightly around his grip. McAllister removed the camera from the tripod, deciding upon a guerrilla style of filmmaking.

"To the people of Britain, you have spoken, I have listened. Thy will be done. I stand before you, my hand strengthened by your votes, by Allah, willing to carry out your verdict, that of..." with this Thompson grabbed Pierce by both the shoulder and his lower back.

"A hung parliament!" Thompson screeched and with a decisive show of strength flung Pierce from the concourse.

Pierce let out a shriek but it was soon cut off as the rope shot taught, the snap of the rope echoing around the room. McAllister dipped the camera following the arc of Pierce as he swung like a pendulum.

After several swaying arcs, Pierce came to a halt unlike his legs which still twitched with convulsed agony. McAllister zoomed in on Pierce's wide eyes, before zooming out, framing his features within a close-up, the light glimmering upon his foaming mouth. On four occasions, Pierce's hands made an effort to rise up and grab at the noose around his neck but he was overcome with agony and panic, the effort a meaningless gesture. Thompson snapped his fingers, a sign to McAllister that he wished to continue. McAllister brought the camera up, briefly correcting his framing.

"It's true what they say... You really can't trust a politician as far as you can throw him. So, to the people of Britain, I ask you; will you go further than this man did? Let me see your desire for change. Take to the streets, take to Parliament. Demand they do the following or I shall blow London's very own fetid soul apart. To the government, I have only this to say, withdraw all military forces from your various conflicts and wars around the world and promptly. I am a patient man and know that this is no easy feat. I am reasonable, so I offer you two hours to provide me with proof that you intend to do as I ask."

"I want a signed declaration of your retreat distributed to the various news organisations of Britain. I wish this to be printed, read out and shown upon live television, we will be watching. If you fail or attempt another incursion; I bring down this building with the hostages inside and with it, I shall detonate my remaining devices around London. People of Britain, mobilise. Like Pierce here, sometimes all you need, is a little push. I advise your government pushes me no further."

With that McAllister cut the live feed and signalled to Thompson that they were all clear. The men waited until McAllister had angled the camera downwards upon his tripod, before removing their balaclavas except for the new edition to the group. Thompson turned to him, removing his own mask and voice changer.

"The sprinklers would have kicked in on the top floor again, not that it will do much good. Level Three is a no go," he pointed upwards and the man followed his finger.

To his alarm, he could see the orange hue of flames flickering, a quarter of the roof also exposed, the night sky now visible, rain entering at a jaunty angle through the jagged hole. Thompson now took the opportunity to look down upon Pierce, noticing for the first time that to his right, on the Ground level, a sizeable chunk of concrete from the ceiling had fallen, cracking the marble floor beneath.

His men had taken cover as they had awaited the breach, in defensive positions. They had been instructed to expect an incursion from above as well as the Ground floor and Level Two. They were confident that the charges rigged on the Ground floor would take out much of the breaching team as well as those upon the roof. They had split into two, much of the force taking cover on the concourse upon which McAllister had just filmed, ready to take out the abseiling strike force or Bravo Team, as his contact had informed him.

"We need Doc. Me and Greaves are going down to retrieve him and establish whether our houseguest has told us anything we can use. If not, we'll prep and execute the exfil. I need you to do one final sweep of this level, Hertz Level One. McAllister you've got the Ground floor," Thompson delegated, the men all now converging around him.

"Shouldn't we just cut our losses; we're cutting it a little fine, aren't we?" the mysterious new addition spoke up.

The other men all glared back at him, taken aback by his insubordinate behaviour. Thompson continued, unmoved by the momentary break in decorum.

"The objective might have been achieved but don't forget the bonus for achieving the other, I don't like leaving unfinished business. We bring this place down, the plans go with it," Thompson asserted.

"Yes sir," the masked man replied reservedly, the red hue to his face as he removed his mask evident for all to see.

He then set about removing the combat trousers he had been wearing and the oversized camo jacket, discarding them, revealing that he had been wearing a suit beneath all along. His top button was undone, his navy tie askew.

"You have your assignments gentlemen; reconvene on the exfil in…" he glanced at his watch, the others reciprocating, synchronising watches, "Twenty minutes."

The men nodded their understanding and fanned out. Greaves made to go, his gait angled, his legs bowed. Hertz had teased him once stating that, *"He couldn't catch pigs."* It had been the first and last time that he ever mocked him.

"Greaves," Thompson caught his arm, forcing Greaves to come to a sudden halt.

"Yes sir," he replied subserviently.

"Any sign of the other one, the Prime Ministers bodyguard?" Thompson pressed.

"No sir but there's no way he survived what Doc and Hertz described, plus add on top of that the roof blast… can't see it myself sir," Greaves reinforced with a slight shake of his head.

Thompson nodded in an ensured movement and gripped both of Greaves shoulders, turning him face on. Greaves eyed his grip nervously.

"Today, is a culmination of what you, Shaw and I envisioned from the beginning. What we set out to achieve, our goal, for Britain to be great once again. It is down to us now. Shaw may be gone but his loss will not be for nothing. This building will be his funeral pyre. Like the Viking he was, he will have a send-off befitting his contribution to the cause. Schematics or not, today ends as it begun, on our terms. The boulder of change has started to roll and all those who stand opposed, will be mown down in its path."

Greaves licked his lips excitedly at the prospect, relishing Thompson's acceptance, his validation.

"Only the patriots left standing in our wake," Greaves bounced excitedly.

Thompson nodded.

"When I found you, the Army, it had taken so much from you, both physically and mentally. You were but a shell, a shell in need of something to contain, an ideal, a purpose in which to strive for. A man who could not stand on his own two feet," Thompson motioned towards the man's lower body.

"You gave me that sir," Greaves replied in a mellowed tone.

Thompson shook his head in disagreement.

"No, no, no. You had it within you; I simply cleared your path. You were once part of the blind flock, a sheep, one of the ungrateful, manipulated masses, as was I once. Today you are the wolf," Thompson accentuated with a slap upon Graves face.

"And you the alpha sir, right at the head of the pack," Greaves excitedly added, getting caught up in the metaphor.

"We have lost much today but in doing so; have gained much, much more. Whilst the hunt is far from over, our pack has been afforded a scent, a scent of victory and whilst it lingers in our nostrils, we must follow it wholeheartedly, track it to its source. I did not fight for the country I love to be discarded by his like," Thompson indicated Pierce, the creak of the rope filling the silence.

"To rot, offering up my beggars bowl in return for a pittance. The new order, it will be run by those very men the government served to alienate and push to the periphery. It has been a long journey but one that has only just begun," Thompson prodded with his finger.

With that, Thompson turned and walked off, intending for Greaves to follow and he did so but only after he had wiped the tears from his eyes, the feeling of overwhelming acceptance and the mission at hand, infiltrating his steely resolve. He would gladly die for this visionary, this man who had plucked him from his obscure pit of self-deprecation and self-loathing. A man of few words with the ability to encapsulate everything that needed to be said. Whilst politicians prepared speeches and liberals whiled away their pitiful existence virtue signalling on social media, Thompson acted. For Thompson understood better than anyone, even more so than Greaves ironically, that a gangrenous limb needed to first be amputated surgically, before the healing could begin.

CHAPTER TWENTY-ONE: THE BATTLE FOR BRITAIN

Tom stooped down by the side of the escalator, obscured by a potted plant which stood before him. He had spotted Thompson too late as he made to round the escalator on Level One, intending to take the neighbouring escalator another flight up. He had held his breath as if it would help. He dared not move, a combination of stealth and fear rendering him immobile. His floral vantage point afforded him the ability to look directly into Thompson's shark-like eyes undetected. Pierce genuflected before him; his eyes telling a vastly different story as Thompson delivered yet another speech. A hazy cloud hung in the air, the by- product of the explosion above offering another element of concealment.

Several seconds after Thompson had broken his line of sight, Tom made his slow and steady ascent up the metallic escalator, relying upon his threshold for pain as he crouched and crept his way upwards towards the safety and obscured vision of Level Two. The escalator might as well have been Everest, his constant uneasiness at potentially being spotted, his back turned to his enemies, plaguing his every movement.

The summit of the escalator fortified Tom with a sense of hope, a small victory overcome. He reached the top and crept forward, edging his way towards the escalator leading to the Third level. He could hear the sprinkler system above him, the crackle of flames now also evident. He found himself praying that the lockers were intact, hoping that his brother's cryptic message referenced the wrapped box he had retrieved earlier that day. Tom's vision briefly clouded with Malcolm's features forcing him to stop abruptly. Just as soon as the thought had surfaced, he compartmentalized it, deciding he may need it later as an additional source of fuel; although he found it hard to imagine himself running on empty. He was running on pure unleaded vengeance, a natural resource of which he was in an abundance of.

Tom made his ascent up the escalator, the smell of acrid smoke and flame engulfing his nostrils. He stopped froze suddenly aware of the fact that he had been doused in petrol; he may as well have been walking, talking kindling at this point. He began to wipe petrol from his exposed skin with the end of his t-shirt before scolding himself for being so naïve, the gesture a futile one.

The low mutter of Thompson's words below could just be heard above the crackling flame but were now discernible to Tom. He stepped onto the Level Two concourse and winced as the smoke stung his eyes. The water from the sprinklers pattered down upon the cold marble floor. The air was damp, a blackened fog trailing across the level. Before him, after a few uncertain steps, the black cloud parted slightly, before Tom's eyes. Then finally, shielded by his hand, he saw the rows of lockers come into his obscured sight. He reached the lockers; the digital read outs affording an eerie red hue of which he was grateful for, the water blurring his vision. He groped along the row of lockers until he found his own read out indicating that his time had long since expired.

He retrieved the key still lodged under his watchstrap, grateful that it had not been discovered upon his body search. The digital display upon the door flashed red with the message that Tom had exceeded his time and that he would have to insert five pounds. He thrust his hand into his pocket and withdrew a fistful of change. Selecting a two-pound coin and three one-pound coins, he slowly inserted the coins into the machine's slot, winching as each coin landed upon the internal metallic housing. A click sounded as the lock withdrew. He yanked the door open, the parcel waiting in the centre of the locker.

Tom grabbed it tentatively, shielding it against the sprinkler's torrent. He turned left and observed that several metres ahead, the concourse was blocked by rubble. He skittered back the way he had come, staying low, minimising the level of smoke inhalation his lungs were subjected to. He took shelter under a coffee shop awning; bright yellow and purple, festooned with the company's logo; extravagant and overpriced, just like their coffee.

It was at this stage that Tom considered the boy again. He turned to his right and whilst through the copious amounts of smoke he could not see along the concourse, he imagined the boy's body now most likely sodden, the sprinklers washing away his blood. He briefly considered going back and covering the boy. He gripped the box tightly, wishing to expel the thought through his very pores. It was a senseless gesture, the boy dead, unfeeling. Besides, looking around there was very little in the way of waterproof material, if there had been, he may have been more likely to take it for himself. Although he could feel the intense heat drying his clothes from the distant flame, he still shivered.

Finally, with clinical urgency, he decided against the idea and instead turned the box over in his hands, once again sensing its weight. The blue tissue paper was slightly damp irrespective of his best efforts in keeping it dry, the stickers that bound it together beginning to peel. With a deep breath he lightly clawed his fingers across the sodden tissue paper. It disintegrated upon touch. A sealed navy-blue box became visible. He opened the lid of the cardboard box and turned the box upside down, allowing the glass, cuboid structure to slowly slide out into his waiting palm.

He could feel his hand quaking under the slight weight. He did not look at the contents until he had carefully laid the box aside. He exhaled heavily. When he finally glanced down with an overbearing sense of trepidation, his worried features receded immediately; a smile burst forth followed by a reminiscent laugh. For the briefest of snapshots during his ordeal, he was content, dare he say it at peace.

The glass box consisted of a mahogany base, detachable from the glass box if prised away firmly enough. As Tom turned the box over in his hands, he felt his fingers dance across a metallic square, flanked on either side by a screw. He examined the brass plaque, upon it an inscription. A lump formed in his throat as he read it, wiping his thumb over the engraving. He chanted the words to himself in a whispered tone, the rising of tears threatening to choke him.

"Let us therefore brace ourselves to our duties, and so bear ourselves that, if the British Empire and its commonwealth last for a thousand years, men will still say, this was their finest hour. With all our love, Anthony and Hawker."

Tom lightly rested his head against the cold marble column behind him, rocking his head in disbelief. Collecting his resolve, he found his hands shake further as he lifted the upper half of the box free prising it from its foundation. Inside contained the Hurricane model that Tom and his Brother had so joyfully played with as boys. It stood at an angle upon a translucent stand, giving the appearance that it was flying. The bottom of the base was finished to look like that of the British countryside complete with hedgerows and farmland. Tom ran his fingers across the fuselage, caressing the ornate detailing, the bumps of the miniature rivets.

He closed his sodden eyes and afforded himself a moment of meditation as he was transported back to a happier time. After several seconds he braced himself for what had to come next.

His fingers came up to the cockpit, trembling, his brother's words scrawled upon the receipt materialising at the forefront of his mind. He delicately slid the cockpit open and immediately noticed that the pilot was missing and, in its place, a memory stick. Tom worked his fingers into the tiny crevice and worked the memory stick out of the Hurricane, which was made even more difficult by his trembling hand. When the memory stick was about halfway free, Tom observed that tied around it was a short length of twine, secured further by a layer of tape. The memory stick snagged slightly as the twine exposed its anchor, a piece of paper rolled up. Tom used his other hand to negotiate it from its recess.

Once free, Tom drew his knife from its scabbard and used it to slice the twine and tape free. He unfolded the note and was surprised to see that it opened out into a sheet of A4, so expertly had it been folded. Tom immediately noticed his brother's elegant handwriting, smaller than usual to afford him as much space within which to write. A tear landed upon the paper of which Tom quickly swept away, wanting to preserve the precious artefact.

He bit his lower lip and read the message:

Dear Tom,

If you're reading this, I am most likely dead and you are left with even more questions. I did not die in Sierra Leone, which by this stage I'm guessing you have already worked out. That is another long story, one that will be answered later. First of all, I'm sorry for the ruse surrounding this situation but upon reading this, I think you'll understand why it was necessary. Enclosed is a memory stick containing highly sensitive data upon it, a blueprint and schematics to be exact. I was tasked with infiltrating a fanatic terrorist cell, one with a military background, largely comprised of those injured or dismissed from the Armed forces. That was my cover. I, along with another operative, was embedded into this cell under deep cover with the intention of both securing the blueprints and a device. However, that was secondary to that of my primary objective, the discovery of a mole within the UK Government.

I have still not discovered the cell's contact inside as of yet but they have been responsible for the leaking of highly sensitive information, one such piece of intel that threatens national security.

I write to you now as I think they are on to me and that I have been comprised. You're one of the only people I can trust with this, Hawker. You need to seek out a man called Robert Carson, the man responsible for establishing my cover. You can reach him at 07759 864261. Upon doing so, quote the security code, Operation: Harbinger. He will update you on how I got where I am today and what needs to happen next. It is crucial Tom that you do not take this to the police or to any of the intelligence agencies, they may be in collusion with the government mole, I have no idea how high this goes. Carson has been updated as much as was safe for me to do so about the organisation and its leader, Thompson. If for any reason he approaches you and identifies himself by name, put him down hard and fast, permanently if possible. I know that may seem drastic but he is the root of my being here, on home soil.

Finally, I just want to say, keep safe and trust no one. I have now willingly painted a target on your back as well as that of my own. I am sorry that I couldn't tell you the truth; I came close so many times. The hardest thing I've had to do in this whole mess of a charade is lie to Mum, Dad and you. When I broke into our own home to plant that receipt, right there and then, it was the closest I'd felt to you all in a long time, since this all began. Leaving was the hardest thing I've ever had to do. Knowing what I was returning to, that I may never make it back to the three of you again.

You have every right to be mad; I only hope that given time; you can forgive me. The RPG attack served as an alibi for my deep cover, part of which was dependent on people being able to corroborate my death and the people I work for thought who better than my very own brother. I love you, Mum and Dad so much and I never meant for things to go this south. I leave how much you tell Mum and Dad, in your hands. It may serve them best if they remain thinking that I died in Sierra Leone.

Keep safe and remember, no matter how this pans out, I've always looked up to you Hawker; you're the best man I've ever known, you reading this, proves that. You always were the best codebreaker out of the two of us.

Love your brother, Anthony XX

Tom folded the earthshattering document, placing it carefully into one of the dry pockets upon his tactical vest before he allowed himself to burst into a fit of tears, wishing he could have helped his brother earlier, considering the fact that he may still be alive if he had. Questions beget questions. Moreover, Tom became increasingly aware of the fact that there was now a larger game at play, one which was more dependent upon his survival than he had first imagined. He wiped his tears upon his sleeve, the sprinklers leaving extraordinarily little in the way of dry material.

The letter served to only strengthen his resolve further. He knew what he had to do now. He had to ensure that none of Thompson's team left the confines of West Acre Point. Even if he were to retreat somehow, depriving them of the schematics, it was clear from his interactions with the organisation that today's attack was just the tip of the spear. Then there was the fact that Thompson had made this personal; Anthony's note only seeking to reinforce this. No, he not only had to play this smart, he had to play to win. They had already seen off the initial phase of attack and had executed the Prime Minister which meant that their exfil would be soon. The cavalry would arrive and soon but not before they had made their escape. He had to slow them down somehow. He begun to flesh out the parameters of his plan when he saw it.

(CHAPTER BREAK)

Gerry swore to himself upon seeing the rubble that lay before him, blocking his path. He observed that he would now have to make his way around and back where he had just come from, ending up on the opposite concourse of Level Three. He had thought he had heard movement on the other side of the rubble where the entrance to the now sealed off Food Hall, resided.

He froze, his body doing all it could at this current impasse to remain upright; he was severely injured. His hearing had largely been impaired by the concussive blast he had sustained upon the grenade going off at such close proximity. His left ear was bleeding and he had come to the realisation that it was most likely perforated, rendering him deaf in one ear. Cocking his good ear, he attempted echolocation, tilting his head from right to left. After several seconds, a medley of irritation and doubt at having heard anything at all, soothed his paranoia.

He grimaced once again; the shrapnel wound he had sustained in the blast all but paralysing his ability to put pressure upon the limb. When he had awoken earlier, he had forced himself to remove it, fashioning a tourniquet from his belt, releasing it every fifteen minutes or so, being careful not to disturb the wound too much. The bleeding had largely receded now but he knew he didn't have long before he yielded to the blood loss.

Gerry began to hobble back the way he had come. He had lost his primary weapon when he had been swept off balance and down the vent shaft. Unadvisedly, he had made his way down to the second level to establish whether Tom had made it to the outlet below, hoping he had been successful in his execution of Plan B. The outlet upon first inspection had been empty until his foot had sent some empty shell casings spinning underfoot. Surveying the scene, he was not hopeful of his partner's chances.

Although, the sprinkler system had now doused a significant portion of the flames, the upper levels were still shrouded in thick smoke. The odds of survival were decreasing by the second when Gerry was momentarily spurred on by the discovery of an M16 which lay beside a fallen insurgent. He had almost fell over the body, his visibility made excruciatingly worse by the smoke. Gerry had checked that the weapon was still in working order although not before ascertaining whether the body belonged to Tom or not. Thankfully, it did not and whilst the M16 clip was empty and undamaged, the lifeless insurgent had attached to his vest two spare magazines.

Upon their retrieval the smoke, disturbed by Gerry's movement, retreated slightly and with it any newfound luck was snatched away instantaneously upon the discovery of the young boy. He let out an anguished groan and stood above the body alone with his thoughts for several moments before draping a piece of metal sheeting that had been dislodged from the roof above, over the boy's body.

"This was never your fight," he whispered, his tone hoarse, the bile that had now risen within him searing his throat.

When the roof had caved in, Gerry had been taking shelter in one of the outlets, seeing to his leg. Thankfully, he had not been cocooned in a concreate tomb as the rubble fell, his second close call at nearly having been blown up. The explosion and the downed helicopter carcass had cut a sizeable swathe down through a substantial part of the second and third levels.

Gerry redirected his anger at the adult carcass upon the floor and hoped that it had been Tom that had taken the man out. He momentarily fantasized about the notion of his newfound partner still taking it to the hostiles, praying he had not been killed himself in the blast. Gerry thanked God, that he had rounded a corner in the shaft just as the grenade had gone off. A split second later and the metallic ordinance would have most likely lodged between his groin, taking both his legs and his pride with it.

Gerry had strapped the MI6 across his torso and was using a broom handle he had found in the rubble as a makeshift crutch. His headache had now increased and with it the sobering prospect that the concussion may fell him before blood loss. It had been around that time that he had decided to once again ascend to Level Three in an effort to afford himself as best an aerial view of the complex below as possible, the smoke thinning more now.

When he had returned to Level Three, he decided to make his way towards the emergency exit, considering whether he would be able to negotiate anymore stairs or whether there would in fact, be any stairs left to negotiate. He had been so focused upon thoughts of the staircase that lay beyond the emergency exit that he had not heard the release of a push bar.

As he shuffled forward, the door swung open and from it a shadow materialised. Gerry painfully squatted behind a cluster of rubble; his injured leg outstretched. Before him, a tall man with close-cropped hair, face heavily smeared with soot and dust, exited the emergency exit to the roof. Gerry trained the sights of his M16 on the man, using the rubble to prop up the ever-increasing weight of the weapon. The man produced his radio. Gerry angled his good ear towards the man.

"This is Jones. I just checked the emergency exit. I could only get about a flight and a half up. The explosion has taken out part of the roof and along with it a good section of the third and second floors. The staircase up to the roof has completely collapsed in on itself; no way is anyone else getting in up there. Permission to regroup on your location, over," the man queried.

He shook the radio slightly, testing that it still worked, the man seemingly agitated.

"This is Jones, does anyone read, over?" he impatiently pressed.

Gerry could just make out the static as the man took his finger off the TALK button. He angrily tossed the radio aside and swore to himself. The radio skittered across the floor, slapping off the corner of the wall to Jones' left, which had been substantially damaged in the explosion. Gerry watched on, contemplating whether to fire or not. Instead, he lowered the M16 and unclipped the strap before testing its length and tensile strength. Satisfied, he coiled it around both hands, the length of the strap about twenty inches in length. With an outward motion of both hands in unison he once again tested the force and durability of the strap. Satisfied, he began to formulate how he would kill the man, his injury minimising his mobility and capacity to approach stealthily.

Jones kicked at a chunk of rubble and approached the radio, muttering to himself. The wall was jagged, the sky visible through the now absent roof. He reached the radio and turned his back to Gerry, bending at the knees. Shakily Gerry rose and began to advance slowly, ignoring the pain in his leg. Jones retrieved the radio and inspected it; Gerry now about three metres or so away, his heart in his mouth. He rotated the coiled strap slightly, making it as taut as possible. He was about a metre away when it happened.

Broken glass crunched underfoot, blown outwards by the various shopfronts. What happened next took both men by surprise. As Jones reeled round, Gerry considered taking cover. However, he quickly thought better of it, his proximity to Jones affording him little protection. He had committed, retreat now not an option. As if to emphasise this is, he threw his makeshift crutch aside and made to charge, coming down heavily upon his stronger leg in a hopping motion.

In the folly of panic, Jones scrambled backwards from the darkened corner already fumbling with his sidearm, his eyes solely fixed upon Gerry. It was because of this that he did not see the sizeable finger of overhanging masonry. Rather comically he backed straight into the jagged finger of rubble with considerable force.

He fell heavily back against the right angle of the wall, the radio tumbling from his hand with a clatter. Gerry froze, as the man groped at his head confused, his eyes unfocused, his balance off kilter. A scattering of dust fell upon Jones as he withdrew his hand, a crimson sheen coating his fingertips. A slow grinding noise came from above, smaller pieces of concrete cascading down upon the man's shoulders and head. Jones made tom withdraw his holstered sidearm, when all at once, a noise like that of an ice skate upon ice, followed by a loud rumble, came from above.

Both men gazed upward just in time to see the jagged metre-wide shard of concreate, a metal mesh at its fringes, come loose. Jones made to scream but with sickening speed, was silenced, his scream cut off by the crunching of bone as he was felled, crumpling under the weight of the concrete. Gerry shielded his eyes as the concrete brought with it a cloud of dust that scratched at his throat and eyes. The last thing Gerry saw before the cloud and concrete encased Jones' pummelled body was the absurd angle of Jones' back as it was disjointed further downwards by the rubble.

The grinding of concreate upon concrete masked the remaining cracking of bone and Gerry had no doubt in his mind that Jones was dead. When the dust settled, he moved forwards. He paused momentarily, pondering whether to take Jones' weapons, perhaps even his tactical vest. The body had all but vanished under the concreate tombstone, the weight of which in Gerry's current state would prove too much in the way of exertion. He decided against it

"Talk about bring the house down," Gerry muttered for his own benefit as he hobbled back to his previous hiding spot, reattaching the clip to his M16, retrieving his broom handle also.

He hobbled onwards, back towards the exit to the roof. He came to a halt and mulled over what Jones had said, *"No way is anyone else getting up there."* Gerry became momentarily fixated by the closed door, his thoughts returning to Tom and the severity of what had transpired since they had struck up their alliance.

With that, he turned left, following the concourse back upon himself to that of the escalators at the other end of the level. He afforded himself a glance over the railing as he found himself on the opposite concourse, now having shuffled his way slowly around it, never taking his eye off the concourse opposite. He did so just in time to see, what looked like Pierce, being flung from the first level concourse below. He watched on in horror, more so out of the vision of barbarism before him as opposed to the fact that he had failed in executing his primary objective, that of keeping Pierce safe.

Even with his diminished sense of hearing, he heard the rope snap tight, Pierce's body bouncing clear of the protective glass of the concourse barrier. He surmised from Tom's earlier accounts that his executioner none other than Thompson. He took a mental snapshot of the man, filing it away.

"Poor bastard," Gerry whispered.

He cocked his weapon and shuffled onwards towards the escalator. He was about several metres or so away when he caught view of a shadow appearing at the top of the escalator, favouring his side of the concourse over that of the one on his right-hand side. No surprise seeing as it was strewn with rubble, impassable in parts.

Gerry got as low as his leg would afford him, using a marble support as cover and waited with bated breath, as the footsteps grew progressively louder. Gerry peered out from behind the column, the man's features still enshrined in shadow. He raised the M16, using the column for support, readying himself, his arm tremoring with blood loss, the sights at the end of the barrel swaying.

The man had been about four metres away when Gerry observed that he too was wearing a suit; the lower half of his torso no longer obscured by darkness. He recognised the brogues as they stepped into the light and his heart, fit to burst, filled with joy. Gerry swapped out his magazine, loading another and placed the old magazine into his pocket.

Jack Wright stepped out in the light, his Glock sweeping the surrounding area. His face etched with concentration. Gerry smiled and rose slightly, lifting the gun above his head in a sign of friendly submission. Wright shot round and levelled the gun at Gerry's head and for the briefest of seconds, Gerry thought he was going to shoot.

Wright dropped his shoulders slightly, lowering his gun, exhaling with relief. He moved stealthily forward, silent yet quick. He reached Gerry and rested his hand upon his shoulder.

"Am I fucking glad to see you," he whispered, squeezing Gerry's shoulder.

"The feelings more than bloody mutual," Gerry replied.

Wright took the man's weight and brought him over to another column. He ushered for Gerry to be seated, so that he could inspect his wounds. Gerry relented willingly, laying his M16 on the floor next to him.

"How the fuck did you get in here? Please tell me you've brought the cavalry," Gerry winched as Wright released the makeshift tourniquet.

"You're looking at it I'm afraid mucker," Wright answered, mustering all the humour he had remaining.

"Beggars can't be choosers," Gerry replied with mock indignation, "they executed Pierce, strung him up like a piece of meat," Gerry winched as Wright prodded a sensitive area within his wound.

"You've done a good job here, you'll survive," he said partially impressed.

"Yeah bloody great mate, tens of people dead, Pierce hanging up like a bloody bauble, blown half to shit, it's a bloody Christmas miracle. Talking of which, how did you get in? This place is impenetrable," Gerry queried.

Wright not bothering to look up, set about dressing Gerry's leg with a mini medical kit that he detached from his belt. He brought out a pristine, white dressing and tape.

"Managed to get in just before the shutters came down, been hunkered down in the warehouse for the duration of this clusterfuck" Wright muttered.

"They took me in there for a beating, I didn't see you?" Gerry probed.

Wright looked up and smiled at Gerry, "That's kind of the point. Plus, I learnt from the best."

"Even so, some good work there. You take any of them out?" Gerry gritted his teeth, as Wright tightened the bandage.

Wright shook his head.

"Negative on that one boss, it's taken all of my training to get me this far, been making my way up the levels, staying hidden. They're everywhere or were anyway, overheard one of them saying that the Prime Ministers bodyguard and some other guy had taken a few of their number out."

"It must be our lucky day; those remaining must be the runts of the litter, practically taking themselves out. I just witnessed one of the twats bring down half the roof on top of himself. I count four or so left," Gerry derided.

"Two a pair if you're up for it. Tom took a good old few of them scalps himself. You hear anything about him? If he's still alive?" Gerry optimistically inquired.

"Too busy looking for you and making sure I didn't cop a round in the back of the head. I'm guessing he was the other guy."

Gerry nodded.

"So, what next?" Wright asserted.

"We formulate a battle plan, take them all down. I suggest I lay down covering fire, take out one or two of them from this vantage point. You take point; make your way down to their level, strike at the same time. Create a panic and pick them off. Then we send up the signal, get the cavalry in to mop up what's left of them, disarm the charges, set the hostages free," Gerry proposed as he rose shakily to his feet, putting all of his weight on the makeshift crutch.

"You almost make it sound easy," Wright sarcastically returned.

Gerry caught his breath and fell against the column once again, the exertion of standing and the rush of blood to his head proving too much.

"You sure you're up for this old-timer?" Wright prodded.

"Less of the old," Gerry wheezed, "now pass me that gun, would you?"

"Sure," Wright replied, stooping to pick up the weapon.

As he did so, Gerry's suspicions rang true. Protruding from Wright's back pocket was a balaclava. Gerry had just begun to come to terms with his utter disappointment when at that point Wright swung round and levelled the gun at Gerry's chest, taking two cursive steps back from Gerry. A look of venom fell across Wright's features.

"This goes down one of two ways. Now, I don't want to even consider the alternative, so let's just talk our way through option one. Thompson, the gaffer running the show, has given me every assurance that if the situation presented itself and I had the opportunity to reason with you, that provided you came round to our way of thinking, he'd let you live. I told them the only one that hated Pierce more than the organisation, was you. Treated you like shit...that you were for the high jump after today anyway. Boss says he'll even cut you in, on one of the other guy's shares; not like they'll need it, hey?" Wright nodded eagerly at this, egging Gerry on, wanting him so very much to agree with him.

Gerry nodded slowly before spitting upon the ground.

"Assurances. Come on lad, I trained you better than that. There's only way out of this for me and that is in a body bag. How long have you been on their payroll?" Gerry hobbled forward slightly.

Wright instinctively took another step backwards, raising the gun marginally higher.

"Stay the fuck where you are Gerry. I'd rather it didn't go down like this but you know as well as I do, you force my hand, I'm putting you down. All we need is the memory stick, that's all; an inanimate object, no skin off of your nose, hey? You tell me what I need to know and not only do we walk out of here together, we do so rich men," Wright pleaded in an overfriendly fashion.

"Were the boys inanimate?" Gerry plainly stated, "the team died because of you! They were your mate's you bastard. They had your back no matter what. You sold them out, all those people down there, for what? For money, some deluded promise from a lunatic?"

Gerry wavered, his anger sending him slightly off kilter.

"I regret that Gerry, I really do but they got to me early. Brenda leaving me, taking the kids and that's not even taking into account the child support. You saw what that did to me and as if that wasn't enough of a steaming pile of shit, I was going to lose my job. A job I've lost my family for. Bled for."

Wright was quite distressed now, swinging his head in stubborn defiance.

"And for what? All because some wet behind the ear's bureaucrat wouldn't let us do our job. Where is the justice in that? I've given this country everything Gerry and what did it get me? A measly wage and a one bed flat in a shitty part of town that makes me question why I even fight for this country anymore."

Gerry opted for a change of tact.

"It doesn't have to go this way Jack. We can end this together; get you set up somewhere else. This isn't you mate-" Gerry's offer was abruptly cut off.

"Save it!" Wright snapped his voice steeped in loathing at being pitied.

He levelled the gun once again and placed his finger on the trigger.

"Jack," Gerry pleaded.

"It's with me or against me Gerry. Rolling in cash or rotting in a shallow grave propping up an overpass. Your choice, now what's it going to be?" Wright raised an expectant eyebrow at this, repositioning the butt of the gun against his shoulder.

"A bullet," Gerry stated plainly, the disappointment etched upon his face.

Wright shook his head, "That's a bloody shame, it really is but you can't say I didn't give you the option, a fair crack of the whip. You can give me that much," he let the statement hang, seeking absolution for sins committed and those about to be tendered.

Gerry shook his head.

"I'm a solider lad, not a priest. If you want to talk to someone in a funny hat, stick your head out the window and wave down one of the hundred or so Old Bill outside."

"You self-righteous prick. Your think your opinion matters?" he huffed, "if that's the way you want to play it, fine. It's nothing personal, it's just business. Not that you'd understand, you've never tasted desperate. I'm like Velcro mate, shit sticks to me. Is it so wrong that I want something better? Something that's mine for once?" he spat, thumping his chest.

"Opinions are like arseholes, everybody's got one lad. It just turns out some of us can tell an arsehole from an opinion and your man down there, Thompson, that's an arsehole that's full of shit. Now, stop the bitching and do it already," Gerry countered wearily, closing his eyes.

This sent Wright into a flurry of anger. He stepped forward and pressed down upon the trigger and with a click, came to the horrifying conclusion that Gerry's gun had not been loaded. Gerry looked up, smirking.

"Dead man's click?" he asked mockingly, knowing full well what he had done, as he lurched at Wright, grateful of the fact that he had swapped out his loaded magazine with the one he had found empty upon seeing the clandestine figure; his wariness had paid off, cautious to the very end.

Gerry fell heavily upon Wright. He tore the gun from Wright's grip and began clubbing him with it. Wright brought his hands up in a defensive posture, trying to parry the blows, his efforts unsuccessful.

"You forgot rule number one you treacherous fuck," Gerry grunted, mid throttling, "always check there's one in the spout."

"And there... was me thinking," Wright jeeringly retorted, as he took various blows to the head, blood now flecking the collar of his shirt, "it was to always... be prepared,"

He withdrew a flick-knife and without hesitation, plunged it deep into Gerry's abdomen. Gerry froze, dropping the now useless M16. Out of instinct his fingers wriggled over the wound, searching for the hilt of the knife but Wright withdrew it and rolled Gerry's substantial weight from atop of him.

Gerry arched over onto his back, clutching at his stomach, his white shirt already soaked with blood, inhaling deeply, eyes wild with pain. Wright watched on, slightly taken aback, not quite knowing how to proceed. That had been self-defence, what came next required him to finish the job, to kill his mentor, his friend, in cold blood. He stood upright knife at the ready.

Gerry used his heels to slide backwards, the pace of which was agonisingly slow. Wright let him continue, following at a snail's pace. His mentors face had grown grey, his vision swimming. He was losing blood and fast. His torso began to grow numb, the bloods' warmth suddenly turning icy cold. Finally, making it to the marble column, he rested, awaiting the finishing blow.

"It didn't have to be this way Gerry. I offered you a way out," Wright ascertained, the bloodied blade angled in Gerry's direction.

Gerry's eyes began to roll in his head. He snapped his head forward, desperately striving to remain conscious. His mouth dry, he thought it best to say something, to keep himself aware, alert.

"This is all on you Wright; don't... try to console yourself, with what you've done here today. You won't escape this. There's a cell with your name on it. You can't outrun that, just... just like you won't be able to...to outrun your guilt" Gerry trailed on in agonised convulsions, the inner workings of his stomach seemingly replaced by red hot shards.

"And I'm not trying to. I will never outrun the things I have seen, the things I've done; part of me knew that when I enlisted. Fuck, I certainly had no excuse when I agreed to work with Thompson. All I want," he beat his chest again, "is some form of recognition for services rendered. Am I not owed a standard of living, some level of comfort after all I've sacrificed?"

Gerry managed a low splutter that resembled a laugh. Wright paused in utter horror, his felled mentor's rabid, blood laden lips turned down in a frown.

"Jesus, you're more deluded than I thought. If you genuinely believed in any of what you set out to achieve today...I wouldn't still be breathing. The only free handouts in this life are eviction notices and P60's," Gerry spat, a large blob of blood enthused mucus slapping the marble floor.

Wright shook his head, stepping forward.

"You always were a cynic, that and an appalling judge of character," Wright sadly stated, "all that aside, is there anything you'd like to stay? A message for your kids before..." he couldn't bring himself to say it.

Gerry simply shook his head and fixed his feigning vision squarely on Wright. He wanted to look the man whom he had held in such high esteem before today, in the eyes when he administered the final blow.

"I didn't want it to go down like this Gerry. I am really am sorry. It was been my honour to-"

Wright's face contorted with astonishment, so much so that he dropped his knife and instead began fumbling for his sidearm. A crack rang out pursued by a whizz. Dumbfounded, Gerry could only stare back at Wright as he now brought his arm away from his sidearm, up to that of his shoulder; the material of his blazer frayed and bloodied now.

Wright breathed heavily, panting in exasperated anguish. He attempted to make a grab for his gun once again and whilst his movements were laboured, his thumb did manage to brush the holster's catch. Gerry was still looking forward when Tom's shoe stepped into his periphery. His eyes came up just in time to see the second, empty shell casing discharged out of the guns chamber.

A second thud came, this time hitting Wright squarely in the centre of the chest. Wright spun round like a ballerina, before falling against the railing of the glass partition, a wild look of confusion etched upon his face. He looked imploringly at Gerry as though his mentor would have been afforded the same degree of mercy had Tom not arrived when he had and made to speak, blood already trickling from his mouth down onto the lapel of his blazer. His hand once again limply nudged his sidearm.

Tom approached and callously brushed his hand away before withdrawing Wright's sidearm from its holster. He flung it upon the floor before sliding it over to Gerry with his foot. Methodically and with calculated action, he then removed Wrights blazer and rolled up the sleeve on his right arm; all the while Wright's head lolled with gurgling chokes. Tom reached into his pocket and brought out a large luggage tag, steadying the man with his other arm. It was plastic with a slip of paper housed within. He attached it to Wrights wrist forcefully and tugged it to ascertain whether it was attached firmly or not. Satisfied, he gripped the back of Wright's head and looked him dead in the eyes.

"You're going to deliver a message to your boss for me," Tom patted the luggage tag as he said this, the words "READ ME NOW!" etched upon it in a silver marker.

Wright drunkenly made to grasp at Tom but he only drew him in closer so that both their noses were almost touching.

"Don't worry about memorising it, I'll be sending it airmail,"

And with that he grabbed Wright by the thighs and in one blistering movement, angled him over the edge. There was the briefest of shrieks before gravity took hold, Wrights flailing arms soon disappearing. Tom peered over the edge, mapping Wright's descent as he plunged seconds later into the shallow depths of the water fountain below. He resurfaced momentarily, bobbing to the surface, about two metres from the Mc Allister who now set about shrieking, the displaced water soaking him in the process. Tom watched on for several more seconds as Mc Allister, who had now stopped screaming, set about trying to pull the lifeless corpse free of the crimson water.

As he grasped at his conspirator's limbs wildly, his hand fell upon the luggage tag. Spooked, he momentarily scanned the upper concourses before pulling hard upon the tag. Freeing it, he scurried back towards the boarded off construction site where Tom had been held earlier. Tom turned back to face Gerry, grabbing Wright's blazer as he did so and bound over towards his fallen comrade. Using his knife, he removed the arms from the blazer, grimacing as the muscles in his shoulder and forearms tightened. Gerry patted Tom's shoulder with a bloodied hand, smiling meekly at him.

"Knew you'd made it," his head lolled.

Tom caught it and held it firm.

"What can I say, Tom and Gerry kind of has a ring to it," Tom winked, measuring the lengths of material, "couldn't leave you to have all the fun."

"You're going to have to... I'm afraid. Silver lining though, you can chalk another ... one up on the board. Jones is down...consider that your Christmas bonus," Gerry spluttered.

"What's up?" Tom hefted Gerry forward, inspecting his wound, "don't have the stomach for it? Taking Jones down filled you up, has it?"

Tom's poor attempt at humour made Gerry burst into a wheezing guffaw, one his body immediately berated him for doing so. Tom mentally rebuked himself for his poor attempt at humour, each chortle pumping out more blood.

"The wall did most of the work," Gerry violently coughed, pointing over to Jones' rubbly resting site.

Tom wrapped the lengths of blazer around Gerry's stomach and tied them tightly, registering an anguished groan from Gerry. He then reached for Gerry's makeshift crutch and laid it across his lap. Animated steps disappearing into the distance could now be heard from below.

"Is there any stomach left?" Gerry wheezed.

Tom didn't need his basic medical training to tell him that Gerry was far from fine, far from recovery for that matter. Instead, he did what most would do in a situation so dire, he lied.

"Enough for what comes next. When we get out of here, together, we'll get it seen to but first, I need your help"

Gerry nodded reluctantly.

"For all the good I'll be. You have a plan?" Gerry croaked, gurning every time his body shifted.

"That's the beauty of it. Down there right now, they're already doing more for us then could imagine. You're my Ace in the hole," Tom prodded Gerry encouragingly as he said this.

"More like Ace with a hole in him," Gerry scoffed.

Tom leant backwards and brought back the M16, positioning it around Gerry's neck.

"Think you can load and shoot this from a fixed position?" Tom hesitantly enquired.

"Just tell me where to point and I'll take care... of the rest" Gerry unconvincingly pledged.

Tom nodded, trying to disguise the fact that Gerry's teeth were now coated in blood.

"First thing I need is you up on your legs, I'll explain the plan on the way down," Tom stated as he made to lift him.

Gerry held up a hand, asking him to wait, bracing himself for what was to come. He repositioned his broom handle before nodding he was ready to resume. Tom took Gerry's full weight and hefted him upwards. Gerry clamped down his jaw and externalised a yelp of pain he had dared not let loose for so long, the need for stealth having now passed. Tom brought his arm across his shoulder and began to walk back towards the escalator.

They had only walked a few steps when Gerry through stifled whines, grunted, "I suppose you think this makes us even?"

Tom lightly laughed to himself, ignoring the burden Gerry was bearing down upon his own wound.

"Kind of, yeah," Tom chipped in, eyes fixed firmly ahead.

"You're lucky, a vacancy for the position as my apprentice just opened up" Gerry stated nonchalantly.

"Oh yeah? How'd you reckon?" Tom replied, glad to be keeping Gerry alert and talking.

"Well, there's the small ... matter that, you just threw the last surviving member of my unit off the top floor of a shopping complex," Gerry slurred.

Tom stopped and shot him a worried, questioning expression.

Gerry indicated he need not worry, "It's ok; I was in the process of retiring him myself. Long story, one for after we get out of here and I'm drugged up to the hilt with morphine."

"We've got this Gerry, those people down there... no more harm will come to them," Tom defiantly concluded.

They were three metres or so from the escalator now.

"Tom?" Gerry inquisitively murmured.

"What is it partner?"

"Where the hell was this guy two hours ago when I needed him?" Gerry probed, gasping slightly.

Tom looked sideways, momentarily recalling the boy and his brother. He swallowed hard.

"This isn't who I am Gerry; I need you... I need for me to believe that. If I'm to get through today, I need to hold on to that. Today is necessity," Tom's voice broke slightly.

Gerry stared back at Tom, shuffling forwards. In that moment he took Tom in for all that he was. He wasn't just a soldier; he was the living embodiment of what those men below actually thought they were fighting for. Their morals, their code, it was medieval, outdated whereas Tom had returned to his fallen comrade in his hour of need.

(CHAPTER BREAK)

"Where the fuck is he?" Thompson screamed.

Greaves offered only a baffled look.

"I don't..." Greaves started.

"That's the problem you incompetent, lowlife, scum ridden..." Thompson emphasised each of the words with a vicious swing of his boot into Doc's corpse, "Parasites!" he ended with an insatiable flurry of kicks to Doc's head.

Thompson bounded free of the pit panting with orgasmic fury. The high Greaves had ridden upon hearing Thompson's previous inspirational words had now all but dissipated; Mr Hyde had returned. Thompson pointed furiously at Doc, his head turned away from the man, his skull now largely concaved by Thompsons steel capped boots.

"Search him for the detonator," he retched, his throat closing, overstretched.

Greaves jumped into the pit and began patting his fellow teammate down. Thompson breathed heavily, pacing like some cornered predator. At that point, a movement came from the mouth of the entrance and Thompson withdrew his sidearm with alarming speed. Hertz and McAllister bundled in, waving their hands.

"It's us!" Hertz screamed; McAllister ducked with a flinch.

Thompson lingered, keeping the men in his sights for several seconds as if contemplating whether to execute them or not, to be rid of them and their blundering antics. He eventually dipped his secondary weapon.

"You have your order's," Thompson spat, baffled as to why the had returned ahead of the designated ERV.

McAllister ran forward with what appeared to be a luggage tag dangling from his grasp. Thompson's heart leapt as his brain began to make tentative links between the luggage tag and Tom. Had his man discovered a hidden clue from the airport, from the traitor within their ranks?

Thompson stepped forward and snatched it from McAllister, Greaves now at his side. McAllister withdrew back towards to the mouth of the pit, Hertz, several metres away, maintaining a watchful sentry of the door.

"Where did you find this?" Thompson hissed, holding the evidence aloft.

"Attached to Wright sir, someone over one of the concourses above into the fountain. He's gone sir," McAllister hurriedly mumbled, as if he were to blame.

Greaves kicked at some rubble, circling Thompson.

"Fuck! And with him, our bloody wheelman! Perfect, that is just fucking perfect."

Thompson shot him an intense glance that told him to cease all noise, breathing if possible. Thompson turned the message over in his hands and read the writing.

"It's addressed to you..." McAllister blurted out.

Hertz shot him a cursory look over his shoulder, scolding his teammate for his continued nervous ramblings.

Thompson zipped the tag open and found inside a folded Polaroid. He discarded the tag by the edge of the pit. He first unfolded the Polaroid and scowled; seething anger solidifying in the core of his stomach. Greaves peered over Thompson's shoulder and shot Hertz a look, mouthing the words *'Fucking hell!'*.

Thompson held up the Polaroid and Hertz took three cautionary steps towards it before stopping dead. The picture was of Tom holding up a memory stick in one hand, in the other he stuck his two middle fingers up. Thompson's eyes fell upon the back of the Polaroid and he read the word's scrawled upon the back.

"If you want the schematics, come alone and unarmed to the water fountain. Leave your entourage behind or I throw it over my shoulder and make a wish."

Thompson crumpled the Polaroid into a ball upon reading the final word and set about muttering expletives through gritted teeth.

"So be it," he spat, unclipping his holster, allowing it to fall to the ground; his upper body had taken to twitching.

"Sir, it's a trap, it has to be," Greaves stepped forward, amazed that his superior was even considering it.

Thompson stopped and angled his head slightly. He did not turn around.

"He thinks he has nothing left to lose, a cornered animal making his last-ditch attempt at reasserting himself at the top of the food chain. He might not know it but the moment he stepped into West Acre Point; he was already a dead man. Look for the detonator you two, check and double check Docherty. The second we blow that, the cavalry are going to come in all guns blazing. Greaves, with me and keep to the shadows, just in case he's armed," Thompson growled, Greaves snapping at his heels.

When the pair was gone, leaving the other two to stare dumbly at one another, Hertz stopped to scoop up Thompson's holster. As he did so he picked up the discarded luggage tag also.

"Guy thinks he's in a bloody Western," Hertz scoffed.

Mc Allister began sifting through the pouches upon Doc's vest where he retrieved a myriad of armaments, a knuckleduster, a flick-knife, a garrotte, yet there was no sign of the detonator.

"Jesus," he muttered to himself as he tossed the items out of the pit, "the guy was like a walking, talking weapons expo."

Hertz eyed up the luggage tag and noticed that there was a small corner of paper protruding from it. He pulled at it and unfolded it twice. He scanned the note and he held it up confused.

"McAllister?" he called.

McAllister turned around, now ten metres or so from Hertz, who now stood in the centre of the pit, scanning the area around Doc, for the detonator.

"What?" McAllister hissed irritably, forgetting himself momentarily and the man before him waving a piece of paper above his head as if it were some golden ticket.

"There was another note folded and tucked inside the tag" Hertz explained, his features twisted in confusion.

McAllister froze and looked up.

"What does it say?" McAllister urged, now frozen to the spot.

"New Years has come early, let's hope next year isn't the pits," Hertz lingered on the last word, "that last bit, where it says pits, it's written in capital letters" Hertz stated, turning the paper over in his hands.

"The pits?" McAllister recited to himself, confused.

Hertz read the message back to himself. Upon the third reading, an icy hand crawled its way up Hertz's back, the slip of paper dropping from his hand.

"He's got the detonator," Hertz muttered to himself.

"What?" McAllister called out, cupping his hand to his ear.

Hertz looked up, scanning McAllister, his thought processes in disarray.

"Oh, fuck me," his head shot up, "he's got the-" Hertz started to bellow but was cut short as he was flung backwards.

The heat was indescribable. McAllister was eviscerated in a vision of orange brilliance, engulfed by flame and rubble, the floor giving way beneath, taking with it Doc's cadaver. Hertz hit the ground hard, instantly knocked unconscious, the outermost flames licking at his legs, the fire's hunger fed by the sudden rush of oxygen from the open pit. Thompson had ensured that there were no gas main's below the target area, his planning meticulous. The blast was remarkably forceful; the enclosed nature of the environment only serving to increase its magnitude, the concrete walls a mere inconvenience to its brute force.

Hertz had sustained a vicious head wound. A light but substantial layer of rubble covered his pelvis and upper left thigh. If he had been a metre or so closer to the blast area, he would have surely been killed outright. The sprinklers instantly set about dousing the flames. They soon began to retreat back into the pit, the crevice now about twelve-foot-deep. The ripples upon the fetid water below began to ebb away also; rubble, debris and viscera now harbouring within it's murky depths.

The surging water from the sprinklers began to resuscitate Hertz, a low mumble of confusion, followed by a comprehension of pure agony.

He sat up as much as the rubble would allow him and surveyed the damage. He brought his breathing under control and attempted to wiggle the toes upon his left foot. Remarkably, they yielded, moving fluently. Happy that his leg was not broken, Hertz hefted the rubble from his leg, yelping out as part of the rubble pinched a substantial amount of flesh as it landed upon the floor. The combat trousers he had been wearing, now bore a slit within the material, which he coaxed apart, ripping the material further. His leg was a violent hue of violet; the leg grazed in places, giving way to a sizeable gash, about five inches in length. It bled profusely but was not life threatening. He reached up and inspected his head, before making his way up towards his ears.

He withdrew his hands promptly upon touching his right ear. Gathering himself, he lightly brought his hand up once again, inspecting the upper part of his ear, which was now missing, a bloodied, serrated sensation where the upper third of his ear had been previously. He swallowed hard. Dazed, he chewed over how best to proceed.

Hertz stared back into the gaping abyss before him, now the burial site of two of his teammates as well as the traitor within the ranks. Had the body been in the pit when he and Mc Allister had begun their search? No matter. It was of little priority to Hertz, the mixture of relief at not having been killed and the thirst for revenge, overpowering all other senses. The mission was now abandoned in his mind's eye; Thompson's desire to kill the man who had caused so many deviations to the plan now rendered obsolete. He struggled shakily to his feet, swaying with giddiness as he did so. He steadied himself against a set of boxes, reinforced with a mound of bubble wrap. He bent down and tore off a strip, using it as a makeshift compress for his leg. He tied it tight and tested his leg. He could walk upon it, although it jarred with pain whenever he exerted any pressure upon it.

He hopped slightly at first, then took to dragging his leg slightly, a pitiful sight to behold. Reaching down, he retrieved Thompson's holster, pulling the Beretta free. He ejected the magazine and thumbed out the bullets, seven in total. He then checked his own sidearm, a M1911 Colt pistol, which held seven rounds also. The men within the team often mocked Hertz for his sidearm, as it was an old model. They called it a relic, an antique. What it lacked in bullet capacity however, it made up for in reliability. There was something he found soothing in such tried and tested weaponry, less working parts, less chance of it malfunctioning, much like himself. He walked in a giddy, slalom fashion towards the light of the door, his deafened right ear, sending him slightly off-balance.

CHAPTER TWENTY-TWO: BAPTISMAL CONDUCTOR

Tom stood alone at the rear of the water fountain, transfixed slightly by the bobbing body within, sailing upon red currents. The liquid was now still, the water only slightly lolling against the edge of the mosaic base, Britannia protruding from the centre. Tom alone with his thoughts could not help but see the symbolism that the fountain was now steeped in; the miniscule body of water over which Britannia ruled an allegorical representation of Britain's all but diminished empire. The water running red with blood, an eternal reminder of the blood spilt in conflicts past, present and undoubtedly yet to come.

Tom focused his mind on the task ahead. If his plan were to work, he would need to manifest a seamless performance. He shifted slightly, his feet displacing an assortment of grenade pins and empty shell casings belonging to a cacophony of calibres, each telling its own story, each in part responsible for a life. He heard the jingle of a shell casing as it skittered across the cold marble and shifted his attention forwards.

He saw Thompson striding towards him, hands aloft in a sign that he was unarmed as opposed to surrendering. Tom trained his attention towards the left and right of the man instead, scanning for any other members within his cohort. Tom kept the barrel of his Sig Sauer aimed squarely at the man's chest.

Satisfied he was alone, within his other hand, he raised the detonator. Thompson paused momentarily, staring back at the detonator, a brief glimmer of bile inducing distain, etched across his features. This quickly broke into a smile and Thompson started a slow, leather clad, clap. A smirk, framed by the ravaged wrinkles of a desert lifestyle, surfaced.

"I must say Tom; you are quite the pain in my arse. First my men, now my detonator, I can't wait to see what you have in store for your encore," Thompson halted, Tom now holding the detonator aloft.

"That's far enough Thompson," Tom directed.

"As you wish, I come only wishing to hear your demands, to parley. I am here to peacefully negotiate..." he spun round lifting the hem of his jumper, highlighting he was not concealing any weapons, "unarmed," he concluded, having gone full circle.

Tom observed that his black combat trousers were securely stuffed into his boots, no evident bulge from a weapon apparent.

"Who said this was a negotiation? I'm here to except your unconditional surrender. No more no less," Tom put forth.

Thompson burst into a deep, growling guffaw. Clapping his knees, bent double, he shot Tom an approving glance. Tom remained straight faced.

"Surrender, that's a good one. Why would I surrender, it's still four to one; Carol Voderman you are not," he scoffed, "I'd rather lose the schematics and escape with my life, live to fight another day, than demean myself before you, before my cause," Thompson confirmed.

"You adamant about that?" Tom queried.

"Unless like you I have lost the cognitive ability to count," Thompson berated snapped in a condescending tone.

"Hmm," Tom replied, his head cocked in bafflement.

He pressed the button upon the detonator and had his confidence bolstered upon hearing the blast of the ordnance within the construction site, smirking as the temporary wooden door to the site was blasted outwards, free of its hinges. Thompson ducked, instinctively cradling his head, facing back in the direction he had just come, smoke already billowing from the site. The hostages began to scream once again.

"You might want to recount!" Tom chipped in, raising his voice to be heard.

The sprinklers began to spray a light mist above them. Thompson slowly turned to face Tom, a murderous glint in his eye, mouth downturned.

"You're going to regret doing that-"

"Never mind what I'm going to regret. Where you're concerned, very little," Tom snarled, Thompson's continued bravado an insult to him.

As if to display this, Tom dropped the detonator into the fountain, the plop of the water serving as a full stop to Thompson's idle threats.

"You think you've got this all sown up, don't you? You coward, with your guerrilla style of combat, sticking to the shadows, not taking us head on. Pathetic," Thompson spat.

"That's not what the jolly green giant had to say up on the roof or the other one, Wright I believe, who betrayed his unit in favour of your bullshit cause," Tom flicked his eyes down towards the body bobbing in the water, emphasising his point.

"You think you can go the distance with me, huh? I'm not going to just roll over and show you my belly as easy as this lot did. You're standing in the way of change, of natural selection at its finest," Thompson began to pace in a sideways motion, "me, I'm a Great White and you; you're a bloody goldfish, hell fucking plankton compared to me! You're at the bottom of the food chain with ideas of grandeur far above your station, boy!"

"Well, I guess there's only one way to find out" Tom hastily replied, holstering his sidearm and taking a defensive stance.

Thompson unclasped his Kevlar vest and removed his gloves.

"Oh, now this I like. Maybe you do have some balls after all," Thompson approvingly nodded.

"By the way, just so you know," Tom stated in an affirmative tone, "this is one-hundred percent personal."

"Of that I have no doubt; I just hope you put up more of a fight than your little Anthony did. The only sturdy bit of him was his eyeballs, took a good old bit of elbow grease to pop them in I can tell you," Thompson jeered, bringing his hands up into an orthodox stance, flexing and cracking his knuckles as he did so.

Tom was overcome with anger; it took all he had to control his breathing, to push the thoughts of his brother's brutal demise from his mind. The scents and sounds of that burned out vehicle were now replaced by Tom's imagined reconstruction of the squelch of his brother's eyeballs, his panicked, anguished cries. Had he cried out for him in his final moments?

Tom held up the memory stick for Thompson to inspection before placing it upon the edge of the fountain. Thompson jutted out his lower lip and nodded, non-verbally authenticating the item that would be awarded to the victor.

"Looks like he had the upper hand over you all along, I'm just here to finish the job, keeping it in the family as it were," he stated, raising his fists.

The men began to circle one another, Tom alternating his arc whenever Thompson came near the fountain and the precious cargo it harboured. Tom was just about to launch his first strike when a bullet whizzed past his head and spat up a segment of the fountain's marble in a plume of dust. Tom dived to his right, taking shelter behind the corner of a large, squared seating area, it too made of marble. Tom heard a second-round bite into the marble to his right, sending up yet another cloud of masonry. He withdrew his sidearm and steadied his breathing.

As the next singular shot came, rhythmic in its barrage, quick and steady, the report of an AK-47 started chattering away, cutting swathes across the floor towards Tom. He watched as the bullets hit the floor before him, a metre or so shy.

"Cease fire! Cease fire!" Thompson screamed, now a sizeable distance to the rear of Tom having also taken cover, bolting back the way he had come originally.

Without looking, Tom calculated that a combination of two separate firing patterns and Thompson screaming for them to cease in their war of attrition, that there must at least be three of them left alive. Tom swore, knowing full well that Thompson would try to outwit him, ever the deceiver. All the better, Tom concluded, that he too, had not been completely transparent.

As if on cue, Gerry let loose a short burst of supressing fire from above. Tom afforded himself a glance around the corner and saw Thompson as well as another man, Hertz he surmised, scrambling for cover, the marble behind them churning and dissipating under the onslaught of Gerry's M16. Tom witnessed Thompson issuing orders via a flurry of hand signals and a brief movement of his lips indicating that he wished for his man to make a move on the memory stick. The man nodded his understanding and handed Thompson a Beretta.

Still, Gerry continued to support Tom with covering fire, offering regular bursts, ensuring the insurgents remained pinned down. Tom heard the clattering of empty shells from the Ak-47, and presumed the owner was not far from his position. He decided to make his move. He swung from cover, firing blindly at Thompson, the other man having now departed. Thompson ducked and let fly a volley of wild shots forcing Tom to return to cover. With Gerry maintaining the high ground and Tom firing from his flanking position it was only a matter of time before the insurgents either ran out of ammunition or sustained a bullet wound.

Tom did not have long to wait. He rounded the corner from his crouched position once again, pinching off three shots. Thompson, who was now sustaining heavy fire on two fronts, had at the time been concentrating his fire upon Gerry. Thompson whirled round to counter Tom's barrage, when a whizzing noise, followed by a wet thud emanated from his leg. Thompson growled, dropping to the floor, swearing as he wheeled about on the floor in pain. The impact of the round had been enough to fleck Thompson's own face with blood.

Tom knew he would have to make this quick, although as loathed as he was to admit it, he wanted to make Thompson suffer. Thompson was already shimmying back into cover, a sweeping trail of blood before him. Tom breathed in deep, ready to round the corner, to fire the decisive round upon an exhalation of breath, when he was distracted by a flicker of movement to his right. It was Hertz, by the fountain. He fired once. Tom instinctively hit the deck, the bullet whizzing overhead.

Tom wildly returned fire as he rolled sideways but still Hertz persisted, discharging a further three shots in quick succession. The marble splintered before Tom, raining chips down upon his head. Exposed, Tom made to propel himself free of the ground when one of the rounds ricocheted off the smooth marble, diverting its course upwards, the bullet slicing past Tom's side. With an anguished grunt that forced him to drop his gun, Tom collapsed back onto the cool marble. The flesh wound instantly sizzled with heat.

Tom lay prone as Hertz approached his quarry, a massive smile upon his face as he moved in closer; the two grenades upon his tactical vest swinging rhythmically with each step. Tom made to act fast, to stand but was instantly felled by the pain, brought to his knees. As if genuflecting before Hertz, Tom locked eyes with his adversary, awaiting the round that would bring an end to the torment of the day's events, nay the past year.

The colt clicked. Empty. Disappointed yet undeterred, a methodical Hertz patted his tactical vest for a spare magazine but found none. Looking at the Colt in a self-deprecating fashion, all seven bullets now spent, he flung it aside.

"Up close and personal it is," Hertz growled and without hesitation, bounded towards Tom.

Tom was counting on it. Whilst it did not take long for his aggressor to cover the distance between them, the wait was unbearable as was the pain within his side. When Hertz was no more than a metre away, Tom barrelled forwards, opting for a rugby tackle. Hertz caught him as he drove into his stomach, his left hand driving deep into Tom's flesh wound. When he withdrew his fist, it was coated in blood.

Tom fell to the floor his weight unsupported, aided by the various paraphernalia strewn across the floor. He was carried off balance, landing hard upon his elbows. Ignoring the jarring pain and in a singular movement, he closed both hands around the floor's contents before hurling a handful of empty shell casings in the direction of Hertz's eyes. Hertz, now momentarily blinded, afforded Tom the time to weakly rise to his feet. With a bellowing scream that was more for Tom's benefit than his aggressor, he let loose a flurry of jabs to the man's face, his opponent's head bouncing backwards upon contact.

Impatient and fuelled by the same bloodlust as Tom, Hertz weathered the blows, driving Tom backwards, gripping at his neck. The fracas caused Tom to lose his footing once again, the momentum bringing Hertz along with him also. The impact was forceful, driving the air from his lungs. Whilst he battled for air, he registered that his back had grown sodden. However, any misgivings that he may have had about this being blood from his flesh wound were quickly diminished by two factors. The first came via the sloshing of water behind his head whilst the second indicator came courtesy of the dead weight upon his chest as it submerged him in the fountain up to his shoulders, the water flooding into his open mouth and nostrils.

Hertz squeezed and rocked Tom's head as he did so in an effort to choke out any last remnants of air. After several seconds, the water parted and Tom's vision cleared slightly, Hertz's toil-ridden face grimacing. Tom made a grab for his vest but was viciously forced under again. What little air he had managed to suck in was expended in simply trying to remain calm, his vision beginning to dull at the edges. He could feel Wright's body knock against his upper shoulder, bobbing in the water. He still clasped his left hand shut painfully, using the pain as an anchor point to the world of the living; the pointed item wrapped around his index finger digging into his palm. Tom broke the surface once again much to Hertz's anger. He countered once again now pushing his full weight down upon Tom, who now gripped one of Hertz's vest straps.

He gritted his teeth, his core on fire as he kept himself from re-entering the water in a plank like position. Hertz was wheezing severely now. It was now or never. Tom reached his hand up from the vest strap, his lungs on fire and grabbed Hertz's deformed ear. His grip wavered, the wet blood laden ear affording him little purchase. Hertz let out a blood curdling shriek, uncharacteristic in nature. He dislodged Tom's tight grip and as he did so, Tom observed within his oxygen deprived stupor that another segment of the man's ear had torn away. Instinctively, both of Hertz's hands shot up as he tentatively fingered his ear, probing it wildly, inspecting the extent of the damage.

Bitter tears gathered at the base of Hertz's eyes and he screamed once again, an animalistic taint to his pupils. Tom sat upright, breathing in deeply. He slid off the smooth marble and landed in a heap, a puddle of reddened water pooling around his resting point. Tom turned onto his front, coughing up water, his throat ablaze. The report from the M16 was still apparent but distant, coming now within shorter bursts. Gerry was running out of ammunition. Onwards he crawled, his gun in sight, four or so metres away. Hertz clamped down on both of Tom's ankles and used the sodden marble floor as a way of sliding Tom back towards him. He turned Tom over and drove his head into his, once, twice, a third time. Tom's head bounced free of the marble and he felt himself slip away slightly.

Hertz lifted Tom to his feet and made ready to finish him, a snap of the neck, now wishing for the clash to arrive at a conclusion. He grinned at Tom, keeping him at arm's length so as to not allow him a purchase once again upon his ear. How the grin soon faded however, when his prey reciprocated, his teeth coated in a luscious red. Tom's left hand came up and with it, an extended left index finger bearing a grenade pin. Hertz instinctively let go of Tom and began patting the grenades upon his vest, tossing them aside. Tom's hand fell upon Hertz's Colt, which he snatched up gratefully, remembering as he did so that Hertz had expelled all its ammunition. Not to be deterred, he detached the slide via the slide's lock safety, relying solely upon the muscle memory drummed into him by his military training. He rose to his feet shakily, Hertz tugging upon the zip of his vest. He made to look up, baffled by the proximity of his adversary but was too late.

Without hesitation, Tom drove the remainder of the Colt, now tapered slightly at the end of the barrel into Hertz's heart. Hertz spluttered, his eyes growing wide. Tom gave the disassembled Colt a cautionary twist, left to right and then let go of the guns' stock and with it, Hertz fell lifeless to the floor. Exhausted and breathing heavily still, Tom gave Hertz a cursory shove with his foot, ensuring he was dead. The man rolled slightly onto his side before flopping back to his original position.

Tom was rooted to the floor, his legs quaking with adrenaline. He considered how much longer sheer adrenaline would keep him alive, the number of near-death experiences now dwarfing any moments in which he had felt he had had the upper hand. He flattened his palms against the cool, wet marble of the fountain, steadying himself, gathering himself for the fight still at hand. He and Gerry were winning the battles, but they still needed to win the war. Their scheme thus far, of sorts, had gone to plan but both men knew that as soon as Gerry's M16 ran out of ammunition, the margin for error and things that could go wrong was relatively tripled. He eyed his Sig Sauer across the way and tracked towards it wishing for the first time, to embrace the safety it offered. As he did so he retrieved the memory stick and pocketed it; it's proficiency as a bartering chip indispensable.

He made to stoop for his sidearm when he heard a slosh from behind him. At first, he reckoned it for the body of Gerry's former now deceased comrade, bobbing under the features steady current. He urged himself to keep it together, not to let his nerves get the better of him. That was easier said than done when unexpectedly, his spine snapped straight, his muscles contorted, convulsing. A crackling could now be heard and the faintest smell of burning material.

Tom's jaw clenched shut, the only movement his body allowed. A static numbness descended the arches of his back; his vision blackened at the periphery. Finally, his right leg gave way sending him crumpling to the floor. The crackling ceased unlike the multitude of nerves that now fired uncontrollably within Tom's body. He lay on his side twitching, saliva trickling from the corner of his mouth.

The clap of heavyset boots upon marble came from behind him. Tom tried to shift his weight, wanting to face the unknown threat head on. Before he could even consider what was happening, he felt a presence at the top of his head, about a metre or so away in distance. He tried to create some momentum, rocking slightly but could not gain any traction; his muscles no longer functioning.

"Allow me," a harsh, rasping tone offered.

A tubular item which resembled a truncheon fell upon Tom's shoulder, black with two prongs at the end. A downward pressure was exerted causing Tom to limply return to his back. He immediately recognised the man, his senses bombarded with shock. The man with the wiry frame smiled down at Tom, basking in his sudden realisation, his hair still immaculately slicked back.

"Remember me?" he mockingly gleamed.

Tom struggled at first to formulate the syllables but after two attempts, did so.

"Don," he stuttered, the double amputee who had earlier been accosted by the Police at the beginning of the day.

"Glad to see I made an impression on you. Shame the same can't be said of you at the time, otherwise I would have offed you right there and then at that checkpoint," the man tutted, a fake air of regret to his expressionless tone.

He walked round Tom, putting himself between him and his Sig Sauer.

"Let's not stand on ceremony though. I mean we're both well past that, now aren't we? The name's Greaves. All part of my elaborate cover, you see. Plus, there is the fact that I feel like we should be on a first name basis, what with me knowing oh so much about you... Tom," he stated, malevolent grimace in tow.

Tom shifted. The tubular device fell upon Tom's forehead.

"Now, now, you've already had a fair few volts through you. Last thing you want is for me to touch this to your old Shirley there," he moved the device down towards his temple, "sure-fire way to get yourself lit up like a Christmas tree. This'll certainly blow a bulb or two and I don't think Santa will be in the business of issuing you with a new brain this year on account of you being on the naughty list. No presents for you," Greaves chuckled impishly, wagging his finger.

Tom rested upon his elbows not wanting to force his adversaries' hand further.

"Your move," Tom conceded.

Greaves sardonically nodded.

"That's more like it, know your place," he smirked, shifting slightly and with it the stun baton.

Greaves motioned over to the fountain with the baton.

"First of all, I want you to stand up and face that fountain, you know, the one with all the dead bodies. Hardly the fountain of youth is it? Shame that," he tutted jeeringly.

Tom wobbled before unsteadily getting to his feet, his hands raised; his biceps still twitching uncontrollably, his legs like lead. He thought it best to buy some time, regather his thoughts as well as essential bodily function. He now faced Greaves.

"How did you lose your legs," Tom probed.

"Does it matter?" Greaves replied in an elevated tone, bemused by Tom's sudden interest.

"I noticed this morning that you had the SAS insignia on your prosthetics. Just trying to piece together what brought a man like you," he lingered "here today? Money, a cause to fight, all seems a bit cliché to me," Tom murmured, feigning interest.

"Get you, right little Nancy Drew, aren't we? What do I look like to you, some kind of shrink? I'm not here to help you come to terms with why we're here or why you're in your current predicament. Your peace of mind means fuck all to me," Greaves spat.

"I was just thinking, those disability benefits, allowances from the Army in short supply; it must be difficult, day to day. Not exactly raking in it are you? Tom sympathised.

"Cut the reverse psychology shit, I'm not in this for the money," Greaves rebuked Tom, disgusted by the insinuation.

"Independent, standing on your own two feet, must be hard that's all," Tom sighed, knowing full well what he was inferring.

The last part of the sentence sent Greaves into a stupor, he shuffled towards Tom awkwardly, his hand raised, baton at the ready. Tom readied himself for another pulse of electricity, tensing his body slightly but instead Greaves swung the device downwards, making contact with Tom's skull. Tom faltered slightly but stood tall. Greaves took the opportunity to grab him by the shoulder and turn him around, now located to his rear. He followed up by placing Tom's hands upon his head pressing down harshly.

"They stay on your head, if you know what's good for you," Greaves tersely grunted.

He wrapped the baton around Tom's neck, holding it at either end in a choking manner. The two stood in this comedic stance for several seconds.

"You think the regiment would be proud of what you're doing here today, acting under the facade of some sick, deluded duty to your country? Or to any of your other cronies, how it went down today? Hardly an honourable death for any of them, they'll be no military honours for you lot, no monument with your name chiselled upon it," Tom pressed.

Greaves sniffed in disgust.

"And where, exactly, is the honour in a soldier's death? There's no pageantry involved when your loved ones get that knock at the door. Nor is there while you lay in a desert four thousand miles away, blown to fuck where the only thing to take your mind off your own suffering is the soldier lying beside you, screaming even louder. Crying out for help, help that won't come because you're being mortared back to the Stone Age".

"And what honour is there to be had in taking the life of some insignificant speck, like you, on the battlefield? Why do we do it, because they're different, because they want what they can't have? There is no honour in being covered in your own piss and blood, caked in the remains of your dead comrades. That's a lie sold by governments the world over, a rallying cry to boost morale in an effort to gain support for their shady undertakings and backhanded deals. You were a solider yourself, open them fucking eyes of yours," Greaves wheezed, slightly out of breath from his verbal tyrade.

"I know killing innocents isn't honourable, no matter the justification," Tom scoffed as they arrived at the fountain.

"No one is innocent! You people, with your hearts and minds bullshit. When are you going to realise that the only thing you need concern yourself with, is your own country? So, some mud shack village, in the arse- end of nowhere gets blown to shit, a country's populace enslaved by some dictator, while they all starve. Who gives a shit? Three quarters of this world had their chance when they had the British Empire and they frittered it away. Their bed, now they lie in it. The new order will be fully self-sufficient. We will want for nothing. If we want something, we'll take it," Greaves tightened his grip throughout his barrage, the baton digging deep into Tom's throat.

The sensation had finally all but returned to Tom's essential extremities or as well as they would do without medical attention. His back yearned for him to lie down but he knew that would spell certain death. He would never surrender; of that he was sure. Instigating conversation, his provocation, it was sending Greaves into a rant, all Tom needed to do was bide his time, wait to kick the soapbox right out from underneath him.

"Personally Greaves... I don't think you've got a leg to stand on," Tom dryly quipped.

Greaves screamed out with anger and withdrew the pistol from his holster, the baton falling to side. Tom heard the hammer as it was clicked back, the muzzle burrowing into his temple.

"Keep cracking wise, I fucking dare-"

"Stop!" an abrupt call came from above.

Tom swallowed hard as Greaves erratic purchase upon his sidearm made scathing indentations upon his flesh. His breathing was irregular; Tom could practically hear the cogs turning in his head, urging him to execute his captive.

Instead, Greaves manoeuvred Tom back towards the source of the voice and was met by Thompson stood slouching over Gerry on the concourse above, he too with a gun to Gerry's head. Tom's heart leapt up into his mouth. Gerry was ashen faced, weakened severely from blood loss. The two men were effectively using one another for support; Thompson's wounded leg hung out to the side, the tip of his boot barely touching the floor. Tom looked up crestfallen as Greaves began to howl with laughter.

"Here's how this is going to go! You hand Greaves down there the memory stick. We kill you both humanely, quick, which is more than you deserve. You draw this out and I assure you, everyone you know and love, will die along with your friend here. And I assure you, I'll make it nice and slow, show you some more of his guts before it's all over and done with," Thompson barked.

"Don't give these fucks nothing," Gerry shouted, instantly receiving a dig to his stomach.

He made to double over in pain but Thompson held firm, raising his head in a manner that indicated that he awaited Tom's reply. Unbeknownst to the others, Gerry had used this as an opportunity to pull from his belt buckle his own retractable knife, short and easily concealed within his palm.

"Ok! Just stop. I'll hand it over," Tom called out before reaching into his pocket rather too abruptly for Greaves liking, who now drove his gun deeper into Tom's temple.

"Nice and slowly, knobhead," Greaves sneered.

Tom shot up a hand, "I'm just reaching into my pocket, no tricks."

"There had better not be," Thompson bellowed.

Tom dug around inside of his pocket and withdrew the memory stick, holding it aloft for all to see.

"Greaves authenticate if that is what he says it is," Thompson pressed, peeking out slightly from behind Gerry.

Greaves inspected it briefly before nodding emphatically, bouncing slightly.

"It is sir."

"Take it from him," Thompson barked.

Greaves removed the gun from Tom's temple and holstered his sidearm, the stun baton returning to the groove of his lower back. Then using his now free arm, he made to snatch the memory stick from Tom's grasp.

Tom looked up at Gerry; saddened by the situation they now found themselves in and for the briefest of moments, Tom could have sworn Gerry winked. What happened next did so with lightning speed, Tom having to react on the fly.

Gerry's hand came up fast, an impressive blur given his current physical state. Tom saw the glint of the knife before it penetrated the forearm that Thompson had been using to keep Gerry under duress. Thompson screamed, wriggling, trying to pull away but Gerry hung firm, swaying the man left to right upon the concourse of Level One, thrashing his arm with the blade like a Great White.

Tom reacted also, bringing his elbow hard into Greave's stomach. Greaves let out a pained exhalation of breath, the severe force of Tom's elbow winding him. He dropped the stun baton, which Tom lurching from his grasp, picked up as he dipped away from his captor. He feigned towards the Sig Sauer but diverted right at the last minute, diving behind the marble seating adjacent to the one he had sought refuge behind earlier, as a regained Greaves withdrew his pistol and fired wildly.

Tom crawled along the length of marble seating, as bullets whistled above. He rounded the corner of the squared seating and afforded himself a surveying glance over the top of the marble. He saw Greaves striding between the rows of marble seats, idly walking past the Sig Sauer that lay in the middle.

Tom glanced at the stun baton and observed that the switch was located about two thirds down the baton. He gave it a test and was comforted by the electric blue spark as it danced in a jaunty, jagged line. Greaves rounded the corner where he had expected Tom to be and let loose a volley of shots. He screamed out in frustration, his prey eluding him once again. Tom rounded the corner once again and began to crawl, separated now only by the metre or so of marble seating, the various foliage in the centre affording him extra camouflage. Tom heard Greaves eject another magazine, replacing it methodically with a new one, the man's breathing wild.

Tom afforded himself a glance up to the concourse above and saw Gerry bearing down on Thompson, holding his knife to the man's neck. Thompson, his stronger arm holding fast, kept the blade from his throat, a bearlike intensity to his stature.

Another series of wild shots. Tom flinched, he was now at the final corner of the marble construct, and upon rounding it he would be able to retrieve his Sig Sauer and bring an end to this rectangular stalemate. Tom made to turn when, a grunt from above followed by a quick movement of black followed. Tom screamed out as Gerry was flung from the concourse above. He landed, breaking through the foliage located within the centre of the marble seating. Tom made to grab his Sig Sauer, to go to his friend's aid when Greaves burst from the foliage behind him, landing heavily upon Tom's back, holding firmly onto his neck. Tom pivoted wildly, sending Greave's gun flying as he swung around giddily; effectively piggybacking his would-be killer. They stumbled frantically forward.

"Squeal piggy, squeal," Greaves hissed.

"You... first", Tom panted as he brought up the stun baton and drove it deep into Greave's arm, pushing the switch.

He felt Greaves go limp. Without hesitation, he dislodged him from his shoulder into the water fountain, the man enveloped by the water. Tom stumbled backwards, slipping upon the floor, his weakened legs once again deceiving him. In a crawling fashion he made his way back towards the Sig Sauer, his hip practically paralysed.

"Don't fucking move!" Greaves hissed through gritted teeth.

Tom reeled round and saw the man standing within the centre of the fountain, sodden, water trickling from his jaw and chin, a substantial cut above his right eye. In his left hand he held one of Hertz's discarded grenades. He smiled, his teeth clamped shut, the pin clearly evident for Tom to see. Tom held the stun baton tentatively by the bottom, obscuring it with his forearm so that Greaves could not see it. He slipped it into his pocket, button end up, not wanting to mistakenly set it off in his pocket.

"One more move and I'm not going to be the only one in here missing limbs," Greaves spat the pin free as he said this, "now, I want you to slowly get up and kick the gun away. Make a move for it and we both go up," Greaves lifted the grenade higher, emphasising the threat.

Tom nodded in compliance and kicked the gun out of reach. As he did so with his back turned to Greaves for the briefest of seconds, he tore a strip of duct tape from his left forearm, grimacing as he did so. The wound opened instantaneously. Tom's stomach lurched. However, he found himself grateful that he had decided to patch himself up in such a crude manner.

"Good. Now with your hands in the air, I want you to walk towards me," Greaves barked.

Tom did so slowly, hands in the air.

"Stop!" he ordered when Tom was about three metres shy.

"Ok, you've got me! I'm unarmed," Tom replied, his voice steeped in defeatism.

"That's the problem with people like you; you don't know what's good for you! You don't know when your race is run. You only understand the firm hand, shock and awe. You lack the spine to act of you own accord. The world needs people like me, to think for you, to act for you," Greaves snarled, patting his chest with the grenade.

"Now be a good boy, toss me that memory stick, retreat several steps and then lay down flat on your stomach. Wouldn't want a water fight, now would we?"

Tom nodded dejectedly. He held it aloft so that Greaves could see it. Greaves nodded his understanding. With a deep breath, Tom tossed the memory stick underhand but deliberately aimed from the centre of Greaves mass, towards the centre of his tactical vest. The memory stick pinged off the torch upon his right strap and ricocheted downwards. Greaves panicked, displaying his best rendition of a one-armed juggler as the memory stick bounced from the palm of his hands. His face was a picture of fear not wanting his bonus to land in the water, rendering it defunct.

Tom acted quickly, Greaves line of vision momentarily broken. He removed the stun baton and tightly wound the duct tape around the n switch, ensuring he kept his hand free of the end. The duct tape, now bound tightly around the tubular device, maintained that the switch remained constantly on. Greaves called out in joy as he caught the memory stick, before holding it aloft, triumphant. It was short lived.

"Sir, I have the blueprints," he screamed with joyful euphoria.

He reeled round, facing Tom once again. The hand that encased the grenade dropped to his side. He smiled back at Tom.

"And now, if you don't mind little lamb, get on your belly," Greaves gloated.

Tom made to kneel, ensuring all the while that the still crackling stun baton remained out of sight.

"On second thoughts, go fuck yourself," Tom chimed insolently.

Greaves sucked his lips and nodded.

"You got some balls; I'll give you that. I can't wait to lob them off and send them to…"

Suddenly, Tom made a bolting movement, tossing the stun baton at Greaves feet. The baton travelled quickly through the air and was quickly shrouded by the sizeable displacement of water. Greaves made to scream but immediately began to judder, his teeth clamped shut, his eyes rolling into the back of his head. The area around his prosthetic legs began to smoke and a sizzling noise could be heard. Greaves fell against the statue of Britannia, which only served to ensure he remained in the water, the ornate metallic finish of the statute only serving to act as a further conductor.

The man's whole body began to spasm wildly forcing him to stand bolt upright like a pylon. It was at this point that Tom recalled that in his left hand he had been holding the grenade. Tom began to edge his way backwards, his eyes never leaving the incendiary device. Greaves fingers were twitching as if he were playing an invisible flute, only ever having no more than two fingers on the grenade at one time. Tom took shelter behind the marble seating, picking up his Sig Sauer as he did so. He braced himself, the macabre vision of a stuttering Greave's foaming mouth sending an icy chill down Tom's spine. Tom peered round the corner. Greaves metallic legs had begun to take on a tapping motion as if he were dancing, the water churning around him, veins protruding from his neck.

Greaves locked eyes with Tom as they slowly rolled down from his skull, a long line of spit hanging from his clenched jaws. He swayed his arm back slightly, indicating that he was trying to throw the grenade in his direction. Tom raised the Sig Sauer and took aim. It was not needed. Greaves fingers betrayed him; his bizarre mime routine abruptly ceased. All his fingers jolted free of the grenade and with them, the grenade which fell into the fountain with a heavy splash.

Tom took cover behind the corner of the marble seating and covered his ears, once again maintaining his mouth was wide open. It had seemed as if he had waited forever for the blast that when it finally did, it almost took him by surprise, the noise deafening. The fountain burst its marble banks and its contents surged out of the structure. Tom made to stand but was swept away by the torrent of water, the marble floor lubricating a trail for him; the water briefly washing over him, sweeping him onto his side. When he finally came to a rest, he peered out at the damage around him. Chunks of marble, crimson water and a medley of body parts and clothing from three separate insurgents lined the floor. Amazingly and although dislodged and on its side, the Britannia centrepiece, was still largely intact.

Tom made to stand up when his hand knocked something. Greaves scorched prosthetic leg, still enclosed in a charred boot, the famous SAS mantra still legible. Tom picked up the metallic leg, wincing slightly upon gripping the warm metal. He turned it over in his hands, facing back towards the fountain. He composed himself briefly, Thompson still unaccounted for, the true scalp of which Tom wanted to claim.

"How's that for shock and awe?" he grunted, dropping the leg from his grasp.

An anguished groan came from close by.

Gerry. Tom bounded over the marble seat before him, parting the foliage with his spare hand, Sig Sauer in the other. He barged onwards; a clearing emerging ahead, snapped branches and flattened foliage alerting him to Gerry's resting place as well as a substantial amount of blood that now coated them. Spurned on, he moved forward quicker still, branches hitting him in the face and upper torso as he did so.

Finally, he broke through a clearing in the spacious vegetation, Gerry now visible. He rushed to his side, squatting down beside him, cradling the back of the man's skull. He lay on a network of broken branches and greenery. Tom placed the Sig Sauer beside him and listened intently, his resolve strengthened upon hearing a low rasping rattle. He gripped Gerry's chin and shook lightly.

"Gerry? Gerry, come on mate," Tom pleaded.

Gerry's eyes rolled up, a fevered gleam, once vibrant, now encased in a grey expression. His dry lips, lightly caked in blood, broke into a weak smile. He reached up and grasped Tom's hand. Tom gripped it back, still cradling Gerry's head with the other, his upper torso upon his lap.

"How many left?" Gerry rasped.

"Just one... Thompson," Tom said with as determined resolve.

Gerry nodded slightly at this.

"The bastard... he overpowered me. Got some good shots in, stuck him in the arm good...his legs busted too," Gerry beamed, much of his jovial undertone now absent.

"I saw that," Tom voiced meekly, scanning the extent of Gerry's injuries.

The realisation of his death began to creep in. Gerry caught his worried, surveying glance.

"Hey lad, it's alright," Gerry said mustering all his goodwill.

A tear rolled down Tom's eye. Slightly ashamed, he looked away.

"I couldn't have done any of this without you. I-" Tom could not find the words.

Gerry shook his head.

"Tom, you rescued me first remember. This, all of it, you've gone above and beyond... none of this is your fault. I'm lying here because my assignment brought me here, you're here because you couldn't stand by... let injustice have its day," Gerry coughed at the end slightly, blood flecking his chin.

"He has to die," Tom stated bluntly.

Gerry nodded slightly, exhaling with a rasping slurp.

"Tom, what you told me, when you found me, what he did to your brother, what he's done here today... the root needs to be dug out, removed. He cannot be allowed to leave... not just for the sake of the hostages or the city..." another violent cough, "because, he can't live another day propagating his bile. After today, people will flock to his cause...his contagion, it needs to be contained at the source."

Tom nodded in agreement, Gerry's grasp faltering slightly. He had envisioned the two of them walking out of here together. A pounding could now be heard off in the distance as well as an angle grinder being used.

"Whatever happens, don't let them rob you of your vengeance. Many will say there's nothing in revenge... a cell's too good for that animal. Bring the fight to him..." Gerry spluttered his head beaded with sweat, his eyes bloodshot and feverish.

"Talking of which, sounds like the cavalry have finally arrived," Tom perked up, turning towards the direction of the noise, patting Gerry's hand.

"Time to get you out of..." Tom turned to smile at Gerry and found his eye's vacant. He tested the man's hand and felt it flop from his grasp.

"No, no, no," he pleaded, shaking Gerry slightly.

His throat began to shake, his eyes engulfed with tears. He tested Gerry's pulse and wept upon finding no rhythmic throb. He tried again to no avail, shaking his lifeless body, urging him awake. Finally, his efforts proving fruitless, he brought down his hand across Gerry's forehead, closing his eyes where he paused in an anguished moment of reflection.

"You... rescued me. Thank you," Tom softly whispered to himself as he patted Gerry's chest in thanks, wiping away his eyes.

He inhaled, steadying his shaking limbs and with that he retrieved the Sig Sauer from beside his fallen companion. As he stepped free from the embrace of the foliage, he caught Thompson as he did so, hobbling in the direction of the construction site ahead, using Gerry's broom handle as a crutch. He disappeared through the wooden carcass of the blown apart doorway, intending to make his escape. Tom was still unsure how he intended to achieve this feat, the local area teeming with various agencies. It mattered little; he would not be given the opportunity to execute the remaining phase of his plan. He strode onwards, tears having now dried, his bloodlust not yet sated.

CHAPTER TWENTY-THREE: DEEPER DOWN THE RABBIT HOLE

Brian fought his way to the edge of the cordon, the throngs of press and spectators hindering his progress. Brian had explained his circumstance to his shift manager and was immediately given compassionate leave, ordered, no matter the outcome, to take the rest of the week, longer if he needed. He had texted Pam, simply stating that Tom was alive and that he had given him a message, a message that he needed to get to the appropriate authorities. He added that he knew he was being obscure but due to time limitations he would have to get back to her, adding his love and reassurance that Tom was safe, slightly embellishing the latter sentiment.

Brian's heart leapt into his throat upon seeing the partially obscured West Acre Point, the structure ablaze. The billowing smoke could be made out even in the pitch blackness of the winter's night, its mammoth silhouette defined by the pyre it had now become. Currently, the corner of the building closest to the crowd, four blocks away, was open-mouthed, smoke and fire being sucked into it, fuelling the ravenous fire. The sounds of additional fire engine sirens could be heard off in the distance, not that Brian imagined they would be able to douse the flames for danger of displeasing the insurgents within.

Brian came within five metres of the barricade, the press facing back in his direction, delivering broadcasts to the nation, cameras illuminating their features. The newsreaders obscured the police officers who stood behind the barricade like blank faced sentinels. Brian stood on the tips of his toes, swaying from side to side, his right-hand waving, trying to attract their attention. It was at this point that a large, armoured police vehicle rounded a corner several metres ahead of the police cordon, the noise causing an excited chorus of speculation. Brian feared what this meant, Tom's words of warning ringing in his ears. His heart was beating away erratically in his chest.

At that moment Brian saw a Police van to his left. In the back sat two police officers, both cradling Styrofoam cups of tea. Brian began to cut across the crowds in a sideways, scything fashion. People muttered to themselves, one even shoving Brian slightly when he stood on the man's foot accidently. Brian was mute to the disapproving masses, with more at play than they could or would, most likely ever know.

Breathlessly Brian made it to the van and sucked in an inhalation of air. The two Police Officers on duty looked up exasperated, no doubt tired at already providing answers to the British public and various news crews, which they themselves did not have. The shorter of the two, a balding man stood replacing his helmet.

"What can we do you for, sir?" the man asked, failing to hide the disappointment at having been disturbed during his break.

"The building... my son's in there," Brian started.

The police officer held up a calming hand and empathetically nodded.

"I'm sorry to hear that sir, if you head over to the back of the crowd, there's a desk that you can report your son's name and description to..." the officer stopped upon Brian waving his hand, still catching his breath.

"No, no listen. My son is inside, he's the one fighting back...against the people who are doing this," Brian spoke quickly.

The officer turned to his respective partner dumbfounded. As if to establish that Brian now had his attention, he placed his tea down with a start.

"Go on sir," the officer urged.

"My son, Tom, he said there's not many left alive, that he was the one responsible for taking a majority of the others out," Brian gasped, his breathing slowly returning.

"Have you got any identification on you sir?" the officer quizzed Brian before turning to his colleague, "Radio this in Stuart."

His partner immediately started muttering into his shoulder radio. Brian wrestled with his wallet, his hands shaking; they had not stopped since he had discovered his son's plight, Tom's phone call only worsening his anxious demeanour. He finally gained purchase of his driver's licence and held it up. The officer scanned it and nodded approvingly.

"Ok, Brian. You say your son is in the centre, that he is fighting back. How can you corroborate this?"

The officer now joined Brian outside of the Police van, indicating for Brian to sit upon the step of the vehicle. His partner handed Brian a fresh cup tea.

"His phone, it was dying but he managed to fill me in, about thirty minutes ago. He's ex-Army," Brian reeled off his response.

The officer nodded, his colleague slid past Brian and stepped out of the van, whispering something into his colleague's ear. The officer nodded, his eyes never leaving Brian.

"How long ago?" he asked his colleague.

Brian looked up nervously, looking between the two men. He feared something was being withheld, the mood now soured by the worried tenor of the officer's voice. The officer nodded and he knelt before Brian. Brian raised a shaky hand to his head and inhaled deeply.

"Oh God, what is it?" Brian whispered.

The officer looked sheepishly back at Brian.

"What your son's doing in there, is fantastic, I mean the guy's a hero," the officer started, working his way up to a point that was taking its sweet time.

He caught Brian's expression, a look he had unfortunately seen many times before on doorsteps across the Capital, the expression of a parent, not wishing to hear bad news but desiring closure, nonetheless. The endless possibilities of what may have befallen their child consuming their very soul.

"Our Commander says that a call was put in around the same time, from a woman, called Anna. Do you know of anyone called Anna that may know your son?" the officer pressed.

Brian thought upon this and shook his head, "No, I mean it's a possibility but... is my son ok?" Brian asked frustrated.

"Of that sir, we have no idea. The Commander just stated that your son, upon checking his phone log with his provider, talked to this woman prior to yourself. The women contacted her local Police station, stating that your son had established that the insurgents inside the building... that they intended to bring it down, killing everyone inside, no matter what. I have to ask this sir, did your son offer any additional information on this matter?" the officer gave his colleague another cautious look.

"No, he just said that they had killed women, children... that he was going to attempt to take down the remaining men. What's going to happen to my son?"

Brian looked back at the officer with complete shock, his son having withheld such information. Brian detected the officer was withholding information from Brian also.

"Between you and me sir, those armoured vehicles behind us..." he pointed over his shoulder in the direction of the armoured vehicles, three now visible, engines still running, "I'm not sure if you're aware but about fifteen minutes ago, the hostiles inside killed the Prime Minister."

Gerry shook his head; he had not seen or heard of any news coverage during his frantic journey over. The journey itself was hazy at best. The police officer continued.

"Given the current series of events that you've just relayed to us, that's more than understandable sir. As you can imagine, this is a first for the nation and many at the top are now very keen to bring the whole mess to a close. We've had orders to evacuate this site and the surrounding area, to give the appropriate people the room in which they need to operate. What I'm trying to say Mr Hawkins, is that they are going to attempt to breach the building again."

"But what about the hostages, the devices around the city? They said they'd detonate them in their message," Brian hastily formulated.

"That's all that I can say at present sir, honestly but I'm sure that they're going to try and save the hostages, as a priority, your son included," the officer empathetically patted Brian on the shoulder.

"Now, what I'm going to do is transfer you to one of my seniors. They'll take care of you sir, probably even be able to shine some more light on the matter for you but we need to get you and the rest of these people out of here ASAP," the officer squeezed Brian's shoulder.

The order had passed down the line and the crowd were starting to filter backwards, unsure, some questioning the Police. The news crews, still addressing their cameras live, were moved from their positions, their attached camera crews, tracking their movement as they were ushered backwards.

The officer gawked back at Brian slightly, the man not moving, unsure of how to proceed. He felt such pity for the man who sat before him; his vacant gaze giving little away as to what he must be thinking currently. Of that, he could only speculate.

"For what it's worth," Brian looked up at the man, the officer's words stirring him from his slumber, "I hope your son succeeds... the nation owes him a great debt, he's a national hero. No matter what happens, when the country finds out...about what he's done, he'll be paraded through the streets," the officer said, uneasy and unsure as to whether he had overstepped the mark.

Brian smiled lightly.

"I just want him alive and in one piece, nation aside," Brian countered, an honest quality to his voice.

The officer nodded back in return, humbled by the man's humility.

(CHAPTER BREAK)

Tom slowly advanced towards the opening of the construction site, smoke still billowing from its entrance. The sprinklers continued their deluge, his upper torso and hands were cold and trembled slightly, largely from the cold, a sprinkling of fear mixed in for good measure. The mangling of metal behind him grew louder, the strike force battering down the doors with what sounded like an armoured vehicle of some sort. He made to enter when a noise startled him to his right. He reeled round; gun readied and immediately dropped his guard. Opposite, a man shook lightly on the metal grill that had been brought down to secure the hostages within the abandoned outlet.

"Help us! Please," the voice whispered imploringly.

Upon hearing this, others joined him at the grill, a chorus of jumbled pleas emanating from within. They reminded Tom of refugees on a charity appeal upon seeing a UN convoy or the Red Cross pull into their village, battered, starved and fearful yet still possessing a morsel of hope.

Tom paused and gave the shutters a cursory glance, the explosive device was wired up about a third of the way from the ground. Tom ushered for them to stop with his hands and stepped towards them, his back angled towards the hostages, never taking his eyes from the open fracture which led into the construction site. He came about a metre shy of the grill when he stopped. Some of the hostages had taken to joyous sobbing upon seeing Tom whilst others paced within their makeshift cage.

Still looking at the doorway ahead, Tom sensing someone to his left, muttered, "I'm going to turn around now but I need one of you to keep an eye on that door for me. Do not take your eyes off it. If you see anything let me know and quickly, there's still one left."

A melody of excited exchanges rose upon Tom's declaration.

Tom was conscious of time and abruptly asserted, "Can someone do that for me?"

Someone shifted to his right and a man spoke up, an East London dialect pickling his words.

"I've got your back son."

Tom turned to meet the man and nodded his thanks. The man looked frail and old but a wild determination to survive burnt vividly in his eyes. His clothes were dishevelled, caked in sweat and a scattering of blood. Tom now turned to face the grill, his Sig Sauer still readied. He made to speak when a man hammered upon the steel grill and Tom shot his hand up.

"Stop, stop, stop!" he cooed.

The hostages inside were a sorry sight in the dull light. All were bound, some by their hands, others by both their feet and their hands. They huddled together, many sullied with blood or dirt, drenched in sweat and a fevered grip of terror. The smell singed Tom's nostrils, many of these people having not been afforded the luxury of a toilet or deodorant in well over several hours. And their eyes, if Tom lived to the age of a hundred, he would never forget the tainted glare of their eyes, the horrors that had befallen them this day, would forever mar them.

"Please you've got to get us out, they're going to blow us all up, and they've put devices all over the place," a petrified man, in a slightly soiled navy-blue suit, implored.

Tom held up his free hand in a gesture of calm before pointing down towards the direction of the explosive device.

"You need to stop banging on the shutter, right now," Tom proclaimed, the cluster of curious hostages staring back at him in bemused. Tom continued, "There's a device attached to the shutter, an explosive one, sudden movements could set it off, so please step back and away from the shutter."

The crowd reciprocated hastily, one woman who had been resting her bound palms upon it, peeled her fingers back through gritted teeth, one by one, until she was no longer making contact, before scuttling off back into the confines of the outlet. Another man made to speak but Tom interjected, painfully aware of time. Tom surmised that even with the extent of Thompson's injuries, they would only slow him down so much. Added to that, the centre would soon be breached and swarming with armed personnel, which would render any chance of him capturing Thompson, allowing him to exact his revenge, unattainable.

"I need you all to listen. The man who was in charge, Thompson, he's managed to get free, escaping through that site," Tom pointed back over his shoulder.

He glanced quickly at his makeshift guard, who stared intently back at the construction site.

"Oh my God," someone wailed.

"Now from what I understand he has a device that he is willing to trigger but not before he has put a safe distance between this building and the authorities. You hear that noise? That's the sound of tactical teams who are breaching and you, along with disarming those bombs, are going to be there first priority. Now I could most likely disarm this device..." Tom motioned downwards with his eyes, "but there is nothing to say that he wouldn't trigger it as I was doing it. Instead, I need to catch up to him and stop him. So, I'm going to need you all to sit tight," Tom scanned the crowd, seeking their approval.

Many looked unsure but it was the elderly man acting as his sentry, still transfixed and unflinching, that spoke up for the crowd.

"I didn't survive the Blitz as a boy to be bombed to buggery by another fascist. We'll hang tight lad and we'll make sure to let the authorities know that you've gone after him and about him detonating the charges," he recanted.

He had a boyish defiance that had been hardened by several decades of hard but honest living, his steely perseverance tempered by the fiery determination to overcome, to not be culled by any aggressor.

At that point, a huge explosion rang out from the other end of the complex and Tom flinched severely. The hostages inside began to wail, many taking cover, cupping their hands in their heads, a panicked euphoria filling the air. Tom stared down the concourse and could just make out a shutter, partially on fire, about three quarters now torn away from the wall. Strong lights protruded, dancing across the floor and furthest wall, illuminating the payload delivered by the sprinklers. Tom swung round, smiling at the hostages.

"It's ok; they just set off one of the devices left by the men with the guns. You're safe; the good guys are nearly through. Now, I need to go," Tom made to leave, some calling from within, begging for him to help them.

As he strode past the shutter, he stopped, the elderly man's eyes burning into the back of his skull. Tom stepped back and turned to face the man, who surprisingly, after all that had happened, still watched the construction site.

"My daughter... she had a little boy with her, my grandson. She's in here with me, distraught. That man, the one you said went through that door...he took him. We're worried sick... we need to know... Is he still?" the man choked up slightly, tears gathering within pools at the base of his eyes.

Tom lowered his gaze; unknowingly, he shook his head gently. The man on the other side of the cage nodded lightly in acceptance, the tears breaking free. Still he kept guard.

"I found him and I tried to...but they," Tom stopped, overwhelmed once again with remorse at his own shortcomings.

Tom repentantly looked up to meet the man's gaze. For the first time the man broke his line of sight and stared back at him through greying, sodden eyes.

"No parent should ever have to outlive their child," he sadly declared.

Tom now realised that the man himself was a parent, his daughter inside the outlet with him, the youngest of their lineage gone. The elderly man gathered his last remnants of communication, his ability to verbalise his feelings now largely obstructed and spoke briefly.

"When you find him...kill him. The world, it's already a bleak enough place... his ability to breathe, it's an affront to all that's good, peaceful," he paused a fresh cascade of tears fell from his wrinkled eyes, "little Harry... he deserved a world better than this one."

The old man broke down into sobs and another captive soothed him, rubbing his shoulder with her bound hands.

Tom froze upon hearing the little boy's name for the first time. The boy's smiling features coming back to him, the face of a boy who had his whole life ahead of him, a soul pure and unsullied by the cruelties of this world. Tom tried to formulate his condolences, to indicate in some way to his Grandfather that he too shared in his grief, his guilt. All he could muster instead were four words.

"You have my word," Tom whispered, he too, guttural with distress.

The fire began to ignite once again in his stomach as despair turned to adrenaline, doubts about what he had done, no longer of any concern. He strode forward, the sprinklers now serving as a cold shower offering clarification, absolving him of his sins, his cause if he had ever been in doubt, reinforced by the words of the bereaved. As long as he drew breath, whether it be several minutes or several decades, he would ensure that Thompson never deprived another man, woman or child of their kin, ever again.

The smoke swallowed Tom whole as he stepped forth into the carcass of the building site. He waited briefly for his eyes to adjust; the room now absent of any light whatsoever. A small fire illuminated the far corner of the room but had been all but doused by the sprinklers. Tom reached up and unclipped the torch from his tactical vest. He gave the room a cursory three-hundred-and-sixty-degree arc, his gun levelled at the same height, his torch clad hand, crossed below his right offering a stable base on which to fire his Sig Sauer.

Satisfied he stepped towards the crates to his left, the location in which he had stored Anthony, encased in bubble wrap. He scanned the area with his torch, disheartened to see that the wooden boxes were slightly blackened, the bubble wrap charred and melted around the edges. Eerily some of the plastic bubbles had popped of their own accord, most likely from the heat.

The area was coated in a vast puddle and Tom's feet slapped upon the floor as he shuffled, peeling back the charred layers of plastic sheeting. The edges had sealed with the heat and Tom was forced to holster his Sig Sauer in place of his knife. He slit the plastic sheeting methodically, cutting a V shape, careful and steady like a surgeon. Satisfied he pulled back the plastic triangle and strangely relieved, looked upon his brother's corpse. He had sustained no further damage. Tom replaced the plastic sheeting. He silently placed the knife within its scabbard, the blade calling out slightly upon being returned to its humble abode.

As he did so, he observed that there was a smaller, charred flick-knife at his feet with the message *'What's up Doc?'* engraved into the pewter hilt. Tom ascertained whether it was still in full working order, of which it was and concealed it within his right-hand pocket. Tom was disgusted by the artefact, the message upon it providing further clarification, if it were needed, of the group's lackadaisical penchant towards murder. That said, he may have use for it later.

Tom ears suddenly pricked up. He instinctively held his breath. A noise that resembled a penny being thrown into a wishing well echoed out, a splash of water deep and hollow, quite substantial in size. He rounded the beam of the torch cutting through the dank darkness. He levelled the Sig Sauer once again and pointed it in the beam's direction, scanning the area around the crevice. There was rubble everywhere, scraps of clothing. Another splash came.

Tom edged closer to the yawning pit, his breathing shallow. He edged the light upwards and was shocked to see that part of the ceiling above the pit had given way, most likely due to the sheer force of the blast. As he eyed up the jagged hole above, he traced with his torch a piece of cement, the size of a fifty pence piece, come loose and disappear within the pit. The piece of cement skittered and cracked off the flanks of the pit before splashing into the water beneath.

Tom edged closer and shone his light into the pit, scanning its jagged circumference before illuminating the bottom of the twelve-foot drop. The water below was murky, a white sheen to the surface as ripples from the dislodged piece of cement still wrinkled the water's surface. Tom's torch came to a rest upon the right-hand side of the pit, a large trail of blood glistening. Seeking further clarification, he moved his torch up and down the pit and ascertained that it must be Thompson's, a trail left by him slithering his way down into the pit. Tom grabbed a loose chunk of cement and threw it into the water. He listened intently, trying to evaluate the waters depth.

He had been so absorbed that when the air abruptly shifted behind him along with a scathing noise as something heavy whistled through the air, it had been too late for him to react. The object came down hard between his shoulder blades. Tom arched his back forward in agony, the Sig Sauer dropping from his grasp and clattering down the side of the pit, its descent followed by a substantial gurgle as the pistol was slowly digested by the stagnant water.

Tom instinctively anchored himself with his right palm as he collapsed to the floor. He made to turn when the second blow came sternly upon his right arm. Tom's kneeling stance became weakened, his kneecaps feeling as though they were departing his very body. With this absurd observation, Tom was knocked off balance and into the awaiting pit. His head took a blow upon the hard-jagged edge of the pit before he was sprung free off the wall, bouncing off the adjacent shafts edge, this time hitting his hip and lower leg. He was spun at a jaunty angle, facing upwards and out of the pit just before he was engulfed by the squalid water below.

The water filled Tom's nostrils and throat, before he lightly touched the bottom, the water proving to be quite substantial in its depth. Tom fought briefly against the weight of the sewage, his eyes clamped shut, his soul feeling as if it were being slowly ebbed away. He felt a surge of water being forced downwards upon his calves and he bobbed briefly to the surface before his frail limbs carried him below again. A foot came down heavily upon his right calve and he yelped out, ingesting more of the fetid water.

Another surge of water came from behind his head, the noise only exemplified by the water. Tom felt a hand clasp around his collar, and he was thrust from the water, choking heavily, sucking in air. His regurgitations battling his urge to breath.

"Am I going to need my shots after this," Thompson bellowed, his voice carried off down the tunnel, audible even to Tom, his hears full of water.

Thompson's breathing was laboured, as he walked before Tom, dragging him clear of the water. Suddenly he stopped and turned Tom around, his features materialising inches from Tom's face, Tom regurgitating once again as he did so. He vomited up a brown liquid, the taste of which burnt his tonsils.

"Breathe it in boy, what a privilege. The veins of London, her sewers, the lifeblood of her fine vessel," Thompson gleefully reported with an embellished tone.

Tom's vison cleared and for the first time he noticed at intervals within the tunnel, there had been placed a cord of temporary lights, housed in mesh cages, the extent of Thompson's planning taking Tom aback momentarily. They had to have been planning their attack extensively and incognito for months, gaining access both to West Acre Point and the sewers below. Tom noticed for the first time also that Thompson was wearing a pair of waders, the kind used by fly fisherman. He shuffled slightly, his wounded leg ailing him. He used one of the wader's braces as a makeshift sling. In his other hand, a Remington shotgun, trained at Tom's forehead.

Tom thrust himself up slightly, his body throbbing and grazed. He made to stand, sickened by the fowl water in which he sat, cautious of the infections and diseases he would be contracting from the open sores upon his body. The water came up to knee height in this part of the tunnel. Had it have been that shallow in the area Tom had fallen, he would most definitely be dead. Tom could not disguise his shocked expression, twinned with utter amazement at the extent of work that had gone on below. His hands slipped upon the smooth face of the brickwork, his knees still weak, the ice-cold water only serving to sap his strength further.

The sewers afforded Thompson and his men the perfect escape route, shrouding them from those above that sought to imprison, maim or kill them. A network of tunnels; countless deviations if they were followed, in which they could lose both themselves and whoever dared follow. A perfect escape: undetected, unimaginable in scale and truly unfathomable, the pandemonium above only serving to further cover their escape. The endless demands, the threat of explosive devices around the city, it had all been done to further establish the men as martyrs. They set themselves up to the nation as not wanting to be bartered with, as people who like so many before, sought no escape, no deals, their façade serving as a smokescreen to the intelligence services and the Police.

"Don't get up. Like the rat that you are, you're going to die down here," gobbed Thompson, wading further from Tom's reach, into the mouth of the tunnel.

"You hang about in sewers for months on end and you call me a rat," Tom discernibly returned.

"Needs must," Thompson snorted, "talking of which, be a good sport and with the thumb and forefinger on your left hand, reach across very slowly and remove that knife safely," he wagged the finger of his injured arm within its brace, "in its scabbard mind! We don't want any accidents now do we. And toss it to your left".

Tom did as he was instructed, all the while never taking his eyes from Thompson's.

"All those women and children up there, my brother included, you going to try and file them under, needs must?" Tom defiantly stated as he removed the knife, an awkward endeavour what with him being right-handed. He tossed it aside.

A loud splash filled the tunnel, allowing Thompson to proceed.

"Immaterial," Thompson stated bluntly, "as am I, as are you. We all have our part to play, some fight, some die. That is how revolution's rocky path is laid. The people are the tarmac of this nation, unless they mobilise and solidify their suffering, seek out a new path, we cannot hope for the path to be smooth and absent of potholes."

"You wouldn't dare try and justify yourself to me! Not after what you've done, to my family, those people up there. After today, the nation's going to see you for what you truly are," Tom snapped, innate of any willingness to understand this man's deluded ideals of grandeur.

Thompson pulled a face that demonstrated he was not convinced, shaking his head slightly.

"I doubt it. All of the evidence, all of the witnesses, you included, will be gone, buried beneath tonnes of rubble, a new foundation, on which to build upon. They'll pick through the wreckage of course... hell they might even find some of my men, what's left of them anyway. Even if they do identify them, they will never be able to conclusively lay the blame at their feet, most importantly mine. I am an unknown variable. The government would much rather chalk it up to some terrorist cell, no survivors left in a Jihadi strike upon the West, conspiracy theories will flourish of course and let them. Resentment will increase in the masses; dissenters left and right will call for the heads of the very government who sought to cover up the massacre of its own citizens. You see Tom, when this building comes down, with it, goes the truth and any social cohesion. My conscience is clear."

"The guilty man always proclaims his innocence," Tom snarled back, sickened by Thompsons absurd ramblings.

"History leaves behind only survivors and victors. There is no place for those who have failed, no one remembers second place, as no one will remember your futile efforts here today, all be they frustratingly impressive ones," Thompson bitterly relented.

"You mean your little club? They were second rate, bargain bin at best," Tom replied.

"They served their purpose and were given a purpose in return. Before I introduced them to the cause, they were broken soldiers, scarred and discarded by the country they risked their lives to serve," Thompson bragged.

"You used them," Tom came back, neutral.

"They were a means to an end, yes. However, I gave them a cause to live on for, one not found at the bottom of a bottle or on some physiatrist's chair or prescription pad. I helped them begin to put the pieces back together," Thompson stated dutifully as if he had fulfilled some kind of civil duty.

"I can't wait to see how you're going to try and put yourself back together when I…"

Tom abruptly stopped as the Remington's barrel was shoved aggressively under his chin, forcing him to look upwards; the stock cradled in the crook of Thompson's injured arm.

"You know you make a lot of threats for a man sitting in shit and piss, some of which is probably your own. I admire your perseverance; it seems there is still some hope left within you after all. But it is misplaced boy. Know that just like your brother, the cause is all. Britain will return to greatness. The cause does not end with me or my men; we are merely the beginning of what is to come. Those institutions people rally behind; the police, the government, the media, we have members within all of them, ready to disseminate and propagate our message through the very outlets the people of Britain and the world revere."

"They will vote us in, gorge upon news coverage and programming we circulate, our cause at the very heart of the mediums they love to fritter their time away upon idly. PATRIOT is more than just twelve men," Thompson twisted the barrel upon each flourish of arrogant pride.

"That's not what your man… Carling said, he said… you were it," Tom grimaced, his neck arched as far back as it would go, a dew drop blurring his right eye as it meandered along his nose.

Thompson let out a bellow. He knelt and brought the barrel of the Remington with him, forcing Tom's head with it, so that he was once again facing Thompson.

"I would have thought you would have learnt by now," Thompson tutted disapprovingly, "our cause, in an effort of conservation, must be preserved, its flames must not be snubbed out before its very embers have had a chance to ignite. Our cause depends upon deception, second truths. Your brother learnt that the hard way," Thompson smirked.

Tom bit down hard upon the insides of his cheeks, knowing full well Thompson wanted a reaction. He stared back intently, not giving the warlord the briefest glimmer of anguish, not affording him the satisfaction.

"Remarkable what the government were happy for your brother to carry out, all in the name of national security. I knew quite early on yesterday however, from my contact inside government that he was embedded, a spy. The head of our organisation wanted him executed upon finding out this news, I convinced him otherwise. There was still fun to be had yet with your brother. The lengths I forced him to, the people he willingly tortured and brutally murdered," Thompson malevolently chuckled.

Tom made a bolt forward at this, the anger now uncontrollable. Thompson effortlessly swung the stock of the Remington into Tom's right jaw and held the barrel across his captive, pinning him against the brick wall, an exerted fervour descending upon his wild features. What was to come next, he wanted to relish, Tom hanging off of his every word.

"Just like your brother, such anger. I really cannot wait to see whether it runs in the family. Will Mummy and Daddy Hawkins put up as much of a fight, I wonder, when I pay them a little house call?" Thompson snarled, a twisted grin forming.

The barrel dug deep into Tom's upper torso and neck, Thompson's full bodyweight exerted upon it, forcing the air from Tom's lungs.

"I'm going to kill you," Tom panted, using up what little air he had left.

"Promises, promises. Your brother made the same one to me and broke it. Tell me, how does it feel to the cherished memories of your brother brought out into the open? Lain bare, the man he became, a pawn of the government and me?" Thompson accentuated with an interested furrow of his brow, the zeal in his voice nauseating.

Tom smiled back, his hand grabbing at his submerged right leg under the water, "If there's one thing that can't be sold or bought in this world, its memories. Not everyone is like you Thompson, so willing to be bought."

This infuriated Thompson and he drew in closer, now only five inches or so from Tom's face, his hot breath washing over Tom's cheeks. Thompson made sure to manoeuvre the gun at differing scathing angles, keeping purchase and inflicting pain as he did so.

"You're pathetic, a mild inconvenience. Trying to play the hero! Look around, your friend is dead because of me! You're an only child because of me! And because of me, you won't get to be the hero! Your only monument will be made of the very rubble of the building you tried to save," Thompson glowered.

Tom sucked in a deep breath and puffed his chest, driving the Remington slightly away, a concerted look of resilience now burning within his eyes.

"I know that. I don't need to be the hero, never did, never will be. And you're right; you have taken a lot from me. But there's one thing you can't take away from me. Something more valuable than anything you can throw at me. Something I'm never going to let you take," Tom pressed.

Thompson relaxed his grip on the Remington slightly, bewildered by his prisoner's omission, having already taken so much from him, his greed necessitated he take what remained of the man and his unrelenting hope.

"And what's that?" Thompson leered.

Tom's hand found purchase, the water-logged movements of Thompson lifting his weight, only serving to aid his underwater endeavour.

"This fuck off knife!" he roared, thrusting his shoulder forward, knocking the barrel askew.

The flick-knife erupted from the water with a blur, brown water cascading from the hilt of the blade. Thompson made to grab at the blade with his restricted arm but it was weak, caught within the strap of his waders. He yelped out, the pain in his arm driving a bolt up through his torso. The knife came down heavily and unimpeded, driving through Thompson's left eye with a sucking squelch, the blood and bulbous matter of the eye already coating the knife. Thompson screeched as he batted Tom's hand away, before discharging a round from his Remington. Tom's ears rang, the proximity of the buckshot being ejected from the barrel mere inches from his face, the flash momentarily blinding him.

He groped at the wall for support, his minimal hearing picking up a deep splash, something sliding past his boot. Tom massaged his eyes, first making out one of the temporary lights and then the shimmer of its light refracted by the rippling, russet water. For the briefest of moments Tom's heart froze, Thompson's form now absent. He rushed to his feet, his scabbard facing outwards with the blade inwards, concealed. Tom flinched upon hearing a booming blast from above, dust falling from the very foundations as the entrance to the sewer breathed in a new sound, a chorus of joyous cheers, boots beating upon the marble floor above.

He blinked the fetid dredge from his eyes, wishing that he could clear his vision with some item of dry clothing, finding none. The tunnel grew eerily quiet, a distant ripple of water could be heard off in the distance. Tom scanned the tunnel, his breathing strangled. He waited, his feet shifting uneasily in the water, the surface of the floor coated in a slimy sheen.

Suddenly the water before Tom parted, a roaring Thompson breaking the surface, squalid liquid filling the already cramped tunnel, only three metres or so in width. However, what took Tom by surprise was that the squealing starts and fits of anguish emanating from Thompson were moving further away from him. His quarry shuffled forward; his hand clamped over his mutilated eye. He used the walls as support, briefly, rather drunkenly, before yielding to their slippery hue. He slid downwards into the water, one arm and leg impaired, the other hand serving as a makeshift bandage. He thrashed, like a tortoise upon its back, unable to right itself.

Tom followed at a safe pace. Thompson regained some resemblance of calm and all the while fearfully staring back at Tom, began shimmying and scooting backwards upon his backside like a dog with worms. The man's howls had now been replaced with a wild panting, gurgled and inhuman. Tom felt the merest prang of guilt, which was soon forced to the back of his skull upon seeing visions of his brother, of Harry, Gerry, all he had lost. He made slow progress through the porridge-like texture of the water below, an animalistic intensity occupying his glare, humanity now absent, devoid of all mercy.

Thompson removed his hand from his eye, holding it up in a pleading fashion, a substantial amount of blood trickling down his palm. Tom couldn't help but smile back in return, his pain had decreased, a warm numb sensation massaging his battered frame. His free hand came up and pointed accusingly at Thompson.

"That's it, plead. That's how you said my brother died wasn't it? How you wanted me to die," Tom encouraged.

"Without me, this nation, it ceases to..." Thompson came to a halt, realising the utter futility of his own words.

"An eye for an eye Thompson and you took both of my brothers," Tom dragged the knife along the wall of the tunnel, now mere metres away from his spoils.

"Mercy," Thompson squealed.

"All out," Tom abrasively retorted, "you're in my hell now. You should know after all, you built it, brick by brick," Tom hammered upon the brickwork with the knife's scabbard.

Thompson changed tact, "I have a device connected to my heartbeat, if you kill me... London goes up."

"I'd believe that if you actually had a heart. You said it yourself; your cause is built upon deception, second truths. Looks like you rubbed off on me," Tom smiled as he produced a memory stick within an airtight bag he had confiscated whilst on Level Two; identical to the one he had given Greaves.

Thompson looked on in confusion.

"I swapped them out, nice little electrical store up on second, in case you didn't know," Tom smirked as he replaced the memory stick back into his tactical vest.

Thompson's right eye opened wide with horror, his hollowed and blackened left eye, barely stirring.

"They'll find you; you know. They'll have some fun with you before they pry it from your cold, dead hands," Thompson exclaimed.

"Let them come," Tom stepped ever closer.

"You must feel pretty pleased with yourself," Thompson nodded, rising to his feet.

Tom allowed it, relishing the thought of the man making it a fair contest. Thompson staggered, finally regaining his balance.

"Unlike you, I take no pleasure in killing," Tom snapped, serving to justify his actions.

"We all have to start somewhere; you would have made a great disciple. That said, you failed to observe rule number one," he smirked as he placed his hand into pocket.

Tom's muscles tensed; his heart sank as Thompson brought out a second detonator.

"You may have taken my detonator for the pit, this however, is my ace in the hole," Thompson gloated.

His eyes rolled upwards. Tom followed. Consumed by bloodlust, Tom had made the error of not taking in his surroundings. Between the two men, upon the ceiling, flashed a red light, its intermittent flashes highlighting the source of the light. A brick of C4, 6 ounces or so in size, attached to a brickwork support beam. Tom' shoulders dropped. He returned his gaze; Thompson brandishing the device the size of a golf ball, waving it slightly.

"You intend to level a building with that amount?" Tom smirked, a poor attempt at hiding his fear, retreating slightly backwards.

"Not a building. No, that comes from a secondary device, not located onsite, a formality put in place by our employer, in case we were compromised. The cause will live on," Thompson moved his finger over the button, retreating slightly himself now, the gloom of the tunnel beginning to veil his features.

"You wouldn't," Tom chided in, the veneer of superiority fading.

Thompson smiled back in return.

"There is a forgotten, nay almost forbidden word, which means more to me than any other. That word is England," Thompson chanted, punctuating the final word with a press of the button, diving as he did so.

Tom reciprocated covering his head as he plunged himself into the water. The room erupted, the bulbs in the surrounding light fixtures blown out by the shockwave. The supporting brickwork caved in, bringing with it all manner of debris. Tom was sucked outwards by the blast, submerged, his face grating against the rough brick façade.

The noise, even below the water was unreal. A shower of rubble projectiles flew out from all directions, one striking Tom across his coccyx. Tom opened his mouth to scream, once again swallowing more fetid sludge. The heat was intense, the expelled force of the blast screaming as it was forced through the enclosed tunnel. It was at this point that Tom blacked out.

(CHAPTER BREAK)

When Tom came to, he was being dragged by the straps of his vest. Men in military garb, shouting back at him, their voice a mere echo. Tom drunkenly searched before him, the tunnel now pitch-black, his vision swimming. Tom lifted a shaky hand and pointed back in the direction they had just come from. Smoke shrouded the area in which Thompson had detonated the explosive charge.

The two men dragging Tom, both with torches attached to their helmets, glanced back momentarily and for the briefest of moments, illuminated the area where he had been standing before the blast. Through the dense smoke and blurred vision, he saw the unmistakable formation of rubble, blocking the tunnel, effectively cutting off access and any potential hope of pursuit.

Tom began to black out once again, only managing to mutter to himself in his hazed state, the words "Don't let him. I need to stop the secondary device. I…"

The soldiers looked quizzically at one another upon hearing this as they made their way to the end of the tunnel, where a stretcher awaited. The men bundled Tom onto the gurney and stepped back, allowing the medical staff to strap him into the plastic structure that was to be winched from the pit.

"You think he's going to make it?" the first said, wiping his hands.

"For all our sakes, I fucking hope so. London, shit, the nation, is depending on him filling us in on the devices we didn't manage to disarm," replied the second.

"You think the disposal unit managed to disarm them all up there? Frank in disposal said they had enough explosives up there to level the entire building," the first repeated uneasily.

"Doubt we'd still be standing if they hadn't. Not all the insurgents have been accounted for," the second concurred.

"Damn, poor bastard looked pretty dinged up," the first concluded.

"I'll tell you this; the press is going to have a field day with that guy, dead or alive. All of those hostages up there wouldn't be here without him."

The first man nodded in approval upon hearing this, both watching as the gurney was lifted delicately out of the pit.

EPILOGUE: LIFE AFTER DEATH

The rain continued to hammer down upon the London streets, dispelling any hopes of a white Christmas. The weather was bitterly cold, cold enough for snow many had thought, however, not cold enough to deter last minute shoppers and haphazard spouses being out on Christmas Eve. The inner pages of newspapers were adorned with many festive puns, further perpetuating the British need to talk about its weather. *'We're dreaming of a whitewash Christmas'*, *'Hailstone and whine'* and *"Weather Woe, Woe, Woe"* to name but a few of the referential, seasonal taglines.

The headlines upon the front pages of every newspaper however, had not changed. In the two days since the attack, the press had gone into overdrive. A combination of leaks and press statements established that the Islamic Brotherhood for Righteous Judgement had all been a ruse. Members within the Islamic community both condemned the actions of the terrorists propagating hate and established a need to eradicate the further establishment of xenophobic sentiment within the Western world. Many on both sides of the divide used the terrorist's façade as justification for their own causes both inciting and denouncing violence and peace processes against Islamic extremism. As of yet, around a third of the terrorist's identities had been revealed via press conferences and leaked accounts, Shaw and Greaves being two of the names exposed.

The key feature on news channels and within newspapers however had been the British spirit during the two days after the attack, many referring to it as a resurgence of a Blitz mentality amongst the masses. Londoners went about their daily lives as normal, establishing their inability to be cowed or intimidated. Many packed the trains on the Monday of Christmas Eve, their last day of work before a well-earned Christmas break with family or loved ones.

Rallies were held throughout the city comprising of all walks of life: race, gender, religion, social status and age were all immaterial within the mixing pot as thousands descended upon the streets of London and Parliament Square. Most importantly, they were peaceful demonstrations that indicated to both the nation and the worldwide community that Britain, London in particular, would not grovel at the feet of tyranny and fear. Even the cold and torrential rain could not dampen the demonstrator's resolve, the attack serving as the highest death toll the capital had ever faced with regards to a terrorist attack.

The death toll continued to rise hourly as emergency services picked through the wreckage of West Acre Point and would continue to do so, expert opinion and on scene accounts expecting the final count to be considerably higher. The news airing countless footage of black body bags being wheeled out of the complex on gurneys added extra weight to this claim. As the sun came down upon London on Christmas Eve for yet another year, the death toll stood at one hundred and fifteen, excluding the terrorists, who themselves were still being accounted for.

The emergency services worked tirelessly throughout the day and night and for many, Christmas morning and the opening of presents would be exchanged for the opening of body bags, the excitement of discovering the contents of ones presents replaced with that of the daunting horror of what would be revealed around the next corner or level.

Thousands had lined the streets for a national two-minute silence, remembering those who had fallen. Thousands too, stood behind the cordoned off area surrounding West Acre Point, a vigil to those who had fallen within the complex. Many held plaques and banners, emblazoned with portraits of loved ones who had perished inside, heartfelt messages and condolences, both floral and written, lined the barricades. When night fell upon London, the mourners and observers hunkered together, weathering the storm, cradling their candles, ensuring their light was not extinguished.

James Braham, under laws previously passed, was sworn into his role as interim Prime Minister, the nation never having lost a serving Prime minster to assassination. When he addressed the nation, he declared both his personal loss, having lost a great leader and friend in Andrew Pierce as well as the nation. Flanked by the London Mayor and Jonathan Benley, he spoke of a nation grieving in its loss, a *'Bereaved Britain,'* as he coined it, which many rather considered, was in bad taste. He spoke of Britain's need to be united, establishing that much would emerge from the various ongoing investigations within the forthcoming days, weeks and months and the necessity for Britain to be patient as well as cautious in its demonization and declarations of blame.

Braham finally went on to state that the nation's part to play within Pierce's death, via social media, needed to be investigated, with lessons needing to be learned. He established that the attack was one the likes of which Britain had never seen and established that contingencies would need to be considered to prevent it from ever happening again.

To the people that took part in the online jury, calling for Pierce's execution, he established that there would be no formal reprimands issued, however, declared the nation and nations around the world should take note of the dangers surrounding social networking and its ability to serve as judge, jury and consequently in Pierce's case, executioner. He established that there would be a confidential number for those who took part in the voting online, where those suffering from feelings of guilt, anxiety or regret, could phone and speak to trained specialists and consultants, impartially and without the fear of prosecution.

The final lines of his speech professed his need for the support of the British people both in supporting his newly appointed role as their new Prime Minister and in picking up the pieces of a broken Britain.

His final lines adorned double page spreads across the nation; *"When the world is coming down around you, you can't just wipe your hands clean and walk away. You must pick up the pieces and start to put it back together, bit by bit, piece by piece. We may lose pieces along the way; some pieces may not fit with others. It may be the hardest jigsaw the nation, maybe the world, has ever had to reconstruct but with the countless pairs of hands up and down this fair isle and around the world in Britain's allies, we will make short work of it. Britain will endure, better, stronger and greater than ever."*

(CHAPTER BREAK)

The former office of Andrew Pierce was devoid of light, a small wood fire, offering little illumination from across the room. The rain scattered against the large windows, the front of Downing Street's exterior hammered by the wind, the wreath upon the door swaying at unnatural, canted angles. A singular, dark figure sat within the leather-bound chair, staring out into the bleak night, Christmas postponed under such circumstances and all the better for it, the wheels of revolution now lubricated and ready to turn.

A well-manicured hand rapped upon the desk, the other holding what many referred to in the intelligence services as a Burner phone. Downing Street was still busy; although, much of the workforce had been diminished with shifts having ended in the evening, spouses and parents off to spend time with loved ones over the festive period.

"Yes, I am fully aware of that," the voice hissed, "no I am not aware of Thompson's current location. As it stands and as you know full well, we can confirm the primary objective was completed, the memory stick however, will need to be revisited at a later date."

A large bolt of thunder cracked from outside the window, distracting the shadowy figure momentarily from the haranguing voice on the other end of the line. The shadowy spectre began nodding profusely.

"Yes, I am well aware of the blackout within the area after we breached," the shadow swung in the chair.

"Yes, I agree. Yes, there is a high likelihood that that was Thompson using the device to aide in his escape," another pause "no, we fabricated our cover with our sources inside the national grid… chalked it up to the concussion of the blast, some damaged wires. Until further clarification, should we get it from Thompson; I would presume it is safe to say that he is still within possession of the device."

The shadowy hand clasped down upon the last remnants of Pierce's possessions, a spare pair of wire rimmed spectacles. The shadow played with the arms of the spectacles, grunts of agreement trotting along with the clandestine voice on the mobile.

"I agree and as I stated earlier, I await your command with regards to Phase Two," another pause, a response considered, "yes the test sites are ready; Project Exodus is in the final stages of experimentation, perfect for human testing to begin."

A bitter taste soured the silhouette's mouth and lower jaw. Unknown to the shadowy presence, their grip upon the spectacles had tightened, the wire rims beginning to yield under the weight of exerted force.

"I agree he needs to be taken care of sir, yes. How we take care of him however, is another matter," the voice grunted disinterested, turning over one of the many daily newspapers before him. The words upon the front page were nauseating; 'Never was so much owed by so many to so few', a picture of Tom Hawkins beside it, taken from what the shadow surmised to be a social networking site, the man having not appeared before the press as of yet.

The picture had been taken from his time in the service, a smiling face, clad in Army fatigues, foot placed firmly upon a rock, in a heroic stance, rifle cradled in his arms. The shadow winced and dropped the shattered spectacles upon the newspapers front cover, sucking at their thumb, blood drawn and dripping onto the cover. The newspaper along with the remains of Pierce's glasses was flung across the desk in rage. The voice at the other end of the line questioned what was happening.

"Nothing sir," another suck of the thumb, "I agree we need to remove him from the picture one hundred percent; however, this man has become a national hero, a symbol, he may be of use to the cause,"

He paused once again to listen to the echoed response.

"If we can't turn him to our way of thinking, sir?" the voice repeated the superior's question.

Another crack of thunder.

"Well, I suggest we first destroy his legend, no longer the darling of the people, instead an enemy of the state. If we kill him too quickly, too absentmindedly, we risk establishing him as a martyr, too many people will dig around the circumstances of his death and conspiracy theories will ensue. Plus given his mental state before the events of West Acre, a staged suicide on our behalf wouldn't be all to fantastical for the nation to believe"

Something brought the shadow from their stupor, ears pricking up with curiosity.

"Sir, I suggest you have your contact at the hospital observe him in a strictly observatory capacity, if possible, an inspection of his belongings, should he have anything of value, incriminating in nature. That should suffice for now. We know where he lives, he won't be going anywhere, the ball is firmly in our court."

Another crack of thunder rang out. The shadowy figure rose from their seat, stature framed by the thunder, a spectre of untold sadism.

"Very good sir, as agreed, I will make the appropriate preparations. Thompson is aware of his mission, if he deviates in anyway, if he should still be alive, he won't be too hard to find. Witness accounts establish he was substantially injured. Mr Hawkins has still not been fully questioned himself sir, quite the beating he endured. As soon as I know the full details, I shall let you know immediately. I will monitor the situation personally and oversee any and all damage limitation myself sir. Our contacts within the media and public sector shall prove most invaluable over the next couple of weeks. PATRIOT shall weather this storm. Of that I have no doubt sir."

With that the shadow hung up and removed the back of the phone's casing and battery with an air of graceful muscle memory that established it had been done many times previously. The sim card was removed and broken in half between thumb and forefinger, before the character kneeled to pick up the pieces of Pierce's discarded lenses and the bloodied newspaper, placing them into a wastepaper bin.

The ominous figure stepped towards the warmth of the fire, crackling away, the mantelpiece above adorned with many a Christmas trinket, festive bunting fluttering slightly. The figure threw both the sim card and the mobile phone onto the hearth, picking up an iron poker, the bin cradled in the crook of their arm. The phone cracked slightly, the plastic melting, the inner workings popping. The poker stabbed at the wood, sending embers swirling up into the chimney. Next, the contents of the bin were thrown in delicately. The newspaper came last, opened fully, the image of the nation's adulation and idolization, staring back at the figure.

"We shall see if you have Britain's best interests at heart, after all, fame is such a fickle beast and the public do love a fallen angel," the voice sneered, before tossing the open newspaper into the fire.

The flames welcomed the fresh fuel, burning the newspaper from the outside in. The shadow strode off, opening the door and departing hastily. The room fell silent once again, all be it for the spectre's whistling as it disappeared down the hall. *'God Rest Ye Merry Gentlemen'*, echoing down the corridors long after the shadow had disappeared.

Tom had been given strict instructions to rest and endless reassurances that he was safe. He had joked with the police officers standing guard at the door to his private room that he did not need them, his Mother who had not left his side since being admitted, was sentry enough. He had required minor surgery on his shoulder with his forearms also having a dozen stitches in each arm. Various cuts and bruises also adorned his body, but these had hastily been treated and disinfected, clean bandages and plasters lining his body. As he sat propped up in the pillow laden seat by his bed, his coccyx having taken much of the extent of the bruising, he took in his surroundings as he waited for his possessions to be returned, the gown and robe he was currently wearing leaving little to the imagination.

Through the glass windows to his room, he could see his father and mother filling in the necessary documentation, allowing for him to be discharged. They both looked as if they had not slept for days. Both his mother and father were of a happy disposition, but Tom saw the pained glimmer that haunted their eyes, their youngest son, whom they had presumed to be dead, now lay in the morgue.

Tom did not remember much of his journey to the hospital. A paramedic had established that Tom, between fits of pain and anguish, would not allow the paramedics see to him without first establishing his brother was ok. He had apparently told the paramedic where his body was, a message was relayed to the search teams within West Acre Point and within minutes he was assured that his brother had been found and would be taken to the same hospital as Tom along with the rest of the injured and dead.

Upon hearing this, Tom promptly blacked out once again. When he awoke, he was in a clean hospital bed, a drip attached to his arm, his mother and father bedside him. He, along with his parents, had broken down into tears upon seeing each other, his mother hugging him so tight that Brian had to practically prise her free in fear of ripping his stitches. His father, upon his mother weeping at Tom's sorry state, chirped up, establishing that, *'He had seen Rugby players leave the field with worse",* to which his wife promptly slapped her husband playfully on the arm. His mother took to lightly rubbing his good eye, the other swollen closed and violently purple in its hue.

The police had shortly entered after that, with an official form from the government. They had asked if Tom was alert enough for questioning, stating that national security depended upon it. Tom quickly established that there were no secondary devices, that it had been another form of misdirection on the terrorist's part, a way to incite panic and cover their escape. After which, Tom recited everything that had happened to him, his mother having to leave the room on four separate occasions, the details of his ordeal too horrific.

To his surprise, upon waking his parents had not launched into a flurry of questions about Anthony. When he came to this part of the story, both his father and, cradled in his arms his mother, stayed; tears streaking both their cheeks, Tom's included.

The men finished by establishing that they would have further questions, thanking him for his bravery. Tom had asked if the final charges within West Acre Point had been diffused and if all the hostages were safe. The governmental representative established that upon breaching the complex, a substantial bomb disposal unit had made short work of the charges, establishing that if Thompson had indeed triggered a secondary device from afar, the devices had long since been deactivated.

The true extent of what Tom had achieved had not sunk in until he had been informed that he had been responsible for saving the lives of over two hundred people. He smiled lightly to himself, considering this statistic as he sat alone in his chair festooned with pillows. His smile soon faded however, as images of those he had not saved, flooded his brain.

Overwhelmed, he broke down, drawing the curtain slightly around him, not wishing for his parents to see him from the other side of the glass. He had been a celebrity upon the ward, afforded the best of healthcare, his own room, nurses and doctors gaggling around him both thanking him and attentively seeing to his every whim. Yet he had never wished to be alone more in his entire life, to be left in solitary with his morose thoughts. He sat and violently sobbed, the pain of his injuries paled in significance to the pain he assumed mourning families across the nation were currently enduring, some awaiting a call to discover whether their loved one was on a ward or upon a mortuary table; his own parents included.

A knock at the door came and Tom palmed tears from his eyes, inhaling the snot and tears back as quietly as he could.

"Mr. Hawkins?" a friendly, feminine tone enquired.

"Yes, here," Tom sniffed as he pulled back the curtain.

A young nurse, no older than about twenty- eight stood before him, smiling, a plastic bag and a large cardboard box in her outstretched hands. Tom made to stand as if to help her with the items but groaned, the nurse ushering him to sit down.

"Rest easy, I have a clean set of clothes here for you. Your Dad went home and fetched you some bits," she stated, laying the items on the bed.

"Thank you," Tom expressed.

"Don't know how he managed though. When I came in for my shift about an hour or so ago, I could barely get into the building, you can't move for reporters outside."

Tom smiled weakly in return, rising shakily to his feet. The nurse made to help but he steadied himself on the edge of the bed.

"I'm fine, thanks."

The nurse smoothed down the side of her uniform and looked unsure of her surroundings, as if she wanted to say something. Tom glanced back at her, removing items of clothing from the clear bag.

"Are you ok there?" Tom questioned politely.

She shook her head lightly and Tom set about retrieving items from the bag again.

"I...I, just wanted to say," the nurse stuttered.

Tom stopped what he was doing and smiled back at the nurse.

"Go ahead; to be honest I'm glad of the conversation. Made all the better for you not having a gun pointed at my head."

The nurse looked horrified at this and looked away bashfully. Tom stepped forward and held his hands up in apology.

"Sorry that was in bad taste, stupid of me to say. Please, fire away," he scorned himself for his latter choice of words.

The nurse looked up coyly.

"I just wanted to say... well everyone here wanted to say, a massive thanks to you, for your bravery and for everything you did. There's a lot of patients and staff in here alike, who have relatives or friends that were in that complex, that wouldn't be here if it had not been for you. The nation owes you a great debt, mine included," she blushed slightly upon finishing.

Tom shook his head.

"You guys are the ones that deserve all the praise. I'll bet you guys have saved countless more lives in here tonight than I did, myself included. I wouldn't be here if you and your colleagues hadn't sewn me up the way you did. It's you I should be thanking."

The nurse shook her head in reply.

"It's our job. What you did in that building ... that wasn't a job. You didn't have to do that. And, as a way of showing the staff's gratitude, the hospital as a whole actually, we had one of our medics on site, follow up on something you kept on repeating in the ambulance, when you were in and out of consciousness" she said as she patted the cardboard box.

"Bloody hell sounds like I didn't shut up. They should have sold tickets," Tom smirked, wincing upon overtaxing his jaw.

The nurse lightly smiled.

"I hope it's what you meant; it's where you said it would be."

The nurse made to leave the room, shooting him another smile as she turned at the door, wishing him well once again. In his dumbstruck state he lightly waved before tentatively pulling the lid of the box back. His hand came up to capture the sob.

(CHAPTER BREAK)

Tom sat atop the crisply made bed, fully clothed now. A loose fitting Hard-Fi T-Shirt, his favourite band and a pair of jeans on. His feet were slightly swollen, so his father had brought a loose-fitting pair of trainers of which the laces remained untied, tucked into his sides. He sat upon his bed, his right hand resting upon the box. His father entered, closely followed by his mother. There was a commotion out in the hallway and his mother quickly shut the door, sighing in exasperation.

"It's a madhouse out there son, you sure you're up to this? They're happy for you to stay as long as you need. The Doctor's practically begged me to keep you in observation longer," his father enquired.

"And miss out on Mum's Christmas dinner? Not a chance in hell," Tom smirked, placing an arm around his mother as she sat beside him, nestled in his shoulder.

"A Christmas dinner with all the trimmings seems like child's play after what you've just been through," his mother welled up once again.

Tom held her tighter, rocking her slightly. He had run through what he was going to say several times before his parents entered but words failed him. He wished to have it out in the open, to leave what was hanging over him in the confines of this room.

"Dad can you sit down for a second?" he asked, motioning to the empty chair beside his bed.

His father nodded, plunking himself down in the seat, an expectant look upon his face.

"Before we go, I want to… I want to discuss what I said earlier, to those men, about Anthony," Tom stated sternly.

"Look son, you don't need to. Get a bit better first, yeah," his father pressed; wanting to be spared of yet further trauma.

"No, Dad, please. I need to get this off my chest, now, and after, if you and Mum want, we'll never speak of it again," Tom pressed on.

He looked at his father who after a moment of contemplation, nodded. His mother sat upwards and held both Tom's hand, tears already welling in her already, tear swollen eyes. Tom nodded ready to proceed, wanting to say what had to be said in one go.

Tom set about telling them all that he knew, establishing that there were still blanks he could not fill in such as his brother's clandestine activities or his need to partake in such a mission. He told them everything; however, he made sure not to tell them about the contents of the parcel left by his brother. He showed them the letter and established he had deciphered its hidden meaning. His father read the letter, the task proving all too much for his mother, who didn't get past the first three words. By the end of his speech, both parents looked on dumbstruck, the fantastical series of events laid bare.

"I told those reporters on the way in, didn't I Brian? No son of mine would be caught up in anything like that! That he was a war hero. You wait until they find out about this!" his mother reeled off, choked up with tears.

His father sat in deep contemplation, deaf to his wife's hysteria. Tom stared back at him.

"What are you thinking Dad?" Tom questioned.

Brian looked up at his son and smiled slightly.

"Just that… in a strange way, this offers us the closure I think your Mum and I were searching for, that we were never given. We always knew you and your brother; were an inspiration, heroes… I mean to us, Army aside. It gives us the chance not a lot of other families get given, a chance to lay Anthony to rest properly this time. Not in an empty coffin, mouthing empty words at some church service. To finally get your brother the recognition he deserves," Brian murmured, emotions getting the better of him.

Tom produced the memory stick from his pocket. Both his mother and father looked at it, a slight distain for the inanimate object that had caused both their son's so much pain.

"There are only currently four people in the world who know about the location of this and three of them are in this room," Tom said assertively.

"Here's hoping it's just three and that that evil bastard is rotting in hell!" his mother shook, an uncharacteristic use of poor language rising to the fore.

Tom gave her another squeeze.

"No one can know about this. People will be looking for it, Thompson's employer for one and if we really want to start over, afresh... I'm going to have to act upon Anthony's letter," Tom swiftly finished, knowing all too well what his parent's reaction would be.

His mother directed a pleading look towards her son and then to her husband. Both men stared back, adamant, in agreement.

"I have to Mum. Anthony entrusted this with me and me alone. This won't go away and as selfish as it sounds, I have questions that need to be answered, if me, you and Dad are ever to be at peace... if Anthony's ever to be at peace," Tom looked upon his mother lovingly as he said this, a slight nod from his mother establishing her resilient agreement.

"Now there's one more thing," Tom smiled as he transferred the box from his right-hand side onto his lap momentarily forgetting himself and his wounded side. He held it out to his father.

"I think this belongs to you Dad," Tom beamed, the threat of tears onset.

His father tentatively reached out, stopping briefly, unsure of himself. He looked to his wife, who urged him on, smiling also. Brian took the box, breathed in deeply and upon exhaling, opened the box. A singular tear instantly registered within his eye and he wiped it aside. He delicately reached into the box and trailed his fingers across the contents, smiling to himself, a distant memory now resurgent. A glass and wooden structure emerged.

He turned it over in his hands, ogling it like a young child with their hands upon the glass of a sweet shop, gawping in at the untold wonders that waited within. He traced his finger over the plaque and his lips moved silently as he read the engraving. He looked up at Tom, his eyes laden with tears.

"Thank you," he whispered, choked by tears.

The rain continued to beat against the window, the room silent. Tom stepped forth with his mother and all three embraced. After a minute or so, Brian nodded to his son that he was ready. His mother helped Tom on with his coat, establishing that they intended to leave via a side entrance, not that it would do them any good with the number of crowds and press lining the streets.

Tom lingered before the maintenance exit, the hubbub on the other side of the door audible. His father gave him a knowing glance before putting his arm around his mother and striding out, his father's arm outstretched and readied to swat away any overzealous journalists. With a deep breath, Tom followed a moment or two after. They were instantly met by a baying mob of camera flashes and excited cheers before being ushered into an awaiting car laid on by the authorities. The uncertainty of what the future held in store subsided somewhat, lost within the surging throng of people. For now, Tom had survived and that was something he would both have to learn to appreciate and come to terms with, in equal measure.

Printed in Great Britain
by Amazon

55356125R00212